ALSO BY LARRY KRAMER

FICTION

Faggots

NONFICTION

The Tragedy of Today's Gays

Reports from the holocaust: The story of an AIDS activist

DRAMA

Women in Love and Other Dramatic Writings
(Sissies' Scrapbook, A Minor Dark Age, Just Say No)

The Destiny of Me

The Normal Heart

THE
AMERICAN
PEOPLE

THE AMERICAN PEOPLE

VOLUME 1: SEARCH FOR MY HEART

LARRY KRAMER

FARRAR, STRAUS AND GIROUX   NEW YORK

Farrar, Straus and Giroux
18 West 18th Street, New York 10011

Library of Congress Cataloging-in-Publication Data
Kramer, Larry.
    The American people. Volume 1, Search for my heart / Larry Kramer. — First edition.
    pages   cm
    ISBN 978-0-374-10439-9 (hardback) — ISBN 978-0-374-71297-6 (ebook)
    1. United States—History—Fiction.   I. Title.   II. Title: Search for my heart.

PS3561.R252 A83 2015
813'.54—dc23
                                                                    2014023449

Designed by Jonathan D. Lippincott

Farrar, Straus and Giroux books may be purchased for educational, business,
or promotional use. For information on bulk purchases, please contact the Macmillan
Corporate and Premium Sales Department at 1-800-221-7945, extension 5442,
or write to specialmarkets@macmillan.com.

www.fsgbooks.com
www.twitter.com/fsgbooks • www.facebook.com/fsgbooks

1   3   5   7   9   10   8   6   4   2

This book is for David Webster

I am aware that many object to the severity of my language; but is there not cause for severity? I will be as harsh as truth, and as uncompromising as justice. On this subject, I do not wish to think, or to speak, or write, with moderation. No! no! Tell a man whose house is on fire to give a moderate alarm; tell him to moderately rescue his wife from the hands of the ravisher; tell the mother to gradually extricate her babe from the fire into which it has fallen;—but urge me not to use moderation in a cause like the present. I am in earnest—I will not equivocate—I will not excuse—I will not retreat a single inch—AND I WILL BE HEARD. The apathy of the people is enough to make every statue leap from its pedestal, and to hasten the resurrection of the dead.

—William Lloyd Garrison, "To the Public," from the Inaugural Editorial in the January 1, 1831, edition of *The Liberator*, his radical abolitionist newspaper

·

History is indeed little more than the register of the crimes, follies and misfortunes of mankind. —Edward Gibbon

·

Novels are the private histories of nations. —Balzac

·

This cultural critic, Theodor Lessing, writing in the tradition of Nietzsche, argued that history, having no objective validity, amounts to a mythic construct imposed on the unknowable reality, in order to give it some semblance of meaning.

—Theodore Ziolkowski, "History as Giving Meaning to the Meaningless"

·

A given datum's status as gossip does not automatically render it false or unimportant. —Hendrik Hertzberg, *The New Yorker*

It is not down in any map; true places never are.

—Herman Melville, *Moby-Dick*

•

It goes on, I see, as my soul prompts it.   —Shakespeare, *The Tempest*

•

Novels are more autobiographical than anything else one could say about oneself. It does not matter how the facts occur in life. It matters how they are told.

—Elsa Morante

•

A wise man should consider that health is the greatest of human blessings, and learn how by his own thought to derive benefit from his illnesses.

—Hippocrates

•

It is my opinion that evil is never "radical," that it is only extreme, and that it possesses neither depth nor any demonic dimension. It can overgrow and lay waste the whole world precisely because it spreads like a fungus on the surface. It is "thought-defying" because thought tries to reach some depth, to go to the roots, and the moment it concerns itself with evil, it is frustrated because there is nothing. That is its "banality." Only the good has depth and can be radical.

—Hannah Arendt, *The Jew as Pariah*

•

Fiction is history, human history, or it is nothing.   —Joseph Conrad

•

Let me say before I go any further that I forgive nobody.

—Samuel Beckett, *Malone Dies*

A Word for My Beloved

"I went to my doctor this morning and received the bad news," the Roman emperor Hadrian writes to his beloved Antinous in Marguerite Yourcenar's *Memoirs of Hadrian*. "I rush to begin and shall spend as much time as I can with the hope I shall finish, even though to do so will deprive me of what I cherish most, to lie in your arms."

There is no one else left alive to tell this history. So far as I know, I am the only person still here who's been on the front lines since the beginning. I write because I know that of the histories that have been written and will be written, none can be like this one, since I saw and heard and knew of much that others preferred not to see and hear and know, or, having seen and heard and known, declined to acknowledge. From that day until this I have felt an obligation placed upon me and indeed have sometimes wondered if I was spared only long enough to complete this work. A history of a plague that has so punished our world and our friends and our families and ourselves: this is the saddest story anyone should ever have to write, or read.

So I, Laurence David Kramer, in my country of death, write this history of the plague, and of The American People before and during this time of plague, and of our people who have died from this plague, and of who and what caused this plague.

I state at the beginning of this telling: I have never seen such wrongs as this plague, in all its guises, represents.

You and I know all this. You have lived this with me. Indeed, I would have been more dreamer than missionary were it not for your presence in my life.

This book is written out of my deep and abiding love for you, and us, and our people, and what I devoutly wish us all to stand for, and to be.

VOLUME 1

SEARCH FOR MY HEART

FOLLOW THE BOUNCING BALL

Fred Lemish is preparing to finish his history of The American People. He sits in his apartment with its lovely view of Washington Square, in New York City, his and Edward's new dog, Charley, the cairn terrier who looks like Toto, chewing a bone at his feet. He faces two 30-inch computer monitors, connected by thick stubborn tough cords to his beloved Mac tower that contains somewhere in its mysterious innards his entire lifetime. He is surrounded by floor-to-ceiling wall-to-wall bookshelves that contain his encyclopedias, his many volumes on this country's history (as well as all the great writers he wishes he could write as well as), and his dictionaries, with his nouns and adjectives and adverbs of the who, what, when, where, and how of life. Close at hand on this enormous desk some ten feet square he keeps, like heaps of ready ammunition, the diaries of his, and the world's, day-by-day life since this plague began. Messy heaps of scattered, torn, furiously scrunched-up manuscript pages lie on the floor his huge desk rests upon, and in several over-flowing, also enormous, wastebaskets containing more of the same, in all of which he's almost drowning.

He's been struggling with this history for many years. He will share his progress with you as he puts it all together in case he doesn't make it to its end, in which case he's left instructions and funds for it to be published as is.

How much did he find out? How much shame and horror at all that was and is being enacted and endured? Shame for whom? He'd always been a hopeful fellow, God knows why, or how. Hopeful fellows, just to get along, often acquire a thick encrustment, to use a fancy word for being blind.

He had not wanted to write this history. He had not wanted to do a lot of things in his life. For a while he didn't even want to be Fred Lemish. Every-thing had always seemed a forging on against awfully high tides of one kind or another. Often it has just been a bad case of feeling sorry for himself, like we all do, every single one of us. But he knows that writing this history is a requirement he must fulfill. He has no choice.

He decides to finally belly up to this assignment on that day when he hears President Peter Ruester refer to "The American People" and realizes that the president of the United States is not talking about him or his people, and that he, Fred Lemish, had best do something about it. A strange and terrifying and fatal disease has appeared in America attacking gay men, including a major number of his friends. Within months of its "first" appearance, twenty years short of the end of the twentieth century, it is recognized to be an epidemic by enough employees of the American government and enough members of the science and research establishments, though in no way will it be identified or treated as such. Within one year this epidemic thus becomes a plague, a plague that unless checked will eventually infect hundreds of millions of people all over the globe, too many of whom will die. Again, no one in authority speaks up, says anything, says boo, most especially President Peter Ruester.

Fred's book will be a history of this plague, which by the way is called the plague of The Underlying Condition, which, as he writes it, he discovers is also a history of The American People.

If Fred's history will seem less unbiased than some would wish, let it never be overlooked that it is no small task to record a history of hate when one is among the hated.

And while one begins at a beginning, as J. M. Roberts, another historian, has written, there is never a beginning, something has always come before.

And as Roberts also said, most people's notions of what is going on are often wrong.

Truths are hard to find, if they can really be found at all. Roberts said that, too. What an honest fellow, Fred thinks, so upfront with warnings usually never posted so early on, if at all.

Fred hopes in writing his history that he'll convince you. But as someone once said, hope is a thing with feathers. Still and all, he pledges to himself that he will write the book he wants to, irrespective of the many obstacles to truth that important stuff always throws up in its wake.

Indeed, had he not, and to be sure, and you can bet your bottom dollar, pledged to offer to all Thomases doubting his suitability for this enormous task these words from an earlier toiler in similar circumstances in defense of his own reporting of an earlier plague (Fred tries to choose good role models):

> In any case the narrator . . . would have little claim to competence
> for a task like this, had not chance put him in the way of gathering

much information, and had he not been, by the force of things, closely involved in all that he proposes to narrate. This is his justification for playing the part of a historian. Naturally, a historian, even an amateur, always has data, personal or second hand, to guide him. The present narrator has three kinds of data: first, what he saw himself; secondly, the accounts of other eyewitnesses (thanks to the part he played, he was enabled to learn their personal impressions from all those figuring in this chronicle); and, lastly, documents that subsequently came into his hands. He proposes to draw on these records whenever this seems desirable, and to employ them.

(*The Plague*, Albert Camus, 1948)

FRED'S SOURCES

Fred has sought, and will seek, the services of many people to help him write this history. Some you may recognize; others you will not. Of course, some of them are fools. It is always particularly important to listen to fools.

More than most histories, this one must of necessity be visited by a host of insistent narrators attempting to be heard. Some are accepted "experts" in their fields, whatever that definition can be proved to mean; some should be and are not; some are useful for little beyond what they can tell us of certain matters; some are more interested in intruding than in sharing what they really know. An overwhelming number will be what will become known as "UC activists."

History is words and most of the important ones never reach paper. People talk. People confide in each other. People gossip. People exaggerate. People lie. It is the good historian's duty to locate and to record as much of this as is useful. Second-rate historians disdain such sources, which is why so much history as written is second-rate. We shall have occasion to argue this case often.

Mention should be made of the two great research libraries in our field. Lady Jane Greeting's library, devoted to "the medical literature of the New Worlde—for is not the beste way to charte a nation's history to tracke how sick it is?" partners, as it were, with the library her husband had earlier established in London to similarly catalogue his homeland. Lady Greeting started her establishment in 1647 in Nearodell, her birthplace and the Strode family estate, on land that would become Charleston, South Carolina. Today this library is part of the University of Southern Medicine and Jewry. Lady Jane Greeting was not Jewish, nor was her husband. The Sir John Greeting Institute of Worldwide Medical Knowledge of All Peoples, in London, is the largest medical library anywhere, and very fussy about the inclusion in all citations of its entire name. The depth and importance of the collections in both these Greeting libraries are priceless. Sir John wanted to know everything about anything connected to the maintenance of the body. By the time he married Lady Jane, rather late in his own life, he had traveled over much of the globe as it was then known, and sent back to London every parchment, pamphlet, prescription, and, if possible, concrete example concerning every ailment, eruption, remedy, and likely deterrent to normalcy that every tribe, people, and settlement might have assembled. The range is quite extraordinary, from tubs for birthing during bowel hot flashes in the Amazon jungle to grinders to turn frozen human limbs into poultices for "dinosaur" bites in Antarctica. Similarly, Lady Jane's own assemblages are as eye-popping. Her interests were primarily American Indian and she catalogued some several thousand tribes. Much of what we know today about early American medicine and treatment we know because of Lady Jane and her obsession. The Sir John Greeting Institute of Worldwide Medical Knowledge of All Peoples continues to add to its collection every day.

The Admiral Mason Iron Vaultum Library of the National Institute of Tumor Sciences (NITS) in Punic, Maryland, is our largest research repository of America's ills and maladies. Who Admiral Mason was, or what an Iron Vaultum was, or what either had to do with each other or a library is to this day a mystery. It is more extensive—i.e., voluminous (bulk mail is, after all, an American invention)—than perceptive. One does not usually go to Vaultum for answers, but rather for clues on where else to look, which should not lessen its value to scholars. Many of Vaultum's contents are embargoed from viewing by the general public. It is top-secret stuff, for one reason or another, often no longer valid, much of it long forgotten, and gaining access to it requires an investigation, a security clearance, many forms filled out in multicopies, and final approval from a federal Chief Librarian (there are currently 1,124). What is inside this library, or was ever inside this library, to warrant such exclusionary behavior also remains unknown; once upon a time Somebody made a rule or passed a law.

As long as acknowledgments of thanks are already peeking through, let us express appreciation to the distinguished lesbian historian Sarah Schulman, for her indomitable compilation of activists' experiences in the ACT

UP Oral History, as recollected here by some members, and to the late Deep Throat, who went to his grave requesting his anonymity be respected.

It is an interesting process—whom to let enter one's history. A history, after all and ironically, is a singular affair. "This is what I think" is compounded from other people's words and deeds to construct a personal house of thought. While any history worth its writing encompasses the activities of too many people and events to succumb to any traffic cop, the good historian is still his own best roving conductor.

So come along. Some of you may remember, as Fred does, the old-fashioned movie theaters, with their "Community Sings," when the huge grand organ rose out of the pit, as it did for him at Loew's Capitol Theater in downtown Washington, D.C. A strange man would pound upon it, and the words of the popular songs of the day were writ large, lined up hugely on the silver screen, an animated orb bouncing along them syllable by syllable. Yes, come along and let America's voices once again sing out in the dark as we respond to that master organist's command: "Follow the bouncing ball!"

THE FIRST AMERICAN PEOPLE

The First American People are monkeys who eat each other.

Who knew?

Histories of The American People do not usually begin with monkeys. As they insistently cast an unwanted anthropomorphic focus on who we are and how we are here, those who have written histories invariably exclude monkeys. They start with Indians, or George Washington, who, indeed, proclaimed, "All history will begin with me!" No one writes about monkeys who eat each other. And who will eat us. As we eat them. (And no one has yet written what, precisely, began with George Washington.)

Well, we are going to begin with monkeys.

Monkey is an imprecise, meaningless, inoffensive word. They will be called orangutans, chimpanzees, gorillas, macaques, guenons, capuchins, marmosets, tamarins, apes (they will never be called The First American People), oh there will be more kinds and species (there is a difference between "a kind" and "a species" but not right here) identified before someone finally pays attention to them, which is still eons and eras away from their first appearance on our stage. Yes, monkey sounds less threatening than sacred baboon or barbary ape or crying tantalus or wretched oyuung or sooty mangabey or *Pan troglodytes troglodytes*, which, this last named, will become a particularly threatening monkey when it's discovered to be related to our plague, or drills and red-eared and Preuss guenons and black colobuses, these last four will one day be discovered to have had bits of The Underlying Condition in their makeup for some 32,000 years! Since none of them form very stable genetic clusters, it is simpler to put them all together and call them monkeys. Or chimps. Or chimpanzees, which has taken hold although they really are a specialty unto themselves.

If we're all descended from monkeys, and it is hoped everybody accepts that we are (although these days in certain states of a retrograde intellectual nature this appears to be less and less the case), then we shall find many who attempt to make monkeys seem cute and sympathetic. But monkeys are not cute. They may groom each other all the time and look clean, but monkeys are cesspools of disease. Believe it or not, disease is a modern concept. Academics now even call it "a modern construct" or "a modern invention," but it's real enough and always has been, and people who talk like that usually have their heads up their asses.

Monkeys are unlikely leading players in any important drama. We shall be discovering that leading players are an awfully big problem in life generally and with history in particular. And that many candidates for anything important are unlikely. Monkeys are even more of a problem because the ones you want are far away, hard to find, expensive to acquire and more expensive to maintain, and messy, very messy, to study.

Not many people work in monkeys and never have. It is not a calling that's called.

Even after the plague arrives it will still be years before anyone notices monkeys. And it won't be until almost the end of this history that their piss and shit will be studied (as Deep Throat literally begged be done at the beginning). Oh, a few scientists will make what other scientists will consider ridiculous claims about monkeys causing this and that. Scientists and their claims have always been ridiculed viciously by other scientists and their claims. Doctors call other doctors "crazy" all the time, so let's get used to that right now. You'll notice that *scientist* and *doctor* have just been used interchangeably. Nobody knows what to call themselves these days. Scientists treat patients and doctors work in laboratories. *Doctor* has become just another imprecise English word robbed of meaning and truth. Sort of like *monkey* itself.

America's monkeys first appear in Florida, in an Everglades that must have looked much as it did in its empty beginnings in the Etrusticene era, in the midst of a lot of tall trees, mostly pines and erovonous deciduous maltreasons, which aren't around anymore but look pretty much like pines. According to calculations from the National Bureau of Geographic Measurements and Standards, this southernmost part of America's landmass is as old as America gets. Dr. Bosco Dripper also believes that you can't get much older than this part of Florida. Many geologists, archaeologists, paleontologists, paleoanthropologists, biologists, pathologists, geneticists, virologists, and just plain anthropologists don't agree. There are so many different "ists" these days, one never achieves consensus. Everyone's got his or her own pet "oldest" American everything.

Well, the Everglades is Dr. Dripper's.

Though for the longest time no one thought to visit El Modesto to locate him, Dr. Dripper knows his monkeys better than anyone else knows his, or now her, monkeys. This is just a fact. Facts are as rare in medicine and in science as they are in history (or, for that matter, anywhere). They last only until the next fact comes along. However, no new fact has come along to lessen Dr. Dripper's importance. Primatology is still not a calling that's called. The current membership of the Primate Society totals thirty-seven, and most of them are women who refuse to work in the jungle. It is very hard to be a primatologist without working in a jungle. The few great ones rarely leave it.

In the middle of the jungle that still exists around El Modesto are several battered wooden buildings hidden in the scrub pines and palmettos and labeled El Modesto Estancia de los Monos Primate Holding Center, or as is painted on its gate, "Yaddah's Monkey House." How does he live such an isolated and lonely and solitary life in a Florida swamp without going nuts? Perhaps he has gone nuts and nobody's noticed. Perhaps he was nuts all along. Craziness, as already indicated, has little to do with anything in either science or medicine and the crazies should always be listened to. You never know. It's not generally known that Yaddah University traffics in monkeys. (Few are cognizant of Yaddah's beginnings.) It's not generally known that monkeys have rights now and are expensive to maintain, and Yaddah, ranked by *Academic Health & Wealth* the richest university in America, appears to be cutting a few too many corners in this laboratory so hidden from view.

Bosco Dripper, D.V.M., M.D., Ph.D., P.S., is America's leading monkey doctor. For many years he was America's only monkey doctor. A monkey doctor is correctly called a primatologist. Bosco has been a primatologist since

1940, when he received his Doctorate in Veterinary Medicine from Yaddah Medical School, the first degree of this nature that Yaddah conferred, although *primatology* was not then a word in use and would not be until 1957, when monkeys finally became of sufficient interest to various cancer researchers to bequeath the study of them a name. It was then discovered that there were few primatologists, anywhere, a major hole in this country's defense system against fatal diseases, and one reason we have so many of them (fatal diseases, not monkeys; we never have enough monkeys). This lack of primatologists persists, which is why Bosco is still considered America's leading monkey doctor and why America still has so many fatal diseases. It would seem an easy lack to rectify until you learn about 1) the politics of monkeys and 2) "the animal model." There are a lot of reasons why we continue to die in droves that have nothing to do with actual physical disease.

Dr. Dripper is a sad, disheveled, cranky man of indeterminate old age, who always wears a rumpled seersucker suit and a yellowed drip-dry shirt and a pale, limp, wrinkled, bespotted pink tie. Like almost everyone else in this country he is overweight. His eyes water constantly. As with all primatologists, a group that has yet to birth their Kluckhohn, their Lévi-Strauss, their Mead or Powdermaker, Dr. Dripper is little known. "Like the deepest secrets in a psychoanalysis, our lives stay hidden, harboring our precious information like a piece of decaying food behind a major molar in our country's maw," he has written. Dr. Dripper can be quite touchingly poetic.

ACCORDING TO BOSCO

EVOLUTION'S SAD

Look at a map. Florida is America's penis and the Everglades is its rectum and the Gulf of Mexico is what we pissed and shat into. All our primeval history started in this Ever Glade. The First American People started shitting their guts out right here. The oldest shit in America is under my feet. The ground here is the packed-down monkey shit of eons.

Fight over this if you want. I don't care anymore. Fight over any of it and all of it. I don't care. Really. I don't.

America's Underlying Condition started right here.

It's been argued, too frequently and by too many, that The Underlying Condition was not originally American, that it came from beyond these shores, brought to this virgin land from Another World. Waste of breath but I say it: we make our own shit. Throw the cream pies and fire the bullets and lower the guillotine. Plenty of other monkey matters are unagreed upon, but this is the big one. Tears us apart. The UC started here and please let's have an end to it. Mad at myself for saying so again. Promised myself I'd stop fighting this battle. I can't. Poor me. Never learn. Well, I wrote my book. Everything I know and believe and have seen. One hundred and sixty-three copies. You used to have to write a book to stay at Yaddah. If you wrote a book they couldn't fire you. Now they fire you even if you write a bunch of books. Books are definitely not the saving grace they once were. Good luck with yours.

They had sex in groups. That's the key to everything. Doing it with lots of others. That's the whole story. Don't believe it at your peril. It's a never-ending growth industry, those who think I'm crazy. Can't prove it, they say. Can they prove I'm wrong? All they can do is call me names. There in a nutshell is what's wrong with history. The Wrongs triumph. Well, it takes a tankful of imagination to have sex in groups. Especially when you're mon-keys. Especially when it's thousands of years ago. Especially when you've never seen anyone else have sex in groups. Without . . . what's that stupid term . . . role models. You get punished for having imagination. I should know.

There are endless opportunities for anything to jump the barrier be-tween monkey and man. That's what you want to know, isn't it? As if that's the whole story. In fact, it's the usual thing for many an organism to do, to pass from what Mirko calls its "animal reservoir" to a human population. Whatever "it" is. Hell, Mirko makes a point of telling us that some Native American tribes pepped up their libidos by injecting themselves in their thighs and pubic regions with male monkey blood for the gents, and she-monkey blood for the ladies. Good man, Mirko. Gets right to the heart of the matter. Mirko neglects to go into details on how precisely they injected them-selves, as the hypodermic needle was not invented until 1670, 1842, 1853, take your pick. It must have been messy however they did it. Mirko was not re-elected to the Primate Society after he wrote this. Join the crowd. Those girls have now managed to get rid of all the men.

Many many many many years ago—no one, I don't care who, can tell you how long ago with anything approaching accuracy—in what will be called these Everglades, in what will be called this Florida, in what will be called our United States, what was and is called a goldmonkey stands in a group of gold-monkeys. Probably not far from this very spot. It would happen soon enough in other places. How come they are in Florida first? The monkeys are running away from something, that's why how come, and get themselves cornered and are unable to find their way out. Just like old kikes and young fairies who come to the penis of Florida and won't piss off.

These goldmonkeys are what today is called a family. They get together because they like each other, not because birth and blood link them.

In each grouping there is usually at least one goldmonkey who is a male and at least one goldmonkey who is a female and a bunch of goldmonkeys who are maybe offspring, maybe relations, maybe friends, maybe just goldmonkeyfolk passing through. They feel connected to each other. They have in fact granted to each other the rights of visitation, and to the biggest the right to host the party. Size counts with monkeys. If you're bigger than the rest you usually get to host the do. Sometimes the hosts are males. Sometimes the hosts are females. Big is big. I'm talking bulk, girth, weight, heft here. Not the size of sex organs.

They don't know why they feel connected. They like each other and they don't know why. People don't often ask themselves why they prefer Manny to Moe. Oh, they could list reasons but usually the reasons don't explain the kind of bonding affection evokes. For monkeys it could be smells, it could be spirits of some sort of animal ancestors, it could be what's come to be known as genetic predisposition. We'll Never Know. No shame in saying we'll never know. More honest to admit it than make up some fancy gobble, which is what academics always do.

The bigger goldmonkeys spring into action if the young or smaller ones get out of hand, or are about to be eaten, or wounded, or attacked, by bigger and stronger Thems, who also live in this jungle, this dark and dangerous jungle, which is where they all live, their home, this jungle which is so thick with growing vines and trees that there is little light from the sky or sun, ever, only the dampness in the earth from the rain that soaks into it and causes a cool moistness that never goes away even though the air is still and humid, dirty, stinky, what's that word? *Fetid.* God, this place smelled. Still does. After it rains. Before it rains. It is the subtle currents of different odors and temperatures that maneuver monkeys from spot to spot and grouping to grouping. It is this fetid and humid atmosphere that also makes their limbs sore and arthritic and eventually renders it harder and harder for them to clamber from trees, so that they have to stay on the ground and learn how to walk upright with better facility. Walking on the ground upright is how they become us. Becoming us is considered evolution. But that's another story. Well, maybe it's not.

Walking upright on the ground proves dangerous. The Chief Intruders from the Thems can eat you and your buddies. That happens every day. Greenmonkeys are the most fearsome Thems. They're monsters. They're terrorists.

The chief chimps patrol around their families and supervise against attacks by Thems. Thems are any marauding intruders, who also live in this jungle, of course, which they love too, a jungle filled with a dampness that spreads the thick smells, the fearful odors of all Others and this steamy heat that makes them have more sex in groups. There is always more fucking when it's hot and steamy. I can't recall any study that's disputed this. (Not that I recall any study that studied it. Outright sex never gets the grants.) There's not much else to do on the ground but to eat and fuck and sleep. And of course to be afraid.

Are you growing restless? No one is as interested in monkeys, fucking or otherwise, as I am, which is too bad. From all you'll be learning from me you might think that monkeys can kill you, that one day a long time ago a monkey ate a man or a man ate a monkey and you could die for it. Well, that's true. You can.

Evolution's sad!

Why are the monkeys I particularly love called goldmonkeys? They're brown. They're called goldmonkeys because they can lead others to special places that are valuable for survival: streams with fish, pools of water, swamps with bugs, dead trees with snakes and rodents, decaying fruit vines. Amazing gift, this. Good sniffers, I guess, though it's probably not that simple, because all species sniff. Why do birds fly? Think it's wings, do you? I'll put wings on you and you won't fly. Then they ate the snakes and rodents and bugs and fish and berries and eventually died because they had no more goldmonkeys to follow. You follow? Probably not. The Thems always eat more than they need to. Lessens the supply, makes everyone hungrier. The fewer and fewer goldmonkeys left don't want to fight back, and so they abandon their big fellows who host the do's. They stop wanting to breed anymore. They stop wanting to live. There is nothing that stops fucking faster even in the heat than not wanting to live anymore. We'll never know about that. Nobody ever really can understand death.

Yes, evolution's sad.

I love to watch goldmonkey babies play. We still have a few of them around here. Boy babies are cuter. Girl babies whine. Their titties aren't producing milk yet and hurt them. Boy babies don't want anything to do with girl babies. Boys spend a lot more time with boys. Girl monkeys are only for babies and fucking, and most times, if there are enough boys around, not even for fucking, and that's the way it is. You think we're off the track but we're not.

Pay attention! Species eat other species. Eat their flesh, eat their young, eat their sperm, eat their cunts, eat their dicks. Once it's out there, whatever "it" is, it's usually inside you forever. You can't just vomit it out when and if it makes you sick. You can't have it cut out. You can't irradiate it or chemotherapy it. You, me, we've got stuff inside us that comes from so once-upon-a-time ago it would revolt you. Gaping Adder. Redendums. Faltnow. Eviscer. Cannantrum. Plooblus. Dreckersluff. Shiessvol. No, you never heard of them. But you're carrying one or another of them, maybe a bunch of them, a bouquet. Yes, you're a carrier. We all are. For instance, faltnow mutated into Drenda fever, killed most of Eastern Europe circa A.D. 800. Could happen again. You could be the one who had the ancestor who ate the faltnow. It was very cold that year and he was especially hungry and he really pigged out storing up as much as he could.

Why can't people believe poison can live inside us forever and ever?

And that the male is its primary transmitter?

Picture this:

There is a Them in the goldmonkeys' midst. A bigger and hairier, taller and ganglier Them. A greenmonkey. Only one. It only takes one. Goldmonkeys are afraid of Others. The greenmonkey is doing something to the youngest and smallest goldmonkey. What he is doing to her is killing her. Her little life movements are petering out.

Her family watch the terrified jerkings of this tiniest of tiny things, of her scrawny legs and tiny feet up in the air, scratching for space, clawing for purchase. The other goldmonkeys around that day, family, friends, passing relatives, stop to watch, and start to poke at each other and scratch themselves, which is the way they express their sadness—goddammit, they don't know death but they do know harm: they anticipate it: they can feel its electricity in the air, which they ground, release, in just this way, scratching here and there, under the arms, under the nipples, scratching each other on their chests, their backs, or reaching their arms up in the air, toward the sky, a sky they can hardly see through the masses of leaves and trees, pointing, grasping at nothing that can be held on to.

Yes, they can feel sad! Oh, the superior posturing of stupid people that denies my monkeys this! They can't remember much, they can't understand birth, death, but they can, for the moment, for a moment, feel sad. No naysaying can prove I'm wrong.

Oh, what is it all in aid of? All my work and rantings. Who is there to listen? I am an aging man howling against the unbreachable walls of incorrect "knowledge" and the silences of too much time. Do you care about any of this? Who are you anyway? Never know my audience. None of us ever does. Talk to strangers, we do. Over and over. Why not? No one else to talk to. Lonely work, this is. Glad you came around.

My poor little monkeys. Who will fight for you when I am gone?

Why is there always someone in power to say it isn't so? Why is it always up to the powerless to have to prove everything only to have it disproved again, "this time irrefutably," by those who originally named it wrong? And who don't have to prove you wrong, only have to say you're not right. All they have to do is say nay. Nay, nay, and they throw everything into doubt. There's always someone to deny the truth. That's the Primate Society for you. It's ruled by Dr. Francine Punic, who is certifiable and used to be my wife.

The little baby girl goldmonkey is dying because the huge hairy greenmonkey has inserted his penis into her tiny vagina and he is fucking her to death.

Her father or protector or familyperson does try to stop the greenmonkey from doing this. This protector tries to stop the greenmonkey from feeling good, from releasing and spreading his genes. This protector goldmonkey snatches his (or her) little baby up into his arms and cradles her and licks her. Saliva is like dog's piss. It's a monkey marker. But the greenmonkey must show who's boss. He'd better do it quick. The goldmonkey is loping away with his baby. The greenmonkey runs after the goldmonkeys and grabs the little baby back.

Now the family must watch as the greenmonkey enters the little baby again. The goldmonkeys see the penis of the greenmonkey grow and grow. This time his huge penis grows and grows to be thicker and wider than the baby herself, and longer. This little baby is impaled like a tiny pigeon by an elephant. Soon the greenmonkey exhibits overwhelming shivers and agitations. The greenmonkey's penis is so engorged that even though it is about to explode it won't detumesce completely back to normal for days or weeks.

The little baby is dead, of course. How could it not be? The little baby is dead but not only from this act. Greenmonkey semen contains a component that is inhospitable to the goldmonkey system. It has something in it that can fell trees, make them die. This component, call it a poison, call it Vel, call it a virus, call it Absalom or Ishmael, one drop of it alone, its pre-ejaculate alone, would have killed Little She without the heaving heavy greenmonkey falling on top of her and smothering her at the same time that his huge engorged unrelenting penis erupted inside her so mightily. The greenmonkey starts walking clumsily, the dead little girl still impaled on his penis. But she is slipping off and his penis is slithering out, releasing not only her but an awful lot of his semen, which comes gushing out onto the ground. It is like he is pissing semen. The pool from this semen, which will penetrate the earth and kill the roots of trees for generations to come so that there will be no more trees growing on this spot, or plant life, only dried arid sandstone, and eventually some of those erovonous deciduous maltreasons, forms a Rubicon the goldmonkeys won't cross. They stare at it as if it contains radioactive magnetic fields keeping them at bay, which in a sense it does. These goldmonkeys are seeing something in the wash of that ejaculate which says Do not cross this line.

The greenmonkey fucker bends and starts to lick Little She clean and then bites off her tiny hand. Which he swallows. How does he know to do that? To take a bite. Only a bite. They always take only a bite of their victim's body. Then he runs away. Greenmonkeys always run away. He doesn't walk. He runs. He runs away.

But he's eaten some of her. Whatever was hers now is his. That is, his ejaculate poisoned her and now he's eaten her. No, he can't poison himself back. That would be too logical.

The goldmonkeys all gather now and take their dead-now once-upon-a-time and they sit around her for several days. Then they too eat her up, as is the custom. Who knows where it came from or how they remember to do it each time. Who knows how to really study memory? So long ago. And as they eat her up, other monkeys, goldmonkeys and blackmonkeys and brownmonkeys and spotted monkeys and striped monkeys and every-which-way-except-greenmonkeys, come from all over this jungle that in not so many centuries will be called the Everglades, Florida, U.S.A., and they stand around in a circle and they jerk off. First they take a tiny bite of the dead baby goldmonkey. That little bite is for them an act of hospitality or acknowledgment of bereavement, like the passing of food at a wake or like eating the Host at Mass. Then they start rubbing themselves with pieces of her bloody flesh, as if they were using soap or unguent or perfume or holy water, which we'll learn to use ourselves one day as invitations of welcome to each other. And then they start playing with themselves, masturbating themselves. All in a group! One big group made up of lots of little groups, going back and forth, changing around, switching partners, tasting each other, a big buffet, a cafeteria, all kinds of foods, boys with girls and girls with boys and boys with boys and girls with girls, yep, a big buffet. And they do all this for days, for weeks, in some groupings I have witnessed, for month after month, and once—yes—for over one whole year. What else do monkeys have but time?

Why don't all the goldmonkeys die from eating the little one, so doused and infused with poison greenmonkey semen? Some of them will. They'll just fall over and their group will move on. The dead ones will be eaten by others. There's never enough food. To be shit out. There's always plenty of shit.

But many of them will be fine. Poisoned they may be, but most of them will just keep having sex and die of old age. We haven't figured that one out yet. Wonder if we ever will.

Sex is what holds the living together. In a group. In a family. Their glue. They fuck all the time, from the minute they get up, night and day, with their little ones often hanging on to them while they do it. Go to any zoo. Take a look. It's their main activity. For a while. They know what it means to feel good. They know that to get together and do this sort of thing makes them feel better than before they do it. We do the same thing! Touch your hard dick or your cunt when it's almost ready to pop and tell me it doesn't feel good.

You want to know why boys and men jerk off so much, often only with each other? They got genes inside them that got to get out. If the ladies won't let them near them, which for long periods of certain seasons they will not, then their genes inside them hurt to get out. This need for release is a powerful force. They've got to release their gism and that's why fidelity is such an ass-backward concept. Sure it's nice. But you die off being faithful. Yes you do. The faithful ones stop fucking fast enough. Their genes stop fighting for release. And pretty much no matter what, one day sadness comes and you don't want to fuck anymore and your line goes thin and then dries out.

Yes, evolution's sad.

Time tells you everything if you know how to look at your watch.

Listen to me! In this very way, in these very ways, was entry of one living organism facilitated by another living organism into another, entry of an organism so invisible it will take every one of all the trillion years before it will be identified, even though it has lived these many eons of monkey years and is still alive and healthy to this day.

Most of the goldmonkey population ended in a *Finnealizestung,* an inability to stop fucking, a perpetual orgy that terminates only in death. It's a German concept. Figures. If evolution doesn't get you one way it gets you another. Stopping fucking kills the line off and too much fucking kills the line off. That's what Pishky and Biggott wrote about in the book that got them heaved out of Yaddah, tenure or no. Have to watch out what we teach, teachers do. Yep, fuckers can fuck each other to death. Just like I hear all them faggots are doing now. In the case of faggots, I hope so. I hope they are doing that to themselves big-time. I hate faggots. In the case of my monkeys, I try not to look but of course I do. It's hard not to look when you love monkeys as much as I do. Although God knows I am looking with great energy for the cause of The Underlying Condition, and trying to be the Christian who can prove beyond a shadow of a doubt that this plague was started by queers, and I don't mean monkey queers, even if they are monkey queers. Maybe you'd call this a conflict of interest. Science is full of them. Just like the rest of the world.

One thing. Don't listen to epidemiologists. Bledd-Wrench is one, no matter what she calls herself. Epidemiology is the science of racism. Government invented epidemiology to protect the rich whities. It demands a yardstick that measures and separates people out only by the bad things they've done, or that happened to them, and then tries to isolate them from everyone else, who are suddenly defined as healthy. No such thing as healthy. Really isn't. Important point. Bet you don't remember it. Everyone's sick in one way or another. Yep, bet you forget that. We're all sickies.

Even if the host is dead, poison lives. Poisons live.

Poisons live forever. The two biggest mouths of the moment aren't telling you this.

But rest assured, eat shit we all have done. How long our journey through life takes depends on which shit we've eaten. In this resides the secret of life and death. When man arrives, monkeys want to be his friend. But man eats them. Which is not a good thing for man to have done. Or do.

There must come a moment when each of us accepts that we are carriers of death. Try getting that into *The New York Truth*. Try getting that into the literature. Funny expression, "into the literature." As if we must be Tolstoys to be heard. Truth. All fuckers fuck each other to death. Carriers. We're all carriers. Secret to life. Secret to death. No big secret.

Prove me wrong.

Remember this: most of our genes had evolved before we separated from the apes and we thus share 99.5 percent of our evolutionary history with the chimpanzees. Mind you, we also share 70 percent of our genetic material with sea sponges. There you have it.

•

STOP PRESS:

> Forget what you've heard about human beings having descended from the apes. We didn't descend from the apes. We *are* apes. Metaphorically and factually, *Homo sapiens* is one of the five surviving species of great apes, along with chimpanzees, bonobos, gorillas, and orangutans. We shared a common ancestor with two of these apes—bonobos and chimps—just five million years ago.
>
> (Ryan and Jetha, *Sex at Dawn*, 2010)

ENTER VELMA DIMLEY

When it is pointed out to Dr. Dripper by Velma Dimley, the intrepid science reporter for *The New York Truth*, at the 7th Annual Conference for Primates and Judaism (not so farfetched as it may seem, but not right now), that his monkeys sound like they're gay, Dr. Dripper, looking from side to side, and behind him, and up to heaven, replies hoarsely: "It's a bind, let me tell you. It's not so black and white, you know!" He has tears in his eyes. "Male monkeys hang out together because females are out fucking like crazy. Hilda Chimp fucked with sixty-eight males in the last three days. That's why males stick together. Fags can call it homosexual. I call it self-protection! Who's got a strong enough sense of self to withstand the competition of sixty-eight other dicks?"

"That doesn't sound like competition to me. It sounds like it's about having enough patience to stand in line." Velma looks up from, as always, taking copious notes.

"No, sir. No, sirree. How big are your boyfriend's balls?"

"That's none of your business."

"Then you ain't getting laid much, I expect."

"What's the size of balls got to do with it?"

"The bigger the balls, the hungrier the sperm. Chimps have got gigantic balls, so they got to relieve themselves or it hurts something awful. You never heard of 'lover's nuts'? If they got no women, what's left but their fellow chimp?"

"That does not sound very scientific." She stops her note taking. She slams her pad closed.

"You still think there's such a thing as scientific? After all I have said and written? Guess you're not one of the hundred and sixty-three people who bought my book."

Dr. Dripper looks very tired. He is ready to return into the mist of the palma negrita overarchers, another favorite tree that has survived the centuries in his part of the Everglades. He starts to leave the auditorium.

But then he comes back for another word with Velma, and with those at every conference who always gather around her in admiring worship, picking up her words like edible crumbs. She is, after all, and will remain, Velma Dimley of *The New York Truth*.

Bosco gets these final words out with difficulty because he is still in tears. "You're going to say that UC comes from my poor monkeys. And my poor monkeys will be besmirched forever. I know what besmirched feels like. It can ruin your whole life. What do I think it all means? I think it means you don't know enough yet to besmirch anything. My ex-wife, Francine 'My Poopsie' Punic, now so generously funded by the University of Southern Jewry, of course is saying just what you want to hear. That Dr. Dripper's fairy monkeys started it all. And Ms. Velma Dimley of *The New York Truth* is here gathering the quotes and making up the story. And Bosco, and Bosco's monkeys, are besmirched."

His eyes are scrunched so tightly that one wonders how he can see as he walks past us all, and out.

QUESTIONS ON THE TABLE

First of all, how do you do?
> **I am very fine, thank you very much.**
> **I am your Underlying Condition.**
> **I am happy to meet you.**
> **I would like to start our relationship by asking the following two questions, which I hope are mature and intelligent and well-phrased:**

Do you really think that a monkey eating a monkey thousands of years ago is enough to start an end-of-it-all plague that will embrace a world as big as this one? That is my first question.

Think carefully before you answer, please.

My second question is this: Do you really think it's possible to single out the murderer and the murder weapon, that mysteries and medicine share such narrative similarities?

You really don't have to answer any of this now. I will find you. We will stay in touch.

These were the years of my early hardship you are writing about. I was still trying to find my voice.

But who was there to hear me? I was only still a kid.

Can you hear me, even now?

Well, let me tell you something.

I was in those monkeys.

How much you wanna bet?

Let me ask you one last question:

Why should you be the only ones to seek immortality?

INTRODUCING DAME LADY HERMIA BLEDD-WRENCH

With a good deal more to say than the usually taciturn Dr. Dripper is Dame Lady Hermia Bledd-Wrench, whom Fred has known since his days in London, where he fell in love with her spirit, her zest for life, and her unquenchable quest for knowledge. Her many-titled name, which she delights in flaunting, she explains thusly: "Because I am prominent and have achieved, I have been honored by my Queen and am entitled to be called Dame Hermia Bledd. Because I married a knight, I am also Lady Hermia Wrench. But obviously I prefer to be recognized for my own name and not that of a husband. So in order to be deferential to both entitlements (being Lady Wrench was no easy gig), I am Dame Lady Hermia Bledd-Wrench, to be called all of which I am aware is absurd. But I enjoy being absurd. I revel in being absurd. The world is absurd and I am at home in the world, as most people are not. Without shocks people tend to fall asleep. I choose to think one of my missions is to wake them up.

"Of course I am never as shocking as I want to be. England allows one to go only so far, which is why I moved to America.

"For you see, I believe totally in the concept of Evil.

"It is important that America learns about Evil.

"You are the fount from which all atrocities flow."

Dame Lady Hermia is a professor on the faculty of the Sir John Greeting Institute of Worldwide Medical Knowledge of All Peoples, in London, as well as its American outpost, the Lady Jane Greeting Institute of Worldwide Medical Knowledge of All Peoples, in Nearodell, South Carolina. She earned firsts from Oxford and Cambridge in the Philosophy of Medicine and History, and in the Anthropology of Science, and she is a pioneer in the field of what is now known as Unknown Law, which she teaches at Yaddah. England prizes itself on such jacks-of-all-trades, polymaths they are often called, although rarely accepting them when they are women, another reason for her transferring her energies stateside. "I also have scads of honorary degrees. Honoraria flock to one like gnats in summer if you are prominent. So few people measure up anymore that the few of us who do are like rare birds that must be found and fed while we still fly. All of this is like armor: it's all very heavy but one feels protected, especially here, in your country, where such effluvia is impressive."

She has always been known in England for *Guess What?*, her exceedingly popular fifteen-minute (and very funny) radio program on the BBC, where she talks about whatever she wants to, which she still maintains is "human nature." It brought her fame, fortune, and her DBE. Fred, during his London years, many of which found him quite depressed, tried never to miss it. It cheered him then and she does the same for him now. She still records her fifteen minutes every day, "seven days a week, we never sleep, from here, the enemy terrain, where I now, as your people succinctly put it, hang out."

Her great text, known and used to this day in academies around the world and into its umpteenth edition, is *The Evil That Men Do: Plagues and People I Have Known and You Should, Too.*

And her husband, Sir Wally Wrench? "I left him in Britain with all the other boring men."

A REJOINDER TO BOSCO, A PLEA TO FRED, AND THEN SOME, FROM "A BIGGEST MOUTH OF THE MOMENT," DAME LADY HERMIA

I must register a few words of protest.

First of all, I hope you can see how much Dr. Bosco Dripper, D.V.M., hates women. I hope you can see that. Louis Leakey, the great paleoanthropologist, believed that women would be best suited to studying primates in the wilderness, in the jungles, because we have greater patience and greater sensitivity to the social nuances of what we would be able to observe. It was he who made it possible for women to get going in this field, no thanks to Bosco Dripper and Yaddah. Jane Goodall had no scientific training and was almost childlike in her sensitivity to the particularity of what she was observing. She followed her chimps over much terrain and over long periods of time. While Bosco joins her in his gift for knowing one from another, not that he gives her her due, or any woman her due, he cannot approach Jane in fully perceiving the close bonds between mothers and their children.

For many years little attention was paid to primate relationships with human beings, as if such relationships did not exist. It was Jane who showed us how much apes could teach us about ourselves. Later observations by Dorothy Cheney et al. would focus attention on baboons' ability to manage and sustain rather intricate relationships in large groups of up to 150 members. Bosco says it can be very stressful to be a male, because to have sex with a female depends on just where the male is in the female pecking order, so to speak, and because the female is better at keeping things in check. It really must be pointed out and underscored and double-underscored what a misogynist he is. No wonder Francine flew his coop. No wonder all those women members of the Primate Society cast him out and asunder.

Bushwah, I say to Dr. Dripper. Bushwah! All male chimps are monsters! They rape female chimps without surcease. After they have chummed around and buddied around and copulated around with each other! They are male bonders par excellence and to the utmost sexist level. As far as they're concerned, females are solely for the delivery of babies, preferably male ones, to add to Daddy's voracious appetite for further buddies. And only an ignoramus would claim that a monkey's homosexual actions and needs and deeds are not homosexual at all and let it go simply at that.

All of this has been made to sound so sweet and Bambi, and it isn't. It is what wretchedly putrid male monkeys get away with, and I say it reeks.

And by the by, Frederick, do you have anyone considering that something predated the Everglades primates? Who is your dinosaur expert? Where did all the dinosaurs disappear to? Did *Tyrannosaurus rex* harbor The Underlying Condition? Surely one of these days an ambitious historian will come up with earlier chapters hitherto buried in some out-of-the-way cave. Sit tight. Someone is always finding a few new old pieces of paper that toss the previous entire course of events right out the window.

Frederick, I hope that you are not one of those who is determined to find wrong in everything, and from the very outset. There is wrong in everything. But you must give cognizance to the fact that there are always other things on the agenda (whatever the agenda is) and that this agenda is always enormous. It is always impossibly arduous to get to the head of the line. Any line. Science and medicine—coupled not incongruously as S&M—are always busy elsewhere, and to redirect them from one agenda to another is akin to personally lifting elephants.

I admire the nerve of your undertaking. I am happy to contribute to what I can already see could be a useful if overly ambitious history of your country, and of this Underlying Condition. I accept your invitation.

SO LET US WEND OUR WAY

I gather, Fred, that you are opening yourself up to the pungent presence of my cousin, Dr. Sister Grace Hooker. Although our family history is intertwined, your American Hookers are not so ancient as our British Bledds by several long shots. The English have always believed that endurance is superior to all. Like you, Grace will no doubt highlight what will be the central controversy of this plague, and that is its irrefutable bonding with the issue of homosexuality.

I must confess that up to the time I settled in America I had given only vague thought to the homosexual aspect of human nature. While I've since discovered that most Americans believe most British men are and always have been what we call poofters, I, who was born there, and lived there in what we may call an active fashion, never gave this aspect of my homeland a moment's thought or notice. When an American epidemiologist at your Center of Disease first asked me, "Well, you have some cases over there in gay men, don't you?" I had to stop in my tracks and say to myself, "Hermia, indeed you must." As we are a much older culture, no one in England thinks much about poofters and fairies, or what you call faggots and queers. Every family has them. They are all over the place. We simply do not think about it. I say this, even though I admit I am not unmindful of an Earl of Dudley's famous outburst to the House of Lords: "I cannot stand homosexuals. They are the most disgusting people in the world. I loathe them. Prison is much too good a place for them."

My continuing education in these matters was really spurred on a few months ago when, upon a visit home, my director at the Sir John Greeting Institute of Worldwide Medical Knowledge of All Peoples, Sir Polkham Treadway, called me into his office.

"Lookee here," he said. "Greeting US wants you to write a definitive history of The Underlying Condition."

GUS is for the moment the world's largest pharmaceutical manufacturer.

"GUS would allow GUK to do that?"

Greeting UK is our institute's parent and principal benefactor. It no longer exists as a separate company, having been bought out so many times that now it is called . . . oh, it no longer matters what it's called. Greeting UK exists now only on paper and only by the fact that the considerable amount of stock it still holds is what supports the work of our estimable institutes. Early in the last century Lord Greeting had founded the company with another American, Tobias Evermore. Greeting Evermore was not a happy union. Each desired to murder the other, which result was prevented by the death of Evermore, allowing Henry Greeting to become Sir and then his Lordship. And even after separation and then the split of American and British (save for the institutes, which remain a joint affair), as in all unhappy families, much bad blood remains.

"It is perplexing," said my British director.

He handed me a letter.

My dear Sir Polkham—,

In my position as Chairperson of the Combined Worldwide Greeting Medical Trusts, and supported by our Ethical and Academic Advisory Boards, and as the Joint Chairperson with you of the Lady Jane Greeting Institute of Worldwide Medical Knowledge of All Peoples, I am authorized by my people here to put forth to the Sir John Greeting Institute of the History of the World's Medical Knowledge of All Peoples a request for our joint compilation and writing of an unequivocal, full-out, no-holds-barred History of The Underlying Condition.

We at GUS are fully aware that such a history must of necessity uncover much that is uncomfortable. But we sense that others are sniffing at our heels, particularly one Fred Lemish, a notorious troublemaker here on our side of the pond, but smart and infamously persistent. It is, after all, a tremendous story waiting to explode in somebody's telling. Why his? Why not ours?

Thus we deem it best to write this history now lest it be worse for our side should others get there first. We would be delighted if Dame Lady Hermia Bledd-Wrench were to be available to undertake this assignment. She certainly would look out for our best interests.

Long live your Queen.

Mt. Vernon Pugh

Chairperson

Combined Trusts

Nearodell, South Carolina

Well, we shall see.

Upon my return to America I found another offer awaiting me.

My dearest Hermia——:

I have the perfect assignment for you! One that I've been searching for forever! It is challenging! It is controversial! It will make everyone hideously angry! And jealous! And you a household word in this country and at last! Which is of course what I have been longing for you! I cannot wait to tell you about my new endeavor! Ring immediately upon receipt and/or return, whichever occurs first!

Eternal love!

Hadriana

I must confess to a certain fondness for this silly woman so many Americans find so fascinating. I've known Hadriana Totem since she was a student, and a most promising one, at Lady Mary's Hospital for the Infirm, where I was on the board. Like so many impressionable girls, she was interested briefly in nursing, before she ran off to marry Lord Totem, rather much older than she. Lord Totem is what we call a "press baron." His many newspapers and magazines are a wretched, tawdry lot, and read each day by a depressingly large percentage of my countrymen. Hadriana, who edited the British *This & That* for him, was offered the editorship of *The New Gotham*, in New York, of course, a particular favorite plaything of Totem's American counterpart, Mr. Swift Merchant. She undertook and proceeded to make it into a rather lively journal, if not as distinguished as it was before Mr. Merchant's purchase of it. When she sensed it was time to move on, she embarked upon the establishment of her own publication, which she insisted upon calling *Scream and Shout*. This enterprise failed. She misjudged by a wide margin America's skills in either activity. There is word that Swift misses her, that he is unhappy with *The New Gotham*'s current editor, Byron Remnant, who has turned her rather jolly effort into a rather bloodless one, and stodgy, quite stodgy. I told you I knew everything worth knowing! I suspect, though, that she had become too full of herself, a quality not unknown in her class and upbringing, and her husband's.

When we met (in the quite splendid Park Avenue penthouse she shares with Lord Totem, who, after attempting several histories of America himself, is now, I am afraid, rather tottering about), she challenged me to write a history of The Underlying Condition that proves it to be intentional genocide, my account of which she would then publish in "its perfect media home, which I am in the process of setting up."

Well, we shall see.

I go into such detail to warn you there are wolves in the hills and we'd best proceed apace and with speed.

Yes, I prefer you, dear man.

You have told me, dear Frederick, that you question my undeniable connection with Greeting Pharmaceuticals, against which you seem to have sworn a very great revenge. Allow me to suggest that this connection may prove of some considerable use to you, especially given the offer I have to write the Greeting History of The Underlying Condition, as well as Hadriana's desired exposé, which does in fact appeal.

Yes, we shall see. Together.

I'm grateful, as I indicated, that you ferreted out this member of the Empire. Challenge is my middle name! I shall try to provide you, to the best of my ability, with the best bang for your buck. Show me a plague and I'll show you the world! It will give me great and inestimable pleasure to prove that your country caused this one.

Again, let us wend our way. Forthwith!

DAME LADY HERMIA TALKS ABOUT PLAGUES

I have been in love with plagues for as long as I can remember. Plagues were the most formative subject of my young life. All that death and destruction seemingly out of nowhere! Could it have been stopped? I devoured all I could learn. All the great books about plagues—Trondheim's *Filth Through the Ages*, Desredorer's *Diary of an Incessant Scavenger*, Knorr and Pugit's *While the World Sleeps*, Peliculosa's *Encyclopedia of Dangerous Diseases and Discordant Deaths*, Irving's *Rambles in Ancient Infected Byways*—were all written by Englishmen. The more recent have been insistent, in dissecting the origins of so many of the world's ills, upon blaming them on others, including you. We have never stopped being sore losers. It's easier to blame others than to face up to how we brought things upon ourselves—for instance, why was there ever an American Revolution?

England has always been the center of the world's knowledge of plagues. Since Britain has been exposed to "every poop and pisspot on the seven seas," as my old sailing great-uncle Silas Wrench-Fergit described the world he'd sailed, it fell to us to flaunt this knowledge. I studied under the renowned Sir Godfrey Klingdot, later Lord Gwelph, at his iconoclastic laboratory at St. Simon's on the Wharf. Among the first to join together the study of social behavior and disease, "attempting," as he put it, "to keep God and the Bible out of it," Sir Godfrey encouraged my love of plagues and made me unashamed of what I'd been afraid was an abnormal absorption in what the rest of the world was avoiding like—well, the plague. It was he who taught me that society and plagues go hand in hand, the latter often springing from an exuberance of what the former is up to and should not have been up to. Additionally, hard as it is to believe, medicine can sometimes actually cause what it's pledged to assuage. Medicine can be very sloppy, inexact, a cesspool of both germs and carriers, its practitioners, in their quest for knowledge, plunging their arms right down to the bottom of vats and pits and bringing forth yet more infectious glop and grunge. Many a medicine man can be a very participant in the illness he's tracking, like a Sherlock Holmes. Grace's Hermatros is certainly one of those, though do not dare to quote me.

Learning all of this, little by little, is what inspired me to add historical epidemiology to my repertoire of expertise. The history of epidemics. The history of plagues. Epidemiology is the study of how disease affects groups of people. It is both dreadfully challenging and, as Grace would say, and indeed has said, and will say again, I am certain, dreadfully full of s——t. It's another one of those "What is truth?" activities so likely to come up with the wrong answers. Like numbers. Numbers are often no more than a pile of rubbish. You can make numbers tell you anything.

But it has become increasingly clear to me that paths of right have most often been walked by the solitary individual, usually when nobody else speaks up. It has also become increasingly and uncomfortably clear that it is not necessarily good history, or better science, or the best mathematics, to believe something to be "true" just because a path has been walked by a group or stampeded by hordes. Ten people can say the same thing or ten people can say ten different things. The conclusion that must be drawn, hence, by any intelligent person (but has yet to be made by even the laziest intellectual) is best stated in these words of Dr. David Byar, the maverick NITS statistician, in *The New England Journal of Statistical Intervention*: "Ten people can lie just as easily as one person can tell the truth." This of course calls into question the very heart of epidemiology, the very methodology of every study—scientific or medical or statistical or what you will—whose author feels it imperative, indeed feels commanded by tradition, indeed bound by it for fear of excommunication, to cite at least several sources for every fact in search of a perfect pedigree. Dr. Byar's calculations are hot stuff indeed, received most frigidly. As I know he has recently died from UC and that you and he were friends, you and I must do him proud in promulgating his revelatory results and following our own parade. If you take the murky essence of what Dr. Dripper has whined on about and add to it the unwholesome nutrients of what Grace will shortly try to feed you, you can see how someone can come to have an intellectual constitution as strong as mine. I believe it's all about that fighting back you Yanks showed me. From the very beginning you have been so good at it! One must say what one must say! One must not be passive and colonial!

Well, we shall see.

Or I must append here, we won't.

Onward!

America has been plague-ridden from the get-go. America has always been extraordinarily deficient in looking after its health. So many of you are sick with things you shouldn't be. I have never been in a "civilized" country where so many inhabitants are suffering from something they can't name, don't know anything about, and refuse to find any help for. You don't like to talk out loud about what pains you, only what bothers you about someone else. Disease, illness—the more serious, the more so—is grounds for the Whisper. "He's got shhhh!" "She's got psssst!" Our noble English language, which we handed to you on a silver platter, doesn't work well in your country when it comes to your health. Most foreign indicia go denied for way too long. No wonder something naughty in the bloodstream such as appears to exist at the present time can spread so wildly unattended to. We Brits are just the reverse: the moment we smell a skunk we raise the alarm. We are a very suspicious people. That is why we have survived so long.

True, doctors everywhere form the principal population of those in denial. God forbid doctors should take sides and render strong opinions out loud. A doctor must always hedge his bets. Just in case. Mind you, the singular lack of curiosity on the part of most people everywhere is distressing, although Americans in particular, and on the whole, are a most incurious people. You consider curiosity impolite. How curious. You stuff yourselves with facts and starve yourself of the truth.

We are dealing with Big Questions here. Your country is not very good at Big Questions. They tend to become little questions after Important People, like presidents, get to work on ignoring, nay denying, them. You'll see.

Yours is a country of death, you know. You'll see.

A few words on "contagious" vs. "communicable." Much has been made down through the ages about the distinction between these two presumably differing modes of transmission. You're supposed to be terrified if something is contagious and only concerned if it's just something you might catch. I have difficulty seeing much difference. Definitions, like statistics, like numbers, are the most malleable of tools and are most often bent out of shape by those with the most to hide (such as their ignorance), or gain (such as from their manipulation of truths). A particle of death is a particle of death, air is air, touching is touching, and the rest is luck. And history. History is really nothing but a history of good luck or bad luck. God forbid anyone should admit this. We would all be out of work.

There have been many plagues of communicable contagion. There have been plagues spread via lessards, and nostremes, and redaltase (all technical terms for conveyance mechanisms). Plagues of dirt and mud and, of course, sex. Most plagues, though, are usually defined by location, which gives us both a certain amount of and not nearly enough information. More and more we can now plot arrivals and (it is to hoped) departures geographically through the centuries. The great plagues of northern Greenland, of the west of Nepal, of the Outer Banks of Upper Volta, of medieval Bruges, of Renaissance Italy south of the river Debbo, these are just a few identifiable plagues that come to mind which are still attributed to unknown causes. Lisbon-outside-the-walls sometime in the fifteenth century, eastern Yorkshire and western Scotland not long after, could these two have been connected? You see what I mean. Indeed, one of these days we may find a way to connect all of these dots. Indeed, dear Dr. Dripper would have us believe that no plague ever ends. And much as I dislike the man, he cannot be completely refuted in this thinking. Everyone has been infecting everyone else since the Garden of Eden. Of course we are all connected! Alas, it is up to us to figure out how and why. And few of us really want to sort all that out. It behooves me to say I have no notion why.

Most people think that tropical medicine, under which rubric plagues are often grouped for intensive study, is about anything unhealthy you bring back from a foreign shore while on holiday. No, tropical medicine concerns itself with the bringing back from there of something—invariably troublesome—that's indigenous to there and doesn't belong here. Rather like illegal immigrants. But it has to come from there. It has to originate there. Someplace other than here. It's a most discriminatory definition, I know: having a special branch just for exotic illegal immigrants is rather dismissive of those legal immigrants at home in Hove. But that's the British for you. If they'd all wanted to stay in Hove they would have stayed in Hove.

And then, of course, once it's been brought back here, what do you do with it? How do you care for it, make it better, cure it even, dispose of it if it's going to be intractable, or worse, deal with it if it's ineradicable? In other words, how do you stop it from spreading? That's the hardest part of all and the part we're all so bad at, even we Brits.

And now we have another plague, The Underlying Condition, of which so much one day will be made and so little, yet again, is known. Where did this one come from? Is there a soupçon of Lisbon-outside-the-walls mixed in with a few drops of the river Debbo? Can its dots be connected back to earlier American plagues?

And has anything from over there ever made it over here?

And if it hasn't, why hasn't it?

And if it has, what is it?

And the reverse: Did anything from here make it over there? Only to be brought back here in return?

With the exception of Bosco and Grace and Drs. Israel Jerusalem and yours truly, why are so few people of prominence studying any of this? Oh, there are a few but they are so inferior.

How do we know there was anything in existence in America so long ago?

I answer: Because if we had them over there you had them over here.

People. Not monkeys. People.

And if we did, how much of what we had became what you had?

Where are those ancient people? Where are their voices? Where are your early people who can write? Why is it only Britain and the Continent that produce entities who pass on information to their future? We have Chronicles from every direction—Anglo-Saxon, French Moribute, Belgian Krechters, Spanish Infitadas, Italian Gothers, Scandinavian Orthods—that never-endingly tell us volumes of what went on long before the birth of Christ. There may not yet have been nationalities called by these precise names, but on the other side of the Atlantic we had divisions of voice and accent long before the first year of the Christian era. You cannot even rouse much of a peep over here before the fifteenth century. What happened to the Voices of America: the voices of those Kennewicks, those Clovises, those Folsoms, those Jomons, those Hopewells, to throw out just a few? How were they silenced so completely? How could you have lost so many people? For they were indeed lost, not nonexistent. Why are you so perennially incurious?!

Life flourished on your continent long before it flourished on mine! Where is the American domination in archaeology, in linguistics? You have bones so ancient they make Stonehenge appear a modern miracle. Mammoth bones in the Yukon 28,000 years ago. Mammal bones in Colorado 17,000 years ago. Tools in Wisconsin mud lakes 17,000 years ago. Basketry in Pennsylvania 17,500 years ago. Blades from Virginia 19,000 years ago. Tools in South Carolina, stakes and carved shells in Florida, stone tools in Florida and Missouri. Human bones in Nebraska 22,000 years ago. Human hair in New Mexico . . . The list is endless and rapidly accumulating. Did these people not speak? Somewhere along the way there must have been, and be still, records of their deeds and thoughts. Somewhere in your earth, deep in your dirt, deep in your heart, there must be emblematic reservoirs of human deeds and thoughts and strivings from all of these eras.

Where is this heart of yours?

Where is it?

These voices remain silenced.

What was it that quieted them?

Plague was plague before America was America. Is that why no one here gives what Dr. Sister Grace calls a hartz? Like Jesus' birth, must your own be deemed immaculate? If you discover even earlier Indians, will more clamoring descendants crop up to claim your cornfields for craps tables? Why are you so uninterested in America before it was America? America was here before America was here and you are dumb Dickies if you don't accept and understand that. Listen to Bosco. Listen to Grace. Listen to Israel. Listen to Hermia. We are all crazy as loons and hate each other's guts, but at least on this point we agree. You and all you came from and stand for and will pass on to the future have been here much longer than you think.

Oh my, there's Ianthe pressing the life out of my doorbell. She's taking me on her Founders' Pass to see our Tate Turners on loan to your Mellon.

But rest assured, Frederick. I shall resume anon.

HOW FRED CAME TO KNOW DR. SISTER GRACE HOOKER

Another double-barreled female dynamo Fred sought is Dr. Sister Grace Hooker, whom he also cherishes. She was, in fact, his childhood babysitter. She is, in fact, as well as in coincidence, a distant cousin of Dame Lady Hermia's.

Dr. Sister Grace Hooker claims, nay guards, her position as "still one of the world's most eminent experts in Infectious Diseases" (*Time*, Oct. 3, 1987; *New England Journal of Infectious Diseases*, March 19, 1997).

She grew up, as did Fred, in Masturbov Gardens, a large garden-apartment development just outside of Washington, D.C. Her parents were dead. She lived on family money but she was not yet rich. She lived alone. She was fourteen when they died in what was said to be an automobile accident; in fact they committed suicide by taking poison and driving over a low cliff in Masturbov Park. Because Grace looked older than her fourteen years and was especially self-sufficient, and did not want to move until she finished Lord of Mercy High School, no one said anything about her single occupancy. Various relatives and lawyer types came and went and vouched for her. There, in Masturbov Gardens, she (and Fred) knew many who would come to be key players in the plague of The Underlying Condition. She knew the twins, Daniel and David Jerusalem. She knew Dr. Dodo Geiseric and did not trust him from the beginning. She knew nasty Arnold Botts and never trusted him either. She was fat and jolly and let everyone pull her pigtails. The kids called her Pudgy Waffle. When they were twelve or thirteen she traded Fred a dim photograph of somebody's erect penis for four Tootsie Rolls, which tells you how little use she had for a penis, even then, and how much Fred did. After she came into the first portion of what would become her great inheritance, her share of Massachusetts Waste Company (renamed First Boston Industries), she moved away from Masturbov Gardens, and the next time any of the gang heard about her she'd become a famous doctor, a great and world-renowned scientist, and a nun. Everyone thought it a big waste, having all that money and not spending it. Somewhere along the years she lost her left arm.

Dr. Sister Grace Hooker discovered Vel, which brought her an additional great fortune. She has won, among other honors, three Radichers, two Venslaws, and yes, one Nobel, for Vel. She is extremely protective of her work, carefully surveying scientific journals on guard against outright pilferage— or just tiny spots of unacknowledged borrowing. "I do not trust scientists because I am one." Before this plague of The Underlying Condition is over, she, with Dr. Israel Jerusalem, will win another Nobel, although Israel will be in prison when this happens.

Mater Nostra Dolorosa Medical Center in the Northeast quadrant of Washington maintains, barely, its fame and nobility because of Dr. Sister Grace, thus helping to keep the deteriorating neighborhood more or less safe. This once-great institution where Ferva taught, where DeMillie discovered radium struts, where seven Nobels were claimed by long-forgotten names, and which has been blessed by four popes, approaches collapse. It really should be torn down, but the diocese, the hospital, and the city can't afford to do it. The Sisters of Most Pious Sequentia are, of all orders, the one that has always trafficked in the greatest adversities—though Grace wants everyone to know "I am a shitty fucking awful nun."

Her habit hides her age. "Let's just say I'm as old as my fucking country," she roars. She has the mouth of a sailor. No, she has a mouth worse than any sailor's.

Her own great work, also extensively utilized around the world, and into its umpteenth edition, is *Science, Medicine, and History.*

COINCIDENCE?

It may seem wildly coincidental that Fred Lemish's childhood babysitter and a chum from London should not only be cousins but both become so instrumental in helping him sort out this plague, but there you have it.

Indeed, Fred has often reflected on the uncanny intersection of his life with so many of those now in a position to affect the course of The UC. There you have that, as well.

THE CAUSE AS ENUNCIATED BY THAT OTHER "BIGGEST MOUTH OF THE MOMENT," DR. SISTER GRACE HOOKER

Amoebas, piss, and shit. The Big Three. And taking it up the ass. The Four Horsemen. That's what this shit's all about, Freddie. It's as all-American as fucking apple pie.

No one knows whether to call me Sister Grace or Dr. Grace or Sister Dr. Grace or Dr. Sister Grace. No one's ever sure, which is the way I like it. And God hasn't confided in me which He prefers, which is the way I like it too. There's something about absolute certainty that closes off real communion. But you can call me Pudgy Waffle, Freddie, just like you used to do.

No, I don't want to go back. Not so many old farts say that, do they? It was butt rot then and it's worse now, so the present needs us more than the past. There's more than enough fucking disease to keep us up to the fucking minute and occupied for life.

Everything I discovered, about life, about me, I discovered in this ancient hive of cloistered cells I live and work in, here, in poopy Mater Nostra. No, that's a lie. I learned a lot before I got here that made me come to live here. But it's been here that I've had the peace to dream and achieve. Beakers and Bunsen burners? Now I have falangers and mefits and conconritons. Some of my instruments are older than I am. I have an original Krusti, for instance, which only has a half-inch spitz, which I still use. They all work. They've had to rewire twice to bring me enough electricity. I may have them rewire again so I can get into whatever's next. They never dare deny me anything. I make them too much money. Sister Perfervid Auchincloss's trust fund has dried up. I'm the only rich nun they have left.

Yes, disease is singular. It's all one disease. There hasn't been a single second of history when we haven't all been capable of killing each other.

I don't agree with that flea-bitten, tick-infested honking fuckface Bosco Dripper, with his obsession that it's only fucking chimps that's caused this. You listen to Bosco and you want to slit your wrists. Him and his fucking goddamn monkeys are too depressing and full of crap.

I try to ransack and learn from the past as much as Bosco does, as much as my dyspeptic dame of a cousin does, but I don't pander to it. I don't hate so many people. Well, maybe I do. It really is all about saving lives, you know. That often requires hating a person or two. I admit it. Shit, I glory in it!

As for Lady Buttinsky, I'm the important one in this particular family on either side of the ocean. What has she discovered to save a single person? Lifesavingwise, her past doesn't amount to what she would call a tinker's damn. If she won a Radicher or a Nobel I might listen to her. But I probably wouldn't. No prize is worth the piddling lead it's poured from, and certainly no prize is worth enough to listen to Lady Fart Catcher. God knows what she'll try to fatten you up with like a fucking Strasbourg duck.

The history of science is not like the history of history. History's too interested in why and science is too interested in what. But consequences are as important as causes. A plague that kills a billion people is a consequence far more troublesome to deal with than looking for some ancient pussy that might have started it all and even if it did, so wanking what? Knowing it isn't going to cure those billion people. Knowing the origin of something is a tool-wanking dead-end waste of time. The door's shut by then. And because people are incurably dumb fucks they are not going to stop doing whatever they're doing that gets them into trouble in the first place just because you tell them what's killing them. Shit, they already know, down deep, and do it anyway. They don't care enough. There, in a nutshell, is the cause of almost all the crap since the beginning of Bosco's baby-chimp twat-chewing long-ago. Not caring enough. And what the fucking, pissing hell can you do with that? Monkeys then and since don't care.

There isn't ever really any beginning, if you want to be philosophically accurate about it. Each day is a new day, forever and ever and ever.

That is not to say there is no cause, no first thing, no First Frigging Principle.

But it is to say that our constant obsession with Fucking Firsts isn't always practical. Or profitable. Or accurate. One day one thing is the cause of a plague and the next day either it isn't or something's joined it. Or taken its place. Which is either worse or better.

And since everything did start a cocksucking long time ago, it's unreasonable to ask this new world to have saved all its pieces of old string and rusty nails so some old English auntie can rant on about plagues. Who gives a rat's ass about her rats' kaka? Today's fact may be yesterday's memory, but it's almost always tomorrow's mistake. Now, that is flowery, but it's true.

You may think I'm just profane, an old crone, an old nun, an old Puritan, an old American, an old bitch, an old slut, and yes an old dyke.

You wouldn't be wrong. But you wouldn't be right.

Now back to taking it up the ass. Dr. Sister Grace is going to tell you more than you want to know about the history of anal intercourse. I tell all my students who are squeamish they are just going to have to get used to the frank language of bodily functions if they want to study with me. All bodily functions. English is a very specific and fucking fantastic language and you have to respect that and try to meet it more than halfway. And listen to what it's telling you.

It's thought that America's belief system started with Pilgrims and Puritans—they're not the same, by the way; everyone uses these names so interchangeably and they shouldn't—but they weren't the first marauders of our land and souls, not by a long shot. The Spanish were here long before the English or the Dutch, and they were Catholics. I'm here to tell you Catholics, and especially Spanish Catholics, are shit-fire big-time killers. Columbus's journey coincided with the Spanish Inquisition, where those spics killed all the Jews in sight and an awful lot who weren't. The Spanish fucking hated Jews. You wonder why everyone goes on so just about Hitler. He's just another example of what I mean when I say, and say, and say again, there is never really any beginning. The Spanish had been over here and murdered half of South America and Mexico and every tribe of Indian they could find ages before there was any Germany. Good thing the Spanish disappeared. Not much interest as to why they disappeared. But they came back. Nothing so awfully shitty ever really goes away.

The early American Catholic Church bears little resemblance to today's. Back then, since it was a lot closer to his time on earth, Jesus Christ was a different force. He was more, how should I put it, suspect. The embracing of Jesus is so totally a modern contrition. I'm not certain anyone has a good answer as to why and how the hated and hateful early godawful Catholic

Church ever got a foothold in America that lasted. They probably bought it. That's how anybody usually gets anything. One of these days they're going to run out of money and an awful lot of men will have much too much free time on their hands. Dangerous, free time on your hands. You can only jerk off so often.

The two Catholic saints most popular in early America that you've never heard of?

Repolto Verginnis. Stupid fartface. He was canonized in the seventeenth century for helping to rid church properties of lust. Extremely practical. He preached that sleeping in a bed without a board down the middle separating husband and wife was a mortal sin. Every man and woman who lived in a building with four walls prayed to St. Repolto at least four times a day or their children would be born with genital warts. Genital warts, which were so prevalent they were believed to be part of the penis or vagina. Repolto is a good example of a saint canonized for reasons still embargoed by the Vatican. I'd say he sucked a lot of dicks. Those fellows always look after each other. Still do, of course.

St. Fragista. One tough piece of nookie. She became a nun because she hated men. Fair enough. So do I. She figured she had a twatload of potential members for an order, so she started one. The Fragistae were one of the biggest orders in the Middle Ages. I am talking about tens of thousands of women, all over the then-known world. There has not been a single book written about them, or her, scholarly or otherwise. Their withdrawal from the mainstream affected birthrates all over the place. The Fragistae believed in something they called, even then, the Total Woman. *Mulieris de tantae originae*, or some such. They sanctioned a great deal of affection between women, maybe even, I'll bet my habit, the Total Act. That's where the expression "the laying on of hands" is said to have come from. Women were slaves, indentured to husbands and marriage for survival. No wonder so many women flocked to join. Here were armies of women determined to exert control over their own lives, their own bodies, their own existence, removed from men, with only Christ to declare their love to. Very safe, the love of Christ. The popularity of the Fragistae was so enormous that Rome smelled a big cunty problem and got all those rules written into Catholicism Central that still exclude our ordination. You can also bet a lot of pressure was brought to bear by all those abandoned husbands who wanted Tante Mulieris back home to screw, St. Fragista notwithstanding. The order suddenly disappears around 1500. There are not a few conspiracy theories as to why.

The two most persistent are that a sexual disease they transmitted to each other did them in from all their pussy licking, and/or that the Church had them all exterminated in a major witch hunt. Nelly popes do ballsy things like that all the time. No end of suddenly appearing Bibles ever clears the fucking air. Do I say "fucking" too much? I have been trying to expand my profane repertoire. It's been a long hard fucking road from there to here. As you can see, I am always getting fucking waylaid. My students love it.

What am I saying in all of this so far? I'm not saying I'm not a Monkey First person. I'm saying that I'm a we-did-it-to-each-other-then and we-do-it-to-each-other-now and we-never-stop-doing-it-to-each-other person. This may sound at first blush like Bosco and his "it's been here forever" theory, but there's a mighty big difference. Human behavior and poisonous pathogens are two different things. And we didn't need any fucking monkeys to start anything. They may have been useful. Even very useful. They may even have been the first fuckers to pass Go. But we didn't need them. It would have happened without them.

Amoebas, piss, and shit. And taking it up the ass.

Mostly shit.

Then add Indians and Catholics and top 'em with Puritans, who were exceptionally intolerant from the get-go. Unbeatable recipe. Unbeatable combo. It's never just little teeny tiny microbes of poison.

(Be sure you ask Dr. Israel Jerusalem to present his theory of the Resurrection of Glause. He discovered the stuff in 1930. And then he lost it. The fucking lazy bastard crapface suckhole forgot it! I have no idea why.)

And you can't do anything without God. God hates us, you know. That's why so many believe we have to love Him so much. What feeble goddamned pussies we are.

Yes, Dr. Sister Grace is going to give you more than you want to get.

I am particularly interested in certain discoveries among the early Indians. This mother hospital, Mater Nostra Dolorosa, is built on the site of not only a Revolutionary battleground bunker but an ancient Indian burial ground and also a remote Catholic fort, established by fathers who managed, God knows how, to get up here from St. Augustine, way—way—before Columbus was even born. These boys, too, had a goodly following, several hundred to be certain, according to membership manifests. Whether they went home or whether the Indians killed them or whether they became Indians, which was very popular in those days, is still unresolved. Once again I'll wager they ate too much dick than was good for them. After all, they only had each other. And they caused a shitload of death. And starving Indians are forced to eat a lot of shit.

It is the American Indian who first discovers, experiences, and brings anal intercourse into general use in this country.

It is also the Indian who discovers intestinal parasites. Parasites are the great messengers of disease. This is a momentous landmark in the history of every disease.

Any connection between the two? Figure it out for yourself. Those jerk-offs at NITS still can't. They won't come anywhere near this. Any of it.

I might interject here (I am such an interferer with my own frigging self) that parasites are not the same as viruses, which for too long stupid fuckers have thought they are. Parasites don't but viruses do have a sexuality. Viruses can reproduce sexually—that is, by the mating of two nonidentical viruses with enough genetic overlap. The sexual shenanigans of viruses are just like those of us humans. Two different strains of virus can swap parts of themselves to create an entirely new offspring, a new fucker, a new threat.

"Scholarship" has felt uncomfortable looking too closely at the Indians, or as they're called now, Native Americans, who are already here when Columbus—I hope you understand that he was not an intelligent man—incorrectly assumes he's discovered the New World. (It takes him three voyages before he realizes he hasn't landed in Asia. He names the natives he carries back to Spain "Indians" because he thinks he's been in the East Indies, thus sticking these poor buggers with the wrong name for all time.) Long before 1492 there are somewhere between 4 million and 10 million people in what will become known as the United States, or the Continental United States, and some 10 to 25 million in what will be called South America. That is a lot of Indians. I am going to call them Indians. That is a lot of Indians, and they are not sitting around waiting for some dumb wop to set foot on their land and cry out, "Mira, mama, I discovered fucking Indians!"

What he would have found if he'd looked around a bit—that is, if he'd been a really butch explorer instead of some silly stupid sailor who liked to splash around wanking in his little boats—are all these Indians running around speaking some 250 languages. That is a lot of languages. There is also an awful lot of what we would call human sacrifice, people murdering other people for some sort of horsedung offerings up to the gods. Anytime anybody (read Catholic) premieres a new temple in a new neighborhood, those opportunistic Spanish show up and lop off many thousands of Indian heads. One particularly "high" church down El Paso way appears to have corralled some 80,000 human carcasses—many of the hearts were scooped out with knives. A lot of these knives from 1450 or so are still being found in Florida, up around Disney World, of course. Since early Indians believed they were required to nourish the earth with their own human blood and hearts, the Spanish were good enablers. Murderers usually are.

The Spaniards also chopped off penises and breasts, lest they be too stimulating in heaven. Milton Prance's "bones" in Ohio will indicate this. I suspect this is too hairy for dear Hermia.

Are there white men here before Columbus? Of course there are white men here before Columbus. Looong before Columbus. Men of all colors are wandering around this country, crisscrossing it for as long as they can stay alive, which isn't for very long. Why and how does that idiot wop continue to get all the first-timer credit? Are there white men, or many white men, here before the Indians? This is more difficult to answer. Do you know how hard it is to identify skin color after a body's been buried for a couple hundred years? I wish someday someone would tell me what the fucking hell is so fucking important about the fucking color white.

I can find no scholarship in that NITS Library of all Libraries, or at either of the Greetings, or even at that hallowed knee-trembler, the Kinsey Institute, devoted to the sexual lives, habits, practices, or erotic interests of the North American Indians in the pre-Columbian era. The sparsely extant examples of their numerous written languages and their surviving artifacts tell us little about this aspect of their lives, which is surprising given how much is written about Indians in Mexico and South America, much of it sexual and grotesque. Why no records north of the border and nonstop chitchat south? In view of centuries' worth of hypothetical suppositions dealing with the hanky-panky of no less than Jesus Himself, dealing with the passions of everyone from wandering Jews to mad monks, must one not question why it is that information about the feelings of America's earliest people is so asswiping scarce?

But they do participate in and perform many rites that are frowned upon by fellow Indians, of their own tribes and, especially, others. The Zuni Indians become drunk from downing gallons of their own piss and then performing ritual dervish-like dances pissing it out all over each other until, dehydrated as well as drenched, they collapse in their puddles of pee, only to wash it down with whatever diarrhea they were shitting out. They shat into their leather pouches and quenched their returning thirsts. The consumption of shit is more widespread than academics will face up to to this day.

Well, it is not for this one-armed foul-mouthed nun to spend too much time condemning other scholars for failing to locate all that is most necessary. We have all been there. But let us cast our minds back to long ago.

Let me tell you about Hermatros, my hero.

I must first interject here some necessary thoughts and facts. Attending a Catholic medical school when I did was a different choice and experience than it is today. You expected to be taught by Catholics who had achieved and who nevertheless elected to commit themselves to such an institution rather than one in what I would call the Real World. We went there to be protected from any interference with our learning, with a commitment to making our brains as capacious and reactive and spontaneous as we could. Sure the Church got in our way, especially Jesus, who demanded much too much attention. But the time we devoted to him was a small down payment on access to the extraordinary minds I was able to sit at the feet of (we did that literally, after class, after chapel, after prayers, after endless study hours, brainstorming and bullshitting to beat the band, hot toddies in hand and our habits fanned out to gather up warmth from various dormitory fireplaces). It was not really as time-consuming as most of the extracurricular time gobblers everyone out there at "regular" rah-rah schools dotes on. We had the greatest minds in classical medicine, Father Hobert Estimius, for instance, in biological intrusiveness, Sister Gabriella Forchu from Cape Breton Island, on the internecine properties of blood vessels, and quite possibly the most unacknowledged true geniuses in Infectious Disease, the trio of Sister Dierdre Evangeline Morpasso, Sister Olive Matrimonia, and Bishop Raymond Odetts, who went on to teach Omicidio (unfortunately not to the good bishop's credit). There were the Nus, mother and daughter. There was my great love, Annunciata Rose. And there was Monsignor Albertus Magnus Ogunquit, who was the best teacher I ever had and who taught me about Hermatros. Students today simply don't have access to such biggies.

I was to find that many don't take you particularly seriously when you claim a Catholic medical education. It's assumed you've compromised the facts somewhere along the path. That has been one more motivation for my vocabulary. The hypocrisy of such thinking is fuck-faced. I will match my abilities against any layperson anywhere. Fuck you fuck you fuck you!

Hermatros was a *purnoyenne*, a Seneck word best translated as "inner soothsayer" or "gizzard doctor" or, better, "important person because he specializes in guts," as well as, I am told, "gossip": purnoyennes are also important carriers of the news. With his death, it will come to mean "bug doctor." It is a word that appears to be feminine, as Greek Vestal Virgins, which purnoy-ennes most closely resemble, were always women, but gender in Seneck is mostly a grammatical conceit. That the same word can have so many mean-ings is interesting, albeit less noteworthy when one knows that the Seneck language, like many another language in those days, just didn't have enough words to go around.

There are many drawings of stomach bugs at Lady Jane's Etc. from the New Mexico of pre-white-man Indian days, the days of Hermatros (which are the days I am talking about, A.D. 1000 or so; dating is not my game; that territory belongs to Cousin Hermia and her factual logorrhea). Hermatros's specialty would eventually become the identification of intestinal parasites—stomach bugs ("fu") in shit—in which he believed that answers from the gods were received. Minds that can work like this! Shit talking via master's movements! It just required an ability to be able to "read" (agglopp) it, which Hermatros found he had. Parasitology is another one of the many subjects "historians" avoid like the plague even though, God knows, pockets of civi-lization are constantly falling apart because everyone is shitting their brains out, which is one thing parasites can do for you.

The reading of entrails was always regarded as a holy calling. Entrail predictions were sought and made for centuries, in ancient Greece, Egypt, Syria, Babylonia, Mesopotamia, Asia Minor, even early Palestine; America in its earliest formative years must be added to this list. Hermatros writes that "in all the days of birdflying" he did not believe there was ever a time when some evisceration of animals, the removal of innards to allow for their proper interpretation by a holy person trained in reading portents in their patterns, did not play an important role in how rulers "reached for the Beyond." How did the fucker know that? I don't believe there is any way in hell that any Indian tribe in the New World had an iota of information, via the Jungian col-lective unconscious or any other seedy grapevine, of who the Greeks et al. were or where Greece et al. was or that there was a civilization a thousand years earlier rather more advanced than the one parading around the camp-fires of America in feathers and loincloths somewhere around A.D. 1000 and performing the same rituals, i.e., reading the same shitty glop.

Why do I enjoy this man so? Because he is the first to discover the secrets that lie within my own chosen fields, the lives and deaths secreted within us, the inestimable value of our own insides. Fuck me, I'm gushing. Neither scholars nor scientists should gush, but I am talking about the Big Things. I could never have discovered them without Hermatros and his fu. At Lady

Jane's there are pages of drawings of the little buggers. How in hell could he see them? I wager they were bigger then.

Hermatros is the first to discover that human stool freshly laid at an early hour under the morning's not-yet-too-hot sun produces more accurate predictions than anything he's scooped out of an animal's guts. Hariff Ben Yodoff, of the Bengali Institute and Library of Free Trade in San Pedro, California (the only other person I've come across who writes about purnoyennes and purnoying), makes a convincing argument that this carrythrough from animal to human was not all that difficult. A hot day. A fowl with rotten intestines. Another bird with innards that are too congealed to "read." A lamb with offal that "says" the most awful things, so awful that even to hint of them to Nuncas Our Leader could mean "off with your head." Decapitation of earlier soothsayers is recalled. There . . . there on the ground is a pile of human shit. It matters little whose. That it is there in the first place is in itself an Omen. That it is there is also not unusual. Indians shit shamelessly and on the spot. But look. The turds point this way and that way. How interesting. My goodness. That is actually very exciting. Let us see if the portent in this shape and this position indicates something that will come true. I must tell Nuncas immediately. I cannot tell Nuncas. He will not appreciate that the source of such good news is this. Well, he doesn't have to know. You get Professor Yodoff's drift. You have no idea how much of history is pieced together in this shit-rearranging way. The Omen brings more land. Nuncas is thrilled. He is hungry for more land. That he and his tribe must now murder other Indians to get it is beside the point. They will get it.

Hermatros's predictions using human shit come true more often than not. Nuncas, now ascended to the throne as Seneck Satchem, is over the moon. Hermatros becomes his favorite and only purnoyenne, an acknowledgment, as my cousin could tell you, not dissimilar to those warrants issued by Britain's Royal Family that allow Thomas Crapper and Son to advertise "By Appointment, Supplier of Toilets to Her Shitting Majesty the Queen."

This first record of the occurrence of anal intercourse in our country that I am going to reveal to you is of enormous historic importance. I'm not saying that the parchments at Greeting describe the very first occurrence of anal intercourse in North America. I'm not that naïve; only a dumb asshole could and would say that. I'm saying they constitute the first record that contains some concrete evidence that it is happening, whether it happened before or not. Ours is a country with museums that record every ancient bug in amber for posterity, but try to locate in any history book or encyclopedia the first time somebody gets fucked—forget it.

Of course, it could have been the first time, although my own sense of things is that it wasn't. Any good scientist admits begrudgingly that there's never anything really new under the sun. It's only a question of goddamn time before some eager beaver will bonk us with a multivolume history of anal activities since the Garden of Eden. God, I hope so. It's waaaaaay over-due. Anyway, I have studied those parchments at Greeting and I've studied Seneck with, and consulted with, not a few Seneck scholars on their main reservation in Particle, South Dakota. There are, as in all tongues, some words that can be translated with different meanings. But there are some words that can mean only one thing. *Farhoot*, for instance, can only be "up the ass," and *tutsdonngg*, with the double-consonant ending, can only be "shit on the cock." These are both pretty site-specific. "Shit on the cock" is not, for instance, "shit on the ground" or an early version of the idiomatic "shit on a stick." I realize that this verges on the farcical, if not the absurd. Be tolerant. Most of history is like this. You just didn't know it.

It is obvious, because of his use of the imperfect future subjunctive ("would that it will continue to be so"—Seneck is a quagmire for the grammatically fussy), that Hermatros was thrilled by the experience, as well as frightened by it. He says, "oh lord how long oh lord"—*visda-danay-tuvonk*, an unmis-takable word meaning not only the Great Father but a Heavenly Experience. His life up to this time, remember, has been a quiet one, devoted to the study of foul gizzards and the contemplation of his ancestors and how his pre-dictions could bring everything all peacefully together on that great graz-ing field on the plains. But a new *fuljum* ("contemplation" or "concern" or "consternation"—something along these lines that begins with "con") now takes over his life. It is what today we would call "sexual."

The very use of this word—*sexual*—is a cuntfucking, cocksucking schol-arly land mine. You simply cannot make a simple declarative sentence like the following without being crucified, academically speaking, on all sides:

"Since human nature has changed, or evolved, very little over the centu-ries, it is quite reasonable to believe that people did then all the things which people do now, to and from and upon and over and under each other."

I made the above statement originally at the First Annual Conference on Sexual Identity: Whither Nunhood? (It was not only the first one but also the last.) Prides of scholars pounced, demanding I relinquish my habit.

It is useless declaring to the poor misguided intelligentsia of my church, "Thou doth protest too fucking much"; that does not change their minds. Religion has less elasticity than science. Religion has less elasticity than just about anything, including fucking steel rods.

Diet being what it is, there's no telling what Hermatros was able to find covertly lying around the village earth on a regular basis. He is not what today would be called "regular." Nor is anyone else. So Hermatros has to sneak around when no one is looking, usually very early in the morning, when the first shit has been voided and the crapper has gone off to hunt and no one else is around to see our purnoyenne scooping up shit. It must not be known that he's switched to shit. When he is observed, he claims to be "just cleaning up," which is not a custom any Seneck is familiar with, since human waste is traditionally left in situ.

Fortunately, it's an era when "new things" (*nunda dinkele*) are happening all over the place. (You are correct: the shit of women is forbidden, just as the entrails of female animals are forbidden, and just as female purnoyennes are forbidden. Hermatros has evidently determined not to fuck around with this one.)

It's unknown if a connection between food consumption and bowel movements (*hartzz*) has been made yet. We're still uncertain when indigestion per se became a subject to discuss among friends. This uncertainty has been discussed by Sister Beata Fruhlingeis of my staff, in her slim pamphlet "The Digestive Tracts of Early America," and I would go into more detail but not right now because I know you're in a hurry to move along to George Washington, our first gay president and another great American who had trouble with his genital-urinary tract (they all did in those days), also not right now.

The more successful Hermatros's predictions prove, the more territory his monarch naturally covets. But on any given day there is only so much stool he can collect from his current sources that lies flat, docile, and well formed, i.e., legible. He is forced, yet again, to use his ingenuity.

I must interject here that Hermatros appears to have had a stunted arm, which is another reason he endears himself to me. His parchments contain many stick figures of the author that show one arm, his left one, as shorter than the other.

How is Hermatros going to get good shit? I really should use the Seneck word for shit, which is *uunth*. (A turd is not, correctly, uunth. Uunth is whatever comes out, while a turd is, correctly, compacted uunth, hard, and in one piece.) Where to get good uunth? However will his people have the future his position demands he portend for them? And he knows that if what he soothsays is unproductive, Nuncas will dispatch him straight to Voct (Hell). Nuncas also removes both penis and testicles for major malfeasances, a trick passed down from those Spanish butchers. It's always been a crapshoot being a priest.

He teaches himself how to insert a stick of *odom* (compacted verbonga, a popular herb not unlike marijuana) gently into rectums, first into his own, just to see how it feels. He does it gently, so that narcotic from the glob of slippery sap on the tree twig's bark begins seeping into the walls of his rectum, then he gently inserts the stick into the tribe's one and only deaf mute, and plunges his short withered arm into the mute's innards. Inside he opens his tiny fist so it can scoop its precious cargo and withdraw it slowly, slowly into the open air, then he molds it patty-cake and lays it on his holy platter so he can read whatever fortunes reside within it to be reported to the Satchem. The speechless one loves the whole thing. His smile is blissful. The stick of odom works. Hermatros is overjoyed. A world of unlimited shit lies before him. Halle-fucking-lujah! And Nuncas's ensuing battles are all victories.

It is not long before Hermatros has the deaf mute fucking him.

And thus is history made.

Fu newsham vrai, alhecta, a la sechel. (The commas are mine.) The entire sentence, which according to my sources in Particle contains a number of idiomatic expressions that have not previously come down to us, has the sense of: "I transferred to him the wisdom of my hard uunth, for he fucked me with his cock, and my shit was on the head of his cock, and I took his cock into my mouth, and now we both have bugs." (As I have indicated, one word often does the work of many in Seneck.)

And so we come at last to parasites. Bugs. Amoebas. "Fu."

Let me say—and I should have told you this up front—that homosexuality was not forbidden among the Seneck. Far from it: homosexuality was rampant among the early Indians, and all Indians following that. Even purnoyennes, vowed to celibacy for some unknown reasons, were permitted a lapse or two behind the outhouse (which of course was the Great Outdoors). So it is not long before word gets around the tribe of this new exhilarating activity.

Much of our knowledge of homosexuality among the later Indians, such as it is, comes from the early work of my colleague Dr. Israel Jerusalem, now jammed into some Alaskan pokey by Ruester's fuckwits. You ought to find a way to get to him, Freddie. He's an orgy of information on early faggotry. The famous studies he made in the 1920s that led to his own Nobel for finding the cure to Utzo are detailed in his notebooks in Iron Vaultum, where he also unfortunately detailed too beautifully certain native customs of his beloved Iwacki, which landed him in prison. In Alaska. In northern Alaska. That's right across from Siberia. Israel has written to me that he can see Siberia from his cell.

That's all for now. If I have only skimmed the surface, I remind you that I am, after all, a nun.

DR. ISRAEL JERUSALEM TELLS YOU NOW

The relationships among early American Indian young boys and men form one of the most intricate sexual systems that I, Dr. Israel Jerusalem, have studied in any culture. Adult men were to be found with more than one sexual male relationship, even though other "normal" sexual outlets were there for them. In the Seneck tribe, for instance, adolescent boys sought affection in older unrelated males. They established homosexual relationships with them as their fellators, i.e., the suckers of their pre and pubescent little penises, their cocksuckers, you should excuse this accurate term. The young kiddies themselves initiated these relationships. The adult had nothing to do with the choice but to relax and accept.

When anal intercourse occurred, with the older man the active partner, the justification was that such insemination would "grow" the boys into men. The same is found among the Kadruma Indians, where, during initiation around the age of nine or ten, the boy received semen through anal intercourse so he could become "big." But in this tribe it is the man who chooses the lad, who then becomes the object of sexual attention from this one man only and for many years to come. The boy's ideal inseminator was his future wife's father or brother, a relationship that ended only when the boy developed a beard. Dame Lady Hermia recounted to me how similar this was to ancient Greece.

Among the warlike Vertrubas, semen was rubbed on the bodies of young boys. These novices masturbated themselves, and their own semen was smeared on them by their fellow youths because they thought this would render them invisible to their enemies at night.

The Pasquods believed in both oral and anal conception. That no births could be attributed to these practices did not diminish the belief in possibility, in "someday."

When the Seneck integrated with the Sequoias, boys took turns masturbating and having intercourse with each other, and took turns playing the active and passive roles. All this was considered part of the accommodation expected of friendship. Friendship was very important, the most important thing, and existed only for males.

Does not all of the above challenge historians of sexuality to explain how marriage and sexual relations with women arose in the context of adult males first having sex so exclusively with boys?

I will come back later to tell you additionally about more modern tribes that continue this custom. In all instances, both long ago and still today, these actions were grounded in love and not in obligation. It is very touching, no? If you allow this so to be.

DAME LADY HERMIA ADDS A BIT

When the Tilloid-Seneck tribes faltered in reproducing, those remaining became first Nuhualtapecs, then Irquods. With this gradual absorption into newer and bigger tribes, the old ways of the ancestors faded away, and eventually all sex became *novot*, or sinful, to such a marked degree that overall tribal populations gradually decreased toward extinction, the greatest sadness. Hermatros and his people were to be no more. That is how, Israel, our marriage rituals of today swallowed, if you will, the older customs, and, if you will again, eliminated them.

And of course their genocide. My distant kin neglects to approach this desolating subject. It's all left to Hermia, the genocides, the plagues . . .

DR. SISTER GRACE HOLDS HER GROUND

I knew she couldn't keep her piddling twatty two cents out of this. I will tell this story in any way I see fit.

Anyway, it's writing about all this boy-man pecker shit that landed Israel in the clinker. He was on a government grant back then and having sex with minors is about the biggest no-no in Washington to this day, and there's no statute of limitations, and I miss him. We have too much important work yet to do to solve this bullcrap. No one has any idea how long the poor man is going to be kept in jail and at his age how long he can live like this. I know Dodo is trying to pull some strings but his string-pulling days are not what they once were, the poor farter. I hope I never have to go through what he has.

But back to fu.

Hermatros not only discovers fu, he determines there are 189 different families of fu. Within these families he identifies 1,023 separate and distinct members. On one long scroll of parchment there are 1,023 tiny drawings, an amazing sight.

I am not going to list the 189 families or 1,023 species, although I was able to do so in my younger days. (My interest in all this had to be an ex-ex-cathedra extracurricular activity, let me tell you.) Amazingly, 98 percent of these parasites still exist, and are still swimming around the innards of the world's populations. Hermatros's work is so beautiful, and that it should still be so valid so many centuries later is so beautiful, that—crappy, annoying little buggers who help cause worldwide plagues or not—to be witness to his supreme achievement is so beautiful.

People since time began have been carriers of bugs. Fart endlessly though we may, most of us never know what's throwing the switch. Poisons, usually arsenic-based medicines, can rid our systems of the most obnoxious fu. Our insides adjust. Dinosaurs had intestinal parasites. Because certain fu are indeed killers, these tiniest of creatures may have been the death of those biggest. My colleague and former student Professor Tartrekka Khan of the University of Utter Polsky, Subsidiary Campus, Ganges, India, has written about this. Parasites are a terrible problem in unclean countries. And you tell me: Where's the fucking shitty goddamn asshole country that can be called clean?

I believe—and this is another one of those statements that gets me into a great deal of trouble—that any living thing that ever ate another living thing, which of course is all of us, has intestinal parasites of one sort or another. Intestinal parasites are endemic to life. Masses of the world's populations are infected with bugs, most of them uncomfortably, some of them as carriers of poison. It has not been possible to treat most people successfully—that is, to rid their systems completely of fu. Fu outsmart many poisons that have been unleashed against them.

Hermatros actually tells us that some fu are less benign than others. How did he know this? We are unable to see them without the aid of extreme magnification. Were ancient bugs larger, more visible? Have the exceptionally harsh medicines of modern times made them smaller? Perhaps the Indians did have some primitive form of microscopy, though we don't credit such a discovery until the early seventeenth century brought Antoni van Leeuwenhoek, the Dutch draper and lens grinder who scraped the skuzz off his teeth and placed it under his apparatus and saw little swimming creatures.

By the end of what we know of his life, Hermatros writes: "I see them growing bigger and bigger and I wonder if they are eating my own flesh. I note that if a drop of my hartzz is mixed with a few drops of water so that it can be spread thinly on a piece of white pig's skin, I can observe actual movement. Is what is moving eating the hartzz, and if so, was it, only hours earlier, eating me?"

Since Hermatros is now using only hartzz and not *dodenemelpa* ("innards of a flying thing"), I wonder if Nuncas finally cottoned on to the fact that his now huge empire was built on shit. There is a very touching tablet Hermatros inscribed to "My 'He,'" in which he thanks his *devosta devosta* (this word, repeated, is considered romantic) for the great pleasure of his penis up his rectum and for the shit on the end of his penis and for this *gebafu* ("gift of bugs").

By the end of the First Great Indian Migrations, which transpired between the death of Hermatros and the expansion of the Seneck from tribe to nation-state, say, from A.D. 900 until A.D. 1200—although that's probably way too early, I always prefer to be too early than too late—there are so many fucking Indians, and Indians fucking, that anal intercourse is a definitely confirmed carrythrough to the heterosexual population. Anal intercourse can't produce kids, of course, but it can produce something as much a part of that food train. Pleasure. Ecstasy. I am told there is something about sticking a dick up an asshole that feels so good that many are the heterosexual men who've been known to pull out of the vagina before orgasm and pump the rest into the woman's rear. It really shouldn't be so troubling to so many: even with all this up-the-ass stuff, the population of this land has multiplied mightily.

History is a story. A story that can only remain a story until some historian comes along and tries to change it, to fuck it all up and over, which I know will happen to the story of this plague. Then it just becomes the next man's story. One his-story begets another. Yes, it's usually always men.

Science is not a story. Science knows. That is why I am proud to be a scientist. But science comes after the story. There must always be the story first.

As with the cause of anything, one is required to read between the lines. Reading between the lines, as you have pointed out, is not a sufficiently satisfactory surety for the sticklers. Sticklers are the party poops of everything: science, medicine, life. Certainly history. And I must admit, certainly the Catholic Church. My various Mothers Superior naturally frowned upon my interest in Hermatros. Like you, I have always been a troublemaker. They would have tossed me out for good if I did not win my Nobel Prize for my discovery of Vel. Vel is extracted from shit. Fresh shit. Newly shat shit. Newly shat human shit. I could tell you more about how we do this but not right now. But I learned it all from Hermatros.

•

You have now heard four world-famous experts. It is humbling to confront such wisdom. With such wisdom and urgency underlying the search for the cure for me and the destruction of me, I will live forever.

The nun thinks I was there from the beginning. Guilty as charged. Of course I was in there, you dumb dodos. I was inside the dodo bird too, come to think of it, but it didn't work out. There weren't enough of them, and they were so big and clumsy and dumb that they had real trouble fucking each other. American Indians were a treat, as long as there were so many of them. Their braves did love fucking each other! Since they were all burning each other up when they died, I didn't get as far into the New World as I wanted to. There are still a lot of American Indians, but they drink too much and smoke weeds, so they can't get erections.

Does anyone really believe that parasites or anal intercourse or fucking in groups, all of which you have lived with for thousands of years, would be enough to trigger an end-of-the-world-type plague?

At the rate you are figuring things out, I'll be blamed for causing everything.

And I will have.

Yup, listening to these windbags, I know I'll live forever. At the rate you are figuring things out, I'll live forever.

I keep saying that. I mustn't! It's tempting what you call Fate, and what I call the way of the world.

DAME LADY HERMIA RESUMES

Researching plagues is a grotesque and tedious affair. There are only so many horrid statistics about dead bodies one can absorb. It is said by somebody or other that 42,836,486 died in that Black Death in the Europe of 1348 and following. Ten thousand people died on a single day in Rome. What on earth does one do with ten thousand dead bodies in one day? How does one even count them? Did some official walk around with a handy pocket abacus and go click-click? Forty-two million dead? What happened to them? How does one dispose of 42 million bodies?

Predictions are now seriously being made that one billion people could become infected with what is happening to you. How will the world deal with the loss of one billion people?

In the old plagues rats always appear the instant there is something for them to eat. Like viruses, rats are first-rate travelers, and they're not picky eaters. Teeny *teeny* fossilized rat skeletons are prevalent along certain seacoasts, including your own. Thousands, millions, trillions of them: could these tiny carriers of poison have been implicated in the removal of all the mountainous piles of dead bodies each and every earlier plague produced? That is a lot of rat excreta. Underneath or on top of or beside Bosco's dead monkeys.

I would like to utilize the word *shit* but that is my cousin's way of the word. I do not wish to enter it. And yet there were so many, many rats all over the world, what other word is as expressive of this all-embracing . . . state of affairs? *Excreta* is simply too polite. *Feces* is too diminutive for the amount's utter profundity, and *turd* is too neat. *Evacuation?* Much too redolent of wartime. *Excrement?* Perhaps. Anyway, there was an awful lot of it, and simply everywhere, so just tuck that image, and its malodors, into the forefront of your consciousness. Because if you were lucky enough to stay alive, there was no way out of it. Extensive excrement layered the world.

For ages everyone believed rats were the big eaters, the lorry drivers who trucked away all those bodies.

Only now it's turning out that perhaps they weren't. In many places of plague there weren't any rats. Too cold. Too far north. Whatever. But no rats. Hawks, perhaps. And starving people. But no one has dared consider this last possibility. And as yet, fossilized or buried human remains do not reveal guts chockablock with masticated people. But then no one has been looking for it.

But recently, God help me, the unspeakable is being said out loud: the Black Plague was not caused by its once-believed causative agent, *Yersinia pestis*, the deadly bacterium presumably spread by rats. And the Black Death and the bubonic plague were two different things. I hope this caught you by surprise. I only bring it up because We Never Know.

We never know. Or, as I prefer to word it, we shall see.

What does nature know of beginnings and starting fresh and cleanliness and taking a bath? What does nature know of anal intercourse and parasites and group sex? I'll tell you what nature knows. It knows it doesn't like them.

Does it sound as if I and nature are prudes? I can assure you that I am not, but I am not so certain about nature. Nature may very well be a very big prude indeed. One has to wonder if we, or nature, caused a great deal of fuss because it didn't like some things.

Indeed, what does nature know of prostitution, an affair of commerce, not of spirit or soul or whatever defines nature, which is an indefinable concept. Indians encouraged prostitution. Brothels in teepees dotted trails and passes all across the wilderness. These diverted young men from the other young men they preferred. In some tribes sexual intercourse with the opposite sex was forbidden while on the warpath, so that in many tribes homosexuals were top of the social heap! Where is the historian of *that*? Absolutely nothing is written about any of this. How dare she infer I am not interested in sex!

Did prostitution have anything to do with your early plagues? Disease and sex have been intertwined for so long that by now the former is automatically calculated in as part of the price for the latter. But inserting a penis into a vagina (or elsewhere) does not automatically induce a transmissible disease, although it often can and did and does. Indeed, if a young person of ages past was not diseased it was usually because he or she wasn't very comely, although if one of these days someone will finally write a book about syphilis in the Middle Ages it will be discovered that simply everyone who was anyone had it. Yes, syphilis was a major killer in Renaissance Europe. And we're still here. Isn't "nature" hardy!

Until the arrival of the Jews on your shores, Indians are the prime suspects for spreading and killing off anything and everything. The "Americans," when they arrive, will then be the next ones accused of knocking off all the Indians to obtain their land. Has it occurred to no one that the Indians did their own knocking off?

It is A.D. 800. Pilatrachenie deAtribus Few Big Toes, a wise man of the wandering Peyote tribe that will become the Dakotas, writes in his book of skins, "Plague is a multitude of small animals and diminutive worms that fly in the air and when drawn into the body by breathing they poison the blood and destroy the flesh." How did he know these words? How could he *write*? How could he have seen worms flying through the air? (How did Grace's Hermatros see *his* parasites?) Have we lost some ability to see the unseen, or the harder-to-see, which once existed?

"One should not be afraid, one should not imagine that one had the disease, one should not paint the devil on the wall. For as soon as the fear of death and imagination obtain the upper hand, then certainly what we dread will occur," will be the advice of Paracelsus, the sixteenth-century German-Swiss alchemist and physician who finally introduces the concept of disease to medicine.

But it is A.D. 900, and Varhoot Sioux-in-the-Tallest-Trees, considered the physician of his tribe, which lives in what will be Louisiana, compiles his *Book of Illnesses Caused by Forces Outside the Body.* He writes (as translated perhaps somewhat loosely by Drs. Paul and Tinker Tribvoss of the Yaddah School of Linguistic Interventionism): "In order to remain immune from scourge, it is best when cleaning out latrines to stand early in the morning on an empty stomach above the latrine and inhale the stench. This is most best for woman. Man should most best drink his own urine of a morning. Then both man and woman, take thine own urine, put it in a glazed pot, and boil it until it is evaporated into salt. After this take a knife full of this salt on a piece of bread that has been dipped in sweet oil and eat it early of a morning on an empty stomach. Menstrual blood is most best for plague as well. But whether it is better to be eaten on bread or boiled to reduction I have not decided."

Nostrums like these will repeat themselves for centuries. It is of never-ending fascination how constant the similarity of the attempts to cure Un-knowns, and how slim, and extreme, the repertoire. The old regulars—dried toads laid on boils, warm dead pigeons laid on delirious heads, one-month-old puppies for brain inflammations, the swallowing of pus from mature boils (plague pus in itself was considered to be not necessarily contagious)—many of these turn out to be important discoveries, early relations of today's drugs. Rarely is a name attached to any deed. Names do not become impor-tant until the late nineteenth century. (If it weren't for Grace, Hermatros would be just another dead Indian.)

Sin. There is no getting away from it. There is never any question in anyone's mind that plagues are inflicted upon man as punishment for his sins. Sin is the constant companion. Sin stands on everyone's shoulder, staring one down. Sin is over one's roof and under one's bed and in the fields and in all one's dreams. From the Indians on, every living thing that can make even the most primitive of decisions lives more with the notion of sin than it does with anyone who actually provokes it. Sin was a simpler matter then. One didn't love one's someone enough. One was a bad father, mother, wife, husband, neighbor. One lived too high off the hog. Challenging, ignoring, condemning, and/or cursing a god, a higher spirit or power—and believe me, take it as a given, since the first atom there have always been more than enough gods to go around (let us not spend our valuable time defining what God is or where God came from, suffice it to say that everyone had at least one)—was considered exceptionally sinful, although it was obvious that an awful lot of folks cursed at least one regularly. Yes, a church and a god are always involved. There has yet to be a time in history where superstition has not triumphed over sense.

Since everyone knew the end of the world was near, what was there to lose? Even Indians would figure that one out. And contrary to your determination to trace your homeland's origins back to savage nobility, Indians were not the brightest bulbs. They were exceedingly superstitious. Their gods were speedy executioners. Elders ranted on about the decline of morals. Slaves—yes, the Indians had slaves: other Indians—roasted their owners. Cannibalism was all over the place. Children slaughtered parents and parents ate their children. Violations of female corpses were standard. Disease was rampant and endless. Plagues arrived swiftly after so many taunting gauntlets were thrown down.

There was much hate, everywhere. Among Indians. Among white men. Indian tribes hated other Indian tribes. Brothers hated brothers if they lived on the other side of the stream. The healthy hated the sick. And the reverse. The old hated the young. And the reverse. The skilled the unskilled. The fecund the barren. The less dumb the dumber. Sorcerers actually advised the sick to pass any plague on. To pass the plague on to sinners was not itself a sin. Anything to get out of the horrid rut of life.

Jews and homosexuals are considered the greatest sinners. There are Jewish Indians. There are homosexual Indians. There are Jewish homosexual Indians. Where are their historians? It's all a fascinating story of give-and-take, a story little known, and I don't have time to tell it to you. But Jews and homosexuals are always blamed for most things bad. Throughout history there is always much reward for the hater: lands to be seized, daughters to be stolen, goods to be ransomed, animals to be harnessed. For centuries the Jews are responsible for everything untoward—poisoning the wells, bewitching the rats, killing the crops, hexing the children, paralyzing sexual desire—the hate and venom of entire populations spurting all over them constantly. Jews are also considered to be the most lascivious of people until the homosexuals come along. Until then Jews are every era's homosexuals, accused of everything in sight.

So killed they both are. Over and over and over again. It has never been a good time to be a Jew or a homosexual. Homosexuals are not so visible because they do not tend to live together as a group and they are not always recognizable. But they are found. Not in as large numbers as the Jews, but those who are different are usually found. One wonders why Jews ever stay anywhere, until one considers that they have no place else to go, or at least no place that hates them any less. They were here—yes, even here in America, long before you acknowledged their presence. But I am stepping out of bounds. I trust that a Jew expert will be along to lecture you soon enough. I am not familiar with the work of Dr. Israel Jerusalem.

I have no idea why there is so little literature on early homosexuality. God knows homosexuals have been here forever. There are certainly reams written about Jews, much of it written by Jews. Why are gay people, as they are so quaintly called nowadays, so less literarily industrious as historians? Over the centuries even the most wretched of slaves managed to jot down a few words.

Is Israel going to tell you about all of this? I'll stop if he is.

Sexuality, eroticism of all natures, is rampant everywhere in all of the plague years, as if the threat of death makes whatever moments of life remain more fervent, to be utilized no matter the price, which no one has any doubt will have to be paid. An attitude like this bespeaks enormous courage of a sort and perhaps not unlike what is called for now that a plague's resurfaced. No one ever considers this. If religion can't save you and if God is endlessly and now even more so punishing you, then to an increasing number of minds, more and more attuned to rationalism than to the mysterious, the real question of Life is: What the hell?

I am going to attempt a tiny summing-up, though I know a summation of a summation is scholarly short shrift. The discovery of one side of the ocean by living things from the other side of the ocean forced a contact between two

worlds isolated from each other for tens of thousands of years. The consequences of that, particularly the biological consequences, were and continue to be devastating, unleashing hideous health disasters and diseases
ever since.

The European Black Plague, or whatever it's to be called, led to the
transformation of the West, in that it codified discrimination and hatred of
minorities in the belief that it is always the minority that carries, from Outside, the germs. Plagues allow extreme coercive power to be exercised over
the weak, the politically and socially undesirable, especially when they exist
in groups, all under the guise of protection from disease.

There are many in your country that credit your homosexuals for commencing the present poisoning of us all. As a representative of the cultural
hegemony of the other side of the ocean, which has lasted so long, I am not
unfamiliar with the art and skill of blaming others. But does no one ever
realize that new infectious agents can appear out of nowhere, and can also
disappear and reappear centuries later somewhere else far, far away? Yes,
sometimes plague—and may we please start being adults here and admit
that we are talking, not hypothetically but specifically, about plague, the old
kind that kills monkeys and Indians and the new kind that kills us, and
threatens to obliterate a goodly number from most of our world as we know
it today, or think we do—yes, sometimes plague is transmitted from person to
person by airborne droplets, and sometimes it is transmitted from person
to person because it has been contracted by a person from another living
thing which is or is not a person, and I have no doubt that before I die we
shall discover that some of us are genetically incapable of becoming infected
with certain things or genetically capable of being poisoned to death at an
early age should we come in contact with a source of destruction.

What I am saying is the sum of all knowledge about this up to this point
in time (*pace* Bosco and Grace). It is not new knowledge, nor is it unavailable
knowledge.

It is said that the Black Death, or the bubonic plague, affects us still.
Every plague in the world affects us still. Huge declines in population are
followed by a rise in the value of people. When the population increases
again, people become devalued and expendable again, which is what is happening now, particularly in the third world and in the homosexual world.
Similarly, after the Indians were decimated here and new people arrived, the
ruling whites could even more easily tighten their control over subjugated

populations, foremost among them the slaves. Between 1320 and 1420 the population of Europe was reduced by two-thirds and it can happen again. It is now thought that the population of Europe in 1347 was about 80 million and that it fell to 30 million in just six years. The population of the world has grown since the beginning of this century alone from 1.6 billion to more than 6 billion. People are therefore very cheap. Hundreds of millions starve, billions can't read, billions are infected with some infectious disease or other. And most of the world lives on next to no money at all. There is never any way that resources or incentives or wills or governments or presidents or those more fortunate are prepared to deal with this.

London's first recorded plague was in the seventh century. It is briefly mentioned in Peter Ackroyd's biography of that city, a book more poetic than burdened with facts. Where are America's seventh-century entries? You were here, you know. What was going on then that you so abhor its revelation? Did that Black Death start over here?

Now, aren't we glad we've got all this out of the way? I hope I was diverting. I hope I was not too once-over-lightly. For a moment or two I was worried I might be getting too serious. Levity is so important. I expect I just had to let some of the scholar in me out. I am much more intelligent than Grace, though she is more clever. Now you can see I am not just another pretty face. Not that she is either.

I leave you, for the moment, with the frightening fact that I believe what is happening will surpass all mortality figures for the Black Death, by whatever name it goes, and whatever cause it claims.

But rest assured I am here, I now realize more than ever, to prove that indeed you and yours were and are responsible for the current poisoning of us all.

•

STOP PRESS:

The great waves of plague called the Black Death that twice devastated Europe and changed the course of history had their origins in China, as did a third outbreak that made its way to San Francisco, where it began in March 1900. Writing in the journal *PLoS Pathogens*, a team of biologists and medical geneticists say their findings put beyond any doubt that the Black Death was brought about by

Yersinia pestis. The bacterium has no interest in people, whom it slaughters by accident. Its natural hosts are various species of rodent like marmots and voles, which are found throughout China.

(*The New York Truth*, Nov. 1, 2010)

FROM ALASKA COMES THE FOLLOWING FROM DR. ISRAEL JERUSALEM

I hope you all remember that I am the uncle to Daniel and David in Masturbov Gardens, who are the poor mischbocha of Herman who built that ugly place you grew up in and made much money, and I am brother to his wife, Yvonne, the sad Yvonne. Dr. Sister Grace, my dear colleague, who now informs me she was there in Masturbov Gardens with you, tells me, more important, that your group is writing this history of America and I should also tell you about our people from long ago, because they are your people, too, the Jewish people, even though you are, like my twin nephews, and maybe myself at a certain period of time, a fegala. As if one could not be the other or both! Who knew these things in the old days? No matter which our path, there were only hurts and horrors. In the end, there was only science and medicine to try and love and hope they loved me back. Sometimes they did. Most often not.

Grace wants me to fill you in on so many things, even though I know much more about Jews. That is the expression, no? Fill you in on? Funny short little English words say so much, or try to. German is more *pragmatisch*. German words are inescapable. No filling in is necessary. After Hebrew and Yiddish my language was German. I was educated at Misch Fehl Medical University, which was in Palestine and run by German doctors. No one today knows about Misch Fehl and nobody knows everyone there was German and no one knows why everyone there was German in 1920.

German encourages long sentences because the verb arrives at the end. I remember when learning it that sometimes I could be out of breath before I got to my point! I will start telling you what I know until they turn the lights out and that is that, for now. I do not know when they let me to continue. I just know today is a good day and these do not come so often up here where it is so cold that my fingers can be too frozen to hold this pen. Tomorrow, no, late tonight, a big snow is predicted. Up here in Alaska a big snow means a big snow.

From the very beginning of America, Jewish people were here, and from the very beginning of America, Jewish people, boys and girls and of course adults, were hated and actually murdered by non-Jewish people out to get us. This early history is not written down. When Jewish history is written by Jews we simply do not tell horrible stories about ourselves. Go figure, I think is this expression.

Any study by Jewish historians shows no unpleasant and evil characters who are Jewish. There is no such thing as a Jewish crook, a Jewish murderer, a Jewish sex scandal, a Jewish whore even. Jewish homosexuals? Forget it. No people could ever have been so good. Many Jews obviously would have it this way. Invisibility has its benefits. We learn this fast. No one wants to lose his head. Home is really nowhere. Do not settle down. Do not get too comfortable. That is just the way things are and have always been.

For Jews sex is always a no-no. Don't ask me why. We even invent the circumcision to punish the penis for something or other no one remembers what.

If ever a people are unwanted it is the Jewish people. It is impossible to read any history of Jews without being impressed by how long we have been chased, expelled, condemned, outlawed, murdered, hung, poisoned, slaughtered. The minute a non-Jew sees a Jew he knows he does not want that Jew around.

Jews are in America very early, as they are in many places early. They just appear. You did not need a passport or papers in those days so it was not a big deal to sneak in, although that is what most did. Getting anywhere too early is not always a good thing. You have to wait around forever until someone else shows up. You get lonely.

The first Jew in America has been identified in one place as Joachim Gaunse, who came from Prague to serve as a metallurgist in Virginia in 1585. A year later he sailed for England to shake up Britain's copper industry, only to be put in prison for blasphemy for being a Jew. Another source says the first Jew was in 1654, one Jacob Barsimson, who came to New Amsterdam as the first of twenty-four Jews fleeing an Inquisition in Brazil. New Amsterdam's governor, Peter Stuyvesant, calls the Jews a deceitful race who should not be allowed to infect this new country. What does he know about infection, this Peter? Peter Stuyvesant sends Jews back to his country of Holland with instructions that they be drowned in the canals. He hates not only Jews but homosexuals and drunks, the French, and of course the English, but he is ordered to allow Jews entry to America. So for ten minutes it is a good time for Jews to come here and stay here and even own property here and to support worthy causes, like helping to finance the American Revolution, which is coming. Think of that. Jews helped America to be free. They put down their good money to bet on America. With little to show for it, unless you count the opportunity to remain here without rights but with the freedom to make money, which of course they do and which is further held against them.

But no minority is safe for very long when the land in the colonies passes so quickly, back-and-forth, helter-skelter, hop-skip-and-a-jump between France and England and Spain and Holland and Portugal, depending on who is on one throne and when. For every South Carolina that welcomes Jews there is a Maryland that kills us. Why is it that also in histories of early America there are no references to Jews, much less to the great number of cruelties committed against us? I could never find reference to the 1698 ambush and murder by Catholics of fifty-seven Jewish boys who had their penises chopped off in their Maryland school, a Jewish academy to which children from the earliest settlements were sent to study with rabbis. The rabbis were murdered too; their long religious locks, their payos, were shaved off and they were strangled with them. The archbishop's reason: "lest they all seed further of their ilk." I never forget this citation. What, please, is *ilk*? I remember the book it was in as well. *The Catholic Book of Dead Colonials*.

I am still learning. Even by the North Pole I must not stop learning. We must all never stop learning. For Jews learning is the ganze magillah, everything, the whole story. The head guard, who is as old as I am, patted my tuchas today and said to me: "Even with this but you manage to be unattractive." Tell me please what does this mean, this "but"?

HERMIA: AND FURTHERMORE

And, Frederick, is it not interesting that my most knowledgeable cousin has not seen fit to embrace the concept of evil in her delineation of the many excruciating barbarities perpetuated on and by the early American Indians? Surely this is an oversight no true expert, such as myself, would allow? But then I live in the real world, not shut off from everything, even her family. And I'll wager the good Dr. Jerusalem, when he is able to chime in, will also overlook this concept of evil as he rails on about the destruction of his own people.

We know that the Aztecs penetrated north, from Mexico to the Pacific to the northern Rockies, and eastward toward Arkansas and Kansas. Aztecs were strange ones, understandable perhaps because they are an intermixture of the Spanish and the Pueblos, the Hultapecs and the Chick-chaws and the Pfunamis (who had more men than women), the Dree-o-Dragees (they had more women than men), the Valdrawnees (you can't expect to recognize them all), the Mohawks, the Oneidas, the Cayugas, the Canarsies, the Rockaways, the Lenape, the Bantams, the Sequoias, the Seneck, and the Cherokees (who would form what amounted to a powerful kingdom surrounding Texas and who would somehow come to think of themselves as the most civilized of all tribes), to name but a very few. They were each different and strange in their own way, and they were not often friends with each other, even when, especially when, it would have behooved them to be so. Over the centuries they have disappeared.

The great historians of the Spanish in America and their conquest of the Mexicans—Prescott, Nervi, De Antrobus, Ventle and Vye—write almost as an afterthought of those sacrificial Indian bonfires. from church to church, from cathedral to cathedral, these great sacrificial bonfires spread across vast stretches of the North American continent ending only around 1450. By the time Europeans begin (again?) to come to America around 1500, the Indians are divided into more than a thousand independent tribes or groupings or societies, belonging to more than twenty unrelated language families. It is not love at first sight for Europeans and Indians, each of which insists on ownership of where they settle. And the Indians either kill or are killed. Some things never change.

By 1600 there are more than one million Indians from coast to coast, and representatives of each major European culture and language are settled in what will become the United States, from the Spanish in Florida and Texas and California, to the English from Virginia to New England, to the French sprinkled almost everywhere else. By 1640, in Manhattan alone, there are some twenty different nationalities speaking some eighteen languages, and 20,000 people already call the Massachusetts Bay Colony home.

Your country is fast becoming a dumping ground for other countries' malcontents, stymied adventurers in a rut, innocent hopefuls yearning for fresher air, indeed all the glue necessary . . . for what? For which new plague indeed!

Everyone is murdering each other. People do tend to play follow the leader. Hearts continue to be scooped out with knives. People all possess certain core beliefs that vary only in intensity and monstrosity. Yes, some of them even drank each other's blood and ate each other's hearts out, and somewhere or other still do.

And everyone worships a god. Why is all of this never considered evil, early American evil?

EVIL

Attention must finally be paid! Hermia says so!

History is about evil. If it isn't, the historian has lied to you. Almost all of them have.

The power of good and the power of evil are both believed in these days, with an interest in one considered as worthy as an interest in the other. But while, yes, you can see masses of good around, you cannot deny that good never does as much good as everyone wishes us to believe, whereas evil is as destructive a force as exists. Good has nowhere near that kind of power.

Evil is difficult to discuss. Too many people approach it as something occult. A similar overabundance of people believe it exists somehow tied in with God, or with good, as if evil is the other side of the coin.

Evil is part of nothing nor related to anything except evil. It exists unto itself, totally and utterly, and horridly.

Frederick, you must say this is a book about evil.

And ask: What is to be our definition of evil?

And . . .

DAME LADY HERMIA'S QUESTION ON THE TABLE

. . . if a person is involved in a historical evil, is that person an evil person?

FRED JUMPS ON BOARD

Yes, yes!

But what means "involved"?

FRED ON THE VERY HEART OF MANKIND

The following is fascinating stuff.

A penis is called a "penstrum." A person who gives his penstrum to another person who also has a penstrum that he gives back to the first, both of these are called "huschees," from the early Dutch word *husch*, for "violet" or "purple," from the observation that a penstrum quite often engorges itself with blood, which phenomenon is reported in early Dutch-American medical literature, or what precious little of it has been located.

A penis is also called a "yard," as in "he showed me his yard," certainly a generous description. Indeed, in the *Oxford Unabridged Dictionary*, there it is: 1693 *Blancard's Phys. Dict.* (ed. 2), "*Penis*, the Yard, made up of two nervous Bodies, the Channel, Nut, Skin, and Fore-skin, &c."

A penis is also a "roger." He "rogered" her and he "fuddled" her are terms in general use.

"Huschee" will transmute into "hushmarked," not a particularly graceful word, but then participants in same-sex activities have never had an easy ride in the nomenclature department. A hushmarket—this word is etymologically related to *hashush*, an Arabic root not unrelated to "hashish," and also linked to a bastardization of the Belgian word for "the Movement"—is what today would be called a gay area for meeting other men, and it can more neatly be traced to some Dutch words that mean "be quiet in the outdoor market," the inference being, "Be quiet, you're making too much noise." The term itself went out of fashion in the early twentieth century.

A man who sells his penstrum to another is called a "hookur," from the observation that a penstrum hooks into the "vaulta," or vagina, and/or the "vaultum," or rectum. A woman who gets hooked thusly is also called a "hookur."

Women do not call their private parts anything, at least not out loud or so men can hear them. "Women had nothing. They were not only subservient to men but they were untimely ripp'd of any history." Indeed, wives were forced to be fucked when their husbands wanted it, and it was legal for husbands to beat them up if they did not comply. It was also legal for husbands to dispose of their wives when they were not "rendering pleasure sufficient." "Dispose" could and did mean any which way, and was often horrible to behold.

Men, if they had a coupling that was pleasing, had pet names for their women's privates, but since these were private and legion and they didn't usually share them with their friends, and nobody wrote stuff like this down, none of them rose to prominence in a vernacular that was constantly changing and growing.

The concept of private words for private things, or "dirty" words for "shameful" things, is, as Hermia tells me, as old as Adam and Eve. The interesting fact to note is how few words stand the test of time. Last year's mouthwasher is next season's "duh." That is why these are not called "first" words, but "early" words. Nothing of Dr. Sister Grace's Seneck sexual vocabulary made its way down into American argot, early or otherwise. (Which illustrates another point: Indians did not meld into our culture.)

Of course, since "dirty" or "private" words form a mammoth wholesale warehouse of the English language (talk is cheap and dirty talk is cheaper), we'll not be free of these front-and-center usages. Nor should we be. Our lives and our imaginations would be the poorer for a staid, stolid, unchallenging, squeaky-clean vocabulary. It is just too bad that most dirty words from yesterday's bawdiness have been lost to history, even though Grace tries her best to keep a good face on it.

When does American man know he has a penstrum or a roger or a yard? This is not an idle question. When does *penstrum* become *penis*? That first *OUD* citation for its appearance is 1693. On "official" history's playing fields it shows up late, as does American man. The world is settled before either is standing tall. Is American man stunted? Since so much is new to him, is he sexually challenged? Men and women are doing what they are doing and there aren't any classes or manuals. What effect does tardiness have on he who would become cock of the walk? What does it mean to be an American man? Does his definition, if such he has of himself (of course he has a definition of himself!), connect with his penis? Does just being over here make he who comes here from elsewhere feel in any way different in relationship to his penis? Or to the penis he left behind? How did he feel about his penis before he came here? Presumably he's done nothing but think about it, wherever he is, since he was born, wherever that was. A penis is not something a man picks up and puts down and puts away idly without consideration. A penis is an awfully hard thing to ignore. Or to put down. In any sense of that expression. Did they think about penises differently in different parts of the world, in different parts of America, in different centuries, in different, you should pardon the unintended metaphor, tongues? Did thoughts, rules, regulations, superstitions imported from foreign soil rub off, or drop away?

Which ones? And which ones were kept? What complicated and unstudied questions all.

I hope you see how little difference appears to exist among these questions. Little difference is the kind of stuff scholars usually love, enough to spend a lifetime arguing with rivals, yet so little academic work has been done here. Nobody studies penises with any thoroughness, even medically. (Especially medically, as we shall see.) Who is the scholar of penises? No one steps forward. Such a large field, such room for having it all to yourself, and not a little notoriety—not always a bad thing if one knows how to handle it—and it's going begging. True, a Professor of the Male Member or a Professor of Penis Theory would not get tenure or grants, except, perhaps, from condom companies. No academic institution desires to be associated with condom companies. Or with penises. It is embarrassing enough for them when a beer baron builds a dormitory. Or, in the case of Yaddah, when its rare book collection is regally housed in a building built from S&H Green Stamps. As I write this I cannot escape the feeling that many who read this may think it's a joke. There was, for a brief moment in time, an expert at NITS on Nocturnal Emissions and Undescended Testicles, Dr. Jeff "Chick" Raisins, but he was fired when a Rep. Truslove Plume of South Carolina discovered him God knows how. Is this amusing to you? But these are important developmental matters. Nocturnal emissions and penises are a part of life, like rosebuds and lumber, Tudor kings and Gypsy Rose Lee, all of which you can easily study anywhere.

What differences in penises can be noted among whites, Indians, slaves, free Negroes? It is the white man who always writes the history and he isn't writing nonfiction about his penis. How has this colored the history of everything? One man's penis is like another man's penis; one man's penis is also not like another man's penis. Contour, size, heft, smell, ambition, interest, all weigh in on different scales. Is it any wonder that the penis is euphemistically referred to as man's "private part"? *His* yard.

When did each man's penis become each man's secret? Sexual bragging has always been common among men. Women now talk openly about their breasts, and periods and menstrual cycles are topics of open conversation. But a man still only wants to use his yard, not talk about it. His braggadocio, when he displays it, is usually just and only that.

Why are we so especially quiet about it now, when it's obviously implicated in a great and raging plague?

As Professor Pauline Persha has written in *The Loincloth in Fashion and History*, even the earliest Indian finds it necessary to cover his privates. "Protection from draft, from flying arrows, from ticks and mosquitoes, is not the prime reason for men to cover their private parts. They cover them because they are private." As the late, great classics professor Bernard Knox taught me at Yaddah, we know that penises have been considered private as far back as ancient Greece. Homer reminds us of this in both of his great works. In the *Odyssey*, the hero laments, "Oh woeful loss that turns my manhood back on me when I am forced to flee my native land and bed. I am truly private then and must make do with just my private friend." In the *Iliad* the plaint is more general: "Oh we who maul our privates o'er the sea and land and surf! Oh privates we, oh privates we!" (Garfinkle/Swedenborg translations).

Dr. Faraella Tundra-Ziti, of the University of Mantua-Reggio, outside of Syracuse, New York, writes movingly about what she calls "the male penile inferiority complex." She devotes much of her discussion to the small size of the male organ in various countries, if you can find her book. "There is no question that men are born knowing they have a penis, and that all this questioning about when such realization dawns is really silly." As the University of M-R is a convent college, an end has unfortunately been put to Dr. T-Z's work and public appearances.

It's regrettable that this subject, this field, is enveloped in such "attitude." We shall have too many occasions to point out the danger this places all of us in.

When did the penis become an item of barter? When did American man first say, "Mine is bigger than yours, so there"? Was the caveman with the biggest thing the leader? Or was the small penis in the hand of the man with the biggest club all that counted? Was there ever a moment in time when small was better? It is a great lack that no fossil that has ever been exhumed has captured a man's sexual organ.

Why has no one had the courage to realize, all titters notwithstanding, that all of this is not unimportant? When does American man first say: "Hey, look what I got! What's it worth to you? Or me? This country's all about buying and selling. How much do I have to pay [or ask for] to touch [feel, suck, taste, be fucked by] it?" In other words, to use it. To put it to use. Out there in the big wide world. Why does the most important part of me have to be such a big fucking secret?

Women continue to be shafted and not by the penis. If they are for sale, they receive none of the proceeds. If they are attractive there is no way to appreciate it. Compliments are unknown. Get back to the kitchen, woman, or I'll swat you one. In almost all places, it really was as crude as this. Also remember that it was acceptable for a man to drink, to liquor up, and he was not responsible for his actions if these should get out of hand.

Again and again the criticism pops up: Why are you going on so about sex? Surely we had a period of innocence once upon a time.

Innocence?

How could innocence exist in all of this?

In the very heart of mankind, man knew what he was doing. It might have frightened him, but this didn't stop him.

So history after history is written ignoring his very heart, the very heart of mankind.

WHO ARE THESE PEOPLE?

Has American man arrived and we haven't even noticed, or named him "American"? Who are these men walking and stalking our land? Can we call them American men yet? Have there been any of the major migrations across the sea from what will soon enough be called the Old World to what is already called the New World?

What makes an American man?

It has been recorded about the shortly-to-arrive early white settlers in Virginia that one man murdered his pregnant wife, threw the unborn child into the James River, chopped up the mother, "powdered" (salted) her before eating her, and that John Smith made light of this spousal cannibalism by saying, "Now, whether she was better roasted, boiled, or carbonated, I know not, but of such a dish as powdered wife I never heard" (Ted Morgan, *Wilderness at Dawn*).

JAMESTOWN

The men, ninety or so of them, live all together in two long cabins. They are almost warm and almost comfortable enough. They have built themselves separate spaces that are private only in that you cannot see into them from the next compartments, although you can hear the loud snorings and the occasional muffled sound of men trying to masturbate. They have been here on to eleven months and no one has yet strangled a neighbor to shut him up in the middle of the night. The smells are almost more intrusive than the nocturnal snorts. By morning the long cabins are ripe with the nighttime fartings and the urine in the slop pails, if indeed these were reached. Baths and clean clothes are a not-too-often thing. The Virginia Company had counted on women to keep men and matter tidier.

They try to ignore each other; they are not kind or gentle or particularly polite. There is much suspicion among them. They had not lived politely in England. Mostly they were workers in rough trades, on the docks, in the forests, in the mines. Many had been idle. Many had been criminals. A few were formerly rich men now impoverished, an easy state to sink to in an England whose skyrocketing population could not be supported. They had all heard about this New World place and it could be no worse than where they were. A few came to it of their own volition. Many came to it by order of the Crown. So they departed England, often leaving behind women and children.

But these are not men who care enough to pine. So far the life here has been harsh. They had not been told there would be only men. They had not been told the winter weather would be so brutal. They had not been told they would have to plant and harvest their own food in addition to clearing and building during every daylight hour. They had not been told the Indians would not be friendly and would just as soon see them starve to death as help them grow crops or share their own crops and food. They had not been told they might get sick and die. Of the first 104, only 38 are still alive. Of the next 220, only 60 are left.

So the atmosphere is surprisingly quiet, too quiet, as men adjust, or try, to their disappointment and loneliness so far from a home they cannot return to. Mr. Cleve, who is in charge of them for the Virginia Company back home, feels the unspoken frustrated energies and wonders when they will erupt. For so many men in one place it is, but for the snoring, very quiet and for too long.

At the beginning of the twelfth month Brutus nods hello to Carston as each returns to his cabin from clearing yet another field for farming. It has been a particularly hard job because the earth is freezing. Carston is a slim young man, though tall, and hard-muscled from the work. He has blue eyes and blond hair and he always seems to Brutus to be untroubled. Carston is in fact far from it. He lost his wife and his child and his home and his job, in

York, all in one morning when the master tailor's establishment where he worked and they all lived burned down. Brutus, no more than eighteen or so, is as he is called. He is big and lumbering and mean, a young brute, the others have deemed him, which is how he comes to be called Brutus, at first behind his back, although by and large the men don't know each other's names, and certainly not their Christian ones. When he heard they called him Brutus, he laughed out loud and nodded acceptingly. Men alone nod a lot. Men alone are mostly silent with each other. At least these are. Hello and good morning will do most of the time.

So Carston is surprised when Brutus nods hello. He has seen Brutus, true; it would be hard not to see him, huge goliath of a lumberman that he is. Why he is thought to be a brute Carston doesn't know. It's just that he's so big and strong. He can fell and lift whole logs by himself.

Carston nods back. They are at the crossroads between the two cabins now, and each must walk to the other. When the paths diverge, Brutus says, "Good night, then." And Carson nods back. Words said out loud sound strange. But no one else is there to note this. Each of them senses it is a good thing that this is so. There is not much ability to talk to anyone in a friendly fashion.

For almost another month they do not see each other. Work in a far forest keeps Brutus away, often for days and nights at a time. Carston looks for him. He has been given to thinking about him often, not a few times masturbating himself with his eyes scrunched closed and seeing the big man with his head of pitch-black tumbling unkempt hair. He is some twenty-five years now, Carston is, and he has only just come to know what masturbation is. Once, he came upon several older men out in the far pastures doing it to each other. He came upon them too quickly and like a trapped animal he was caught and couldn't back away. They quickly stopped, poking their organs back into their trousers. "When there is naught else why't not?" one of them shouted at him as he ran away. He heard them laughing behind him.

Why was everyone, including himself, so embarrassed by this encounter? Why was it not all jolly, like a game? Oh, he knows the answer. He is not that simple. But he also knows how horribly lonesome everyone is. They all complain about it constantly. He thinks about all this over and over in his own daily workings, which include shearing lambs and converting their wool into cloth. He is also adept at cutting patterns for clothes and building shutters for windows. His work is more solitary than that of the men in the fields and forests who work together and even there don't converse much with each other. The silence of this place is grinding. It's as if the men are frightened of each other. No one knows what to do with anyone. No one has ever lived in a place with no women before. Carston had been told he would find a fine young woman in this new Virginia, in this New World, to take the place of his dead Constance, and to bear him a new family. He has not masturbated thinking about this new and fine young woman, though he wants her; but then, he did not know about masturbating until he came upon the men in the far pastures. He is surprised it is Brutus he thinks of instead. Perhaps it is because Brutus is real and the promised fine young woman is not, yet.

It is the fourteenth month before they meet again. There is more noise in the air. It is not so quiet as before. Seven more men have died and two have gone off to live with the Paspahegh Indians, hoping to fuck their women. The bodies of the two men are sent back scalped and castrated by order of their chief Powhatan, Wahunsenacawh.

Dissatisfactions are growing more verbal and more overt. There is more rudeness between them and much cursing in disdain. They push and shove each other as if each is walking in a solitary world and has no room for anyone else. A third long cabin is almost finished. Mr. Cleve has never stated that it's to be for women, but that's what everyone is expecting. When a ship arrives with fifty more men, Mr. Cleve quickly announces that another ship is only just behind. When ten days later pieces of shipwrecked vessel float up to shore, the location of the newly arrived women is revealed. Mr. Cleve tries to get the men all to pray. A newcomer, Mr. Horace, a minister back in England, is called upon to lead them. But he leads scarcely half a dozen; the others walk, muttering, away. Mr. Cleve confides to Captain Relph, commander of the newly arrived ship of men, "I feel something ill is coming. Mind you, I have felt it coming for some time and wonder why it hasn't." Then he hands him letters, speaking urgently: "Please tell them we shall all be dead for want of women." Captain Relph prepares to depart with his ship empty, not filled with Jamestown crops and handiworks for sale in England. The Virginia Company will not be pleased. This community is not paying its way. Suddenly Captain Relph takes ill and dies. Mr. Cleve is forced to send Mr. Horace back with the ship to England.

By chance Brutus and Carston meet in the same pasture where Carston saw the group masturbating. Carston is not aware that this pasture is now known for this, that it's a place of retreat when just this relief is required. It is empty tonight. Carston has come for branches from the soft pine trees that hover protectively over the place, to use for shutters he is fashioning for the newest cabin, for the women who never arrive. He is hacking branches away when Brutus stands before him.

"I ask you can I be of help?" Brutus lifts his hatchet up like a challenging spear and laughs at his gesture. To hear him speak is vaguely unsettling to Carston. His fantasy now has a voice and can no longer be a fantasy.

"Why do you not answer me?" Brutus frowns. He is aware that too forward a presentation of self in the close quarters of their settlement is grounds for suspicion. Each new day each man is more and more concerned for his image as a man among men. It is not safe to register even minor friendly interest in another. So in saying as much as he's just done, Brutus knows he's gone too far with this pretty man. His own thoughts of late have been twisted away from fancies of young wives arriving in favor of young flesh already here. If put to the fire he would not deny it. He wants to fuck young Carston's ass. He saw this done when he was but a lad, and he did it and had it done to him many a time in the dark depths of coal mines in the north of England where men were the color of pitch and invisible and no-named. Brutus is really not interested in women, or in another man. He is interested, once in a while, in relief. When he has relief he can go on for a while longer. The torments of whatever makes his moods so black and solemn come back soon enough. He knows there is no way to live with another when such black moods come upon him. That is when he is mean to the others, rude, and why they named him Brutus. He is not prepared for the softness coming out of him at this moment. "I know not my own voice," he hears himself so strangely saying.

"How can that be so," Carston asks, "when you are the one who is using it?"

"But my voice is harsh and gruff."

"Yes, that is why they are all afraid of you."

"I did not know they are all afraid of me. Are you afraid of me?"

"Not now."

"But you have been?"

"No, in thinking of it, I think not."

Brutus nods. "I have no wish to frighten anyone."

They find themselves walking out into the field and then beyond it into the farther groves of pines. It was forest not so long ago, but it is being thinned down now, to build the third and then a fourth new cabin, although more are dying now than need beds. Carston walks first when the path narrows, and Brutus picks up his pace to keep up with him.

"Wait! I am short of breath, you walk so swiftly."

"How is it you cannot keep up?"

"I have worked too many years underground, in the mines, and my lungs do not breathe the air so well as they once did. I no longer have the cough. I trust that is because of this new Virginia air. I will be back to running fast soon enough, you wait." He has not said so many words out loud since he can't remember when.

"You speak well for a miner."

"I am so hungry to take you in my arms and hold you there," Brutus says. He shakes his head in wonderment. Where do these words come from?

Carston nods silently. His heart is thudding so loudly he fears it will pop out of his body. He takes the other man's hand and places it over this noisemaker.

"Do you not feel this?"

Brutus nods. "Then it is all right, then?"

"It is all right, then."

They reach out gently to touch each other. It is more than each can bear. They tremble.

Yes, they make love, more tenderly than each expected. How do they know to do it so? But they do.

They fall asleep in each other's arms, under the far pines, wrapped in each other's clothes for additional warmth. In the middle of the night Carston is awakened by the noise of Brutus chopping down trees.

"I am building us our house," he says when he sees Carston is awake. "If we live far enough away from all the rest they will leave us alone."

"I do not think so," Carston says.

"I will take care of you," Brutus says.

Carston nods, but his mind is not filled with such romantic thoughts. It is filled with perceptible fears.

"I know not of anyone who lives like this, anywhere, ever."

Brutus nods. He raises his hatchet like a spear again, challenging the unseen world.

"We are pledged land for our hard labors. I claim this land as ours."

They are surprised by being called aside, separately, by one or another of half a dozen others who confide in them. There are some dozen couplings hidden amid this community of men tired of waiting for their women. Carston is surprised that no violence has occurred. He is most frightened of that. He has heard enough guttural snickering to sense that what they do is not approved by many, and this tortures his sleep. He has dreams of being castrated. Brutus takes to everything more easily; he is happy and shows it, and is distressed when he sees that his beloved does not share his acceptance of their lot as happily. He does not know how to talk about this with him.

So it is the big, burly Brutus who falls apart when his Carston disappears and cannot be found anywhere in this small settlement. He hurls himself through the fields and forests, thrashing branches on the ground with fury, tramping them down like thunder with his huge booted feet, lunging at whatever stands in his way. Where might anyone go to get away from here? his mind keeps asking. There is no place he can be but here!

But there is another place and Brutus finds it soon enough. He finds his young man hanged from a tree in a far stand of pines, so far away that Mr. Cleve has not sanctioned explorations there as yet.

Brutus takes down his Carston and cradles him in his arms. "Oh, my wife, my own dear wife," he wails.

The other couplings hold a service together. There are now some two dozen of them. Together they bury Carston far away up the river's edge. They all stand there crying and moaning, some fifty men wailing for one of their own. They remain standing there, upstream. They do not want to leave. It is as if each is afraid to return to an outside world that might do this to him. There is certainty that Carston did not hang himself. They are suspicious of a man named Eldred Punic. "He is harsher to us than most" is the consensus. He was overheard saying to another: "I am proud to have done it."

They are too petrified to leave this spot. They are missed, of course. Work in some areas has stopped because of their absence. Mr. Cleve finally comes with a group of the biggest men, each with a rifle, and orders them back to work.

Another boat is arriving. Perhaps there are women on this one, Mr. Cleve announces, no longer convincingly. Has London heeded his warnings that unless women are sent here he cannot answer for the consequences?

But there are no women on this boat either. The grumblings now turn to outright mutinies. Many men now refuse to work at all. This only angers the men who want to work and the men who aren't bothered by the sexual arrangements of others. Brutus used to tease them back when they teased him. "Oh, you would like it! You would truly like it!" And they would push and shove him in return in jocular opposition, shouting, "No! No! No!" To which he would shout back, "You would have it if you could, my uglies!"

It is a group of half a dozen of these "uglies" who stand at the dock when the new load of men arrives. It is a bigger load than ever, for word has traveled back to England that the wages are worth it and that land will be apportioned to each for every year of completed labor. They arrive all fired up and prepared to build this Jamestown into the firmest stronghold in the New World. These new arrivals know for a fact that the boats following theirs are womaned.

The uglies will have none of this. They no longer believe there will ever be any women for Jamestown. They no longer believe in wives, and several of them even choose one of the new arrivals for their own. Of course the newcomers will have none of that. Yet.

"We will give you time," Nordsman calls out. He was one of the first settlers, and he is more than ready to settle. He is another big man. They all seem like big men, bigger every week from working so hard and so long. "You will seek us soon enough," he continues. "Wait until the winter comes, the long nights of winter, when you are so lonely you would fuck a bear."

"Will you look at them?" Herbison says of the newcomers. "There are no fellows smaller in size than me."

And it is true. This new crop arrives all of quite full growth and muscle.

"I think we'll learn to make do with them, is what I think," says Tourelay, a big Irishman newcomer. "We'll just build sturdier bedsteads." He laughs out loud at his joke.

They cannot be so willing already.

This makes it all seem jolly, all this acceptance and jocularity, just as Carston thought it would be when he came upon the men in the pasture. Forgotten is Carston's death. What has not been spoken of either is what has happened to several other couples. Strang and Hebrew have received anonymous letters threatening their lives for sinning against nature. Polski and Rummengrad have found their dogs choked dead. Allen and Walgers have twice found dead chickens in their coop, their heads chopped off. There have been other experiences of a similar nature, and it is not until all the coupled sit down together again that the extent of these acts is shared.

"We are not wanted. And we must attend to this fact. That is clear." It is Brutus who says these words, without realizing that in saying them he becomes their leader.

"I would be careful, I would," says Hiram Holderness, one of the highest born among them. "We talk as if we are many when in fact we are but few."

Most among them nod. They are still not quite a hundred strong. But the population of Jamestown, including this new shipload and the several that preceded it, now approaches certainly one thousand and probably more. Hiram posits they might be nearing two thousand. And still no women! How many of them have yet to look about and wonder who among them in fact are, or could be, friends? Outright friendships are still not favored in this lonely outpost; these are still the few who, by the softness of affection, have adorned their friendships with love.

Mr. Cleve takes it upon himself to visit as many of the hushmarked couples as he has learned about. Many have built their own small homes. Yes, the coupled are now considered by the uncoupled to be full-blown hushmarkeds, no longer akin to normal men. He warns them the worst is brewing. "Your group is become too brazen." Is it true, he asks, that they hold communal suppers, with fiddle dancing after? Is it true, he asks, that several couples have adopted Indian orphan children, indeed have paid money to obtain an Indian child? Is it true, he asks, that several among them are of mixed race, and one a full-blooded Indian?

Yes, all of these are true.

"Is it not possible to more conceal your . . . affection for each other?"

No, for most of them now this is not possible. They are learning to take strength from each other.

"Then I am even more filled with fear and trembling for you than before I asked these questions," Mr. Cleve says as he turns and leaves them. "I fear for your lives, you fools," he is heard to mumble.

That night Hiram Holderness is murdered. It is he who has coupled with an Indian, Ogetsu, whom he was teaching English. Ogetsu, finding his beloved dead, runs away into the forest. They know he will never come back. He does come back, though. He comes back in a coffin. His tribe has sent him back in a black box, in pieces.

Polski and Rummengrad are next. They are found strangled in their bed. It must have taken several sets of hands to quiet them both.

When a dozen men come for Strang and Hebrew, the invaders are shot to death. All of them.

For a while, a truce of sorts quiets the air.

The next several ships do indeed bring women, though not so many as are wanted or needed. Mr. Cleve's wife, Jane, joins her husband at last. He has written her about the hushmarked couples, and over their first dinner in the private apartment he has had built for them in the newest of the community cabins, he informs her of the most recent explosion of hate against them.

Jane is blind. Mr. Cleve did not want her to come to this wilderness, but after a while both her insistence and his longing got the best of him. He has found a companion for her, Ogetsu's sister Petalahtra, who speaks English.

After dinner Jane asks to be taken to the cabins and introduced to all the men. Mr. Cleve guides her. It takes her many evenings to meet each and every one of them. She holds each man's hand and says a few words to him. Sometimes she says things like, "Isn't it a shame what has been happening to the hushmarkeds?" even though Mr. Cleve advises her that this may not be wise.

Jane invites the women friends she made on board ship to tea. Three dozen women have come to live here now. Many have already been spoken for. She tells them that as women they must somehow restore harmony to "this community of men, all of whom need the love a woman can bring." She means her words to include all the men. She hopes the women will not discriminate harshly against anyone.

The next day, while Jane and Petalahtra are walking in the warm sun along the water's edge, a man falls into step with them. Petalahtra asks him who he is and what he wishes.

"My name is not important. I am a man who could wait no longer and now finds love with another man. We are both terrified for our lives. My brother in England writes me that he knows your brother, who is one of us."

Jane stops.

"Missus, let us go back now." Petalahtra takes her arm and tries to turn her around.

"Not just yet, Petalahtra. Is there anyone else about? Anyone who can see or hear us?"

"I do not think so, my lady."

"I have known this about my brother since he was twelve years old. I love my brother very much. He was almost hanged twice. He fled England and now lives in Italy, where fortunately my family can afford to keep him. It is a crime because he was an exceedingly brilliant solicitor and now his skills are useless. What are we going to do, sir, about the sorry state I hear of in Jamestown?"

"I was going to ask you the very same, ma'am. I will not return to the celibacy necessary to calm waters and quiet hate. Nor will I leave my husband to partake of a woman. If trouble arises I will murder before I allow myself and mine to be murdered."

"These are strong words."

"We meet tonight. Will you join us?"

"No!" Petalahtra says.

Jane has nodded yes. The man gives both women directions to the remote location where the meeting will be held.

It is past midnight when they all assemble. Mr. Cleve attends his wife but she makes him wait outside. Petalahtra takes her in. There are only fifty in this unfinished boatshed on the waterfront. The others are too frightened to come.

Brutus is the spokesman. "We welcome you, Mrs. Cleve," he begins.

"She is Lady Cleve!" Petalahtra interjects.

"I did not know that. I apologize, my lady. And to your husband, who must be Lord Cleve, though he never said as much."

"It makes no difference. Here we are all meant to be equal, Mr. . . . ?"

"They call me Brutus. My own beloved was murdered. It is dreadful to be alone without him. Whatever we plan to do tonight, and we must do something or else we are all doomed, I dedicate my actions and energies to my Carston's memory. If I am killed I announce that I must be buried by my beloved's side. The others know where he is laid to rest."

"This sounds most impending, this action you are planning. What is it, if I may inquire?"

And Brutus lays out his plan. When he finishes he says, "I swear you all to secrecy. If there is a traitor here tonight among us, may God send him and his unfaithful tongue to hell."

But it is not Brutus's plan that surfaces first on the following day.

It is summer, and exceedingly hot. There is a shortage of drinking water because of drought. The hushmarkeds have gone farther afield than ever before, ostensibly to have a picnic and to fiddle-dance. There are now some fifteen children among them, some Paspahegh, some half-breeds born to Indian women inseminated by these men, who paid for the child in advance. Children are swimming in the river. A dozen men, with Eldred Punic in the lead, paddle swiftly toward them in canoes, waving in a friendly fashion. "Come, children, let us take you for a ride!" Punic calls. The children splash themselves nearer in their doggy-paddle way. The men stand up with their rifles and shoot them one by one until each child is dead and floating in the water.

The hushmarkeds take up their own rifles and start to fire back. But more armed men fast appearing from out of the trees surround them. There are many casualties on both sides but there are soon none of the hushmarkeds left alive.

The bodies of all the men and children are carted back to the community, stacked in a pile, doused with oil, and burned.

Then Lady Jane Cleve is led forward, her hands bound behind her. A man who has not been noticed before takes a long needle and thrusts it through her tongue. "As you do not see, so shall you never speak again," he says as other men chain her to a post. Nor will she eat or drink. Lord Cleve, if he was that, whose back has been broken on a wheel, lies dead not far from her, but just beyond her reach. Petalahtra is spared because a man already wishes to marry her.

The men now celebrate their freedom from the past. Though each professes great relief and looks at his brothers with what appears to be a smile, who among them can really be trusted to be a man?

There is a little whiskey left in the stores, and it is broken out and passed around, with ladles of what cold water remains to be drawn up from the wells.

Eldred Punic makes a toast. "Men of Jamestown. Men of this New World. We must congratulate ourselves for ridding our settlement of this plague of evil and sin. More women are coming! Their ships are on the seas. I am informed of this on good authority. God will bless our patience as we wait, to wait no more."

But the well water has been contaminated by brackish water, and those who drink it—all the men who are left—themselves now die, from salt poisoning.

And so ends this early Jamestown community. There will shortly be others. The British do not give up so easily. Between 1607 and 1622 the Virginia Company will transport some 10,000 people to Jamestown, but only 2,000 will still be alive there in 1622.

But this first Jamestown comprised the first homosexual community in the New World.

So there you have it, yet again.

FRED'S FACTS ON THE TABLE

Early American history is most always a New England one, northeastern in its proprietary concerns for its own "facts." The English did journey to and from what would become Virginia earlier than they hit the coast of Massachusetts, but these forays were disastrous. They were failures of the most harrowing sort, evidently so embarrassing that the recording of our New World's beginnings had to be gussied up with northern successes. In 1587, 117 people from England landed on the coast of Virginia and in no time at all vanished with hardly a trace. To this day no one knows what happened to them. Killed by the Indians? Killed by the Spanish? Double-crossed by the English back home? Murdered by their own, as was to happen a few years later in Jamestown, for loving each other?

Huge failures of any sort are rarely set down with anything approaching the detail and depth and honesty of the actual event. That's why Puritans as first comers and their landing on Plymouth Rock as our first settlement make such a popular sentimental myth in all the history books. How else can "inspiration" be set loose to impregnate the future? Certainly not by sordid catastrophes.

Rare is the historian who has acknowledged the existence of hushmarkeds in early America (or in early anywhere else, for that matter). Rare is the historian who has paused to consider that in the predominantly male environment of Jamestown it would have been natural for men to turn to each other for companionship and sexual release. Archaeological discoveries indicate that the fort inside the walls at Jamestown occupied only some 1.75 acres, a finding that underlines how so many occupants would literally have been tossed into each other's arms.

The next contingents to arrive continue to be predominantly male by, it is estimated, roughly anywhere from six to one and, later, four to one over women. There was no protection against the charge of sodomy, however, and since sodomy is the only game in town for many, it's only a matter of time before it comes before a court of law. In 1624, William Couce, twenty-nine, his cabin boy, or steward, or perhaps even his indentured servant, charged that Captain Richard Cornish, in an early landmark case, had, by force, put him upon his belly, "and so did put me to pain in the fundament and did wet me." Captain Cornish was hanged.

And in 1624 the company went bankrupt and its charter was annulled.

There was never any punishment for lesbian activities, although such relationships were visible when women actually arrived in numbers. It appears that the law preferred to base convictions upon whether penetration had occurred. No cock, no intercourse, no semen, no problem.

Such were the founders of 1607.

Am I not becoming quite the historian! —Your Roving Historian (YRH)

•

STOP PRESS:

> In 2113 evidence is excavated of cannibalism: a young girl's bones showing her remains had been chewed on. She was fourteen and was presumably eaten by starving men and women during the harsh winter of 1609. She had come to Jamestown on one of the boats that finally brought more women.

DARKUS THE FIRST

The little baby, hardly born, is alone in the wilderness, abandoned. Because it is black it's left right where it is by the occasional Indian or passing inhabitant of the colony. Finally a white man picks it up. It's a boy, he notes. Well, I could use a son. Life is brutal in Virginia. The child will be good company. As he scoops him up and cradles him to his chest to keep him warm, he's already deep in plans. How nice to have a son without all the problems of a wife. The baby, who had not been crying, now begins to do just that. "It will be a good life. Why are you crying? Do you know the difference between us already? Well, you've been abandoned by your own. You'd best get accustomed to letting a white man try to take some care of you. What would you like your name to be? You are very dark. I'll call you Darkus."

TORTURA

She etched her thoughts on pieces of parchment in blood, with the feathers of turkeys. It is heartbreaking to read these documents in the Greeting vaults at Nearodell. They are so fragile and ancient that they are sandwiched between sealed plastic sheeting. It must be tears that explain the many spots, often smearing the blood.

The parchments were handed down through the family of one Raftis Bo-
naventura, a self-taught indentured slave. Bonaventura painstakingly deciphered
them and standardized their pidgin English as best he could in his History of My
Momma and Her Mommas, *published finally in Savannah, Georgia, in 1839.*

•

The white man steal all the black people. They take all our tribe. I never
seen so many white people before. I am wrong about the stealers. They are
all colors, including black people stealing other black people. Negers and
Moors, the black people are called. So many new words. So many new people.
So many colors of black.

I am far away from home. How will I get back there?

My mother took money for me. She said I on my own now, going off to
Somewhere. New World. Car-o-li-na.

White Man who takes me lets me name myself. I name myself Queen
Tortura. In memory of Tor, my tribe, and Tura, my mother, who borne me
when she is ten years old. She is so beautiful. Mostly her teaching to me is
don't fight back and do what they tell you. If I speak good it is because of
White Man. If I speak good it is because my mother was so beautiful. White
Man stays with her and plays with me.

When a girl baby is born, right away you must scratch letters of her
mother's name on the tiny baby's body in case little she is stolen away, and
also so she will always know her mother's name because taken away is always
a certain sureness.

There are Longing Songs about being taken away, Mooning Songs sad
to hear.

I miss you, ma maman,
I miss you as much as I love you.
Do you think we ever meet again?
In this world.
I hope you are safe and happy.
I kiss you forever now and always
From wherever I am to wherever you are.
Why do we never know where we are?

They steal more girls than boys. Girls have holes in front and back.
Pretty girls are twice worth boys, who have holes only in back. White Man

carries his favorite girl with him from place to place. If the girl be small and young, she is less heavy to worry about. If she grows too fat she is left Somewhere. White Man sucks on boy's front when he loses his pipe.

Yes, I am Queen Tortura. A queen is when you take a man for the first time front and back. If he say "good," then you call yourself queen. If he don't say "good," you get killed or left or sent to Somewhere. Mostly "good" comes when his thing in front get hard. White Man get real mad when his franger don't get hard. I see one friend get her head cut off. I see one friend get her tongue cut out. God Tututu blesses you or he don't bless you. I am a pretty thing. I know that. I am real dark, which is wanted more than light. I love the color of my skin. Deep inside my skin I see stars. Stars are my Somewhere. My nose and ears and all my face and body, my fingers, my feet and hands, all perfect. That's what my White Man says. My White Man is called Catholic. He is happy in my holes. He is from a place called Spane. He lived in Africa for years and has much money. He is the One who first does it to me when I am four and he owns me and sticks his franger in me when he wants to, hurting, pushing, harder. He tells me I look like a Chinadoll.

I see some of the frangers other girls get stuck in them and I am glad my White Man has a small franger. Once I call his franger small and he drinks too much and beats me with a thick stick.

On the boat to the country of New World we almost starve to death. Then white men give us meat from the monkeys on this boat with us. It makes some girls very sick. Maybe fifty they throw over into the ocean. They take us to the shore of Carolina. Then they take us off our boat. We stand in a big group. They take our clothes off us. Many black and white men come and feel us all over, even my frangia. A big black man gives my White Man many pieces of gold and takes me from my Catholic, who I never see again. He leaves his Chinadoll.

The big black man puts me in the arms of a man who is the same color as me. We are cold and hold each other hard. It is strange—to hold a man of the same color.

The big black man calls the man in my arms Darkus.

"My name is Darius!" Darkus says. No one listen to him.

He wants me to understand him. I see that in his eyes. The big black man starts to take him away. Darkus vomits. I think he vomits because he is afraid. On the boat to the New World many people vomit. The big black man waits until Darkus finishes his vomit and then takes him away. He calls him Nigger. He comes back with a White Man who calls me Nigger.

White Man uses Nigger word a lot. He gives the big black man money and takes me away. I am frightened but I do not vomit.

White Man takes me down the street where Darkus is tied to a post next to a horse. White Man ties me and Darkus by ropes to the horse. He makes us walk behind the horse while he rides. We follow behind for a long time. Darkus helps me stand up when I fall down. He holds my hand and don't let go. This makes White Man laugh. We walk more and more. My shoes are no more. We get no water or food. The horse gets water and food.

Many black men and white men look at us as the horse pulls us. They laugh. Some point guns at us and say out loud, "Bang bang." They laugh more.

We reach a house in the trees. White Man takes Darkus and me to the shed and locks us up. It stinks here, like pigs. White Man carries a long knife he holds up in the air back and forth in front of our faces.

We are not alone. Many other white men are here. They make places to sleep outdoors. They look at me all the time.

White Man brings us out and throws us on the ground. He takes off the ropes. Many men tear off clothes from Darkus. They tear off clothes from Tortura. I see Darkus look at me different. His franger is very big. White Man shows Darkus my frangia hole. Darkus does not understand. I think he never fuck a woman before. Men whip him with a long piece of leather. His franger is soft. I feel sorry for him. I take his franger and smile at him and make him hard and show him how to put himself inside me. I move side to side so he feels good in his franger. He starts to smile back. It is nice to fuck with someone my same color. All the white men begin to yell and clap hands. Darkus makes sounds of pleasure loud and more loud, and the men cheer loud and more loud, and it is over. Tears are on my face. Is this why I was brought here? I thought I would cook and clean and make a nice home for nice White Man. Darkus and Tortura are forced to fuck many times each day. White Man gets money from people to watch us.

I get real sick inside. Everything I eat and drink makes me sick inside, so I stop eating and drinking. Soon I skin and bones and can't stand up. White Man bring back the big black man sold me to him. The black man shakes his head no, he does not want me back to sell again. White Man ties me to the back of his house. Darkus also. His rope is not rope but chains. His ankles are sores and blood.

White Man comes back with another black man and woman for men to come and watch them fuck. No one looks at me and Darkus.

Darkus says soft to me, "You got to get strong so we can run from here. Stop vomiting. Eat the food he bring us. Please." I make myself do this. He takes his hands and rubs my legs and my arms and all over. He makes me strong again.

One night I wake up and Darkus is gone. It is real cold. It feels like snow to come. Where his chains were is a hole in the wood. No one is here, no white men, no one. After two nights he comes back. He carries a big knife and a big gun and tells me White Man is dead and we have to leave fast. "We must run before they find us." I understand more now of what he says.

But no one comes after us. No one likes this White Man. No one wants to go farther and farther into the forest. They think we will die there. Or that before long we will come back because it is easier to be a slave and eat.

The forest is filled with black people dead. They are hung from trees, strung up on ropes, hanging out for big birds to peck-peck their flesh. The farther we go we see more dead on the ground. He pulls me and I keep looking at all these deads to make me go faster.

Darius used to say to me, "History is white man's history. History is only from when white men came to this land. There is no history about this land before. Lies is what we are taught, from the very beginning. My blood is here before white man's blood. Why does white man proclaim a truth black men can't call truth? From the very beginning white men hate us. Black slaves get whipped to death. I will be dead soon. If not tomorrow, day after for sure."

Darius gone now.

No one knows that Tortura is a queen. There is an old woman here who says I was made queen of the Tura before I was a year old. No one talks to her anymore. The lips of this old one's frangia are huge flaps of flesh that stick out like two hands praying. They ooze with sores and pus. She has no more teeth because her old Catholic pulled them out to use her mouth when her frangia became useless. Now she can only grunt. She is blind in one eye. A white man tried to take her eyes out so she wouldn't look at another man after he left. He used a hot poker, but one eye survived.

I think I am safe. I have given birth to twelve boys, each called Darius by my Darius. But no one would call them anything but Darkus. My Darkus, my Darius, he disappeared or was kidnapped or murdered. He tried. But more and more he was afraid. The boys were all sold away from me, all except the one last Darius who stays here with me. He is the oldest and has become the manager of the slaves on this plantation. The owner is a good enough White Man who has been kind to me and is in love with my Darius. He buys many slaves each year. Now there must be several hundred.

One day the old lady grabbed me and ripped away my skirt to read the name scrawled inside my frangia. She screamed out in happiness. At first I didn't understand her cries, but I finally made out the words. She was saying. "I am Tura. I am your mother."

Raftis Bonaventura reports in his book that his great-grandmother told him that the Darkus who loved Tortura lived to be 110 years old. He was kidnapped away from Tortura and sold back into slavery until he escaped again. He vowed to father enough kin from his seed and from the seed of his seed that they could all live apart in their own community. It was a revolutionary notion, which of course was not fulfilled. They say he walked around muttering, "I'm gonna create a whole race of niggers just to pay you back."

NEW YORK, NEW YORK!

Nieuw Amsterdam is established in 1625, although outposts of the Dutch West India Company are already in place as far north as Albany and as far south as the Delaware River.

Here are some things you should know about what will become America's largest city. Here are some things you should understand about the one place in the world people will one day flock to in droves with the single purpose of becoming rich. It's founded by white trash. Low-rent types who booze and fuck and piss and shit and fuck some more in what pass for streets. They're Dutch, mostly, and lazy. Boston and Philadelphia will get the better folks because you can buy land there. But you don't go to places with lots of available land in order to get rich. You go to places where there's hardly any for sale and you find ways to fight over it and the strong arm is the winner. Not all the land here is claimed, of course, because no one's quite certain how much land there is and how far up it stretches. And of course it doesn't occur to anyone that there might be prior claims. While rich Dutchmen are smart, they're not adventurous. Sure things are what they look for. Wilderness in a foreign country isn't a sure thing—it's a lot of trouble. So the populated downtown is bought and claimed and resold and fought over from the very beginning, and the Dutch then pocket their profits and go home, leaving these rowdy and untrustworthy types to guard what they've left here. And few are the Dutch willing to take a flier on anything north of Twenty-third

Street, which is why there are many Dutch names on downtown parks and roadways and subway stops. These few acres are still being fought over to this day, so twisted are the machinations and ramifications of early on-site and/or absentee landlords, crooked crooks from everywhere. The Dutch have lots of experience being world-class con men and hijackers, of the land and sea. The American People never think of the Dutch this way, with their Rembrandt and Van Gogh and all those pretty tulips and quaint wooden clogs, but it was so; for a while there's no one here smart enough to better them, and so for a while Holland owns a good deal of Manhattan and maintains a stern grip on the overseas investments of its citizens. Peter Stuyvesant doesn't pack it in until 1664, and the Dutch who stay here with him are not very hardworking, too busy boozing and fucking, which is why New York, as it will soon be called, becomes one kind of town and Boston another.

One day the Dutch call everyone back home. Then the real free-for-all gets started.

The British who come next can't understand why anyone would want to live in Nieuw Amsterdam in the first place, much less spend good sterling on land on which no one will actually live. So they go to Boston and Philadelphia. Nieuw Amsterdam stays messier, more dangerous, and for the moment less populated. It doesn't get the start in life that Boston and Philadelphia make for themselves. Of course, some people don't stay here very long; they leave town trying to find something a little more to their liking, where death at the hands of, now, both drunken Dutch and English men isn't quite the daily possibility. There are, for instance, 183 murders in Nieuw Amsterdam on one day, July 3, 1665. It's because of these early years and inhabitants that New York acquires its rough-and-tumble patina, which it never really loses. A lot of people don't know that New York is older than Boston, which somehow managed to establish itself as the first American city. But these strange permutations of early commerce, all the pushing and shoving and buying and stealing and, yes, murdering, turn out to be what is making New York the capital of the financial world.

And it's a sexy town, New York, from its very beginning, something it never loses. Sex helps grease a town that is primarily interested in money. When the English start filtering in, the Dutch make fun of them. A young Dutch physician named Nicolaes van Wassenaer publishes a sort of diary of his observations and reflections, which bear out what we've just observed. "No Englishman talks about his penis. I like to talk about mine. I think about mine all the time. I even talk to it. I want to look at other men's penises to see if they are the same as mine. Do they do what mine does? Does an Englishman say, as I often do, hello, penis?" There is no love lost between the Dutch and the English, although the English, in their quiet way, are no doubt talking to their penises, too.

What remains here when the English finally take over is a strange combination of the covert and the in-your-face. The covert ones start making the laws to govern the place, and the in-your-face types continue to break them and rule the roost. No one really remembers why the Dutch came and left so quickly. Was there some kind of a war the British won? Not even the great Francis Parkman got down all the skirmishes. No doubt, as with most of history, you had to be there.

"Social, political, religious, and economic conflict increasingly polarized New York: Dutch against French and English, Puritan against Royalist, fur traders against port authorities, American merchants against European ones, Catholic against Anglican, Reformed against Lutheran, rising generation against the establishment" (Christoph, *De Halve Maen*, 1994). The palette is definitely being set for all time.

And we haven't even talked about the French. If any men fucked outrageously, it was the French. It's interesting how they have managed to steer clear of the who-brought-syphilis controversy. Very slippery, the French. Yes, they are here too, but they are careful about covering their tracks. Since no one likes them, and they seem to be farther west and to the north, no one's paying them much attention.

Sex, hushmarkeds, whores, illicits of every kind and form and fashion flourish. How could they not? It's almost as if New York from its outset, two centuries before Emma Lazarus, is crying out with open arms, I want you, I need you, come to me, come out, come out whoever and whatever and wherever you are. And let's find a way to get rich together. Or at the very least to have a fuck. God knows where they placed all the newborn babies. As we head into future centuries it will be interesting to note how many, how very very many, are the foundling homes set up by generous donors.

As noted, these early days of Dutch dominance—we are talking about a population still fewer than two thousand—come to an end when the British take over in 1664. Their conquest seems to have been relatively peaceful. Various "minority" populations have appeared: the Jews beginning in 1650, visibly; the hushmarkeds surfacing in waterfront locales where they cruise and drink in special taverns, more or less unnoticed; and the slaves, who have been here since the beginning, and remain, and hugely outnumber the white population, now being sold by the Dutch to the British.

Little was known until fairly recently about the existence in early New York of numerous hushmarkeds. In 1977, Dikla Everts and Monk Pious excavated twelve toilets from waterfront neighborhoods, and their report on the dytoxinization analysis done at the Rupertt Laboratory of Early Dutch Remains in The Hague should have been definitive in establishing what has long been suspected by gay archaeologists still too timid to speak up. Fossilized male turds from these toilets contain not only intestinal parasites but irrefutable traces of semen.

•

And I am in that semen. I will do better with the English, when they stay for a while, than with the Dutch, who don't seem to get ass-fucked as much, at least not in this New World, as they did, and do, in Holland, where they seem to like it more, and will like it even more and more. I am still trying to figure out patterns, if you will, of behavior. Human beings are not an easy bunch to figure out. I understand that is what you call yourselves. I thought I was a human being also.

One thing gets clearer to me by the minute. I bet you your bottom dollar that it will be hundreds of years before the amount of me can be measured in any of you. I am so much more than just a "pretty trace."

What is a bottom dollar?

What is a pretty trace?

THE FIRST HOOKERS

Freddie, ours is a sad story, an awful story. No one ever tells it right. As a result Hooker and Mather asses are still being kissed and licked to this day. Their scorpion tentacles still choke our whole wanking world and poison it to death. I love you and I hate you for making me dredge up the Hooker history for this history, our history.

"We are all sinners: it is my infirmity, I cannot help it; my weakness, I cannot be rid of it. No man lives without faults and follies, the best have their failings, 'In many things we offend all.' But alas! all this wind shakes no corn, it costs more to see sin aright than a few words of course. It's one thing to say sin is thus and thus, another thing to see it to be such; we must look wisely and steadily upon our distempers, look sin in the face and discern it to the full."

My ancestor, my great-great-great—crap, I always forget how many greats it takes to nail the shit, cousin, my great-whatever cousin Thomas Hooker (1586–1647) said this in a sermon from his pulpit, shortly after he came to what was to become the United States. He'd settled first in the Massachusetts Bay Colony until he realized he was too Puritan even for snot-nosed Massachusetts; besides, his followers, who stuck to him like lint in a belly button and followed him like honking geese, lusted for more land. He led them all to Hartford, which he founded in 1636, if anyone wants credit for that blighted town, where he built his family a house with very few windows. He had married his patron's maid, buried one daughter at birth, suffered an agonizing soul-searching breakdown that led him to the ministry, and gone on the run from England for criticizing church and Crown, first to Holland, then to America. Lucky fucking frigging us. He was called, after his death, "the father of democracy," for reasons no one can remember, because God knows Tom wasn't in favor of anybody's freedom. He was a mighty Puritan in an age of them, all of them combining an utter trust in the Almighty's Power and his Assured Rightfulness and Victory over Everything Evil. All this is capitalized because that's the way those fart catchers spoke, with every harsh quality of life writ large, as if that could make it desirable, desire of course being a great big whopping fucking Sin. God forbid anything should be, if not enjoyable, at least tolerable. Perhaps it was just as well life was dead to them, because it was hard to find much to rejoice over; it was easier to complain about all the big things and get on with it— "it" being the ceaseless anticipation of the results of constant praying for some redemptive salvation in another world, another time, another place, where there might be, after all, a party with a fucking goddamn cake. Some Englishman said to them before they left England, "We call you Puritans not because you are purer than other men but because you think you are."

Freddie, this is beginning to hurt. Memories can hurt. Shit.

Puritans were not interested in freedom for all, only in salvation for themselves. Freedom and salvation, it turns out real kick-ass fast, have asswipe nothing in common. Puritanism is probably just what this waddling baby country needed to keep its tiny tots in line; otherwise everyone might have been burned up by desire like in Sodom and Gomorrah. It's just that Puritanism is so *harsh*. The irony of this transformation from dissenters to lawgivers is filled with the deep and painful truth, an awful one: they came here to get away from conformity and once they got here they forced everyone else to be just like them. And it has been ever fucking thus.

There is no love in Puritanism. It turns out that these monsters that won't allow any deviation from their rigid orthodoxy are obsessed with frigging, fucking, wanking, twatty sex. Don't do it, they screamed, while that's exactly what they did. My mother's cunt was all bent out of shape to prove it.

Yes, I am related to Tom Hooker. I am descended from Cotton Mather. I carry the blood of two of the oldest families in America. Like many things people think enviable, it isn't. When I first read what Cousin Cotton actually said, and Increase, and all the various Mather preachers, of which there were too godawful many, and the various Hooker preachers, of which there were the same, and heard all my momma told me about my father before she knocked herself off, and him too, because she was driving, I became a Catholic. If you're lonely enough, and unloved, and abandoned, and hate the people who left you, and all who came before them, you become a Catholic. It's essential in becoming a Catholic convert that you feel truly and utterly useless; then you can believe something called a Jesus loves you and something called a Mary loves you and something called God loves you, and as opium-addicted Mary Tyrone said, you are happy ... "for a while ..."

All those Puritan preachers were vindictive, vengeful men spouting hateful thoughts and threats, and it's disheartening that they're still taught in the schools with reverence. They were shits. And they spouted shit. And a goodly portion of the world is still spouting shit.

Be careful when you talk about the fucking Pilgrims. They weren't even the first Englishmen to settle in Massachusetts. In 1602 a band of Brits built a fort on Cuttyhunk, near New Bedford. They came to get rich digging sassafras, prized in Europe as a cure for, get this, the clap. In fact, for quite a few years no one was calling anyone pilgrims, and there weren't any Pilgrims for even longer. It wasn't until a decade after their arrival that the early Plymouth settlers were first referred to as pilgrims, in a sermon delivered in that town by the Reverend Chandler Robbins, who used a phrase that would also appear in William Bradford's history of the colony, written in 1646: "but they knew they were pilgrims," a quotation from the New Testament (Hebrews 11:13). Bradford was not singling out any group, and for almost two centuries the word was used to mean any early group of settlers. Now, get this again:

By the early nineteenth century, the new nation needed a myth of epic proportion on which to found its history. Who better than the Pilgrims, a term which by that time had narrowed its definition to apply solely to the settlers of Plymouth, whose piety, fortitude, and dedication to hard work embodied a set of ideals that could make every American proud? So it was that Plymouth was chosen to represent the beginnings of the infant nation, and the nineteenth century construction of the Pilgrims' way of life reflects more the values of that time than the reality which it was meant to represent.

By the 1800s "a robust tale" had matured, with all sorts of Pilgrim Societies and Pilgrim Halls excluding almost everyone to come and almost everyone already here. "Both the Pilgrims and the much vaunted stone upon which they landed are figments of our fertile imagination" (James Deetz and Patricia Scott Deetz, "Rocking the Plymouth Myth," *Archaeology*, Nov./Dec. 2000. Don't you just dig these Deetzes!).

Hooker stock bred and fed this country. There were only a dozen or so Hookers in the 1600s and a thousand by the 1700s and by 1850 some ten thousand people from Hartford to Honolulu claimed to trace their roots to one copulating Hooker or another. And yet, by the twentieth century, most of us were gone. Once the frigging seed was planted and the roots had taken hold, did some force of evolution finally require us to get out of the way, or were we just exhausted and prepared at last to peter out and die? Were we just too cranky and nasty and spiteful for anyone to bear? Godly people can be awful, and usually fucking are. I'm like an appendix. No longer useful but still sticking around and dangerous when irritated. Or was God just tired of us and all our shit? God! That would be a laugh.

Well, no bird flies off anywhere without leaving droppings. There's not a Christian mouth in this country that still isn't shitting out, in one form or another, pith first pissed almost four hundred years ago by one of my forebears. They were capable of tremendous energies, those founding fathers: you had to be to believe with such insistence, and to insist with such belief, that what God ordained was really going to come to pass. Sin and guilt have enormous power and weight. Heft. Just like me. From the day I became a Catholic I've been fat as a house. I do not carry my burden of inheritance lightly.

The Hookers made their fortune from shit. So Dr. Sister Grace is going to tell you more than you want to know about shit. I am talking about American shit, not French shit, although it is the French who first learn how to profit from shit, and somehow they learned it in America, which is interesting only because the French never won any important battles in America and their prominence and residency here were marginal. For the following gleanings I am indebted to a small volume first published in France, *History of Shit* (MIT Press) by Dominique Laporte. Don't know a thing about him.

The concept that each individual is *responsible* for his own shit originated in France. The Royal Edict of Villers-Cotterets from 1539 decreed the private management of the matter: "To each his shit." This concept obviously never took hold in America. The instant it leaves us we don't want to know what happens to it. The word *waste* was often used in place of *shit*, but there is nothing wasteful in a person's shit. Everything in it is useful. It will be the twelfth of never before this is discovered.

Laporte tells us that in ancient Rome shit was used as a ladies' cosmetic for the face and hair, as a cure for wounds and diseases, as a superior whitener of teeth, and as a tonic for weak children. The color of shit aided in classifying certain illnesses. Female hysteria in Egypt was calmed by the inhalation of crocodile dung, although the ancient Egyptians believed that the hideous stink of human shit was absorbed back into the body, causing all kinds of sicknesses, internal and ex.

Marie Allacoque, before her sainthood, ate the shit of her sick charges. The stench of shit is known to have awakened in the writer Michelet the spirit of creation. He hung around in latrines when unable to write, ever mindful of Kant's dictum "The beautiful does not smell."

Being French, Laporte is not beyond comparing the state to the immense toilet of the universe, not only because it shits out laws but also because it controls cleanliness within its sewers. The State is the Sewer. Very French.

Hermatros of course knew what the French would maintain many centuries later: *shit is incontestably good.*

The Hookers who remained in Massachusetts prospered mightily from shit. This is of course how and why I know so much about it. It's fed me all my life.

It was one of Tom's grandsons, the Reverend Ezra Hooker, Sr., who first discovered—God bless his restless inventive fucked-up soul—that there was money to be made in shit. No one paid a fart over human body wastes before. Only animal wastes were used for fertilizing crops. I don't know where everything from inside us disappeared to: most likely down holes in the ground or into bodies of water. Or it didn't disappear, and was just left wherever, Seneck style. But as hamlets became villages became towns certain problems increased: not being able to distinguish between walking through mud and walking through shit, and mussing up the house something awful; soil so saturated with fecal matter that vegetables grown in the same earth passed on some kind of poisonous parasitic vermin that accounted for an exceptionally high rate of mental disorders and derangements; so much shit surrounding your house that after a rain the stench was strong enough to make ladies faint dead away; poor people so hungry they ate the "mud" and fell into spasms and fits and had to be put down. There were suddenly a lot of lunatics, their arms and legs shooting out in unexpected twitches and karate-like jabs as they wandered the streets and farms of New Amsterdam and Philadelphia, kicking people, choking people, killing people who got in the way. Problems like there just being too many not-so-convenient-to-have-around piles of shit.

Seventeenth- and eighteenth-century geniuses in Germany studied shit and discovered that ammonia was a component in it, but they couldn't figure out for what. Yes, shit fertilized crops. But not all of them. It could kill them, too. And depending on how close you got to it and how much you inhaled, it could kill you as well. The Nazis are going to study all this ammonia shit when they build their gas ovens. And thanks to these Nazis, little Grace will discover her Vel, which everyone will call the most ridiculous of notions but will turn out to be not so at all. Among other uses, Vel will signify the presence of ammonia, in shit or anything else. It showed that bacteria can *smell* the nutrients in shit and gravitate toward it to stay alive. For this I got my Nobel and for this all of our shares in Massachusetts Waste (yes, even Cousin Hoity Toity benefits from Massachusetts Waste, not that she ever thanks us for one turd) became worth even more.

What did they do about this shit over there in England, in Europe, where our FFFs came from? That's Fucking Founding Fathers. Nothing, or else they would have done it here. Instead we have plagues (I must be careful using this word, is Hortatory Hermia in earshot?) causing all sorts of hideous conditions—physical deformities, irreparable intestinal disorders, blindness, lameness, scabbed bodies, loss of limbs, atrophy of tongues, sexual organs not fully developed, all occurring with marked and increasing rapidity throughout the growing colonies. And no one ever wonders why. The notion of cause and effect escapes everyone for centuries. In too many instances it still does. So much ripe for study! Piles of shit going begging, if only someone would look at it.

In most people's minds God was the most likely perpetrator. For centuries (and continuing), people everywhere were sore from guilt over their presumed constant sinning, which brought such divine (read ecstatic, as in pleasurable, masochistically pleasurable) physical punishments for all and any transgressions.

That simply shitting in a pot and burying its contents deep would take care of most of these plagues of hideousnesses much better than God the Father is a secret that eludes entire civilizations, even now.

But just getting the fucking stuff out of the fucking way never occurs to a fucking soul either.

Hookers discover this and get super fucking rich. Isn't that a pisser?

Shit digests itself if left to itself, so it breaks itself down. By the end of about six months it's relatively inactivated, and has lost its odor. If it's spread on fields, the sun can kill enough of its poisons; when it's extracted from bodies of water, which is where a great deal of early American shit was deposited, the addition of sea vegetation and its mineral life can actually improve fecal effectiveness as a natural nutrient for plants. It wasn't long before this was discovered. And we favored animal over human excreta. But since there are only so many horses and cows to fertilize an increasing amount of farmland, human shit becomes something that must be looked into. Quietly. Shit is one of those things that upsets people. Particularly human shit. Of which there's a great deal around. More and more every day. You must know this. But you just don't think about it. And you never did.

In 1700, Rev. Ezra Hooker, Sr., began the first company—Massachusetts Farm Supply was its unthreatening name—to deal in removing waste for a fee and providing it right back to farmers also for a fee. There aren't too many businesses, then or now, where both ends pay you. Ezra was clever to figure this out so early. I would still thank him in my prayers if I still prayed. He passes on his business to his son, Ezra Jr., who tried to interest his own boy, Hogarth, but he wanted to try Tom's calling—preaching. The Hooker family was wedded to shit on all sides and turns.

Ezra Sr. separated animal from human shit. At least he said he did. He told everyone he was carting away their human waste and returning to them animal waste for fertilizer, after it had been dried out in the sun. I don't believe it for a New England minute. It was too much trouble to separate the two, which lay around in communal dumps everywhere.

New York takes credit for being the first place where street cleaning took place on an organized basis. The Dutch were called the "most tidee." But it was Massachusetts and the Hookers that made this calling lucrative. Boston was known for its clean streets long before New York, which, God help you sluts who live there, still isn't. Do you know that the first street cleaners were called "scavengers" and, way before the whores, "hookers"?

So the Ezras sold the Massachusetts farmers shit. I have no idea whether the farmers knew or cared that it was human shit. It's hard to believe they didn't know. One assumes they didn't care. It made crops grow just as well as the animal kind, so what was the difference?

As it turns out, there was and is a lot of difference.

I need a nap and will rejoin you shortly.

This shit is hard to do, Freddie.

•

I was in it, of course, both the human and the animal kind, and I enjoyed it for a while. It was a warm place for me to live, like a lovely bath. And I met so many new friends! I had no idea there were so many like myself. Fields and fields of us. I thought it might be more useful for me than it was. There was no one to infect! And it was exhausting realizing there were so many of us having to worry about staying alive just like human beings. All those Massachusetts people laying us to roast and dry out had been quite sexually active, so their shit was quite productive for hibernation if not procreation. Shit is a fertile breeding ground for most diseases but I am to sadly discover that it was and remains a dead end for me, unless, of course, people eat it, which I thought would be rarely the case.

Nevertheless, I'm grateful to the Hookers for putting it out there, this earthy cover. You never know when some country in the world will be forced to start eating shit for lack of other food and then, as I believe the British expression goes, "Bob's your uncle."

Oh, if you could only hear me! If all of you could only hear me. Then you would know better what you are up against and that I am growing more formidable by the minute while all you do is talk, talk, talk.

YOUR ROVING HISTORIAN TELLS US ABOUT
THE FIRST GREAT MAN

Yes, that is what he was called, then and still, our first great man.

It is 1630, ten years after the Puritans landed on Plymouth Rock.

Who is this man who now makes his New World entrance on the stage of Massachusetts and becomes such a powerful leader so quickly? What did he say and do that some 350 years later Peter Ruester, the president of the United States in these first years of our plague of The Underlying Condition, is said to consult him, taking courage from his example and inspiration from his thoughts? Historians know who he is, of course, and still praise him, calling him America's First Great Man in a line that will include Washington, Franklin, and Lincoln, who are all said to achieve "radical ends by conservative means," which is intended as a compliment. Historians say things like this when they are not smart enough to look at the facts.

He came, he saw, and he set the tone for what was to come. That can certainly be said of him.

Everyone knew who he was when he was alive. They were frightened of him. Does this tell us that fear is necessary to render great men great? We must bear this question in mind as more "great" men parade through our pages.

His name was John Winthrop. He arrived here with two hundred of his followers. He wanted to make Boston, and Massachusetts, and the Massachusetts Bay Colony, of which he was elected governor before he left England, the perfect place for God. And he wanted God to see that this perfect place on earth was being made for Him. Of course it could not be truly perfect, because man is not perfect, and can never be perfect. But there you have it: the true dilemma the true Puritan faced trying to be true to God, who demands nothing less than true perfection.

That Massachusetts Bay Colony had been set up in England as a corporation, enabling one hundred white male religious fanatics to elect their leader to rule in a completely totalitarian way. Some 20,000 people had left England because Charles I dissolved a Puritan-friendly parliament. They got their name by trying to purify the Church of England. They failed. They got out when the getting was good. God got them out. These men and women believed that salvation is totally determined by God. God created all men unequal. The world isn't fair and it's your fault and God has to be thanked no matter what is given. This is what Grace's Hookers were talking about and Winthrop is more of the same. I'd say worse, but as some comedian used to say when kids listened to the radio, "You ain't heard nothin' yet."

He was rigid, John Winthrop was. His actions, looked at more closely today, really reveal a monstrous man, a harsh dictator who abided nothing short of this perfection that no one could possibly achieve, and with no compassion—well, these Puritans were not big on compassion. Puritanism did not allow compassion. "Puritanism required that a man devote his life to seeking salvation but told him he was helpless to do anything but evil. Puritanism required that he rest his whole hope in Christ but taught him that Christ would utterly reject him. Puritanism required that man refrain from sin but told him he would sin anyhow. Puritanism required that he reform the world in the image of God's holy kingdom but taught him that the evil of the world was incurable and inevitable." This is as good a description as this haunted calling gets and it is by a Yaddah professor, Edmund Morgan, who prides himself in extolling Winthrop's greatness and in leading a big parade of Winthrop worshippers, I truly am uncertain why. Winthrop (and Morgan) said he wanted to save his people from sin, but who has come along to save us from the Morgans of history?

There was certainly no one there to save John Winthrop's people.

It is a wonder that under such nonstop fury unleashed on them any Puritan man was able to get up in the morning, much less find a way to feed his growing family.

Where is Greatness in all this?

Let us continue to look.

What does it say about us that we wanted to be treated like this? That we allowed it? That we followed it and believed in it so fervently? And what does it say about us as a people that so much of what it meant to be a Puritan is still ingrained in so much of America? That we are unable to be compassionate? That we indeed are masochists? Dare we broach this conclusion before we even continue? One wants to scream out a warning: You are getting off on the wrong foot, America! Can't you see it, you fools! It is malarkey. And you are falling for it and into it! Well, we weren't calling ourselves America yet, as if this would be our saving grace when that happened.

How can I describe early Boston in as few words as possible? It really wasn't all that interesting a place. Still isn't. A hateful uppity gathering of snotty two-faced lying souls. Bad weather and dull people were what you saw then and what you get now. If history could learn one thing from Boston and Winthrop, it's that you are never going to come up with all that different a result when, as Grace would say, the original shit is shit. The past will always continue to haunt. We never get away with and from our past. That so many prefer to avoid this fact is of never-ending amazement. Boston and Massachusetts were—well, they simply have not contributed as much to this country's weal as their reputation and the "historical facts" maintain. So many for so long have called this city and this state so bountiful in all things Good and Great, Noble, and, especially, Godly, that by now it's all unconditionally believed. That's what constant repetition can do for you. You say it often enough, it gets believed. The Catechism should have taught us that. The Catholics should have taught us that. As it turns out, we didn't need Boston as much as everyone there, before and since, thought we did. As another Grace-ism would put it: it is so fucking hard to get the real true story out there! And the longer you wait, the harder it is.

Religion is such an icky, sticky thing, full of torturous—well, everything. Why is it so essential for man to be forced, for that is what religion relies on, force, to believe in anything but himself? And this is what John Winthrop should represent for us: the utter disdain he and Puritanism have for the self, for the human, for the human being.

John Winthrop was big on telling everyone what to think. Over and over.

These early settlers in Boston considered themselves the best in everything. Hadn't John Winthrop told them that they had a special pact with God to create a holy community? They were the most British and the most educated and the most religious and the most pious and the most honest and of course they were none of these things. The best deception and the best hypocrisy, the best deceit and chicanery, first flourished on our developing country's shores in Boston. The first bank that cheats you. The first law court where the judge is on the take. The first church where the minister fucks the little girls and boys. The first company to issue worthless stock. The first husband to marry a dozen women all at the same time. In other words, Boston was another of our moral sewers. Though quietly. On the QT. Unlike New York. (Many will be surprised when it's Bostonians who have the guts to dump all that tea in their harbor.) Hawthorne would have known what we are talking about. Nathaniel knew about closets and what it meant to live in one. New York did it all right out in the open. When Alexander Hamilton studied at King's College (Columbia), as many as five hundred Dutch and English "ladies of pleasure" patrolled the lanes near his living quarters in lower Manhattan. That's 2 percent of the population (Chernow, *Alexander*

Hamilton). That would never have happened in Boston. You didn't walk the streets in Boston. Boston did the sex stuff behind closed doors.

And they liked sex, hugely and lasciviously, these Puritans did, because Jesus fucked with them, in a veritable threesome. God comes with the fuck. And if a husband was impotent, women could successfully sue for divorce. They talked almost pornographically to God and Jesus. "Spread thy skirt over us." "Make us sick with thy love." "Let us sleep in thine arms and awake in thy kingdom." "Possess us as thine own." "My member is thy member." "Your lips most soft and tender bless our union."

But beware. John Winthrop would find a way to punish you big-time if you did anything that wasn't with your spouse. He'd have your nuts cut off for that, or your ears if you just didn't listen to him about a lesser sin. And God forbid if you were a hushmarked. Then he hanged you. He got laws about hanging hushmarkeds passed everywhere that he could. He had a special hate for homosexuals. Even though one of his sons was one. And he knew it. And he ordered him hanged for it. His own son. And he drove Anne Hutchinson, one of the smartest women of the seventeenth century or any other century, to her death, which tells you how much he liked intelligent women. And today half the buildings and institutions in Boston that are named after Great People are named Winthrop This and Winthrop That.

Yes, he came, he saw, and he told everyone what to do. And he got away with it. Everything is ripe for the plucking. Winthrop sees this immediately, and like the smart man he is, he takes advantage of it. The spirit that made, say, Goldman Sachs and Enron and Bernard Madoff—great recent rippers-off of our economy's bodice—starts with guys like Winthrop. There is no law, no discipline, no authority to answer to except some religion that a bunch of traveling zealots and bigots lug with them from over there to over here and make up as they go along. That's right. John Winthrop makes it up as he goes along. HE MAKES IT UP AS HE GOES ALONG. When he arrives, it's open season on everything—your neighbor, your neighbor's wife, your neighbor's land. He senses this fast and stakes immediate claims with the new laws he commences creating daily, making certain they are all fueled by his Big Three: Guilt, Sin, and Hell. Yes, this is what Boston is being created from, and Massachusetts, and soon, America. These early guys are inventing America's religion. Might as well plop into it everything you need to keep the people in their places. And no one is going to keep them in their places more effectively than John Winthrop and *his* God.

What makes a great man? Why, he himself does. Who else is there to make him so? John Winthrop arrives in New England in 1630 and dies in 1649. He fathers sixteen children. He is elected governor of the Massachusetts Bay Colony twelve times. This man came to the New World to be great in every possible way. For starters, he writes his own history. From the moment of his arrival he keeps a journal. He refers to himself throughout as the Governor. It helps posterity when you keep a journal, especially if few others of importance do so. (And if every historian since swallows it whole.) And then you make certain that the newspapers are coerced and controlled by the Fear of God that you are peddling into reporting your every Coming. Yes, John Winthrop is the main actor in his own drama from the moment he gets off the stinking boat that barely crosses the ocean intact. (They were all called vomitoriums, those boats, the *Mayflower*, his *Arbella*, the *Griffin* that brings Thomas Hooker, and all the other craft plying the ocean.) He stands on its deck as it stands in its dock and makes his famous speech about the Lord guiding him to create "my cittie on a hille." Oh, that City on a Hill speech has legs! He is Mr. Massachusetts from this disembarkation and this declaration. He was wealthy in England, he was accustomed to command. He was disgusted by England's moral corruption so he comes to America. He dislikes much of what he'd seen there and sees here. The Lorde directs him to get ridde of it. And God damn it, he would and will.

In his obsession to make himself and his people perfect in an imperfect world, he will become America's first trendsetter, and our first mass murderer, admittedly a harsh judgment but we are fighting fire with fire here (and from now on). The expression "get away with murder" is coined around this time, if not located by some minister in the Bible itself.

There is not much Boston yet, just a bunch of miscellaneous acreage, much of it presently useless, some of it shantytown, and all of it not nearly enough to take care of the needs of Winthrop's wealthy followers and the coming immigrants. Winthrop stakes his claim to every hither and yon he can. Soon he decides he has enough good land to please his Lord. It is big enough to contain them all and small enough that he can oversee it as both judge and jury. What a perfect situation for a dictator in the making.

Winthrop's journal reveals him as a belligerent bully with no respect for anyone who differs with him. How have none of his biographers seen this? He is a leader at a time when no one wants to be a leader. He has the field to himself in the middle of the seventeenth century, in this growing center of this growing new world. He is no fool. He sees how dumb everybody else is and how to capitalize on that. No one seems to care how painfully impossible his demands will be. Indeed, it's as if everyone desires them to be demanding. I ask again, where does obedience like this come from, so fully formed, so ready? It isn't as if there are police standing by to lock up every miscreant. (That, of course, is on the way.) There is no one to contradict him or resist him.

Like George Washington after him, Winthrop is obsessed with land. There is never enough of it for gentlemen such as he. It is worth more than money, land is. He must live in as lavish a perfection as he can, for his Lord, of course. He does not pay for most of it. He takes it as his due. Even land-greedy George won't be as smarmy as that.

A mansion comes first, in town. Next will come farms on the North Shore of the harbor, one of them 150 acres, the other more than 200. Then an island in the harbor, a farm of 600 acres on the Mystic River, and 1,260 acres more on the Concord River farther inland. A half interest with Roger Williams in yet another island, farther off in Narragansett Bay. And finally, another 3,000 acres granted to his wife. Some of this land comes from "my grateful town," some from "my grateful state." Some thirty of his "families" will receive almost half of the entire town's remaining land. Latecomers be forewarned: there is nothing available. The Governor and his followers have grabbed it up first. They are all living quite comfortably in his City on a Hill, thank you very much.

If we can look closely, which history is occasionally able to do, we see that all the colony's land is taken from the Indians. Winthrop's excuse is that the natives haven't "subdued" the land and thus had no "civil right" to it. Never mind that he kills them off first before he takes it. He authorizes the smallpox-them-to-death trick, and he brags about it. Starting in 1492, contagions claim nine Indian lives out of ten, many of them from infected blankets laid on them by Puritans as gifts.

But look: slowly, year by year, his people seem to be cutting back on God. Have they got John Winthrop's number? Are they just exhausted? Was this Roger Williams guy and his campaign of revisionism working? Roger Williams was crisscrossing the Colony, speaking at every pulpit and would-be pulpit he could climb upon, tearing the Puritans to pieces. By 1645, of 421 families, 128 are no longer attending church. And this number of stay-at-homes is increasing. What does the Governor do to keep his colony from slipping away, from falling apart? How do you get these folks back into the saddle of the Lord?

You get meaner, that's what you do. You make harsher laws and you punish the disobedient and you imprison them and you cut off their ears and you place them in stocks and you banish them and you hang them too. There are lots of things you can do when God is whispering them into your ear. And you encourage everyone to rat on their neighbors to alert Winthrop and his fellow preachers, or teachers as he calls them, of anything "bad" seen or heard or suspected. It was early blacklisting, that's what it was. It appears that we have been very good at this from our beginning.

For "Disrespect of the Lorde's Day" and "Absence on the Lorde's Day" some two thousand fines are collected. This works out to a fine on more than half of the households. "I have lette matters slippe too much. Never againe."

There will be more than one thousand harsher convictions credited to Winthrop during his nineteen years in Boston.

Two hundred cases of adultery are punished annually. In at least two-thirds of them it is the woman who is put in the stocks. In at least a dozen cases the woman is hanged for not being sexually available to her husband on demand, although, thank the Lord, "thus free-ing up the husband to marry again and return to the bosom of the Lorde." Many couples are punished jointly for not accepting each other under God. This is where his nut-lopping comes in. "If you are not to love each other and not to part, in order to try elsewhere, what use to you of these but as a remembrance of what the Lord had wished?"

One-fifth to one-quarter of all offenses in the records of the Massachusetts Bay Colony are for homosexual acts. As indicated, hanging is the punishment for sodomy. Each and every year at least thirty-five men are hanged. At least fifty are put in the stocks. At least a dozen are banished. Why the difference in the severity of the punishments is not noted is perhaps because of payments to Winthrop. Yes, Winthrop has "a special hate for the sodomites." Yes, one of his sons comes before him for this crime. His own father orders him hanged, and never knows that the young man is set free by his mother and allowed to run away.

A man named Philip Morgan comes to live near Boston. He and his younger lover, Paul Morton, find themselves happy here. They acquire land far away from staring eyes and they farm sufficient to their needs. Yes, life is hard; storms, wolves, starvation, and diseases are rampant. "But we have each other and we are safe," each tells the other all the time.

The Boston Latin School has opened. Philip is engaged to teach. He tells the boys, of whom there are no more than half a dozen, about "the great

Greek philosopher Socrates, and Alexander the Great himself." He wants to tell the boys what he knows in his heart about both these men. He does not, but he is discharged for telling them what little he did. Ancient Greece already has a bad reputation for "licentious behavior."

What he had written down to tell them was more complete. "In ancient Greece, a man might be attracted to a woman not his wife. He might be attracted to other men. When the Greek army defeated a Persian army ten times its size, the power of love among comrades could be seen to be the heroic power it was. The great philosopher Socrates taught that physical beauty and moral excellence went hand in hand. The greatest warrior of all time, Alexander the Great, was such a man beloved by all men, including the one he bedded with each night." These words were found on a sheet of paper beneath their bed.

Although hushmarked behavior was illegal and sodomy punishable by death, this is one of the first recorded instances in the history of The American People in which a private house is entered so brutally and the sleep of the inhabitants interfered with so vigorously:

"It is with sad occasion that 'twas necessary to invade the household built by said Mr. Morgan in the Roxbury Woods, and here it was discovered that he lived not alone but with the young man Paul Morton, some years his junior. And here they slept in one narrow bed together, and here were the sheets investigated and found to contain stains of a male nature. When caught unexpectedly together they were found to be naked of clothing and in each other's embrace, involved in that act which is so repugnant to God in Heaven and which is condemned in the Scriptures of Our Lorde."

The case is open and shut. Philip Morgan is hanged on two charges of "indecent morality both in his teachings and in his ungodly desires." Paul Morton could not be found. "The young lad managed somehow to disappear afore arrest was sent to fetch him to the gallows." (Above from *Additional Annals of the Massachusetts Bay Community, 1630–1649*, vol. VII, pp. 245–53. Massachusetts Historical Society Annex, Duxbury.) John Winthrop personally signed Morgan's death warrant.

Also found under the bed was a letter Philip had written to Paul: "We all want desperately to believe we come from and are a part of the best that ever was." He went on to give Paul directions about how to get himself to a safe place many weeks away due south, "where it is warm and safer. Go, with my everlasting love." Did Paul know about this letter and its contents?

It is the commandment "Honor Thy Father and Thy Mother" that John

Winthrop uses to rid himself of the biggest trial of his governorship. "If we should change from a mixed aristocracy to mere democracy," he wrote, "first we should have no warrant in scripture for it: for there was no such government in Israel. A democracy is, amongst civil nations, accounted the meanest and worst of all forms of government. [To allow it would be] a manifest breach of the 5th Commandment."

A woman, a housewife named Anne Hutchinson, begins preaching in the Massachusetts Bay Colony against the basic principles of the Puritan religion. She aids new mothers, helping her best friend, Mary Dyer, with the midwifing, and she starts leading the women in regular Bible study in her big house, which is just across the street from Winthrop's. She believes that no one else is responsible for her salvation, no church, no preacher, no teacher, not even the Bible. Her relationship with God is hers and hers alone. This is blasphemy to the Puritans. She is accused of luring and then harboring people into secret "conventicles." Anyone can be saved when one feels saved is her feeling and she will be exiled for it. She is nearer to our Protestantism, which would be anathema then as well: a dangerous disregard for so-called expertise, for authority. It is all quite petty, these differences, and utterly cruel. Anne was challenging the Bible, she was questioning it. She knew what she was doing. She was crying out against enslavement, of women, even of the Indians themselves. She challenged the concept of original sin because it blames women.

Winthrop also has to contend with Roger Williams, that other preacher from hell, as he would call him. Williams is also obsessed with God and his own determination is to completely separate church and state. He is single-minded in his attempt to point out to Winthrop and his followers that a civil state should allow all kinds of religions and should not have jurisdiction over the soul. Let us not kill each other; this ending will come soon enough.

It is interesting to note that John Cotton (Cotton Mather will be his grandson), and Thomas Hooker himself, have arrived. Each will be called by Winthrop to judge both Anne Hutchinson and Roger Williams. Each will condemn them both. The great Thomas Hooker describes Williams as "from whence the infection would easily spread into these churches." Cotton says of Anne, his former dearest friend, "You are a woman not fit for our society."

Roger in his single-minded zeal has never stopped hammering at Winthop's God. "It is a false peace" when the state inflicts punishments on people who question it. Such talk is considered a contempt for authority, and if he doesn't recant Williams will be punished.

In 1637, Winthrop has a court order issued "to keep out all such persons as might be dangerous to the commonwealth." Once again one shudders to see Christians setting in stone powers that permit them to persecute other Christians who disagree with them. "We are your judges, not you ours," Winthrop says to Anne Hutchinson at her trial.

For Hutchinson and her followers are accused as not only enemies of Christ but of society, of everyone, of the entire population of the Massachusetts Bay Colony, and are to be imprisoned until Winthrop decides where to send her.

An earlier sin had been discovered that was the clincher. In her midwife days Anne had delivered the stillborn baby of her friend Mary Dyer and, with John Cotton's blessings, secretly buried its fetus, claiming, when later queried, that it was "a monster." Winthrop has it exhumed and indeed it was so misshapen a monster that Winthrop blames this consequence on the mother's friendship with Anne. Cotton denies his participation in the cover-up. Mary Dyer and the Hutchinsons (her husband has just died and Anne is pregnant for a fifteenth time) escape before the sentence is delivered and head for Rhode Island to join Roger Williams. Rhode Island allows them, along with Jews and Baptists and Quakers, outcasts elsewhere.

What had Anne said and done that was so awful? Being a good person was salvation. The Holy Spirit in the hearts of true believers relieves them of the responsibility of obeying the harsh laws of Puritanism. Its ministers were deluding their followers by declaring that good deeds would get you into heaven. But Anne was the unauthorized minister of a dissident church discussion group. She held Bible meetings in her house. She invited her friends and neighbors, at first all of them women, but soon to be joined by men. Participants felt free to question religious beliefs and to decry racial prejudice, including enslavement of the Indians. She explored Scripture much in the way of a minister, allowing different interpretations. She had a strong concern for women's lack of rights. It was also charged that by attending her gatherings women were being tempted to neglect the care of their families.

The General Court of Massachusetts, presided over by Winthrop, brings her to civil trial. She is forty-six and advanced in this fifteenth pregnancy. It is whispered that one of John Winthrop's congregants is the father and that he raped her in an effort to silence her. She is forced to stand for several days before a board of male interrogators as they try to force her to admit her blasphemies. She is condemned, awaiting Winthrop's disposition. The First Church in Boston on its own conducts a religious trial. They, too, accuse Hutchinson of blasphemy. They, too, accuse her of "lewd and lascivious conduct" for having men and women in her house at the same time during her Sunday meetings. "Your opinions fret like a gangrene and spread like a leprosy, and infect far and near, and will eat out the very bowels of religion," her old buddy John Cotton, who had taught her to listen to Jesus speaking within her—"the Spirit of your Father that speaketh in you"—now condemns her as she is consigned to the mercies of the wilderness. She suffers a miscarriage. The Puritan leaders and preachers, from all their many pulpits, gloat over her suffering and that of Mary Dyer, who also suffers a miscarriage, and call it the judgment of God. When Dyer becomes a Quaker, and goes back to Boston to recruit others, she is hanged by Winthrop for this. A real troublemaker Hutchinson was, with her implacable self-certainty, and now, because of these two Johns, the most hated woman in America.

The Colony continues to persecute Hutchinson's followers who don't go with her to Rhode Island, where, with Roger Williams, who's already there, she became the first woman to found a state. Winthrop and all who stood with him sanctimoniously cited her subsequent tragic misfortunes—her deformed stillborn baby, and the scalping of six of her fifteen children and her own murder by Indians—as proof of God's judgment against heretics.

This was a great man? *A Modell of Christian Charity* is considered his "great" work, the one that includes that "cittie on the hill" baloney.

Looking back, it can be seen that John Winthrop and Roger Williams were two strong, smart, obsessive men challenging each other's beliefs, trying to chip away at them, without success, which made their bondage to each other (for that's what it was) even stronger. The irony is that in this battle they somehow loved each other, because of this very fight. Their correspondence and dealings were not dissimilar to how Melville and Hawthorne will dance the same ritual dances around each other, each in awe of the other, each afraid of the mightiness the other's passion represents, Hawthorne incapable of saying anything out loud to him at all, Melville imploring desperately, I want you with me, please, I need you, and together we could make the world understand. Winthrop did do something for Williams he'd never done for anyone, not even his own son: he tipped him off in advance of the verdict against him so he could escape his imprisonment and get to Rhode Island safely. Those letters Roger wrote to Winthrop sound like the ones Melville wrote to a terrified Hawthorne, imploring Winthrop for his love on his, Williams's, own terms, not God's, but man's. Williams calls the Boston church "the dung heap of this earth." Hawthorne surely knew what this was.

"THERE IS EVIL AT THE CORE OF LIFE"

That is what Hawthorne will tell Melville. All Melville wanted was Hawthorne's love. Not this pearl of wisdom. But that's all that Hawthorne gave him. And pretty much all that Melville found anyway, on his own. What a sad, unappreciated life he led. It was a hundred years before someone took him seriously.

THE FIRST PLAYWRIGHT?

You would not note me walking down a street [he wrote] unless you are one like me, or you desire to see me perhaps only when you are drunk or far enough away from pervasive and disapproving eyes. I look like any other man.

You might even want to know me. I am friendly. I walk with unthreatening gait. I'll shake your hand firmly and with neighborliness.

Yes, I am willing to know you. I am lonely, as all Others are, and desire a Friend.

Indeed, my eyes will look at you most beseechingly to know you. To accept you as you are, if you will do the same for me. Yes, like every Other, I am lonely. These days, loneliness is ill spoke of. Folks do not know what the cure may be. Folk are frightened of that which is full of pain. Loneliness has not yet come into its own as Blight. There is no cure, is there, for Blight, or Sadness? Cure is a word perhaps too new.

For now, the sad Loneliness of Man is called, only, an ill-Humour.

There is a cure, of course. Another body's warmth.

Where find the ones who will not savage your soul, or pilfer your purse, or take a knife to your member or your throat? Where find the ones to talk to? The ones who are able to love?

Where find the One?

Where are the words to explain such feelings as these? Who understands these things?

I am a Playwright!

I speak Tongues rich in variation and innuendo. So easy is it for me to summon the Feelings of Mankind.

I have been Performed! I have heard my words spoke before a crowd and seen tears and heard laughter and, most joyously, cheers. How grand are the feelings that swell inside one when people shout and cheer. Applause! Is there anything so full of balm? Then pride sweeps over one—, yes, pride in the power given me to summon words and devices to string these words together and evoke such Wellcome.

But Wellcome does not come from all. In this new land, filled with new people who are frightened of the New, there is often opposition to the Play, to any Play. There are places where arrests are made, where incarceration comes from performance of the written word in public by actors who speak such lines as I do write. More and more laws are made against "Publick Performances."

I do not know what to make of this Chagrin. Not to earn a livelihood from the Calling of the Heart and not to make a marriage from the same are great woes.

And so comes the loneliness.

•

This boy is dressed most proper neat, as for some school far off.

"Are you lost, my lad?"

"I am, sir."

"Can I aid you home?"

"I don't know, sir."

"Where do you live, then?"

"I lived in Stuyvesant Square."

"Are you then Dutch?"

"I am. And you are English?"

"We are all from somewhere. What brings you to St. Tom's?"

"It is a peculiar story, sir."

"Will you tell me?"

"Would you like that?"

"Why, to be sure."

"I was witness to a signing most important. A treaty, my father said. To pour the wax, and to emboss it with the signets of all our family, required my parents and my aunts and uncles to withdraw into a chamber distant from the main altar, where I was left and told to pray. 'You must wait here for my summons,' my father told me. 'You must kneel.' And so I did. 'You must pray.' And so I did. For ever so long. But no one returned. I ran in their direction. I searched each alcove and behind each door, until there was only street beyond. So far, you are the only answer to my prayer."

"That I will try to be."

"I confess a certain fear, sir. And I am tired and I am hungry and I am chilled and near to tears. I am too old to cry, do you not think?"

"There is never an age too old for that. Come, let us look together."

The elder holds this Youngster's hand as we march forth. Does that not sound Promising, and Grand? Out of the churchyard we start to walk, away from the tombstones, toward some Light of Day. The elder's thoughts fill with the Youth:

I would kiss your lips. I would kiss you a thousand times. Everywhere. Everywhere. I would hold you in my arms, but would you return my embrace? How would you receive what these feelings, my tremors, my needs, must certainly convey to you, of warmth, of loyalty, of devotion and conviction and reality, of—who knows, perhaps of Love?

"Are you still frightened, lad?" We are still within the churchyard's walls.

"Sir, I am."

"Is it I who frighten you?"

"You, sir? No. Though I am puzzled by your . . . agreement."

"What means you by 'agreement'?"

"I don't know, sir. I don't know what I mean by this word. I don't know whence it came, though I spoke it. I think I mean that I sense you and I are like."

"You are no more than a dozen years and I am twice that."

"I am made of other things than years. And I am a full fourteen."

"Speak more of your thoughts. Fear not."

From what depths came what I felt, to make my heart a thumping drum?

The lad looks me full in the eye. "I perceive why I have been abandoned by my own. I believe my family has left me and shipped back to Amsterdam, now that my father has made his fortune here. I am justly amazed that you come in their stead. Tell me, from your heart, please, what you want from me." He has his fingers on my lips, reaching slightly up to touch me. "I want such honesty as you have never uttered, such that there is nothing more pure within your being."

He is most provocative, and precocious, and perhaps mature, my new fourteen-year-old friend.

"I offer you, young gentleman, a love." I say these words softly, and I say them fast.

"My mother always spoke of love." He is being wily.

"It is a different kind of love. A love of Own for Own. Do you know of such?"

We are still in this damnable graveyard where New Amsterdam buries its bodies. There is a rain. Since time began I'll wager there is always a rain here.

The lad is silent. As Playwright, would I not provide Youth Soliloquy here!

"Yes," the Youth replies at last. "I know of such."

"And you do not walk away?"

"Where have I to walk?"

"You could run."

"Yes, I could run."

He speaks this bravely, this Youth.

It is I who try to hide the tears.

"What do your tears mean, sir?"

"I promise never to abandon you."

"A promise, and so soon." He looks at me carefully. "I am suspicious of promises. I have heard many promises of the Everlasting. And those who made them are gone." He smiles. "You silly man, you have no idea how to ask your questions of me."

I shake my head, perplexed. "You are indeed most mature, and I the elder."

"But I am only just alive. I know why I have been abandoned. I have been named One of Them. I have been named Sick, and Ill, and Diseased, by my own father, who took me to his bed and put his body into mine, then to throw me down in his after-drunk."

Now it is his turn for tears, and he lets them come. We are just outside the graveyard now, in the open. We hold each other close.

"What is your name, lad?"

"Thaddeus, sir. Thaddeus Ignotum Harsh Arbuthom Lees. It is a long and posturing half-English and half-Dutch name that brought me much embarrassment in school."

"Now that you are about to begin again, you may choose any name you wish."

Such anticipation brings him a happy look.

"Then might I choose a new name, yet again, as often as I desire?" He sounds like a little boy.

"I see no reason not to." I feel like a little boy.

It is he who takes my hand. It is he who leads me out of the graveyard and into life.

It is this lad, barely grown toward a man, who teaches me, at last, to love.

"I shall start as I am, as Thad."

Thad. Tad. We call him both and either. Tad. My little bit. My little bit of Everlasting Love.

•

The soliloquies I write for him turn into an Ode.

What happy Circumstance of Fate brought each to each? Why was I there, in a graveyard? And he, just rising from prayer? What messenger sent him to my arms? What utter cruelty disallowed his return to those who bore him there, and thence to me? Will those who sired him reappear? Were they, too, guided by some Higher Force? No. No Higher Force looks after them as it does Thad and me. Should they, or those who act for them, ascertain our ardour, would they have me—us?—removed and killed forthwith? My boldest question yet remains, as ever it must. What brought such Beauty to my arms? How did this boy decide, here, now, at this moment in Time and of our History, beside this monument to God that is one step only down from Heav'n, to wellcome Everlasting Love and bring the same to me?

Such an Ode of Questions!

•

I took him, first, to where I lived, my small retreat from the Outside World, my home, at Number Three, Revender Way, which is by the Wall Street, and by foot only moments from City Row, where I earn my bread.

I say "first," for the instant his hand was in mine, before I even tasted his lips or sucked his flesh or licked him top to toe like some mother cat, I knew that I—that we—must betake our precious cargo from this world of danger. I am no fool. I know that what we do is Death, not only in these parts, but I surmise—No! I know!—in most others as well.

I do not know where Safe Harbour lies. Every town and direction, every country, I have heard is Woe. I am only twenty years myself, and have known my direction since no more than five, and have practiced my proclivities, albeit covertly, for one learns early what is Deemed and what is Demon. But since the Age of Tad, I have done so, I now see, most recklessly and fearlessly, uncaring, then, if Death should come my way.

Now Self in me cries out: Beware!

I have never felt as this. Great love comes so entwined with fear to test it.

There were, this very year, in these territories alone, so I have heard, some hundred deaths for Self-Love. There is no official name for what we do. Some say we see only half the world, and from such so-called blindness do we lose our sight. This punishment—the banishment of sight—is the most commonly rendered. One sees the blind men walk the streets, young in years, their spirits dead, their hands reaching out for warmth and comfort and wellcome, of which there is none. It is beyond pity, it hurts so to see. There is many another punishment. To be boiled in a vat of oil. To be skewered through and roasted on a spit. To be cast into a bottomless pit. To be hacked to pieces and thrown to wolves. To be sold as a slave to places beyond Far. To be thrown into Prison, or Bedlam, and be buggered to death. To be bled to death by chopped-off Member. To choke to death when forced to eat this Member. To be tongue-tied by rope to toe. To be tongue-cut. To be throat-cut. To be rendered deaf. To be beaten to death by clenched fists of hate. And burning. There is so much burning.

These deaths are always most dramatic, so that all may see.

There is no such thing as easy death for Love of Self.

Yes, this must be punished most theatrically.

Why? Why? Why? So many Whys.

How did They find these Hundred Self-Loves? Does some Invisible Ruler pay an Army of Spies? How high the Bounty on these Heads? What does the Law require as Proof? What cares the Law at all?

Rarely is there more than one man's Word for Condemnation. Rarely is there more than a claim by One against Others. I know of those killed for what they did not do, nor are.

Now I am frightened.

Where can we go?

"Be careful," comes the Warning from the Master in New Fleet, he whose journal of daily news and happenings I do my remunerative writing for, who is my only Friend among Them. "You walk most dangerously. The walls have ears. The walls have eyes. Not only for such as you and yours. For us all. In one way or another."

Such parlous Times. To try men's Souls.

Where can we go?

New World indeed.

"At least my father let me live," says my Tad. "Where I was born, in Holland, one of my friends, one too of my brothers, together were boated out beyond the dike, and thrown in the sea, and drowned each with a hundredweight after they were found each in each other's arms as you and I are here together now. What we do in the face of all these punishments is most brave indeed, do you not think, my William? I am proud to be most brave with you, in this new world."

New World indeed!

The last name of William, our first playwright, is never known, but a play, Facing the Music *(author unknown), was performed throughout the colonies for some fifty years beginning in 1648. (See* When the American Theater Was Young, *by Steiner and Steiner, published by Rittenhouse Trinity, 1934.) The first white man to be hanged in Virginia for sodomy, in 1670, is a playwright named William Haythorn. Also, in New Amsterdam, after an on-again, off-again attempt to do so, it's once again prohibited to put on, write, and appear in a play. The penalty is imprisonment. For writing a play. Even a comedy. The first playwright so imprisoned is named William Hawthorn, in 1670. Authors remain shadowy figures, with good reason. We know the titles of 1,500 plays performed between 1590 and 1742, of which only a few hundred survive. Did our guys know about what had happened in England, where Christopher Marlowe, a gay playwright, was murdered in 1593, the same year that the playwright Thomas Kyd was tortured? After the great Ben Jonson had his thumb branded for being too opinionated, it is said that Shakespeare himself kept a low profile.*

•

I must tell you that America is boring me. I have more energy than you let me use. I do better in other places like Arabia. Talk about people who kill each other! They are always going after something they call the yellow-bellied heathen hordes. The men fuck other men a lot. They also rip each other's guts out. Arabs are not so much fun as you guys. Just scarier. But they're not looking for me or going after me, thank goodness. They hate hushmarkeds even though they fuck each other a lot.

Much to learn still. Much to learn.

Trying to keep an open mind.

Some doctor lady in America is going to tell you soon enough that she figures the transfer of me from chimps to humans occurs between 1590 and 1760, with 1675 the most likely date. Boy, is she late for the party. Her name is Dr. Gudrun Organo and she is at that Southern Jewry place. Funny they study me with Jews. I have a hard time infecting Jews. Don't know why. Ask Gudrun if she knows why. Go on, ask her. Dr. Gudrun, is there something UC is not doing correctly when it comes to Jews? Let me know.

They have these cut-off penises, Jews do. I wonder if that's it. Makes me slither. Can't grab ahold. You got a lot of them hanging around? I wonder if I can come up with a work-around for them. Hope so. That is, if you got a lot of them.

That Jesus fellow had a cut-off penis. Was he a Jew? Or an Arab? Those Arab fellows are circumcised, too. Does this mean they're related? Jesus and his buddies fooled around a lot. Got to check my record book which ones I got.

I wonder what I look like in 1675? Cute and desirable?

You keep going on about hushmarkeds being hanged for fucking each other. Am I missing something? Hard for me to keep accurate records of me.

And this Dr. Gudrun lady doctor is crazy. I crossed over much longer ago than she says. I thought you knew this.

You certainly are spending a lot of time on me, guy. Why don't you listen when I tell you it's a waste of your time? I will be what I will be which will be me. Call me a microbe. Call me a gene. Call me a cell. All one and the same. Zillions of me in each of you.

Tell your guys to please get to work and mingle more. Living dangerously can be fun!

AN IMPORTANT DATE

Dr. Gudrun Organo at the University of Southern Jewry will pin down 1675 as the likely date that The Underlying Condition crossed over from monkey to man. She will not accomplish this until 2009. It is said to be an amazing bit of scientific detective work and not possible without the equipment that by then had come into use.

No one will remark that, even knowing a date for this, how much does one know?

It's too bad Bosco won't be alive when this happens. I hear him saying, "I don't want to say I told you so but I told you so. I knew my stuff and I was right. Gudrun was another one of those women who hated me."

YRH TELLS US THE HISTORY OF YADDAH, FRED'S ALMA MATER

OK, I went to this place, and I tried to knock myself off at this place, and I tried to change this place Big-Time, which of course they wouldn't let me do. So I've had perverse pleasure piecing its revelatory history together for the delectation of all.

Yaddah College (to become Yaddah University in 1702) is founded in 1512 or 1634 or 1701. It's not as if they couldn't make up their minds, but there are official histories by the shelf of Yaddah College and Yaddah University, and of Yaddah Medical School, and there is a lot of major disagreement. There are the old histories and the mid-century histories and the centennial histories and the bi- and tricentennial histories and of course countless revisionist histories. They agree on little. Yaddah's history may never be fully unraveled. "Founder fathers" come and go, ordaining him and him and proscribing this and that. They do not appear to have got on with each other very well. Presidents and chairs and fellows are always being pushed out or leaving of their own volition, some with unexplained hastiness. They are all men of God, of course. God is what is taught. Religion depends on an educated ministry for its perpetuation. *Educated* is perhaps too generous a word, and this last sentence should be fashioned thus: "Education depends on a devout and God-fearing ministry for its perpetuation." In any case, twelve books written by these founder fathers laid everything down. Or were there thirteen? Or only ten? Is there a lost book? It is said there is a lost book. And is the handwriting in the "original" mission statement really the work of one hand? What could be so complicated about starting a school to teach religion that leaves no history, to this day, quite agreeing with any other?

If it is 1512 or 1634 or 1701 from which all blessings flow, does it matter much? Does it matter much if there are three first students or a dozen, or if it is Harknettle who is the first minister to teach God, or Seymour the first founder from Old Nestor Township who moves his class and small library from there to settle in New Godding, to seed America's first—what? School? Academy? But is it really our first? What about the University of Southern Jewry? What about Elizabeth and George? What about Tradumpha? What about Harvard, which was our first college? Why and how does Yaddah always manage to usurp such pride of place? Yaddah has a proprietary and presumptuous way of proclaiming itself the oldest and/or best of everything and getting away with it. There are no arguments, no counterclaims; there is no one to dispute Yaddah's primogeniture, preeminence, and impertinence. Yaddah has always been able to claim a "history" that covers all bases, and no one ever cries foul to this day.

Our new country wants so much to have schools, as evidenced by a circular distributed in the early Massachusetts Bay colonies, "Please Eddicate Our Children." We don't want to bow down to England or to import a way of thinking that most men have sailed away from. The Founding Fathers want everyone to be educated, but in a new way. What is this new way? Well, it will be different from the old way. A grand desire, this, to forge a country's education, as ambitious a scheme as creating the country itself, without knowing how in the name of God to do it.

Unfortunately, our country had no great early thinkers doing our "new" thinking. They were solid, stolid, boring, and intensely conservative, with limited imaginations and curiosities. They were more conservative, as we have already seen, than those who were left behind in England. How could anything new come of that? Elisha Yaddah reads books, true. He has made money, though none of the histories is certain how, which is always a suspicious shortfall. Accumulations of capital in those days tend to go unnoticed because they are usually kept secret by their accumulators. Money is a very secretive thing. Elisha has books sent to him from all over the world. He pays scribes to copy anything new and interesting. He accumulates a lot of books. It is his library that forms the basis of the first Yaddah, and Elisha's name is bestowed upon it in exchange for this gift of his books.

Elisha mentions in his diary the Brothers in Zvi, that elusive organization said to have been responsible, back in the snows of yesteryear, for the establishment of a worldwide network of Jewish whorehouses in accordance with the sacred Zordah, which wanted Jewish men to fuck only Jewish women when they were out on the road. "I read books before and after I fucke," Elisha writes (thank goodness so many diaries are kept by so many people). "I fucke men because the business of brothels is distasteful. It has besmirched womanhood forever. To touch a Jewish woman's private parts knowing men all over the world are paying money to Zvi to do the same is enough to make me glorye in the touch of a man who I know touches only other men, and for free, and reads books." What an unusual excuse for homosexual behavior. No wonder there is a missing book or two in Yaddah's history.

To think that Yaddah was founded by a homosexual! This will be news to all the legions of Yaddites!

This diary entry is particularly upsetting to Semplish et al. because it is the one piece of written evidence that Elisha Yaddah was a homosexual, and by inference a Jew. Reynard Fasswuss of Cambridge has written, in his own *History of Yaddah* (1998), that Elisha Yaddah left no diaries, and the one that has been found is fake. "This whole queer business is very hard to swallow." That's pretty strong language from an academic. "There is always a historian or two or twenty who cry out at some point, fake!" cries out in response a rival camp headed by Dr. Endicott Klemm of Oxford, in his *Encyclopedia of Whorehouses* (1999).

Fasswuss does not dwell on Elisha's private life, only on "his animal interests." Indeed, there is no sidestepping that part of Yaddah's "history" which records that it began life as Deacon & Caplan in 1589. Or 1673. Or 1702. "Documents" of incorporation can be produced to support each date. Mr. Caplan's heirs consistently maintain that he most certainly wasn't Jewish, and that "Elisha Yaddah" is a misreading of "Yalish Caplan" and hence really not that person, i.e., Elisha Yaddah, at all, and that somehow various genealogies became inadvertently intertwined, from bad handwriting perhaps. Caplan, by whichever name, was what we today would call a veterinarian, but one specializing in monkeys. He came to America a rich man. He had spent much of his life in India. "Deacon" was what America's early settlers called the organ grinders whose monkeys danced for peanuts. In one of the Twelve Books of Yaddah there is mention of D&C as "an institution of knowledge important to all humanity's welle-being." Fasswuss concedes the founder's "animal interests" but leaves out any details.

To think that Yaddah was founded by a homosexual veterinarian. A monkey man! This will be juicy news to Yaddites near and far.

Not only a homosexual veterinarian but one who collected and peddled monkey blood. Now, which story of which founding of Yaddah do we like more? There are others.

Fasswuss devotes little space to the private life of "our founding father," whom he does name as Elisha Yaddah. "Elisha Yaddah was rich. That he was a single gentleman is not much cause for interest. He came and went quite often. He traveled from his house to other houses. He journeyed from one town to another, indeed from this world across oceans to others. He desired no outsider to pierce his nature." Like all heterosexual biographers of homosexuals, Fasswuss does not go anywhere near the heart of his subject. He does not, as it were, go the whole nine yards. Elisha did write in his diary about his very long penis.

A point that has eluded all historians of Yaddah's beginnings is that Elisha Yaddah did not make a secret of his life. He did what he did and if he was seen, so be it. The men who came and went from his house also came and went from his bed. This is a strong statement, that the founder of Yaddah, vet or not, was a practicing and open homosexual. It will not be verified until 2001, with the attempted establishment of the Frederick Lemish Initiative for Lesbian and Gay History at Yaddah, when one of its visiting scholars, while rummaging in the Globb Memorial Library, is led by a gay librarian to Elisha Yaddah's diary, lying there on a shelf, all those centuries later, just waiting to be discovered and read. Shortly after this discovery and its release to the world Yaddah abruptly shuts down the Frederick Lemish Initiative for Lesbian and Gay History at Yaddah. No legions of even gay Yaddites come to rescue it, or me.

New Godding is on the Connecticut-Massachusetts border, and at one time or another each state—much as Maryland and Virginia still claim credit for Washington, D.C., as carved materially from their flesh—has tried since Yaddah's establishment to usurp it. It is "halfe a horse" to Boston due north, and "halfe a horse" to New Haven due south.

New Godding has a tough time in the history of early population centers. Perhaps because it is equidistant from so many places but still on its lonely own, sexual offenses outnumber all other categories of criminality handled in its courts. There are many convictions for "drawing out his yard." There are many flaps over "obscene conversation" and public behavior perpetrated quite deliberately to embarrass and shock pious neighbors. Men masturbate ("self-immolate," in the act of "self-pollution") in public, even unto seminal emissions while praying. Indeed, ejaculations at prayer by some groups are commonly considered as offerings to God. Other men just do it to show off. Quite evidently, life is boring in New Godding without a lark or two.

For all its fame as a center of education, which is certainly one of man's higher callings, New Godding comes to represent as well another side of man's increasingly complex nature. As ministers and magistrates agree that each decade sees more numerous offenses, Yaddah draws to its ivied courtyards more and more men of God. Morrissey, Goldnerstas, Davenity, Winthrop (even here), Adams (there is always an Adams), Edwards, Elliott, Davenport, Silliman, Timothy Dwight, Jonathan Edwards, the list of theologians is end-less. These men of the cloth rush to "bring" respected young students into Yaddah's mix, and the students pay for this privilege. As with Socrates and Plato, instruction in the search for perfection encourages youngsters to go out and search for it on their own. And so Yaddah is from its earliest years, whichever ones you choose, a most ungodly Godly place. Education in the use of genital organs is certainly constantly denounced and a Mather pulpit is never far away, but Yaddah boys will be Yaddah boys.

New Godding's infamy gets lost soon enough in the rush of Godly edu-cators to join the band. There are more and more sinners than saved, but there are more and more people everywhere who claim they want to be saved. It is a growth industry. No one wants to get left out of whatever is all the spiritual rage. It is not long before Yaddah this and Yaddah that begin to grease up the intellectual circuits of The American People. To have Yaddah any-where near your name means you're a class act all the way. Yaddah will become America's preeminent center of all learning. It will seed the world with its enormous and ever-expanding network of scholars and their publications, all those men sent out into the world like the missionaries they are, clutching their valuable tubes of rolled-up sheepskins.

If carnal exuberance or its squelching occasionally erupts in such an exalted center of learning, which is the worse for wear?

When institutions of learning are exclusively male, what higher good do they have to offer, when all is said and done, than the love of man for his fel-low man?

It is only in 2014 that acceptable scholarly verification of Yaddah's life and story appear in *Elisha Yaddah: Merchant, Collector & Patron* by Scaris-brick (Oxford) and Zucker (Harvard). Born in America, he went off with a well-to-do father, who was a merchant and attorney, to London at age three, and to Madras in southern India at sixteen to be a clerk for the South India

Company. As Madras itself grew from a small fort when he arrived to a population of some 300,000, he became governor and then returned to the small country town in Wales where he retired and died in 1721, at age seventy.

New Godding had been too tame for the father and London too little for the son. He saw no available opportunities interesting enough. He wanted out, on his own, and saw the newspaper advertisement for the South India Company, a guild of merchants and stockholders that traded back and forth on their own fleet. From being a clerk, an office boy, a bookkepper, his excellent work slowly took him to the top. He married a widowed woman with a title who slowly went crazy in India and took herself back to England with their daughters. She never returns to India. The widow of his Jewish diamond expert became his mistress, more for her knowledge of her late husband's contacts. There was some fuzzy stuff about a young man who started out as Elisha's son and became his lover before he too left Madras and was shipped home.

No matter the wretched heat and foul sanitary conditions, Elisha obviously found it difficult to leave Madras because of two words: "tremendous profit." He became many times a millionaire in various currencies. He accumulated a huge collection of very valuable items, diamonds (foremost), rubies, emeralds, gold, works by such as Rembrandt, Rubens, Breughel, Dürer. He returned to England with some seven thousand paintings. Trunks full of all kinds of fabrics, of course, for which Madras and India were famous. One hundred canes, five hundred rings, fifty-four tobacco boxes, all fashioned from one kind or another of something precious. Every kind of watch imaginable. Ivory. Pearls. Coins. Medals. Mathematical and surgeons' instruments. Firearms. Swords. Cabinets of rare wood. There were more than ten thousand articles that were shipped back. There were thirty-four days of auction sales, with the hope that no market would be wrecked by such a sudden and lavish infusion.

And books. Erudite, learned tomes about the natural world, the law, history, philosophy, the beautiful maps in the twelve volumes of Pitt's *Atlas*. He gave 449 of them to the group from New Godding's Collegiate School looking for funding. Mutual friends there put great pressure on him to contribute in accordance with his great wealth and to match, at least, gifts to other places of higher learning. So he added two trunks of Indian textiles and a portrait of George I. The books earned him his name over the front door of the no-longer Collegiate School. He never saw it and he never went to New Godding or indeed back to America to see it. He had promised more but died before the will had been legally approved. The total value of the gift amounted to something less than $30,000, about the same as John Harvard paid to get his name on everything half a horse away.

In the elaborate and embroidered clothing he wore, it was "too hot to partake too often" in comfort, his diary tells us, even though, as in Edinburgh, as in London, Bombay, Calcutta, there was a House of Zvi to welcome him in Madras. In fact, he owned its lease and wound up finding his generosity challenged by their bad business. There were not enough English, and too many poor Indians, and certainly hardly any Jews, to keep the place on its own two feet. "Besides, I am not interested in women," he honestly and boldly states. And as will be with George Washington, Yaddah's foppish attire, the clothing and jewelry he always wore, were a bit too much and spoke volumes to those who could read.

Leaving Madras to retire home, Elisha burned down the House of Zvi and sent the women—and men—home. Yes, Elisha Yaddah had placed his possible harm's way out of harm's way, right next door. He had enjoyed going out at night occasionally for a visit with one of the beautiful young Indian men he'd placed there. It was said this is why his wife had her breakdown.

As noted, Elisha Yaddah is hardly mentioned in all those earlier books about Yaddah's history. He disappears from sight or further fame after his death and after all of his valuable estate was disposed of. But the name, if not the man, remains, along with the slogan perpetrated on banners all over New Godding to this day. "When better men are made Yaddah men will make them."

AN IMPORANT PUBLICATION IS LAUNCHED

The *New England Journal of Spots* claims it was the first medical journal in America. It continues to this day. It is indestructible. No criticisms or lawsuits can dent its mighty armor. Why is it so named? Because all illnesses were originally known, seen, viewed, identified, as spots, of one kind or another. *NEJS* was published in Boston. Its founding editor was Dr. Ralph Measlee. The first copies were written in longhand. It was the first of what will be many New England journals, whether they originated in New England or not. There was great trust in all things New England. To this day these journals are routinely cited first and foremost in all discussions and dissertations and disseminations of medical and scientific "knowledge."

The first issue of *NEJS* comes out when spots are spots and spots are all there is: you find a way to remove them by rubbing them away, by cutting them out, by somehow making them leave you. When they don't go away you are considered sick. And you usually die. "He died from the spots" is a familiar statement in the annals of early America. Had it originated anywhere else in the country, the publication would have updated its name when the scourge of spots subsided, but *NEJS* it remains, to remind us with each issue, its masthead blazing that it has been serving the well-being of the world through the dissemination of the most accurate available medical knowledge since 1713, that it has seen a lot of spots.

If it's in an NEJ it must be so, and if it isn't it mustn't. Dr. Measlee, whoever he was, set the rules, the parameters. These rules for acceptance and inclusion are strict and they will stay intact, these rigid, biblical rules set down by an otherwise unknown doctor and at a time when next to nothing about anything it writes about is known.

The words and worlds of all the NEJs continue, to this day, with their corruptible incorruptibility. This is science. This is life. This is The American People. We know better than you do. We're from New England.

Does this sound like a police-state publication?

It is meant to.

Perhaps this is too harsh.

Perhaps it isn't.

It isn't.

A MOST IMPORTANT STATEMENT
FOR OUR HISTORY

We are overdue in trying to pin down some definitions of some words and terms, indeed principles. The word *gay* has been used. The word *homosexual* has been used. Neither of these words will exist for a great many years to come.

No, there was no right word for it that you wanted to use for it if you were doing it. Buggery and sodomy connoted anal penetration and were in many places punishable by death.

Death.

Death.

DEATH.

So you have to be careful what you call it, if you call it anything, which—not doing so—is probably the safest bet of all.

So men learn how not to talk about our very own hearts of mankind.

That does not mean that men did not know that they were gay, to use today's word, did not know what to do with their cocks, did not know when they were smitten with other men, did not know where to go to find them, did not know what it meant to be violently rejected, or the reverse—in other words, the whole gestalt, to use another of today's terms. A penis has never been something that anyone picks up and puts down and puts away idly without consideration. This has been noted earlier. It bears constant repeating. Men knew what they were and what they wanted and what their penis was. It may not have made much sense to them, if they thought about it, and if they thought about it they knew it would cause them heartache and trouble as well as occasional joy. Yes, it was *complicated* (a word by the way not yet in general use). But so were so many other things.

Do you know that same-sex love does not require the sexual act to qualify as homosexual? *The American Heritage Unabridged Dictionary* lists two definitions for *homosexuality*: the first, "sexual *orientation* to persons of the same sex"; and the second, "sexual *activity* with another of the same sex."

In other words, it is not necessary, nor should it be, for a person to have sex with another of the same sex in order to be a homosexual.

Why, then, do most academics—indeed, why does everyone who isn't gay—insist on the second definition over the first? This definition makes it all but impossible in many cases to say that a person is gay. Thus is gay history eliminated, as if it never existed. Perhaps that's why this second definition rules.

What does *orientation* mean?

" . . . a tendency of thought; a general inclination."

OK. This historian can go along with that.

Just because academic research has not uncovered smoking cocks, that doesn't mean that loving male friendships weren't shooting themselves off all over "pristine" America and the thirteen colonies and into the Louisiana Purchase soon to come. It seems reasonable to assume this, no?

Reason and *assumption* are dangerous words.

How does any historian know the intimate male friendships he or she uncovers in early America were sexually chaste? There is no more evidence to prove it than there is of orgies in colonial beds. The argument goes both ways. If one side cannot wave Monica Lewinsky's semen-stained dress, neither can the other side wave immaculate bedsheets.

Your present historian believes that homosexuality has been pretty much the same since the beginning of human history, whether it was called homosexuality or sodomy or buggery, or had no name at all. "What's in a name?" old Will Shakespeare, who certainly knew what it was, has Juliet ask us. "That which we call a rose / By any other name would smell as sweet."

That few other historians agree elicits from this one, after many years of his own struggles to fight such stupidity, a simple response. Tough shit.

No "established," "famous," "heterosexual" historian, scientist, academic, journal, no mainstream anything will be caught dead agreeing.

This will prove enormously, tragically, destructively evil, as we shall see.

YRH is sorry he's waited so long to say this. I should have put it way up front.

But I wasn't a historian then.

IANTHE ADAMS STRODE ATTEMPTS HER OWN GENEALOGY

There are sloppy records (that any records from those days can be found at all is luck) indicating that she owned property under many names, Marjie Destog and Nuncie Bledd, for two. The name she used when she arrived in New York was Vitalia Strode. Different families fought to claim her when they learned after her death that she was so rich. The Dutch Destogs and the British Bledds fought so ambitiously that by the time her estate was settled, well into the nineteenth century, there wasn't anything left to divvy up. But no one knew she'd seen to it that most of her wealth had long ago been directed where she wanted it to go.

Most lives are based on incomplete information, mine own certainly. You will meet me soon enough and I'm speaking out of turn because I was an Adams. We used to be all over the place. But I was born too late to pal around with the big ones, and I was stuck during my peak years with a Strode, nice enough, and with a certain power, but not nearly strong enough for this smarty-pants.

That original Strode was a strong and effective woman. And indeed she strode into the New World and never looked back.

There is no place in London, or anywhere over there that she can see, for an ambitious woman to achieve on her own terms and in her own right. She arrives in 1737 with a bit of money. She says her husband died and she had to get away. He was older, she says, she was his second wife, and she's still young and vital, *spunkie* is the word used by interested gentlemen, of whom there are plenty when they hear her husband was not only old but had died. She loved him and she was faithful to him and she feels betrayed when he leaves almost everything to his two sons by his first wife. Worse, they make it clear they will fight to keep her from getting what little he does leave her, certainly much less than her due.

She dresses too well and she wears a valuable jewel or two. Everyone knows London is dangerous, and she travels with a bodyguard armed with a hidden blade. The bodyguard looks to be a man but isn't. Her name is Leakey. She dresses like a man and has a low and threatening voice. She is over six feet tall. Strode is five feet six or so, a strong height for a woman, a height that can stand up to most men, look them in the eye, and say, "Get out of my way, buster." *Buster* is a word in use already. To bust is an action fully understood.

There was a large Strode family in England then, of sufficient wealth and enviable position. There was a Sir Henry Strode who died in 1735, and he was older indeed. He died at eighty-six. He left a young wife, one Dinitia Ianthe Bledd Strode, of a good family evidently.

She is to write, "You won't locate any news of me. When I saw that his two sons were not going to take care of their stepmother in the manner she wished to be cared for, I snatched all I could gather, converted it to cash, and boarded the first boat to this America place I'd been hearing of. It caused them to turn upon each other. They had a duel. Each killed the other. Then I got all that was left."

Since there are still a lot of Dutch in New York she calls herself Marjie Destog. She gives herself a Dutch accent but refuses to speak Dutch. "I am in America, gentlemen!" She gets away with it. Should anyone be suspicious, Leakey steps forward and reveals a few inches of blade.

It is an interesting blade. More scythe than dagger or short sword. Slightly curved. With a sharp-edged hooked end that could rupture your insides to shreds. On the voyage over Leakey uses it several times. "His" mistress is an attractive woman still, about thirty-five years of age, and trim, and she is much leched over by captain and crew and passengers. The three murders are all executed at night; all three intruders into her Lady's cabin are dispatched overboard. If they are later missed their absence is not questioned. Drunken sailors and officers, even passengers, are thrown overboard all the time. It is not an easy voyage to America. An inconvenient man can be lost on land with equal ease. There is no such thing as a detective or a missing persons bureau; there is hardly any such thing as law. Luck is the main reason people stay alive. New York is into its second century and it's still its old cussedly rambunctious self. Boys are still being boys.

It is interesting that so little fear is visibly expressed. People go to bed early, with locked doors and windows and a lantern left burning to discourage outside interest. Guns are becoming less frequent as constant companions. But any sense of the danger of everyday life as a damper to the daily excitement of a new world aborning is seldom manifest. People keep their scaredyness inside of them. Perhaps old people are more fearful, but there are not so many of them. It is a young person's world, this New World. And this settlement of Manhattan is nursery and playground and jungle gym to it all.

She loves it, Strode does. Or is it Destog? She buys a small house on Rector Street. She buys another small house on Divinity Street, around the corner. She wins a house, on Trinity Place, around the corner again, in a card game. Property is cheap, certainly compared with London, where the stifling lack of anything much for sale keeps prices soaring. Within six years she has sixteen small houses, all under rent and bringing in enough income to finance her continued forward march. She has no idea how much she wants to buy, or what she is buying it for or toward. It is like a game where the dice always come up winners. She and Leakey now travel with a third person, named Quadree, who carries a tiny firearm obtained from France. Quadree, too, is a large woman posing as a man. Again, no one seems to notice this. Perhaps Leakey and Quadree are that expert at their disguise. Or perhaps there are just so many unusual beings walking around Manhattan that no one takes much notice. I opt for the latter. It's not that much different today.

Lower Manhattan is gradually moving north. So move north will she. She knows the British will be here for a while. And she knows them well enough to know they won't last here. America will scare them half to death. She now starts buying property in the name of Lady Nuncie Bledd. It is not such a stretch for her to take this name. She claims her husband's name was Sir Optley Bledd. The British, for all their vaunted superiority in colonial management, are sloppy record keepers, as sloppy as every other country at that time. Again, if paper proof is what you're seeking, a certain caution regarding its worth, when "found," must be uppermost in your mind. It has never been difficult to manufacture paper legality. The expression "not worth the paper it's written on" has been around for a long time.

Strode's English self loses its charming Dutch accent. Her metamorphosis happens gradually. By the time she is fully British again she owns some four dozen houses in lower Manhattan, just short of fifty, which she has determined will be her cutoff, after which she'll do something else. She acquires two more houses. She's hit her goal. Two more "ladies" bearing arms join her growing group for additional protection.

I guess one should pause to ponder where she found these women. As with your hushmarkeds, there is no proper word for lesbians, for it is no doubt this is what they all were, including Lady Nuncie Strode Bledd Whatever. It's an early history not much written about, as I discovered when I came to write this paper for a course in My Family History when I was at Smith and still blushing when I heard words like *pussy* and *clit*. There have been many times throughout my life when I wished that women did excite me sexually. Men are simply not very good at it, and from many lesbian friends I've discovered we who aren't are missing a great deal of pure and simple pleasure. Of course we can take care of ourselves getting more pleasure than any man's second-rate fuck can give us. But one can do that for only so long before its essential component of being solitary dribbles into loneliness. As with gay men, they obviously found each other.

Our Lady now fancies an enormous swatch of land that extends from river to river at Twenty-third Street. It is the Fallingsworth Farm and it is owned by Sterling Fallingsworth, a bachelor of some sixty years, tall and rugged still, and handsome. All these years he has avoided marriage so assiduously that lewd jokes are made about his solitude. How could a single man with so much land to farm and oversee have done it by himself, with only serfs and slaves? Men need wives. At least men who have wives say that men need wives, although there is not always unanimity from the wives themselves. A wife's lot is little better than that of one of her husband's slaves. Many a wife would just as soon not be one. Grace and Hermia have both remarked how annoying it is that so few women in distress down through the ages have written about it.

Sterling Fallingsworth is not interested in selling his extensive holdings. True, he is interested in passing these holdings on to some possible future generation of Fallingsworths, a point Lady Bledd, in her pitch to him, forces him to concede. Is she suggesting a marriage? he asks her. She is attractive to him and he is surprised he is so bold now, after so many years of shyness in the face of woman.

No, she is not suggesting that. She is suggesting a merger of sorts. She will place all her holdings into an equal partnership with him and his.

"To what end?" he inquires. Her mind amuses him. He has never met a woman so bold and so imaginative in the ways of business.

"To the end that if we join together we shall be among the largest land-holders in New York."

"And to what good?"

"Why, the good of having enough to bargain for yet more and more, much more than either one of us could fashion."

She thinks him a trustworthy enough fellow. She and Leakey and Qua-dree and now Eleanot and Forbes have discussed his trustworthiness. There is little save looks and instinct to go on. No bankers or security men yet give assessments or writs of bond. Instinct is all.

He agrees to her arrangement. The papers are signed. In celebration he offers the neighborhood a mighty feasting afternoon and night, capped by his drunken attempted seduction of his new partner, in front of all the guests. He seems intent on proving that at last he's found his woman. She will have none of it. He does not subside easily. Nor does she. His continuing importun-ing, accelerated by yet more hard spirits, becomes so obnoxious to her and so visibly upsetting to the guests that it can end only in the way that it ends. Quadree shoots Fallingsworth dead. There is no one present who would not agree that his dismemberment—for she shoots him in his groin as well as his head—is well deserved.

The law is swift and concise. The entirety of their joint landholdings now belongs to her. Whatever her name is.

Five additional large women in men's clothing now are added to her ser-vice, for a total of nine. When she purchases more adjoining farmland, both north and south, this cadre grows to thirteen, a baker's dozen. Thank good-ness her diaries are kept up to date on matters that matter to her.

These women are exceptionally protective of their mistress. She has given each a freedom they have never known. Each has a story not dissimilar to another's. Each had been in a vile marriage to an abusive man, from which there was no possible escape. But here is this remarkable woman of many names who somehow has found the nerve and pluck and luck to play the man's game in this world and win. Of course they are all devoted to her, Leakey and Quadree, Eleanot and Forbes, and Georgius (who will change her name to Georgia) and Ishmaela and Nottie and Manila and Ruthhanns and Serenus and Nodotla and Achilla and Zenobee. They are all protective of her, and soon enough, of each other, too. Each knows a good thing. Each has endured enough unpleasantness in a former life to guard her present one with firm agility. They are a remarkable group. And they all know it and treasure it, and her. And no "gender studies" "historian" has yet to write about them or what they represent, this (so far as is yet known) first group of America's lesbians. Mr. Lemish's attempt at an excursion into this neighborhood at Yaddah is woefully indicative of the lay of this land. So I found it generations earlier at Smith, where my professor Newton Arvin was imprisoned for being gay.

Such a group, remarkable or otherwise, cannot go forever unnoticed in a pioneer community, no matter how many freaks are parading by. Strode, Destog, Bledd represents to any man who wants to call himself a man too much of an unresolved nature. There is much talk heard, and growing in volume, of this woman's rise much too high for the good of man. Many women are just as strong in their jealousy. How is this woman and her cadre allowed to live so high off the proverbial hog when there is not a family among them? Is she fucking with all these men who protect her? That, too, is certainly whispered about, also giving rise to jealousies.

Soon it is known that all her guards are women. Somehow this secret has been let out. It was bound to happen. She knew it was only a matter of time.

She now considers hiring some armed men to help them. But a vote among them determines this is not what's wanted. More women? More women might only exacerbate what is now a growing threat to their continuing safety.

Bledd determines upon a surprising next move. She sells everything at great profit and divides the receipts equally with her thirteen protectors. One day they are all here and the next day they have all disappeared during the night. No one has seen them leave. No one knows where they have gone. Once again they have been most clever. Where will they surface? Will they split up or remain together?

Let us pause to consider the possibilities. Where can fourteen women go with a hope of safety and success? They are not farmers. They are not wives and mothers. They do not want husbands. Most important, they are rich. These are days when there is no safe place for cash. There are no banks to speak of, certainly not for travelers. They all have an enormous amount of cash. It is no wonder that their sudden disappearance elicits such interest. If these girls are out on the open road, then that is of supreme interest to the marauding male. There are not a few who set out to seek trails that might lead them to their fortune.

Where did they go?

There is no news anywhere of a group of fourteen women glued together as one. Had they been remotely visible, someone would have picked up a scent. This is a land of many newspapers filled with any and every scrap of gossip to alleviate arduous and boring lives. This is certainly a story for them, but they don't get it. Strange as it might seem, or perhaps not so strange, newspapers and reporters considering this story do not pursue it. Their own historical files admit to this, with "grave disbelief bordering on the hokum."

Our own story picks up a few years later in southern Delaware. Delaware has had a personality problem not unlike New York's. It was Dutch and then British, and still occupies an uncomfortable and unwelcome secondary position as part of the land bestowed most generously by Charles II, in one of the largest land grants ever, on William Penn, who, even though he wanted frontage on the ocean, nevertheless favored the portion that he'd named Pennsylvania. Delaware is an area more abandoned than popular, though those living here are known to be of hardy stock.

Yes, she was a Nuncie and a Marjie and a Strode and a Bledd and a few others besides before she took up her new life and calling here in Delaware. Now she is known as Lois, a simple name. They are all together still, Lois and her thirteen protectors. Now they are even safer because of a small army of men in their employ who guard their fort, for that is what they have built here in this wilderness. They make spirits from the local water, and they send the men out to peddle them to the countryside. They pay them well and supervise them with strict attention. The men are not allowed inside the fort. They do not know what goes on inside. They obey because they are paid to behave. (When did women stop behaving like this!)

Lois was inspired by reading the Bible story of Nadie. Not the Christian Bible, but the Bible of the Anapalpa Indians who are their neighbors and partners in this new endeavor. Nadie was a woman who protected herself with her own tribe of women warriors, who in turn were protected by a tribe of men. Lois is impressed that this tribe of Indians is still ruled by women.

Yes, almost without knowing it, Lois has started a strong tribe of women with a fearlessness that is solid and invincible. She decides to expand on a good thing by welcoming additional women agreed upon by all. There are many women longing for what they have to offer. Every woman in this New World lives in some kind of unhappy slavery. Carola and Zantippe are the first to join. They are the youngest and they convey their enthusiasm to the others.

The women take to birthing their own children. Many different sires father these children. Carefully picked men are invited in occasionally, one at a time, to do the honors. They have a birthing ward where the women tend each other lovingly. If a boy is born he is sent outside the gate to live among the fathers. Only the girls are kept inside, and by now, with all of them going at it as fast as they can before they dry up, they have some hundred females. The number increases, but increasingly slowly. They feel that so many sons out there with their fathers only gives them more protection for their lives and their desires. Lois comes to believe that some of the men outside the walls have taken to loving each other as the women do inside them.

The women believe they are safe: they are now a self-perpetuating community of women. Lois knows now that this is what she wanted from the day she left England. There is now a story of Lois in the Anapalpa Indian Bible. The Anapalpa revise their Bible as they live. *Lois* in their tongue now means "mother of mothers."

It is amazing how lavish and generous the fineries they allow themselves. They sleep in beds fully garbed in linen and lace, on pillows stuffed with feathers from their softest geese. They wear clothes woven with the finest threads, and shoes fashioned from animal hides that are soft but strong. All of which attire is decorated with bits of gold. Their combined money now totals over $500,000. New income arrives daily with the sale of more spirits to farther regions by their army, now composed of their boys as well as their fathers.

Suddenly Lois dies. She dies in giving birth to a girl she was too old to bear, named Eve. Eve brings no happiness. For with her mother's passing, and after the great moanings and mournings of her devoted family, there is such a void that no one knows how to fill it. Strode she so deeply into all their lives, this woman of so many names, that no striding by another can fill her place. Oh, several try. They hold elections and choose one or another. But no hearts are in it. It all seemed so easy when she did it, whatever her name was, whatever they call her now. They decide indeed to give her one name once and for all. Elena Delaware. She will be buried as such and worshipped as such, for she is as good a god to recognize as any.

Lois's death is kept a secret from the men outside the gates. It is better, is it not, that her passing be unknown? How long such a secret can be kept begins to worry her survivors. Fear, which has been unknown for years, returns. Leakey and Quadree, as the two longest in residence, attempt a joint management, and for a while they are successful enough. They are still strong enough to keep the others calm and the men outside at arm's length. But there is an epidemic of some sort outside the walls, and many of their sons and their fathers die. The women inside sense immediately the vulnerability that these losses bring. Soon there are not enough men out there to peddle their spirits. Soon there are not enough men out there who knew Lois, and who understand, albeit naïvely, enough to let her family be. There have been times, in this country's wilderness, when a certain respect was allowed to difference, if only because no same is ever everywhere the same. Indeed, people in Delaware have prided themselves on this. Are these times coming to an end?

Slowly, as months turn into years, it would seem so. Their male protectors are fewer in number. The stills are allowed to slacken off in their productivity. Even the Anapalpa are moving westward. Our women must go into the outside world to perform chores, and they go bearing arms. Inside the walls they are not so loving and attentive to each other. They try to discuss what they come to call "our deterioration as a people," but talking gets them nowhere, and there is no Lois to be the beacon of enlightenment. Their treasury is diminishing. Their treasurer, one of the newer women, Anolpha, becomes depressed and infirm and less attentive to her duties. She has what we would call a nervous breakdown and tries to slash her wrists.

Eve is now eighteen. She is old enough to claim a leading role, and she does so. She, who has her mother's sense and strength, if not her calming ways, does well enough, invents a plan to attract some of the increasing number of men always wandering the wilderness of this country, rootless and aimless, yet hopeful for some answer that will still their restlessness. Word gets around again that there is still money to be made working for an army of women who are living armed, so don't get any wild ideas. Many men come to investigate.

One of the men who appears is more handsome than any Eve has ever seen. His name is Arundel, a last name he says without offering any first. Leakey and Quadree, who have seen so much, recognize in Arundel a courier of trouble. They see in Eve's eyes the hunger for something they had thought was long bred out of them. It had been easier for some, more difficult for others, but had they not all weathered their sisterhood with nobility enough?

Now it is Arundel's moment to know a good thing when he sees it.

Whether he loves Eve or not, or respects the sanctity of Harmony, he makes known his desire to move inside and live with her. Eve, on her own, agrees. There is much upset that she takes this decision upon herself without consulting all. When confronted, she nods but says nothing. She is not enough her mother's daughter to realize there are times when the group must come first.

Once inside the walls, Arundel can't believe the good fortune that resides within. It is not only the money, coins now worth close to one million dollars, but also the hundreds of hungry eyes, now set free by Eve's capitulation. He can have his pick, and does. Eve does not take this easily or well. When is all this happening? What year is it? How long has everyone been here? There are few anymore who know, they have been sequestered from the outside world for so long.

Soon enough Arundel is followed into the once-forbidden haven by other men. The delicate balances observed so harmoniously for so many years are gone. Male babies are allowed to remain inside, and family units begin to form, at first at one end of the fort but soon expanding throughout. Within a dozen years or so the women who remain together and with each other's love alone are laughed at. The first time this happens Quadree disappears and is found dead from drinking a draught of poison. She is buried but with no hint of the nobility that attended her beloved Lois's passing. Few remember Lois or that moment anyway. The other remaining originals, Georgia and Ishmaela and Nottie and Manila and Nodotla and Achilla and Zenobee (the others must have died by now), bury her quietly and with many tears.

The men entering now at an increasing rate do not loot and kill and run. The established way of doing things is too fertile a gold mine. There are a few of them who want to kill off all the lady-lovers but they are overruled. Arundel, to Eve's surprise, takes decent hold of matters. He convenes the first Council of Elders, all of whom now of course are men, and they determine that the remaining single women may withdraw a share of the treasury and go off where and when they will. Georgia and Ishmaela and Nottie and Manila and Nodotla and Achilla and Zenobee do just that. Each leaves with a heavy sack of coins. They go out once again into the wilderness on their own. They are robbed and murdered, as they knew they would be. Word of their deaths at the hands of the very men inside the compound reaches Eve. Soon the walls of the fort come down and the official founding of the village of Arundel, Delaware, is announced. Arundel pronounces himself its mayor and erects a statue in his likeness and in his honor as the founding father.

One day Atona, a daughter of Nottie, becomes sick with a strange illness. Nothing can stop her coughing and then her vomiting of blood. She dies, but not before her "husband," Franklin Gorsby, begins to vomit blood as well. In fast order that entire quadrant of what had been the west end of the compound, but is now open to the world, becomes a violently retching population of fast-expiring men and women and babies. Eve herself patrols this quadrant and has the sense to put up barriers to keep others from coming near. Then she herself falls ill and dies.

One of Eve's daughters, Alicia, now faces up to the rage that is growing inside her. On the day of the Arundel Banquet to officially celebrate the town's founding, this young woman awakens from her afternoon nap and goes into the communal kitchen, where she covertly deposits into that evening's meal poison sufficient to kill everyone who eats it. She summons every one of the fifty-seven remaining women to her chambers and asks them to bathe her and to plait her hair with flowers, and to perform these same acts upon each other. She addresses them. "My sisters, the name of our true founder has been lost to history. We must return our community to the life that was led here when once there were walls tall and strong enough to protect us. Our husbands and men now return from their travels carrying back the sicknesses of the outside world."

To her amazement and relief the women support her plan.

Alicia, her grandmother's true heir, has taken care of the future as only her grandmother could. She advises the women to refrain from eating, and the following morning they begin to reestablish their domain and dominance. The bodies of all the dead men are burned in the hope that whatever disease they brought would be purged along with them. Once again the high walls are erected and sealed, built by arriving men who are given the take-it-or-leave-it arrangement of an earlier time.

Thus are the names of Harmony's founder and the noble qualities she stood for returned to history. Alicia Strode, a vital, vibrant bearer of her grandmother's spirit, ensures this effective memorial to her presence on this earth. Harmony, Delaware, is rechristened in her honor. And, in 1787, this very state will become America's first.

I was young when I wrote all this, a junior at Smith. It wasn't a bad piece of work, and when I showed it to Strode after we married, he said it did seem to touch some chords of remembrance. "I always thought every woman around me was a bit strange." I wish he hadn't said that. What woman has a man who can say all the right things? That wasn't the response I was seeking, but that's what a political marriage was, and still is. Abigail Adams was one lucky puss. It took me a while not to sound so timid. Indecisive. Wimpy. The me I've cherished building myself into.

GRACE: This is the fucking pussy stuff you promised me? God, Freddie, you're moving along so suckhole slowly, I'll be dead before you can really give us equal time.

FRED: I hadn't thought to include lesbian inclusionary equality, as Grace directs me to call it, because UC has become so gay-male identified that co-joining lesbians into its history seemed a bit presumptuous. I certainly didn't think they'd feel discriminated against if I left them out. I was wrong. Gay men never know much about lesbians anyway, or women either; that's just been a sorrowful given. I remember many a meeting where the lesbians actually asked gay men to leave the room while they conferred on their own. They always considered themselves light-years ahead of us in terms of enlightenment and self-empowerment, and they were. Gay men were only interested in getting laid. It was almost as if there were two different opposing teams on the same side, if that makes any sense; we were joined together by a word, *homosexual*, and not by much else. Loving the same sex almost didn't seem part of the ball game. No, lesbians have always seemed something . . . well, another country, if you will.

UC will change all this. We'll get along better and many walls will come tumbling down. But at this stage in our history, we're a long way from that.

GRACE: This shit is not good enough, Freddie. Sweet, Freddie, sweet. And dear Ianthe, my dear D.C. buddy, nice try for a het. I don't believe for an eighteenth-century minute that those girls weren't brutalized at every block and corner, bodyguards with shivs or not. Among many other things, the smell of money turns men into pigs. Not enough real pigs in this story.

THE GREAT AWAKENING

In Enfield, Massachusetts, in 1741, Jonathan Edwards, who has been called too many times by too many people "colonial America's greatest theologian and philosopher," reaches heretofore unparalleled heights of oratory and rhetoric with his famous sermon "Sinners in the Hands of an Angry God," in which he describes man as abominable in God's eyes, a sinner so hideously wretched that eternal damnation is the best he can hope for.

The coalescing of Edwards's fans into a movement of fanatics begins in New England in 1734, and grows onward and upward, despite fierce doctrinal disputes among his competition over just how abominable is abominable. No previous preacher among these early Puritans goes as far as Edwards in calling men shits, and the huge crowds he's packing in certainly don't go unnoticed by the other traveling God shows. But there's no one out there who preaches or wants to preach or is capable of preaching at such a peak of nihilism as our man Jonathan. Across New England, at first in church after church and in meeting halls, and then, when no building can contain him, at crossroads, in fields under sunny and thundering and downpouring skies, Edwards ignites combustions. Souls explode. Screechings abound. Bodies writhe and limbs bend out of shape. Faces contort. Weeping's supreme. Agonies of every sort display themselves unbridled and uncorseted. Shrieks of terror, in terror, convulse young and old into visions and swoons.

Faith, long dwindling in popularity and becoming increasingly rote for all—forget the Hookers and the Mathers, timid fellows—is now passionately resuscitated. Too many are the scholars of this sort of thing who look upon the Edwards phenomenon as nothing short of "a landmark of American religious history," as too many biographers and historians also note. Would that someone called his gatherings orgiastic. Laundresses and all those who washed clothes report men's underpants as semen-stained and the periods of women brought on prematurely. This guy is tuned in to his crowd and is giving them what they want.

"The God who holds you over the pit of hell abhors you." Yes, there is something about this blackest of appraisals of man on earth that evidently appeals and no one questions it, then or since. It's not so much that the soul's poisonous vapors are vented, freed at last from interior captivity, as it is that Edwards seems to know something no one else does about his audiences and their fears and souls, indeed their needs and desires, careening unmoored ever since this lot of The American People first set foot in America. The previous lot of preachers evidently didn't do the trick. Yes, sir. The American People have not been yelled at, hell, excoriated effectively for almost a hundred years now, and here comes the Reverend Jonathan Edwards to snap the newest conscripts back into shape. He is telling each man and woman:

You are a piece of shit. And each man and woman is answering: Yes, I am! I beg for mercy! Yes, I am a piece of shit!

Hate, fear, these are what have always kept the troops in line and they haven't been planted, watered, and fertilized for too long.

Oh, the blackness of it all. Oh, the willingness of it all. That self-hate can come so easily to the souls of The American People. However are we to be saved—from this?

Why, just to hear his words, just to have their worst inner fears confirmed, the masses weep, they pray and plead piteously for help and hope.

But Edwards never ends on a note of hope. He leaves them weeping, crawling, mewling, orgiastically begging for mercy.

For some perverse reason this period in our history is called the Great Awakening. Who thought that one up?

Cleverly, Edwards's prescription for living each day is less physically exhausting than any earlier Puritan preacher's. Perhaps this is its appeal. (His wife was Thomas Hooker's great-granddaughter and his daughter married the father of the future Aaron Burr: few major characters in American history escape being effectively related.) Numerous Hookers told you what you had to do for punishment. It took a lot of time. Edwards just tells you you're a piece of shit and go home and live with it. Numerous Mathers told you that God hates you unless you do this and that and x and y. Edwards just tells you that God hates you. Bad deeds, evil thoughts, sex and carnality, all equal a wretched life "in after death." Hookers and Mathers told you to stop doing them in this one. Edwards tells you you have them, you do them, and you will never stop, you hideous person. But you don't have to go out after church and *do* anything except feel awful.

America's population is growing rapidly toward its first million. Imagine: that at this time and place, which we still choose to see today in our minds' eyes as a landscape scarcely populated, there are so many here already! And no one's even counting the Indians. Or the slaves. Or the hushmarkeds. But then no one knows what they look like; they can pass even better than most Jews. Is the secret to our success that nothing keeps folk working harder than feeling so bad that only work can cure the pain?

The number of home incarcerations of family members deemed crazy after hearing Edwards is impressive. After his appearance near the town of Litchfield, Connecticut, out of a population of 3,412 in 1745, 567 family members are confined to their rooms "for reasons of unhealth in mind and spirit," according to the records of the Congregational Church on the Green. If sex is the great sin, how can a young country procreate its future? Why is procreation acceptable but the pleasure that attends it not? Are people having trouble telling the two apart? You betcha. As Dr. Sister Grace has said, "I know these are questions that have been asked by every age. I add one to them: Why has no one answered them satisfactorily? Does that mean people want to feel terrible? Does that mean no one has brains enough to shout out, 'Fucking hell, enough already!'?"

This new America is a hell on earth and it is proud of it. Go figure. Edwards will come to be held in high favor by East Coast academicians, particularly at Yaddah, which he entered at fourteen and graduated at seventeen and at which he was a tutor, and where one day a dorm will be named for him. Yaddah is proud of this man.

Here is part of his sermon given on Northampton Green in 1749, as reprinted in *The Complete and Unedited Sabbath Sermons and Diatribes of the Good Reverend Jonathan Edwards* (The Presses of Yaddah at New Godding and Guilford, 1845).

True, God loves you. True! True! True, God hates you! More true! Do not fool yourself this hate of God's is love in some disguise! It is Hate! True and fearful Hate! And you deserve this Hate! Your thoughts each day and night, through sleep and work, through toil and sweat and dreams are wretched thoughts, filled with carnal desire for every other living thing. You lust for her, you lust for him, your lust and need are indiscriminate and everlasting and impossible of eradication. You are doomed to lust for life and unto death, when only bitter peace will come at last to sever pain before you are consigned to everlasting Hell, and for that we thank you, Lord.

We thank you, Lord, for barring all escape.

I list here the names of all our brethren I have seen or heard to lust since we met last. I name Ogilvie, John, for lusting after his neighbor, Aberdeen, Richard. I name Stiles, Martin, for lusting after his oldest son, Stiles, James. I name Murano, Philip, for lusting after his fellow student, Underling, Tom. I name Fewling, Adam, for lusting after his fellow student, Ash, Anthony. I name . . .

There are one hundred men named in this way, all lusting after other men.

Then begins the listing of lustings of men for women. There are four hundred of these.

Then begins the listing of lustings of women for women. There are forty-five of these.

The sermon and namings are followed by another sermon, after which begins the listing of lusting children. There are mercifully fewer of these, but their naming takes longer because mothers faint. A certain pride in the ability to faint with honest, loud, repentant fervor is considered a plus. Fathers, of course, fiercely and loudly slug their kids.

In the wake of each Sunday's bleatings, there are also "some dozen strokes, conniption deaths, and suicides, each and every week with sureness" among the faithful flock (see *Records of the Towne of New Haven, Colony of Connecticut, for the Years Before the Declaration*). On one particularly arduous Easter Sunday, the naming of names and the callings to the Lord take nine hours and the death toll following the service rises to forty-two, in part because a number of parents stab their sinning children to death as gifts to Jesus. Three young Negro children are also found dead from stabbing.

By 1750, the Awakening has been put to sleep. Liberal members of Edwards's congregation, along with an organized opposition no doubt whipped up and controlled by rival preachers tired of empty pews on Sunday, joined by a growing number of people returned to relative sanity and able to speak out against Edwards's single-mindedness in damning simply everyone as so confoundedly awful, force him to resign his calling in the east.

But that doesn't stop him.

He goes west.

Edwards is enamored of the philosophy of the German Meister of Lehmbruck. The Meister's beliefs involve such surrender *to* God as to convulse the body until a sign is received *from* God. What this "sign" might be is not specified. In Germany some followers summon snakes, others speak suddenly in strange tongues, yet others succumb to what can only be called orgiastic fervor, usually imprecisely described but often said to involve immolation and dead bodies. "You will know it when you are called to it," the Meister is said to have counseled, "just as you will know those only pretending to be called." Religion as excessive orgy thus receives a resuscitating stimulation from this Meister of Lehmbruck, with his coreligionists now arriving in America in increasing numbers and commingling with Edwards and his lot. It is this combined group of zealots that then travels farther and farther west, establishing wilderness settlements to accommodate their increasingly fervored and fevered lettings-go, farther from the view of whatever leavening civilization is settling in more eastern states. I'm talking about such northwestern outposts and townships as Fedenta, Roundabout, Sequentia, Snake Pass, Revolta, and later Partekla, each and every one still there to this day. Partekla, in what will become Idaho, close to the Canadian border, will prove to be of singular importance to our plague. Stay tuned. Follow the bouncing ball.

Jonathan Edwards is a handsome firebrand, a movie-star type of his day, with piercing eyes. His wife is a dog, and all Jonathan can say about her is that she is "always full of joy and pleasure," neither of which he appears to approve. He genuinely believes he is preaching love. "Salutary terror," he calls it, quoting from Revelation 21:5: "Behold, I make all things new."

Why does it not occur to anyone that what Edwards goes on about so is harmful, and accomplishes little that is good? "I am ready to say," Yaddah's Professor of Early American History Perry Miller gushes, "that the Great Awakening was . . . a transformation, a blaze that consumed the theological universe of the seventeenth century, and left the American wilderness to rake the embers for a new concept of meaning." Perry Miller is held in his own great esteem for rescuing all these preachers from obscurity, in the literary and cultural sense. He thinks they're just swell. Why do so many "great" teachers and scholars and academics fail the test of reason, of perception, of the true sense of the hideousness they are extolling for its originality, for its transformative energy, for its "newness," for its contribution to our becoming The American People? When is anyone of any repute going to start saying "Hogwash." Newness is not enough, never ever.

It is not to be. The religious duties and obligations of The American People are being codified and set in stone. Preachers spring up everywhere, no longer needing the college education of their colonial predecessors. The never-ending revivalist movements—to be called the Second Great Awakening—undermine the old established religious orders of Congregationalists and Anglicans and create a religious world dominated by evangelical Methodists and Baptists. In 1811 alone more than three million Americans will attend revivalist camp meetings.

By the beginning of the twenty-first century, Jonathan Edwards is a hallowed name. He is assessed as full of humanity, a loving man and husband, and possessed of "an awareness of joy." "The famous image of Puritanism as 'the haunting fear that somebody, somewhere, might be happy' is a caricature that needs laying to rest, however amusing it might be." What rock did this Brit who wrote this in the *Times Literary Supplement* live under? Amusing? Well, YRH is not amused.

Let us move on, battered but unbowed.

Now, and next: Who asks, If God is so terrifying what else is left but money?

But how can money, and the seeking of it, and the acquisition of it, be made less sinful?

We shall see.

•

I've got to say business was pretty good, here and there, but it was spotty. Lots of you guys went to these Great Awakening things but when you got home you were all tuckered out, as I heard you describe it, and so I still could not get the purchase, the traction, the grab-on, the hold on you that I need to make a really big-bang all-out all-American winner for me. So my cases were scattered hither and yon and nobody paid much attention to me or the cause and effect of it all when some people did catch me and leave their life on earth.

Your "straight" men are terrible fuckers. Up and at 'em and into her and out of her and all to sleep in five minutes. I give a top-quality job and that takes more time. I have to prepare myself and go into his dick and slither and grease hither and yon in his immune system, and I am the only one at present who even knows what an immune system is. Not that this makes any difference to what I'm trying to say here. Just wanted to stick it in. Sticking it in is the problem. There is for many early years in your New World a real problem with really sticking it in. Men have a fearfulness about plunging in too deep for some reason, maybe for fear of hurting the missus, or like some kid afraid to go into the water lest it to be too deep and the tide will swallow him. Also the missus, she is not so comfortable with being penetrated too deeply herself. Afraid of possible pain, of getting hurt, of "being cleft in twain," as I'd hear some of them say, or probably just of getting pregnant yet again. Neither one of them, man and woman, had learned yet about the pleasure principle, the let-yourself-go-and-it-feels-better principle. As I say, no one seems to be enjoying themselves or know how to.

A VERY IMPORTANT LECTURE

What makes a rich man? What makes him worthy of remark? What of envy? And how does he get away with it? God does not like the greedy, or so we are told.

Silver, not gold, is what it's all about in colonial America. Most of the gold has been looted and sent to Spain to finance more of whatever they're doing over there at the moment to make the rest of the world, including their own people, miserable. So silver it is, and fortunately there are big strikes around and about (the biggest in Bolivia, which Joseph Conrad will write about in *Nostromo*), all south of the border, or what will one day soon become the border, but it trickles north, the silver does, since things of value never stay in one place for long. Silver becomes a currency of sorts, but not in the form of coins: coins won't come along until we have a Constitution that authorizes a U.S. Mint. Silver in bulk, in lumps, something of heft that can be weighed and transported, that's the ticket.

Believe it or not, things are not moving as swiftly on the other side of the ocean, where you'd think they'd have had their money organized centuries ago. "The honor of creating Europe's first freely circulating banknotes goes to the Livonian Johan Palmstruch, who founded the Stockholm Banco in Sweden . . ." but that was in 1656 (*Money: A History*, edited by Jonathan Williams, 1997). The British send over lots of "bills of exchange" for trade. And France will soon issue a ton of paper promises to help finance the American Revolution. But silver in lump form is in short supply and the colonies are desperate for some sort of local circulating currency. The big year is 1690. The Massachusetts Bay Colony puts out some paper bills.

Money is at last, as the British say, "to hand."

Not much has been written about the role of wealth in early America. The concept of money, the sense of entitlement, the jealousy of the have-nots, all categories dear to the heart of modern economists, remain relatively unexplored by historians of our beginnings. We forget that many settlers arrive well-off, or well-enough-off, to have the necessary stake to become even better-off. It is difficult for a white man not to earn decent money. There is so much to do! Land needs to be bought and tamed. People need help. It would be the laziest of men who could not move forward, if only bit by bit.

To be considered rich a man would have today's equivalent of $40,000. A very rich man would have access to money, land, and goods worth hundreds of thousands of dollars today. It is difficult to pin down precise amounts.

There are no banks, or when there are, no one puts everything into just one. Bookkeeping is private, and ledgers are often stashed away with valuable family papers—a Bible, a marriage certificate—and hence quite often lost to time.

What becomes increasingly visible, albeit so gradually that not much oohing and aahing goes on, is the *manifestation* of money. Houses become bigger; they are built with more-elaborate materials such as imported bricks; they are furnished with more things made by artisans who are closer to artists than to carpenters. Families have been so accustomed to living in barren saltboxes, with little room for comfortable chairs or sideboards or bedsteads, that when it dawns on the father of the house that there is now enough money for him and the missus to have their own bedroom, he adds one. All of this is, as The American People will find themselves aware over and over from this moment on, an idea whose time has come.

It is a simple notion: to spend the money one is accumulating.

Up and down the East Coast, and increasingly inland, villages and towns are accumulating handsomely. Most visible wealth belongs to gentiles. Jews try not to show their worth in any way, going so far as to live humbly, if not wretchedly, to attract less notice.

Where are the hushmarkeds? Well, they are not called hushmarkeds for no reason. And there are no run-down neighborhoods yet for them to reclaim and redo and move into.

From few pulpits in the land are the accumulations of wealth condemned or chastised.

Pause to let this last statement sink in.

How does it happen, in a population approaching 2,250,000, that there are at least 7,300 households with assets worth today's equivalent of $100,000 (*The London School of Economics Handbook of Worldwide Wealth*, 83d edition) and few men of God are screaming, "Cease, you worshipper of Mammon!"? What gives? Are these God über alles guys on the take? More likely they want to spend their own money, if possible, guilt-free.

There are two distinct and divergent schools of economic thought at play here. One school holds that from the start there is plenty of everything for everyone here in America—raw materials, land, good soil, good growing weather, food, timber, and of course freedom from interference—so everyone prospers mightily. (Today's foremost exponent of this view is Britain's Paul Johnson, called by *The New Gotham*'s Adam Gopnik "just too far out and cranky.") The opposing school maintains that life is hard, labor is scarce, weather is defeating, Indians are untrustworthy, soil is rocky, crops are sporadic, and everyone is poking their nose down your throat and saying, "You can't do that!" and if you get through to next week, much less next winter, you'll have nothing but more of the same. It's a hard life, it remains a hard life, and it won't be long before the poverty and depression of urban areas, which all of the above failures drain into, will blight the growing nation. (The popularizer of this view is Howard Zinn, "too to the left for even the most rabid Marxist," according to Professor Howard Lamar Guthrie of Yaddah University.)

The first Perdist Poll, in 1790 (we're jumping ahead for half a tick) (we'll meet many a Perdist Poll along our way; we're still doing them!), attempts to find some answers. Polls are unheard of, and why and how Brutus Herakles Perdist comes to conceive of such a notion is lost to history. He takes a pencil and a notebook and asks the same several dozen questions to assorted neighbors and strangers along his route as a self-appointed inspector of what passes for a mail service in rural Massachusetts. Actually, it's not a badly constructed what today would be called "sample." He discovers more Johnson than Zinn. This land and those who dwell here are doing very well indeed. Very few people gripe. Many answers are embellished with statements like "heaven on earth" and "the only way you could get me to leave this country is in a coffin." America, it appears, is on its way to becoming the richest country ever, but its population is still too small to produce enough volume to be heard.

And we do want to be heard, The American People. "We want for everyone here, yes we do, because more will lead to more," advises Brutus Herakles Perdist in the preface to his study. "America is still too lonely, and if it is facts and figures that will bring them here, then here ye, hear ye!"

Thanks to Alexander Hamilton (also still down the road apiece), it will be the pursuit of wealth, not excellence, that will form and inform The American People from their official beginning (yes, we're getting there, but not yet). This wealth will become, like Mick's Rolling Stone or Sisyphus' boulder, increasingly visible as it gathers negotiability. Everyone will soon realize that everything is and can be and will be and really should be for sale.

And all of this, miraculously, is now all right. God is keeping His lips sealed in His Holy Temple.

For a bunch of religious bigots who conceive of the Lord as a wrathful punisher of overreaching, where in God's name does such permission come from?

John Locke.

Yes, a man named John Locke, who wrote a lot of things that many think they understand when they do not, a man no one reads anymore, a man who lived in England and Continental Europe from 1632 to 1704 and never came to America (although he helped to write a constitution for the Carolinas), this man has more to do with forming the soul of The American People than any other preacher's God.

These are some of the things he said, stood for, and believed (with grateful acknowledgment to *The Blackwell Encyclopedia of the American Revolution*, *The Blackwell Encyclopedia of American History*, and *The Blackwell Encyclopedia of British History*):

He wrote, in 1690, *Two Treatises of Government*, which played a large role in the debates leading to the Declaration of Independence.

He believed government is a voluntary creation of self-interested individuals who consent to be governed in order to protect their personal rights to life, liberty, and property.

He believed the unlimited acquisition of money and wealth is neither unjust nor morally wrong.

He believed men are moved to community by a common "moral sense" that produces sociability and benevolence and a more rational perception of the common good, which is informed by sentiment and affection, not by fear of eternal damnation.

A "moral sense," John Locke says, is innate in all mankind, giving us all the intuitive knowledge of what is right and what is wrong.

For Locke, "or else" means you don't eat, not that you go to hell.

Now, in the most fundamental sense of all, because of this universally shared moral sense, all people can be seen to be equal, because all people have the moral capacity for sociability and benevolence, for sentiment and affection.

"God is love" is now "Man is love."

It is rich to be rich.

All this is certainly a far cry from Cotton Mather's "We Must Live on God's Love Alone." Locke's very Protestant God commands men to work the earth, true, but in exchange comes not a fleeting respite from eternal damnation but the right to possess what they work for. Since God gives "different degrees of industry" to men, some have more talent and work harder than others, and it is entirely ethical for them to have as many possessions as they want.

This is crucial to America's emerging ideology. If individuals are to define themselves in terms of what they achieve in the race of life, and if this sense of achievement is seen increasingly in terms of work and victory in a market society where talent and industry have their play, then the earlier Christian moral barriers to unlimited accumulation have to fall. Achievement and sense of self are now measured by economic success.

Take that, John Winthrop! Take that, Hookers and Mathers all! Take that, Jonathan Edwards! The cosmic struggle is not between God and Mammon but between industry and idleness.

Yes, this is the beginning. Those who came here to preach self-sacrifice and defilement are swept along? away? farther west? The concatenation and tintinnabulation of damnation must now fight it out with the purrs of comfort and the grunts of greed.

The philosophical decks are now cleared for America to be on its way to being the richest place in the world.

So if you are rich and have no guilt, John Locke is the man to thank. John Locke made you rich, keeps you rich, and will bury you rich.

And if you aren't rich, it's nobody's fault but your own.

But if you think the Devil has been banished from this earth, think again.

THE STATE OF THE (STILL NOT QUITE) UNION

The early Americans are subject to the same appetites, suffocated by religious hypocrisy though they may be, that accompanied their lives where they came from. God may inhabit the house, but bedrooms and crotches have their visitors. True, matters had got out of hand back in England, where licentiousness was a way of life. There was ample reason for the concerned to be concerned. The London that has been left behind is smutty and scurrilous. But once the immigrants are over here, why is there such denial that anything much is happening save for the worship of God?

The South is way-out-of-control permissive; it is much too far away for law and order to hold sway. South Carolina is filled with scum. "Devil-may-care degenerates," as one historian describes them. The tough guys wind up in South Carolina. The Mid-Atlantic is rowdy and free-for-all, though perhaps with self-appointed civil magistrates more plentiful here. There is rarely a shortage, anywhere, of neighbors eager to tattle on what they see or believe they see. In the major population centers of Boston, New York, Philadelphia, each with its growing abundance of hungry adults, as well as a superabundance of men of the cloth spouting God and sin, things are held better in check. Sort of.

This is not to say that Philadelphia, for many years our largest "city," is a spick-and-span kind of town. As we shall see.

Bawdiness. It sounds a rather old-fashioned and sophomoric word, doesn't it? But it's the one attached to most offenses. Many are the complaints about and punishments for bawdiness. There are bawdy houses and bawdy almanacs. Ben Franklin's *Poor Richard's Almanack* will be filled with swipes at loose women and cuckolded men. But then, Ben never did like women much. And there will soon be more newspapers in the New World than even in the Old World. And newspapers will print almost anything. And do.

Yes, God may be in His Holy Temple, but earthly thoughts are never silent. Miscegenation in the forests (big-time in the South). Bigamy in the towns (ditto in the North). Unwanted babies, abandoned or murdered, more of the latter than the former, pretty much everywhere. Self-pollution (i.e., jerking off in public). Bestiality (i.e., fucking animals). Dirty talk. Foul language. And adultery everywhere. Fucked, rogered, fuddled, or yarded, these folk are hungry! There are not enough magistrates to marry and not enough law enforcers to enforce. The statute may be on the books, but there is usually little save a neighbor's testimony to go on when it's disobeyed.

So it can be safely said that while righteousness is galumphing through the pulpits, sin is slithering supremely in the alleyways. Everything that we do now they did then. Don't you let any boring historian or chronicler tell you otherwise. Don't let *anyone* tell you otherwise! There has been little new under the sun in this department.

Let us press on.

It's time to finally meet our Father.

•

It suddenly occurs to me . . . you do understand . . . and I don't think that you do . . . that I have three completely different sets of problems in dealing with all of you. There is a penis, which you know a little about, and there is a vagina, of which you are most ignorant, and there is the asshole, which Dr. Sister Grace is so fond of profaning. *Profaning.* That is a new and big word for me. I learn from you. But you do not learn from me.

Working with you is like taking ocean voyages to three entirely

different continents. I think it will take a very long time for you to understand this geography of your own bodies. Good. I like long voyages. They are relaxing and refreshing and I meet so many new and interesting people.

Who is this Father you speak of? I look forward to meeting your father.

GEORGE WASHINGTON: A RECONSIDERATION

"All our history will begin with me," George Washington will say again and again, "and all our history will happen here," he will say, referring to the town being built to honor him.

To read what is written about him, George Washington is among the most boring presidents that The American People will ever have. Everything written about the man is as if from a catalogue of spare parts, *The Great Men Catalogue*. There is no warmth, no blood. There is only his "icy majesty" (Rhodehamel). And he is a snob of the highest order. He is always cognizant of who is above him and below him. For a man who liked to get fucked up the ass he certainly is uptight.

"Washington eludes us, even in the city named for him," Garry Wills begins his peculiarly unsatisfying biography, illustrating our theme:

Why is George so eternally elusive?

How mysterious to have our very first president so invisible and The American People so bereft of human knowledge about him.

Surely someone must have known him a little bit.

Apparently not. Or not so that he thought so.

"I did not desire to be known," he will lie. "And no one knew me," he will lie again, in some final notes Hamilton finds and which make Alex cry. They had been in love with each other, mightily.

He did have beautiful handwriting, exceptionally neat and pretty. It's hard to get to know someone who writes like the best girl in penmanship class. For a man who kept every scrap for the posthumous record of his life and saw to it that each was stored carefully away, he is surprisingly difficult to pin down. Amusingly, the relative who inherited these papers passed out free samples of the great man's handwriting to anyone who asked for a souvenir.

George reminds one of Peter Ruester, another famous president hard to know. He, too, wrote reams of pleasantries, passionless records of events that were passed around for souvenirs.

George is said to be tall by some and short by others (David Abshire nails him at precisely six feet three, one wonders how), and pasty white, not a healthy-looking chap at all. Not only biographers and historians but also artists have found it difficult to transmit a revealing portrait, to locate an essence. One painting by Trumbull shows a weak and effeminate man who begs for affection's return. Ceracchi's model for a stone rendering (called by Madison "an unrealizable project for a bombastic marble allegory") is of a veritable movie star, an action-adventure favorite, the John Wayne of our early frontier; this man is so handsome that he is not meant for commerce with mere mortals. Surely by artist's license, he is presented as six feet three indeed, with a huge bull neck, large feet, and long legs, muscled calves. He is the quintessential heterosexual; in no other "likeness" is he so starkly attractive and masculine. Houdon's elegant bust (1787) is a likeness as no others; Rhodehamel names it "the finest portrait ever achieved." Most other representations show an aging impersonal man in a wig, with cheeks sucked in and mouth somewhat pursed; you sense those false teeth in there, hiding a tongue that probably smacks when tasting food. Or cock.

The eyes, it is the eyes. No artist is able to get his eyes.

None of the many famous well-known portraits hanging in every American public library and classroom are ugly, like so many of Benjamin Franklin's are ugly, but none much resembles the others. Rarely do they appear to be of the same person. In the most famous of them, like the one by Thomas Sully, he looks as distant and enigmatic as in all the others. There is one sort of sweet portrait, by Charles Wilson Peale, circa 1779–80, where George stands on one leg, the other cocked before it, in beautifully made uniform and regalia with sash and epaulettes, all color-coordinated. He is high-booted (over rather skinny legs), with a tiny bit of a paunch showing, an intimation of genital endowment, and a sort of nice half smile (a tidge of pudge in the cheeks and jowls), his left hand leaning against and rather caressing a very bold phallic cannon's spout. A cute young subaltern behind him holds his noble horse, both lad and horse at the ready (the horse has particularly adoring eyes; no trouble for the artist with the horse's eyes). George is trying to look regal and patrician. He also looks to be not terribly intelligent, and like someone too much enjoying dressing up in such a costume. Again, his head does not look big enough for his body, particularly with such a wide expanse of barrel chest, or is it stomach girth? Yes, it is rather a big barrel belly disguised by that sash. No one has ever portrayed him as fat! He does not look like a man who will become the president. He looks like the stand-in for such a person, an actor trying out for a part. (This portrait was sold to an anonymous buyer on January 21, 2006, at Christie's for $21.3 million, setting a record for the sale of an American portrait. According to Christie's it was expected to bring "only $10 million to $15 million.")

Peale paints another portrait, of his head and shoulders alone, in 1787, with his cheeks rouged up. This, too, is a peculiar likeness, of a man with no eyes and an inscrutable, almost imbecilic expression, the man in the beautiful uniform, the gay man all dressed up but offering nothing real. He does not welcome you, he does not repel. He just . . . is. A portrait by Rembrandt Peale, Charles Wilson Peale's son, of 1795, could be of another person and from another family entirely.

All these faces. All these bodies. Yes, he is so elusive.

Is he frightened of anything? We don't know. Is he in love with anything or anyone? We don't know. (Well, we do now.) Obsessions? What are they? (MEN!) Even the goals for his people in his turgid prose seem rhetorical, too studied, too bloodless, no doubt well thought out (by Alex), but still.

Try as anyone may to make him interesting, the results are usually leaden. There is not one biography of the man that can be called gripping. He is a cold chap you wouldn't want for your father, though no doubt you had one like him. Perhaps he set the mold for every uncommunicative cold fish of a dad who has cursed the development of this country ever since. Who knows how to be a good father, even yet?

As a general, George is a strict disciplinarian. Deserters are hanged and incompetents are sacked. There are many deserters and many hangings. These are never detailed or even mentioned by the many historians who worship George, who do not tell us that these portraits are elusive and passionless, that his prose is turgid and passionless, and, of course, that he was homosexual.

He is not talkative. As has been said, he is not comfortable with the spoken word. He is a terrible soldier and an absent leader of them. He is a wretchedly inept fund-raiser better equipped to starve his men than locate the bread to feed them. He is appointed commander in chief and put forth as president because nobody else with a sufficiently impressive profile, or fortune, wants either position. It is not that he is the right person at the right spot at the right time; he is the only person at a time when this country is filled with men who aren't interested in stepping forward for an infant country that may not outgrow its crib. And then he sort of plays hard to get, co-quettish. That makes America want him even more.

Listen to Thomas Paine: "He had no friendships. He is incapable of forming any. He can serve or desert a man, or a cause, with constitutional indifference; and it is this cold, hermaphrodite faculty that imposed itself upon the world and was credited for a while, by enemies as by friends, for prudence, moderation and impartiality."

No, Paine did not like Washington. He accused him of abandoning the cause for which the Revolution was fought. He thought he was a phony.

A hermaphrodite? Did Paine mean sexless or an equal-opportunity employer?

John Rhodehamel of the Huntington Library writes in *The Great Experiment* (1998): "Every passing year makes him a less accessible human being."

Yet, despite all this, he remains monumental.

And yet "he never seemed to have very much to say," Rhodehamel tells us. People who talk to him were "often disappointed."

The strong, silent type? What better repository into which future historians can channel their own GW?

Much has been written over the centuries to the effect that he is a clever duck, crafty and quiet, seeking opportunities to extend his family fortune. Gore Vidal sees him as our first great selfish venture capitalist, presiding over the country so he can buy it up cheap when his government puts huge parts of it up for sale. The man does seem to care most about his land. He is making a living as a surveyor at seventeen. Many are the occasions throughout his lifetime that he returns to the wilderness, alone, save for those cute young Indian fellows, or that sweet young French morsel, Gilbert Lafayette, who visits often.

He meets Martha Custis, a widow with children, when he is twenty-seven and proposes to her on a second meeting. She is very wealthy, and it is hard to conclude that he marries her for any other reason. She is evidently pleasant. She is an unattractive woman one year older than he. This is not love, or passion. It is, at best, companionship. What more could a syphilitic hushmarked ask of any woman?

Yes, like Lincoln, he has syphilis. Boxes of dried sassafras accompanied him all his life. The Indian braves? Syphilis is rampant among his troops, among all troops. Do they joke about it as they fuck each other? Sodomy is also rampant among his troops, among all troops. Who else is there to fuck, for goodness' sake?

No one (except Gore Vidal) has ever called him what he is: a young man so obviously on the make that in seven years he goes from "poorly educated younger son of a minor planter" to "one of the richest and most famous men in America" (Rhodehamel). By then his landholdings—and yes, his slave-holdings of more than three hundred—are immense.

He has an insatiable appetite for acquiring land. With Martha's money he is able to do so. Is this his only visibly naked hunger? His years of survey-ing in the wilderness have given him this appetite for more and more land. His enemies say he wants to own all of America for himself. If this is so, it is by far the most interesting and honest human quality about him.

One wonders why Martha destroyed all her letters to and from him. What could possibly have been in them to prompt such a strong reaction? Were they too boring? But then, she would have had to have been intelligent and tasteful enough to recognize them as such, which she was not. She was dowdy, frumpy, uninteresting. So what could they have contained? Sympa-thy for his physical illness that made lovemaking impossible? Sadness for their lack of children? Would either of them have committed such feelings to paper, to words? The marriage has always been presented as a good one. But what actual hard information has been uncovered to tell us anything about what passed between them? What was there to hide that might cast doubt on this pleasing picture? Well, several possibilities have just been pre-sented to you. He was fond of her. And she of him. But like Mary Lincoln, Martha knew that his interest lay elsewhere. Mary also destroyed almost every letter from her husband. Mrs. Herman Melville did the same. This act alone bespeaks more loudly than anything else the determination of these women to keep the world from knowing the paucity of their emotional lives with these men.

We'll continue to consider this peculiar man and the country he will rule, and that will let him rule it—we want him to rule it!—twice.

THE AMERICAN REVOLUTION

The American Revolution is the first successful colonial war of indepen-dence. This unprecedented success is achieved against one of the most powerful nations extant, a country that is the greatest naval and financial power in the world. It should have made us feel good.

It is important to know, as the most astringently vital of all lessons about the early history of The American People, that the American Revolution is not what it's cracked up to be. John Adams said that a third of the people didn't even want independence, a third didn't care one way or another, and the rest were probably faithful to the Crown. Indeed, some 50,000 Americans are said to have fought on the British side. And one out of every five Americans traces his roots to Africa. In the port of Charleston alone between 1672 and 1775 nearly 90,000 black slaves enter this country, and their masters have better work for them than to be shot dead defending a country that isn't theirs. So this 20 percent of The American People don't fight at all, or give much of a hoot.

Brutus Herakles Perdist, ever vigilant to locate the soul of his people, confides to his diary, "I fear for us how we shall get through the coming fray, for it shalle be a fearful fray, a fray of frays, with nary enow of us to fight back. And even should we fight back we have no power to Staye Firm and spitte in the enemy's eyes. We are not angry enow. We want too much our soup and porridge. We want our land and barnes and cowes and ducks more than we wante our freedom from the masters who enslaved us once before and return to do it again" (Historical Archives Division, Admiral Mason Iron Vaultum Library).

The British over there care even less than the people over here about soldiers getting killed. Many of the soldiers, on both sides, are mercenaries. Mercenaries are paid to get killed. Indeed, they are among the few soldiers who do get paid. Stories of filthy prisons and crude amputations and no medical attention, never mind harsh medicine (such as it is), lift neither patriotic fervor nor enlistment.

The soldiers of The American People run away with regularity, back to their farms and shops and families. They have no guilt about this: they were roped into service in the first place, with too much wine, a rousing speech in a pub, and a few coins for joining up. So what if I signed a piece of paper? My wife needs me more than my country, whatever that is. While George and his staff are at their parties and horse races and gaming tables, those who remain in his forces are half-starved, half-frozen, and entirely unhappy. There is no record of George noticing this with sufficient concern.

Rich people want to stay at home and poor people can't afford to leave it.

Poor people? A growing class of poor people is finally appearing. It's about time they are noticed, even if they most certainly aren't attended to. Between 10 and 20 percent of the inhabitants of Boston, New York, and Philadelphia are genuinely poor. While it may have seemed a good idea for them to join up, for the sake of food, shelter, shoes, when these run out the bodies once enjoying them do as well.

Some of us fight, of course. We even have rebels. "Mobs," they're called, a radical fringe. And there are popular "upheavals" wherein country folk, town and village people, short of joining up, pitch in and do odd good deeds to help the growing cause. Not that many can yet enunciate what that cause might be. Don't they want to be free? It's not a concept that many have given much thought to yet. They don't like those damn taxes, that's for sure. We have the Loyal Nine and the Sons of Liberty and the Friends of Moses Brown. We have the Sons of Caleph and the Sons of Seneck. And of course there are the Minutemen of Massachusetts, so called because they're pledged to come in a minute, the joke among the men soon arising whether the name describes their readiness or their ejaculations, so close a bunch in affection are they. As for the men who have signed up, they are discovering that boredom in the army is a big, big problem. How do you occupy an army that isn't fighting, or if it is fighting doesn't want to be fighting, and either way is short on food and clothing? It's a logistical mess on all fronts however you mention it, and no one ever mentions it, really. Another case of our wanting our history pure as the driven snow. Well, the snow was filthy, all winter long and into the spring. And this went on for some eight years. How do you hold on to, much less amuse, troops away from home for so long a time?

So it's a wonder we had any army at all. They don't tell us that, all those other historians. Much too much has been made of our noble defense of ourselves. If we won it's because we got lucky. Nothing to congratulate ourselves for so endlessly and for so many centuries.

As Hermia keeps saying, plenty of British are against the war, too. Britain is a rich place and, as such, sloppy in its accounts management and, as noted, in constant need of ready cash. Their biggest argument against the war: don't bite the hand that feeds you. America is a good customer.

As she also points out, the Brits are not about to let us slip away through the very fingers they keep showing us how not to eat with. They try every which way to corral us. The Molasses Act, the Currency Act, the Stamp Act, the Quartering Act, the Sex Act, the Coercive or Intolerable Acts, the Manchester Act, the Townshend Act, the Foreigners Act, the Hemp Act, the

Barrel Tax. When the British treasury needs more money they pass more Acts. They add to colonial asperity such ass-kickers as the Second Molasses Act, the Third Currency Act, the Fourth Stamp Act, the Fifth Quartering Act, the Grenville Program, the Fifth Coercive Act, the Intolerance Act, even something called the Bedding Act. It becomes difficult to remember what each one demands from suddenly diminishing incomes that were not much to begin with. There is also a Sodomie Act that allows Britain to export to the colonies all those so inclined or caught in the inclination, as well as just your general rowdies. How many are actually sent here? No one is counting, but sent here many are, much as prisoners will shortly be shipped off to Australia. England knows how to clean house and is fortunate to have many far-flung closets to sweep her unwanteds into.

All these Acts are ostensibly pursued to extract much-needed revenue from us, her ungrateful children. Sir Robert Walpole, a shortsighted and short-of-cash chancellor of the Exchequer and Britain's first prime minister, had railed: You must never forget you are our citizens, you belong to us, and you are British subjects! You need our permission to journey forth to attempt your fortunes. "We were unfortunate he was such a stupid ass," Hermia says. "Our history was punished evermore."

Although there are perhaps some 200,000 Indians from some eighty-five different Indian nations living east of the Mississippi River, it should be no surprise that few are willing to fight in any war for any white man's burden. (Some fought for the British, but they were paid more than American troops were.) They never "surrendered" their lands to "The American People" in the first place, and the news that Britain has or had dibs on their territory comes as something of a shock. So many acts of injustice white men are capable of! Such acts go even further when the victorious Americans show up with papers maintaining that since they defeated Britain they are entitled to *all* the Indians' land. This claim causes many defensive and futile acts on the part of tribal nations seeking to protect their ancestral homelands. If year by year there are fewer Indians, there will soon be even fewer. White men will take all the land they can get, any way they can get it. Their means are bloodier than the Revolution's, and, obviously, than the Indians'.

Statistics are still scarce for this war. Dead Americans: 4,435 out of 290,000 soldiers. Dead Brits: 10,000 out of a much larger fighting force.

But these statistics do not tell the real story: that "roughly nine American soldiers succumbed to disease for every one killed by the British," as estimated by James Flexner in *Doctors on Horseback*. Indeed, from 1775 to

1782, *Variola major*, the virus that causes smallpox, killed more than 100,000 people in North America, maiming even more. Measles, influenza, mumps, typhus, cholera, plague, malaria, yellow fever, scarlet fever, whooping cough, and diphtheria caused their own revolutionary devastations.

So yes, the Revolution is a big win on paper for our side, but against pretty low odds and with the forces of fate most cooperative. Few wars in history have won so much and cost relatively so little and then been entombed in so much hoopla. That dramatic a fracas it wasn't. *Noble* is not the word to use, for either this war or so much death from disease and sickness. The American People do need their glorious history, like an addict needs a fix. When you haven't got much decent history to begin with, noble it up.

How did we win? In a nutshell: the enemy was lazier than we were.

By the time of the Declaration of Independence five generations had lived here since the first settlements 150 years or so earlier.

The most little-observed fact about our revolution is that it was the first time American men held each other in their arms as they were struck down, as they died, the first time they cried over each other's bodies and kissed so many comrades goodbye. Men had not seen men behave like this. Men had not known they could feel and act like this. And it did not shame them or embarrass them. These feelings, and these acts, burrowed their way into their hearts, their bones, their minds and souls. And remained there, searching in vain for safe ways to get out. Yes, America, the United States of America, is born out of this.

But we are now free! What does it feel like to be free? What do The American People do when they are free?

•

I cried too. Please give me credit for having a heart. I lost many I loved. It is part of the wicked curse that fate has placed upon all living things. I fall in love and lose, just like you. I have left little bits of me on all the major battlefields. Why, at Yorktown itself I had a mini-epidemic going. But it sputtered out. So my influence is only imperceptibly increasing. People don't understand about soldiers. People don't see that men-only groups are the wellsprings of many contagious diseases, including me, of course. Strange fevers and purple-spotted bodies are cropping up here and there. So I do manage to leave a few of my calling cards. Perhaps someone will notice me. I want to be famous, too.

I have a lot of time on my hands. But I can tell you from personal experience that you have many more hushies than anyone can know. I am doing my best to meet them as fast as I can, but they are still too spread out across your mighty land.

THE ADJUDICATOR

The Adjudicator, who is not made known as such to the men, the better to observe them, wrestles with loose ends that do not knit themselves into whole cloth. He sees too clearly how harsh life is for these men who are not officers. They daily endure living conditions so wretched it is a wonder more of them don't desert the job, the cause, the general himself, whom all profess to worship. The least one can grant them is a look-the-other-way when same-sex comfort is sought.

But the list grows longer. Caleb Halstead, the new Adjudicator (the previous one having been shot to death by, it is [incorrectly] thought, an enemy sniper in the forest on a recent skirmish), young and handsome and himself an occasional recipient of Hamilton's cock inside him, faces a tormenting question: How can he order the death by hanging of men whose only crime in the face of death in battle is to love each other so briefly?

Yes, the list grows longer, of those he has caught in the act, or about whom he has "information" from the ones who are always there to provide it, for whatever reason, to please the mighty boss: jealousy, ambition, vindictiveness, just being a shit. It is not difficult to "catch" the "perpetrators" in performance. The quarters are squalidly intimate, and after the rations of rum, which are meant to appease the troops, men are not so concerned about the noise they make. After so many, so very many months, lengthening into years of life together thus, it has become for many of them a joke. "There they go again," that sort of thing. It is only when the "perpetrators" are repeat performers that Caleb notes their names down. Then he begrudgingly sees this as not good for the morale of others not blessed by any couplings. Would that it was not so awfully cold so they could all go screw each other outside.

But Caleb is discovering that actually turning them in goes against his nature. And Caleb is aware that one Norwood Punic knows what he's not doing.

Washington had asked Hamilton to be the Adjudicator; Hamilton had refused and suggested Caleb. "Sir, young Halstead will understand what this is all about." Apparently Caleb wanted more of Alex, and Alex is too infatuated with Jack at the moment; indeed Jack might notice, or worse, want a taste of Caleb himself. Jack is John Laurens, the son of a rich South Carolina planter, educated abroad, and the great love of Alex's life.

Yes, the general knows what's going on. He is no fool when it comes to understanding how bodily needs, one way or another, can take a mighty hold. If he did not have his handpicked group to observe, and touch, and invite to sleep by him throughout these years, throughout these battles, he would go crazy. That, he knows for certain, would mightily pain him.

Just as watching Alex and Jack make love mightily pains him.

Just as watching Alex sodomize Jack mightily pains him.

George has no intention of hanging either one of them.

Alex and Jack are in the inner circle of the general's inner circle, the general's direct daily company, along with the young Lafayette, whose particular passion is for the general himself. Perhaps I am not so old after all, the general cannot help thinking when such an adorable youngster is all over him with hands and arms and embraces, and that double kiss, one on each cheek, which the French evidently bestow. Yes, George has assigned young Lafayette to his personal staff as well. He likes his hand held, he likes his cheeks double-kissed, by this effervescent young man who brings such profound enthusiasm for what his general is accomplishing in this New World. Has not this richest young man in France come with his own army, to join in this fight for freedom? Why, he has defied an order from his own king in coming to America. George, the general, his general, has actually referred to him out loud as "the man I love." Alex and Jack, who serve as translators and teachers for "Jeel-bare," as the young Frenchman pronounces his first name, hear the general throw these words out casually. Thank goodness the old boy has found someone to entertain himself with, for the nonce.

But there is a war on.

And regulations are being flouted all over the place.

And Caleb Halstead is confronted by Punic. "I have witnessed you, sir, as you make note of all these disgusting couplings. I wait. I listen. I look. I do not see these malefactors hanged by their necks until they are dead as General Washington commanded, and is of course demanded by the very law itself. Why, sir, is this? I shall pen a letter to the general myself."

Which he does.

The general summons Halstead to his tent.

"This was your first test, young Caleb. I am sorry you have failed it. You have provided me with no names."

Caleb is relieved of his commission and of his rank as well. He commits suicide. He falls on the ceremonial sword his father gave him when he became an officer.

Alex dares to broach the matter with the general.

"Sir, there is in all this something greatly askew."

Washington will not discuss it.

Hamilton is accustomed to this silent Washington. He boldly takes his George's hand. He holds it without letting go. George does not remove it, but he will not look into Alex's eyes.

The mighty general is mightily moved. Would he not cry if he knew how to? There has never been a moment when George Washington has not wanted to take Alexander Hamilton into his arms and into his bed exclusively and, yes, faithfully.

Turbulent experiences of intricate male intimacies are not unknown to either of them. Alex had his cock sucked by an older man when he was—how young he was he can't recall, but he was very young. George, as an infant and throughout his earliest years, had his cock sucked and fondled by his old queen neighbor, Lord Thomas Fairfax, who couldn't keep his hands off him. Neither boy had a father he could love. George hated his, and Alex was never sure who his was. Alex quickly learned that he was handsome enough to cause men to want him physically. George learned that his pockmarked face required powder in public, as did his peculiarly reddish unflattering hair, and that his sagging body required increasingly elaborate corsets and tailored adornments of disguise. Each learned that handsomeness is a commodity. Each knew which of them had it and which did not. Great playwrights such as Euripides and Racine wrote great tragedies about this. Alex knew these plays. Did Alex know that sadness was the incorruptible foundation of his life, that his life was even tragic? Did George? No one has ever considered George tragic, much less sad. These are muddy waters that biographers of the truly great men won't inhabit, lest "their" men appear less manly. How could anyone as poor as both Alex and George have been—the one in background and birth, the other in self-knowledge and regard—not have felt some indefinable hunger along their journeys, George from his primeval wilderness and Alex from his impoverished tropical islands, to the very sleeping quarters of this soon-to-be-first president of the United States? Is this the stuff of tragedy? It is when it informs such harsh inequities of the heart that disallow the man to be the man he wants to be. It is doubtful that George Washington ever experienced a fully happy day in his own skin. But he didn't want the moon and Alex did, and that he could never have it hurt, which in turn hurt George.

Once there, once so instructed by life, what is there to do with a love like this?

Alex will go and fuck his Jack once again. He will fuck men and women throughout his short life. He will have a scandal or two along the way, usually because of a woman; scandals with men are never reported, of course. Sometimes, as with George, he will manipulate these encounters to guarantee his own devices. His vision of America is not everyone's, and it is his that will prevail, in the process winning him the enmity of Thomas Jefferson, who wants the states to run the country instead of letting the country run itself, and who is a complicated and most expert and manipulative politician himself, claiming to be Hamilton's friend while in fact his enemy.

It is Alexander Hamilton's America we live in today, much more than Washington's or Jefferson's. Or any Adams's. Or Madison's. Or even the great Lincoln's. Alex gave us banks and money and international trade, commerce, and solid national credit, and America über alles. He talked his George into everything he wanted, Alex did. When he dies it will prove to be an impressive list, such that one wonders what George—or America—would have done without him.

THE TWO ALTE MARIAS

The general is having tea. He looks up to see before him the other "old Mary," the baron, Frederick Steuben, who is older than George's forty-four, but only by a couple of years.

When they first meet he announces himself as "Lieutenant General Friedrich Wilhelm Ludolf Gerhard Augustin Baron von Steuben" and declares that he held high rank under Frederick the Great, "who really was an Alte Maria." And just in case, he adds, "An old queen." And then he dares to add, "Just like us." George actually laughs.

"Dat is vat we are called in Austria. Alte Marias. It is blasphemy, naturlich."

Yes, Washington laughs. This silly old poofter makes him laugh. They understand each other at once. Why does George put up with him for so many years? Because the baron has made his army a joy to behold! He has taught the platoons of rough stragglers how to coalesce and operate in unison. No one has seen such an accomplishment before. So this is how they do it over there.

"Will this make my men fight with more skill and attention, and of course, success?" George had asked the baron.

"Naturlich. Did I not do this for Frederick the Great?"

The baron, this queen, this poofter, this sodomite, this bugger, this hush-marked, will write "Regulations for the Order and Discipline of the Troops of the United States," the drill manual still in use today. He understands the male body completely. He particularly understands how asses and crotches will look all aligned in the tight and tailored and effusively bedecked uniforms designed of course by George. George and the baron are creating America's first love affair with drag. They are creating what the historian Charley Shively has called "the masculine equivalent of the female chorus line." Go to West Point or Annapolis and watch them march. Yes, they understand each other immediately, these two Alte Marias.

"Naturlich. Dat is vhy it is done. To make men march together in all ways. Dat is my gift to you." The baron is learning the vocabulary he believes essential for his own maneuverings. He is grateful to this man for taking him in. He has been thrown out of his own country, his own army, and other armies and countries too, ignobly, no gratitude for the scores of young men, generations of them, that he trained into the precision and perfection so prized by Germans and Austrians. He, too, has been caught in acts of love. He, too, would have been hung had he not escaped from Europe. George Washington knows all this.

"What should I do?" Washington asks him now, setting down his teacup.

"You do not hang them, naturlich."

"It is the law. John Winthrop made this the law in Massachusetts, and it has been followed everywhere with alarming speed."

"Vhy ist diss alarming? Komm into das . . . world. You are prepared to hang until dead Hamilton and Jack Laurens? You are prepared to hang until dead the child warrior Frenchman Jeel-bert with his own private army? More important to attend to your Baron. I am not paid since I arrive here. I am given no contract as promised. I live and eat here with you and at your command. I am grateful. But I am not so very grateful. Please to keep your promises."

"I am pleased to note the great improvement in your ability to speak my language."

"Alex has taught me. Jack has taught me. They are so sweet. They flirt with each other in Greek and Latin and French." Hamilton will look after Steuben's financial affairs until he dies. The baron is a spendthrift, and his business of decorating the homes of the wealthy is an idea before its time. "But tell to me, do you have just for yourself a special close and tender tie and not one but two?" Washington says nothing and the baron wonders if he has overstepped himself.

That is more or less that for this late afternoon. Steuben realizes it's time to leave. He does know that George wants time to consider and select the young men who will sleep near him, in this place, in whatever place, be it a tent or an actual warm room with a fire, as here. Both know the boys are waiting to hear who the lucky ones will be this evening. What does he do with them? Steuben always wonders. He is certain that he, and they, do *something*. No, George will never be hanged.

Enough, enough. George gets up to remove his uniform and his underwear and his corsets, and make certain that there is still sufficient powder on his pockmarked skin to disguise him. His hair? His teeth? It is an ordeal, dressing and undressing. He is behind on sending to London his own new designs and his new measurements. He is putting on more weight. He has spent a great deal of time and thought on what new buttons and braiding and laces and buckles he desires, and whether gold or silver. The lanterns have been brought in, and the candles lit. He's had his bite to eat and his warm milk. He will waddle around in this nightshirt that is now a bit too tight for waddling, although he had it cut particularly full. He will go to his bed or to the portable sleeping cot he's designed for the field, and watch the four or five men he's selected enter his presence, watch them in the lantern light as they remove their own uniforms and lay them out neatly by the sleeping mattresses on the floor beside him.

He will watch them as they strip down. Some take off more than others. Some even sleep naked. They know this pleases him most of all, to see them naked. It has been discovered that he sometimes promotes the naked ones faster. Indeed, he himself has noted that more of them are now sleeping in the buff. Too bad it will soon be much too cold for taking off anything at all. Then they will all begin to smell from never taking off anything. Some of them are already sweating too much.

They know, these fellows, that George is watching them from his bed.

They doze off, but not so much as to be unaware of which of them George summons to his side and what sounds might then be forthcoming.

It is all quite electric, this gay mess. This college fraternity before there's such a thing. They are all in a pageant and George is the leading man. He lives every day as if he were the lead in a dramatic play of great moment. Which indeed he is. How does he look? Are his pockmarks showing? Blow out a candle or two if they are. But then he will not be able to witness fully their naked chests, their young skin, their sexual organs, which one has hair on his chest. He has heard that Benjamin Franklin has invented eyeglasses with which to see better. But how does one wear them in bed?

By now he is seeing the world in his own image, just as the world, in a few years' time, will say that it visualizes a country based on him, and be completely wrong. Herein lies his greatness, this pretense, of which only the best actors are capable, although no historian would parse his life like this. For the need to look up to him in glory will eviscerate the much stronger need for the truth about him, which The American People do not want to grasp.

Yes, he does think about his men, his other men, the enlisted ones, the ones dragooned into service, the soldiers he sends out first to be killed in battle. In his first years he has nightmares about young men being run through by bayonets and blown up by muskets. He has seen heads severed from their bodies and has done the same. He is not so self-centered and uncaring as not to be affected by his doses of actual battle, when he does step into one. But these bad dreams pass. He knows there is criticism that he is too often an absentee leader. He knows he is accused of attending balls and parties and foxhunts and gambling at cards with the rich when he should be with his troops. It offends his sensibilities to see so much bloodshed and ripped flesh, and yes, so much mussing up of his beautiful uniforms.

Where in the world did this general come from? How has his life led him into this? To slice off heads. Not much is written about swordplay and the slicing off of heads, as if somehow killing a man this way is more sacrosanct (or repellent?) than via shooting him. Swords hold a talismanic spell, though, possessing an impressive lineage. He and Alex and the baron have studied warfare as waged by not only Frederick the Great but Alexander the Great and Julius Caesar and Sweden's Charles XII and the Duke of Marlborough. The baron has pointed out that all of these were Alte Marias too. "Is it not interesting," Alex once said, "that we who love men so much should become such fervent murderers of our own?" George does not like to think like this. And so he doesn't. All his men use swords, carrying their dangling weights into battle until the baron convinces him they are too clumsy and bayonets do the job more efficiently. "Let your boys run free mit bayonets. Dey kill besser mitout swords." So swords come to be used mainly for dueling. And bayonets run through many an enemy's body.

He always lies awake long after his boys, including the one nestled beside him, have gone to sleep. He will look down on them from his bedstead for many hours more. He would like to lie beside every one of them. Even the smelly ones. Perhaps especially the smelly ones. He would like to lie among them all in some sort of fevered mass orgy such as he has heard occur in those increasingly popular religious convocations. He wonders what to do with that unpleasant Punic. With luck he will be killed in action. But George knows it is never the disagreeable ones who get killed. They are too busy hiding behind the other soldiers.

No, he is not lying in bed thinking about his life, as so many might do, or about the days just past or the days to come. There will be few thoughts about the long, awful months at Valley Forge when 2,500 of his army of 10,000 die from disease, or his losses at Long Island, Manhattan, White Plains, Brandywine, and Germantown (Monmouth was a draw) or the victory at Saratoga, or even the aftermath of Yorktown, when the British can finally leave and the killing can stop. His dreams are not riddled with the faces of his boys under fire, or of Cornwallis or Burgoyne or Howe or Gates, or of Braddock, the handsome Braddock, who had made such a mess that he should have been discharged; George was smitten with the older man and anyway was under him. Truth to tell, there have been so many battles both won and lost that he can't keep track of them all. Alex can. Alex does. Alex catches him in his mistakes before he makes them.

Indeed, if George managed to keep his army alive, it must have been for other reasons. He loved them, or he loved the ones who counted, his officers, and they knew it, and were happy to accept it, like the young men waiting in their cots now to see who is on tonight.

JEEL-BARE

The time comes, the date, the evening, when George can no longer abide his loneliness in this midst of so much desire, when he wants more than just a naked nameless officer's body beside him. When he reaches out, actually reaches out, to pluck a fresh one for himself, caution be damned (no, that is not correct, there will be only the two of them in camp tonight), it is young Lafayette he chooses to let fuck him, after he has tried to fuck the lad himself. This latter has never been easy for him, for some reason he cannot fathom. It was the same with the Indians. Fucked he could be, but rarely the reverse. He chooses Gilbert Lafayette because, yes, it is time. The boy has been after him since his arrival. He has already bundled up the lad like a young puppy dog inside his great coat in the cold and slept side by side with him on the battlefield at Monmouth, where the young man kissed his face from side to side and up and down. "I am most happy when I am with you!" Gilbert says effusively yet again. He worries constantly for his general's safety, and the kisses are for good luck in anticipation of another battle's successful outcome, which is far from guaranteed.

They dine alone in a civilian home that has been billeted for the general on the eve of what will be Lafayette's first battle commanding a brigade by Washington's side. He is hardly past twenty years old and has been begging for this chance (Which chance? The battle or the bed? Both of them!) since his arrival. Can you imagine a nineteen-year-old arriving with his own army and his own ships? Who is also the richest man in France? (He has a yearly income of $800,000.) He is in love with the idea of America and with George years before he gets here, longing for a major piece of this action; he has been in the military since he was thirteen and his family's military service to the king goes back seven centuries. Barely months after his arrival he is living in George's house; weeks later he is riding at George's side on parade; another month and he is riding with him into battle; and now at twenty he is to become one of George's generals. At last the general has given Jack and Alex and Gilbert battalions beside him against Cornwallis, whom they will trap into defeat in the coming days. The candles on the table, beside the food, beside the wine, flicker and reveal to Gilbert the encroaching intimacies that he hopes the general is now considering.

Neither of them is a physical prize. George seems "to be composed of damaged spare parts, a nose too large for his pockmarked face, eyes too small for their sockets, a mouth slammed shut over decayed teeth, enormous hands and feet and outsized hips" (Gaines). Gilbert, already losing his sandy red hair, with a long pointed nose, a bad chin, has "a certain birdlike aspect" (Gaines again). And yet, and yet, as even Douglas Southall Freeman, George's multivoluminous chronicler of his not-quite-every burp, writes, "Never . . . was there so speedy and complete a conquest of the heart of Washington."

It is the youngster who, sensing this change in the general's temperature, is the aggressor. Frenchmen know about these things, and George has counted on this because his own inexperience troubles both him and his erection. The casual touch of fingers as they both reach for bread and butter. The wine and the toasting as they hold each other's eyes. Gilbert cannot believe the good fortune awaiting him, and his impatience leads him to hasten the outcome. He practically jumps George before the roast is eaten. He puts his hand over George's mouth so words will not mar the moment.

George takes this hand into his mouth. He clumsily licks it, then kisses it and holds it to his cheek, hoping the powder doesn't rub off. They are on the bed in no time, Gilbert peeling off his general's commodious wardrobe down to his pale and lumpy nakedness. He has many layers to remove, many buckles and belts and strings to disengage. Gilbert tries to perform these activities with a flourish that will accentuate their ardor. George's body is not so beautiful to behold as, say, Alex's, or Jack's, both of which Gilbert has seen, and celebrated as well. Was it not a night of nights when the three of them did it all together! (It is of note that both Lafayette and Laurens left pregnant wives abroad and years later had still not seen wife or child.) Gilbert then strips his own skinny body bare. He makes a lame joke about his being covered with freckles. Each notes the other's amplitude, or lack of it. The French lad is skinny, too, in his member, though it is certainly hard. George momentarily wonders when a bigger cock will fuck him. George's balls are huge, and his dick large and soft. It is such a waste, but he will do his best to work around it. Just as he will do his best to work around Jefferson's growing enmity for his Alex. There are so many considerations to juggle all the time.

So Gilbert makes entry into the precious interior of one of the greatest men in America's history. Over succeeding years they will retire many times to George's cabin in the Virginia woods. When Gilbert returns to France, George Washington, for the first time anyone can recall, is visibly in tears.

•

By now Georgie is already infected, more or less, even though small dicks never provide a satisfactory penetration. A little penis going into such a large bottom does not allow for a complete-enough dose of ejaculate. His big bottom will also protect him when he is fucked by Jeel-bare, as it will protect the Frenchie, whose penis is not much larger than an Indian's. By rights Jeel should have caught me from George. But Jeel was lucky, especially because he was not circumcised. In studying my success rates over the centuries, I discover that

I can insert myself between the foreskin and the glans and stay there for quite a while, particularly among those who bathe so little. All American men, except the Hebrews, of course, will remain uncircumcised for quite some time. This will help me and not help them. But I am ahead of myself here, daydreaming of victories yet to come.

The small amount he has of me inside him will not kill others. I will never be able to control how much of me I can pass into bodies. It is only when there is enough of me inside someone that I can truly claim victory. Your Dr. Omicidio will know all this. He just doesn't want to tell you.

I'm glad I didn't really kill George. I wanted to spare him and I did—my gift to the birth of America.

Alex was circumcised, being the son of a Jewess. I spared him, too, but Burr won't.

THE DEATH OF LOVES

George Washington is aware that over the years of his presidency some four dozen men are hanged for sodomy. This may pain him, as it pains Hamilton, but neither lifts a finger to save one of them. Washington has worked out for himself the notion that "loving the boys could be perfectly acceptable as long as it remained within certain boundaries" (Shively). He has established America's first version of President Boy Vertle's twentieth-century ignominy, Don't Ask, Don't Tell.

Jack Laurens is murdered by Norwood Punic during a useless skirmish with the British in August 1782, and thus not alive to receive the latest of the many love letters that Alex, now married, has sent to him. Jack has just returned from a successful mission for Washington in Paris when Punic literally shoots him out of his saddle and gallops away. Punic has been waiting for such an opportunity. He is not seen or heard of again.

Jack is the great love of Hamilton's life. Alex's passion for him exceeds by far what passion he feels for his good wife, Eliza, who bears him seven children. His own voluminous papers, which are often starkly honest (he "suffered from excessive openness," Chernow writes), reveal numerous dalliances through the years. Many of these are with young men. According to Kenneth Anger, in one of his *Hollywood Babylon* series, the movie star Errol Flynn wanted to play Hamilton. "He would fuck anything in sight, and so do I," Flynn is reported to have said to the great British filmmaker Alexander Korda.

Alexander Hamilton commits suicide on July 11, 1804. He is either forty-nine or fifty-one years old. His papers reveal that he knew he would not fire at Aaron Burr, and that Burr, an expert marksman, would fire at him with great accuracy. (Ironically, Alex's eldest son, Philip, had been killed in a duel in the very same spot three years earlier.) His George by now is dead some few years and Alex's life has become more and more uninteresting. He is depressed, and increasingly so. The battles left for him are petty and boring, his life too bourgeois. God forbid he should wind up like George himself, up there on that hill with only a Martha to talk to. He has come to hate the law, which he must practice to support his large family and his wife. He is mourning not only George and Jack, but also his lack of interest in anyone and anything else. That he even bothers to annoy Burr (and the argument on both sides is about petty things) so much that Burr feels he has no option but to call for this duel is an indication of just how depressed Alex is. And what an opportunist Burr is. Alex just does not care.

Indeed, what is left for him to do, and for whom could he do it? He's created for his George a strong central government, an effective tax and tariff system, a national bank (because of him the country for the first time can actually pay its bills), the U.S. Mint; he's written, with Madison, the Federalist Papers, which would mold the Constitution itself; he's started the Bank of New York. He battled hard for every single one of these against major opposition, working day and night for as long as he can remember. Now there is no one who even offers thanks to indicate a job well done. There is no one left to do anything challenging for. Yes, he misses George, mightily.

Several days before his death, he comes across his correspondence with Jack and his files on Maria Reynolds, the hooker who years ago had obsessed him to such a degree that the public exposure of their affair put paid to any notion he could ever run for president, even should he be able to manipulate the Constitution to make that possible. He did not want to be president anyway. George wanted him to. George had been his goad throughout his adult life, the father he never had. He loved George. Jack had been his greatest love. There had never been another like him. "Mind you do justice to the length of my nose," he wrote to Jack, *nose* being code for "cock." He also wrote, "I wish that it might have been in my power by action rather than words to convince you that I love you." They joked about marrying each other somewhere, on some distant shore. He sent his last love letters to Jack before he knew that Jack had been shot dead. They were returned to him unopened.

He never forgot his receipt of the news that Jack was dead. It was said that he howled so in pain and anguish it was as if the winds would carry the echo of his helpless cries throughout the world.

He must have pondered all this before he faced Burr in that duel and aimed his pistol at the trees.

GEORGE AND THE JEWS

The American Revolution is financed in large part by Jews. In 1789, George Washington visits Savannah to deliver personal thanks to them. In the large classical temple the Jews have built for their worship, he says to them, "I am amazed how many of you share the notion that this country will be great and rich and wide and free for every man. The belief that America is the future is the food of many men's wishes and dreams." He gives Jews credit for having been in one Promised Land and journeying so far to be a part of another. He talks to the Jews as if they have just arrived, when in fact many of them have now lived in America for several generations and consider themselves Americans. Some are suddenly frightened: What has their financing of the American Revolution bought them after all if he talks to them like this? He cautions the Jews against greed and urges them to control their usury. Several men get up and leave.

He goes on to suggest that the western part of this country is where dreamers should go, that the South will fail under the burden of slavery and rigid social codes, and then, rather pointedly, he advises that "those with large landholdings in the South may find their investments circumvented by new conditions birthed by America's new laws." More of the congregation walks out on this.

SLOW TOLL THE BELLS OF SEXUAL TRUTH

Martha Washington is not a journal keeper. But thanks to excellent sleuthing by Mary Lefkowitz in a piece in *The New Gotham* in 1996 called "The Wandering Womb," we realize that she did leave behind some information, in the form of her dirty linen. Many of her garments, her dresses, gowns, and underwear, are available in various collections, chief among these being the Smithsonian's. Curators have long been puzzled by the fact that all this stuff is invariably soiled in the area of her crotch, and that these stains, when microscopically examined, are discovered to be composed of fecal matter. It is also known that Martha had a great interest in medicine, and that she made many visits to many people she'd heard mentioned as medically skillful in varying areas, including specialties of the Orient and the ancient world. Her personal library at Mount Vernon includes books on Egyptian and early Greek remedies, one of which, as both her stained wardrobe and Professor Lefkowitz also attest, is a small volume on the use of "animal excrement" as a "vaginal irritant," and of "dried human excrement mixed with beer froth" as a salve for women's "affected organs." Lefkowitz goes on, "Greek doctors, for their part, prescribed cow or goat dung, or bird droppings, often in combination with fragrant wine or perfumes like rose oil. (Cures derived from animal excrement are used today: a form of the estrogen used in hormone-replacement therapy is extracted from the urine of pregnant mares.)"

What were these cures meant to cure? There was much fear of the "wandering womb," which, it was thought, "could move about in a woman's body, putting pressure on other organs and so causing serious illness, and even death." One of the cures prescribed for diseases of the womb was sexual intercourse. Poor Martha. Her husband was unable to fuck her even if it might save her life.

Lefkowitz does not go far enough. She fails to allow us to consider the possibility that George and Martha knew George was syphilitic, and knew that China and the Orient sometimes used feces as a protective sheath. As a condom protects modern man against venereal disease, so was earlier man's own shit thought to accomplish the same.

If George then *was* fucking Martha, it would appear that this Oriental cunning worked, in that Martha, so far as we know, did not become infected with syphilis or, for that matter, become pregnant by him. But it might be said that she never again conceived because she was never fucked. Or that shit is an even more protective sheath than even the Chinese maintained.

Did George Washington have The Underlying Condition? On his deathbed he had very small purple spots on his face and flesh. He called them his "old spots," because he'd had them and hidden them for so long.

SO ENDS THIS RECONSIDERATION
OF GEORGE WASHINGTON

No. Not yet. His life cannot be told chronologically. He is a cold fish with many tadpoles swimming inside him. He is an actor who plays many parts intentionally. He knows what he is doing and what he doesn't want you to know he's doing. He is enormously admired from that day until this. There has never been a period when Washington Worship has been out of fashion. Nary a dissenting voice. Beyond criticism, 'twould appear. You've got to know that no man was as great as this. Even those Jews kept their mouths shut when George easily gobbled up every bit of new land they thought was contracted to them. That he has come to be considered a great man and a great leader and a great mind is a remarkable testimony to the vicissitudes of history, society's need, cowardly and unimaginative historians who can't put one and one together. There is not one single extant biography of this man that paints a convincing portrait of a *person*. All his biographers fall in love with what they think he is, and what they think he did. And after a few years the cement is set. He is another one called great because America has become great and this must have come from someone.

His best biographer is a historian few have heard of. His name is Charley Shively, and he labored for many years at the University of Massachusetts Boston, where no one paid much attention to him or his remarkable work. He made his great discoveries about Washington (and Lincoln and Walt Whitman) and wrote them up only to discover no one would publish them because he said these men were all, distinctly, homosexuals. So his stuff was published by a little rag in San Francisco called *Gay Sunshine*, which was happy to have it. He was the first person to claim Whitman was a gay man, now widely acknowledged as such, and of course he was much maligned for saying so. Indeed, there are still academics who refuse to admit that Walt was gay. "It is so fucking hard to tell the truth," Charley wrote to your present historian. As for his claims about Washington and Lincoln, well, not even malignity greeted them. They were completely ignored, perhaps because of shock. How do we know that Shively's biographies of these men are accurate? How do we know that Gibbon's or Herodotus' or Thucydides' versions of all their men are accurate? "It's only by being shameless about risking the obvious that we happen into the vicinity of the transformative," said Eve Kasofsky Sedgwick, an interesting straight woman who wrote much about people in the closet hiding their homosexuality.

After George Washington dies, in 1799, there is no outpouring of support for him or his city, in which no one wants to live. So certain has he been that his people would flock to join him that he'd bought options on much of the land. The American People do not wish to acknowledge him. At least not in as celebratory a fashion as he would like to be remembered. He had not touched anyone's heart. That would only be manufactured later.

Yes, the remote hero dies. "My success came because of silence, pride, and wealth. No one shall ever know me and that is as I want it. Let them think me cold and distant. That is true. Although there has been more than that, no one is to see it." He sounds like an early version of the alienated man, something out of Beckett. You remember his face until you see a different portrait of him. He is carved in stone, but what were those eyes like?

He is remembered, of course, but strangely absent from anyone's memory.

The Great Man dies with but two additional beside him, his two favorite Seneck braves who have lived on his land since youth. They who bathed our first dead president remark, yet again, on his most large and hanging sacks.

•

I can see that you don't like each other as much as you should.
I guess we are all having what you call growing pains.
I need you all together! In every way that you can.
Poor George.
Well, I loved him.

THE SONS OF THE POCAHANTI

After George Washington's death, Baron Steuben, whose idea it is, and a number of Washington's officers come to John Adams and suggest that a society be formed, one that will last through time and tide, and that the membership in this society be restricted to those who knew George or served under George, or knew Martha or were related to those who knew her. Rather than call this society after the Washingtons, for there are already a growing number of those named after one or the other or both of them, Washington This and Washington That and George This and Martha That and George & Martha This and That, it is suggested, quite amusingly it is thought, and seconded and ratified by the officers in attendance at the first and founding meeting, that the society take its name from an earlier moment in American history, as a joke really, because she was a joke, a coarse Indian woman who took off her deerskin and put on a dress and went to visit the king and appeared at pageants and opera houses all over the world to show herself off in brocade: Pocahontas.

"But let us masculine be, as well as plural," General Kurtzbogg further suggests. "Let us call ourselves not the Society of Pocahontas but the Society of the Pocahanti—no, even better! the Society of the Sons of the Pocahanti—and let us as our annual rite don deerskins with beads and war paint and feathers. And let us call each other 'Corn Huskers,' one hundred Corn Huskers, because that is where she came from, the cornfields on some old plantation. And let one hundred comprise the total membership of the Society of the Sons of the Pocahanti, now and forever."

And so it was. And is.

Thus comes into being America's most elite gentile male secret society. One hundred founding members start it up and one hundred members only is it to this day. Presidents, Supreme Court justices, military brass, governmental bigwigs, millionaire and soon billionaire tycoons, flagrant heteros and closeted queers and queens flow through its ranks until they die and are replaced by more of the same. It is a much-coveted membership. It brings with it much power.

When the papers are drawn up for final ratification, Lieutenant General Friedrich Wilhelm Ludolf Gerhard Augustin Baron von Steuben is excluded from membership. Some say it is because he is foreign-born. But everyone knows it is because he was an Alte Maria. Naturlich. He dies shortly, still full of amazement about these Americans and their hypocritical ways, so like everywhere else he'd ever lived.

THE END OF AN ERA?

We have come to the end of an era. Of sorts. We have been born. We have had a period of youth. We have won our freedom from a domineering parent. We have started our own country. We have elected our first president and watched him die. We have grown enough in strength to carry on.

We want to learn.

Don't we?

I wonder. Hermia has been chiding me lately. "I am annoyed to note that you believe that almost everybody is either a homosexual or a repressed homosexual or a homophobe. Is this what your history of The American People is to be? Surely heterosexuals have a more central and forceful and guiding position in the world. Your world. My world. Any world. *The* world. How dare you be such a usurper."

Although Grace's response to this is "Shut the bitch up," I think I must never lose sight of this question. Am I writing the history I want to write? It is certainly history as I am coming to understand it. I claim time is short. I claim I miss retiring in these possible final days to my lover, Edward's, arms. I claim a lot of things, but now that I am actually collecting the evidence, is it sufficient to convince? Is it building to what will be an undeniable and airtight case that will hold up in a court of reason? After all, straight people never do understand gays. The Bible, the most beloved story ever told, is far-fetched. Wasn't it given to us somehow as a kind of novel, with a beginning, a middle, and an end? Whether it was true or not, wasn't it accepted as a believable story? Eventually.

But real history is not a story. Stories manipulate, and their characters are at the mercy of their cruel creators, who tell it their way. So aren't good historians permitted to string together a more sophisticated form of narrative, one in which there is more than one kind of thread to follow, to pursue, each of them, of course, suspect by somebody? Isn't this closer to the truth of actuality?

All I have so far are bits and pieces. I have no alternative but to press on. I am not dissatisfied. I see a bouncing ball that I can follow. Do you? Can't you? Why not? It's all becoming much more clear to me.

So far I trust my instincts and my nose. If I am as faithful to my beliefs as a Parkman or a Gibbon or a Macauley or a Herodotus, the greatest originator of us all because he was the first (the older the historian, the fewer his attributions for his "facts"—Parkman has almost none), why should I not be as believed as they are?

Of course, one must always be harder on oneself! But does that mean falling into the same pit any old historian faces when the evidence is not so stone hard as the enormous world of Unbelievers demands? I hope not. I must always ask myself, Am I being too timid? Somehow I don't think this will be a problem. And God help us if I become just "any old historian." They are why we are in so much shit.

Can't you see and feel the superfluity of Hermia's evil that has been perking from the get-go?

So far, isn't it enough for me to ask you, "Bear with me"?

PHILADELPHIA

My name is Hogarth Hooker. I am son to Rev. Ezra Hooker, Jr. I have written these words about my life.

I studied young and hard and long to be a doctor. I wanted to be a doctor because I am the son of a famous and hateful father, from a family that hurt so many people.

But my father's father had been as hateful to him, and his father and the father before him, old Tom Hooker himself. He had been a fervid monster as well. I wondered if this meant there was no hope for my own happiness, for any future Hooker's happiness.

In 1787, when I was twenty-two, I was invited to Philadelphia by a frightened group of doctors, several of whom I had studied with at Yaddah, where I was first in my class. I think I was chosen for two reasons. First, because I can pay my expenses out of my own fortune, their treasury being insufficient to pay for much of anything, certainly not anything to do with health. And I have made a small name for myself because in Massachusetts, where our family business is the collection and removal of human waste, I have been instrumental in attending to its safety. The doctors here are bereft of any other "expert" to talk to. They claim to have consulted many, with no success.

Philadelphia appears to be a sick place ever since Mr. Penn birthed it in 1682. There are epidemics regularly, and much resultant death. The place is all set on marshy grounds, its weather excessively hot or freezing cold. The great Dr. Benjamin Rush reckons that there have been plagues of the smallpox here in each of these years: 1731, 1736, 1756, 1759, and 1773. And still it is the largest town in America. It is almost impossible to fathom why people still live here when this disease alone has carried so many hundreds away.

I come to Philadelphia as the Constitution of the United States of America is on the eve of being forged here. There is great hope in the air. Can these men create an America that will please all?

A number of people are dying from something that looks, to learned eyes, like syphilis. But syphilis, while it has been seen for centuries, has never been seen to be so immediately fatal. And yet it does look like syphilis, and is like it, too, in that the act of sex appears conjoined with these new cases, or so these learned eyes which summoned me have said.

There is no word for what I am trying to teach myself to do. I call myself a sanitarian. I say that I am interested in the health of the public and in how we infect each other, but secretly I am most interested in what men think of their cocks, which is to say, what they think of themselves as sexual beings. *Sexual* is a new word for us, an actual word for what our men of God condemn with such contempt.

A first walk around reveals the town is putrid. The streets are overflowing with filth, as is the river that travels through the town's backyards. Amputated limbs floating down the De-La-Ware are not uncommon sights. The houses, bigger and bigger the closer to town one comes, are fancy in front and full of shit behind.

Philadelphians do not collect human waste as we do back home in Ontuit, in loads, by horse and dray, for removal elsewhere. They say there is too much here to collect, if they are not too ashamed to talk about it at all. When confronted with the absurdity of their position, the doctors respond instead with questions of their own. "How do you dispose of the waste of twenty residents in one house alone? Or twenty houses side by side? Or twenty streets in this same neighborhood? Or twenty additional neighborhoods? Or the whole of Philadelphia itself? Your Ontuit is but a speck on Philadelphia's size! Why, we would be buried in piles of shit were it not for the river to dump it in." Boston and New York both have more capacious river basins that are for the moment performing adequately in this regard. How does England deal with so much shit? I am asked. As you do, I say, but the river Thames moves swiftly. This De-La-Ware is a stagnant swamp. Stagnant water is dangerous water. It alone can kill you.

Twelve whores calling themselves the Peabody Sisters live in a lovely house on Chestnut Street, "the best street," as they advertise it. Another dozen live in a hovel outside town in Vanderberg, on the river's edge. They call themselves the Sisters of Chestnut, and are fond of quipping, "We're the girls who fuck our founding fathers." Seven whores and three customers were the first to die, some from each house. Now there have been half a hundred various, and from places other than these two. This is a great number from something so strange and unknown. A number of the dead bodies are found in the river. No one comes forth voluntarily to identify any of the dead, even, I gather, their own families and relatives. The dead bodies, I should state, are often hideous in their disfigurement, in limb and skin especially.

My great-grandfather and my grandfather and my father all predicted such would happen in a sinning city at such a sinning time. I must prove them wrong, if only for my own salvation. Medicine must overcome the idiocies of the pulpit.

I am questioned vigorously by the doctors, late at night in a makeshift sequestered ward—the town does not yet have a hospital—filled with moaning men and women. I venture to suggest that the products of the body— disease, blood, feces—are interconnected. "How can they be interconnected?" I am asked. How can they not be? That is not a satisfactory answer. "You are too young," they tell me. "On what basis do you even make this ridiculous statement?" The older ones are the most dismissive.

Several younger doctors whisper to me. "Some new kind of pox is rife and no one wants to speak of it or let it be known. For who will come to Philadelphia then?"

There is much mumbling. "It is not an easy death. It is not an easy death." Dr. Clement John Norris has seen his own son die but several days ago.

Three more of the whores and six more men now die. That is the highest count so far for one day's dead.

"Thank you, Dr. Hooker, and good night."

The assembled doctors have had enough of me.

I attempt to appeal to them.

"Our history is coming of age!" I tell them. "The stuff of our lives is accreting, like a snowball. Things are beginning to stick to each other: neighborhoods, lawyers, merchants, tailors, greengrocers, doctors. We all mingle with each other, unavoidably. We must look at these sores as windows on our selves and our future. How can we stay together?"

I fear I am not expressing myself clearly. I am still trying to work out my philosophy. I cannot answer any of them. I am obsessed with blood and with disease and how it transfers from one to another person. And sex as a part of these. But these cases I am seeing do not tell me how to stop deaths occurring because of them. My hands are tied by ignorance!

Invasive surgery as a cure has found a home in Philadelphia. The esteemed Dr. Benjamin Rush is called our first great doctor, the greatest among us all. I call him the King of Bleeders. He believes that every sickness comes from excited blood vessels and that a good bleeding makes the sickness go away. These past weeks he has been proved wrong again and again. But no one remarks upon his useless and dangerous acts. The sum total of the knowledge of these prescribers in Philadelphia is hot mudpacks and leechings and teas steeped from pulverized plants and these idiot bleedings. Dog blood is being given to humans in Europe. They are trying adventurous new things over there! Why are we so timid? I do not want to go to my grave remembered as the shit man from Massachusetts.

I do not like Mr. Benjamin Franklin. I am suspicious of men whom everyone worships, like Dr. Rush, like all my preaching Hooker kin. Franklin is everyone's friend and I try to be no one's, for fear of bondage to false gods. He claims to be a scientist, inventor, diplomat, politician, moralist, wit. That is too many things for one man to be good at. For all that is said and known about him, no one knows with certainty what it is he does. Several of the Peabody girls say that he is a womanizer. He takes opium when he is with them because he is in pain from heaving such a fleshy frame. He does not strike me as a man who is interested in women. He is a very good champion of himself alone.

He has asked to meet me. We walk around his town.

"Look, over there," he says to me, rambling as we walk, "two men slipping into the house of Laurinder Tresh. They will say they are attending a reading club, and each will show some book he has brought to share with other men also arriving to read. The hushmarked. If Hamilton could diddle the cock of our commander in chief, why not these men who say they read books?"

It is as if he is conducting a tour. "Even in France I never knew of such a lot of single and lonely ladies as are here. They all come to find a husband. There is no patience. Should a woman see a man of interest, she does not think it rude to inquire immediately, often to his face, of his availability. 'Time is precious' are words of explanation given for almost all behaviors. Girls come to town from everywhere. Philadelphia is like a magnet whose force of attraction is money. A man in a suit with his hair slicked shiny and his boots not caked in mud is money. You cannot deny the atmosphere here, the whisper, the belief in the destiny of tomorrow. It is believed this town will be the capital of the world, the richest place ever to be. A piece of land that costs ten dollars today is one hundred by a week. And next month upon it will be built a house that will be joined in another month by two, then ten. And then all will be sold for a dozen times their cost and the recipient of this bounty is on his way to more. It all happens like lightning. And I am a man who knows his lightning.

"So many have come to this country with every conceivable baggage save common sense. That is why they revere me. '*You* are Mr. Common Sense,' they say to me. And so I am. I am. Where are the intelligent? Right here in front of you. I am the sum total of all knowledge in this town. William Penn himself warned that reading books is not so good as praying. We will become a dumb country. Mark my words.

"Oh, it is a terrible burden to be right," he concludes, or seems to be doing so, but he goes on. He goes on. And on. I have captured as much from my memory as is necessary to paint him.

Finally he demands, "What have you discovered since your arrival?"

"Pus, pustules, sores, scabs, dementia, fits of raving and wild thrashings preceding seizure and death, rarely seen here before. Convulsions most florid, fevers most elevated, chokings more apoplectic than any recollected."

I see him wince with each mention of these unpleasant matters. I continue.

"Uncontrollable voidings of the bladder, intestines, and stomach. Tempestuous bowel movements continuing uninterruptedly even when no intake occurs. What of remedies? Salves? Bloodlettings? Plugs up the rectum? There are in your town champions for each. As well as the cutting out or sewing up of vaginas, the severing of penises, the stitching up of rectums with gut. Each, I gather, has been quietly performed, or as quietly as such pain allows. In one case a woman exploded. And . . . and . . . should it indeed be syphilis, there are not sufficient sheepskin sacks or makers of them as are routinely found abroad."

To which Ben Franklin responds, "This is a country of differences which everyone demands be made the same. I fear this is only a magical idea. Still, I remain an old man of pride and curiosity, a constant observer of one and all, a roamer of the universal realm. But you are young."

To which I more fervently reply, "Sir! I add to the foregoing more alarming symptoms: bodies entirely scabbed, fierce howling not unlike a wolf's, the urination of blood, shit containing bits of intestine, ghastly suffocations, ghastly fevers that burn men up. And still your doctors do nothing but leech and bleed."

To which Ben Franklin responds with amazing speed, "Young man, my town is filled with men come here to compose this new land's legal foundation. George Clymer, John Dickinson, Elbridge Gerry, William Johnson, Rufus King, John Langdon, Thomas McKean, Thomas Mifflin, Charles Abner Pinckney, Charles Cotesworth Pinckney, Pernnilius Abraham Pinckney, Edmund Randolph, Ebenezer Punic, George Read, James Wilson, Matthew Thornton, William Whipple, Francis Lewis, Israel Clark, William Ellery,

George Wythe, John Morton, William Pacah, Caesar Rodney, William Blount, William Few, Jared Ingersoll. I know their names as those of honored family. Whipple and Blount seen walking together provoke small girls to rush to them and curtsey. Our Constitution proceeds. We shall be free and independent. There is much to do. God give us the strength to do it all."

"Sir, there is no time!" I finally intrude upon his performance. "This town grows filthier by the day. The riches you describe lure multitudes more to augment this filth I beg to bring to your attention. I cling to the notion that could we all but talk aloud about it, matters would not be so dire!"

To which he replies in most unexpected fashion, "Have you heard that jest is made about my yard? 'Old Ben Franklin has a dripping cock,' they say, 'but better his cock run off than his mouth.' Yes, I hear all this. I hear everything. I hear that many find me intolerable, unbearably pompous, with a pretentious unasked-for opinion about everything. To have worked so hard and given so much and to be laughed at for reward."

Mr. Franklin sighs wearily. As he turns to walk off, he says again, "It is a terrible burden to be right."

A fair is under way here. It is being held on a field far removed from the center, in a pasture once used for visiting preachers and their Puritan awakenings, no longer popular in a town of Quakers, but now adjoining a graveyard for the indigent. I have heard about the fair from the Peabody whores in Vanderberg. A number of foreign lands have dispatched representatives to bring best wishes to the new Americans who have abandoned those lands to come here. It has not been well received and those attending are few. Walking through the fairgrounds I am approached by a sailor, a mammoth black and bearded man.

"I can sell you something that can destroy all mankind," the sailor says to me, holding forth a small package wrapped in paper.

I am startled. "Is it Mr. Borstal, now?"

"Yes, Dr. Hog! I had heard that you were here. It's good to see you."

Mr. Darcus Borstal is a shit shoveler I had met in Boston, a jolly young man with a smile for everyone. He had shoveled shit in London originally, where he was born and raised by a nobleman from whom, as I recall, he ran away. It is one of the few lines of work in which a Negro can travel without being arrested or indentured. How did he get from London to Boston to Philadelphia?

"Ah, there is a dramatic story in that. The heart travels across the ocean with the body."

"And what are you attempting to sell me, my good man?" I have taken his package and unwrapped it. It contains two small vials.

"As I have said, something that can destroy all mankind."

I clap him on the shoulder. "I very much doubt that, for since my birth I have heard men promise the end of the world, yet here we are. But I shall buy it anyway. What is it?" I am holding one of the vials up to the sun. Inside is what looks to be a chunk of rotting flesh.

Mr. Borstal looks around to make certain we are alone. "That is my cock," he says, and lowers his trousers. He is indeed without a penis.

The suturing has been most well done. There is a metal straw, which appears to drain fluids into a leather pouch ingeniously strung around his waist.

"That is a fine job," I say, my medical curiosity having overcome my shock. "Where and by whom was it accomplished?"

I am holding up the other bottle, which appears to hold a piece of spotted skin floating in what he says is gin.

"Is that pox? These are not spots I recognize."

"It is the pox of the wife I left in Paris. She it was I gave it to. She is dead. What do you think? You get the moon when you buy the stardust."

I give Mr. Borstal several coins and rewrap the vials clumsily and prepare to say goodbye. "I wish you well with your injury. Might I inquire how it came about?"

"As I say, the heart travels across the ocean with the body." He hands me a letter. And he is gone.

My grandfather Abstruse Mather believed in the supernatural. He looked at cabbage roots and deemed them capable of miracles. He would eat them. He dug up red earth and mixed it with wine and offered it to God, before consuming it himself. He preached about the terror of swords in the sky, and his parishioners saw swords in the sky. "Those swords are the unloosed passions concealed beneath your trousers," he would warn them; "and these passions are the most terrifying part of human flesh; they can spear you to death." The weak in heart would kill themselves when he frightened them so much. After hearing him, they often determined it was safer to be dead. Abstruse, of all the Mathers and Cottons, claimed the record for these.

Is there no man alive who is at ease with his cock? Why do preachers never preach on this?

I continue to confer with sundry medical and municipal authorities and to walk the streets. I study the eruptions on the bodies of those willing to reveal themselves to me. Fourteen more deaths in only several days elicit another private convocation of these medical fellows. A gentleman has just been pulled out of the river behind the Peabody house, his throat twisted from some last gasping for air. He was a gentleman known to these doctors.

Again we meet late at night at what now passes for the central infirmary, claimed like so much in this town by Franklin to have been started by himself, that many-sheeted moaning room in a large warehouse basement. The dead gentleman is laid out on a table, naked for all to see his tortured body. The fear in this place is palpable. "He is one of us," one doctor says, "from Upper Bucks. Dr. Carlisle. Tom. What if we are somehow the ones at fault? Some say the fault is ours for our great ignorance. Doctors are not trusted as it is."

And they all turn to me.

I say what little I am able.

"Are you asking me if it is a plague of the pox? I do not know. Are you asking me if an end can be put to the current outbreak? I know not. Are you asking me if it is fair to lock up the infected, for now, for life? No, that is not fair. But it is reasonable, though this conclusion must come from your own deliberations. I will say that I think it will do but little to stop the culprit. If this culprit is some new pox, it is out there and it is going to stay out there for far longer than we all shall live. The only safe course is for everyone in the world to stop mingling. I think this unlikely even if any of us knew how to bring it about. All in all I do not think I can tell you anything beyond what your common sense should by now have considered.

"Yet I ask you to reconsider. It is always what is most obvious that we blame and often what is least obvious that is at fault. I extend an invitation to you to come walking with me around your Philadelphia. Let us go at dawn tomorrow, when all is quiet, and watch the day begin."

The doctors show interest. Perhaps there is something to reconsider.

"Doctor, please! We must first take a vote." The voice is not one but several, soon joined by others.

Their vote is unanimous. A quarantine of all infected persons, and suspected infected persons, and all persons suspected of being prone to infection because of their "known habits of life" is to be placed into effect tomorrow noon.

Benjamin Franklin, who rarely misses a meeting of anything, nods approvingly. Dr. Rush—he who thinks that Negroes are black because they have a kind of leprosy—agrees as well.

At dawn the group of doctors, with the addition of a few civic authorities and local dignitaries and the curious who have heard, accompany me on my tour. It is a long walk out here and many have come by horse and a carriage or two.

"Here, gentlemen, is the source of your plague. It has been here some several months' time. I believe that your first cases date from the very same."

"Where? Where? Where?" Everyone rushes about, wondering where to look. They step across puddles and small pools and dark-colored streams. Boots are caked with mud and shit, if their walk out here had not already accomplished the same.

Atop a platform, so elevated it is almost out of sight and certainly almost out of focus for the elderly, to the accompaniment of loud drumbeats and trumpet screeches, is what in the dawn's early light appears to be a skeleton moving, swaying. From the same height comes a loud voice through a horn.

"Friends of Dr. Hogarth Hooker! Good citizens of Philadelphia! Pray silence whilst you attend on this performance arranged especially for you!"

More drums and horns and then the skeleton falls forward, as if pushed into falling forward, and drops toward a tiny pool of water encased in a wooden frame on the ground. As it falls and twists, the skeleton is seen to be a human being, arms and legs now tumbling out from a carapace painted with white bones. Screams of alarm erupt among the spectators. "It is alive!" And then, "But there is not water enough in the tub!" The body lands, and splashes what little water is in the tub out, and now this tub is empty, save for flesh and bones disintegrated, splintered and splattered into specks and spots and pieces and drops of blood that fly out over the crowd. "Stand back! Stand away!" I cry in warning and many move to do just so. But far from running from this hailstorm, many others scream and rush forward, reaching for pieces of bloody flesh, grabbing them, clutching them, folding them into handkerchiefs and sticking these into pockets and sacks, "as mementoes of this spectacle"! Drops and rivulets of blood spatter many faces. Many tongues automatically lick the blood away.

"There. There is another source of our plague." I point to the licking, darting tongues.

"But what you are showing us has nothing to do with the intercourse of . . . coupling," protest several of the younger doctors.

"How has such a demonstration of death been allowed?" asks an angry Dr. Rush. "Mr. Franklin, do you know?"

"I do not, sir, and I resent your accusatory tone. How have you not heard of this yourself, as you claim to serve so many patients everywhere?"

I hasten to regain their attention as I answer the young doctors' protest. "Indeed. While I do believe there is syphilis in your town—it would be a rare town that did not have some—I do not believe that the whorehouses and their customers are the only cause of all your moaning deaths. Do you know how many dead bodies are catapulted from that parapet each day? And who they are? And where they hail from?"

The dozen or so bodies that are hurled from on high six times a day into the evening come from a local gravedigger credited with creating this act. Wandering around behind the scene, I watched the gravedigger haul each body up from a pit with a pulley till it reached the sky. I discovered that all the dead bodies were male. Studying the stacks of waiting corpses, I noted that some of their necks were twisted from gasping for breath, with mouths caked with blood, some limbs and torsos mutilated by ropes and whips and knives. Some penises had been severed and some tongues removed. These men had been tortured somewhere first. "Where did you obtain these corpses?" I asked the gravedigger, when I found him delivering more. "They do not look like they have been exhumed from the earth." He would not answer me. "From many watery graves," he finally replies when I put a coin in his hand. Mrs. Peabody, the mistress of both of the whorehouses, most vehemently denied the dead to be her customers. "Had I so many visitors I would be rich!"

Although Mr. Darcus Borstal gave a letter to me with his two bottles, I must confess to only remembering it after being asked, and not too politely, to continue my journeys elsewhere. Briefly, I was not believed. Dead diseased bodies hauled from the De-La-Ware to poison the town? "Do not test our patience any longer." I was given neither an honorarium nor a parting gift. Indeed, no one of these many doctors would even shake my hand.

The letter from Mr. Borstal read,

"Dear Dr. Hog, I saw you with my Ben, walking and talking. He no longer walks and talks with me. I love him like I love starlight and moonlight and he took my love and took it and took it, and now he takes it no more. He gave me dripping cock. My Ben has a dripping cock and sores and pus and now I have them, too. He said I gave it to him. In Paris he took me to the doctor, who sliced mine off. 'We must see if this will cure us,' my Ben said to me. 'And if it will now go away.' But it is my Ben who goes away. Now I have fits and monsters in my eyes. I sleep and wake up mad and crazy. I see bears and lions and tigers growling at me, ready to eat me up. Then men come to throw me out of Ben's. They tie me up and throw me in a room with locks and bars and many other men tied and shackled, pus and scabs and whip marks o'er their bodies like a second skin. I ask for Ben. Bring me my friend Ben. Bring me my friend Ben, who taught me so much of what I know. Bring me Ben, who took me from Boston to London and Paris, promising me the moon and starlight. The men laugh and laugh and laugh. I kill the man with the keys who comes to feed me at night. I break my ropes and choke him to death with my bare hands. I run and run. I see my Ben. He points me out to a guard man with a gun who is with him. I run and hide. I come to the fairground and I become friends with the circus men. They are hushies too. The king of England threw them out of his country, my country too. They are crazy and dizzy with spells like me. Some are very mad like me. Some scream. Some bite and hit. The maddest ones are hauled up and fall down from up high. Some even happily jump, screaming out in laughter. Some are pushed. By the time you read this I will be dead or crazy or both. Please remember me. Panther."

I leave Philadelphia, distraught, disgusted, and sorely disappointed in myself for not having stopped the despair. By the time I depart, some three hundred men and some one hundred women are dead, and the fairground show is still performing, but now to crowds of people, often mobs.

•

Yes, the bodies thrown from above were all diseased with me. A most unusual way to dispose of my partners, but they were useful for my propagation nevertheless. No one, I am grateful to say, comprehends any of this. Dr. Hooker is certainly trying his best to make me clear, but once again, thank goodness, the natural ignorance of The American People, as you now call yourselves, allows me to continue to live and breathe and grow. Like all the grand and learned men gathered here in this town to make a country come into being, I believe I have a future.

BENJAMIN FRANKLIN'S REAL ALMANAC

Hog tried to tell them and nobody listened. Disappointed mightily, he set out for the long trip that produced the journal that was to be his life's work, wondering what hell his country would become. To this day you can never erase a history that found Rush bleeding people to death and Carthwaite insisting that syphilis and gonorrhea are caused by the same thing—two leading doctors with their heads screwed on wrong. This is the home where purging through poisonous enemas, "powder-nostrums" (inhalations of fine white powder thought to cure catarrh but causing cancer), are for far too many years the standard of care and the backbone of its knowledge. A city, and by extension the country that houses it, doesn't live down facts like these, not for a long time. That "city of brotherly love" becomes much too quickly one of those places—of which this country will never-endingly have so many—that is old before it's young. It remains stubborn and rigid and unable to keep up with the times. No words can express the sadness of the useless-ness descending on this city that is America's biggest, and which, this use-lessness, continues to this day. Yes, it becomes our new country's first center for the study of medicine, but surprise surprise, it turns out to be a wretched place for medical progress. Baltimore and Washington and Boston and, finally, New York take its place.

Many blame Ben Franklin for this lacklusterness. "He gave us too much hope," they say of Ben, when in fact he gave us much too little. "Common sense," which he was so fond of calling up, is not hope.

Why were and are The American People so completely in awe of Frank-lin, whose continuing unblemished adoration has always been perplexing to me? Why do we always fall for the head and ignore the slop pail when he was afflicted with what even one of his most gushing biographers, that miss-the-boat guy previously mentioned, Edmund S. Morgan, calls "a prolonged fit of political blindness"?

For most of his adult years, certainly the years of his greatest physical and mental energy, he attempted, with a relentless determination that is in-comprehensible, to turn Pennsylvania into a royal colony. He hated the Penn family, to whom the king had given the huge grant of land. In the face of major opposition, Ben stayed fervently intent on royalizing his state. He didn't care that such an upheaval could easily endanger the fragile new liberties of the colonists. For Ben, the British monarchy came first, long after anyone else stateside stopped giving a fart for the king or his goddamned country. It was a strange and inept stand, even traitorous. "America" had already been here for more than one hundred years, and he wants it to go back to its ice age. The guy had lost his marbles. Nobody talks about this to this day. They don't talk about a lot of things about Benjamin Franklin.

By the time he returned to Philadelphia, when Hogarth met him, he had been away from home a long time. The worshipful attendance paid upon his every belch and fart in England and France was less in evidence. A lot of the younger crowd didn't know him at all.

He was having such a good time in England hobnobbing with the titled and the rich that he was reluctant to return to America even when his wife, Deborah, informed him she was dying, had not long left, and begged him to come back so she could see him one more time. He dithered and dallied, so she died alone, in 1744, while Franklin was in London. She had not seen him for some twelve years, during which he sired a couple of illegitimate sons.

Amusingly, if you can find any humor in this, he did not like or get along with John Adams, another patriot of the era who is also the object of unbridled adoration. The dislike was mutual. John thought Ben vastly overrated. Ben said of John "that he means well for his Country, is always an honest Man, often a Wise One, but sometimes and in some things, absolutely out of his Senses."

No one yet has the goods on John Adams, but Benjamin Franklin not only abandoned a wife, had illegitimate children, disinherited his son, and was one of America's earliest published writers and purveyors of pornography, but he had a black man murdered for loving him.

So, in fact, this man did not offer hope. He will prove prescient, though: "I believe . . . that this [the form of government envisaged and guaranteed by this new Constitution he helped to birth] can only end in Despotism as other Forms have done before it, when the People shall become so corrupted as to need Despotic Government, being incapable of any other."

The bile inside him gives him this insight. Washington didn't believe the new country would work out either, saying that "it would not last twenty years."

How is it that two hushmarkeds have such morbid insights into our future?

Ms. Stacy Schiff, in her book on Franklin in Paris, *A Great Improvisation*, reports, "he made regular late-afternoon visits to a white, canvas-covered barge that floated on the Seine opposite the Tuileries. Pot-de-Vin's bathhouse was not Paris's most luxurious establishment, and Franklin was surely unaware that it was the city's premier gay bathhouse." Every day? And he didn't notice all the naked men cruising on the river? Oh, please, Stacy dear. She suggests that Franklin needed a place where he could confer with his spies. Oh, pretty please. This bathhouse stuff is of monstrous historical importance. Schiff has a case of what YRH calls Ron Chernowitis, of Doris Kearns Goodwinism, denying a truth writ so large she should choke on it.

To say that Benjamin Franklin was not a nice man is putting it mildly. To the list of his personal failings mentioned earlier let us add some more.

He hated women. He brutally fucked them. He probably passed on syphilis or gonorrhea to all those "cousins" in Philadelphia when he came back from France with his dripping cock. Yes, he was a pig of a womanizer. But what he really liked when he'd had one too many were his evenings of being fucked by black men.

Grace writes, "History is sad, Freddie. It can tie up the tongue forever and render a vocabulary mute. I am, of course, in receipt of a cranky epistle from Our Lady of the Discontented, the bleeding Bledd-Wrench. 'I am distressed to note that Mr. Lemish believes Benjamin Franklin to have been a homosexual.' Etc. Fuck her."

Hog was on to something. He just didn't know it. I quote from a report from 1846 in London, where similar conditions existed along the Thames, an equally foul waterway filled with floating humans: "Whenever animal and vegetable substances are undergoing the process of decomposition, poisonous matters are evolved akin to ammonia which, mixing with the air, corrupt it, and render it injurious to health and fatal to life. If provision is not made for the immediate removal of these poisons, they are carried by the air to the lungs, the thin delicate membranes of which they pierce, and thus pass directly into the current of the blood's circulation. The consequences are often death within the space of a few hours, or even minutes."

THE PENIS AND THE RECTUM: SOME THOUGHTS OF DR. HOGARTH HOOKER FROM MY BOOK OF FLESHLY THOUGHTS

Where comes the knowledge from, how gets it into our fibers, how to use these parts of us for events other than waste and exit? From a wretched wounded sailor, I hold now in my hand, halfway around the world from whence they were once whole, tiny pieces of flimsy flesh that would be rotten were it not for their being soaked in gin and pearce. Each day I look at them. What do I hope to perceive? As from some crystal ball am I to be the recipient of some omens locked up within these tiny bits from cock and cunt? How talked they into this tiny vial of glass?

When did man first know that rubbing his thing brought pleasure? Adam must have discovered that fact, and told Eve, who rubbed herself and discovered likewise. Then they learned how to fit their pleasures into one. Stick the stick into the hole. "But I have two holes," she one day must have said. So the hole in front and the hole in back must have been a field of choices for the stick of Adam. Did this make man, from his beginning, feel somehow less? Did woman tease man: You have only one hole and I cannot use it because I do not possess one of your ridiculous sticks? And laugh at man in a haughty and superior way?

But wait. What about the mouth? Surely this qualifies as a hole? So that would give her three holes to his two. For by now they must have discovered that to taste each other with their mouths is pleasurable also. That still leaves man lacking by one.

But he has a cock. A cock is better than a hole. It is big and strong, indeed like a stick. Her pleasured parts are all inside of her. You can *see* a cock. Is it this advantage, more than any others, that gives this self-assumed supremacy on his part, to the man?

As for the rectum used for fucking, I wager it is the shit coming out that Adam and Eve found most strange. I believe the rectum to have nerves of pleasure, but then comes the shit. "Surely, Adam, comes this odor from this stuff that pleases not my nose at all." "But, dear Eve, perhaps it is important that it comes to view, that it falls from inside of us, that it comes each and every day, as if God wishes us to know that He is with us each day."

What would ever make people believe that shit and sex and religion are inter-mix'd? This question haunts me.

·

Such is the book of philosophy I try, and try again, to write. Now that I have writ this small portion, what can I say?

These thoughts are most peculiar. And yet I have them.

The world is a peculiar place in more ways than are considered.

Is that not what I learned in Philadelphia?

Causes, and the effects of them, are not what we want to see, or know.

What, then, do we want to see, and know?

Whatever the answer, I fear it is a great secret I am striving to see face to face.

Who will want to know that the penis is the secret to the world and the key to all its actions? For that is what I think I shall find.

How do you tell such a secret to the world?

Do others have such unvoiced thoughts? How am I ever to know?

The maid who cleans my room asked me to read her what I was writing. I did so. I was asked by the proprietor to leave Toobeloo forthwith. In fact, he escorted me to the stagecoach depot with a rifle and sat there with me for some hours waiting for it to arrive. He did not take his eyes off me. I tried to engage him in conversation, to no avail.

CONCORDIA, EASTERN SHORE, MARYLAND, MARCH 12, 1790

I wonder if semen and shit share anything in common. I must research this matter when I return to Ontuit.

I am not gifted sufficient in science to locate the answers to all the questions that plague my mind. There is no one with whom I can share my thoughts. When I talk I frighten people. Well, I come by it honestly. I am a Hooker, after all.

My nanny used to tell me, "If your semen can birth a baby and your shit can help grow corn, then a man is not a useless thing."

Wandering this country I must perforce live with myself. I have never been alone with myself for such a long time. I find it is a struggle.

Here in Concordia, I have fucked with my first woman. She has been a long time in arriving! At last I shed my shyness and timidness. She was wife to the local collector of clams. Her hands were rough from shucking them, but her face and eyes sparkled. We did our coupling in a shack on the shore and we lay on a bed of clamshells! It was most pleasant, if a bit peculiar and filled with humps and bumps. I was happy, and yes, proud.

I fell asleep and when I awoke she was gone. But a man of great height and wide shoulders and strong arms stood over me, his penis out of his pants and erect. He was waving it in my face to indicate I should take it in my mouth. He was not threatening me. Indeed, his face was most kind, and welcoming. So I did what he desired. His penis was noticeable for its saltwater taste. He did not take long to deliver his semen into my mouth. It too tasted of salt-water. When he was finished I invited him to sit down so we could talk.

"Tell me about yourself," I started.

"What more do you need to know? You have fucked the wife and sucked the husband." He roared with laughter.

"Does this happen here often with passing strangers?"

"We do not see many passing strangers, but if we did it would not go amiss. Is such behavior strange to you? Then you must live in a place of many people, not like here, where it is so lonely it hurts."

Before I could respond, he took my cock and made it hard and then put it into his mouth so that my pleasure returned once more.

I was urged by both of them to stay for dinner and I tried again to discuss our unusual couplings. Men talk only when they are hard and ready for pleasuring, and not always then. And a woman is quiet in front of her man. So they were not much interested in a discussion. They had done what they had done and thought it not much to talk about. We all drank wine and went to sleep separately and in the morning I sensed that it was time to say goodbye. They had much work to do with clams.

I recall as I went on my way how he had made me laugh when he wanted a second act of sex and his cock was slow to harden. I was to see this often, men talking to their penises, as if to another being. "Come on, George!" "Let us go, Peter!" "Come to Father, John." If their members do not respond they hit them.

NORTHERN TERRITORY, TERRA HOTE, NOVEMBER 3, 1790

This place is flat and small. There are people who speak French and recall the Indian war.

Traveling the roads into the heart of this country shows me that there is not much people do but for work. Joy and sparkling eyes are fleeting. When I try to discover their thoughts, I am told, "We have work to do. Our lives are hard. Goodbye."

In small towns or outposts like this one men get drunk a lot. Women do not come to these places to live. There is naught but the hard work of clearing the land, which is overgrown with nature, high and thick. I asked one man if he stayed here to forget. He looked at me with nary a glimmer of understanding. Fearing I had insulted him, I moved on.

At night the men repair to a tavern set up in a log cabin. Here, after a while of drinking, they perform on each other without shame or concern. They need relief from their needs, I hear them say, and, since they do the same most every night, their needs must be most strong. Their faces are blank, as if they are watching wind or rain. There is no joy apparent in the performance. But then there are few smiles during the daytime either.

I spent the past many months working in a camp for logging men. The work was especially hard and I was always very tired. I am not certain why I did it for so long. I expect I thought being in the midst of so many men would give me information, but they were all as tired as I at the end of the day and not interested in talk.

There was much coupling among them, always swift and necessary, like removing mud from boots before entering a new room. I saw no affection exchanged. Always eyes were tightly closed and britches swiftly hoisted when the act was over. Insofar as I could avoid it, I did not partake. The harshness of sex with these men was not appealing. Few want to do anything but have their cocks inside an asshole. Not everyone is comfortable with this. There is much fighting for supremacy, like roosters, I guess, or dogs. Few are interested in using their mouths.

One night the owner of the camp—a man of seventy or more, I would say, tall but still most muscled in his arms—pulled off his shirt and grabbed me in a rough embrace, kissing me and using his tongue to taste me. He had protruding tits that sagged like an old woman's and he was trying to get one of them into my mouth.

"Suck! Suck! You bastard man, suck my tits! Suck, goddamn you! I own this place and I order you to suck my tits!"

Around us were gathered the men I felled trees with by day. They were drunk now, and they took up his words. "Suck, suck, suck!" they chanted, stomping their heavy work boots on the floor of this cabin where we also ate and slept.

I had little choice but to take his tit in my mouth. Well, I had tried other peculiar things before, and I reminded myself that that was a principal reason for my journey. He smelled terrible, like the dying men in Philadelphia, and there was liquid oozing from the tit that I surmised to be a bodily poison of some sort. With a mighty surge of strength he threw me up into the air, and

I would have fallen hard but for the men closest around us catching me. I would have been relieved of my distress had they not immediately relieved me of my clothes. Six or seven of them pinned me to the floor facedown and proceeded one by one to fuck me. There were some thirty of them in all, and each took his time coming to his climax, or not. I wanted to lose consciousness but I could not. One or two of them passed out in drunkenness while still inside me. When all was silent at last, the old man picked up his rifle, shot them all dead one by one, and motioned me to go, his eyes filled with tears. "I am sorry," he said to me as he turned the rifle on himself.

I recovered my clothes. I located a small glass jar and squeezed into it some of the juice from his tits, tucking the jar in my pack with the vials containing the flesh of Borstal and his wife.

I knew I had to leave before all the dead bodies were come upon, but I could barely walk. I stumbled to a small shack where we left the tools, the saws and axes, and collapsed on a pile of seed bags. I passed out for I do not know how long, but I know I had a great fever that kept me tossing in sweat and nightmares. When at last I had the energy to get outside and feel the cold air in my face, the cabin was gone, burned to the ground. There was nothing but the smell of charred flesh in the air.

It was a long and painful walk to the next township. The roads were coated with snow. The wind whipped me forward. When I arrived I was greeted with suspicion as the new face in town. I was accustomed to that look. I found a poor accommodation to sleep in and eat some food.

It took me some time to mend. I was afraid a serious injury had been done me, either of the flesh or through some infection transferred to me, but after several weeks I felt almost myself again. I worked for meal money and a cot in back of a schoolhouse, ignoring the teacher when she inquired why I did not sit down "to take a load off your feet, sir."

•

I then begin a course of longer wanderings wherein I know not the dates nor make entry of them. I am lost and I know I am lost. I feel a failure in everything I've done. I have not loved or been loved. I have not succeeded in any fashion, and Hookers, if anything in this world, are meant to excel at something, if not godly at least measurable for decency and respect. I just walked and slept and ate and shat and found labor to make some coins and walked some more. People who talked to me received no response. I begged sometimes, I even stole when I was able. My bearded face I know was sinister and so I was more left alone. I knew I stank from lack of bathing or any hygiene. My God, what had become of me, I was able to ask myself again and again. Looking back I note that, not by design, I had stayed away from any beaten path, large and growing places, prosperity, and even merriment. All I saw were people working hard and bent over from exhaustion and, yes, lack of joy. Most surprisingly there were few churches and no Great Awakenings here. I had thought Puritans were everywhere and had taken over everything. The few churches I went into, to keep warm, were sparsely attended and the preachers often had not shown up. I remember pledging to locate a smile on a lovely young woman's face, and I looked and looked but I could not find her. No, I saw no joy. Not in faces or smiles or in gratitude to anyone or anything, certainly to no deity. I visited places of healing, tiny . . . *hospitals* is too grand a word. Clinics some called themselves. There are never any doctors. We must be too far in the wilderness for doctors. "We get sick and we just die," a nurse of sorts told me. "Isn't it the same everywhere else?" When I told her about Yaddah Medical School she said it sounded like heaven and where could this town get "one of them who learned there." I turned and ran away. How long this lasted, and how I beat it out so that I came out of it, I have no idea. But I did. One day I knew that once again I could see clearly. I was ravenous but not for food. The one thing I was most hungry for was to fuck a woman. I start talking again to men and this time I am hearing answers. Men are most angry when their penises do not do what they are told. "If you are a doctor like you say, then give me something guaranteed to make me hard!" I hear this over and over, so many times it hammers itself into my brain. If there is one thing that most men want it's this.

CHARLESTON, SOUTH CAROLINA, JANUARY 2, 1792

From a doctor here I learn there is a term for this thing so dearly sought.

Aphrodisiac.

"The man who discovers one will become the richest man in the world and bring much joy and happiness to all mankind as well."

The doctor says he believes it possible to find such a thing in nature and ingest it.

I wonder if I would have given this much thought had I not encountered these past years of wandering with the problem myself. Many a lonely night I wanted to comfort myself, only to find the more I wanted to use my cock the less it wanted to be used. More and more I am not always its master.

Charleston is a lovely place. I walk its streets day and night and find women willing to take me into their beds. These are poor women, often Negro, all of them unclean and not put off by my being the same. They take me into hovels or into their master's homes when they are not there. I realize that it is only diseased women I want to fuck. I become consumed with fucking and fucking and fucking. This is my research, I say to myself. Why have I wasted so long avoiding it? What better way to investigate disease than to become diseased?

I wonder if I am passing on to them any disease I surely must have by now myself.

But I am not diseased, at least not so I can see or feel.

I go out of my way to locate women who are in some way infected, with pox, with clap, with any ailment of the cunt or blood. It is not so difficult to find them when you know what you are looking for. This lovely town is diseased more than it can know. Like Philadelphia, towns with prosperity most often are. This very challenge excites me. I see in it a way to find myself and bring me back to life as it is lived, and most of all, to do good for my fellow man. It excites me sufficient as to make my cock hard all the time I am fucking a woman of ill health. The more I remain free of pox, the harder I must work. I am determined to make myself poxed!

The more I fail, the more I begin to suspect that I have become invincible and that within me must reside something of great import.

I traveled through the southern regions, where it seemed to me there was more pox. I fucked white women and black women and mulatto women. I fucked American women and Indian women and Chinese women and Jewish women. I fucked them front and back and in their mouths. I am so obsessed with my challenge that sometimes I become quite brutal. I did not see that I was becoming a man I no longer knew. Anyway, that man is gone.

NEW ORLEANS, LOUISIANA TERRITORY, AUGUST 1792

I had heard of a hospital here for venereal diseases, which are rampant in this place. I arrive only to discover that it has been closed for some forty years. It was started by royal physicians from France because matters were so bad here, and there too. Apparently it did not improve them. The soldiers were so licentious that the epidemic could not be stemmed. I could find no one able to tell me much about it. The building had been burned down to destroy any possible contagion.

But here it was that I met the woman who would become my wife, Margatula Abagale. On the still partially charred grounds of this once-hospital she maintained gardens for the city. She grew flowers and she was allowed to sell them. She was a Creole woman, tall as me, and strong. Her skin was like highly polished burnished wood. French was her first language, but she spoke English, too. I was admiring her herb garden particularly, there were so many kinds I had never seen.

"Don't touch them. Come with me."

I followed her into a large shed of everything needed for her work. She filled a great tub with water. She took off all my clothes. And with her strong arms and shoulders she threw me into it.

"Now I can see what you really look like," she roared with laughter.

She made me remain in the tub while she washed my clothes and I shaved myself and she set my clothing out in the sun.

And here it was that after I fucked her seventeen times and fell in love with her my penis would not erect again, no matter what I said to it or how hard I tried to slap it into sense.

I had learned enough, or too much, or more than I wanted, or not enough, so I married Margatula Abagale and determined to take her home to Ontuit.

The week before we were to depart, I met Hiram Punic, in one of those taverns where men fuck each other when they are drunk enough. I had gone to see if my cock would still work here. I struck up a conversation with this Hiram Punic, an ordinary-looking man about fifty, and to my surprise he was eager to be interviewed about his penis, and invited me home so that we could talk privately. He was a person who never stopped talking and he said he had many interesting things to confide. He took me to Mon Petit, outside New Orleans, to a small farmhouse that was filthy and stank. I could see that he was lazy with his hands and barely getting along, but his brain was busy enough.

Hiram Punic was an evil man. He wanted everybody to fall sick and die, and he told me so. For some while now he had been going to this or that town a few days away by horseback, and then a few weeks away, and finding a church social to attend so that he could pour a poison powder into the punch. With great pride he spread a local newspaper before me, with a headline that read, "Mysterious illness results in deaths of 34 ladies and gentlemen." He brought forth more newspapers with similar headlines, from all over Louisiana, and from Alabama and Mississippi.

I think Hiram Punic might have killed off all of America had he not met me.

Hiram told me that he always had a few animals on his farm that were sick from something strange, something Hiram didn't recognize. He took the oozing pus that came out of a duck's ass or a chicken's or a pig's and he put it in the food he gave his healthy animals. Soon they were sick too. The larger ones, the horses and cows, discharged much more pus before they died. Hiram collected all this in a bucket and poured it on a big flat rock and baked it in the sun until it turned to powder. He gave the powder to his cat and she died fine, so he knew he had what he wanted. He saddled up and galloped off to his first town, Veronica, Louisiana. There isn't any Veronica anymore. He laughed loudly as he told me, and when I looked skeptical, he barked, "Come with me!"

We rode to a town close by. It appeared to be a holiday of some sort. There was a big outdoor picnic, with what looked to be everyone in town in attendance, including many children. The people were laughing and singing in Spanish and French and not much English.

"I would not ordinarily go so close to where I live," Hiram said, "but these people are a particular annoyance to me because they are so many different colors. They should be white. They must fuck each other every which way to produce such unnatural results. It is not as God intended."

"I am amazed you speak of God," I ventured. "Surely He would not approve of your activities."

"He would. He certainly would."

"What is your heritage, sir, if I may ask?"

"You may. You certainly may. I am of strong British stock, sir, through and through."

He had prepared small packets of his poison powder, which he deposited covertly as we talked and walked. In a water tank. In a large vat of sauerkraut heating up. In the horse trough, in the many large bowls of fruit punch laid out here and there. He performed his handiwork with skill. When I cautioned him that he might be witnessed, he replied, "No matter, there are many chefs walking around adding last-minute ingredients to their stews." Again his jolly laugh. "And we shall be off and gone before the height of the festivities.

But I must work out a better plan for ridding the bigger places, like New Orleans itself. Yes, I will enjoy that."

As we were leaving, an old woman fell down dead in a fit. People started screaming and rushed about in growing fear as more and more fell down and were seen to die so quickly, struck in spasm and choking to death. The children, of course, went even faster. One little girl, a beaming blond-haired child, was offering me a candy when she suddenly expired.

Yes, I watched him do all this.

I wanted to kill him on the spot but I was not finished with him yet. He still had more to teach me.

We went back to his decrepit house and I made him fuck me. It was not easy, because his shriveled cock was lazy, too, nestled as it was in awful-smelling britches. I sucked it hard. I made myself make his penis hard so he could fuck me and I could continue my experiment. Surely this man must be infected with something that would transmit itself to me.

"That was good," he said when we finally finished. "It has been a long time since the last one. You must come around more often. Where are you staying?"

Instead of answering, I coaxed him to show me where he worked and tell me if there was anything else I should know about his powder.

"Yes, it is more than just the pus of sick animals. It is shit and piss from them, of course, and from me, too, and rancid remains of food. Everything I can lay my hands on that is putrid I throw into my stew. There are no secret ingredients. It is all things nature and God give to the world to use as we see fit. Here, take some home for yourself." Then came that awful laugh as he filled my hands with the tiny packages of his poison.

Suddenly he had his own spasm and fits of choking and fell down dead.

That was when I knew I was infected with something.

Or was I?

I took Margatula Abagale and went home to Ontuit.

THE LAST DAYS OF HOGARTH HOOKER

I have traveled many years now. I claim I did it to learn, for knowledge and experience. Perhaps some of it was too extreme, but men who push themselves to the extreme to learn are building this country and I considered I was doing the same.

No man knows what to do with his cock. Most men do nothing with it. "I do not pleasure myself," I was told many times when I asked. No man looks upon his penis as his friend. In fact, I think for most, his penis is his enemy. Men too afraid of sex? Men being afraid of women? Men being afraid of men? Quite possibly it is all three and Hooker preachers have been smart enough to make strong meat of this. I would like to locate that aphrodisiac but I look back and see that my investigations were just the reverse: I tried to locate what poisons were in play, so that what happened in Philadelphia could not happen elsewhere, and in trying to poison my own body I could discover how to mend it. I wonder how presumptuous all this was, and whether had I been God-fearing I would have been any more miserable than I am now. I don't think I have much time left within me to change horses in so late a stream.

I do know that men do not know what to do with their thoughts, so they don't even try.

That is what I discovered.

How many years and how many questions and answers has it taken me to adduce this? It all seems so obvious now. How many miles did I walk to locate only this?

I have aged much since Philadelphia. There I was a smart upstart, a fresh young man who thought he knew all the answers.

My brain is clogged up. I know not what to do with my own cock, much less the one in this bottle here. What have I to show for all my wanderings?

In all this time Ontuit has not changed much. It is still quiet and small. My servants and slaves are all still here. My Hooker cousins have tended my land carefully. My hateful father, Ezra Jr., still is hateful and still hates me and considers my life unworthy. My kindly brother Lucid looks at me with imploring eyes. Please tell me what has happened to you, I can see he wants to ask me. I wonder why he doesn't come right out and ask. But now I know he is no different a man than all I've seen. We are all lost, like every Hooker has said.

I believe I am slowly going mad. That is what can come to the man who has not found his place in the world.

I experiment with tubes and herbs and barks and plants and roots and all that kind of stuff that since the beginning of time people seeking to unlock the strange forces of the universe have believed they must explore.

I keep staring at my little glass bottles that hold the sailor's severed penis and the piece of his wife's cunt and the tit pus from Lester Noggins and my most recent powder from Hiram Punic. I no longer harbor excitement about the future or a goal of great deeds to be done. I hold no belief that tomorrow will be anything different from today. Thinking like this makes me sad. Soon I never leave my rooms. After a while my own wife scarcely misses me.

I still have come down with no illness.

And no experiment I have tried in my laboratory and on myself and with my blood and spit and shit and piss has revealed anything to me.

A young Negro serving girl cuts herself while moving my glass slides in my laboratory. This girl and I have fucked. She wishes to fuck yet again. We do so. Enormous heavings now come suddenly upon the girl. She is groaning and crying out in passion and lust and trying to scratch my eyes out with her nails. She is so overcome with shuddering from my cock going in and out that I can barely keep inside her. The thrashings of her body are so harshly violent that were Tom Hooker still around he would cry out, as I hear him do, for he is always with me, "The Devil is inside her!"

I do not release my semen into her. Instead I withdraw and collect it swiftly in a bottle of its own. When every inch of her flesh breaks out into sores, and these sores void great amounts of pus, and this pus forms new scabs all over her like some second, reptile skin, I scrape everything I can from her surface, from her skin and her cunt and inside her mouth, and I mix all this together, and mix my semen with it too.

The young girl dies screaming so loudly the entire town can hear. She is by now so encrusted in a hard outer coating of scab that when lifted to her coffin she is as heavy as a tree.

When my serving girl smeared my head with her pus, taking it from between her legs upon her fingers and running these fingers over my forehead and cheeks and the very lips I kissed her with, as if she were etching some pattern or design upon me, I thought her paint was poison. And yet I live!

I still do not fall sick. I wait for it. It does not come. One year, two years, three, I wait, fully expecting the killer inside me to claim me. I study myself thoroughly every day, every inch of my flesh that I can grab or see. I strain my urine through the finest sieves and study its clarity. I boil it to see what it reduces to. I spread my stools in the sun to bake. Nothing happens when I feed the results to any animal on my farm. I cause my blood to be introduced into pigs. One pig dies, but an animal who feeds on garbage is not fair evidence, particularly when the other pigs live.

But what is fair evidence? That is what haunts me. How do I come to be healthy when I suspect I should be otherwise? I have no answer, except that the serving girl died.

And what am I looking for? Something that kills people or something that makes penises hard?

I have poured enough poison into myself that I must have found the cure to something.

I have two concoctions now. The powder from Hiram Punic and the mixture from my slave and my semen. The first I know can kill. The second I have yet to try. I mix the two and consume them.

I go to my wife's bed and body. I return to sex with my servants. Three die, two serving girls and one houseboy. All three die with thick scabs covering their bodies like armor.

One day, Margatula Abagale, who has not shown any signs of illness, begins thrashing and retching, her vomit purple with the blood that heaves out of her in buckets. Before she dies she says to me, "My life was not happy with you but I loved you anyway."

And still I am not sick! What is in me that I escape? Why am I protected? How? Why am I exempt? Which of my many acts has granted to me an . . . immunity? Can such a deadly poison yet feel so safe inside a host that it wants to stay there, and arranges to stay there, rather than kill its master and be forced to find another or die itself?

It is when I hear this thought that I know I must end my own life. I am a killer and I must stop living because of it, lest the poison live on.

Once upon a time I was called brilliant. What has this brilliant man done with his life? Why have I never journeyed out again? I have walked no more than several miles since my trip until now this day. How long must I wait for something that never comes?

I am fifty now, but I am as an eighty-year-old man. I am as an eighty-year-old man who in his head is still the young boy running up Beecher's Hill. I want the energy to ignite my old age one more time. I seek an everlasting erection!

I crave to discover what this End of the World that Borstal the shit shoveler spoke of is like.

I break open his bottles and extract the shriveled pieces of flesh. I break open the bottles and packets with my other potions. I mix it all together and swallow it.

I eat you because there is nothing interesting left to eat. Why do I now think that these remains might contain within them the qualities necessary to fashion anything? Because diseases are caused by something. Some iota of something. Some sop of something that soaks up the qualities of the disease. The hungers of the disease. If the disease be a disease of sex, of fucking, why could not the iota be this quality liquefied or transfixed or reduced or quartered out, or isolated? If this is so, then how to isolate it further, bring it forth, and make it what it wants to be, which either is its passionate extension or its cure?

HIS BROTHER LUCID TELLS ABOUT HOG'S ENDING

He dies in March 1815. He is fifty years old.

He dies a crazy man, demented beyond anything yet seen by the community of religionists and relations still willing to surround him, no strangers to the sight of crazy men in throes of one kind or another. Hog dies by his own hand. His nails have grown into talons. He rips out his own heart. He wanted us all to see it, and we did.

I watch from the doorway. As does my son, Lucid Hooker, Jr., born this very year and held in his father's arms. We are all with Hog when his body finally explodes into a million pieces.

In the family Bible he entered these words: "Strange deaths I have seen and in a most quiet fashion tasted. Neighbors I have partnered with. And with my pigs and dogs and sheep and roosters. Local dens of witches and men with masked heads and all of us eating neath the full moon strange dark earthly roots. Strangers naked coupling unendingly till dawn."

Also inside this Bible are pages and pages of scribbles, formulas, lists of strange ingredients and theories. It would take another crazy man to make sense of them.

REACTIONS TO HOG'S ENDING

DR. SISTER GRACE: Hog was one fucked-up, mixed-up cookie. Or was he? Could a smart doctor have been anything else in those days? Or was he suffering from the same Hooker Hubris that I suffer as well?

DAME LADY HERMIA: Man is capable of as much atrocity as he has imagination, though he be reaching for the moon and stars.

•

I needed him dead, can't you see? He was getting closer and closer . . . to me.

I am proud that I was able to kill him at last. It took me too long, I agree, but I was learning how to get better control of my hosts.

He had infected many, of course. Which was very helpful.

And no one was able to see any of this, which was also very helpful.

STATE OF THE (AT LAST) UNION

Because we are now united, more or less, scandals of sex and bribery and corruption and of people in high places fighting increasingly bitter battles over new beginnings, new rules, new ways to make a new country and a new buck (although this term is not in use yet) begin to arouse attention. Day by day more men are seen to want more things and find more ways to try to get them. And day by day more other men come face to face with the harsh stone walls of impossibility. The Haves and the Have-Nots now enter our history as definitive categories, not just as random tales from out of the wilderness, tales of good luck or bad.

Now commences the passionate, angry, divisive, contentious, exciting America that in these regards will always be with us. From now on nothing will ever be completely boring, those long stretches of time when nothing happens will be less. That's what a growing population does for you (3,929,214 according to the first U.S. census in 1790). If you're bored from now on, it's your own fault.

Everyone has ideas and desires, but few yet have enough of what will come later in our growth: ambition—the hungry need for fame and power, achievement and success, on the part of the many and not just the few. People are still a bit too polite, or too timid, or just plain frightened. Or there aren't enough "role models" yet.

Mr. Hamilton, Mr. Jefferson, Mr. Burr, these have been the big three, interacting effectively until Mr. Burr shoots Mr. Hamilton, the beloved of George Washington, dead. Is this an omen for the new America? Mr. Burr is wellborn and well connected and wealthy and educated. Mr. Hamilton is the poor boy from the sticks. It is Mr. Burr who is having the incestuous relationship with his own daughter. Mr. Hamilton's male lover was long ago shot dead for being a hushmarked. Is this an omen for the new America? Or which of these are omens for the new America? Dare we now say "all," as in All-American?

The American People grow in number from some 5,300,000 in 1800 to around 8,750,000 in 1817. "Probably no great people ever grew more mature in so short a time," writes Henry Adams in his *History of the United States During the Administrations of James Madison*. Of course, what we didn't know then, there were, around the world, around and about, already some one billion people.

Mature? Were we once upon a time mature?

Annual sales of western land increase from one hundred thousand acres to half a million as tens of thousands move westward in the decade or so after 1800, occupying more land than in the 150 years of colonial history. A middle class is materializing. By 1810, 24 million copies of newspapers a year are printed annually as reading becomes a necessity.

As more land is cleared preachers are still springing up everywhere. In 1811 alone some three million people go to revivalist camp meetings. Religion still rules everything, of course, certainly everything to do with the body. Yaddah's professors teach that reptiles are descended from the ones on Noah's ark, and the "medical" building at the College of William and Mary has a roof that leaks on opened cadavers; medicine and science are only subdivisions under God and obviously very far down on His list of Greatest Hits.

Medical knowledge is still crude at best. It's hard to teach much when nothing much is known. This has been said before. It bears repeating. Little energy appears to be expended to rectify this lack of knowledge. Ignorance is bliss. If we're sick, we're sick. Doctors, of whom there are still too few, do not seem to be questers. The story of Hogarth Hooker has made the rounds. A doctor is not the respected man he'll become. He is still barely one step up from what we would call a quack.

One thing, though: there is a dawning awareness that the body has its own rules and regulations, requests and requirements. You can't eat just anything, for instance. Eaters begin to stay away from stuff that gives them discomfort. There is something called "health" that people wish for in their prayers. That's new. It connotes a sense of possibility. Feeling good, or at least a little better, might just happen, because so much else is happening. The blissful state of possibility is rooting itself, hard and firm. Indeed, it is not giving anything away to state that The American People will never lose this belief in the possible.

Little is known about blood beyond the obvious fact that something red flows through us. What is in it, what can be done with it—this is still some time away. It is thought that to lose too much of it is not good and when too much is escaping it must be stanched. But it is thought that to lose some of it when one is sick is good. Go figure. Bleeding people, still in order to drain off the "bad humors" thought to cause every problem, is even more prescribed for relief. Several times in the last century blood from a sheep has been put into a human. It doesn't work. When blood from one person is given to another person, the recipient dies. Philadelphia's first medical school, founded in 1765, and Yaddah's, in 1782, have not progressed much past bleeding people to death. Oh, Yaddah killed a few monkeys and then sheep but then they didn't know what to do.

As for information about particular organs like the heart or liver, these are still strange and foreign countries and completely misunderstood. Attempted transplants of animal hearts into dying humans are certainly imagined and crazy surgeons try heart transplants all over. A doctor in New Hampshire is finally shot dead by his neighbors after trying unsuccessfully thirty-eight times to perform this operation in the village of Manchester. If doctors are quacks, surgeons are butchers.

Feeling worse follows most "cures." Despite centuries of observation that diseases can be transferred from person to person, and that feeling bad can be transferred from man to man, precautions continue not to be observed. If someone had said to a man, "Keep your mouth away from that woman's polly," an earlier word for pussy, he would likely have said, "I like the taste," or "Mind your own business," an expression more and more coming into general use as there are more and more people to butt in.

Nobody writes about sex. Doctors don't talk to their patients about sex. Yes, this medical silence started then and has been faithfully observed ever since. And couples don't talk to each other about sex. There is such an overwhelming lack of talk about sex that one wonders if feeling good from sex doesn't really last all that long.

Chains of whorehouses continue to proliferate. Whorehouses are great businesses because if men don't want to talk about sex there are plenty of them wanting to perform it. The good feeling may not last all that long among these men either, but that only increases the hunger. Jew Louie, in the records of her Washington house, lists one "Robert Ackenace" as a regular who visits each morning and evening for the twelve years she's in business. "I wish there was more like him," Jew Louie writes, understandably. "He says he would come more often if he could make his work that way."

Indeed, this particular holy grail will become the holy grail that men rush after for fortunes, and that will eventually be the cause of—well, we shall see.

A FIRST HELLO

The overlooking or complete ignoring of hemophilia as anything of concern well into the twentieth century will have a historic and tragic effect on the history of The Underlying Condition. Will Fred Lemish be alone in believing this led to the plague of UC itself? Let us begin to follow it more closely.

The transmission of hemophilia from mothers to sons is described in 1803 by Dr. John Conrad Otto, a Philadelphia physician who writes an account of "a hemorrhagic disposition existing in certain families." *Hemorrhagic* means "bleeding." It is he who names them "bleeders." He determines that this particular bleeding condition is hereditary and affects mostly males. He manages to trace it back through three generations to a woman who settled in Plymouth, New Hampshire, in 1720. It is astounding research and there is little information of how he achieved it. Dr. Otto was then an apprentice to Dr. Benjamin Rush.

The word *hemophilia* itself is first used at the University of Zurich in 1828 by one Friedrich Hopff, a student, to describe inherited blood disorders. A report from a surgeon, Samuel Lane, in *The Lancet* in 1840, described his control of this bleeding by administering fresh blood from another boy with severe hemophilia. While this, too, was an amazing discovery, a lack of understanding of blood groups and basic transfusion methods prevented further development.

Excessive and unexplained bleeding has been seen since ancient times. Dr. Israel Jerusalem writes, "In the Talmud it is written about the mother: 'If she circumcised her first child and he died, and a second one also died, she must not circumcise her third child.' This is because the excessive bleeding from the circumcision pointed to the mother. Women from the beginning get the raw deal."

A VERY GREAT UNREQUITED LOVE

The country is ours now, more and more of it. Jefferson buys even more, and then determines to send out an expedition to tell him what his new Louisiana Purchase looks like. The land included in the purchase comprises around 23 percent of the territory of the United States today. Can we get from the Mississippi to the Pacific by water? Jefferson wonders. Surely there must be a river running through us. He will be mightily disappointed to learn there isn't.

Meriwether Lewis and William Clark co-captain the expedition. It departs in 1804 and comes to an end in 1806. Lewis, a lifelong bachelor for whom the company of other men is more congenial than real life, is a heavy drinker, a manic-depressive, and very much in love with Clark, whom he personally chooses to accompany him. This love will eventually destroy him. He will become a complete and lost drunk, and he will commit suicide when the expedition is over and he is permanently deprived of Clark's presence.

But only after their magnificent journey is completed and America learns what America is and will be. Oh, it is a mighty journey, a mighty achievement, from coast to coast, finding places on a map that they are drawing as they traverse them. Lewis and Clark and their expedition are the first white men to see so much of us.

Clark, the perfect second in command, is insensitive to Lewis's love, and to the love of York, his mammoth black slave, who is indentured to him as his father was to Clark's father. What is it about this ordinary plodding explorer that excites lifelong passionate devotion from his two closest male companions?

Lewis and Clark set forth with their party, nearly four dozen young men (there is disagreement about the exact number and whether it should include York and the Shoshone Indian woman Sacagawea, who shows up with her infant son). They are "robust young Backwoodsmen of Character healthy hardy young men, recommended," as Clark describes them all, between the ages of twenty-nine and thirty-three. As piece by piece they uncover and witness the pristine voluptuousness of a wilderness still unpopulated save by animals and Indians, whose willing women are offered as gifts along with the syphilis they carry, these men and their leaders are passionate about their challenging endeavor. Many of them are having sex with each other as well; their leader is particularly unable to do anything with any of this passion but get drunk and lash out with his own particular frustrations at his men. In their close quarters they hike yet more miles into the heart of America, none of them to talk of certain feelings, or write about them, so that it is left to any deft historian with sense and insight (are there any such?) to read between the lines and point out what should have been obvious to anyone who grew up on a farm or in a large family in the woods. Or to anyone at all.

What is it about historians such as Stephen Ambrose, who in his much-overpraised biography of Meriwether Lewis, *Undaunted Courage*, leaves the most courageous courage out? How can any sentient person read anything about Lewis without realizing the man was gay? Not a little bit, not just sometimes, but totally and wholly gay? We'll encounter a similar obtuseness on the part of Abraham Lincoln's many blind biographers, as we already have with George Washington's worshippers. How is it that "learned" tomes are written about the syphilis rampant among soldiers with no one figuring out that they are getting it from each other??

No wonder hushmarkeds have been granted no place in their histories.

God save us from the heterosexual historian!

IDAHO

The men of the Lewis and Clark expedition are thought to be the first white men to gaze upon this peculiar state, so let this be our introduction to it. It is 1805. Much of what we'll encounter in our history of Idaho will be unpleasant, and will happen much later and much farther north, in the aggressively rugged uplands, in the overpined mountains that glower and guard some of the most remote and impassable territory in our whole United States. The Idaho Territory will be bigger than all of New England. If ever our wilderness is frightening, it's here. It's almost as if it belongs to another country. Perhaps in view of what will happen here, it would have been better if it did. But no, it had to happen in America.

For now, a deserter from the Lewis and Clark expedition breaks off and heads into this unfriendly state. He is part Seneck and part southern hillbilly. His name is Partekla. He has been the victim of one of Meriwether Lewis's cruel whiplashings. It was common for a soldier to be lashed by Lewis to within an inch of his life when he got out of hand. Partekla was often ordered to masturbate a very drunk Lewis and was brutally punished afterward. Along with a Chinook squaw the expedition has been given as a gift, Partekla bolts off into the night and they walk and walk until it seems they are at the edge of the earth where the forest gods live. Here they build a cabin and he stakes his land and names it Partekla, a place that, as indicated, will play much too important a part in this history.

FEBRUARY 12, 1809

Charles Darwin and Abraham Lincoln are born on the same day.

THE HOOKER ARCHIVES, CONT.

Fred has warned me that my narration of this part is a shit pie in the face of Her Damehood, who has claimed the whole history of medicine for her tinny pie pan. I think, though, in this case, and Fred has succumbed to my reasoning, because I am the Hooker archivist who has all the papers about our earliest days, that I've got squatter's rights on certain topics. Anyway, really, when you come right down to it, all this shit was Hooker born and bred.

To trace, to follow, to try to understand the history of disease in America is, most importantly, to study, from this point on, and carefully, indeed assiduously, in the most determined way, the history of the National Institute of Tumor Science, a pimple sewer. The official history of NITS will not mention that it was in its beginnings the Hooker Home for the Syphilitic. The official history of NITS will not mention that these beginnings caused the massacre at Fruit Island. Both of these occurrences are just too fucking juicy, lewd, lascivious, and disgusting for Hermia or any other would-be chronicler to get their polite bite plates around and properly masticate.

Let me tell you it was not easy resurrecting this shit (in any sense of my favorite word). I am a scientist, not a historian, not a linguist, not a lot of things (which *she* says that she is). It has been no easy task becoming as proficient in Seneck as I am, say, in microbiology. I have no interest in Indians, all men of all races and of all castes being horrid. I was not particularly interested in human waste, either, though I came to surmise this by-product of ours is an important component of what we must come to terms with if we are going to end a plague, and besides, it pays my rent. "Shit as a Surrogate Marker," the title of an earlier and overlooked paper of mine, could very well be the overall and encompassing title for any major study of The Underlying

Condition. Shit *is* a surrogate marker. I have much left to teach you as I continue to study it myself.

From this country's birth, wouldn't you just fucking know that neither branch of the new Congress sees fit to consider, even casually or marginally, anything pertaining to the actual health of the country's new citizens? But because so many soldiers and sailors are returning from sojourns diseased in some way and contagious as well, their lack of health becomes increasingly difficult to ignore. In 1794, Alexander Hamilton, almost as an afterthought, and unofficially, sets up a "Soldiers' and Sailors' Health Service." He co-opts a clerk in his Treasury Department into collecting twenty cents per month from the wages of each soldier and seaman to cover the cost of keeping the boys in shape. It is an unsatisfactory arrangement, not only because no one is using any of these services, whatever they frigging are (it's been impossible to find out; were they actual clinics with doctors?), but because sailors, particularly, object to paying for them. Shipowners, even if only managing vessels owned by the government, which is often news to a government that doesn't know what in the fucking hell it owns, object because they don't like the government butting in, even though, per Alex, this is not officially the government. So sailors, and let's just concentrate on the sailors, keep getting sick. According to Fred, the young fellow who had enjoyed a brief fling in New York with Alex had died, causing Alex to set this thing up in the first place. Those accumulating twenty-cent payments in no time flat prove not nearly enough to cover such services, as the various contracted establishments are billing a government that knows nothing about any of this (not to mention that the contracted establishments aren't performing these services anyway). Well, you can see that it is and will remain for quite some time one big frigging seafaring mess, with no idiot in charge.

Much to everyone's surprise, it is discovered that Dr. Hogarth Hooker's will—quite generously—stipulates the establishment of a Hooker Home "wherein men and women with diseases of the sexual tracts are to be studied, solely and for no other purpose"—i.e., solely to find out whatever it was that Hog had thought killed them. His shares of Massachusetts Farm Supply are by now worth a bundle. Interestingly enough, Hamilton had tried to define the Sailors' Health Service as "created to coupe up all pox'd heads and render them away into a home until they are cured."

But what the fuck means "diseases of the sexual tracts"? Syphilis is the only one any of the Hooker family can think of, and they're not so pleased to see the messy assortment of houses and outbuildings, a mad scientist's laboratories, that Hog also left behind. Nothing would have gone forward had not Hog got his wishes into his own lawyer's hands.

Other Hooker lawyers are going at it, as best as possible, to sidestep the embarrassing and the inconvenient. When it opens, the Hooker Home bills itself as a "safe haven to tend those who suffer from illnesses God sent to punish man for his willful waywardness." No doubt a Hooker conference call came up with this one. There was, of course, much discussion about whether, with God's imprimatur or not, the damned place should be opened at all, but piety plays its trump card and God wins. Once a goddamned Hooker, always a goddamned Hooker. So the Hooker Home finally opens in Ontuit, not all that far from the cursed church old Tom Hooker preached from in the first place. When word gets out in town, no one wants it around. "Every clap-ridden pervert from anywhere will be traipsing to Ontuit!" Lots of encouraging and Christian letters like that in the archives, winding up with too many vomitus versions of "How could you!"

How do we cut to the chase? For a bunch more years, new cases, gradually increasing in number, come and go each day into and out of the Hogarth Home, sailors, whores, orphaned children, the abscessed, the poxed, the near-dead, and, yes, the dead, delivered in their coffins. The treatment, God knows what it was, is free. Had Hermatros been around he, too, would have recognized many a parasite. Bugs from the four corners of the globe are visiting Ontuit, Massachusetts, with impressive free-floating aloha abandon. They've also come to stay. Thus is more and more shit of all natures and nations added to the wagonloads Ezra Jr., now in charge of Massachusetts Farm Supply, carts out into the world.

A bit of genealogy to keep ourselves going: Ezra Sr., who was Thomas Hooker's grandson, had the original idea of collecting shit. His only son, Ezra Jr., turned the idea into a company, Massachusetts Farm Supply, with shares of stock. It made a shitload of money. It wasn't easy for Ezra Jr. to live in Ontuit and see what his own crazy son had got up to since his return. It wasn't easy for Ezra Jr. to take care of said crazy son and watch his body blow up in smithereens. Ezra Jr., what with a crazy dead son and a business collecting shit and a home for the syphilitic, is understandably now cracking under the strain.

Who is the mother of all these Hookers? As is often the case with early America, she is never mentioned. What a strange fact to report. How can a whole family of fucking Hookers be motherless? No wonder women always felt like shit. Oh, Tom, Tom, what a fucking awful drum you started beating.

The clap, the pox, syphilis, these terms are interchangeable. Over the centuries syphilis is called the "French disease" in Italy and Germany, and the "Italian disease" in France; the Dutch call it the "Spanish disease," the Russians call it the "Polish disease," the Turks call it the "Christian disease," and the Tahitians call it the "British disease." It is called "great pox" in order to distinguish it from smallpox. Americans just call it the pox. Whatever it's called, it's all over the fucking place and Ezra Jr. begs his other son, Hogarth's younger brother, Lucid Sr., to help him, please.

Lucid Sr. is a good man, a bit on the timid side, who fears God mightily as Hookers are meant to do. He bathes the sick who come to the home and tries to make them rest, which isn't easy when they are out of their asshole minds. His son, Lucid Jr., won't go near any of it, neither the shit nor the pox, and shortly after his wife dies birthing *their* son, Lucid III, Lucid Jr. runs away in the night. I don't think he was ever found. Lucid Sr., now having lost both a brother and a son, is close to destroying himself. He lacks any skill to keep anyone, it seems, alive. Why, he begs his father, in all our Hookers, has no one pleaded with God "to teach us what all this is! Will not somebody come here to teach us?" Fucking A!

It is Lucid III who will introduce us to Dr. Maurice Punic, Sr. I believe it was Dr. Maurice Punic, Sr., who found him.

Dr. Maurice Punic, Sr., like all the Punics in Fred's history, just appears. Not everyone has a history that fucking fatal fate allows to be known. Dr. Maurice Punic, Sr., will be the first official director of the Hooker Home. "Teach us what all this is" is what he says he aims to do. To collect all the syphilitics in America is a kicky-wicky kind of calling, ambitious in the extreme. Many discreet placements in publications such as *Police Round-Up, Soldiers' and Sailor's Life, The Happy Traveler,* ask, "Are you the victim of a disease from coupling?" and direct those caring to respond in the affirmative to Dr. Punic in Ontuit, where the good people, finding it increasingly impossible to walk on their overcrowded sidewalks, will soon cry out, Enough, you shitheads! Enough!

Dr. Maurice Punic, Sr., writes in his journal: "New York saw a cheap way to deal with one of its biggest problems and leaped at the opportunity for Hooker to house all of its clap-ridden. The House of Sores, I hear we're called. No sooner does a bump of pus appear in Manhattan than it's shipped to Ontuit. We are so overburdened that I grow frightened."

He sends long memoranda to various government offices, never knowing quite which one to write to or even which ones are there. It's an era when the concept of federal government is solidifying, but Washington remains such a disorganized crapshoot that power does not congeal, as it must to hatch results, or even a reply. He has sick patients, Dr. Punic writes to them. He needs help, he writes to them. His sick patients' bowels are working nonstop, he writes to them. Washington still doesn't answer. Who is there, then or now, who will respond to an unknown doctor in a Massachusetts village who's complaining about syphilis and shit?

And yet, coming into focus in this wretched genealogy of honking, barking, spewing, puking goddam germs is a cesspool about to combust.

Our fucking Hooker archives fucking runneth over. And I am sore ashamed.

I wish to fill in some gaps about my Hooker family. More of this might have been presented further forward but I didn't want to. Piece it together as you will. I'm still trying to do the same.

My father, Lucid Hooker VI, was one of New England's most active sadists. My mother was addicted to cocaine. They died when I was fourteen. He was often called in by the police for questioning whenever they found some mutilated young woman's body; he'd show up wearing his preacher's frock (there is *still* a congregation in Boston with "a Hooker pulpit," meaning no one else can hold it or rant opinions from it), view the remains, invoke a curse against the devil, "lest he triumph," and return home to stick his penis into another corpse (for indeed it had been he who'd done the mutilating). He had a lot of free time on his hands: no one much ever came to his church— Puritanism might be the ethos to which this country answers, but actually worshipping it in an edifice has always, like hula hoops, been an inconsistent trend. Though not as rich as he wanted to be, he was nevertheless very rich, perhaps the first of the Hookers to have such unlimited wealth. Ezra Jr.'s Massachusetts Farm Supply, now called Boston's First, had become prodigiously profitable. We all own parts of it. Every bowel movement from Plymouth Rock to the New York border flushes a few pennies into a Hooker bowl. One share of stock purchased for a dollar in 1801 is worth one million shares *each* worth one hundred dollars today. And it is all still privately held, not a small amount by myself and a larger amount, unfortunately, by the weasel brothers Table, to whom we are in no other way related. When the Boston cops got too close, we moved to Masturbov Gardens. Pop had got a gig as "staff spiritual adviser" at NITS. NITS had long ago subsumed the Hooker Homes.

I wish I could say that I had the vaguest notion of what my father was all about. I've skidded lightly over this sadist shit, as if I were talking about daisies in green pastures. Very little is written about the effects of the grotesque on the very young. Kids see much more than adults ever want to remember. I can see my father fucking strange women on a floor, and I'm certain I've been psychically wounded by it no end of ways, but I hardly knew the man and he paid no attention to me, and I had some sort of survivor's instinct that kept me going with my self-preservation intact, along with ambition, intelligence, and a sense of right and wrong. You'd say: "God knows how," and I'd say: "So what? I'm here. And I've had a pretty decent life." Sure he was a shit. But he was like going to a scary movie. I had bad dreams for a while. No, I'm not being blasé or naïve, or even a bad feminist. Some people are blessed with better psyches or poorer eyesight than others.

No, I never saw him mutilate a woman. That I only heard about. That would have made a difference, I'm sure. Hearing about it and seeing it should produce some hatred. Mother Superior uses a word to end all conversations she senses can come to no resolution: "Interesting," she says. "Next!"

A personal drama had a great deal to do with my path. When I am twenty-two, a fellow sister, Annunciata Rose, kisses me on the lips. The kiss is a wet one and saliva drips from her lips and onto mine. I worship Annunciata. She is beautiful as I am not: in her habit and poise and intelligence and honesty and directness she is every nun I wanted to be. When she embraces me and kisses me, I know this is why I became a nun. I embrace her back and I feel our tongues touching together, tasting each other's saliva instinctively. I know that this is why I was called to become a Sister of Christ. I know this is the way of my world.

Sister Annunciata Rose is in the last stage of a fit of a disease called mismitosis, some kind of perverted cell division. She is on her way to the next set of symptoms, which are drooling spasms. She will shortly lose her mind. And I, some eight years later, will lose my arm.

This is when I truly fall in love with her: when she gets really sick.

Annunciata! This is physical love I am talking about. Lust! Licking pussy! Licking pussy after lights out and sleeping in another woman's arms. Oh, the warmth and ecstasy that Annunciata slathers me with. It makes all that Bride of Christ shit, all that married-to-Jesus shit utterly irrelevant. One love feeds the other. Our only common ground, in genes as well as human hearts, is desperate loneliness. I am the cute new girl and mighty are the flurries of intensity to discover who will get Grace. Well, Sister Annunciata gets Grace. Six feet tall and big-boned, let me tell you she was one big girl. To lie underneath her, to have her lie on top of you, was, whether you were hungry or not, a physical feast. Is there ever, ever, *anything* like the taste of first flesh with your eyes closed?

Then this big beautiful buffalo starts walking around the nunnery mad as Ophelia. She screams out blasphemies in the middle of her catechism and when all of us sit at silent supper she starts slugging other nuns, just hauling off and slugging them. I take her off to one of the Hooker residences, the gorgeous summerhouse in North East Harbor, Maine. It is the single most beautiful place in the world where I know for a fact that I was happy, for a bit. For a month Nunce calms down and I let her love me so intensely my body still shivers. You know how your body feels after you've made love and made love and made love some more? You feel weak in the most outstanding way. I can feel it still. Then she starts that drooling shit. And she dies in my arms. And it is mismitosis. What happens to old diseases? Where have all the years gone? They have gone with Annunciata. And my arm. She died, that big gorgeous buffalo, and it was she who taught me to find love in myself for myself and to face up to the fact that my religion is no theological jackpot that I or anyone else with a brain is ever going to win.

The one thing she taught me is that old diseases never completely fade away and disappear. They just come back again and again and usually under different names. This, of course, opens many a Pandora's box. There is no dogma without sniveling unbelievers. But it's what I know and have always known instinctively, almost like hearing voices inside me crying out from earlier centuries: "What I'm enduring has been gone through before and before and before." Of course, that is what Catholicism is all about, which is why it's so comforting to so many like me. I know that hearing voices is a sign of a crazy person. Well, I say that there has never been an important discovery in any field where voices are not heard. You show me a sane scientist and I'll show you a scientist who will never discover shit.

Mismitosis is not seen much anymore but it was thought to be something like rabies—transmitted usually by animals in fits, which of course was totally incorrect. Through many centuries of plagues and lesser poisonings that devour flesh, it has not been until quite recently—with the arrival of the ability to calibrate various blood chemistries facilitated by my discovery of Vel— that we have had an accurate measurement for bodily poison. Most diseases have always been described as caused by some sort of poison that has entered— somehow—the body. In the old days fits accompanied illnesses more often than not. *Contagion* is a relative term. One person's infection is another person's death. What can kill a horse can overlook a mouse. The nature of poison is ephemeral and complex, and if not always subtle, not always brutal either. Many are those attempts at murder that go afoul because of incorrect dosage, or unknown protective immunities, or an unsympathetic knowledge and sense of, feeling for, the nature of this poison. Thus, many that have come to be called "poisons" are often only those potions and powders that always work: the arsenics of this world that are "so brutally frank that they brook and harbor no gainsaying," as Dr. Lydgate Hill, the famous eighteenth-century ernthologist, has written. "If one only had a decent familiarity with the nature of poison, its very nature, then one could use poison and not kill. Then we could have little oars that guide the voyage but do not sink the ship. Then we could have slightly bigger dippers that topple the mast but do not fell the fleet. That way lies cure and help and life, not death." This quotation is from Hill's *Terrestrial Infirmities: Poison as a Way of Life.*

The entire medical system of the entire world is now based, quite comfortably, and quite incorrectly, and quite tragically, on the testing of blood.

BLOOD CAN BE FULL OF SHIT!

My Vel confirmed this.

That, unfortunately, is my conclusion, so far, of my life's work. (I'm not dead yet, but no matter.) It has taken me some fifty years to find it out. I couldn't believe it when I discovered it. It's Israel and his goddamn glause that made me see that blood is only blood. That the world's foremost expert on blood should, almost in a deathbed confession, tell the world that blood isn't worth everything as a marker, as a tool, as the guaranteed lifesaver everyone believed, as anything other than some sort of water that runs through our veins, not as a nurturer but as a conveyor belt, is pretty important news to anyone who's interested, which I hope is just about every doctor and researcher and scientist and person who goes into a hospital. However, I know better. My truth will lie right here as dead as Lydgate Hill.

There are poisons that are undetectable in the blood.

There are poisons that are undetectable in shit.

And, goddammit, I am going to sort this out before I croak. And I think this UC shit will take me there.

You can measure blood until you are blue in the face but you may be missing the root cause of the disease, any disease. Poison is not always represented in blood. That's why a Vel test is so important. It cannot tell you where the poison is or what it's doing, but it can tell you if you have poison in you or not and how much of it there is. There is no other test like this. And as life proceeds further toward new centuries on earth, it's become medically evident, statistically irrefutable, and alarmingly relevant that more and more people are testing positive for Vel. This is a state of affairs as frightening as the fact there's no information to tell you about what you can do when you discover that a Vel test indicates you're positive for poison. All of this parallels distinctly this woebegone Underlying Condition.

I was taught it's the Lord's question, Alone, to answer: why people remain alive at all. Well, I wanted to answer the question myself. Still do. I suspect most scientists are the same. It's amazing there haven't been more plagues than there have been, and it's amazing that we're still here, and I want to fucking know why. One thing I do know is that it doesn't have anything to do with the fucking indomitability of the fucking human spirit. My cousin says it's either good luck or bad luck. I think the secret to life is nerve. You really have to be able to say, Go fuck yourself. Humanism? Forget it.

After Nunce's death, I began to speak another language. As you've seen. And will continue to see as I catch a second breath.

THE MASSACRE AT FRUIT ISLAND

My name is Lucid Hooker and I am the third Lucid Hooker. Lucid Hooker III is what my Bible calls me. This is how I got to Fruit Island by way of Sagg.

How did I come here? Why do I stay?

He desired our home in Ontuit, our "patient load," he called them, did Dr. Maurice Punic, Sr., the father. He offered us $500 hard cash for title, name, and bodies, which was not stingy. Old bent-over Ezra was glad enough to relieve our family from this burden, this "diabolikel disablement," and which burden was enjoined upon our family by Hogarth's will. "I have done it from respect for the dead, for the love of Christ, but no more. I no longer hear any call but that of weariness over the putridness of man. No more, I say, no more!" So spoke Ezra when he approved the sale.

Ezra, like all of us, was wallowing in shame and guilt. Shit. Hogarth. Syphilitics. What had Hookers come to? I was glad to get away from home and him and them and that! Moreover, since Uncle Hogarth held my infant hands and kissed my lips goodbye in death, I feared I had been exposed and was facing a fate like his unless it suited the Lord to send a cure. Toward this end I was happy to join with Dr. Maurice Punic, Sr., to save my self and soul. I had the chance to leave with Dr. Punic, to travel on a boat far from the stench of the Hookers, and I grabbed at it like food for the hungry frightened child I was.

It is painful to be adult now, to see how enchained I was from so early an age. A bondage caught so young is like a body buried alive in a tomb.

Yes, I am the living dead, and my record of these years will prove it. I do not want to live beyond the completion of this crude journal of a cruel and fantastical history. I shall die before its receipt into the world as Truth.

As helper in Ontuit, I saw that there was puke and shit most everywhere, and it was left to me to cart it all away, to the bay itself, which was soon brown and black in color. Massachusetts Waste would have none of it.

Uncle Hog left us all his notes. Acres of gardens are our yards and my childhood playground, made up of herbs and plants from everywhere around the globe that he had read or heard or dreamed about. He grew them all. Forks of plantain, stalks of Nervil, roots of ashforth, wormwood of Labe, pages of these magic names, sounding so of the far-away, we try them all, our local Dr. Pleasants and I, but in the end so useless. There came a time where there was naught but the voidings and ghastly stomach cramps and violent wretchings of dozens upon dozens unable to hold anything inside them. Many lost their minds, their words nonsensical and their eyeballs rolling backward. Was it blameworthy or in any way un-Christian that I longed to leave? Dr. Pleasants could not look me in the eye when I sought his opinion, and I could see he would be leaving himself. "There is a limit, lad, beyond which even the good Lord cannot push us further."

I wanted to leave for other reasons much more private. I knew that with the Hookers I could find but woe. Each uncle and cousin seemed more bereft of sense. Uncle Hogarth had pushed Hooker patience too far. I feared I was also carrying inside me the poisons of my ancestors and the sins of which I could never be free, so strong their pull, so intractable their power to drive me to perform acts of "human kind" and "charity."

How many years of this I can't remember since each day was as awful as the next. Thomas Hooker was indeed punishing us for Uncle Hog.

Dr. Maurice Punic, Sr., looks me up and down. He betakes me into another room and makes me undress for him to see my nakedness. Then he nods yes. "I will include you in my purchase." I don't know why I feel relief.

Lucid Jr., and his grandfather Ezra Jr., open wine to celebrate. They speak of Dr. Punic as "our reward for Grace." "I am free," I say to myself as we help lead the inmates to the harbor, now stinking too, where we board a boat that will take us down the coast and across the Sound to yet another new world, Dr. Punic's, a new world in a place called Sagg, where the Sailors' Institute has a big house for us paid from Mr. Hamilton's twenty cents per sailor all these years. The Hooker Home in Ontuit is no more. Long live the future Hooker Home in Sagg. Dr. Punic hands me a glass of rum "to drink to tomorrow and all that will come of it." It is my first glass of hard liquor and I am soon drunk. I am so very young when all this starts, when I leave home at just on fifteen years.

Dr. Punic says he will apprentice me to be a doctor. "Wellness is possible," he tells me, and I am most excited and impressed. He sounds like a man possessed, so intense is he in his feelings. I cannot tell you even now his origin or native place. Punics have been here forever, he says. Why then does his tongue twist strangely on many words? He sounds most foreign to me. But he promises to teach me everything he knows. I have prayed for so long for God to save me. I feared this could never be.

We leave before dawn, because no one wishes the world outside to know of our departure or our destination. There are no faces of friends from my lifetime to wave goodbye and Godspeed. I say a prayer that health and well-being will return to this benighted place with our departure.

On crossing o'er the water my gut wretches up more than I believe can be inside me. Finally comes blood, from my mouth and from my end; but I should not say finally because my innards spew forth still more: yellow bile and green water and I think the very linings of my being. Dr. Punic stands in his long yellow rubber coat and watches me from an upper deck. He offers no aid. When finally my heavings and evacuations stop, with my rear end hanging over portside, and I stand up and let the whipping wind and rain wash me off as best they can, he nods and comes to me and tells me that God has cleansed me for the days ahead. Now I am ready, he says. I nod back, wanting to believe him. Indeed I do believe him.

We arrive in Sagg with one hundred of the poxed from home, fifty more than we'd housed, but word had already got around and other poxed showed up just as we sailed. We are to live in a large house situated on the bay, already prepared under the supervision of Dr. Punic's, son, Dr. Maurice Punic, Jr. They are doubles of each other in height and weight and quiet demeanor, distinguishable only by the years that line the elder's face. Their hair is black, their eyes are gray, their skin a palest white. They do not know how to talk in loud tones. To hear them I must lean up close. They are somber men, which loans them depth so they give off an air of trust. Around the house the Punics tour, Junior pointing out this and that to Senior, so that it becomes clear that Senior has not been here before. Father nods to son, pleased with what he sees. I do not especially notice that Dr. Punic Jr. is no more than twenty-five years to my fifteen, because the paleness of his skin renders him older. There are many bedrooms but four at least must berth together.

I am to be chief attendant and my duties are to serve them both as trusted confidant. More staff will shortly come; the finding and the hiring is to be the son's task; indeed he has commenced already and in a matter of weeks he promises completion of "our new family in this new chapter of our lives." More doctors, certainly, will come, though once again the son makes the same promise as his father: I am to become a doctor trained "just like me," he says with his own smile of pride.

More patients come, lining up outdoors almost before we settle. Day after day and night after night come more; indeed, many are the nights when knockings are heard, and soft moans of "Let me in, oh God, please let me in!" Within three months our first one hundred are increased twofold. Where are we to put two hundred people, young and old and male and female, able and lame and near to death? This house with many rooms was once a grand hotel when Sagg was sought for fun, when healthy sailors stopped here only for their ships to unload all their oil from whales. But fifty, even a hundred rooms cannot our multitudes bear, so perforce additional rooms are quietly found and rented around town. Before long it is a secret little held that we are Sagg's biggest tenant, and this is not a part of that town's history it wishes known. Many have found room and board for themselves and come only daily to the clinic but those who require shelter continue to mount up. By the first year's end our patient load of two hundred has increased to five hundred, Dr. Punic Sr. claims. I am not certain I believe him, although it does seem as if every sick sailor and whore from the entire world has found our door and clamors for help.

In addition, from whales and their oil Sagg is overwhelmed with loose money and sailors constantly drunk, with unspent energies waiting to be discharged. The town never sleeps. The streets of this small village around the bay teem with fevered activity from dawn till dawn. The tiny rooms in the tiny shacks and the small rooms in the small cottages and the large rooms in the grand villas on Main Street are busy places indeed. We see many of them go into one house and then weeks later come into ours.

But there are simply too many here. Mumblings turn into churnings of loud complaint. Often patients come in with bruises they say are struck upon them by their fellows, shoving for a better place in line or a bed. "Is there no God in Sagg?" is more than once the plaint.

When Dr. Punic Sr. chooses the certain ones he wants, he bathes them with Special oils and tinctures that color them pink as babies from a bath. I often see them walk out most healthy, though a few of them come back most awful shriveled. The ones he chooses to bathe are always young and strong, "and better for my cure," he says. I am forbidden to help him and I am especially forbidden near the Special bathing liquids. How will I ever learn, then, I wonder, though I fear to ask him. What he does he does behind locked doors, with only his son providing the aid he once said he needed me for.

Dr. Punic Jr. asks that I copy some of his father's notes for him. In leaning over my shoulder as I write, he bends close. I hear his breathing almost stop in this scant space between us. He smells of I know not what—of distant lands, of cloves and oranges and perfumes that are not feminine, but that I never knew of for men. His hair is hard and shiny, waxed down so that it never is in a mess like mine. When I raise my pen to show him how I write, he takes it, and my hand with it. He smiles at me and I smile back. To other men this feeling might seem goodly, and Christian, as of a brotherhood in Christ. To me it is not from God but from some strange unfed hunger in my gut. I cannot say it is good or bad. Just strange. And when he goes away, my new friend, and lets my hand fall back to earth, no appetite is slaked. I only feel sad, and as before, unworthy. I hardly understand what I have written down.

Help from several nurses and a few male attendants, newly arrived, is strangely circumscribed. They, too, are not allowed inside that inner room. They are wanted only before and after the treatments. But we are busy enough, from ushering in each day's new choices and trying to maintain order.

Those picked to join our staff are a motley lot. The women are bleak and dour and barely speak. I think a few of them are unable to talk, that they possess no vocal cords or are otherwise impaired. I have no proof of this beyond their constant silence, but I never hear so much as a gurgle come from some of their throats, even when words are needed or expected. In charge of all the staff is a stern, unsmiling, tall, and obviously physically strong woman, Mrs. Horvath. I do not exist for her. Keys always dangle from a locked belt around her waist; evidently she has been entrusted with something I have not.

There soon is a staff of several dozen. The available supply appears to be plentiful enough. If one departs a-sudden after breakfast, there is another in place by midday meal. From bits of talk I do pick up 'tis clear that staff is found most often in distressing places, prisons and hospitals for the mad and such. The male attendants are big enough and strong enough to control the troublesome and to carry out the writhing or the dead. No one wants to be friends with anyone else. I do not know where they take the dead.

Yes, there are often dead to be removed. It is a token of the regularity of this that it almost slipped my mind. I hardly have time to learn a name or face. I am told it is to be expected. "The poxed die with predictable frequency," the elder Punic tells us. "It is the wishes of the Lord Our God Who takes His children home to rest." The aspect of those who die is such that death indeed seems best. The vision of these deaths builds within me its own dismissal. After a while it is not noticed much. "That is the way good doctors operate," Dr. Punic Sr. tells me, congratulating me on my "fine composure. It is best you do not become too close to those we care for."

From behind the doors where the Punics take the younger poxed, I often hear noises such as groanings, screams, occasionally cries that sound like moans of pleasure, which I take to be a sign of hope. How strange a word to enter here. Dr. Punic Jr., whom I call at his urging Maurice, tells me, "Those sounds you hear and will come to hear more often are sounds of improvement, of progress, of well-being come upon our charges." One day he says, "They are sounds of ecstasy." He pronounces the word in a drawn-out fashion, mouthing its syllables as if savoring its shadows. It is plain he likes the word. He smiles when he says it and so I smile too, though I cannot say I understand what meaning this word has beyond his liking of it. In leaving Ontuit my studies at Boston Latin were cut short. Once again he gives me that smile of brotherhood. "One day you will know," he says, as if comprehending my unvoiced ignorance of its meaning.

One night when we are drinking in a local tavern, Dr. Punic Sr. tells me he will be leaving soon. "It is time now to trust you and to trust your trust in me." Then he says, "My son is not so strong as I wish him to be. He will need your help. I wish I had taught you more. I wish you were my son." To hear such words from him likely has more to do with drink than with the truth. I have heard his disappointments before and try not to put much stock in them.

•

It is now almost two years into my stay in Sagg. During this time there have been established, so I am told, ten more Hooker Homes up and down Long Island, one even in New York City, as well as the main Sailors' Institute on a place called Staten Island convenient to the ships. Ten Hooker Homes! I wonder if each one has so many hundred poxed? I wonder if each one has more patients than they can care for. I wonder if each one has rented rooms all over town to house the overflow. I wonder. I wonder. Five or ten thousand poxed! What is transpiring? What have Uncle Hogarth's riches bought?

I have little more knowledge than when I left Ontuit, for which wretched place I begin to pine. No medical skills have been imparted to me. I sometimes think my food and drink are drugged to make me as docile as the patients. That is the word of what is done to them. No, I do not want to go back to Massachusetts! It is easier to deal with people than only with their shit. I can put a name to many now, and often they smile and talk with me though I am little more than a servant.

When they talk it is most always of some long-ago lost love. A man or woman who has left them. A person made out to be too perfect for belief. *Worth* is the word I hear most often. "She was worth it." "He was worth it." "It was worth it."

Sometimes when I am special blue, I go down to the bay, beyond the harbor, up and around the bend, and watch the gentle waves come rolling up the sand. No one ever comes to see this lovely view. I pretend to build my own house upon this point. I pretend the view is mine and ever will be mine.

I have money to spend and more sums hidden away. I hold in my name many shares of stock in Massachusetts Waste. I court a local girl or two but none will have me for fear of where I work. This game of trying with them amuses me. But my father who disappeared never loved me, so why should they? Never did I see love within a Hooker household. Oh, I heard words about love spoken all the time, but never did I sense any passion such as brought all these sailors to Sagg. It is as if people live in different worlds.

'Tis passing strange but I no longer fear Contagion. Despite all my touching of the sick, I do not have *It*. Several servants and nurses and guards do die. We are told it was not from *It*, but I will wager it was.

That is what all call it now. It.

Dr. Punic Sr. always sternly instructed all, "You will not catch this pox unless you couple your body in some way with theirs! Unless you kiss them, and I know you will not. Unless you fuck them and I know you will not. Will you?"

One day, just as he warned, Dr. Maurice Punic, Sr., is gone. His son tells me his father has departed for another Hooker Home, started by another son never earlier mentioned. He tells me that from this moment forth he himself is a doctor. "I am Dr. Punic now. My father's wisdom now resides in me. He gave me all he knew in all his books and all his notes. I ask for your blessings and your aid." At first this angers me. Was he not a doctor before? If a doctorship passes from man to man so easily, why am I not a doctor too? Then he takes my hand, and holds it hard, and begs me with his eyes, saying, "I cannot run this place alone." I am a fool for pleas and supplications. I nod my head and squeeze his hand in return. His nice smell comes back to my nose. His father did not smell nice. Only now as I write this do I dare allow myself to consider that they were not father and son at all.

From the day of his departure, "father" is never mentioned by "son." Within a few more months we have another hundred or so. How Dr. Maurice Punic, Sr., had managed is a secret not left with us. Whatever goes on behind closed doors, there are fewer and fewer called to enter. Dissatisfied mumblings increase in volume. At last the town sends official letters of complaint that we are a disturbance. Outside our doors churchwomen march back and forth, holding signs demanding that we leave. It becomes an embarrassment to walk out into the streets and be accosted by a chorus of hissing cats. They are afraid of us and if we come too close they scurry back in terror, their looks of hate and fear so mixed they are as one. That others think me toxic is a feeling now too often upon me. My sleep is troubled. I dream most often of fires and conflagrations, huge gusts of orange and red and yellow and black, and then all black. My dreams burn me up and wake me in a sweat. Some mornings I try to confide my fears to Maurice, but he is less friendly to me now. "Call me Dr. Punic," he says. I even try to talk to Mrs. Horvath, who seems unchanged by anything in her unsmiling sternness. She never talked to me before, and she is not starting to talk to me now. How she manages to keep her rough brutes as assistants, I have no idea.

One night, when everyone has been put to bed, Dr. Punic tells me we are moving. The Sailors' Institute and the government of our country are giving us a bigger hospital for our very own. It is more remote but it is very big indeed, he says, with rooms enough for many thousands. He has arranged a fleet of boats to take us there. Comes the night of our departure, we make our way, small group by small group, from every street in all of Sagg it seems, into rowboats out to the big-masted boats that are berthed in a cove removed from the harbor's edge. It is a lovely night, with enough breeze to get us off. The harbor itself is more crowded than I remember it ever to be. It seems as if of late vessels from every nation in the world assemble here to unload their cargo, as if all the whales of every ocean have been siphoned of their valued oil at this one same moment and brought to Sagg. Great prosperity has returned here. No wonder they want us to leave. They jeer at us as we row to our ships. They cry out awful things about us, hateful Godless things, taunts and filth and curses. Not one cries out Godspeed, God bless. I see so much hate in so many eyes that I believe I am leaving hell.

I do not know why but I know it is I who did it and did it purposely. I know I have not been happy here, and now it seems so clear that I have not been happy anywhere or anytime on earth. It is that clear to me, this knowledge that I will never be happy anywhere or anytime on earth. In earlier years I was told that the Devil was inside me. I want Sagg to burn. I want it to burn to ashes. I had heard of earlier burnings of this place and how quickly they repaired it. Well, they will have to do it again. I light a match as we pass the last of the many ships of oil. They combust one by one as we sail away. The harbor is soon no more, and much of the town. High on the hill I can see our grand hotel is particularly blazing bright, as if an omen to me of good riddance and farewell.

So much destroyed, so fast described. This deed is to be as naught compared to what does lie ahead.

We journey by our fleet of boats to an island far off in the sound, between Long Island and the Connecticut coast. A most lonely place it is, this island, with little of interest to lure outsiders. Its few inhabitants have lived here from birth and are stunted in mind and body from intermarriage and untended diseases. They meander around like misshapen dwarves, looking at us through crazed eyes and mumbling grunts and groans. When they see us they run and disappear. I am never to see them again.

The island is named Fruit Island, both because it is owned by a Dr. Frucht and because it is not one island but three: Peach Island, Cherry Island, and Plum Island, the latter being the largest, some thirty acres. Each island is connected to the others by small wooden bridges or often just by proximity, as they are so close that all that is required is a jump from here to there. I do not know who Dr. Frucht is or was. Dr. Punic thinks he was a war hero of some sort.

The doctor leads us from the boats in a large group, across the flat land of Cherry Island, across a small stream and a grassy plain and up the hill to the large building on the highest point of Plum Island. As we near it, he stops us and welcomes us "to our new and permanent home, where we can deliver unto you the latest in treatment and care so that you may have hope the Good Lord will repair you and heal you and send you back into the world should you wish to return." There is much happy cheering and clapping, even from the guards, for no one of us has heard our doctor speak in such exciting words of a new future no one ever dares to think about. I am overwhelmed to see us all together in one group for the first time. We cover half the hill. How is one doctor alone to care for all of these? Dr. Punic tells me more medical staff is coming and my new education is finally to begin.

The building that is waiting, empty, immense in size, was once called the Great Hospital for Foreign Heroes, for we find a sign torn down that says so. I will discover that it was built after the War of Revolution, to imprison British soldiers and deserters, a great number, in a place where they could not be found and where they could be starved to death in tiny cells. There is a new sign and a new name, presumably for us—the Great Hospital for the Wretched and the Destitute. This seems unkind, and hopeless. Dr. Punic disclaims knowledge of its maker. Something else, too, is new, and that is the presence of a number of uniformed guards carrying muskets.

Then he says that because there are so many of us and because our new home is so large and because we are now under a contract with the United States Government itself, he is unfortunately required by law to have on the premises guards carrying arms to be used only in the event of emergency or danger from the outside world, which is unlikely, so remote are we. There are noddings of acceptance among the patients; I sense that far from being distressed by the presence of armed guards, as I find myself to be, the patients take comfort from it.

I realize there are not enough guards and muskets to protect all of us. I realize that this is a fearful place. There is no mainland here. We are in the middle of nowhere.

I have never seen a building so big. Not even in Boston was there such a place! Whence came so many with the skills to build and hammer and nail and roof an edifice of such great size? No church in America, no cathedral in the lands our families left, could be so huge, so high, so long, and so far away from life. I will learn it was built by the labor of indentured slaves.

No description can do justice to the horror of its innards. Endless walls of peeling paint and corridors with windowless dank stinking cells poking off them like the rotted teeth Indians string into necklaces to ward off evil spells. Into these tiny cells, with no water or food, are locked our many hundreds and hundreds of poxed, several to a cell. I note for the first time that there seem many more here than the number I thought we left with, and many faces of strangers. Were other shiploads dropped here first? Are these new ones from those other Hooker Homes? I ask a few of the unfamiliar faces where they hail from, but as always among this lot no information concerning former lives comes forth. Everyone is too afraid, perhaps. Or too sick and tired. Or most likely all.

It is peculiar that locks on the doors are all in working order, as if our government sent men on ahead to attend to this repair alone. Why did they not clean the cells? Or give them mattresses or straw at least to rest on? Or sweep the halls? Or tidy up the kitchen, which looks beyond any use? At night I tour the halls for hours and try to count the rooms. I count some eight hundred doors. None of the rooms are numbered. The halls are a great maze. Have I walked in circles? I wonder. When they are let out, how will the patients find their way back to their rooms? Quickly I find that they are not to be let out. No air. No exercise. No interchange with any but their cell mates. "For their own good," Maurice tells me. I have decided that I cannot return to calling him Dr. Punic, which makes him frown. "We are trying new ways here." He calls it "quaranteen." The idea is to keep them clean from the others lest contagions ruin all. It sounds sensible, and yet I have worked with many poxed and remain in good health.

Within several weeks, after several more arriving boats, I am certain we have three thousand poxed. I will be told this number is inconceivable when the very population of Long Island itself was still so small. Yet, though I vouch not for these figures, these numbers will tally with ledgers and records found later for this period at some national institute. The guards, with no shame or compunction, stuff the newcomers into cells already filled. When I complain to Maurice of these severe conditions, he says, "The fear of pox is loose in all the land. From state to state and territory to territory and sea to sea. There is great fear out there, of this, and of us all. There is little sympathy for what you and I would call their 'human needs.' The government now controls us. I have no choice. I was compelled to sign a contract to get this home for us. I have been ordered to lock all up and feed them through holes in the wall and make them slop their waste through holes in the floor. If they die, they die. That unfortunately is the unwritten directive communicated to me in so many words by my superior in our new capital, Washington, at a place called the Department of Health and Disease. If I am to continue, if *we* are to continue our experiments, with the hope that God will bless our endeavors and increase our knowledge, if *we* are to continue using our patients for our testings, then *we* shall now have to do so under these constraints. Let us recommence our work and see just how far our work will take us."

"Tell me what it is you hope to find."

"You know it is a cure for pox."

"How goes your progress toward success? Tell me in honesty."

"Some days I think it right over there. Other days I think 'twill never be."

At this moment he looks so human and so sad that I reach out and take his hand. He steps forward and puts his arms around me in embrace. "I would kiss you were I not afraid, no matter what I say, that I carry death."

I understand.

The screams begin, the agony of the newly incarcerated going crazy. And still we pack them in. Each week brings yet another boat with more. Bodies are spirited along by the guards in dark of night and housed I know not where.

Maurice now shows me the contract with this Department of Health and Disease conjoined with the Sailors' Institute, "a contract with Dr. Maurice Punic to look after the health of certain American people." I was not aware of the government's financial involvement in his work. I read on quietly about the "fee structure" for our work. Then I walk in the darkness among the huge trees with their heavy branches that populate these islands instead of people. I have learned that we are paid one dollar for every patient admitted, and then two dollars for each one that dies. The scant five cents per patient per day allotted to feed and clean and clothe them is absurd. Indeed, it is all too obvious that it profits us to see our patients quickly dead. Is Maurice supervising a charnel house?

On come the boats and the poxed. The only thing as sure is the stench of human waste and rotting flesh. And piss. The smell of urine grows more awful by the minute.

And the hideous never-ending screams, barely muffled within the stone cells by thick walls that cannot contain the horror.

And I am richer for it. Hundreds of dollars come wordlessly to my hand each month from Dr. Maurice Punic, Jr. There is a look of terror in his eyes that I will abandon him and leave him here alone if he's not given me enough, and so each week he gives me more.

More than money now comes into my grasp.

He gives me each day my pick of women and men to fuck. I fuck and fuck and fuck and fuck and if I were to write the word as many times as I did the act there would be no more paper for I don't know what. I had never fucked before.

My cock is always hard.

There is a reason.

Tincture of salving oxide is mixed with ore beads and melted and mixed with propholoxis fercurochrome, falidia trice, sassafras, and salt, all of which is stewed with green medicinal herbs such as mint and frankincense, chamomile, rebid, and lyre of Jew. Some of these I recognize from Uncle Hogarth's notebooks. Then it is reduced to a pulp and kneaded to a salve with whale blubber so that it can be spread upon a cock or rubbed into a cunt or up an asshole.

Yes, I come to use all these words as freely as my ever-aching cock. I come to know these constituents of our unguent and to gather them and mix them and knead them, and to write it all down.

I cannot describe the feelings excited by this salve. It is as if explosions burst and burst again, so warm and vital and taking me to the top of life. Last week we—for Maurice now partakes of all of this with me—discovered that when the salve is inserted up a nostril the pleasure increases even more, although I had not thought more pleasure possible until it was reached. Each day and night and in every conscious moment do we, Maurice and I, grease our cocks with this and stuff our assholes and our noses, and we go and choose our women and men, for in these passions' heights it matters not which sex, and we salve them up too, and then none of us can stop. Whence comes such strength, and for so long, and without sleep or proper food, though some of this has arrived, for us? It seems sometimes as if we fuck for days.

Yes, I partook, and partook, and partook, and partook, and partook. I deny it not.

Once we do it all alone, Maurice and I, just the two of us. I have never known such pleasure. Yes, it is that ecstasy he promised I would one day know. It takes us two days and two nights until we finally climax. We sleep in each other's arms for two days more.

Maurice Punic is refining the world's most perfect aphrodisiac, he tells me. It seems that in the course of purchasing the Hooker Home, Dr. Maurice Punic, Sr., either found or was given Uncle Hogarth's notes, and added these recipes to his own growing knowledge from experimenting in his travels. From this invention we will become rich, Maurice says, rich beyond any king or kingdom or crown. I am to be his partner in all we make. I believe him. I have no time not to believe him, because there is something in this stuff that stays inside me, so that my cock demands repeat only hours after climaxing. If I do not fuck over and over again, my muscles and bones ache most horribly, and my brow grows fevered with heat and sweat, until my cock must touch and enter another's flesh or I think I shall lose my mind. Oh, this is the most insidious of masters! After entry these fevers vanish, to be replaced by lust so fierce as make the fevers seem calm. For time beyond reckoning my cock pumps and pumps, even when the rest of me cries out for sleep, for respite, for surcease.

Maurice says we must have patience, that each day and week his experiments bring him closer to perfection of "our" recipe; that it will soon be possible with a smaller amount to achieve a lesser passion, but a grand and fulfilling one nevertheless. Then he goes into his laboratory, sometimes for hours, sometimes for days, while I wait outside, yearning for more, like the most depraved eater of opium. I hammer on his door until finally he must let me in to join him. And we start again. He confesses he is just as much enslaved. So much so that he barely concentrates on his work as a scientist. A cure for pox? This is what has come of the cure for pox. We cannot stop! I cannot stop. God help me! I think myself better dead. Until we start again. And then I am in heaven.

And yet it does appear that there is perhaps something in this salve that *prevents* disease. Naturally, Maurice says that is part of his plan. Neither he nor I have become remotely poxed, however much we fuck with the poxed. If indeed there be some sort of protection in our salve, then it will be a gift to the world far greater than any aphrodisiac! If we can discover how it works, then sure we will be saints. Saints made of gold.

All that is why, highest upon my list for my defense, I join him in all of this. That is what I tell myself. That is what I tell myself.

May God have mercy on my soul.

Maurice summons no more bodies to be bath'd. We confine the poxed we'd fucked with to their cells. Let loose they are likely to kill each other, they are that hungry for the salve. There are now numbers of patients so demented that they can summon up huge energies to become unpredictably violent, as if they know it is not worth staying alive and madness is a gift given them to dwell in. They scream all day and they scream all night and they rattle their cell doors and hurl themselves against them with inhuman energy. Bedlam swirls around us. We do not notice that slowly, bit by bit, in certain corridors of the hospital, the screaming subsides, then ceases.

Now I see Maurice himself going mad, his cock hanging out all the time from his trousers or undergarments, if he troubles to wear any. It juts out permanently erect, like a branch from a tree. When he cannot stick it in me he rushes around looking for someone else to stick it in, but he is unable to find anyone since Mrs. Horvath has assumed complete control over all the keys, Maurice being in such a state and I not much better. She keeps her distance and has her own guards now.

Maurice desperately wants his cock to go down. He looks upon it and begs it to soften. It will not. He cries out that he has succeeded with his invention only too well and the punishment for his success is not fair.

His lab when I enter it with him is a shambles of broken bottles and vats leaking on the floor, where we fall down and roll in this mess, so that we might feel ecstatic again.

I think of the women and men we fucked and how grotesque they came to look, with twisted bones, and noses eaten away by constant inhalations, and eye sockets running streams of pus, now with altered bodies like one buttock swollen ten times larger, or toes fallen off. I fear to catch sight of myself and pass by any mirror or glass as if it is not there.

And then I think of the babies, the hardest to view, scabrous, infected, screaming malformed bundles of flesh which bite and scream and kick and spit like tiny sharks. How did they come to be this way? Surely no one fucked them! The matron in charge of their "nursery" wing of cells had died, sprawled out on the corridor floor, and they got out somehow and were crawling around trying to eat what remained of her pitted flesh. I had fallen upon them when I lost my way and was nearly eaten alive.

I barely remember sunshine. I realize that when Dr. Punic Sr. came to call, God cursed me with the perfect punishment for all past Hooker sins. Hogarth Hooker is responsible for all the syphilis in America, and I for perpetuating his legacy. And Thomas Hooker, the progenitor, the father of us all, for making Sex the Sin. Had he not trumpeted so against it, who would have wanted it so much?

I grab Maurice on the floor. I ask him where the latest formula is written down. Maurice shakes his head. "No, I am not going to give it to anyone. It is still too strong." He shakes his head again. "You are going crazy," he blubbers. "I must not follow you into madness. I must finish my work. Without you. Away from you. There is no one to be trusted except myself. Maurice, Maurice, Maurice."

He puts his hand to my face. "You are passing into another world. You were once so handsome and filled with promise. Now you look like an ancient cow." His eyes are staring into nothingness. He screams that he sees me crawling on the ground like a snake and spitting venom. I am crawling on the floor, and I see myself doing the very same. He is also affixing his mouth to any part of my flesh that is exposed, which is all of it, trying to suck it as a baby does a mother for food. Even for air to touch his cock, which still sticks out hard like a rock, makes him scream. He jumps up and rushes from one side of the laboratory to the other, from the ice chest to the kettle on the stove. First he applies cold compresses of ice to his penis, then, screaming in pain, he runs to pour boiling water on it and screams appallingly louder. Then he tries to push me against a wall and sit on my hard cock. But this only makes both of us scream out in pain. We simply cannot be touched now.

With the key on the chain around his neck Maurice bends forward to unlock his safe. He withdraws his salve, uncorks his vial of inhalant, and tries to stuff it up our noses again. He finds a knife and tries to rip his throat open. I think he is trying to kill himself to ease his agony and I see that I must not let him.

With all my strength I tie Maurice against the post that holds the ceiling up. "I have not endured for so little recompense." I look all over and can find no records. Maurice must be working in some secret room, perhaps in a basement or an attic or in another part of the building, or even in some other place on these grounds I do not know about. I continue my search. I fear I am indeed going crazy and must not allow it. I find the enemas he uses for his concoction. Are these enemas his secret to life? I had watched while he siphoned bits of this and that into the liquid he pumped messily up his ass. When he was flying he would scream, "I have found It!" Every salve and mineral and element and salt I find on Maurice's shelves, surely the world's bowels cannot absorb these ingredients. But I will steal the formula by putting them all together! In this tiny laboratory, I give myself a dozen enemas a day, flushing myself out over and over again, not caring that blood pours from me, my hair falling out, my eyes becoming, if not sightless, useless, as I see only blazing suns. Sleep is lost to me. Time is meaningless. The room is nauseating. I am too crazy to notice that my cock has finally shrunk nigh unto invisibility. That my passion for sex has been rendered nil.

Maurice, still tied to the post, has long since been hanging there limply. Is he even alive?

That it is about to become even more awful almost stops my telling it.

I swear to all that this is true remembered, and I write this at a time in my life when calmness has returned.

I had untied him free and returned to my search, which took me out of this cabin. When I return, Dr. Maurice Punic, Jr., still naked, has gouged out his pelvic area. His male organs have been replaced by a woman's vagina (it belonged to Mrs. Horvath) that is stitched to a rope tied around his waist. With his hands holding his penis, impaled on a long stick, up in front of him like some banner of freedom or cross of Christ, he runs crazed from the hospital. There he puts down his bloody penis so his hands are free to remove from the leather pouch around his neck a spoonlike implement that he inserts into his exposed guts. He scoops more of them out, to place beside the severed penis what feces remain inside him.

Behind some trees not far from him, I, Lucid Hooker, also naked, am thrashing myself with branches, flagellating myself in punishment for my never-ending sins. "I condemn myself, I condemn myself, I condemn myself for my failures and my acquiescence."

"I am the teller of all futures and all fate," Maurice intones in counterpoint.

Maurice is shaking and finding it difficult to stand. He falls to earth. As I come closer to him I can see him looking up at me. He is dying. His hand reaches for mine. In it is his bloody severed penis.

"It has gone down at last," he says.

He presses this gob of flesh and shit into my hand. Then his head falls from him and I see his eyes rolling on the ground, staring into me.

I am crying, sobbing, violent sobs that soon become racking spasms of abandonment and fear.

"Goodbye," I finally manage to spit out.

Then I believe I hear voices from each side of me. From Maurice's clutches I seize the leather pouch that contains the record of all Punic experiments and many small vials of potions and salves and the lump of blubber that is the aphrodisiac itself and clutch all to my heart as I head into the night. Like my progenitor Hogarth I carry with me another man's severed member out into a hostile world.

DAME LADY HERMIA STARTS DIGGING IN

Frederick, what my research is uncovering about this man Furstwasser is important for both our history and my history and will get us both murdered. We can have a double funeral. That said, here, as nonjudgmentally as possible, is what I have learned:

Considering he makes such an indelible mark on your country (I guess it is my country now as well but I shirk from such possessiveness when it turns up such as what is turning up), it's peculiar that his name, Furstwasser, an Ezra or any other, isn't found in any earlier record located thus far. He has come to America to join his brother, Gideon, also Swiss, who has claimed to his employers that he is an American by virtue of his wife, Nephtalia, whom the two brothers (?) had already quietly murdered? disposed of? unloaded? before they arrived here. (Ezra, so far, is single.) Gideon is sent on an official visit to Fruit Island as a representative of the Department of Health and Disease in Washington to its contractee, the Great Hospital for the Wretched and the Destitute on Plum Island. Any government contract requiring the paying out of so much money must be adjudged for its worth and value, and of course its truth. Gideon was already employed by HAD when he hired his brother Ezra to work with him. I do not know yet how Gideon got the job in the first place.

Fruit Island is situated in an area described by the U.S. Department of Land and Sea, Division of Storms and Weather, as "laden with weak alluvial banks," i.e., what are known as swamps, particularly on the south shores, which, because of "Tidal Disturbances and Concomitant Sediment Irregularities," are dangerous.

A Mr. Bernhardt Krebs, who is director of the Office of Disease Disbursement of HAD, brought this unruly situation to official attention. HAD contracted the hospital to Dr. Maurice Punic, Sr. Providing care to 2,700 patients "with disease" has come to $26,543.76 thus far, which amount is considered excessive by Washington and requires an on-site investigation by Gideon Furstwasser, its director of Receipts and Disbursements. According to the admission records sent to Washington, the Great Hospital actually houses "two thousand, nine hundred adult syphilitics, plus additional seven hundred twelve children under age twelve years; oldest syphilitics eighty years and youngest infant babes," and Punic is claiming additional monies due him.

His report for HAD, dated 3 Aug. 1838, signed by Gideon Furstwasser, although he has been disposed of? unloaded? murdered? disappeared? by the time of its receipt in Washington, is as follows:

"We arrive in our boat at night because it takes much time to sail from Sagg. No one is here to greet us. We march on to the Hospital. No one is there to greet us. We go inside what is identified as 'Office.' Again no official with greetings. We pass down corridors and we look into the many tiny windows of doors. All doors are locked. Much stink comes from the tiny rooms, packed two, three, four, five to each, with the people inside them screaming like banshees or dead. What to do with them? This is not a question I know how to answer in comfort.

"Further investigation reveals no one of authority in evidence. In Switzerland I was a man accustomed to be in charge. What would I do in Switzerland? I ask myself.

"I make a list. There is no one in charge. There is no food. There are ten soldiers with ten musket guns fit to kill jungle animals. I do not believe any jungle animals are here. Options include finding food and feeding people in tiny rooms. This is no option since we can find no food or keys. All cupboards are bare. We are on a tiny island. Options include burning whole place down and removing people from misery. I am not permitted by God to make such Judgment and perform such acts. Options include going back to Sagg and seeking help from another source. But this takes time and storms are coming. If the storm kills our boat what will happen here?

"I and Ezra determine we must set these people free. But we find no keys. Then a woman appears in night robe who names herself as Mrs. Katherine Horvath, Chief Nurse. She takes us to the office of Dr. Punic, whom I have been looking for, and locates keys to the tiny rooms. She is bleeding and excuses herself. Then Ezra Furstwasser and I unlock the doors. It takes us many hours and dawn comes by the time we finish. The soldiers hold up their musket guns so the inmates stay in line as we set them free outside. They look terrible. They look almost dead. They lie down on the grassy banks and fall asleep in the fresh air.

"How many? Two hundred. Three hundred. Not thousands as we are told and as says the official reports sent to our Department. But they are possibly dead and disposed of.

"Outside is also the body of Dr. Maurice Punic hanging from a tree."

This is the end of his report, a copy of which I tracked down at Iron Vaultum.

As Ezra's official biography issued by the Disciples of Lovejoy (Mother) Church of Montrose, Missouri, states: "As he surveyed the diseased hordes which, mingling under this moon, were to become his first flock of followers, swaying already in thralldom to this new leader, he, Ezra Furstwasser, received his First Call from God. He is told that it is now his time. He must redefine his name. He is given the choice, to be either Furst or Wasser. He elects to become Ezra Furst and Gideon accepts his new calling as Gideon Wasser.

"The Angel then says to Ezra, '*Furst* means Prince too. You are hereby the First Prince of a new religion that God and Jesus are birthing.' Gideon immediately kneels down before Ezra. 'My brother, I pledge you my fealty!' The Angel causes lightning and thunder to announce this fealty of brother for brother."

A later official biography, entitled *Our Prince*, describes in more elaborate detail and more polished English how Ezra Furst led "my faithful three thousand" out of bondage and into the Promised Land. Their march westward across America, eventually to the Nehigh Basin in the as yet unclaimed and unnamed western provinces, is to become known as the Great Migration.

This is the account of the Great Migration given in *Our Prince*. It is told in the first person, as narrated by Ezra:

"I returned to the now-empty Great Hospital and I set fire to it. Such a house of horror and unkindness to humanity and the human spirit must no longer stand. I had wondered how difficult it might be to do this. I am a man not given to deeds of destruction, no matter what reason for it, but I feel that God is lighting this fire with me. Indeed, so willing was this fire to inflame the heavens that the night breezes fan the tiny flames into bigger and bigger ones in cooperation with this Holy Spirit that is guiding me. This was to be the Great Consumption that we shall celebrate each year, along with the Great Migration, as part of Our Festival of Our Beginnings. God was my fellow torchbearer. A mighty bonfire it was, growing to so huge a height and making so loud a clamor for importance that I am told it could be seen and heard on all far shores on the entire coast. I am in awe of my deed. Yes, I see my act as one of sweeping this filthy earth clean. I knew I was now God's co-worker.

"Yes, it was here and now that I felt my first call to be God's leader. Right here and now I heard my name called out loud by God. As these new hordes prostrate themselves before me on this Great Lawn I kneel with them and we pray. Oh Lord Our God, oh Jesus your son, give Your Blessings to this New Calling to which You summon me. And these new servants before me raised their hands to me and to our Lord and his Son. With the conflagration behind us making ever-louder tintinnabulations, my new people, racked by hunger and lack of love, gallop like some terrified herd of cattle released into the freedom of the only thing safe before them: the Unknown. Three thousand strong in total, they pound down the hill in the dark night. Closer and closer and faster and faster, as one we reach the water's edge.

"Yes, we wade into the water of the Great Bay, like Egyptians walking into the Red Sea. I, Ezra Furst, their Moses, lead them and part their waves. It is low tide by now, for God is on our side, and He makes for us to walk on the firm sands He now provides for us, leading us to freedom. We set out across the wilderness of this country's deserts and plains to find, finally, on the two hundred and twenty-second day, that the Lord hath delivereth us, my people and me, now at last and for all eternity, to our new home, Montrose, where God tells me this is where He wants us to be, and we will be, and that is where we stop, to be joined by Tom Lovejoy and his followers and to be knit by our Lord into one.

"In all this journey does He take but one of us, my beloved Brother, Gideon, who, in crossing the wilderness, succumbs to a rare illness that he has carried from his own partnering with another man on Fruit Island and with which God wishes to fell him. In this death, from this disease, God has given our new religion its first fervent mission: to crusade against the evils of the flesh in all the many guises of its proliferating sinning, most particularly the one that he has spared my people but not my brother. God wants us to be Clean and we pledge ourselves to oblige Him in all ways we can."

So many biographies of Ezra Furst, and of his brother Gideon Wasser, and of Tom Lovejoy, have been written that such "facts" as there are are now codified by "scholars" and "historians" and "ecclesiastical experts" into a legendary inspirational scenario of early awakening to piety, a stumbling, fraught, but eventual triumphant struggle against temptations, all leading to unbounded happiness and an exceedingly important spiritual life of constant communication with "Our Saviors," Jesus Christ and God the Father and all the Angels.

The murder of his brother's wife and the disposing of his brother are not among these "facts," nor is there any mention of the Massacre at Fruit Island, at least not in any resemblance to the various versions of that event now coming down to us, all lacking in agreement as they appear to be.

LUCID CONTINUES

The two new men who came to this island fucked Maurice Punic, Jr., to death. They both took of the aphrodisiac. Maurice was still clutching a little bottle of it and he was still alive and he stuck it up their noses. The few prisoners left, maybe fifty of us outside, stood around and watched. And then all the others rushed forward, not abiding by the volleys of shots from the guards with their muskets. Their bodies were hungering for more of the magic sex potion and they tore Maurice limb from limb and ate him, believing that he was made of his aphrodisiac. They were crazy. One of the new men was fucked to death by these hordes, and the other new man would have been done to death had he not grabbed a torch and set fire to the hospital while those outside rushed down to the water where many were drowned in the swamps. I was hiding there and I saw it all. Three thousand people still inside were burned up!

I see the voiceless lad who is shaking mightily from so much fear as I am and we go into the forest together.

VOICELESS

I find another new lover. We hold each other tight and when it is darkest he takes my hand and we walk into the forest and we disappear. He says he will lead us out to freedom and safety. How many months or years passed I here? Two of the four of us in our cell had long since died. My living cell mate would softly chew their flesh. And then he died too. I was alone with three dead lads.

Those of us left alive and then let free rushed out and many died in the swamp.

HERMIA CONTINUES

The dead were never found.

A check dated June 25, 1840, for $63,987.09 was made out by the United States Treasury to Amalgamated Medical Holdings as full payment due under its contract with Dr. Maurice Punic, Sr., "for services rendered at the Great Hospitals in Sagg and on Plum Island *inter alia*." A further payment of $35,398.54 was made to Dr. Maurice Punic, Jr., for "professional services rendered to the needy." Both payments were sent to the Schroederer-Lutz Bank in Zug, Switzerland, for the account of the Brothers of Lovejoy, Ezra Furst, Principal Disciple.

Dr. Maurice Punic, Sr., was a poor Furstwasser who came to the New World, went to work for the United States Government in Washington, discovered a way to take advantage of a loophole he discovered, brought his smarter cousins Ezra and Gideon over to help him, and almost made a fortune. There is no record of his name after this. Perhaps he returned to Switzerland to spend his money, quite a decent amount for those days.

FROM THE PEN OF DR. ISRAEL JERUSALEM

I put in my own ten cents.

According to Mr. Plutarch, at the Battle of Chaeronea one hundred and fifty pairs of lovers from Thebes pledged to defend themselves against the invaders. They fought and died to the last man. They were all found dead in each other's arms.

These men on Fruit Island had come in hopes of meeting others like them. Sagg was on the water, it was summer, what better excuse and place for a holiday? Sagg was a port, so there would be sailors there as well. What better! They were certainly not all poxed. But it was hard not to see no one wanted them. Wherever they went, wherever they were, they were sniffed out by dogs and sent away. If they were not hanged by some government for schtupping each other. Straight men do not get hanged for schtupping a special tootsie. Even not so special. Even a kurvah. A whore. There is in this country never a penalty for fucking a whore.

Yes, many went to Sagg because word had got around that there were others like them there. True, some went to Sagg because word had also got around that there was money to be made by participating in experiments. Those infected convinced themselves a cure was being perfected that would save them. They put their trust in Dr. Maurice Punic, Sr.

In either case, they all gave the most precious thing they had to give, their bodies.

This is an early example of a Tuskegee experiment—that is, one in which the government on purpose allows the infection of unknowing subjects. I believe this to be the first example of what will become the backbone, the foundation, of all future scientific research in America, what is called the "controlled clinical trial." Controlled, my tushie. These hushmarkeds, then, are participating in history, the first of a long line of homosexuals that our government will get its hands on. NITS will become the world's chief home of the Controlled Clinical Trial and, in due course, of The Underlying Condition, which will be their man who came to dinner who never leaves.

They are then told they will be safe on this far island, on this Fruit Island, with some famous Dr. Punic no one ever heard of. By this time, from all the experiments they had done on them, and from all their couplings in the excitement of meeting so many like them, they had come to be afraid that they were dying. If this were so, well, then they would die in each other's arms as in ancient Greece.

And so they did. They died in each other's arms.

•

My first massacre. My debut. You think it was pox or clap that infected them all? You insult me.

You have now met me in my growing glory.

A FEW GOOD MEN

"All, all are dead, and ourselves left alone amidst a new generation whom we know not, and who knows not us," Thomas Jefferson, such a good talker, laments before he dies. He has seen what is happening. He senses what is coming. "Notable geniuses and great-souled men" are no longer around to lead. From here on in, the string of America's leaders should shame The American People, who voted them in. Martin Van Buren, William Henry Harrison, John Tyler, James K. Polk, Zachary Taylor, Millard Fillmore, Franklin Pierce, James Buchanan, one is almost worse than the next or the preceding (although maybe not Polk, who got us California, Nevada, and Utah, with Texas and Oregon thrown in, thus doubling the size of our country albeit hastening the Civil War). And then comes Lincoln and we murder him. To be followed by another string of mediocrities just as long.

In 1831, Alexis de Tocqueville and his boyfriend Gustave de Beaumont come from France to travel around America, to take a look, to size it up. Alexis is only twenty-five years old but he writes a book about us that many say is still smarter and tougher and more prescient than almost anything any American of any age has ever written. He predicts, for instance, that the danger of the "tyranny of the majority" will cause great troubles, that the majority will trample on the minorities, the people "reduced to nothing better than a flock of timid and industrious animals, of which the government is the shepherd." He also says, most frighteningly, that he knows of no country with "less independence of mind and true freedom of discussion."

Alexis, inspired by Gustave, has written America's first reality show. "It will be given to America to teach the world about good and evil, not because the world wants to listen to anyone so young, but because America will not know how to do anything but show them."

The love letters between Gustave and Alexis have only recently been discovered. But that is a French affair and this is an American history. Just know that Alexis himself is so highly sexed, as one of his annotators puts it, that his wife destroys all their correspondence, always a suspicious sign of such high-sexedness, and that Gustave and he jointly share a preoccupation with young women, but also with each other, and so to take advantage of their distance away from home they vow celibacy, which leaves them free to spend each night only with the other. Such abilities for clearing the decks in this way for the important things are particularly French.

In later years, after his two volumes have been published and he's lived longer and observed us more from over there, Alexis becomes increasingly disillusioned with the United States. This is rarely written about by his many champions in their determination to extol his praise of us. He is proved correct in his prediction that slavery here would not be abolished without a civil war, if then. He now more fully realizes that it is money alone that makes our world and the "loudmouthed ignorance" of our politicians and public leaders go 'round; and that the general population will be reduced to "sheep-like dependency" on a state that saves them the necessity of thought and destroys their will. He has already predicted "the lonely crowd" where individuals will find themselves alone in the midst of many and unable to think any differently than this multitude, and that religion will attempt to make us good citizens, although all "attempts to relieve the distress of the poor would destroy the economy." Oh, he got it all, eventually, although his "great" work contains little of the prescience of his later years that would and should have been written and published by him as volume three (Damrosch, *Tocqueville's Discovery of America*, 2010; Alan Ryan, *NYRB*, Nov. 2010).

From 1829 to 1837, Andrew Jackson, the shaper of the modern Democratic Party, is president. We know he was a pisser. He needs more said about him than this history is going to say, though it will say this: He was madly in love with his wife, who died quickly. What we did not know was that the popular portrait painter Ralph Earl climbed the back stairs of the White House to Jackson's bedroom, and he would stay by his side until Jackson died. Yes, they were lovers. For many, repeat: many years. As there was in short order no Mrs. Jackson, Ralph had a long run playing the part. How could this not be seen and known, recorded and remarked upon?

While we are at it, from 1853 to 1857 there are two more gay presidents in the White House. Franklin Pierce is an alcoholic from Vermont who was roommates at Bowdoin College in Maine with another famous American not yet recognized as the homosexual he was, Nathaniel Hawthorne. President Pierce is married and has lost three sons. His wife, Jane, faints when he announces his candidacy and spends much of his term isolated in an upstairs room writing letters to a son dead only two months in a train accident. Pierce is lackluster and ignoble and leads us closer to war, one of those northerners who favors slavery, or rather opposes it not enough. He is exceptionally handsome. He drinks himself to death. But Hawthorne loves him. It is the great hidden mystery of this mysteriously hidden, i.e., closeted, great American writer who ran in terror when our other great American gay writer of this period, Herman Melville, moved to Salem to be near Nathaniel, to woo him, and to somehow win him.

And in 1855, an outrageous gay poet publishes a book of passionate odes called *Leaves of Grass*. He loves men furiously, and with great hunger, and too openly. No one knows what to make of his poetry, which is ravishingly homoerotic, and so hard to conceive of as anything else that it is assiduously overlooked, as is its author. And what a symbolic title, *Leaves of Grass*. Is it meant to mean . . . what? That men in love are everywhere, as plentiful as grass?

Another gay president! Two in a row! Pierce's successor, James Buchanan (1857–1861), is a bungling, unattractive Pennsylvanian also too fond of slavery for the country's good. What did he and Pierce before him do in Washington for eight years? How does a country piss away eight long and entire years? Where is everyone and anyone?

Three homosexual presidents, Jackson, Pierce, Buchanan, almost in a row. (Our fourth is on the way.) What is happening and why is it happening now? Even today, there is not a major piece of historical work about these three gay presidents that makes mention of the foregoing revelations. And here is YRH, hurling them at you one-two-three, and upsetting our chronology.

What all these revelations should tell us about The American People during these years is that many male citizens from every segment of society are now engaging in sexual relations with other men. Because they know that their nation's leaders are hushmarkeds (hushmarkeds recognize their own), they feel in some small way sanctioned. Washington, and by extension other large centers on the East Coast, is becoming the center of more than government.

Where is the cadre of historians this true history of early America requires? Nowhere, with the early and honorable exception of a small volume published in Athens, Ohio, in 1929, *Garish Grandstanding: The Role of Faggotry in 19th Century America*, by Mae Blossom Yangtzee, purported to be a wrinkled old lady in a tiny Midwestern town. It is a pretty racy book to come out of Ohio during any era. Mae Blossom Yangtzee was evidently a man, Howard Akins Kree, a lawyer and drag queen who performed in Oriental garb at private functions. The world he so briefly describes flourishes only in an occasional miasma of rumor and whispers, visited by few and those few frightened by their adventurousness.

Oh, also by the way, although known since the beginning of the seventeenth century, the hollow needle and syringe for injection of fluids into the body makes its appearance in its first convenient handy model, constructed by Dr. Charles Pravaz, in France in 1853. By the end of the year it is being used everywhere for a faster introduction into the body of opium. Indeed, it becomes a necessary bit of paraphernalia for parties among a certain and ever-widening set. It will also prove an invaluable tool in medicine.

There are some historians who maintain that de Tocqueville did not really "get" America. Not even having left New York, he writes to a dear friend that America was "a society without roots, without memories, without prejudices, without routines, without common ideas, without a national character." He'd made up his mind that this was what he would see and write about. In the opening lines of his finished work he declares, "Among the new objects that attracted my attention during my stay in the United States, not one struck me more vividly than the equality of the conditions."

And as said, lovers they were, Alex and Gustave. Nobody has "got" that, either.

WANDERERS

Voiceless and I wandered for several years after we got free from Fruit Island. I had noticed him there, and the more he clung to me, the more he broke my heart. First we headed south. Then we tried north but every place we went we got tired of what was there. What was there was us, Lucid and

Voiceless. We thought if we should go far enough away from all we had known, we might find another us. It was as if we couldn't shake the horror of what we had lived through and escaped from. Somehow we had to kill off our old selves before we could become new, but we didn't know how.

Oh, we tried various things. Once we jumped into a river and left a note goodbye. I signed it Lucid Hooker III and Voiceless indicated he wanted a new name, so we gave him one, Messie. He chose it himself. "I is in one big mess." He was learning how to spell his thoughts in letters. I had taught him the alphabet and he was a quick study. But we didn't drown and no one found the note so far as we could tell when we camped out farther up the bank and spied back. At least now we had a name to call him.

Then we went to Maine and then across to New Hampshire and Vermont. We must have cleared many dozens of acres here and there and built some thirteen cabins here and there. But no peace arrived. Still I heard in my head the screams of Fruit Island and felt in my groin the mingled pain and pleasure of what the Punics had mixed and what I'd helped them mix and what we had sniffed. Still I felt the agony in my penis of how long and fierce we had fucked there, Maurice and I. It was not a feeling to be rid of so fast.

And Messie still had nightmares of how Dr. Punic Jr. made a hole in his throat to drop in a cure that never came. I know he is fearful that because he will never talk again, no one will ever know all that happened to him except himself inside his head. He was all of fourteen years old when that happened to him forever.

But we comforted each other well enough in the middle of the night when we woke up frightened. He held me in his arms most dear. Soon it was that I hugged him back as he held me. We did not partake in sex but I knew that what came upon us now was love. I am not ashamed to say that for the first time in my life I felt the feeling of true love.

No, neither one of us wants sex anymore. I do not know how long this will last, but for right now we just work our energy off by clearing land and building cabins and marching on, trying to be as brave as we can be. He is a strong lad, growing already past my height, muscled now from our labors, and blond hair on both of us from the sun. I find I am noticing his body more and more, so perhaps my penis will want to work again. We sell the cabins when we leave them, and I have money from Maurice. Too, I have the formula that Maurice said would make us rich, though I do not know how to bring this feat about, or even if I want to. It seems I am always sitting on a bag of questions and a keg of powder. It is enough to keep us moving on and on.

BLISSFULNESS

Upon an ever-widening horizon, stage, panorama, platform, whatever do we call this landscape for our ever-growing dreams as The American People push out and forward with hope into our ever-expanding universe?

Ethel Prance is a large-boned woman of short stature, approaching forty. She is not unattractive. She has black hair and black eyes. She stands on sturdy legs. Her bosom is generous and would appear welcoming but for her intensity and forthrightness, which tend to make onlookers nervous and keep them at arm's length. Her ever-present smile does not hide her firm sense of determination, because this smile also informs you that it's her way or no way. Ethel is a resolute woman, far ahead of her time.

Such a stance and demeanor are difficult for a woman interested in men. Men simply do not like her kind of woman. They are unfamiliar with her sort, for a start, and they have too much else on their minds. So the men of New Bliss, Ohio, pay Ethel little mind or heed.

Even though she is voraciously interested in men, she does not possess the self-awareness to change. Few people do. Self-awareness is still at least seventy-five years away. She contents herself with the knowledge that her father adores her, utterly, and that this father, Milton, is not only the mayor of New Bliss, the small and hopeful town in central Ohio where they live, but also an amateur archaeologist who studied at the Copenhagen Museum with the great C. J. Thomsen and J.J.A. Worsaae, and is convinced that New Bliss is resting upon a fortune. These are truly great men, Thomsen and Worsaae, who did groundbreaking work in the Danish peat bogs and funerary mounds, and New Bliss would have heard of them if it cared a whit about archaeology, which it doesn't at this moment of concentrating on its future, not its past. In the nineteenth century, ruins were turning up everywhere, vestiges of everything.

Milton Prance owns much of New Bliss for the simple reason that, courtesy of C.J. and J.J.A., he knows his ruins and runes and believes that New Bliss sits on top of a Hopewell Indian mass burial ground, and courtesy of his wife's money he has bought it. The Hopewells, who will one day be discovered to have lived and roamed throughout the central American plains from the Gulf to the Michigan peninsula, will also be found to trace their ancestry to the time of Christ. Here is one American man who is both interested in our past and rich. Dame Lady Hermia would be thrilled to know that such a smart American man ever existed in Ohio. "I am not very keen on the possibility that the American male brain is as inclusive and capacious as they constantly maintain," she has written in one of her own early great works, which should have been cited previously, *The Rose and the Ruin*. Milton is a partner of Mr. Charles Goodyear and they are very involved in making wheels from rubber. Great riches are not only underfoot but just around the corner.

Ethel is the first lady of New Bliss. How her father thinks ancient Hopewell bones can be worth money he has not confided in her, which is just as well because Ethel finds bones all very boring. For Ethel, today is today. New Bliss is now, not then. She is a modern woman. All those Indians knew was how to kill and eat each other. They did not know bliss. Ethel will know bliss. Ethel is accustomed to getting what she wants.

Ohio helps. Ohio is a hopeful place in general. Ohio is turning out to be one of those places where there is more right than wrong. If you were to ask anyone in Ohio, there isn't much wrong with Ohio. From early on it is one of the first places where most of the people feel this way. They have pride of place, a quality sociologists will one day identify as particularly Ohioan. There are not too many states or territories where the people are quite so chauvinistic so early on. Yes, Ohio is a little pocket of state-love from the get-go, which is a good thing because it is deficient in attributes such as weather and topography compared with, say, Virginia, which is much more beautiful, or Massachusetts, which has more variety, scenically speaking. There's not much to look at in Ohio. It's more what you feel than what you see. The American People have already learned how to move around when they don't like where they've landed, but when people land in Ohio they tend to stay put. That says something about something.

So whatever Ethel has in mind to do, it's easier for her right now to do it in Ohio. Women and men may not be equal but they are more equal here. When you think well of yourself, and well of where you live, well, then the sky's the limit, isn't it?

But while the population of 5,400 in New Bliss is not a bad size, it's been a bit stagnant of late. People have stopped stopping by and staying put. No one notices except Ethel, who worries that growth is being stunted and the place will fill up with old people. Her father founded New Bliss when he got lost looking for a lost lake, and Ethel is determined to see that the town will stay here forever, lake or no lake, as a monument to him, and to her mother, although she ran off with someone when Ethel was only three (her mother, too, was uninterested in lost lakes and old bones), and to herself, of course. Once she does something memorable. Which she will do soon. She knows she will.

There are old-timers here now, but not so many as in nearby Ashton Grove or Appleyard Corners. Their young people have been running off to towns that are becoming Toledo and Columbus and Akron and Cincinnati. When young people traveling around looking for a place to live stop here on their way to somewhere else, it is important that New Bliss look good, with lots of people their own age, so they'll stay. That's the ticket. More young people.

Most towns in America are born this way. Stopovers become stay-puts, and if you were to ask them years later why they stayed they would likely answer, "You know, I can't remember, but it hasn't been all that bad." Not all that bad is about as good as it gets most anywhere. Ethel's been pondering this very subject. About as good as it gets is not good enough for Ethel.

Nobody in Ohio and thus in New Bliss gets worked up about much of anything, so when Mrs. Sary Peyser opens her home no one gives it a second thought. In this, Ohio is different from almost everywhere else in our still new country where people are up in arms swiftly and loudly the minute anything unusual damps down the morning dew. In Ohio people shrug it off and wait another day to see if whatever is troublesome is still around. Usually by then it isn't. How Ohioans come by their good sense is a mystery, but they are a patient lot.

Ethel Prance is not patient. She has come up with something, and she fears that what Mrs. Sary Peyser is doing will cast a pall on her idea.

Mrs. Sary Peyser could not care less what anyone else thinks. A dogged sense of get-up-and-go and can-do does not reside in Ohio exclusively within the bosom of Ethel Prance.

Mrs. Sary Peyser, a childless widow only thirty-five years of age, has opened her house in New Bliss to little boys.

There are a lot of little boys lost in the landscapes of our expanding country. It is a growing problem no one notices, and it will become much worse after the Civil War, fast approaching. Where their parents are and where they come from are questions most of them cannot answer. Oh, they probably knew once, but a few months in the harsh wilderness of running away erases memories, especially of parents who abandoned you. Then you want to pretend you never had them. There are adults who try to take the little boys in, but often these men and women are stern and unloving, even downright cruel, and if the boys are able they run off as fast as they can into the woods and forests. There they learn to live on berries and leaves and water from streams and fishes speared with sharpened poles and eaten raw. Most of all they learn how to evade emissaries of the law in the few places that worry about wandering children and try to capture them. Once in a while there's a good meal, perhaps at a church dinner in a town they're sneaking through, or in a farmhouse along the way, but too often the momma or poppa wants them to stay and gets too fervent in the determination to make them do so. There are lots of grown-ups who want kids of their own when they can't make them. In some places runaway children can be forced by a local law enforcement person to stay if the adults claim them, saying the children are their own kin when they're not.

Mrs. Sary Peyser evidently has the touch, because little boys come to her house and ask to stay. Evidently her interest doesn't threaten them and she's a good cook. She has a large house with many bedrooms. Her late husband was a carpenter with hope. Both husband and wife planned for a very large family. Her husband died during her first pregnancy, which she miscarried.

She has noticed how the little runaway boys who show up at her local church suppers are painfully shy in their dealings with adults and with each other. They blush and turn away, as if caught out in a wrong. She is touched by their behavior. Why are they so nervous? How can I make them more comfortable? She knows that each has fared so harshly in journeying to New Bliss that trust is as grains of sand in their small hands. They do not know how to be friends with anyone. She will teach them how to be friends with each other.

She decides to ask some of them to stay with her. She is careful in her choices, seeking boys who seem kind and gentle. Before long she has a full house of some thirty boys, bunking three and four and five to a room. She can tell they are hungry for friendships and uncertain how to establish them. Once when one of her boys runs up to a new boy at the church supper and hugs and kisses him, the new boy is so surprised he cries out, "What am I to do!" And Mrs. Sary Peyser answers simply, "Why, hug and kiss him back." Even her pastor, Rev. Tillman Tighe, smiles on this interaction. Mrs. Sary Peyser is one of his favorite parishioners and he would not mind moving in with her and all her boys himself.

She makes up stories she thinks will further her boys' friendships and banish their blushing nervousness, stories about little Billy and little Bobby Bunting types, where little Billy and little Bobby wind up kissing and hugging each other and moving to their own little farm and raising their own little crops together for life. She is surprised to find a few books of this nature in the tiny town library that is just getting started. These little books are quite popular in the Midwest in the nineteenth century; it's known that mommies and daddies have little enough time or imagination to make up stories, so it's nice that someone (in this case a Mrs. Sidney Lovitt in Worcester, Massachusetts) has thought to compose these virtual self-help guides for what unfortunately will one day be regarded as "the natural sodomy of the womanless plains," as Dierdre Hand puts it in *A History of the Abnormal in Children's Literature of the American Mid-West* (Akron, 1955). The boys love hearing Mrs. Sary Peyser read to them from these books by Mrs. Sidney Lovitt, and at the same time she is teaching them how to read, too.

Then all the little boys go to bed kissing each other and hugging each other and falling asleep in each other's arms, just like Mrs. Sary Peyser tells them to do and Mrs. Sidney Lovitt tells them to do.

Mrs. Sary Peyser's bountiful existence is exclaimed over by many a neighbor woman who is barren of such joy herself. Her charitableness is lauded. There are so many homeless children roaming the country that it is heartbreaking to many who possess maternal instincts. But Ethel Prance, who has yet to find herself a husband in a place where husbands are not as plentiful as straggly wandering ruffians, and who is coming closer to her own notion of how to put "her" town on the map, finds herself more and more annoyed. There is something unnatural to her about so many boys living together next door.

LUCID AND MESSIE IN NEW BLISS

One day Messie and I come upon a town somewhere in Ohio, with a white church and folk who invite us to take supper. A nice woman by the name of Mrs. Sary Peyser invites us to stay with her. She says she has not been well and she trusts our faces. Her house is filled with many young boys, all under the age of fifteen, and it is plain she needs help. I am older, she says, and so can be most useful to her. It is Messie who sees the good in this place first. The boys take to him so fast that in no time I see he will not soon leave. They do not care that he cannot speak. He shows them things, like how to make knots from pieces of rope and how to carve logs and stray branches of trees. His face reveals a smile I have never seen on it. How he sensed that the love here was so strong and firm I will never know, but he did, and what else had we now to do but stay?

We are here but a few months when Mrs. Sary Peyser dies. She has been very brave in keeping her pains to herself. She signs over her property to me on her deathbed, in the presence of her preacher, Rev. Tillman Tighe. "Take care of my children and welcome more when there is room and teach them how to love each other" are her instructions to me, in the Reverend's presence, and to the Reverend himself, who has been most attentive to Mrs. Sary Peyser in her terrible decline. He blesses her as "a great gift from Our Lord." When she dies, he asks if he can move into her bedroom and live with us. The boys take a vote and decide against it. The Reverend Tighe is not a man who smiles much. Messie points out to me that he has seen him fondle some of the boys in too familiar a fashion for someone of his age and calling. Then I see it too.

Now comes forward a Miss Ethel Prance. She comes through our front door without so much as knocking. We have not met officially, although we know she lives next door. She embraces me and kisses me and without so much as a condolence for Mrs. Sary Peyser's passing. She tells us the time has come for all of us to visit her in her community of love. "My House of Blissfulness," she calls it. She and her family and friends live in several large houses not far from here. No one in this town lives far from any other. We have seen in our travels that in towns everywhere houses are built close together. Why, with so much endless land, do people use so little of it? I fear people everywhere are afraid. I understand.

Miss Prance, still holding my hand, tells us she is concerned that all our young boys are a drain on the community's peace of mind. "You are motherless now." She squeezes Messie's hand to emphasize her words. It comes clear to me at this moment that she would like to be our mother and to combine us into her House of Blissfulness.

My boys are suddenly frightened of her, as am I.

OH, ONEIDA!

Like some steam valve screwed on too tightly for too long, the strict religiosity of Puritan New England is finding new ways to blow its head off in this newish nation. In Massachusetts, Ralph Waldo Emerson is writing, "We are to revise the whole of the social structure, the state, the school, religion, marriage, trade, science, and explore their foundation in our own nature . . . what is man born for but to be a reformer, a Re-maker of what man has made; a renouncer of lies, a restorer of truth and good; imitating the great nature which embosoms us all."

Like many great thinkers, Emerson leaves out the details of How, What, When, Where, and Why, and, of course, Who. You know, the Basics. The nitty-gritty. He leaves out his subtext too, that he is in love with a young man and it pains him mightily. Revise and reform and remake and embosom indeed.

In 1838, in upstate New York, John H. Noyes starts his Oneida Colony. He is twenty-seven years old and had studied divinity at Yaddah, where he had been refused ordination because he did not believe in sin. He had reduced the Gospels to sinlessness. He fills in a few of Emerson's blanks. What John Noyes is saying is this: The fear of, and sense of, sin is the cause of all the world's ills. People must be freed from sin. (He was to run his colony until 1881.)

Indeed, in the air there is increasing talk about the dissatisfactions with established religions of which Noyes speaks. Is this to be the death knell of Puritanism as we have seen it?

It should not be wrong to love one another, Noyes is saying, fully and completely, and that includes brothers and sisters and children. Men and women should be free to love each other without benefit of marriage, he is saying. "The marriage supper is a feast at which every dish is free to every guest. There is no more reason why sexual intercourse should be restrained by law, than why eating and drinking should be. I call a certain woman my wife; she is yours; she is Christ's." This is hot stuff: communities should be established in which all are free to couple and to raise children jointly, overthrowing such outmoded notions as marital fidelity and incest, and hushmarkedry. He is saying that all this is natural and fundamental and eternal and that Jesus would approve.

Yes, in upstate New York, John H. Noyes is saying all this. "I am conquering the devil's last stronghold. It has got to be taken down." It is 1848 when John flings open his doors in Oneida. Some three hundred people will eventually join him. Soon there will be similar places in Wallingford, Connecticut, in Newark, New Jersey, in Putney and Cambridge, Vermont.

To repeat: John H. Noyes is saying Oneida Colony members are required to exchange partners. He is saying: Equal Access to All for All. He calls what he is espousing Perfectionism. And, let it be noted again, he is saying that Jesus would approve.

Oneida is a complicated place. Everyone can fuck with everyone, but men have to control their ejaculations lest too many children be born. Boys entering puberty must confine their intercourse to postmenopausal women until they can prove their ability to control their ejaculations. The young girls are introduced to sex by the older men. Too much love is frowned upon, and exclusive romantic or sexual relationships are frowned upon. There are lots of rules, with twenty-seven standing committees and forty-nine administrative sections.

It doesn't sound like much of a fun place. "Spirituality" is what binds them together and "spirituality" can turn out to be as big a problematic bummer in Oneida as it was for all those Puritans. And is for those once again wandering Disciples of Lovejoy, led by Tom Lovejoy its founder and Ezra Furst his second, who have been expelled from Montrose because the locals find them just too weird. But not before Tom Lovejoy is murdered by several of his own and Ezra Furst has declared himself the First Disciple of the Church of Lovejoy. Yes, Tom Lovejoy, who as a youngster wrote out on golden plates the religion he dreamed of, is murdered and martyred. This will be one of many examples of what YRH will come to call the "Fuck the Founding Father" syndrome, which becomes so much a part of The American People.

It takes a few years for word of what's going on in Oneida to trickle over to the ears of Ethel Prance, farther south and west in New Bliss, Ohio. All of it is heady stuff to a strong woman desirous of coupling, desirous of children, desirous of increasing her town's population, desirous of having her own way in a bigger arena. She figures she can do without all those committees, and put a little less emphasis on Jesus as blessing all activities, and be in charge of everything herself. She shivers as she establishes her house of free love in New Bliss, which she naturally can't resist calling Blissfulness. She calls herself the Foundress. She can tell she has a good product when one by one and two by two and three by three newcomers settle in New Bliss and sign on, even though they are members of Milton Prance's large extended family whom he has invited "to join in Convocation of our New Desires, as the great Transcendentalist Emerson has urged upon us."

But the existence of two neighboring New Bliss households embodying, in essence, free love can be nothing but trouble. Ethel just knows that all those boys next door are sleeping in the same beds and coupling with each other. She is right. They are all coupling with each other, at first simply lying in each other's arms, but these embranchments lead naturally to coupling fully and completely. No one inside Mrs. Sary Peyser's house makes much of it. Messie, who is familiar with the behavior of young boys in groups, smiles benevolently. Oh, boys do have crushes on each other, which occasionally presents problems when the crushes move around from boy to boy. Consistency is not a trait of youngsters. But all in all, what's going on is working well enough, just as it should in Ohio, where nobody thinks that anything much is wrong. That what is going on in Mrs. Sary Peyser's house is not antithetic to what John Noyes is espousing up there in Oneida is immaterial to Ethel Prance. What she smells in the full house next door is competition.

Apparently she hasn't noticed that the ambulatory amatory couplings in her own house are causing much more fuss. Many are the fits of screaming that waft through the New Bliss air from the House of Blissfulness. It's a wonder the neighborhood doesn't complain, but that may be because a few of the neighbors have joined Ethel's movement. Messie observes a number of people from around town dropping in on the Prances. Lucid and Messie try to shut the boys' ears to all the racket, but closing the windows doesn't work. When they're not fighting in the House of Blissfulness they're having sex, which of course is louder than the fighting.

Lucid determines that enough is enough. But how to approach this touchy subject? He is uncomfortable in Ethel Prance's presence. Each time she passes him on the street she grabs him in an embrace and invites him "over." Lately her kisses have come to involve her tongue and her saliva. Their last encounter elicited from her demure mumblings about "affiancement," whatever that is.

Matters come to a head when six of Ethel's adults kidnap six of Lucid's boys while they're out playing kickball. "I am just borrowing them," Ethel calls over to Lucid from her yard, waving her hand as if it was nothing. "I need them for our next Voluntary." Lucid, standing there helplessly, wonders if he should summon the Reverend Tighe. As he is starting toward the church at the end of the town green to do just that, Ethel bolts out and announces loudly, "I would not make a fuss if I were you. God is on my side. It is against the law for young boys to be kept in houses without parents."

Lucid hears the ring of Hooker vocabulary. He comprehends the position she is putting him in. He comprehends that in so casting her cards down on their connecting greensward she is endangering all the lives that he has come to love.

She turns back sweetly and yodels, "If I were you I would come and visit."

When the boys don't return for supper, Lucid pays a call.

"What do you want?" demands Milton Prance.

Ethel's father is standing in the frame of his front door, barring Lucid's entry with his own big frame. He is dressed in a flowing white gown adorned with gold braid and pearl buttons and billowing down from his shoulders is his cascading white hair. On that hair is perched the headdress of a Hopewell Indian chieftain, scarlet and orange feathers pointing up to heaven. Ethel, sans headdress, is wearing the same voluminous and she believes voluptuous robe, as is her sister-in-law, Millicent Fardue, a tall and skinny lady who has come from Akron with her husband and four grown unmarried sons, all gowned and gilded and headdressed, though with not so many feathers as Uncle Milton. They all stand in a phalanx confronting this new young man whom Milton may or may not be letting in. Twenty or so others, all dressed similarly, bring up the rear.

Let us recall that Milton Prance has studied abroad, in Copenhagen, in Scandinavia, in a part of the world where, even then, the exchange of bodily tempests is better coordinated into daily life. Let us recall that he studied with world-famous experts the important bones buried in Denmark's bogs, imbibing not only the excitement of such discoveries but also the dream of untold riches and fame. Had not the Drs. Thomsen and Worsaae been knighted by their country's sovereign and handsomely pensioned off for life? Had not their good student married the lovely flaxen-haired beauty related to one of them, with her huge voluptuous Scandinavian breasts (a trait he identified, from his own fieldwork, as indigenously Scandinavian)? And had she not deserted him after some dozen years in the New World of boredom and bonelessness, leaving him with a harridan of a daughter and a bit of her fortune "to muddle through with to the end of your dull and dreary life"?

Milton Prance is more than ready to embrace his daughter's House of Blissfulness. He will outdo the Danes, as he remembers them from his youth. He will out-Oneida Oneida. Free love, here he comes!

Lucid cannot sight his six young boys. When he inquires of them and declines Ethel Prance's invitation to enter, the door is shut in his face.

The "Voluntary" that Lucid and Messie watch through a side window astounds them. Its sheer perversity reminds them of Fruit Island. As far as they know, no one here has been infused with potions, though everyone is participating ambitiously. The participants seem very assured in what they direct their bodies to perform. There is not so much nervousness as one would expect, even in Ohio. They must have been practicing.

Milton Prance, now completely naked and featherless, his big ungainly body all covered in brown bumps and lumps, stands on a long raised platform on which sits an exceptionally large bed. He summons to the stage his three sons and their wives and Millicent Fardue's four sons and of course his daughter, Ethel, as well as several townspeople new to the neighborhood (yes, word is getting out). Each drops a plain white robe and approaches Milton in nakedness. He taps each head with a wand of startling heft, and each then goes to stand encircling the bed. Ethel, also a bit lumpy without her clothing, steps forward and lies down in the center, and leans back into the many pillows as if she is a queen.

"I choose first my brother Alfred," she proclaims loudly. She points to him.

Alfred, the youngest and best-looking, nervously steps forward.

Milton taps his head and he lies down with his sister.

Ethel lunges and kisses him full on the lips, to scattered applause from the crowd.

But wait. Alfred cannot achieve an erection. His impatient sister takes his penis in her hands and attempts to make it hard, which it soon is. Then she sits up and sits on it and Alfred begins to get into the swing of things. Ethel is not a quiet woman. Nor is the audience, increasingly more vocal.

"Gaze upon this wonderful act. Look! Look upon it!" Milton proudly announces. "We shall never have heaven till we can joyously witness this beautiful exhibition on our stage of life. Look upon it without shame!"

Oh, how this group now hollers its approval. Lucid is familiar with the mysteries of group dynamics.

Milton Prance removes his son and takes his place. He fucks his daughter. He has no trouble with his erection. He is beyond exhilarated with this discovery. If it takes fucking his own daughter to finally give him such a firm and strong and lasting erection, praise be to John H. Noyes.

"Atta girl!" Milton is heard to cry out several times.

"Daddy!" Ethel shrieks as another daughter-in-law, this one from Chicago and named Trish, leaps up and pushes Ethel out of the way and takes her place. Milton's violent arched lurchings and thrustings never miss a beat. Occasionally he leans over to kiss his sons, one of them Trish's husband.

Lucid watches (he has sent Messie home as "too young to witness this"). He sees his six young boys ushered in to kneel before the fucking couple. They are painted bronze, their faces covered with Hopewell markings. Each wears a crown of local apple blossoms. Each wears a loincloth and carries a small tomahawk. The first is summoned to strip as a woman appears to draw him into copulation.

Milton Prance bellows loudly when his orgasm is finally reached: "I dedicate my gism to John Noyes and his valiant pioneers in our neighbor Oneida!"

AN END TO BLISS

The next day at dawn Rev. Tighe comes to our door to return our six young boys. Their war paint is streaked and their bodies soiled. The Reverend will not look me in the eye. I inquire if anyone has complained about the ruckus last night, but he does not answer. Later in the morning a large gentleman in a black uniform arrives, identifying himself as "an officer of the law in this county." Behind him stands a stern woman, also in black, who the officer tells me is "in charge of orphaned children in this county." He says that we are to be evicted from this house, that I am not its rightful heir, that Messie and I must leave New Bliss this very night, and that the boys have been declared wards of the state and will be removed to the care of the Prance household next door. "Orphaned children must be placed in parented homes," the stern woman pronounces. "It is the law." They try to come inside but I prevent them. The officer says he will wait outside while the children gather their belongings, by which time he will be joined by other officers and they will enter by force.

Twenty boys have been living here. Last night ten of them ran away, frightened that fear has returned. The remaining ten are determined to fight. "This is our house!" they all yell. "Mrs. Sary said so! Forever and ever!" I cannot convince them that we have but moments to make our escape.

There are two rifles hanging on the wall over the mantel, and down they come, into the hands of two boys. Peter and Paul? John and James? I cannot keep all their names straight. Only Messie knows them all.

I try to take the guns away. I have never held a gun. I know that guns are of increasing importance and that I should by now be proficient with them. I know that in releasing my hold on these guns as they leave the house in the arms of my boys I am inviting death.

What ensues is an armed war between my boys and certain citizenry of New Bliss. Eight of the boys are wounded and are carried away howling by the police. The remaining two turn their rifles on themselves.

Messie has been shot dead by Miss Ethel Prance. She approaches me, still wearing her white robe. It is stained with blood and semen.

"You will come and live with us?" she asks somewhat sternly, implying that if I do not, it will not go well for me. Again she tries to take me in an embrace. I stand quiet and wordless.

Now she says awful things. I am sick and I am illegal and I am a molester of little boys and an "incentor" of little boys, and much else I need not catalogue. She offers me "one last time, salvation in my House of Blissfulness." She promises, "I will program a Voluntary just for you." When I still do not speak, she attempts to have me arrested. But the officer says I am free to go so long as I go now, and far away.

I lift up my dead Messie and head out. I bury him under his favorite wantag tree, in the dead of night when no one will see where he is laid to rest. I sneak back and set fire to the empty house of Mrs. Sary Peyser, a torchbearer again.

One of the boys catches me up under the rising moon. He has managed to escape. He has managed to collect Messie Voiceless's ashes in a tin box. I had buried him too close to the house. He takes my hand. He asks me to call him Messie too. When I start to cry he puts his arms around me tight. He is young and I no longer am. Getting us to our next chapter is now my goal and gives me strength.

DAME LADY HERMIA REACTS TRUE TO FORM

Why do you constantly do that? Why do you take a perfectly well-meaning experiment in social progress and manipulate and corrupt it into such vibrant hues of hate and horror? The Oneida Colony was, in essence, a lovely thing. Or it wanted to be. It lasted many decades, nigh unto the end of the century. So far as I have been able to discover, New Bliss, Ohio, ceases to exist, so far as extant records are concerned, by 1860. I have no idea what happened to it. One day it's there in the records and the next day it is not. If you are trying to intimate that New Bliss ceases its existence because of its failed attempt to emulate what obviously had only been heard about but not witnessed firsthand, i.e., an attempt at communal living with, yes, if you must call it that, "free" love, then that is one thing. But I am beginning to take note, and exception, to the way that you focus the entries in your history, which more and more strikes me as perverse and leaves very little to the benefit of any doubt. It is either perfection or nothing. No, I take that back. It is either homosexual or nothing, and by nothing I mean exclusion from your history. I know what you are trying to say—that we are where we are because of what we did once. It is just that you are so, well, heartlessly specific about this. No shades of gray for you! Perhaps that is your point, too. Indeed, perhaps I am coming to agree with you. And I do not like myself for it! Yet.

But rather than belabor my point, or your efforts, which despite my remarks I find riveting and extraordinarily illuminating, I will shut up once again, take a deep breath once again, and prepare myself for my next appearance, be it as narrator or as pain-in-your-arse, probably both.

My dearest Fred, carry on.

WESTWARD HO THE WAGONS!

Preceding and concurrent with the activities and disappearance of New Bliss is the journey across America and settling-in of Ezra Furst and his growing band of followers. We shall come to it soon enough; it is a hoary, hairy story, filled with holes and hopes, with much enmity and jealousies and vyings for control (seven Lovejoy brothers will wind up killing an eighth to obtain Tom's place at the head of God's line, only to be checkmated by Ezra). The mythologizing needs this respite before it commences its hardening into belief.

When Ezra comes to allow the release and sale of Tom Lovejoy's Bible to the public, it will be seen to include Tom's story of America's Indians as the remnant of the Lost Ten Tribes of Israel. When Milton Prance's Indian bones are eventually exhumed, ancient Hebrew phylacteries (or *tefillin*) will be found buried with them. Crucifixes were found as well, giving rise to the legend still believed by many that Christ Himself had come to the New World.

•

Everything you are about to learn concerning your most revered president is true and you are not going to believe it, or me when I say I was there.

Yes, I was there. I watched very carefully.

No, I could not get myself into Abe. My problem is that he was not consistent. He spurted furiously forward in his younger days, and then he would back off when he was too busy and then he would do nothing before starting up a bit here and there. I need consistency. By now I have discovered that to be the most important thing. The very essence of my existence is the consistency of yours.

"AND THE WAR CAME . . .": THE HOMOSEXUALITY OF ABRAHAM LINCOLN

As a youth Abraham Lincoln had sexual encounters with a number of boys, young men, and mentors. He went through puberty quite young. He was uninhibited in his sexuality with other males. He saw someone he wanted and he got him. It was no big deal to him, or to the others in these small Illinois frontier towns of New Salem and Springfield. Such actions were not unexpected among young men, or even younger lads; there were no other sexual outlets, certainly not with women. Men were much more likely to have emotional attachments and sexual experiences with other men, though they kept quiet about it, perhaps because it was so commonplace that it did not have to be discussed. In any event, Abe was not interested in women, and never would be.

His first partner was young Billy Greene, who was fifteen, and then Abner Ellis, seventeen. Both of them worked with eighteen-year-old Abe in a New Salem store. New Salem was a very tiny outpost and would fold up shortly after Abe moved to Springfield in 1837. He and Billy shared a cot and made good use of it. "When one turned over the other had to do likewise," Billy, who initiated the sex, would write. Billy was particularly enamored of Abe's thighs, which "were as perfect as a human being could be. He was well and firmly built." He particularly liked to stick his penis between those thighs. Abe had other encounters, with Horace White, Trunker Awll, Thurgood Franks, who was a slave, Michael Botter, Noble Vernoose, Cat Nottinks, Nat Grigsby, and Tom Simpson. These were all country kids and wouldn't count as important encounters if Billy and Abner and others hadn't followed. Abe and his law teacher, John Todd Stuart, perhaps the person most responsible for Abe's choice of law as a career, often polished off their studies with a sexual encounter. Similarly, Abe and one of his early law associates in Springfield, Henry C. Whitney, with whom he traveled on the local court circuit, often bunked together. "He slept in a short home-made yellow flannel undershirt and had nothing else on. I don't know certain if that was a constant habit or not, but that is what he slept in with me and I could see what he had to offer and we enjoyed each other. He didn't care where he slept or who he slept with. None of us did. If the bedmate was young and didn't smell too much for need of a bathe, we often fucked with each other before we went to sleep. It helps you sleep better. I would say something like 'I cannot sleep,' and Abe would say, 'Want to give me a poke?' " John G. Soto's tabulation of historical sources in *The Physical Lincoln Sourcebook* shows that Abe slept with at least eleven boys and men during his youth and adulthood.

His great awakening to the power of other male bodies to arouse him occurred when he and Billy Greene went off and joined the army to fight the uprising of the Black Hawk Indians in 1832. It was a short war and a small battalion. (Jefferson Davis was also one of the soldiers.) Abe was elected captain by acclamation, the first time such popular recognition came to him. It was also the first time such a wide variety of so many naked young men was visible around the clock. He was twenty-four years old. He was six feet four and weighed 214 pounds. He was still immature and unsure of his place in the world and his career. He was beginning to sense that his social graces were primitive and not sufficient for what might be out there for him. Joshua Speed, a rich man's son from Kentucky, would come along shortly and educate him mightily in these and other areas.

Joshua Speed will be the great love of Abe's younger years, indeed of his entire lifetime.

A man knows when the sight of another man interests, no, excites him. He may not understand it, or why it is occurring, or what to do about it, but he usually knows what he is looking at and how it makes him feel. True, nudity among men in our young country was a more natural thing then, but body parts, their sizes, their erotic content, are of little interest unless you know what it is you find yourself staring at too often. Of course men don't talk much about all this, but they know when they really want to see another man.

A hushmarket is what today would be called a gay area, a cruising area for meeting other men. The word itself, along with *hushmarked* for a gay person, disappeared very quickly after the arrival of *homosexual* in the late nineteenth century, perhaps because it was an unpopular word among those to whom it applied, just as *homosexual* itself would later become an uncomfortable word. Today these areas would include bars and beaches, hotels, streets, or entire neighborhoods. In the earliest years they were less visible— under certain trees or at distant farms or in remote fields or parks, often only at preordained nights on waterfronts; they were always in less fashionable areas where the more prominent would be less likely to be recognized.

But they were there. From the beginning of time, they were there. From the beginning of time, of people-in-groups and people-in-crowds, there are such places. Why, oh why, has it been impossible for us to accept such an obvious fact? That there is so little record of them is a testament to what must have been a nonstop effort bordering on the superhuman to eradicate all traces of their existence on the part of city fathers, and of course historians, and sadly, no doubt on the part of the hushmarkeds themselves. No town, or family, or hushmarked, wishes such information to be known.

There is an interesting local guide to male nudity by one "Adam Adornment" that is "published private" in 1830, "by the banks of the Wabash," and written by a man with a remarkable eye for observation of his fellow man. Adam Adornment writes, "men work together and when it is hot they work together naked as their births. There are traveling groups of men who ride to view such sights, going down the back roads where white men work the farms, or down other roads where Negro men are the preferred objects of inspection." Amazingly, these groups of gazetteers often travel under the banners of such organizations as temperance groups or various Christian alliances that are conducting studies along the lines of "God and the Working Man." Often these traveling men converse with the Working Man. Often they offer words, as it were, each to each, after the visitors stand for some time on the edge of the field noting who is who and who is noting whom back. Then arrangements are made for further discourse, usually at a campsite where the travelers are, well, camping out. Larger groups of men camp in the wilderness to be with each other exclusively and without interruption.

Men travel in groups for safety. A few of them are certainly armed. One thing that is abundantly clear is that there exists a network, haphazard and not particularly organized, but a network nevertheless, of the like-minded. There is little now that was not done then, determined though so many historians are to deny this. It is not much different today but for the numbers. And these fewer who are venturing forth with thumping nervous hearts into a relatively unknown field of public social activity are indeed courageous pioneers. There are laws for their arrest and even extinction on the books of many localities. No doubt they know this; for some no doubt it is part of the adventure. As year after year goes by, men are learning, somehow, to live with constant danger.

Men are not yet generally for sale to other men. They may own other men back home as slaves, but that is another matter. That hushies are not yet paying for each other could mean a number of things, the most important of which is that the sense of "wrong" is not controlling any sort of barter for choice, wrong usually connoting that one of the parties, or both, hates himself for what he's doing. Does this mean there was no sense of sinning, or fear of being blackmailed? Can the times be so innocent? Or so advanced? Answers to these questions remain, sadly, incomplete. This area of our social history joins the others we are enumerating on our journey as lacking their own decent historians.

Here is a circular letter from the spring of 1832:

"Dear Fellow Traveler,

"The summer is near upon us and your correspondent in Freshwater Depot, Kansas, is once again writing to enquire your interest in joining our group of friends for our annual holiday journey, this year by the back roads into our neighbor, Illinois. So popular was our tripping last year in our neighbor Missouri that this year we are prepared to accept several dozen gentlemen of manners and concern and also hardy-ness to camp outdoors for a week from August 23d. Please let the undersigned know by the mid-of-May whether you wish a place reserved among these gents, and biographical particulars you wish to share. Costs for all expenses will be equally divided. Last year they amounted only to some $4.00 total each."

The letter is signed "Dapper Dan."

It is known that Abraham Lincoln as a young man worked as a surveyor, traveling the back roads constantly, as did young George Washington. (It is a misnomer to call them "back roads." Few were the roads at all, back or forward.) No doubt he often came upon such groups of traveling men. And no doubt he came upon groups of the men they were observing.

From August 23 to 30, 1832, Dapper Dan and a group of twelve gentlemen of manners and concern and of course "hardy-ness" make their excursion to Illinois. The list includes "Abraham L." from New Salem. Abe has lost his first run for public office. He also for the first time has some cash in his pocket ($124.00) from his army enlistment in the Black Hawk War. He writes the following when he is nineteen and before he turns seriously to the study of the law.

•

I responded to "Dapper Dan" that I desired to journey with him.

He was not so old as I anticipated, not so much more than thirty years, with huge mustaches that almost covered the bottom half of his face. He laughed a great deal, which was agreeable at first. But after I heard him guffaw for several hours it seemed too hearty to be genuine. For myself, I found less to laugh about. It is uncomfortable laughing when one is learning so much about oneself.

The others appeared to be older, and men for whom the several dollars were not so arduous to part from. I think I was allowed to come for one dollar only because I am young. Many a hand I felt on my shoulder, clapping me a hello, and then falling down my back to my waist and then ending on my backside. I had to step away from many a hand. Although I was happy to talk to these fellows, one of whom came all the way from a northern Michigan territory I desired to hear about, —he says it is most growing fast there in northern Michigan—, talking is one thing and going off into the trees is another. And many are so lacking in experience of the world as to make what they have to say of little interest to me; I have enough of little interest about myself as it is!

By day all went well. We traveled and saw many a worker. I found it not so interesting as my companions claimed. To watch others work so hard is not a pleasure, be they naked or not. Slaves particularly are difficult to witness because they are not free. But until I am more certain of myself in my own mind, I have learned not to express an opinion as radical as this!

Nighttime was more troublesome. Then the liquor came out to coerce the wants of lonely men into fulfillments of which not all wished to partake. It was known almost immediately that I was "not an easy lad." I might have been more so for one or two of them but for the raw hunger visible on their faces. Surely it must be possible to maintain balance and equilibrium as one seeks companionship. I think that what I see there was naught more than I have seen everywhere: life is hard and painful and for two people to find each other in some sort of harmony and comfort and, yes, passion is not easily achieved. This makes me worry for myself, whatever my hungers settle down to be.

The last night out was "banquet night," which sounded safe enough.

Our group was joined by other groups of similar travelers, as if by pre-arrangement with other Dapper Dans. There must have been near a hundred of us, a formidable lot. It was a pitch-black night with rain approaching when our wagons deposited us by a roaring bonfire in some unfamiliar woods. Liquor and food and farting and belching were the order of the early evening hours. I had to smile at some of the couplings sneaking off: for example, mister six foot six with mister five foot naught. Some several guests played on banjos and sang songs of lost loves found and found loves lost, and occasionally something more spirited about new days coming. The moon did appear, and more and more hungry fellows withdrew further into the forest.

After a long while, during which time the rest of us stared more at the ground than at each other, our thoughts for conversation having long since petered out, a long table came into our midst carried by four naked muscled Negroes. Drumbeats from somewhere announced them so that many of the fellows returned from behind the bushes and trees. Everyone rushed to gather round the table, as if they knew in advance what I was now to witness.

A young Negro boy, no older than I when Billy Greene and I first partook of each other, was led out from the woods and placed upon this table. Then the four Negro men proceeded to perform on him. I find it difficult to detail more than this. It was both repellent and exciting for me to watch. I knew what those men's hands upon my bottom were feeling for, but now I could see in detail what use hungry human equipment can be put to. I have known for some time that my own member is well suited for competition. Playing around with Billy and Abner showed me that. But here was a competition that most men would lose. It was compelling to watch, no matter the size. I could not take my eyes from the entire event. Indeed it brought to mind the several times I begged Old Joe Watkins to let me watch his stud stallion perform upon a mare. I could not take my eyes off that either, and when it was over wished to witness it again.

Yet I also felt my heart go out to that young lad. His pleasure did not seem as great as that of his audience. I wondered if he had choice in this matter. If he had been forced to perform, that would be a painful fact to know. Later I asked Dapper Dan and he guffawed yet again and said, "Oh Mr. Abraham L., do not concern yourself with the petty problems of our black-skinned slaves."

During that week we slept outdoors and swam naked in a lake. We bathed in front of each other. We were all even more visible to each other than even in my Army encampment. I have seen many men naked. But to see many men washing their genitals with soap and water, or doing the same to others, and the rest of the crowd looking on with great interest, and noting as well the many erections, including my own, was educational for me in ways I had suspected but not considered. I did not know how to integrate this information about myself as well as about this world, for it was indeed another world. I even noted penises shorn of their foreskins. I assumed their possessors were Hebrew. I had not met Hebrews before, in any company. The young man from northern Michigan must have been one. How did a Hebrew get to northern Michigan? I would have asked him had he not been so eager for my friendship.

Most of the naked bodies parading around would have improved with clothes to cover them. Several of them, though, were mighty men, big and burly and hairy, which I confess I found exciting. I had never seen bodies so covered in hair. My own body is so pale, my frame extended beyond necessity. I stared hard at one man without consciousness that I was doing so until his penis erected as he stared right back at mine in its similar state. He tried to converse with me later. Again, my inability to find words and thoughts to exchange rendered me all but mute. I had been day-dreaming of burrowing my face into all that hair upon his chest.

In all, my excitements were satisfied several times in hasty ways at the hands of a few men who wanted to "love" me and to take me back home with them to wherever they were from. I became confused. I too am lonely. I want to go forward into life but know not which road leads where. But how can a man swear eternal love on such swift terms for a fellow man?

There are many questions akin to this that the trip forced my tired brain to consider. What joins men in unity? Is it only that our penises erect themselves, and relieve themselves and then their flaccid owners pass on? To what?

I do not wish to live such a life.

Surely there is a better life for men like me to live. What means "men like me"?

How do I find it, and with whom, for certainly I do not wish to live my life alone.

I began to realize the power that these feelings can assume in those who own them.

I would dearly like a life free from secrets.

The next day on our continuing journey we saw the young Negro hanging from a tree. He was being cut down by a group of angry white men who heaved his body on a burning pyre. The four older Negroes were in chains awaiting a similar fate. They were much ridiculed and called "Niggers" and "Rent-Marys." I want to stop to find some sense here but Dapper Dan is quick to restrain me and hustle his group along with much more speed. I notice that none of the gentlemen could refrain from looking upon this scene.

I had thought once, when dreaming of my election to some office, that I would fight for the freedom of one as the same as the freedom of all.

I begin to see this will not be possible.

We are not all the same, at least so that this can be told out loud.

In battles and in victories one must make choices. I know that. But what if you know that the choice you make is somehow wrong?

JOSHUA SPEED'S REMINISCENCES
OF ABRAHAM LINCOLN

I write this in memory of what was and might have been. I write this as a beaten man. My once Abraham has been taken from us, and the memories I hoped were gone come flooding back still. The peace I thought I had away from him I have not, still these long years later. I guess I will never have it. It is with trembling that I confront the terrible sadness that remains in this. For all these years I believed I had made myself safe, had made the right and only choice, and I sequestered myself away from the world lest it discover the reality of what we, and I, had done. And now, as death is all that is left to me, this safety still remains not to be so.

Billy Greene sent him to me. In New Salem, Billy was a partner in his store with Abner Ellis, who was partner with me in Springfield, in my store. We all fucked with each other at one time or other. Indeed, the spare bed I had was home to Abner or Billy, or both, when they were in Springfield. Billy was younger by several years than Abraham and much enamored of him, particularly his thighs, which he extolled as perfect to fit his cock between. They were all New Salem boys, Billy and Abner and Abraham. Abner's father in fact did business with my family in Kentucky. When Abraham joined me, I was happy for it. I admit it. I sought him. I had heard him speak. I could tell he was marked for great things. He already had done important political work, like getting Springfield made our capital.

From the first night we met I held him in my arms, each night for going on four years. And he held me in his arms even tighter. We were both big strapping young men and my big bed took quite a beating. If Billy came upon us, or Abner, in the middle of our occupations, they would throw a pillow at us. Oh, how we laughed, all of us. Those were happy days.

Abraham was twenty-eight. I was twenty-two.

But I was older. I had lived in many ways that he had not. It was for me to take him into society, and even dress him, early on.

His long bones and muscles did not always join together properly. It often hurt him just to stand. To ride a horse from town to town to trials in various county courthouses was agony. No, he never complained, not even to me. I could tell, though, in our bed, where it was hard for him to shield his discomforts as he tossed in bad dreams or attempts to find sleep. Then I would get up and fetch Dr. Mervin's Extended Elixir and rub him down until he could sleep. I could tell he was finally asleep only when his hand, which was wrapped around mine in his unease, slowly released its grip. I confess that I looked forward to his attacks of spasm so I could tame them down, and tame him as he slept beside me, so handsome to me then especially in his need, even in his melancholy and his gloom that others claimed made him a sad-looking man. Some saw him as a long, gawky, shapeless man. Some told me they thought him ugly, which I never did, although I wondered how I came to entertain him so passionately, forgetting that he was muscular and lithe and supple like a willow tree or a birch. He never asked that anything be extended to him especially. Even when we loved, he never specified a favorite means or a more comfortable position, content to go along with my own desires in this matter. I do know that all his physical needs, his sexual wants, his bad back, his various ailments, were not attended to much by others after I left him. Mary was only interested in Mary. He put up with the pain of her—and yes, the pain from the loss of me—for the rest of his life.

Yes, I left him. I was not so kind to him as I should have been. I was punished for that for the rest of my life, to use those pathetic words again. For the rest of my life.

He was so needy. That was attractive to me, his inexperience so childlike. But after a while it became annoying, and a burden I did not know how to carry. I could not give him what he wanted, whatever precisely that might be, for neither of us knew. We were both walking on unknown ground. Perhaps I was the more confused of us two; we could not live like this; we had to get married, each of us. Neither of us knew what to do about that, or about each other. Where were we going? Where could we go? He was just starting his legal career. How could he, and we, fail to be seen for what we were and what we did? How could he succeed with the world knowing what we were and did? He would not answer any of these questions I demanded we talk about. It was almost as if he did not care, as if my concerns were just bits of dander to be brushed away. Yes, it turned out I was the more confused and Abe was never confused about anything in his entire lifetime!

No two men were ever so intimate. I can say that now. I knew it then, for a few years. He knew it until the day he died. I did not. I did not. Now I wish I had.

He fucked me immediately. And I immediately invited him to live with me. And he immediately accepted. Springfield was a town of very few women and many young men and much fucking among us all over the place. There was this electricity in the very air. And there was electricity between Abe and me and we both knew it. I made him tell me all the boys he'd sexed with and he questioned me about mine, almost as if I were on the witness stand. It turned out he'd had more than I had! When I mentioned a woman or two, whores I'd visited, he said he wanted one, and would I take him with me next time. I wouldn't, and he went anyway, and had not enough money to pay her, so he left even though she offered herself anyway. It was I who later gave him syphilis, not the whore whom I have heard blamed for this.

He was like a great big boy in my arms. I called him my countess because I thought it suited him, a man so tall and seeking the deference of others. I could picture a tiara perched upon his head. "You would be most dashing in a regal gown, with a train. Oh, yes, with a train!" He did not like me to talk this way. He kissed me when I teased him, to shut my mouth. He would grab me up in his long arms' embrace, and like a clinging vine. He was needy of affection, and demanding of it too, in his intense and quiet way.

Sometimes I think I was there but to be both mother and father to him, so that when he grew up, which he did in our bed and in our embraces and with his cock in me, or mine in him, he could go out and stand as tall as he really was. When I teased him he would get so riled up he would pound upon me as if I were a drum. Then I would hold his body at bay and bend to kiss his face, his mole touching the tip of my tongue as I licked at his rough skin. He had no beard yet. That came later, and while it was I suggested it, I did not much favor it.

But I had long since forsaken his kisses by then. I separated myself from him for many years. I was a fool. We both were. Both our marriages were as barren of love as we had feared. Had I not grown too hard a man to cry, I would cry now, although it is too late.

He was rarely one for pitying himself or his beginnings, though he never forgot their poverty. When I took him to my family's home, he could not believe its luxury, or that any family could be as old as ours, seven generations away from Great Britain. "That people live like this!" Again he cross-examined me, question after question, about my upbringing, and every member of my family, all my ten brothers and sisters, and what it was like to be rich. Always he was stingy about himself. I tried to question him just as pointedly but he was a clever one. Oh, I had seen him speak. I knew something of his style, tall, upright, so honest that it hurt, because I could tell such honesty came only from hurt. I could never be so honest! But what he told the world was his great rhetoric laced with sentiment, and what he would not talk about was the pain.

You might say I knew in advance what I was out to get, and got it, and from that first fuck determined to keep it only as long as I liked it. That has always been my way. I always had only what I wanted for only as long as I wanted it. "Mighty fine" is how he sighed sometime after we finished bringing each other to pleasure. He was not more adept than this for talking about what we had done. So when we were losing each other because of me, nei-ther of us knew how to talk about it.

I asked him once, "How many others are there like us, do you think?"

He answered, "I think that many things that feel so fine are ruled pecu-liar for that reason, and by those who cannot feel so fine."

I said, "I know full well there are many like us. I know full well."

I do not think he thought us other, as I did. We might suffer from what he sometimes called our "nervous debility," but he also pronounced this "ut-terly harmless." For he was only one, within and without, one whole person undivided and unable to think otherwise. That is why he could not bear to conceive much less allow what he called "a house divided."

He became exceptionally able to think for himself and for his needs. Like so many who come from the poor, he knew how to find food when he was hungry.

Once he said to me, "Speed, if there are so many others like us, perhaps they need a lawyer." This was his humor, but as with everything he said there was a part of heavier weight. He was concerned about the rights of all. He did not think that hushmarkeds lacked rights. I knew we never would have rights. We were too invisible to have rights.

"Could you be our Jesus, to lead us to the world of glory?" I once asked, knowing full well he believed in God only as He who created the world and then abandoned us.

"It is not right to have to hide" was all he said. "What law, exactly, has been broken?" He would never join any religion.

We both worried for each other. We both shared our one great burden. We knew we were meant to marry. When our feelings about this tried to find their way into words, he closed his eyes rather than look at me. But after a time he would lean forward and kiss me. His lips were rough, as if a carpenter were needed to plane them smooth. And then we would do with each other that which we were frightened of with women. And fearing it so much made us perform on each other with even more boisterousness, and yes, love, as if it were ours alone, for now. But underneath, that was the question always on our minds. What would happen next? We tried to console each other that all would be fine, that each of us was ready for what we felt we had to do.

He let me love him. I am not certain he knew the effect he achieved on me. No, that is not true. He knew well and good what effect he achieved, on me and others, and he knew how to effect it silently and without a comment. This was an amazing gift I have noted in no other, this ability to possess a want, a need, and to obtain it without expressing or demanding it.

In the end, he wanted all his slaves to be free.

THE END OF A LOVE AFFAIR

Between 1837 and 1842, Abraham Lincoln and Joshua Speed are lovers. Springfield, just over twenty years old itself, is a small place of hardly several thousand mostly men who come, as Abe does, to start their lives. Indeed, as the young and growing San Francisco will shortly be for the young Samuel Clemens, many young men come here just to be with a lot of other young men.

Surely their relationship must have been known, witnessed, talked about. How could it have escaped the notice of customers, women coming in to do the cleaning and laundry, to wash the sheets? Such a deep friendship must indeed have been known, and even accepted, by many a friend and neighbor and fellow citizen.

The Speeds are a wealthy Kentucky family. Joshua is trying his hand at running a dry goods store as an experimental lark, trying out "trade" before he decides on this or something else, which is what it will be when he elects, like Abe, the law. Because of Joshua, new shirts come to Abe, and new shoes, and enough food, and a warm home, no small gifts for someone who has always been so cold and hungry. They will also sleep in a big, wide, clean bed, another luxury for Abe. He is taken into society as well. But more than any of this, Abe has obviously been ready to fall into another man's arms and stay there. The desire for warmth involves more than just a big wide bed, wood in a fireplace or coal in a stove, and two or three square meals a day.

What happens, then, to end this friendship, at least the sexual part of it, and separate Lincoln and Speed, and send Lincoln into marriage with Mary Todd, a woman he certainly does not love?

Speed determines it is time to leave Springfield, sell the store, and return home. His father has died and his mother has asked for him and indeed has inquired with growing persistence why he remains a bachelor. He conveys this news to Abe on January 1, 1841. Abe's response is awful. He has a nervous breakdown. Indeed, it appears that he has several, perhaps three, no sooner recovering from one than another replaces it. Speed finds him several times with knives and weapons, as well as strong medicines, all of which he removes. "Lincoln went crazy," he writes. "It was terrible." He takes him back to Kentucky and there for many months he nurses his friend back to health. They even take an eight-day Mississippi boat trip, and return to stay at a friend's house in Springfield, where there had once been happiness and a touch of permanence. Joshua stays with Abe for many months, neither of them ostensibly performing any business but to be with each other.

Then Joshua does a terrible thing. He takes Abe to a hushmarket. The two men were back again at the Speed mansion. They had been discussing Joshua's marriage to an orphan, Fanny Henning, consoling each other that, yes, it is now the right thing to do and not so fearsome. Joshua takes him to a gathering of hushmarkeds in a tavern on the other side of Louisville. There Abe sees Joshua embrace another man and kiss him passionately in a far corner and then go off with him to a private room upstairs. "I was not accustomed to such feelings of deprivation and jealousy as I knew that night," he is to write to Joshua many years later. Abe makes haste to return to Springfield.

What transpires for many years to come is a fitful correspondence between them, with emotions couched in heavy armor, as Abe attempts, at first painfully and feebly, to concentrate on the law and his career in politics. Of this period Abe writes, "I am now the most miserable man living. If what I feel were equally distributed to the whole human family, there would not be one cheerful face on earth. Whether I shall ever be better I cannot tell; I awfully forbode I shall not. To remain as I am is impossible; I must die or be better, it appears to me."

Joshua weds Fanny and writes to Abe that he has consummated the marriage successfully. He is lying. Abe conveys his congratulations, particularly about the successful consummation. Speed will never consummate his marriage with Fanny. Abe, of course, must now marry the unpleasant Mary. If Joshua can fuck a woman, then Abe can, too. He will in fact impregnate Mary on their wedding night, and have four sons, and constantly invite Joshua and Fanny to visit them in Springfield, and then in Washington, but to no avail. Joshua refuses all invitations or ignores them altogether. Abe will offer Joshua positions in his government (one of Joshua's brothers will accept one of these), again to be refused. Many of their letters appear to have disappeared. Like Mrs. Melville and Martha Washington, who destroyed all the evidence of their husbands' homosexual yearnings, Mary Lincoln destroyed a large number of her husband's papers. How long she'd known, and how much, we can only guess. One thing is certain: she did not like Speed, never had, and she was unfriendly to and suspicious of Abe's many close male friends over the years. Just seeing Abe with one of them could lead her to one of her punishing orgies of riotous consumer spending, almost, as it were, to pay him back. She may not have known, but she knew.

No sooner is Speed married than he commences his many years of creating a new narrative to deny the old one. His version of how they met is far from what transpired. For one thing, he tells William Herndon, Lincoln's first biographer and his law partner (who had his own reasons for protecting Abe's sexual history, of which he was more than aware), and hence the world, only that Abe showed up one day, a perfect stranger who could not afford a room, or a mattress, or indeed a sheet. Why someone who had been the lover of the president of the United States could not live with this fact and indeed cherish it would today mark Joshua Speed as a very strange man indeed.

Speed will write to Herndon, "One thing is plainly discernable—if I had not been married & happy—far more happy than I ever expected to be—He would not have married."

He will write in his *Reminiscences*: "This thought occurred to me while gazing upon Abe in his coffin. This lie of mine."

THE PENIS OF JOHN WILKES BOOTH

Among Speed's papers is a drawing identified as "the penis of John Wilkes Booth." The penis is markedly bent, so that it must have been awkward, even painful, for Booth to use it in normal positions of insertion. This abnormality of Booth's was also noted on the autopsy after his hanging (bodies in rigor mortis often have erections), validating the drawing among Speed's papers and his descriptive notes underneath remarking on this physical deviance. One can only assume it was drawn by Speed, both because the handwriting is his and because of the scrawled words of greeting, "For Abe: How about this for a twisted fellow? Your ever alert Audubon, JS." Was there another copy that he sent to Abe?

Papers and interviews with family members turned over to the government by one of Booth's brothers indicate that Booth spoke of his torment from his malformed penis. "I hide myself when I am with another, lest they laugh or run away. Some become so frightened when they see it that they call me 'Devil!' and I am forced to bind them to a post to keep them near to me so I can love them." He writes this to his older brother, the great actor Edwin Booth, who, on several occasions, was called upon to extricate his brother from the results of his brutal behavior.

That he does more than bind them is also confided to Edwin. "Like many others I almost killed him not so much because he laughed at me, or because I performed on him acts he were not accustomed to, but because my cock with its wretched hook did him internal injury, so that blood came spurting out his rectum. I was worried he would soon be dead from this cause and thought I best try to end his agony more quickly. But he pulled himself up and ran away. How am I, with this, like this, ever to love, ever to hope to love, ever to have a person of my own?"

In Speed's own handwriting: "He caused me much lost blood. It was vanity on my part to believe, as he claimed, his extreme fondness for older men."

Such abnormal curvature of the penis will become known as Peyronie's disease. It is caused by the buildup in the soft tissue of hardened fibrous lesions that develop under the skin of the penis. The cause of this fibrous tissue is unknown, but was thought to be caused by trauma or injury to the penis through sexual activity. It is now considered to be an autoimmune disease, meaning that the body is attacking itself. The Underlying Condition is an autoimmune disease too. Peyronie's only gets worse and makes intercourse difficult, painful, or impossible, much less erections. The stronger the erection, the more acute the pain.

Abe, of course, knows none of this.

Lincoln's third and final visit to a gathering place for hushmarkeds is to a room in the Willard Hotel, just around the corner from the White House. A special suite is arranged for a Mr. Brown. Abe by now has been unhappily married for twenty-three years, a marriage he knew before he entered it that he shouldn't make, a marriage that is a hideous parody of that word and institution and that ruins every minute of his life he spends with Mary Todd Lincoln.

He is fifty-one years old, our president, when on the eve of his second inauguration he agrees to meet Joshua Speed, who arranged for the room.

WILKES AND THE FATAL MEETING

John Wilkes Booth was born in 1838, a year after Joshua and Abe began their own relationship.

He was not tall, not as tall as everyone then and forever after thinks he is, or really should have been (after all, he murdered such an important person; surely a shrimp couldn't have done all that leaping onto the stage); but no, he is not tall at all. He is only five feet eight inches, at the most. Mind, he wears lifts in his shoes. Even the tall ones do, like his brother and father, each more famous than he, each, he knows, a better actor than he; but with his lifts and his ambitious determination to remove the president of the United States, he can become, to his own mind certainly, a much taller person indeed.

He has many ideas about how to do it. They are not so well thought out as they should be, but he doesn't know that, although he is twenty-seven years old. Is he dumb, perhaps, not to have figured his plan out to a degree that might give it half a chance of succeeding and him a chance of surviving? But he always was a spoiled kid who did just what he wanted. Doing what he wants to do will certainly change history, which is what he wants to do. But that's just it. He doesn't know how he wants it changed beyond getting rid of all the niggers. He doesn't realize that's not enough. So in this sense, the sense that he has this one bold notion, to eliminate the president, like everything else in his life he will have enough but not enough.

He is of course crazy. Historians haven't known what to do with him, because he left so little beyond his actions to speak for him, for his heart, for his dreams, for his *reasons* for doing what he did, so as usual, and as we've seen again and again, and as we'll continue to see, our historymongers refrain from naming the obvious truth. There are holes miles wide in every history written of his terrible deed, so many questions unanswered. Killing Abe does what? Getting rid of all the niggers accomplishes what? How do you get rid of them? What do you do with them? Send them all off somewhere? Then what? Does he really think the world will be a better place for him then? Who will do all the work? Who will look after well-enough-born people like him, even with their crooked cocks?

And what has been so lacking in his world, anyway? He is handsome and talented and as rich as he wants to be if he works regularly, performing for the worshipful crowds of women around the country who are his greatest fans. A doctor in Philadelphia told him he'd seen other cocks like his and it was possible to live with them, depending on what you did or didn't do with it. "Gentleness is all, I would suggest to you, my dear man, in sex as in love as in life."

In the future such a deed as he is planning, executed successfully or not, would immediately bring the charge that "ulterior forces" are involved. Foreign enemies, perhaps. Someone(s) dreadfully and terribly rich who hunger ravenously for power. At the very least, associates in the crime who are not so ragtag as the ones caught and punished after Lincoln is murdered. What a motley crew of misfits!

"Niggers out!"

That's all it seems to be about. Get rid of the niggers.

When does the prank turn from cogitation to all systems go? What pulls the trigger in the mind of this Wilkes, who doesn't even go by his first name?

As it all stands now, still stands now, after an enormous number of books about it, it doesn't seem enough, doesn't add up. What aren't we seeing? What's missing? Motive? Enough of a motive actually to murder the president? Is it enough just to call this Wilkes crazy? Deranged? A crazy young actor playing a mad Richard or an obsessed Macbeth or Othello off the stage as well as on? What about all of the others?

Who is this Davey Herold who hangs around Wilkes like a lapdog, an idolizer, a fraternity pledge, a thing, a very slave himself, who never leaves his side even when he knows that if he remains he won't get out alive? What's he about, this Davey Herold?

Who is this Lewis Powell who is so magnificent in his handsomeness, to equal Wilkes in this regard, indeed to surpass him? He is a young Marlon Brando, broodingly posing all over the place, even in prison as he awaits the gallows. Without question he'd be a movie star today the minute a casting director caught any sight of him. What's he about, this Lewis Powell?

What he is about is that he is the beloved of John Wilkes Booth. Why has no one ever fathomed this fact? These two handsome, strapping, indeed gorgeous men, the only attractive couple in this ragtag lot, are bound to each other in a tortured way that neither understands nor can speak about. The brooding referred to as Powell's dominant mien belongs to a man trapped by forces that can only silence him. He has fucked up his assignment to render the vice president, Andrew Johnson, unto death; he has never been much successful at anything except being pretty. As he faces death, he welcomes it. That brooding stare says as much as "You will never know and I will never have to tell you." It is said that he and Booth have known each other for a number of years, ever since Powell, as a handsome Confederate soldier, saw a photo in a newspaper of Booth, a handsome actor appearing that very night, and went to see the production. He was so taken with Wilkes that he went backstage and introduced himself, thus commencing this "friendship."

These six main conspirators, Herold, Powell, Samuel Arnold, Michael O'Laughlin, Edman Spangler, George Atzerodt, how are they all connected? To this day no one seems to know. Was it really so helter-skelter as it has been made to sound? They all look much of a muchness. A certain look. Acceptable-looking. Except for Powell and Booth, nondescript. To this day we don't know how they all met and/or were connected to Wilkes. A couple were perhaps friends from school days. None of them appeared to have strong political beliefs about anything. Did he seek them out? Was he paying them? Why did they join him? If they did join him. How did they all wind up dying for his misguided deed? Once again: it just doesn't add up. Why is so little known, from then and until this day, about this group as a group? Everything written about them is unconvincing.

It is at this last meeting between Joshua Speed and Abraham Lincoln in this Washington hotel that Lincoln meets John Wilkes Booth. Amazingly, hideously, Speed has brought Booth along as "an inauguration present" for the newly reelected president. If Abe still longed for a return to Joshua's arms—for indeed he had never stopped thinking about him over all these years—then this night must have been a nightmare. Speed's notes accompanying his penis sketch allow us to fill in some blanks. "I told Abe that we were two old men, and here was a youthful ass to fuck, enjoy it! I was astounded by his tears. It was as if he were that child again who came into my arms that day in Springfield when we both were young. He was so needy for my love then, and apparently still. I envy any man who can love so deep and long. Abe whispered to me now, 'Oh, Joshua, what you have not learned about the human heart! You who left me for Fanny, whom you never loved and lied to me about it, you who in my very sight gave yourself to another man, and now this—do you not understand how such acts warp and destroy the love I've managed to hold in my heart for you?'"

Speed scrawls his defense in handwriting that is blotched by tears: "I believe he said these things to wound. It was his own growing ambition that rent us apart! I wrote to him once, 'You want a lifetime of importance and I do not. You want a place in the sun and I do not. You want others to hear your voice and I want mine to be a quiet one. I could not say nay to your desires in these regards.' All these were lies."

And then Speed writes in bolder script, "I only brought Booth to be looked at, for he was most unusually endowed. Abe had told me he admired his acting. I brought him to be a treat to look at! Yes, I had thoughts of the three of us naked together. Yes, as old as we both were I wished to see Abe naked again. My life had been a sham of everything and he was the best I ever had. But Abe dismissed him, demanded that he remove himself immediately from the room. Booth did not take kindly to such treatment. This act, of his, of mine, of ours, is what sealed Abe's fate."

•

Lincoln is murdered on the night of April 14, 1865. That he, "the leading actor in the greatest and stormiest drama known to real history's stage," as Walt wrote, "should sit there and be so completely interested and absorbed in those human jackstraws, moving about with their silly little gestures, foreign spirit, and flatulent text," with the audience watching "the scenes of a piece that make not the slightest call on either the moral, emotional, aesthetic, or spiritual nature," while "the actual murder transpired with the quiet and simplicity of any commonest occurrence—the bursting of a bud or pod in the growth of vegetation, for instance" is not the complete story. There is a different story, known to Lincoln, Speed, and Whitman. But the times, ah yes, the times, always the times, never allow the whole truth to be revealed.

Walt Whitman knows John Wilkes Booth, the murderer, "his face of statuesque beauty." He knows that Booth, an actor, hounded the boys and young men in the acting companies he performed with, hounded and seduced them. *Seduced* is too kind a word. There are dead bodies along the routes of Booth's theatrical tours, missing kids who aren't found because Wilkes disposes of them. He burns them up. One or two he only butchers into pieces. Several are older men. By the time he murders Lincoln, he doesn't care if he gets caught. His dash for freedom is haphazard, twisted ankle or not. *"Sic semper tyrannis!"* he shouts at Ford's Theater, but the end of tyranny does not mean Lincoln, the obvious interpretation. Like the serial killer grateful for the electric chair as the end to his miserable contortions, John Wilkes Booth, as he performs his greatest role on the stage of history, is finally able to play a part for which his talent rewards him fully and completely, with the self-immolation that his misery longs for.

Yes, Walt knew of Booth's activities. Walt certainly knew of the world of young boys, having been sent packing by angry parents of a Long Island school or two for being too attentive to their offspring. Walt had even been interviewed (and rejected) by the Milton Academy, north of Baltimore, one of the boarding schools to which the young Wilkes was shipped off. "Oh, wretched transpoiler of the air I breathe, oh you of poison'd thought and deed" is an early barb of complaint aimed but not sent to the principal of a school in the Menemsha Marbledale Pequod district of Nassau, Long Island. Yes, Walt knew this world of young boys and their educators and their despoilers. And their protectors of which he considered himself to be one.

THE FINAL LOVE, THE FINAL WORDS

Abe had written: "I wish a certain knowledge to be known that there was no duplicity, a word itself that pains me, for I meant no double motives to my actions, but that the man himself, your brother and my dearest precious friend, had and held all of which my friendship was capable. I believe he does know this and that he too felt the same and that he too kept his secret from the world all these years."

These are the great man's words. They were written to Joshua's sister Susan some years after the two men parted and she, who had been half in love with Abe herself, demanded to know why.

Abe's final lover had been Captain David V. Derickson, of Company K, 150th Regiment, Pennsylvania Volunteers, Second Regiment, Bucktail Brigade, who was chosen by Abe to be his bodyguard. Captain Derickson was a twice-married man (his first wife died) who had fathered nine children by the time he began his relationship with Lincoln. He was five feet nine inches tall, with a husky build, and at forty-four was nine years younger than the president, with whom he slept in the White House when Mary was not in residence, and whom he accompanied everywhere else. These facts are not unknown and indeed were commented upon in local gossip columns of the day. The affair lasted about eight months, ending amicably, the captain requesting a transfer, which Lincoln granted along with a promotion.

The duration of their love affair, during 1862–1863, coincided with some of the worst battles and casualties of the Civil War.

"Such was the War," Walt writes. "It was not a quadrille in a ball-room." No, the real war will never get in the books.

Nothing became Lincoln more than his removal from life. Nothing ensured his belovedness more than his murder. It took John Wilkes Booth, a hustler, to make Abe into a god.

In his Second Inaugural Address, Abraham Lincoln said, "Both parties deprecated war, but one of them would make war rather than let the nation survive, and the other would accept war rather than let it perish, and the war came."

THE CIVIL WAR

The Civil War is the single most hideous event that ever happens to The American People.

The Civil War is one of the bloodiest, meanest wars in human history.

Six hundred and thirty thousand Americans die at the hands of other Americans. "And this is surely an undercount," writes James M. McPherson, "for the figure of 258,000 Confederate war dead is arrived at from incomplete data and does not include the unknown (and unknowable) number of Southern civilian deaths indirectly caused by the ravages of disease, exposure, malnutrition, and inevitable disruption of a war that was fought mostly in the South and destroyed much of the Southern infrastructure." Fifty-one thousand are killed at the Battle of Gettysburg alone, which John Rhodehamel describes as "the deadliest encounter in American history and the biggest military encounter fought in the Western Hemisphere. It is our Waterloo, our Stalingrad."

The Civil War is the supreme manifestation of everything that was, is, and will continue to be appalling about America and The American People. That so many volumes by so many "intelligent" writers should claim this internecine bloodbath as some sort of noble enterprise is unbearable. Yes, it ended slavery, but did it really?

America from the Civil War on becomes the America we know now. By the end of the Civil War, The American People commence becoming greedier, more idealistic, more ambitious, smarter, ceaselessly *more*, more innovators and accumulators of bank accounts and progenitors of children and everything else under the sun. There is much obsession for land. There is little visible desire by anyone to consciously do the right thing, after all, and at last.

What is it about this war that unleashes such energies, pent up or newly formed? Is guilt the subtext, from brothers murdering so many brothers? As if by ambition and enterprise alone a past could be buried, the foundation, true, of a better future, but a cursed foundation nevertheless?

As with all pasts, it will never be buried, no matter how great any good fortune to emerge from it or how high the golden temples to be built on hills.

No one considers this: that the whole point about the Civil War is Hate. Men were told to go out and murder each other and they did so with the fervor of righteousness they never knew they possessed. That it was about freeing black people was almost beside the point: most soldiers didn't care about slavery. It was just an excuse to go out and kill. It's amazing how many turned out willingly to fight their own. Releasing years, perhaps even centuries, of pent-up energies was the result.

Such hate as lay at its rotten core, and in too many hearts—where did all that come from?

Did we see this coming, all this hate? Were we warned of it, all this hate? Could we not have seen it coming and aborted it, all this hate?

Could no one see that it's a war that need not have happened? Thinking like this is considered naïve. But no war should ever happen.

And does it still remain, this hate?

We should never stop talking about the Civil War. It's what made us what we are today. It did not unite us, however much it's proclaimed that this is what it did. Brothers murdered their brothers. Some 630,000 men died in battle. What a hateful people we are visibly turning out to be. Or were we like this from the very beginning and we didn't notice? Had Puritanism served a worthwhile cause after all?

"The first Battle of Bull Run in August 1861 had shocked the nation with its totals of 900 killed and 2,700 wounded," writes Drew Gilpin Faust in *This Republic of Suffering.* "By the following spring at Shiloh, Americans recognized that they had embarked on a new kind of war, as the battle yielded close to 24,000 casualties . . . By the time of Gettysburg a year later, the Union army alone reported 23,000 casualties, including 3,000 killed. Confederate losses are estimated between 24,000 and 28,000; in some regiments, numbers of killed and wounded approached 90 percent. And by the spring of 1864 Grant's losses in slightly more than a month approached 50,000."

The total figure "is approximately equal to the total American fatalities in the Revolution, the War of 1812, the Mexican War, the Spanish-American War, World War I, World War II, and the Korean War combined. The Civil War's rate of death, its incidence in comparison with the size of the American population, was six times that of World War II. A similar rate, about 2 percent, in the United States today would mean six million fatalities." Fifty thousand civilians were killed "as battles raged across farm and field, as encampments of troops spread epidemic disease, as guerrillas ensnared women and even children in violence and reprisals, as draft rioters targeted innocent citizens, as shortages of food in parts of the South brought starvation. The distinguished Civil War historian James McPherson has concluded that the overall mortality rate for the South exceeded that of any country in World War I and that of all but the region between the Rhine and the Volga in World War II. The American Civil War produced carnage that has often been thought reserved for the combination of technological proficiency and inhumanity characteristic of a later time."

And yet, once again, boys, men, cry for each other, in each other's arms, over each other's bodies and graves, as they have not done since the Revolutionary War.

Yes, the Civil War ended slavery. But did it really?

The living remain'd and suffer'd—the mother suffer'd,
And the wife and the child, and the musing comrade suffer'd,
And the armies that remain'd suffer'd.

WALT WHITMAN

WALT

During the four years of the Civil War, Walt Whitman writes that he visits more than fifty Washington hospitals six or seven days a week, some six hundred visits to "80,000 to 100,000 of the wounded and sick, as sustainer of spirit and body in some degree, in time of need."

He is there when no other major American writer is there. Twain and Henry James and Howells and Melville and even Hawthorne appear unable to write about this war or address it meaningfully in their work. Henry James, in fact, condemns Walt: "An offense against art," this other great hush-marked writer lashes out, venomously or in secret jealousy. Walt visits the wounded, writes their letters, brings them little items to cheer them up, holds their hands, and kisses as many of them as he can. He believes in physical contact, the magic of touching, and is always on the lookout for pain and suffering. He will do almost anything a soldier asks of him. He is forty-one years old when he starts these ministrations. He is one of nine children, and devoted to his mother and his family.

Of course, in all of this, he struggles with his sexual attractions, struggles to govern himself, to be careful when he and another or others sneak off into the latrine at the end of each ward's hall. The city is full of sights that turn him on, walking the streets, riding the streetcars, seeing so many men everywhere, touching their hands daily, buying them clean underwear, kissing them, kissing them, kissing them, saying goodbye, saying goodbye often just after saying hello. Most nurses love him. A few do not and suspect him of just what he is trying so hard to control. The dying walk with him all his waking hours and in his dreams.

Leaves of Grass, one of the greatest works of art an American has ever produced, is first printed in 1855, and then in many subsequent editions as Walt writes and includes more poems. It sells a few copies, attracts a few vice squads, but mostly arouses no attention at all. It is amazing to see how openly homosexual Walt's poems are, how full of outright and unconditional love of man for man. Few notice this either. He gets away with it. (Walt's words selected here are extracted from *Now the Drum of War* by Robert Roper.)

> *We are fully aware of the lack of a word to describe us and how we*
>   *feel.*
> *A spirit of my own seminal wet.*
> *This is no book,*
> *Who touches this, touches a man.*
> *(Is it night? Are we here alone?)*
> *It is I you hold, and who holds you,*
> *I spring from the pages into your arms.*

Come closer to me,
Push close my lovers and take the best I possess
Yield closer and closer and give me the best you possess
Give me the drench of my passions!
I am for those who believe in loose delights—I share the midnight
    orgies of young men.
This hour I tell things in confidence,
I might not tell everybody but I will tell you.
Who goes there! Hankering, gross, mystical, nude?
This is the meal pleasantly set . . . this is the meat and drink for natural
    hunger.
It is for the wicked just the same as the righteous . . . I make
    appointments with all,
I will not have a single person slighted or left away,
This is the touch of my lips to yours . . . this is the murmur of yearning.
O Drops of me! Trickle, slow drops,
Candid, from me falling—drip, bleeding drops,
From wounds made to free you whence you were prisoned . . .
Stain every page—stain every song I sing, every word I say, bloody
    drops.
Bloody drops of me.
And I found that every place was a burial-place,
And fuller, O vastly fuller, of the dead than of the living.
Union losses at Fredericksburg for the day were thirteen thousand,
Confederate five thousand.
Said Lee: "It is well that war is so terrible—we should grow too fond
    of it!"
A heap of feet, legs, arms, and human fragments, cut, bloody, black
    and blue . . .
I was fired for writing a dirty book.
Mercury-based meds, the most destructive of all meds, ipecac,
    strychnine, turpentine, castor oil, belladonna, lead acetate, silver
    nitrate, bleeding, purging . . .
These young men meeting their death with steady composure, and
    often with curious readiness.
Cherish your American experience! Emerson advises all hopeful poets.
I believe I weigh about 200 and as to my face (so scarlet), and my beard
    and neck, they are terrible to behold—I fancy the reason I am able

*to do some good in the hospitals, among the poor languishing &
wounded boys, is that I am so large and well—indeed like a great
wild buffalo.*

Quicksand years that whirl me I know not whither.

Years that trembled and reel'd beneath me!

A thick gloom fell through the sunshine and darken'd me;

Must I change my triumphant songs? said I to myself;

Must I indeed learn to chant the cold dirges of the baffled?

And sullen hymns of defeat?

All is shaken, eluding,

Only the scheme I sing, the great, possess'd Soul, eludes not . . .

One's-Self, need never be shaken—that stands firm . . .

Out of politics, wars, death—what at last but One's-Self is sure?

Lovers of me, bafflers of graves,

To anyone dying—thither I speed!

Many want apples.

One wanted a rice pudding which I carried him next day.

Two or three some liquorish.

*One poor fellow with his leg amputated I made a small jar of very nice
spiced and pickled cherries.*

One lad in bed 23 had set his heart on a pair of suspenders.

I took him a pair of suspenders.

There is a new lot of wounded . . . long strings of ambulances . . .

*Mother, it is the most pitiful sight I think when first the men are
brought in—I have to bustle round, to keep from crying. Mother,
I will show you some of the letters I get from mothers, sisters,
fathers &c. They will make you cry.*

I lie to him about how serious is his case.

*The amputation, the blue face, the groan, the glassy eye of the dying,
the clotted rag, the odor of wounds and blood.*

*One must be calm & cheerful, & not let on how their case really is . . .
brace them up, kiss them, discard all ceremony, & fight for
them . . .*

*Mr. Lincoln passes here every evening, his complexion gray, very sad.
He has a face like a hoosier Michael Angelo, so awful ugly it
becomes beautiful . . . him I love, the sweetest, wisest soul of all my
days and lands.*

We have got so that we always exchange bows, and very cordial ones.

Dear comrade [this to a young soldier named Tom Sawyer], you must
not forget me, for I never shall you. My love you have in life or
death forever. I don't know how you feel about it, but it is the wish
of my heart to have your friendship, and also that if you should
come safe out of this war, we should come together in some place
where we could make our living, and be true comrades and never
be separated while life lasts.
Ambulances . . . hundreds, I don't know but thousands, constantly on
the move . . .
. . . what I see probed deepest . . . bursting the petty bounds of art. The
hospital part of the drama deserves to be recorded . . . over the
whole land . . . an unending, universal mourning-wail of women,
parents, orphans—the marrow of the tragedy concentrated in those
Hospitals—it seem'd sometimes as if the whole of the land, North
and South, was one vast central Hospital, and all the rest of the
affair but flanges. States plentifully represented. New York and
Pennsylvania have their offspring here by hundreds, by thousands.
Ohio and Illinois and Indiana and Michigan and Massachusetts
and Maine. My soiled and creas'd . . . forty little notebooks,
forming a special history of these years, blotch'd here and there
with more than one blood-stain.
Chant the human aspects of anguish!
620,000 dead. 360,000 from the North. 260,000 from the South.
Poor boy! I never knew you.
On, on I go
The crush'd head I dress (poor crazed hand, tear not the bandage
away);
The neck of the cavalry-man, with the bullet through and through, I
examine;
Hard the breathing rattles, quite glazed already the eye . . .
(Come sweet death! Be persuaded, O beautiful death!
In mercy come quickly.)
The wounded—They are crowded here in Washington in immense
numbers, their wounds full of worms, many afflicted young men
are crazy—they have suffered too much & perhaps it is a privilege
that they are out of their senses—Mother, it is most too much for a
fellow, & I sometimes wish I was out of it.
The hurt and the wounded I pacify with soothing hand,

I sit by the restless all the dark night—some are so young;
Some suffer so much—I recall the experience sweet and sad.
Many a soldier's loving arms about this neck have cross'd and rested,
Many a soldier's kiss dwells on these bearded lips.
. . . the dead, the dead, the dead—our dead—our South or North,
*   ours all, (all, all, all, finally dear to me)—or East or West—*
*   Atlantic coast or Mississippi valley—some where they crawl'd to*
*   die, alone, in bushes, low gullies, or on the sides of hills . . . our*
*   young men once so handsome and so joyous—the son from the*
*   mother, the husband from the wife . . . the clusters of camp graves*
*   in Georgia, the Carolinas, and in Tennessee—the single graves left*
*   in the woods or by the roadside . . . corpses floated down the rivers,*
*   and caught and lodged . . . the infinite dead . . . the land entire*
*   saturated, perfumed with their impalpable ashes' exhalation in*
*   Nature's chemistry distill'd, and shall be so forever, in every future*
*   grain of wheat and ear of corn, and every flower that grows . . .*
The living remain'd and suffer'd—the mother suffer'd,
And the wife and the child, and the musing comrade suffer'd,
And the armies that remain'd suffer'd.
Poor dear son, though you were not my son, I felt to love you as a son,
*   what short time I saw you sick & dying here—it is as well as it is,*
*   perhaps better—for who knows whether he is not better off, that*
*   patient & sweet young soul, to go, than we are to stay? So farewell,*
*   dear boy—it was my opportunity to be with you in your last rapid*
*   days of death—no chance, as I have said, to do anything particular,*
*   for nothing could be done—only you did not lay here & die*
*   among strangers without having one at hand who loved you*
*   dearly, & to whom you gave your dying kiss.*

•

Half of those that die in your Civil War die from disease.

I killed one half of this one half.

I am getting into the swing of things. It took a little cooperation on the part of your people but once that was in hand it was all systems go. This war has helped me.

You are my homeland. My rock and my redeemer. You are my people, my lost tribe.

Before this war I almost died a number of times. During this time I

have only been able to survive in a very few of you. But I survived. I endured.

I have now established my beachhead where brothers murder brothers.

I can suffer pain. My own cells murder each other every day. I had given it no second thought. But I see that you have not felt half so sad at this destruction of your own as I do of my own. You human murderers are as adept as I am. I must be on my guard. You will come after me soon enough with a vengeance.

If you are going to continue to kill each other I can save you a lot of trouble.

HERE BEGINS THE HISTORY OF
THE MASTURBOVS

Doris Hardware will meet Abraham Masturbov in 1925 and bear his son, Mordecai, in 1934. Mordy Masturbov will grow to become a central figure, the incubator, creator, generator of the climate, atmosphere, dare I say history? again precise words fail me, of the plague of The Underlying Condition. I don't know what to call him because after all these years I can still remember that young body which I'd pined for so at last in my arms, and he was also the rich landlord's son who was also our cousin. But Mordy and *Sexopolis* are to provide the signal Petri dish for this plague to nurture itself into worldwide growth.

On one long dark night still some years away Doris will have a breakdown and tell Abe her own family's history. Since chronologically Turvey belongs here, here he is placed.

This, then, is Mordy's future mother talking, to his future father, about her own father, and her own father's father, and her own father's father's father.

If you can handle another sneak peek at the genealogy, Abe's father, Herman Masturbov, will be born soon, in 1880; his own parents, Yissy and Truda, will be prevented from celebrating his arrival in even a modest way because they will be getting massacred in a pogrom in Russia (many of which in fact are going on at this very minute), but not before making certain their newborn son is spirited away in the arms of a distant cousin who is on his way to the New World.

TURVEY

My great-grandfather came to America from Croatia and immediately went west, ostensibly to escape conscription in the Civil War, but actually to sell women. I don't know where he got the idea. He'd read a lot about America. It was hard not to, even then, when the exploits of the white men, with their Winchesters and Colts, were coming to define masculinity everywhere. And the gold rushes! Everyone had heard of gold rushes. The whole world believed America's streets were paved with gold.

He chose Colorado because it sounded nicer than Arkansas or Arizona, which are harsh words. He was a lonely man, taciturn. He hated to talk, even to his family, perhaps especially his family, which was enormous, as he fucked his way across America, keeping a careful record of who his children were, promising to make things right when he made his fortune. He enjoyed sex, coupling with women and playing with his penis, and when drunk he boasted that he masturbated a dozen times a day and produced as much semen late at night just before going to sleep as he did in the morning upon arising and doing it for the first time of the day. He held contests to prove it and he always won. It's said he never lost at anything. And he probably never did.

Turvey was his first name, though it sounded like his last, which was never used, which was Hartinckwarjender, which no one could pronounce or spell or even remember, even in a country where so many names were unpronounceable. That's why we became Hardware. In this country and the old one he had a dozen children by his first wife, who finally died in childbirth. He deserted them, plus the fifteen or more he had by other women. He did leave notes saying he intended to send for them, and that he knew some would die but that everyone would die if he stayed. He'd seen more than enough of how dirty life was, and how dishonest. He had a sense that he would make a lot of money somewhere else. Some people just know this from an early age—you probably do, Abe, or did, or will.

It was a good thing he left when he did. There was massive conscription into the army, no matter where you were, the Union or the Confederacy or Croatia or Timbuktu. On his way west he had to dodge skirmishes of this civil war. His English was poor, and he never knew which side was doing what to whom. All the way west he was stepping over dead bodies in abandoned fields or standing on hills looking down on bands of children manning cannons pointed at other children. What were they fighting for? What were they fighting against? What was the prize? It all seemed to have something to do with people who had black skin and whether you could own them or not. Like many Middle Europeans who regarded colored skin as exotic, he couldn't conceive that so many white people would kill each other because of it. No, he would say, it must be something else. They must really be angry about something else. This slavery business must be hiding something deeper. "More deep." He got caught and thrown into makeshift prisons in Pennsylvania and Kansas. He was evidently freed because he refused to speak English and they figured he wasn't an American. Nobody else in the prison was either, so far as his ear could tell, but they were all lined up and shot because they'd tried to talk English and he talked gibberish, like a child playing foreigner would make up and spew out, and it saved him.

Over the years he wrote down bits in the secret ledger he kept of his illicit businesses, which all had to do with sex. He wrote, and he was very rich by this time, hugely rich, that he hated America, every second he'd been here, he hated a place that did precious little to help good men and women honestly feed the families every religion was pressuring everyone so endlessly to bear. He wrote that this was why he'd found no difficulty in breaking a law, any law, all laws, gladly. "This hypocrisy was America, is America, and will always be America," he wrote in that ledger, more than once.

He wrote that he had seen in prison men covered with sores, on their arms and legs and trunks, men whose mouths were pocked and swollen with disease, men whose semen was black or green or speckled with blood. He said men were so hungry for sexual release they didn't care when or where or who saw them do whatever—masturbating, screwing each other, taking each other in their mouths, fucking stray dogs. When they were intimate with each other, though, they would call each other endearing names like "Little Lamb." He was very touched by these scenes. American men seemed so hard the rest of the time. Even if one man came before another there was much solicitation on both sides to see that the other had been satisfied enough. These were the only instances of tenderness Turvey encountered until he set up his women and saw how they, too, tended each other. But the women needed no sexual excitement in order to care.

He'd seen men with men in Croatia plenty, which was not what was surprising to him; what was surprising was how much men in the growing cities needed sex, so much so that when they didn't have women they might do anything at all with and to each other. And when they had their women in view, they would scorn and ridicule and often beat and maim their former love mates, denying their coupling had ever taken place. Yes, this was more hypocrisy for Turvey, but it gave him the idea for how to get started on his fortune.

I said he sold women. That was before the whorehouses. I wasn't around until the whorehouses but I want to give you plenty of front-and-center information so when I make my entrance later you can understand me, which I want you to do, Abe, so badly, because I can't, not right now at any rate, and I need you to.

Men needed wives most of all. That's what Turvey learned in prison. They didn't want them. They needed them. They needed them to have their release, and the law and God said they couldn't have that release unless there was an official piece of paper entitling the bearers to have sexual intercourse legally. "That's all it was," Turvey wrote. "Why can't people realize that's all it says?" All this civilization built on the piece of paper. A piece of paper! which says the law is *love*. But all he'd heard every man in prison say was *fuck*. "That's where and when I learned the difference between love and sex. The difference between a piece of paper and truth. The difference between truth and lies. Hypocrisy!" *Hypocrisy* was a word, once he learned it, he used a lot.

Before he left Kansas he posted a broadside outside a grocery store. He was in a town called Nordick; it wasn't very big, a few hundred people or so. He said he was looking for single women to take west, where he guaranteed them husbands. Ten women showed up at the Pony Express depot, suitcases all packed. He hadn't the vaguest notion how to find those husbands, how to do anything he'd said he would do, or even how much to charge them for their new wives. He just had a hunch men out west needed women.

Of course he was right. Getting them together was "damn good fun." The women were all ages and shapes and sizes. He evidently sampled not a few of them on the journey. One of them got pregnant. When the baby was born, after he'd sold her, she sent it to him in a box, dead, killed by her own hand, she said, lest she be reminded of its father, who had delivered her into a slavery she'd never imagined possible for a white woman. In the beginning he got a few hundred for most of them, more for the beautiful ones. He mainly sold them at an auction in Fairchild, Nevada, a central mining town where women were indeed scarce. When he came to open one of his houses there a few years later, it was the most beautiful one—Torrence, she called herself by then—who became his madam. She'd shot the husband dead three months after the piece of paper. Whatever her motive, it must have been good enough because she was acquitted at what passed for a trial, by a magistrate who came through town every few months on horseback and rendered judgment, and whom she said she'd fucked for her freedom.

Turvey made twenty or thirty more trips and sold maybe five hundred women. "I made several hundred thousand dollars," a startlingly large amount of money in those days. "I wasn't proud of it," he wrote. "I wasn't ashamed of it either. Maybe that don't make sense to some. But it does to me."

Turvey hit Colorado on his way back east to buy another lot of stock. He decided he was tired of traveling. Over the past years there had been numerous gold rushes, beginning in 1859 at the Comstock Lode, so by now many places west of the Rockies were filled with hungry men. "I understood hungry men." Denver, which was one of the first places folks seemed to arrive at, was rowdy and young, a place men wanted to get to on their journeys, a goal: "Let's go to Denver and have us some fun!" When he hit Denver and heard all this, Turvey knew what kind of fun was going to swell his fortune.

Why did he do it? He hated prostitution. In Croatia his own mother had been taken into prostitution as a young wife. Hosta. Hosta Hartinckwarjender. Hosta was literally grabbed away from her husband and imprisoned in a whorehouse for a number of years. Only when she had lost her looks was she released. By then she'd evidently given birth to several dozen children who were put to death immediately by the madam; when she got out, her husband, Turvey's father, had died, and all her half dozen children, except for her last born before entering the whorehouse, Turvey, had grown up and moved on, to where she didn't know.

Turvey had waited for his momma. She came back to their tiny town in northern Croatia and there she found Turvey, alone, carving wood and planting potatoes, and he held her close and told her how much he had missed her, and bathed her and found her some of her former clothes, and showed her all the money he'd managed to save up from his carvings. He told her they were going to live in the New World. No sooner had they hit New York than Hosta met a man on the street and walked off with him. Turvey was in a boardinghouse checking to see if they had any cheap rooms. He never saw her again. He said that's when he stopped talking much to anybody. He walked the streets of New York. He walked to Philadelphia, but he felt crowded there, too. Then to Scranton and Allentown, where the mines were. Mines he recognized. Croatia had mines and he'd worked them and he went down inside the earth once more, which evidently gave him some sort of comfort in his misery. Yes, he sent for the remnants of his family when he got rich in Denver, but there was only one son who responded, perhaps the only one who survived, Horace Sr., my father's father, who got the letter when it arrived in Pennsylvania some fifteen years later, and who answered the summons. Horace Sr. must have been a lot like the Turvey who waited at home in Croatia, through thick and thin, plague and famine, death after death, for his parent to return from somewhere.

By the time Horace Sr. arrived, Turvey was living in a hundred-room mansion and was richer than God. Every single room was filled to overflowing with Things. Big Things. Paintings with scenes that needed whole walls to hang on. Furniture that also stretched from wall to wall. It wasn't awful taste that was out of control, just acquisitiveness nurtured by a life of being hungry, by the sheer need to purchase, the way starving beggars scratch for as much food as their fingers can hold and eat too much when they get it. You know how rich men can never have enough? Like that. The son looked questioningly at the father, and the father took him by the hand and drove him in the buggy downtown to a whorehouse. Horace laughed out loud when he found out what his father had done to make his fortune. I should say here, because I realize I haven't, that Turvey was perhaps all of thirty years old by now; Horace was sixteen. That's how much life had been packed into lives then. Turvey had been all of fourteen when he fathered his last lot of kids; he must have started fathering them when he was no more than eleven or twelve. He was fifteen when he shepherded his first lot of women out west to sell. And now he'd been in the whorehouse business for fifteen years. It's hard for us to imagine how young people were when they did things in those days. They probably figured they might not be around for long. We wait forever now, don't we? Well, perhaps not you, Abe.

"This here's mine," the father said to the son in that first whorehouse. Before the son could respond, he was led back to the buggy and driven to the northern outskirts of town and deposited dab in the middle of another bustling house of hookers and food and drink and ragtime piano and noise, lots of lusty noise. "This here's mine," the father said again.

This little tour went on for several days, around and around the territory, to over two dozen houses, the last one so far out in the wilderness that Horace thought he must be in Canada or Mexico. Turvey asked him, "Now do you understand how rich we are? Do you got any qualms about becoming my partner in this particular business?" And Horace roared again. "Hell, no. I can't wait," he said.

And he couldn't. He later claimed to have screwed every single one of the hookers in all the two dozen houses. "I had to try them all out, just like any businessman should know his wares. I had to taste them and judge their quality." He decided he wanted a new name, so he and Turvey somehow settled on Hardware. Horace Hardware. I've always thought they were making a bad joke about the women, all of them getting such hard wear. But no, you can sniff the original name in it. The girls all loved Horace, as they loved Turvey. You've got to realize these places were an important part of society. They were places where men could have fun, and most of the women were having fun too, more fun than they'd be having most anywhere else. I asked Horace how and where he and Turvey found so many women. "There were a lot of girls down on their luck everywhere. Husbands dead. Killed by Indians. Never came back from some war. There were always little wars one place or another. Men they was engaged to never met them at the train. Poor girls who just wanted to eat. Bored girls who couldn't wait to get out of their boring little towns. Lookers who wanted to be admired. Dames who genuinely liked to get screwed. And don't forget: all of them, I don't care what they said, were looking for a husband who would set them up in a house with a hundred rooms. A few of them found that, and so the hope was always kept alive."

Guilt and God still lay outside and down the street. But they were coming. Church groups were starting up, and different moralities were taking hold and growing tentacles, and all those sermons about damnation from the East were not so softly beginning to be heard across the land. Turvey ignored them all.

When I was a little girl, my father, Horace Jr., had one hundred whorehouses. He could have had more, but he said he'd stop when he reached one hundred and he did. I used to play in them. Grandfather Horace still collected all the money himself. He was driven around by his bodyguards, and one by one he went to his houses, and was handed the bags of cash, and stashed them in banks, a different one for each house, in case any bank went bust. He took all the ledgers home and stayed up all night studying them and verifying how much each girl had turned. If a madam cheated she was fired on the spot, and if a girl wasn't popular he found some other work for her, in the kitchen or the laundry or as a maid, if she wanted it. It must have been a prodigious task, going to one hundred locations; hundreds of miles separated them; but he did it all himself, and like a father confessor he heard all the complaints the girls didn't want to tell their madam. They trusted him, and he never, so far as I know, let them down. He loved his women and he was happy to pay them. Honest work for honest wages, he said, and he believed it.

Turvey died from some disease that sounded like syphilis or elephantiasis. His whole sex area . . . His genitals and testicles all swelled up to enormous size, and then sort of got rancid and infected, until he was pretty much one huge pus-filled sore. The doctor was repelled. He'd never seen anything like it. He didn't know what to do and no one he talked to knew what to do. Turvey's stare frightened many a man, and that was part of how he held power so long without getting in trouble with the law, with politicians, with any group or religion. He claimed he never paid anybody off. It's not hard to believe that this fear alone gave him such power, so that even his own doctor was so afraid of him he couldn't tell him properly that he was dying.

Remember, don't forget, that Turvey never stopped hating America, and really, if you think about it, hating women, for it was his mother who abandoned him, and in America, and whorehouses and hookers were just about the most vengeful thing he could think of to get even. He loved his girls, but he never forgot what they were. God knows what made Horace Sr. always cheerful. It was probably that he'd starved for so long and then been led to El Dorado and told, "It's yours." That would make anyone happy. Sometimes I wonder if certain traits just skip a generation. My father was just as filled with bile as Great-grandfather Turvey, although he loved his girls as his forebears had.

This is how Turvey died: he was punctured with a huge needle so all the pus and poison and bad bile inside him that had puffed him up could drain out. The doctor said he recommended it to keep him alive. The doctor said he never thought it would kill him. But Turvey knew it would, and it did.

I guess that's all I want to tell you for now. I need a break. You'll see why.

AN AGE OF HATE

It is both appalling and perfectly understandable how and why a wretched human being like Andrew Johnson becomes president of the United States following Lincoln's assassination in 1865.

The Age of Hate is what a sympathetic supporter named his book about Johnson, which claims him as the good guy and the wronged one, against mountains of evidence to the contrary. He was a pig, a bad man in office at an especially wrong time, when The American People, all 35 million of them, desperately needed better. Instead they got a man who led us in every wrong direction.

Johnson was indeed poor, very poor, "the poorest of any man who ever reached the White House," writes the Columbia historian Eric Foner in *The Reader's Companion to the American Presidency.* Johnson gloried in telling you that he rose from the dirt, to become a tailor, to become a president.

Here is a brief sampling of pertinent clips from Foner's essay.

The first president ever impeached . . . one of the least successful American chief executives . . . he owned five slaves . . . Johnson defended slavery against the abolitionists . . . he did not believe blacks had any role to play in Reconstruction . . . indeed he harbored deeply racist sentiments toward the former slaves . . . Johnson would insist that blacks possessed less "capacity for government than any other race of people," and when left to themselves showed a "constant tendency to relapse into barbarism" . . . the terms Johnson laid down for the South's readmission were amazingly lenient, especially for a man who had spoken so insistently of punishing treason . . . he ordered the return of abandoned plantation lands to their former owners when parcels had already been divided among blacks in Virginia, South Carolina, and Louisiana . . . Government had no obligation to assist the former slaves . . . clothing blacks with the privileges of citizenship discriminated against white people . . . Clearly Johnson envisioned no sweeping social revolution as a sequel to emancipation. He compared himself to Jesus Christ and at one point suggested that divine intervention had removed Lincoln to elevate Johnson to the White House. He believed that "the people of the South, poor, quiet, unoffending, harmless, are to be trodden under foot to protect the niggers . . ."

This then is the president of The American People after Abraham Lincoln. It is as if Lincoln never lived, which is obviously how a good portion of The American People want it to be.

BLOOD AND SHIT

With dead bodies piled everywhere across the landscape, problems with blood begin to assert themselves. It's all over the place. You can't get away from it. It's on the ground, in the dirt and mud, on bushes and tree bark, on doorsteps and porches and building doorways. It is on furniture and floors and on beds and linens, should there be any of this last item left after years of bandaging. It's on clothing, everywhere and everyone's. Animals carry it from their snoots to their assholes. They roll in it, eat it, shit it out.

It's on almost every man's hands. Somewhere on his body he carries it. It's impossible to wash it off. It's under nails, in body cracks, at hair roots, inside ears. People are constantly infected and infecting each other. No one has ever seen so many people sick with something. No one knows what to do. Certainly no one in authority knows what to do, since there is no one in authority. Most of the doctors are dead from the war or so depressed that they're useless.

There is so little to eat and drink that blood and shit are ingested accidentally or otherwise. At the notorious concentration camps at Percyville and Andersonville, huge bloodlettings are effected regularly from the dead for drink, and shit is consumed daily as a primary food. It is mixed with mud and wild berries and fried in animal fat, an old Indian recipe. There is no other food.

No one knows what to do. This is an incredible statement, and an incomparable indictment. How are we ever going to become anything at all if in the face of such grotesque treatment of each other daily, and in the wake of such grotesque treatment of each other on the killing fields, no one knows what to do? The new president, what is his name? Well, that's what it's like. If ever a country needed a great leader, this is that country, and now is that time. And it doesn't have one. And it isn't going to get one for a long, long time.

That NITS was established is irrelevant. Such buildings as were built to house it are empty. Not only are all those dead doctors not replaced, no one wants to be a doctor anyway.

Why is it that The American People never have a great leader when we need one, or if and when we have one we don't let him lead for very long?

WANDERERS

From 1865 on, an entire country's set of values is turned upside down and sideways and every which way but straight.

For too many people, the accumulations of a lifetime are now gone. Robbery becomes a way of life. Even murder becomes, in certain places, an accepted means of . . . what?

America will never again be the same.

A lot of men don't come home, not because they are dead, but because they don't want to. Many just go wandering in the wilderness. Many are genuinely lost. Many take new names to start again. Many don't care who won. Or why. Or who they are. Or what the fight was about. Who shot me? A boy from where? Many don't understand. Anything. Anymore. Many feel free now. Maybe for the first time. They can start over. But too many are just plain depressed. And scared. Frightened. They are not ready for freedom.

One thing should be certain, but of course it isn't. Trust of brother for brother has been destroyed in America forever. Few would understand this, or use this word *destroyed*, or *forever*. People don't think in terms of forever except in church. If they go to one. Forever, for now, will be just another naïve dream for another time, another place.

Yes, so many men have loved each other, at first out of fear of being confronted by the horrors of having to kill their own, having to actually murder someone just like themselves, that for many now it is as if they only want to hold and feel each other, somehow.

Wandering men of many ages form small groups of their own to live together in who knows what kind of harmony, seeking some kind of peace. "All I know is I do not want to see anyone who did not fight in this war, be it father or mother or sisters or any men other than my brothers-in-arms" pretty much sums up the kind of letter many a son or husband sends home, if he writes at all. Many folks back home think their boys are dead when they aren't; these sons and fathers and husbands just don't want to see anyone who could possibly have done anything at all to have caused this hideous war of brotherly hate. Many of them are beginning to cotton on to just what they had been obliged to do.

No one pays much attention to this loss of trust. No one pays much attention to the ones who are frightened and depressed. For too long too many people have believed that all we have to do is start over, move on, look to tomorrow.

The only thing not in short supply is inner emptiness.

How do you stay alive after a war like this one?

How do you rebuild a self on emptiness?

How do you stay curious and interested and positive and full of beans?

How do you get anything done?

Few are happy. The country is filled with blood. This point, already made, can't be made enough. You can't imagine it, but that's what the country is. Filled with blood. Few aren't bleeding. It can't be said enough. Blood is everywhere.

Blood is everywhere.

There are bands of homeless orphaned youngsters roaming the wilderness, going nowhere in particular, just moving. They are unable to stand still. They don't stay anyplace for long. It is not the first time we have seen this. Now there are more of them. And they are more wounded, in every conceivable way.

Some of them perform strange acts like flagellating themselves in public to atone for man's sins, for brother killing brother. There are more of these than you would think. Something about the act, the public display, the pain, draws many to join these bands of wandering flagellators. Only by our sacrifices can the anger of Christ be appeased, one sign says, carried by a child whose name, which he can't remember yet, is Clarence Meekly. We carry our scourges as Christ carried his Cross, another sign says, carried by a young man, Horatio Dridge, who remembers his name, but not where he comes from. Some wear only loincloths, even in the freezing cold. They sleep all in a heap at night. They prostrate themselves on the ground in the form of a great cross by day. They go from town to town. At first they shock people so much that they are fed and prayed with. But after a while they become too scary, or too annoying, or too numerous, and they are sent scurrying away.

Many of these wandering young ones continually sob and cry.

Many of the older ones do as well.

Some know they are lost. Some do not.

Yes, the wandering wounded are everywhere. Many wander to Washington, as if by being in what is now firmly recognized as the capital of America they will receive a Sign that will tell them what to do or where to go or how to lead a life.

These tragic human beings are very sad. There are a great many of them. They are the orphans of this war.

A MOTHER

Did I weep when we looked back at Georgetown as I tried to stop my boy's own weeping? It was a terrible place we left. How could he cry for it? He would not stop. You know how it is when a child weeps for a dead pet, well, that is how he was, only he is some seventeen years and he stays and stays weeping and weeping so much that I have no breath left of my own. I am gasping for him, trying to grab breath for him. I wanted to keep running so as to flee that swamp where his friend lay dead from something called ogloop, at least that is what I think I heard it called. His friend is in the long swamp that runs outside the back doors of the houses all side by side and sinking in muck. His friend, his friend who was all the world to him, his friend who was the only thing in the world to him, certainly more to him than me, the wife to his father, also dead in that swamp from the funnyname disease. He wants to run back! I tell him we cannot stop running away, because the plague that killed his dear friend and also his father in that swamp in this terrible heat, runs after us fast and will catch us dead if we stop for even a moment. The doctors are saying so. They are saying, run, run, run for your lives, for the plague from the swamps is upon us!

"Please, Mammytoo, please let me go back!" and I yank and pull him from all the poisoned dead not only in that swamp and around our house in that place called Georgetown, but everywhere we run forth to, he tries to stop and run back from. He begs me over and over as I yank him forward with all my might. We run without breath and now without shoes and always without food. We run past many dead boys, dead boys from the battle with holes everywhere, in their heads and their legs and their stomachs falling out. So many dead someone's sons. They lie often in each other's arms last-comforting each other.

"Mammytoo, Mammytoo, please I want my Davey!" the boy wails on and yet he runs with me now. He must know that life is not for standing still. He cries and cries and he will not eat the berries I grab for him as we run, not even suck them for their sweet juice to feed his running. Oh my child my child, I choke just as you for what is out there for us, where do we go to find what?

Where are we going?!

A LAKE

The lake is wide and shallow and hard to see for all the brambles and brush fallen upon it, all the dead tree trunks and heavy brown-leafed branches. But it can be seen, through all this, that there is water there. Liquid. As no sun shines in this heavily wooded area, the water's color is dark, a not unusual characteristic of the many creeks in this part of northern Maryland, and of all the dirty bodies of water that harried and desperate soldiers are called upon to visit. For the parched and filthy this lake is like an oasis in a desert, a mirage come true. Just to be in sight of it perks up spirits and quickens steps. In we go. In we go.

Not all of them come back up. It depends on how much energy is left in their war-weary bones. If they are exhausted, as most of them are, they drown in the heavy water, which appears on the closer experience of submerging in it to be thick oozing muck. In reality this lake is filled with blood, thick blood, blood clotted with bits of persons, flesh blown to bits by cannons and balobustumes, new forged rifles of Russian design made in France by Averva and imported by a War Department that has heard good things about them. This lake is proof of how effective an Averva balobustume is. The rifle was first introduced at Antietam, just down the creek. There were one hundred balobustumes only and more casualties were suffered at Antietam than anywhere else. The North could have had them first but the general in charge of ordnance, Otis B. Jarman, refused to pay extra for them and so his soldiers used the infinitely inferior single-shot muzzle-loaders although the lever-action repeating rifles were available to and used by the Confederates to mow them down. This lake is full of dead bodies. This lake is nothing but blood.

Here comes another harried band of the wounded. One-two-three in we go. Four-five-six they all jump in.

In the blood. In the blood.

They bathe, they drink, they drown.

EVERYWHERE

Dead bodies are a dime a dozen. It's impossible for children to play in wooded areas without stumbling over a dead body or two, and difficult to ascertain if the corpse is a murdered man or one dead from battle, or from some illness or disease, or starvation, or suicide, not that people can tell the difference. There is no one around to differentiate or to care about which is which. Not much has been written about how commonplace unburied corpses are. Or about the lack of law enforcement. Or the singular absence of pure curiosity about who's doing what and whether it's legal. The American People continue to grow along the path of Who Cares? Whatever it is, it's somebody else's problem. No, no one is in charge of burying dead bodies. How can they be allowed to rot in plain sight for so long? There may be drums beating for the coming of the railroads, and for greed, there are always drums beating for greed, and a fresh new day, but it's all frosting on a cake sitting on plates of maggots crawling over mountains of decaying flesh. Talk about cesspools of disease!

Something called the Morgens Report appears, which presents the frightening "fact" that at least four out of five soldiers killed at least one other person.

TWO OF OUR LEADING CHARACTERS
MEET EACH OTHER

Another one who can't remember his name. Or where he comes from. Or what he did before. His body tries to tell him its history. He looks at his scars and scabs and spots and rips and bumps and stitches and holes. Where did he get these? Were they here before? Before what?

He's very lonely. The war was the first friends he ever had. The war was men who spoke to him nicely. He doesn't want to take off his uniform. He runs into other boys in uniforms. He reads a magazine in a library. In West Virginia. It's about a war. He doesn't recognize much of anything. Maybe the names of towns. He knows he was in some of those towns.

He'd not known he was strange before the colonel came and offered ten dollars and a uniform to anyone who joined the Western Kansas Territory Freedom Brigade. He was thirteen years old then. His skin is pale. He is short and skinny. His mouth is small. His voice is high-pitched. When the war started he learned that he was strange. Too strange for the others, who would not talk to him. He got used to silence. Even when the guns wouldn't stop he couldn't hear them. He was lost already.

He knows he can't remember anything. He was able to before. He could list all the places where he fought. He caressed the heads of dead men many times as he sat beside them, holding their hands, leaning over them too late to hear their last words, these first men who ever talked to him. They looked frightened even after they died.

One day in Ohio he sits on a rock and looks at a creek and talks out loud to himself. "Clarence, you must get a hold of yourself." Why is he calling himself Clarence? Is his name Clarence? Why is he crying? In Missouri he talks out loud to himself again. "Clarence Meekly, you must get a hold of yourself."

He's in Indiana. He's in Kansas. He's in Missouri. He's in Georgia. "You are entering . . ." "You have crossed . . ." Hand-painted signs stuck on stakes trying to tell you where you are. America's very quiet. No one wants to say anything out loud to anyone. When books start to be written about this war no one ever talks about this silence. Perhaps everyone still alive is finally ashamed. That often causes silence. Somewhere in Virginia or Delaware his money starts running low, the severance dollars he was handed along with a piece of paper that says someone named John Doe is discharged. He was told he'd get more dollars if he sends a letter to Washington. He just keeps walking. It's so quiet. Ohio. A sign says Ohio again. He walks around and through and out of Ohio. Whatever he's been looking for, it doesn't seem to be in Ohio. When he thinks he must be in another state he sees a sign that says Ohio. He sleeps under trees. He eats berries and eats leaves. His uniform is tattered almost into dissolution. He is filthy dirty. He runs into other soldiers walking alone, just walking, in one uniform or another, it doesn't seem to make any difference any longer which one anyone is wearing. It's like the whole army was the same army, just wearing different clothes. He reads another magazine in a library somewhere else. He doesn't recognize the battles it writes about either. It tells about a war he didn't fight in, except for the names of those towns. Yes, he was in some of those towns.

He is crying again. It seems he has been alone his whole life. He can't remember where he came from. And he never will.

He wants a friend to talk to who won't die in his arms.

He's fifteen years old when he meets Horatio.

Young Horatio and young Clarence meet in Washington. They are in their mid-teens now, and each has gone through puberty and is filled with unexplained hungers. They meet at a march for homeless children that has spontaneously erupted. Word has passed, almost nationwide, that all the homeless little boys and girls, though there are mostly boys, will march in Washington on July 4, 1867, "in order to break the hearts of The American

People, to let them see how many of us are without food or clothing or work. Come! Come out of the forest! We must break their hearts!"

How many arrive to march? There is no written record of this event, only the memories of hundreds who talk about it over the succeeding years as their lives' paths cross: "Oh, were you there, too!" In memory the hundreds become thousands, become hundreds of thousands. And perhaps indeed there were. That is both the sad and the wonderful thing about so much of history: we will never know for certain, and therefore we can suppose, we can wonder, we can dream, we can hope, and in doing so, one day, perhaps . . . what? We can believe?

Horatio sees Clarence first and falls in step beside him. They talk, each of them as if for the first time in years, with animation and growing excitement.

And then, as often happens in parades, in crowds, in love, they lose each other at a turn in a road when mounted policemen on horses break up the crowd.

Each turns to look for the other with growing desperation. Each is overwhelmed with a new fear, a new trembling, but with the same familiar grotesque devastation, which had disappeared for a few brief moments. Each sits down by the side of the road, hoping the other will reappear. He does not. Suddenly life, which for a few hours had seemed worth living, morbidly returns to seeming not worth much at all.

KLANS AND KNIGHTS AND ORDERS

Strange small groups wanting to get rid of assorted folks that they find bothersome are quietly proliferating. Oh, there always have been such since the beginning of time, but now, particularly in certain parts of the country, mainly in the South and the Midwest, one begets another, and there are more of them, and they are larger. Negroes of course are the objects of most, Jews are the obsession of a number of others, but these groups now join others in displeasure of homosexuals. Unnamed as such homosexuals still may be, though they did not go unnoticed during the war, when so many men fell in love with each other. Some people must now know what one looks like. And spies are everywhere, writing down the names of those hated by someone in order to sell their names.

The Ku Klux Klan is only one of a number of secret organizations founded solely and purely on hate. (By the 1930s it will have some two million members.) These guys hate all Negroes and Jews across the board. The KKK is already scary and powerful. The Knights of the Golden Cross and the Knights of the White Camellia are two others that now appear, pledging themselves to the elimination of the Negro population. The Order of the Brothers of Jesus devotes itself to the hatred of anything Roman Catholic, while the Affectionate Order of Abraham's Bosom expends its considerable energies solely on hatred of Jews.

And almost out of nowhere, we now have Ezra Furst's vitriolic hatred of homosexuals entrenching itself firmly in Washington itself in his newly established Tally Office. How has he managed to obtain such power in Washington? He bought it, with secret Disciples funds. At the office's official (secret) opening, the staff drank champagne and sang "The Battle Hymn of the Republic." Who are these Disciples of Lovejoy and why do they hate homosexuals so much? For that's what Ezra's intent on doing, getting rid of all the hushmarkeds who murdered his beloved brother at Fruit Island. And with the death of Founding Brother Tom Lovejoy, who proclaimed all love is equal, Ezra now controls a growing and mighty group who follow his every word.

There is much overlap among these groups. Their representatives meet regularly to compare notes. Every group has its own Pushnow, out there being a spy-in-chief for something or other. It is difficult for some people to hate only one "other" at a time. Hate is surprisingly contagious. Or is it just communicable?

AMERICAN RED BLOOD ESTABLISHED

Some people are trying to be nice. In October 1867, Mr. Clarice Ding of Geneva, South Carolina, starts American Red Blood in the ruins of Atlanta. It is an organization meant to show everyone, North and South, that Someone Cares. Volunteer women, quite a large number of them from the South, start banding together around the country and try to help somehow, if only with a friendly voice. "You're going to get out real soon, you hear?" they promise those still in hospitals as they wash their faces. Mr. Ding's heart has been broken many times as he wandered around all the battlefields, every one. He is gratified that so many others are appearing to heed his call, even if most of these are women.

Before the war, Mr. Ding was a wealthy playboy who longed for a cause but refused to let the Confederacy be that cause. He often goes by the name of Dr. Ding because of a degree from Oxford and believes that such volunteerism, what he comes to call "social work," will become an important activity in this postwar world. He becomes quite caught up in his vision of what might be. Perhaps there might even be a way not only to collect information about enlisted men but also one day to collect blood and distribute it to those who need it. Mr. Ding is on to something here, but it's a good idea way before its time.

Many people now know, or sense, that blood is important, if only because so much of it is visible and so many clearly lost so much of it. Now, if we could only learn what to do with it, in or out of us. And if we all have it, then when we lose it there should be some way to replace it. But blood is still too mysterious, and its properties are elusive. "With the Lord's blessing, one day in the future American Red Blood will help discover what blood is all about," Clarice Ding writes in the Atlanta *Plantation*.

In the meantime Ding forms a board of rich southern gentlemen, with many of whom he and his late father have been in business, of one kind or another. These men are all getting richer. After the war, even in the South, especially in the South, there is much money to be made, once again in one way or another. Reconstruction, it's called. Money suddenly gushes like all that blood. Railroads are being started all over the place, for one thing. Clarice Ding will be very big in railroads. The Ding & Virginia & Ohio Railroad will shortly be of major importance. He doesn't know all his partners on this one, and that will be a problem.

American Red Blood remains just a name for the time being. If it's too early for blood, Mr. Ding also has a notion that there might be a way to take shit and turn it into food. Why do so many folks find this possibility interesting? There is certainly plenty of shit around, particularly along the excavations for his railroad, where more and more men come to work and sleep outside. And there are certainly plenty of people starving. But no one knows quite what to make of this idea yet either. If it seems to the reader that there sure is a lot in this history about shit, s/he's correct: there is, and not idly or irresponsibly so. There is a Mr. Gobesh Table, a Moroccan Jew who has a small hotel in the West Virginia wilderness, who writes to Dr. Ding expressing interest in this shit conversion. He receives no answer, but then mail delivery is really bad.

It is not long before Mr. Ding's board of directors decides to get rid of Mr. Ding. He is a single gentleman of a certain age in an age when such men are becoming increasingly more suspicious. They should be at home with a wife and making more babies to replace all the lost soldiers. It is implied that he has been too involved in the lives of a number of "my builders," the army of workmen stringing tracks from coast to coast. Several of them have been paid to testify as much. In fact, one of them had been Clarice's lover. Northern partners water the stock and clean him out. One of his northern directors even gets up at a board meeting and tells about Ding and his interest in shit. So Clarice is voted out of office of the very organization he started in his living room, and his name removed from everything. Clarice Ding goes bankrupt. In short order the Ding & Virginia & Ohio Railroad shortens its name. Mr. Ding is lost from the history of both business and blood. This breaks his heart and he commits suicide. When American Red Blood develops into the dominant and hugely important organization it will become, Mr. Clarice Ding's name is nowhere near it. A nurse, Clarice Hummingbird, is located and is placed in charge. "At least know your new Clarice to be a real woman and mother to pain and suffering," she announces in her acceptance speech. Her name had really been Polly O'Neill but she'd been renamed for this occasion. To this day it is she who's given credit for founding American Red Blood. She never ceases bad-mouthing the original Clarice Ding. "I think his views were most absurd about wars costing too much; how could anyone who wanted to reduce suffering want to make war less costly?" She always refers to him as "that little man from Geneva." For some reason she thought he was Swiss.

Over the years it has been rumored that American Red Blood collected and sold blood. Even though no one knew what to do with it or how to keep it "alive," this was a rumor from the very beginning and continues until the present day, when we do know what to do with it and how to keep it alive.

Blood is a cesspool and will always be one. It is certainly still a cesspool many decades later when Mrs. Rivka Jerusalem goes into the District to work for the national headquarters of American Red Blood and Mrs. Algonqua Lemish goes to work for the Franeeda County chapter in Hykoryville.

LUCID IN WASHINGTON

Arrives in Washington on the night of the very parade, Lucid with his two Messies. He has not come to Washington to march. Lucid has another mission to accomplish here. He has survived an earlier war.

He's brought his beloved Messie's ashes to Washington because he read there is a cemetery where beloveds can bury beloveds who were killed in battle defending their country. Certainly the giving of their youth to their country upon such battlefields as Fruit Island and New Bliss, Ohio, qualifies them both. He has come to think of the Massacre at Fruit Island as part of the Civil War. New Bliss is not exactly a Civil War battlefield, but no one has to know exactly where his Messie died.

He has come to think of the ashes in the can as his beloved, much to Messie Too's chagrin.

They are older now, a bit the worse for the unrooted restlessness that has taken them from Ohio to many other places, which, so unwavering are their wanderings, become nameless to them the moment they leave them. What is it that makes their feet refuse to stay in place? There is not a town or rooming house or bed that holds them for more than a few days. It is not that they grow bored. Indeed, there are many places that Messie, particularly, would like to explore in more peace and detail. But Lucid just can't do that, as Messie comes to realize soon enough into their journey from Mrs. Sary Peyser's in New Bliss. Messie also realizes that he wants to stay with Lucid, even though Lucid has a tendency not to see things that are there to be seen clear as day, like how much Messie Too is in love with him and in hurt from his not knowing this.

Lucid wants to bury his can of Voiceless in this cemetery in Washington, and when he is ready he will lie down beside him and they will live side by side forever. It does not take him long to discover that people in offices all over town look at him like he's crazy when, fumbling for the correct words, he tries to make his wishes known.

"I have the ashes of my friend here and I want to bury him in the government's cemetery for heroes."

He faces a grim elderly woman in the office of the Department of the Army. She is eyeing the container of Messie uncomfortably.

"There is no such cemetery as of yet."

"When will there be?"

"This is not known."

"Where is he, and we, to rest for eternity, then?"

"We?"

"Yes."

"You wish to be buried together?"

"Yes. Side by side."

"You are kin?"

"We are family to each other."

"But you are not related by blood?"

"No."

"What are you, then?"

"We are two dear friends with great love for each other."

"Yours is an unusual request that is not for this department to answer."

"Why not? We fought side by side and he died in my arms. What department should I go to?"

"I do not believe there is one."

He stands there staring at her. He does not know what to say next.

"Nor do I believe there should be one," says the grim woman. "You should be ashamed of yourself."

"Should I? Well, I am not. And you are saying more than you have been called upon to say!"

Then he follows this up by saying: "And of course there will never be a place for one man to lie down beside another man, no matter that the war was fought by nothing but brothers. Well, I am a brother who will fight to protect his brother even after death!"

The woman looks at him piercingly. He is much more intelligent than he appeared. She is moved by his words. She would not say so. She is not accustomed to dealing with intelligent men.

"I am sorry there is no place for you and your . . . brother to lie down together."

Out on the streets he finds himself smiling at his courage. He is proud that he stood up and spoke out and did not falter. Messie, the voiceless and dead one, has given him his voice.

Does Lucid realize he has crossed a new bridge? That there was indeed a war in which he can honestly claim that he and his Messies were heroes?

He tries to conceive of a way in which his request might not be perceived as peculiar. As he goes to more and more departments, of the Navy, of Health, of Dying, to the bureau of this and that and the office for this and that, he refines his technique so that his desires, in their abbreviation, become more rather than less obvious to the listener.

"If my reading of your situation is correct I think you had best leave this building, sir, for you are against the law of God."

He is to hear this often. There is that God again. He is all over the place. After several weeks without success he feels dirty, a failure, and ready for death himself. He doesn't even know how old he is, but he believes that his life must be near to over.

"You are afraid of something," Messie Too says often enough, never receiving an answer or affirmation of this quite correct suspicion. "Why won't you ever tell me anything? Isn't that what love is meant to do, help and be a balm?"

Such concern, attention, devotion, makes Lucid cry when he is alone. He does not want Messie to see his tears.

What precisely is Lucid afraid of? Of Punics, pursuing Punics come to poison his insides even more, come to reclaim the salve he still carries hidden deep inside his traveling pack. When he and Messie Too were on the road it was possible to outrun pursuing Punics, but now he is losing steam and he feels them catching up.

He knows he is being followed. He knows not by whom, but he senses it. He has been subjected to enough horrors that he knows when another one is near at hand.

That is why he never confides in Messie Too. One person's fear is more than enough for either of them to deal with.

He misses his first Messie, his Voiceless, very much. He carries his ashes everywhere, or rather the portion of the lad's body that Messie Too had managed to salvage from Mr. Milton Prance's mastiff's jaws. This vicious cur had been set loose by their "neighbor" after Lucid and Messie Too set forth from New Bliss never to return. But the dog's howling in the quiet night air forced Lucid's cognizance of the gruesome act in progress and thus impelled them back. Messie Too shot the ravenous animal, and together he and Lucid rescued as much of Voiceless from the clawed-up grave as they could before more of New Bliss rushed forth to try to incarcerate them once and for all.

Farther on, under the moon, they burned the remains of Voiceless. It is these ashes that Lucid carries still, in the little metal box.

Thus it is that Lucid is not available to Messie Too for physical passion, causing the new lad to suffer much painful unsatisfied desire. They had made love only once before the mastiff roared.

In Washington, in yet another unsmiling and unhappy room, when the lad goes out to explore, Lucid takes out his box of Voiceless and achieves the only erections and orgasms of which he is now capable, holding the box to his heart with his free hand.

The young man becomes too sad to bear it any longer. One morning when Lucid awakens, Messie Too is gone.

Lucid never even misses him. His box of his original Messie is enough. There is no point to moving on, he thinks. Where is there to go? There is no home anywhere, no childhood home, no safe backyard in which to bury Messie. Lucid decides to stay in Washington. It is his country too, so it is his capital too, and he will make it his home whether all the unkind and unhelpful government workers he has encountered since his arrival welcome him and his Messie or not.

He lives in a small cabin on the outskirts of town, toward Maryland. It is country here. The owner of the house does not live near. There is a bed and enough crude furniture, and a big fireplace. He can chop enough wood outside his door. It is a lonely area but this is what he desires. He feels most comfortable being lonely. It is ingrown in him. He knows no other way to feel. He counts up his money. He has managed frugally, and yes, there is still enough left, though he is not certain for how long. He has noticed that things cost more each day and week. He should look for some kind of work. But doing what?

When he no longer has the energy to maintain the necessary firm erection for his communion with his dead ashes, he does what he knew he would one day do. He takes out his pouch with its tin of Punic salve, the aphrodisiac that has already caused so much death, and he dabs some of it up his nose. Now he can get a big erection, fine and firm again, and make love to his Voiceless again, with the great passion his memory refuses to relinquish. He has used the salve only once before in Washington, after that big march, when he had met a very unhappy boy named Horatio Dridge (how could you forget a name like that?), who had lost his new love and had clung to Lucid earnestly, imploring him not to leave him too. They went into the forest of Rock Creek, and to cheer him up Lucid gave him a dab of Punic salve and jerked him off. Then he performed the same acts on himself and they fell asleep in each other's arms. When Horatio Dridge woke up he walked off into the night, taking a sample of the salve with him in a little tin from his chewing tobacco.

Lucid often wonders if Horatio ever found his lost friend.

PUSHNOW

It is in his small cabin that Pushnow finally catches up with Lucid Hooker and murders him in his bed in the dark of night and leaves his body, with the tin of the ashes of Voiceless, and its additional contents, the Punic salve and notebooks, no longer clutched to his chest.

He is not the first Pushnow nor will he be the last. Pushnows have been here forever. They have always ferreted out and bought and sold secrets. There are always secrets and they are always for sale. There are always Pushnows to buy and sell them. Pushnows even sold and continue to sell their very name, which has come to have its own stature in the world of secrets, conveying its own special fear or awe or respect among those who know about, or traffic in, these things.

So the salve has now gone out into the world, via Pushnow, via Horatio, and yes, via Messie Too.

GERMANS

We have not been keeping track of the Germans. We neglected to mention that 1,800 of them arrived in 1710. (There were only 103 Brits on the *Mayflower.*) There were only 6,000 people in New York City then. Where did they all move to, these Germans? Today more Americans claim German ancestry than any other. And we haven't been paying any attention to them! Well, there was no work for most of them in New York and they went up the Hudson, and then westward, to settle into hard times. We can trace dim patterns of their settlements because they named things after themselves. Fahrt Seed and Grain. Schmuck Wine and Liquor. *Fahrt* means a drive and *Schmuck* means a decoration, only they sound much better in English.

FROM WALT WHITMAN'S JOURNAL, 1869

"I cannot say I did much good though that is what I desired to do, solely. Though some thought I was only there for the boys, which of course was a truth undeniable and unrepentant. How could it be otherwise in an arena full of dying young men, and anyway what was the worse for the look?

"There is no pleasure in this. There is naught but surpassing pain. I at least am not ashamed to look upon all and be pained, and mortified, and full of unapologetic love, and sadness that this is my country.

"I am still punished for my looking and loving. I am denied the right to teach. I am forced to move from place to place because of untrue things people say about me. My books are made mortified and burned to crisps."

"I have just been informed by an old law partner of my most-missed Abe that he saw my talent right on, and would read aloud from my *Leaves of Grass* to people in his office, and told many that great things were to come from me. He took my book home, only to return with it next day saying if he left it home the womenfolk would burn it.

"My heart cries. It never stops."

HOMOSEXUALITY

In 1869 the word is first used by Karl Maria Kertbeny, a German-Hungarian doctor campaigning against the criminalization of sex between men in Prussia, which is about to adopt the infamous Paragraph 75, which Hitler himself will continue to invoke. In 1871 the Reichstag will officially pass the Imperial Criminal Code, which includes a law prohibiting sexual penetration of one man by another. Kertbeny writes a letter to the German minister of justice arguing that the state has no business entering people's bedrooms. Prior to his coinage of the word *homosexual*, gay people were called Uranians or the intermediate sex. Havelock Ellis and Richard von Krafft-Ebing usually get the credit for first using *homosexual* a little later in the century (the latter's hugely influential *Psychopathia Sexualis* comes out in 1886). No doubt earlier examples will be found, but Kertbeny is the earliest uprooted thus far. The word travels around the world with speed. There is much hunger for it. In Chicago, another Hungarian-German doctor, Grody von Eyssen, writes a letter to a minister of justice in Pennsylvania literally copying Kertbeny's wording. This act is taken by some gay historians as the beginning of gay activism in America. Von Eyssen is never heard of again and homosexual acts, in Pennsylvania and state by state across most of America, have already been declared a crime.

But now hushmarkeds have a name! We are are here officially, although an article in *The Journal of Modern History*, "The German Invention of Modern Homosexuality," gives one pause; it maintains that modern conceptions of homosexuality began, ironically, with this 1871 German antisodomy law.

A CELEBRATORY WALT!

When I heard at the close of the day how my name
had been receiv'd with plaudits in the capitol,
still it was not a happy night for me that
follow'd;
And else, when I carous'd, or when my plans were
accomplish'd, still I was not happy;
But the day when I rose at dawn from the bed of
perfect health, refresh'd, singing, inhaling the
ripe breath of autumn,
When I saw the full moon in the west grow pale and
disappear in the morning light,
When I wander'd alone over the beach, and undressing,
bathed, laughing with the cool waters, and
saw the sun rise,
And when I thought how my dear friend, my lover,
was on his way coming, O then I was happy;
O then each breath tasted sweeter—and all that day
my food nourish'd me more—and the beautiful
day pass'd well,
And the next came with equal joy—and with the next,
at evening, came my friend;
And that night, while all was still, I heard the waters
roll slowly continually up the shores,
I heard the hissing rustle of the liquid and sands, as
directed to me, whispering, to congratulate me,
For the one I love most lay sleeping by me under the
same cover in the cool night,
In the stillness, in the autumn moonbeams, his face
was inclined toward me,
And his arm lay lightly around my breast—and that
night I was happy.

LESBIAN

The year 1870 seems to be when the word *lesbian* is first used to differentiate a female homosexual. There does not appear to be as much etymological history available for the actual first use of this word. As with Germans, we have not been paying "lesbians" sufficient attention. They were not considered as dangerous as their male counterparts. However, one of those Cottons, John, tried to get them punished, and Thomas Jefferson, of all people, in 1779 tried to pass a law stipulating that a woman, if caught in such activity, would be punished "by cutting thro' the cartilage of her nose a hole of one half inch diameter at the least." Havelock Ellis (British) and Richard von Krafft-Ebing (German) seem, again, to be the first two doctors to officially discuss this activity of female same-sexuality, and perhaps they are the ones who named it after Sappho, the great poet who lived in 600 B.C. on the ancient Greek island of Lesbos surrounded by many women; but one hesitates to give these chaps that much credit for worldly knowledge, particularly when Krafft-Ebing has already bracketed homosexuality with insanity.

MEDICAL REACTION TO THE OFFICIAL IDENTIFICATION OF HOMOSEXUALITY

How does this new nomenclature and the pursuant visibility of this new "class" of people affect the medical establishment?

This is a topic that will form a good deal of the remainder of this history. Without the ability of the world to identify homosexuals, or their ability to identify each other, there would be . . . what? A different world? No Underlying Condition?

DR. PAULUS PEWKIN IS ASKED HIS OPINION OF EARLY HOMOSEXUALS

Over the decades, nay the centuries, the attitudes of the medical establishment (and all other establishments) remain remarkably consistent. In the early 1980s, when Dr. Pewkin is asked his opinion of early homosexuals, he has this to say:

"I am chief at the U.S. Center of Disease. The appearance of homosexuals is always a kettle of smelly fish. I have my Ph.D. in Communicable Diseases from Yaddah. I am an expert on syphilis and every other kind of claptrap humans can give to each other. I'm a scientist. I'm an expert in public health. I don't understand literature or history, both of which imagine all sorts of things and pass them off as fact. In science none of this is fact. I have at my disposal at NITS the Admiral Mason Iron Vaultum Library, the entire record of this country and its medicine and its hospitals and its illnesses and diseases, and I tell you that in all these books and volumes and records—and I know because I have asked that this matter be researched thoroughly in light of the current hoopla by a few people over all these homosexuals dying today— there was only heterosexuality until the twentieth century, when something dire went wrong in the gene pool or some kind of pool and homosexuality oozed out. Nobody in their right mind did it before then. How could they? They'd be dead. People would murder them. Quite rightly. It's obviously happening all over again. They got too big for their britches and they're dying again. It's got nothing to do with bigotry. It's got to do with pragmatic practicality. We have to breed! Breeders don't like their breeding interfered with. Otherwise there'd still be Indians. Damn, we'd probably *be* the Indians."

INTERVIEWS WITH AND ABOUT HOMOSEXUALS

The following appeared in *The Louisville Advocate* on October 21, 1870.

So that is what I am called. All my life I have had these feelings without a name. I cannot say I feel better with a name. The name is not pleasant to hear pronounced or see in print, especially here in Louisville, Kentucky. I do not know what good it is to have a word for me. A man came up to me in the market on Saturday where I shop for my weekly food. I cook for myself and live by myself and I think this other man does the same because I have seen him shopping here before. "So," he asks me, "are you a homosexual too?" I pretend I don't know what he's talking about but I do know and he knows I know. When I don't answer he is most impolite. "Don't you think you might be a little more pleasant now that we are brothers?" he says. I hit him. "You are not my brother," I yell loudly. People look at me and move away from me and I run into an alleyway a few stalls up from the vegetables. At the beginning of the fruit I start to cry.

People passing by look even more strangely at me. "Why are you crying?" one old woman asks me. "You look like a strong man who should not have to cry." I go to another market to buy my food now because I do not want to see that man or that woman.

Who is going to read what you write in your newspaper? Please keep my name out, and any description of what I look like. I am sorry I agreed to this. Your paper wrote that anyone willing to come forward and talk about it would be paid two dollars. Now you tell me that you will not give me my two dollars unless I can prove I am one of them. How? You cannot tell me? I must prove it myself? I don't know how. I'm going to cry again. The doctor who wrote your article asking for volunteers said this new name would make us all happy. He said it would make us feel like we have our place in the world at last. It doesn't. It just makes me want to go home and lock my door and pull down my window shades. Perhaps I must move to another place. Cleveland or Detroit or Minneapolis. But they are all too cold. It's cold enough here. Suddenly I want to be some place where I never have to be cold again. I wonder if there is such a place. Why won't you give me my two dollars you promised me?

Around the same time, a diversity of homosexuals are interviewed in various publications around America: Carroll Cameron, a photographer, one of this country's first professional ones (*St. Louis Post*); Natasha Kilbogen, a lab technician in a hospital laboratory (*Seattle Post*); Reynall Murphy, a haberdasher in Ohio (*The Sandusky Post*); Arthur Adelphi, an actor in Philadelphia (*Actors' Weekly Report*); Horstus Schoensten, a dentist in Versteht, Wisconsin (*Milwaukee Heimat*); Ogunquit Chou, a medicine man of the Ogunquit tribe in Maine (*Ogunquit Tribal Journal*); Sarah Fidalmeh Toobin, a Brooklyn rabbi's estranged wife (*Jewish Forward*); O'Ransky Triall, a ninety-year-old veteran of the Irish-Mashush Wars that destroyed a good part of Galway in 1825 (*Four-Leaf Clover*, Queens, N.Y.). There are interviews with some two hundred "former hushmarkeds" in the Mansion Clare Foundation archives, all appearing between 1869 and 1871. There is not a man or woman among them who likes the new nomenclature.

Stories about the deaths of homosexuals, particularly from suicide, also begin to appear in the press. "Now that they have a name for themselves, homosexuals can no longer hide, and they often cannot bear the light of day," declares an editorial in the *St. Louis Post* in 1872. One particularly unpleasant paper, *Raw Reports*, in Baltimore, runs a regular tally of men (and women, too, although women are rarely included in any public discussion of this new topic) who commit suicide, or disappear, which *Raw Reports* believes amounts to the same thing. The tally runs every Monday. Weekends are evidently ripe for "disappearances."

Suddenly many Pushnows are everywhere to round up these wayward lads. Some are even under contract to the Tally Office. One Pushnow broadcasts the instructions to his network, which sound kindly enough: "Try to catch them up before someone gets them."

That Tally Office is rounding up and collecting as many names as it can. The Disciples of Lovejoy love to collect names. They want to collect the names of everyone who ever lived, anywhere and everywhere in the world. Their religion says they must consecrate all people who have died, because they do not believe anyone ever dies. They have determined that they will not consecrate homosexuals. But they will have all those names when the time comes for . . . what?

This is not the place to go into this remarkable activity, but when we do you should know that *Homo sapiens sapiens*, which is what we are, began to appear about a hundred thousand years ago; ten thousand years ago the world's population was a little over 5 million; by the beginning of the Christian Era the population had risen to between 200 million and 400 million; by 1750 the world's population can be estimated with 20 percent accuracy to have been around 800 million. (Thanks to Dame Lady Hermia, and *The New Gotham* and Alex Shoumatoff.) And these Lovejoy folks are going to collect *all* their names and *all* the info they can on each and every one of them. It is now enshrined as a cornerstone of their religion.

The first federal census was only taken in 1790, with new ones conducted every ten years. For whatever reason no president has ever allowed detailed information gathered from these censuses to be divulged. What is that all about? What did they reveal?

Anyway, so it is that many American people now read about this new breed of American people called homosexuals. There is a flurry of newspaper interest in the new name and the newly named. This is a whole new category of news. Homosexuals. There are tens of thousands of newspapers in America. Hushmarkeds are no longer hush-hush. How do The American People react, if one could embrace them all in a generalization?

AN OFFICIAL MURDER OF SOMEONE DIFFERENT

The first arrest, detention, and conscious, intentional extermination of a homosexual by an employee of the United States Government (that is, the first that can be located as such in an official record) is that of Paul Evenrute, who is asphyxiated in a small cell in the Milwaukee County Jail on January 1, 1875. In the deceased's records there is a "work order" for a "smothering to death." George A. Ockton, a "behavior guard," performs it. The records contain no indication of Evenrute's behavior or misbehavior. Evenrute was twenty-four years old and worked for the Schlitz Brewery as a hops jumper, someone who throws bags of hops from wagon to vatside. He was well liked by his fellow workers. When his homosexuality was revealed in an interview Evenrute gave voluntarily to the *Milwaukee Record Arbeiter* for twenty-five dollars, there was no apparent communal displeasure, according to the town's mayor, Helmut Wolfe, who professed surprise at Ockton's action, which occurred shortly after the interview.

Although there is an "official request" in Evenrute's file that he be killed, it is not signed with a recognizable signature, and when the whole matter becomes public Ockton is fired. Subsequently he is hired by Schlitz and remains there for the forty years left of his working life. He will never speak about the "smothering" beyond being heard to say that he could not find a woman to marry him because his two hands had been used to choke someone to death.

In June 1875, Ockton is sent a commendation by the Idaho Association of Healthy Men, one of several early fronts now financed by Hesiod Furstwasser I, according to research conducted by Hamilton Moyne-Lebber in his groundbreaking 1984 study, *Emerging Hate: The Early Homosexual Revelations, 1869–1900.* According to Moyne-Lebber's important book there are 447 prison deaths nationally during those three decades, all following similar voluntary revelations of the victims' homosexuality in the public press, and all accompanied by "official requests" that are unsigned or bear illegible signatures. It is almost as if someone or some group is going around the country following up on these newspaper confessions and stirring up activities inside the prisons. After Ockton leaves the jail, other "behavior guards" and indeed other prisoners take up killing homosexuals, now that they have a name and have been described more or less recognizably, an activity that is still a major problem in institutions of incarceration. So a certain pattern is being set. The IAHM becomes the National Association of Healthy Men, which, as we shall see, even as it changes its name again, and then again, and then many times more in its attempt to outrace any possible government or public outcry (which never materializes, anywhere), remains in the forefront of virulent hatred of homosexuals with, at last report, forty-three paid lobbyists in Washington and various state capitals, as well as innumerable and uncounted less-visible chapters, most of them underground. Its headquarters will move from Partekla, Idaho, to Trebla, Idaho, and then to Verstehen, Utah, and finally, in March 1912, to Washington, D.C., where the Tally Office, established and run by the Disciples, is up and running in the office next door.

As little by little the faceless Tally Office gains its grip on its "mandate," there is growing terror in the land of the homosexual. While it is not difficult to sense when the forces of evil are abroad in your land, it is frightening when you cannot see your enemy face to face. Or perhaps you can, or could, if you were experienced in recognizing evil, which of course few are. No one understands there is also safety in numbers. Fear grows.

So far, there is only whispering and mumbling among homosexual men. It appears no one has suffered, *appears* being the operative word. There is only scuttlebutt about a friend of a friend who . . .

AND ALSO . . .

In 1895, Teddy Roosevelt is put in charge of the New York Police Department and determines to clean up this "city that never sleeps," this "island of vice." The streets are so filled with offenders that they are virtually impassable to the clean-hearted. Why, on West Twenty-seventh Street alone there are whorehouses at numbers 101, 103, 105, 107, 109, 111, 119, 121, 123, and across the street at 104, 106, 108, 122, 126, 128, 130, 132, 134, 140, and 142. Between the Civil War and World War I, the city's population just about quadrupled. There appears to be work, certainly something to do, for all. Many jobs and pastimes are of course against the law, but try to find enough law enforcers to monitor and punish it all. By 1897, Teddy gave up and went to Washington hoping to find something more rewarding for a career.

RUTHERFRAUD B. HAYES

There was a disputed election in 1876. By promising to remove the troops that were keeping order in the South, Rutherford Hayes defeated his Democratic opponent, Samuel Tilden. As a result of this removal of law and order, the hard-won rights of the black citizens proved worthless, blacks returned to their former servile state, and the civil rights revolution was stalled until the twentieth century. The Civil War might just as well not have been fought.

SEVERAL NINETEENTH-CENTURY MEN

So many have a similar profile: young men born into a growing and struggling country where people were still lucky just to stay alive. They might have large ideals but they have, as well, large experience of hardship and need and, most particularly, the lack of affection. Mothers, fathers sire too many offspring and then die young, or disappear, or are so ratcheted into God that freedoms—of expression, of emotion, of love, allowing oneself to be, without so many restrictions of right and wrong dictated by so many invisible forces to which one can't talk back—are frowned upon and hence usually never taken.

Men and women simply do not know how to love each other. However would they or could they learn? How do they really know what love is, and means? We are told that they did, in the many paraphrasings of their lives that continue to be manufactured for us. But there were no great romances for them to emulate, no TV or movies or even bodice-ripping volumes to point the way. There is only some peculiar God who is harsh and punishing and exceedingly ungrateful for all the devotion offered to Him. No one, it would appear, knows any other way. Where is the historian of all of this truth, the continuing lovelessness of America?

FRED SUMMONS T. HEWLING DUPPERS

Fred has generously invited me on board for a change of tone. I am a professor of American history who writes about the boring stuff. I am often called in when a course instructor isn't up to it because whatever it is is so boring. Kids got to be taught a lot of stuff that's boring. It turns out I'm your man. If I didn't have tenure I doubt I'd still be here (on my retirement pension). I'm one of the few fairies Yaddah didn't axe back in those '60s when Mendenhall and Griswold ruled the roost and hated fairies, fiercely. My pal Newton Arvin, who courageously wrote about the homosexual subtexts in Herman Melville, committed a certain kind of treason up at Smith, of all places, and

Joel Dorius, with whom Fred studied, damn near did so because charges by the Northampton police ruined his career, too. And he was only visiting Newton. They and a few others were accused of looking at pictures of men in bathing suits. That's all that male porn amounted to in those days. Bathing suits. Not even with erections bulging out of a crotch. Some police in Northampton without any legal permission broke into Newton's home and located a bunch of pictures of men in bathing suits. Bathing suits. Boxer-style. Not even Speedo. Anyway, my name is Trenton Hewling Duppers. That's a good boring name. I hope you won't say it too loudly. You can call me Hugh. The walls in this place still have ears. It's really like Soviet Russia here. To this day, you can only teach so much stuff at Yaddah and go so far. Like I say, I got my pension and I guess they can't take that away from me; but I wouldn't push even that too far at this place. Fred says it's like Soviet Russia, too. I guess he said it first, at least out loud.

In the case of these two particular important boring men Fred wants me to fill you in on, James Abram Garfield and Anthony Comstock, he says it is their sexual lives that got them into all their trouble. Well, that's certainly a treat for me. Academics aren't usually allowed to tackle sex lives. I hope you realize that Fred is going way out on a limb to include all this in his book. What fun! Although I think these two clinkers are getting in under the wire and rather it is the hypocrisy surrounding their lives that is the issue. It is not easy to teach kids (or the world!) about hypocrisy. Or irony. (I call them the yin and yang of history so at least a few kids can identify.) Both hypocrisy and irony are more and more prominent among the underlying conditions (if I may borrow this name that I know Fred favors so much for another human uncertainty) with which history must increasingly deal. Comstock only jerked off all the time and Garfield got assassinated by a crazy man because he was gay, neither of which is especially sexy, hypocritical, or ironic, in and of itself.

Mind you, the crazy assassin certainly had a peculiar sexual history as well. But then, everybody has a peculiar sexual history, in the sense that it is special to him, though if the person is boring, as these two are, then their peculiar sex lives tend to be boring too. C'est la vie. And if that's the bottom line for Fred, he's going to churn out a book longer than Gibbon and Herodotus and Thucydides combined. Perhaps that's what he wants. I know size is all to many gay guys but I hadn't thought Fred was like that. All those guys are a bitch to teach to kids today, especially, I find, Thucydides. Very cold bugger. Let's get started. The quicker we start, you'll see what I mean and you can take it or leave it, I'll understand. I'm not certain who comes after my two guys. I'm an easy act to follow. Anybody is more interesting. I think it's Sam Clemens. Now, I could make him boring for you too when I point out that I don't know why everyone loves him so much. He wasn't very lovable. But then, most people aren't.

JAMES ABRAM GARFIELD (1831–1881)

James Garfield might have been a decent-enough president if he hadn't been murdered. Mind you, the competition for most useless leader during these late-nineteenth-century years is great (Rutherford Hayes in office before, Chester Arthur to follow Garfield).

He always worries that he is not man enough. His ambition for himself is compulsive and never-ending. After many a tussle looking for salvation, through God, through educating youth and then administering their schools, he becomes a lawyer, a decent one, if overly and intentionally concerned (because it is less controversial; it is safe) with issues of little interest to the masses, such as monetary policy, which make him appear more boring than perhaps he is and I can make him. He believes it wrong to hold slaves and wrong to free them. His fellow Republicans said not to meddle with slavery, and he will go along with that.

He is righteous, that's to be sure. He is some 200 pounds, and quite tall, six feet, but with short legs, which give his massive torso an off-balance presence, which goes well with his objective of tilting himself slightly forward not to miss important things, when he knew what they might be. This aggressive personality is sometimes overpowering, often rude, always proud. He discovers that all this makes people look at you. At last. You've got to keep them on their toes.

He, too, was born in a log cabin. He, too, had a strong mother and a father who died young and a stepfather who was unkind to her and him; so all his growing up was nothing but unhappiness, not, as mentioned, unusual in growing America, even in Ohio. That he is constantly drawn as a teenager to the wharves of Cleveland, where he listens intently to the exciting tales of the seamen, does begin to indicate a certain interest in their half-naked bodies displayed so vigorously and unselfconsciously before him.

He attends a tiny Christian biblical college, the Western Reserve Eclectic Institute, in the tiny town of Hiram, where, like Lincoln, he begins his difficulties with the opposite sex, courting them, then retreating, not fully understanding why he does so, nor, it would appear, even wondering about it. Like Lincoln, he will finally find one, Lucretia, and marry her; she is decently well-born and patient and supportive and all-suffering (she will bear him seven children), and she is there for her Jamie until his end, not all that very far away.

After Hiram he will study at Williams College in the East, which will polish his rough edges enormously. Like a growing number of other institutions of learning, it is on its way to becoming more materialistic and less spiritual. He gets invited back to Hiram to be head of his former school, and he accepts.

At both Hiram and Williams and back again at Hiram appears one James Harrison Rhodes (1836–1890). Harry is a short, attractive, neat young man who, like Garfield before him, was a student and instructor at Hiram and a student at Williams and then a fellow professor at Hiram. It is hard to pinpoint just when this similar trajectory becomes a joint journey and they become inseparable and begin to live with each other, sharing sleeping quarters, writing each other letters, calling each other "My Love." "Dear Harry," Garfield writes him in 1858, only four months after his marriage to Lucretia, "I would that we might lie in each other's arms for one long wakeful night and talk not in the thoughts or words of the grand old masters, nor from the Bards sublime, but in that language whose tone gushes from the heart."

You may well ask, where oh where oh where does a man learn how to love another man? There were certainly no great American romances of this kind for them to emulate. Whatever the inherent turmoils, they do not appear to trouble the lives of either Jamie or Harry. Each leaves diaries with evidence of their love and no mention of their difficulties in owning up to it. Harry will be at Garfield's side for the remaining years of his life. He, too, will marry and father children (one of whom, obviously homosexual, will become a prolifically successful playwright). Sound business practices, good contacts, and timely investments will make Harry a very wealthy man.

One wonders why Charles Guiteau (1841–1882) feels compelled to murder James Garfield, thus committing the second of our presidential assassinations. There is no doubt that he is a crazy person. He, too, is the product of a loveless marriage between a father who believed in a vengeful God and a frail mother whose own sanity was not secure and who, two deceased infants later, took her leave from her unhappy life when Charles was only seven.

For James Garfield was a compulsion for Charles Guiteau. He stalked and followed and notated as many movements of Garfield as he could. He felt fated to rid the world of this man; it was a "political necessity." For he knew that Jamie Garfield and Harry Rhodes were "unnatural" lovers. He had been a janitor at Hiram. He would hide in adjoining rooms when they covertly met to kiss and embrace and "hold each other, to last us till tonight," as he often heard Jamie say to Harry as he lowered his trousers to get his hand around his lover's penis. "I had a muss in my pants from watching them and I did not like this at all," Charles wrote in one of his endless diaries. He was fired for making advances toward a young maid (he, too, had a history of being rejected by women) who cleaned Garfield's rooms. "I was only trying to gain entrance and learn more about this nasty man," he also wrote in his confession, which, at several hundred handwritten pages, was so long that no one ever read it, certainly no lawyer defending him, or judge who condemned him to die.

Undeterred, Charles Guiteau, his obsession with Garfield unrelenting, now becomes Garfield's biggest booster. He will become such a big booster, and make so many unsought speeches on Garfield's behalf as he runs for various political offices, that he becomes convinced he is entitled to a counselor position at (preferably) the United States missions in Vienna, Paris, or Liverpool. Garfield must give him this, if only to shut him up.

Years earlier, Guiteau's father had heard about the Oneida Colony, not for its "celebration" of free love but for its heavy emphasis on Bible study. His son, he thought, must go there. That would put him right in his own head. Charles finally agrees when he learns they practice this "free love." He cannot believe his good fortune when he discovers all its aspects, not only with women but with men, only to discover they are not so free for all and certainly not for him. Rejections abound. He is thrown out, not once but twice. John Noyes, the founder, bases Guiteau's final expulsion on the young man's losing battle with masturbation, a forbidden activity at Oneida, indeed at every God-fearing habitation in America. Charles is to write, "Men are not allowed to touch their things. What am I now to do with it?"

Somehow he had managed to eke out six years of attendance at Oneida. He then tries to sue Noyes for a $9,000 reimbursement. Noyes lets loose with the masturbation charge and Charles returns fire with the charge that Noyes was manipulating all the Oneida women to do his personal naughty wiles. "All the girls that were born in the Community were forced to cohabit with Noyes at such an early period it dwarfed them. The result is that most of the

Oneida women were small and thin and homely." His vehicle for this exposure is a newspaper that he himself writes and gives out on the streets of New York, where "even before my eyes they are sent to the gutter." His father, refusing to notice that his son is going insane, or is already there, or always had been there, prefers to believe that what is destroying him is "the free exercise of his unbridled lust."

Somehow the son manages to find a woman who marries him. They move to Chicago, and he tries a few cases badly, calling himself a lawyer. He beats his wife up and escapes many creditors as he goes back east, now calling himself "a man of God now called by God," and conceives of the tactic to bring Garfield into his ken, his orbit, to win the undying gratitude that can only grant him his embassy appointment abroad. He writes a speech pointing out that Garfield must be elected the next president: otherwise a return to the Democrats can only bring a resumption of the Civil War.

Somehow it works. He is asked to deliver it again and again at various gatherings as the forthcoming elections hover closer. He prints it up in broadsides that he distributes in New York and now in Washington, to which he moves so he can further press his case after Garfield is elected. His message has hit home. Whether or not it elected Garfield, as Charles is convinced it did, Charles is on the spot to demand his due. In those days you could actually get into the White House itself. He'd go there, crazy Charles Guiteau would, looking for anyone who would listen to him. He becomes quite adept at siphoning out Garfield's staff and collaring them, and even the president. Everyone by now knows the guy is nuts. His own father is to write, after his son's hanging, "I have no doubt that masturbation and self-abuse is at the bottom of his mental imbecility."

Of course, the job abroad never arrives. He writes an "Address to The American People": "I conceived of the idea of removing the President . . . I conceived of the idea myself . . . gradually the conviction settled on me that the President's removal was a political necessity, because he proved a traitor to the men who made him, and thereby imperiled the life of the Republic . . . This is not murder. It is a political necessity . . . The President's removal is an act of God."

He buys a revolver, he practices with it on the banks of the Potomac, he goes to the railroad station from which Garfield is to depart for a vacation, he has his shoes shined there, he even hires a hack for transfer to the District Prison after his arrest. He fully expects that his country will be grateful to him and that he will be pardoned. He fires two shots at President Garfield. President Garfield takes two and a half months to die. His tenure has been two hundred days.

It is now believed that he died not from Guiteau's bullets but from the wretched medical care he received, the doctors turning tiny rips into major excavations in their efforts to retrieve the bullets. These became infected.

Charles Guiteau believed that too. He thought he should have been acquitted, and was planning a lecture tour of Europe. After all, the president died from malpractice. But Charles was hanged. He had written a poem that he delivered in a loud and clear voice. "I am going to the Lordy. I am so glad. I am going to the Lordy. I am so glad." Etc. In that long prison confession that not even his lawyer had read, he'd written: "Tell my Pappy I masturbated muchly because it let me think of Jamie loving me instead of Harry whilst doing it."

ANTHONY COMSTOCK AND
HIS COMSTOCK ACT (1873)

"Be it enacted . . . That whoever, within the District of Columbia or any of the Territories of the United States . . . shall sell . . . or shall offer to sell, or to lend, or to give away, or in any manner to exhibit, or shall otherwise publish or offer to publish in any manner, or shall have in his possession, for any such purpose or purposes, an obscene book, pamphlet, paper, writing, advertisement, circular, print, picture, drawing or other representation, figure, or image on or of paper of other material, or any cast instrument, or other article of an immoral nature, or any drug or medicine, or any article whatever, for the prevention of conception, or for causing unlawful abortion, or shall advertise the same for sale, or shall write or print, or cause to be written or printed, any card, circular, book, pamphlet, advertisement, or notice of any kind, stating when, where, how, or of whom, or by what means, any of the articles in this section . . . can be purchased or obtained, or shall manufacture, draw, or print, or in any wise make any of such articles, shall be deemed guilty of a misdemeanor, and on conviction thereof in any court of the United States . . . he shall be imprisoned at hard labor in the penitentiary for not less than six months nor more than five years for each offense, or fined not less than one hundred dollars nor more than two thousand dollars, with costs of court."

Whence cometh such fervor?

Those words and this act changed the lives of The American People forever.

This Comstock Act of 1875 was brought into being, rather amazingly, since he was such a nerd, by Anthony Comstock, and nobody liked him and many made fun of him as he rushed into premises all over New York to "catch you in the act" of whatever he'd been tipped off about, including sticking a condom on your dick in the privacy of your own home.

He jerked off a great deal. It bothered him a great deal. He knew he was a sinner. He just couldn't stop. No matter how much church he went to. Just couldn't keep his hands off himself. We know this because the chap kept a private diary every day of his life. "This morning was severely tempted by Satan and after some time in my own weakness I failed." There were a lot of days he did it more than once. "Again tempted and found wanting. Sin, sin. Oh how much peace and happiness is sacrificed on thy altar. Seemed as though Devil had full sway over me today, went right into temptation, and then, Oh such love, Jesus snatched it away out of my reach. How good is He, how sinful am I. I am the chief of sinners, but I should be so miserable and wretched, were it not that God is merciful and I may be forgiven. Glory be to God in the highest. O I deplore my sinful weak nature so much. If I could but live without sin, I should be the happiest soul living: but Sin, that foe is ever lurking, stealing happiness from me." His penis must have been sore as all hell. He must have located some decent goo to protect it. Wish he'd written about that.

In one way or another the law or portions of the law or updated versions of this act that Anthony got passed are still in healthy working order all over America. That it is a clear act of censorship, a clear violation of privacy and freedom of speech, only makes a lot of people feel safer. Really, it's not so far removed from what Jonathan Edwards had been raging about a hundred years before. Keep it in your pants, fellow Americans, and don't send anything through the mails. (Well, Edwards didn't say anything about those mails.) A lot of The American People actually want to be censored and protected against anything "dirty."

From a too early age Anthony was very upset seeing anything pornographic, when in New York City, at this moment in time (although it had been the same for many years before this moment in time), you couldn't walk two blocks without your eyes being offered something pornographic. That one man's dirt is another man's art, or passion, is almost beside the point and has also never been decided with any definitiveness, which is probably just as well. (I'm not supposed to go on so. Fred told me keep it short and he's not paying me full rate.)

What do we know about this Comstock who brags about destroying 15 tons of books, 284,000 pounds of plates for printing "objectionable" books, and nearly 4 million dirty pictures? And don't forget his 4,000 arrests and the at least 15 suicides of people he was closing in on. And the 60,300 "articles made of rubber for immoral purposes," 5,500 sets of playing cards, and 31,150 boxes of pills and powders ("aphrodisiacs"). Yes, he brags about them all. And about his arraignments over the years in state and federal courts of some 3,697 persons, of whom 2,740 pleaded guilty or were convicted. Among these were a number of persons of intelligence and moral fiber concerned for free speech or the right to disseminate knowledge respecting birth control.

How did this guy bring about this monumental change in America's law almost all by himself, because, you know, most people don't like to talk about any of this in public? We could infer that Anthony was a sensitive soul but he wasn't. Women and children were to be protected from men's lusts at all costs; their innocence was the ultimate example of God's wisdom and grace, and must be preserved from male desire. Anthony was all about decency.

He was born in Connecticut, one of ten children, three of whom died; his father had land, a sawmill; he also farmed and was well-to-do, until he died, when Anthony was ten, but that's okay because his devoted mother was ready to gobble him up. She didn't know why he went to church a dozen times a week but she approved of it. Even when he was briefly in the Army he found a way to go to church every single day. His fellow soldiers thought he was unusual and didn't want anything to do with him, which didn't bother Anthony, already very much in the "I'll show them" school of American entrepreneurship. He worked in a dry goods store, which was the only regular-paying job he had. It was the only job he ever had. For forty years. A clerk.

He certainly doesn't know anyone in Washington. He is a volunteer for the Young Men's Christian Association, just revving up in New York, where he corners a couple of stern-faced fellows on its board and convinces them he has something important to say. He's prepared a full report for them on his own, you see. This is a man with a mission. (This is a pleasant irony, if you believe in any such thing, because the YMCA, whose official history claims it was formed in response to "the craving of young men for companionship with each other," would shortly become the biggest meeting place for homosexuals in America, and probably still is, with its gyms and cheap rooms and shared toilets and showers for the traveling man on a limited budget, or rather, with an unlimited appetite for meeting other men; but that is still a few years down the road.) Anthony outlines for these YMCA board members his plans for cleaning up the city. They are not a larky group, this board; they rarely smile. They all look more or less like Anthony, tall, big barrel chest, with effulgent muttonchoppy whiskers that make their bald heads look much balder. These guys have the friends in Washington. And Anthony can be a very convincing salesman, for the health and welfare, of course, of The American People. The bill gets passed. As noted, we still live with much of it. In parts of America they live with all of it. Anthony is appointed secretary of the New York Society for the Suppression of Vice. It all becomes, God help us (and of course in this area He doesn't), very heavy-duty stuff from this moment on.

One should always wonder, what would have happened without the Comstock Act? Kids would see a lot of dirty pictures, which can't be all that bad for a young person starting out on the road of life, and men would be free to use condoms so that the 676,009 illegitimate babies born in New York City alone during the years of Anthony Comstock's living there might not have been conceived.

Let us be clear: the Comstock Act has hauled into court the likes of Shaw, Dreiser, Dos Passos, Faulkner, Joyce, Picasso, Lawrence, Aristophanes, Lysistrata, *The Canterbury Tales*, O'Neill, Balzac, Wilde, Odets, Steinbeck, every painter who painted, gasp, nude women or sculpted them, even worse, and me. Even anatomy textbooks were prohibited from being sent to medical students by the United States Postal Service, for which Comstock was now an unpaid director. And this dry goods salesman remained a dry goods salesman for all of the forty years he wielded his censorship power.

He may be laughed at but his picture is in a newspaper regularly, which pleases his mom no end. He has married his "Wifey," quite a bit taller than he is, as well as ten years older, and she weighs only 65 pounds but Mom is in residence too. Mothers are very important to crusaders. Wifey bore a child who shortly died and from a dying prostitute Anthony stole a newborn baby just for Wifey; she wasn't very bright or healthy and eventually they had to put her in a home.

Before his death, Comstock attracted the interest of a young law student, J. Edgar Hoover, interested in his causes and methods. Hoover asked for a meeting and tour and pointers, "any help that you can give me because your heroic stands in New York should be followed across the nation," he wrote to him. One wonders where Anthony took him? Perhaps they discovered a shared interest in beating off. Hoover is cut from the same cloth as Comstock, only nastier. Interesting how all these guys find each other.

At this point, classy historians like Bledd-Wrench reach for a final "summing-up" containing a major statement about history and life. The Comstock Act as "a great dividing line," that sort of thing. It certainly succeeded in making the federal government an intrusive oppressor of the personal lives of The American People in an unprecedented way. It would be particularly hard on males. Private life had been much simpler before it. Male sexual outlets would come increasingly under assault: prostitution, pornography, age-of-consent laws, same-sex relations—all were areas where males up through Lincoln's time had an easier time of it. Yes, indeedy, something happened to men by the twentieth century that altered their relationships with one another. Anthony and his harsh "morality" put the nail in the coffin of the "after all, we're all human" outlook on life that some people, who one day I guess will be called liberals, were just beginning to speak up about.

He died in September 1915. No one remembers his name.

Me, I'm not a major-statement person. The astonishing fury of this man's creation is a major statement on its own.

So long, for now. I wasn't really all that boring, was I?

YRH PIECES TOGETHER THE LIFE
OF "MARK TWAIN"

Mark Twain wrote the first gay American novel and nobody paid any attention to him. "I wrote this book and tried to tell the world about where my heart resided. I thought long and hard about doing this because I knew not all would want to hear it or have sympathy for it. But I also knew by then that my words could change people. That was the most exciting discovery I ever made. I told them all about the Bible, how it is full of interest, it has noble poetry in it; and some clever fables; and some good morals; and a wealth of obscenity; and upwards of a thousand lies. They slapped their thighs in laughter and agreement."

I can't be the only homosexual writer who at some time has felt the same cleft into two, the same "I will write this and not tell you that," the identical fear that Sam Clemens has, that if I tell you, the world out there, too much, you'll punish me for my thoughts and deeds.

If ever a great writer put one over on The American People it was Sam. He changed his name to get away from us. He thought it was because he didn't want his momma to know some stuff. He was what some guys he hung out with called "a real pisser"; in his exuberant needs he pissed every which way on truth. He recognized he was getting away with it. People loved it. They laughed and laughed. This made him frightened. It did not make *him* laugh. But it made him rich.

All the others his age went off to fight in a war. Well, war was not for him. Two weeks and he left it, just walked away. They want to go and knock each other's brains out and kill each other, just shows how stupid man can be. He felt lucky that he discovered early enough how stupid they all were and how smart he could be not to be like them. It probably saved his life. And Sam liked black people, especially if they were young boys. Young boys had a mystery for him, and always would. It was a way for him to dream about the youth he never had. Yes, he dreamed. Sam's first pseudonym, which he dreamed up while still a youth in Hannibal, Missouri, was "W. Epaminondas Adrastus Bab." Well, Epaminondas, for real, ruled Thebes with his male lover, and they maintained their power through a fighting unit called the Sacred Bond, 150 pairs of warrior-lovers. How in the world did Sam know that?

He thought he could live as two people, but you really can't, you know; two people are twice as hard to live with as one. Harder, even. But if his momma never knew the pisser of a life he was leading as Mark Twain, then he figured that was the main thing. And the money pouring in would impress her mightily, which it was meant to do. She never thought he'd amount to much, running off so young and uneducated. He sent her money to shut her up. And so his path was clear then to love all the men he wanted to. In his own mind he fucked as Sam Clemens and wrote as Mark Twain and it would be like that for his entire life.

But it wouldn't take long before he could see there would never be any freedom. Well, Mark Twain would make them all laugh about that.

The biggest pisser is that Sam lived his life in the open, right out there in front of them, in front of whatever world he happened to be lying to at the moment, and that no one's ever noticed, then or now, this life he really lived. He lived his life right out in front of all of us! He took his men with him. Every single one of them. They boozed and fought and fished and even dug for gold together, side by side. They slept each night together, side by side too, from north to south, from west to east and over the oceans. He took them where he found them, or when and where he wanted them. Abe Lincoln had that gift too. Funny how, as with Abe, of all the people who'd write about him nobody noticed a bit of this when it was as plain as his face.

He was to make a fortune writing about how America and Americans didn't see a thing. Didn't see that Huck and Nigger Jim were lovers, that Tom and Huck were his country's first gay rock stars, and that the only love men really ever had was for each other. Huck and Tom and Jim were forged from the love Sam had for the boyhood of men, for the young flesh of men, for the sad innocence of youth that made men men. He would never write a woman, not because he didn't understand them, but because he didn't care about them.

Oh, he settled with a nice young rich wife, the emphasis on rich. Many great men marry for richer, starting with George Washington. Sam loved most people who adoringly took care of him; he wasn't so dumb as to bite that hand. That all his living children turned out to be girls, well, he figured this was his punishment from some unholy god he didn't believe in anyway. So he adored these little girls as if they were precious gold, as unrepentant sinners often do, in case there's a God up there after all.

He had never seen so many men in his life. Well, that is why he went west. For once, what he'd heard was no exaggeration. He was already a big believer in exaggeration. He was just finding out what he wanted to write about, and discovering what he had to write with. He'd never dreamed particularly of being a writer and never knew, or thought, much about it. He just started doing it. The people he and his brother mixed with out west read and wrote for newspapers, so it might just have been the company and the first men he bedded down with there who got him to do it.

This much he knew already. He didn't much believe in truth. And his life had been too hard to want to remember it or honor it for real.

The men appear to start in earnest around 1862 when Sam lives in Virginia City, Nevada, and then in San Francisco. Between 1862 and 1865, Samuel Clemens engages in a series of numerous wild romances with men. He is twenty-seven years old in 1862. He's a late bloomer, that's for sure, but most people were, if they ever bloomed at all.

San Francisco during this period has a population of about 100,000. Over 90 percent of it is male, all on the whole remarkably well educated, half of them in their twenties, many of them from wealthy families back east. Like Sam, more than a few had left the Civil War by moving to California. It was all the rage, from New York to here, to be "bohemian," to find a place with much drinking, much dressing up, much pretense, and a high tolerance for sexual ambiguity. Men often walked around dressed as women ("Puddy got a job selling men's clothes in Gramp's and he was told to wear a dress to do it"), as did Sam upon occasion, or the men he was with. The Left Bank of Paris, already the model, was extending itself to San Francisco, which was happy to follow suit.

Virginia City had 2,500 women to 45,000 men, and it was also wild, but for twenty-four hours a day instead of just the nighttimes.

The two places weren't all that far apart, and Sam and his friends went back and forth, often to get away from someone or other.

Sam writes this about the mining country: "It was an assemblage of two hundred thousand *young* men—not simpering, dainty, kid-glove weaklings, but stalwart, muscular, dauntless young braves, brimful of push and energy, with every attribute that goes to make up a peerless and magnificent manhood—the very pick and choice of the world's glorious ones. No women, no children, no gray and stooping veterans—none but erect, bright-eyed, quick moving, strong-handed young giants . . . It was a splendid population . . ."

It was in San Francisco that he learned about men, about men's bodies, about his own body, about what men's bodies could do together. At first he would go home from walking around the streets and bars and he would masturbate. It was not long before he went home with another fellow who told him, when he started jerking off, "Here, you don't have to do that by yourself." And so begins his education. "This is a real man's world, out here," another fellow tells him when they go to his room. The city is filled with small rooms that are rented to the many men who parade around looking for each other. Yes, there are jobs some do to feed themselves, but he cannot feel any sense of ambition parading on his strolls. That kind of ambition is over in Nevada. Here he feels only the ambition of men to grab on to other men, much of it for sex, but not always just that. There's an almost tangible feeling that they're in on the beginning of something out here, no one could tell you what it is, but it feels different from back east, that's for sure. Here, quite simply, men are men, and they all seem to know it in a way he's never seen before, and to somehow glory in it, in the sweat and the grit and the hard labor of finding themselves and each other, even in dresses. Sam understands.

No, he doesn't know what he is going to do yet, for real. He noodles with lots of thoughts and he makes notes of—for him—perplexing incomprehensibility. He does not know that he's forging a distinct style in what he's scribbling about what he's seeing, although he does not think he'll write about what he's really seeing, and he knows, already, that this is dishonest. What's the point of writing anything if it isn't about what you're really seeing? He hears voices like this as he looks down at his hand full of semen from jerking off while thinking of that young guy he wants. He looks at his hands, all sticky. He looks at his hands all full of, well, nothing yet. At least he knows it's all complicated, and that's a start.

But you can tell he loves all this, those gold and silver fields of the West. When he gets around to writing about it, you can taste and smell it just like he did—that is, if you understand the lingo. No Twain scholar has ever understood the lingo, not this lingo, not Mark Twain's lingo. Those many men who wrote and still write about Clemens never see the Twain.

These are some of the men Sam gets involved with: Clement T. Rice is a rival reporter in the Nevada towns, from whom, for a year or so, he is never separated; indeed, they go to San Francisco together, shack up in the same room, upsetting one Don De Quille, an earlier bar buddy with whom Sam was involved. Something happens between them; Rice upsets Sam and Sam cuts him out of his life completely and returns to De Quille; the two move in together, furnish their two rooms lavishly, with only one bed, "the snuggest little bedroom all to ourselves," Don writes; "here we come every night and live, breathe, move and have our being."

A threesome develops with the arrival of Artemus Ward, a successful columnist of humorous pieces who influences Sam and falls for him as well. These guys drink an awful lot; "this place is a wild, untamable place, but full of lion-hearted boys," he writes to Sam. But he must return east, and Don and Sam continue their constant companionship. "My life was so full of stuff I didn't want my Ma to know that when I turned in my next piece to *The Enterprise* I named myself Mark Twain. I had been looking around for something to hide behind; I'd earlier used 'Joshua' (not certain why) but it hadn't set quite right. They all say that I hid behind my new name to run a bar tab or a gambling debt but it was because of Clement Rice; we had been inseparable for unto a year, starting out in Virginia City, coming here to run away from 'Dan De Quille,' which wasn't his real name either. I don't know why I ran from Dan except that Clem was more fun and Dan wasn't anymore. But Clem got to be a handful and annoying and Dan was back, and so we hitched back together again, in a two room apartment but one bed for the both of us, like we liked it, except when Artemus joined us. Artemus wasn't his real name either and I missed him when he died young: he taught me how I could be, like him, a writer and do a comedy show as well. He was more courageous than I, sending up Walt and writing right up front about counter-jumpers, which is what they called us queer ones. I got to say I was nervous when I read that piece. I had given Mother a subscription to *Vanity Fair* where this appeared as he is its editor. His letters to me always started and ended, both, with, 'My Dearest Love,' and I miss him mightily. He made Dan jealous though, which I enjoyed to watch. By now Dan and I were always moving from place to place and raising hell. *The News*, up in Gold Hill, ran a piece, 'Dan De Quille and Mark Twain are marrying shortly. About time!' I roared, but I was glad it was Mark Twain and not Sam Clemens. I made that name change just in time."

Enter young Steve Gillis. Short, wiry, scrappy, a pistol, a lethal barroom fighter who weighs 95 pounds, and Sam can't get enough of him. He is small and compact like the Tom Sawyer whose voice Sam already heard in his head as he would hear Huck's and Jim's and he would show us without telling us about their love. They have barely met when Sam agrees to post his $500 bond for shattering a beer pitcher over the bartender's head for pushing patrons around. Unable to pay, the two hightail it to Steve's brother's tiny cottage in the next county, where they shack up for a not inconsiderable time, and then to San Francisco, where they go from hotel to hotel, carousing mightily, even, according to one landlady, brandishing pistols. The Gillis log cabin in the woods, to which they go back again, is no doubt one of those lifetime experiences for Sam; it goes on for many months, maybe longer, when they are alone together in a tiny, two-room, one-bedded place. Yes, they are on the run from the law because of that bond money. How convenient.

Then he is out with one Higbie, with his "brawny muscles," camping on Mono Lake for quite some time. "Higbie and I went to bed at midnight, but it was only to lie broad awake and think, dream, scheme. Each new splendor that burst out of my visions of the future whirled me bodily over him in bed or jerked us to a sitting posture just as if an electric battery had been applied to me." They become prospectors together. They become rich. Then almost overnight they lose it all and part.

Then, who was "Johnny K," the rich man's son from Ohio? They went out to Tahoe together. He was there for recreation. He got it. They both got it, falling so in love with the experience that they jointly pledged to buy three hundred acres. Sam writes, "if there is any life that is happier than the life we led on our timber ranch I have not read of it in books or experienced in person."

Talk about truth, he knew Wilkes Booth, he'd fucked him, he'd seen his dick, he knew what he was all about, and he knew that the war, as far as Booth was concerned, was about the North not being available as the haven for hushies that he wanted it to be even as the South was on its way to becoming, with Richmond and Atlanta, like ancient Greece. Now, there's a whole bunch of truths he wouldn't write about, no sir. It won't surprise him when Wilkes will shoot Abe Lincoln. Hell, Booth tried to stick a knife in Sam's asshole when his dick got stuck in there and he couldn't get it out. Too strange to write about that, that's for certain. Hell, half the fairies out here in San Francisco will claim to have fucked with Wilkes, with not a one of them talking about his screwed-up dick. So much for truth. That's why Sam couldn't believe in it. Wherein, in all of this, lies truth? "Lies" indeed.

Tell the truth? For what, by the end of his life, he's discovered is this: that many men, many of the best men, many men period, are as he is, in love with other men and bound hand and foot and mouth from showing it. Who can become an honest man like this? And how? Steve Gillis let out whoops of joy regularly and Sam joined in with him, letting himself go as well. He'd never allowed himself to do that before, let go. And soon Steve Gillis was . . . well, after a while Sam couldn't recall. Until he wrote *Tom Sawyer.*

"What is it that strikes a spark of humor from man?" Twain is asked, or asks himself in one late interview. "It is the effort to throw off, to fight back the burden of grief that is laid on each one of us."

Charles Warren Stoddard, whom Sam continued to see all his life, is hardly acknowledged in Sam's biographies, or Twain's. Stoddard was as flamboyantly gay as they came. "I thought him sad and sensitive and he touches me," Sam wrote at the time. He was a successful travel writer who fell in love with the young boys in the South Seas and actually wrote about it in a widely read series (especially widely read for some reason by the Disciples of Lovejoy). Once, Charles decided to try to get rid of this passion by going back there and walking alone by the water's edge in the moonlight. He reported back to Sam of his failure to lose this ardor: "it didn't work. I was back in their arms, which they offer to older men so profusely." Over the years Sam would call upon him for . . . what? Stoddard was one of the few writers Sam listened to, though he might not follow his advice. There is no question the relationship was touchingly sexual in the midst of so much of San Francisco's "heaving and ho'ing," as Stoddard called it. "Charles is tender and he touches me in spirit as well as body," Sam writes. By the time they're aging men in London they're really like kids cutting up as only old friends can do, comfortable in the release of feelings they could still reveal to each other. Yes, it was complicated, but no more so than any gay man will tell of. Once, Sam and wife Livvy are in England and she gets sick and Sam takes her home on the boat and the boat docks and Sam sees Livvy and the kids safely off it and on their way, only for him to immediately reembark, now with Stoddard on board, back to London. He accompanies him not only to London but on the rest of an extensive tour. Both called Stoddard his "secretary." Both liked to dress flamboyantly in grand hotels, Sam all in white, making entrances down dramatic staircases. "I think he is the purest male I have known," Mark writes in his autobiography.

"What liberating personal magnetism did he possess that moved his contemporaries to forgive him for traits and tendencies that biographers of a later time have found deplorable?" This query goes unanswered by he who raises it, Ron Powers, in *Mark Twain: A Life* (2006). What indeed? To what traits is he referring? Is he suggesting he knows all that's been divulged above but found too deplorable to include in his well-received book? Powers, needless to say, leaves out the most powerful "liberating personal magnetism" of all. Yes, Sam's undoubted homosexuality has never been explored by *any* of his biographers. Powers can somehow still locate other "liberating" experiences, including Sam's presumed besottedness when he was twenty-two with fourteen-year-old Laura Wright, whose disappearance into "the vagaries of fate" is "crushing" to him. This nonsense is not dissimilar to the sudden appearance after Lincoln's death of a presumed broken heart over one Ann Rutledge, which bears no truth in actuality and was indeed launched by protective friends of Lincoln who knew he was homosexual and felt compelled to disprove it for all time. "The Lincoln of our literature," William Dean Howells claimed Sam to be, in his own influential *My Mark Twain*.

Yes, Sam Clemens changed his name.

Mark Twain means "safe water."

FIRST AMERICAN HOMOSEXUAL RIGHTS ACTIVISTS?

That first spate of homosexual exterminations (yes, there is already a gay grapevine) inspires a young Sault Ste. Marie man and his "beloved friend" to travel around the country delivering what are believed to be the first public speeches in America in defense of homosexuals. Their real names are unknown; at first they go by Peter and Paul Ulrich, in honor of Karl Heinrich Ulrich, a German who delivered and published in Munich in 1867 what are believed to be the first public speeches in defense of homosexuality anywhere in the world. Wherever in the country Peter and Paul go, they stand in public squares and attempt to present their message: "We are homosexuals and we have come to introduce ourselves to you and show you that we look just like you." They seem to have instinctively grasped that the perceived legitimacy of nonhomosexuality is based on the unquestioning acceptance of its universality. (The use of the word *heterosexual* is not noted until 1892, in *Psychopathia Sexualis*, that book again, by Richard von Krafft-Ebing, that identifies everything imaginable that can happen to the mind, soul, psyche, and sexual organs, including heterosexuality, to be something that is sick.) Their appearances, mostly in the central portion of the country, from Milwaukee to Chicago and environs, and in Buffalo, are met with discomfort at first, and then with growing hostility as their notoriety grows. It is not long before they are both found dead, floating in the Erie Canal.

Were the Ulrich Brothers, as they briefly came to be known, the first two identifiable gay activists in America?

There has also been talk of a man in the West who went by the name of Virgil Vindicator.

•

The "germ" theory of disease is discovered by the German physician Robert Koch in 1882. He demonstrates that a particular bacterium can cause a particular disease. I am just such a particularity. This should be a very important discovery. But it is discounted or ignored, particularly by American medicine. I am having such increasing luck in your country!

THE CAMPS OF AMERICA

It behooves me, my Frederick, to take us down the road I am now compelled to follow. This is a crucial marker in the wretched history of your country, shocking and painful, and to my knowledge never revealed by anyone heretofore. That it takes a Brit to be the one to uncover and unravel this deep vein of your poison says more than enough about a basic understanding of history that you and yours simply do not share. It is the placid, some would say boring, nature of our personalities that allows us to perceive with a clarity, indeed an honesty, that does not come easily to such a frenetic land as yours.

I talk of camps, of the camp movement, because it is a movement, an ardent activity that is now growing in size and taking hold of a certain part of the American imagination and landscape and that will prove unstoppable: the "putting away" of those who are troublesome, or unwanted, or considered in some way unhealthy, and therefore deemed "un-American." The world has never been at a loss to have such imaginings, or indeed such locales, flourish secretly. My chum Anne Applebaum, in *Gulag*, has written magnificently about the history of encampments. But these are later camps established by Russians and, as she tells us, Germans, sometime before the Nazis, who will become their prime facilitator in the twentieth century. In all cases people are rounded up primarily because of who they are and secondarily for what they might have said. In an almost copycat manner continuing until today, camps take root in locations all over the map. It is as if, once a camp is heard about in country X, its very nature excites duplication in somebody's perfervid imagination in many a country Y, transcending boundaries with amazing celerity. I don't want to say that you are first, but you do predate Applebaum's amazing discoveries. Indeed, The American People are continuing on their roll, their nonstop and never-ending revelation of the sorry state of human nature and behavior, particularly but by no means exclusively toward those who love their own.

Various groups of self-appointed and almost always secret vigilantes, most often in isolated areas of the country where they can operate as they will, begin more and more to take control of local "law and order." Secret documents certainly have turned up: tallies of inhabitants, instructions regarding their treatment, advice on to how to perpetuate the place and its activities when a current "administration" has passed on. Many little black notebooks are found in basements and boxes and trunks, filled with not always decipherable scribblings (but clear enough), and are duly turned over to historical societies, which of course don't know what to do with them but throw them into other basements and boxes and trunks. Timid historians—almost all historians are timid (and/or, for the sake of this history, heterosexual)—are loath to document such horrifying discoveries; they write history so they can hide behind it, in their own closets. Yes, many are the historians who shrink from writing about certain activities, even when they are known to have transpired. This is always history's greatest failing, its inability to believe what it sees, what, almost always, someone sees.

These camps are filled with people who are forced to stay there, a device that will be most successfully put into widespread utilization in Russia after their revolution in 1917, when that country is overwhelmed with too many people and not enough food to feed them. Starvation and freezing to death are the chosen methods to deal with them. Camps are hidden away on land so remote as to be unblessed even by the weather necessary to keep living things alive. Many great Russian writers have told this awful history, Dostoyevsky, Chekhov, Solzhenitsyn, to name but a few. No newspaper of that time, and few afterward, would write about it. Indeed, *The New York Truth*'s reporter in that country won a Pulitzer for not writing about it.

The incarceration of those one doesn't like is, of course, an old and dishonorable calling, but it did not take firm root on an expanded scale in America until the nineteenth century. Very distant outposts do not bless this country; Russia has a vast and endless wasteland to its north, replete with far-flung islands where church and state send many a dissident to this day. Britain and the countries of Europe also have many possessions where they secret their unwanteds, without note or notice. People get shipped away into oblivion. But America is wide open. How could so many shards of your unwanteds get lost here?

Herschel Mentone, in his classic *Unkind German Behavior Around the World, 1875–1945*, a groundbreaking work that remains unnoticed, corroborates Applebaum's reference to the early British concentration camps in South Africa, which were based on camps set up beginning in 1895 by the Spanish in colonial Cuba. Applebaum incorrectly names these as "the first modern concentration camps." She can be forgiven if only because of what she then tells us, which is quite a shocker. In 1904, according to Applebaum,

> there are a number of strange and eerie links between these first German-African labor camps [that the Brits set up in South Africa] and those built in Nazi Germany three decades later . . . The first imperial commissioner of Deutsche Sud-West Afrika was one Dr. Heinrich Goering, the father of Hermann, who set up the first Nazi camps in 1933. It was also in these African camps that the first German medical experiments were conducted on humans: two of Joseph Mengele's teachers, Theodor Mollison and Eugen Fisher, carried out research on the Herero, the latter in an attempt to prove his theories about the superiority of the white race. But they were not unusual in their beliefs . . . the notion that some types of people

are superior to other types of people was common enough in Europe at the beginning of the twentieth century. And this, finally, is what links the camps of the Soviet Union and those of Nazi Germany in the most profound sense of all: both regimes legitimized themselves, in part, by establishing categories of "enemies" or "sub-humans" whom they persecuted and destroyed . . .

And so was it to be attempted here.

It is disappointing that Applebaum did not look farther west for antecedents and accompaniments to her findings. It is Mentone's belief that Germans in America would have known about all of these efforts in South Africa that Applebaum details. Incarcerated people freeze to death in the snows of Nantoo, Abbator, Partekla, and other such camps in America before they freeze to death in Kolyma and Siberia or are gassed in Auschwitz.

"In certain . . . camps, at certain times, death was virtually guaranteed," Applebaum tells us.

Here, too.

There are not-yet-states in America, territories they were called, that are vastly underpopulated and unguarded, with enormous stretches of unoccupied, unfriendly terrain. These house many unfortunate secrets about their past, waiting to be believed.

DAME LADY HERMIA MAKES A BIG DISCOVERY

The Disciples of Lovejoy have been in the Utah territory since 1847. For some time it was uncertain whether they were in fact in Utah or in Idaho. Idaho did not become a state until 1890. Utah did not become a state until 1896. Ezra Furst, still in power at this juncture, still mighty in his determination to make the Disciples of Lovejoy the biggest religion in America today, and tomorrow the world, will shortly be summoning into Secret Chambers the Fifteen Men of Superior Wisdom to elect his replacement. Ezra is very old. His son, Ezra Jr., covets this leadership, though he knows he is still too young. Old men rule this religion. Ezra's refusal to step aside is reaffirmed by the Fifteen Men. Ezra Jr. must find another path to climb to the top of a mountain, so impressing his elders that he can one day run what is legally named the Princely Bountiful Pearl of the World Trust.

Tom Lovejoy had written polygamy and the physical love of man for man and brother for brother into the catechism of his religion. Incest was added by his son Jared, whose first son, Aaron, married his own sister, Gibbonette, who died bearing him triplets, all of whom died during their delivery. To see to it that he would not have a lonely old age, Jared, at eighty-four, impregnated a young cousin, Deirdre, who bore several of his children. She took them with her, however, when she ran away from Oxonia—which, finally, was what the Council of the One Hundred Holiest Elders determined to call their Holy City—in a successful attempt to prevent any more Disciples from, as it were, screwing her, one way or another. They are a fecund lot, which is their stock-in-trade, although in these early years they murder each other a lot, which I am not going to go into here. They break off into sects, which for brief periods loathe and kill each other, only to regroup and pledge eternal love. Year by year the Disciples of Lovejoy becomes an increasingly complicated religion, filled with much mumbo jumbo, unusual undergarments, and new "traditions" they claim have been dictated by God. It is not surprising that it's difficult to trace a good many things, which is just the way they want it. At present they are stuck with all those wretched physical acts that Tom and his son ordained, homosexuality, polygamy, and incest, which turn off not a few prospective converts. How to proceed?

Enter the Ku Klux Klan into a secret partnership with the Disciples. The Klan, with its own unusual attire of conical hats and long raiment of sheeting, and masks, and which shortly will claim six million members, is at present falling apart. Founded after the Civil War, the Klan targeted freed slaves and their allies; it sought to restore white supremacy by threats and violence, including murder—thousands, many thousands of murders.

For whatever reason, toward the end of this nineteenth century, the Klan is falling apart. It may be able to claim four million members in 1920 and six million in 1924, but now its haters are too busily involved with various forms of graft in the Reconstruction period.

Enter one Nigel Rotbart, Grand Wizard of the North and South Carolina chapters of the KKK, both states holding records for killing the most Negroes in the country. Rotbart meets Ezra Jr. at a conference in Washington entitled "How Do We Rid Ourselves of Our Unwanteds?" Each smells in the other not only a kindred spirit but money willingly flowing for services expertly rendered. Nigel Rotbart is put in charge of the Tally Office.

THE CAMP AT ABBATOR, TEXAS

The camp at Abbator is built and ruled by Cord Rine, a mammoth white man of indeterminate ancestry and accent. He is said to be deaf. Sketches of him in period newspapers indicate a man with stooped posture, almost Neanderthal in aspect, with jutting brow and recessed jaw and bulging deep-set eyes.

Cord comes down to the Texas panhandle from the KKK chapter in Ogetts, North Dakota. The landscape he settles on is all long stretches of hard sand and crabgrass and nothing for a cow or anyone else to eat. It's soil that doesn't lend itself to growing, swept by winds whipping tiny pinpoints of sandy pain into your eyes night and day. Cord has chosen this location wisely. With the assistance of invisible financing he builds a compound of high walls capped by spikes. Inside there's nothing but a gaping pit. He tries it out himself. No, he can't scale the walls. No, he can't dig under the walls. No, he can't force the gates because there aren't any gates. No, from inside he can't see what's going on outside. Yes, it's a huge gaping hole, a yawning mouth ready and waiting hungrily to be fed.

The camps that come into existence in the post–Civil War years blend into each other as part of one long chain of emptiness. Indeterminate dates. Undetectable locations. Invisible owners. Wandering people ready to be captured. Capable criminals ready to do the capturing. Smart, greedy wastrels who have learned how not to do what is expected of human beings, especially ones who have survived a cataclysmic war or a trek across the country. Indeed, it is veterans of this war who are among the most successful at greed and anger and hate. It is amazing how a country that has just suffered so much can continue to wound itself unendingly. Perhaps it is not so surprising. Will America ever be a country that knows how to repair itself?

Cord throws his first faggotty nigger into the pit around 1870 or so. A dozen of them are delivered under guard by a Pony Express wagon. Cord's rigged himself a rope-and-gallows affair with which he can put the noose under a young man's armpits and haul him up and swing him over and drop him in. Inside the pit the young man, and the other young men who are regularly dropped into this hell, receive occasional kegs of water and packets of seeds. A couple of dozen young men realize they'd better plant these seeds and water them and hope they grow fast. A few of the youngest boys are eaten before any of the seeds bear anything. There must be forty or so men inside before they can stop eating each other. For a while. By the time there are one hundred there is no amount of carrots and potatoes that can feed so many, so they devise what they believe is an equitable solution. They draw straws. The loser is knocked unconscious by the strongest fist, and then his body is ripped into its various parts and those hungry enough eat them. Everyone is hungry enough eventually. Whenever the supply of flesh appears to be sinking dangerously low, another batch of what are presumed to be homosexual Negroes is delivered by another stage and posse from the Tally Office.

Cord was said to be deaf, because the screams from inside his pit must be monstrous. He sleeps in a little hut outside the wall. He never looks inside, but he keeps a detailed tally of how many men he drops in. He gets paid per body. Every so often the Tally Office sends a representative who climbs up on the gallows, makes some sort of calculation, and pays Cord cash on the spot. There isn't a day goes by since the first body was tossed in that the vultures haven't greedily circled the sky and swooped down for their feed. It must be difficult to count how many bones equal a body equal a payment. God alone knows where Cord hides the money. By the time Virgil Vindicator and Domna Radiance finally arrive on horseback with their own posse of armed homosexuals, Cord is dead. He must have collapsed one day and the vultures ate him, too. The vultures didn't eat his tally book, though, so Virgil and Domna are able to figure out what happened. A few of the captors had survived and lay side by side or in each other's arms while awaiting death.

Cord Rine's tally book is in the Lady Jane Greeting Library in Nearodell. You can see it there, though few want to see it, it makes for such sick reading.

THE CAMP AT NANTOO, OKLAHOMA

The camp notion grows more fevered and poisoned. It is the women Disciples of Lovejoy who conserve and maintain Nantoo. The camp for women in Nantoo, Oklahoma (Oklahoma didn't become a state until 1907), is ruled by Philice Abingdon, an Australian woman. No one knows how she got to America. A Tally Office representative at about the same time as Cord, she sets up her camp. She calls her charges, who are all lesbians, Negro and white, "pussy-suckers," and they call her the "Hateful One." Her population is smaller, it was originally thought, because it is more difficult to locate lesbians. However, recent evidence indicates that the Tally Office sent out female spies to visit places where women gathered: church groups, sewing circles, civic meetings, group picnics, even nunneries. It's never clear what criteria were used to identify a homosexual man or a lesbian, or who was doing the identifying, although people like Philice and Cord always claimed, "I know one when I see one." The financing sources of this hate are legion. There is not a religion that does not wish good riddance to those "who do not act and think as we do." There are also Catholic and Jewish secret organizations. It is just that one does not associate such brutality with them. One is wrong.

Nantoo's landscape is almost as desolate as Abbator's. "You look into forever. Even the sun is unreliable. The only thing you can count on is the deep dark of night. You could probably run away in this dark if it weren't for all the snakes, coyotes, foxes, and vultures," one of those who did escape wrote in her diary. One wonders how she escaped: Philice has the best guards nature can provide. She also makes a point of leaving around a few dead bodies of adventurous women, bitten and chewed and poisoned to death.

Her place is evidently cozier than Cord's. There are long bunks where the girls sleep with each other while she watches them "suck each other out," as she writes in one of her reports to the Tally Office. She lets her charges live too long, something she will regret, but she wants the company. She kills only the ones she doesn't like, "mainly the niggers." When she gets tired of a girl, she has one of her big-boned lady guards shoot her in front of the others, and the next day there's stew for lunch. One shudders as one relates this, Freddy.

Although the landscape of Nantoo is harsh it's slightly more congenial than the Texas hellhole. "Flowers grow. The sky makes pretty colors and the clouds make pretty patterns. How can I kill them off when the sun shines so brightly," Philice writes in her reports to Nigel.

Thus does she find herself with a population much too large to handle. "Be careful you're not too easy on them," Nigel replies. "Such softness can turn against the caretaker. We lost our camps in South Dakota and northern Florida. Our representatives lost control. Please get to work." The Tally Office leaves the means of killing off the inmates to each camp's caretaker.

One day, two new Tally representatives appear unannounced. The men look around. They ask Philice why so many of "these hideous homosexual sinners" are still alive. They berate her for her "unconscionable breach of the rules" and add: "Clean house. We have many backed up awaiting their assignment. We shall wait outside while you do." These two Lovejoy officials are Turpa Diamond and Eagen Odemptor, who will work with Nigel at their Tally Office well into the forthcoming century. They will both live to a ripe old age and die in office. They will claim that by then the office will have been responsible for the "disappearance" of many thousands of homosexuals, men and women, black and white.

How does one eliminate fifty women to make room for one hundred more? Philice has grown quite fond of a few of them. She is tired of killing the ones she doesn't like, and she is tired of eviscerating them and making those stews. She writes about her growing discomfort movingly. "It is just getting too difficult for me to control, house, feed, police so many in such an isolated place. My new guards, too, are uncomfortable with shooting those trying to escape and bringing those bodies back so terribly mussed-up. And I can no longer ignore that while I am paid modestly to keep this place going, I shall be paid a great deal more for cleaning house and I should like to retire. But I grow too attached to some of them. I have been in love with several."

Ruskin Nancey, in his *Some Deranged Inhabitants of the Early West*, a book that is more or less disappeared (read "purged") from stores and libraries, uncovered some of this history. Philice Abingdon was murdered by her guards under orders from Turpa Diamond and Eagen Odemptor, made into one of those "stews" but with poison among its ingredients, and fed to all the prisoners, cleaning house indeed. Replacements followed until statehood was achieved in 1907, thus making further activities of this nature illegal. The place was burned to the ground, as were all the other camps, some fifty of them according to Nancey, when their locations became officially part of The American People.

Ben-Ezekial, the erudite and pontificating Yaddah historian of this religion and almost any other matter you could possibly want to think about, predicts, "The Disciples of Lovejoy fully intend to convert the nation and the world. They will not falter. And it will be a good thing." Well, any group that hates so passionately and claims such hate as the word of their God must be dealt with. These new Americans who, quite literally, make up their religion themselves as they cross a country that once belonged to others, are of stellar importance.

There are certain historians who make other historians see red, or purple, or black and blue, or cause lightning flashes of anger to strike when merely in the presence of one of their tomes. Professor Ben-Ezekial is one of these. He is very special to your country. We can claim many blowhards but few who blow so hard. Be patient with me, please, as I not only summon every bit of my courage. This is too important a subject for me to be too flippant. Tiptoeing in discussing a major world religion is delicate. I have not made my name from being delicate.

WOMEN

Your Roving Historian is aware that he hasn't dealt much with women, their lives, their specific issues, in gathering the history of this plague. This is because the plague is initially and for many years remains a plague of men. When it crosses to women it will be because men give them this plague as well. And by then it will be much too late to do anything about it beyond marveling at how much human behavior has passed under so many bridges to flow into the swollen river of cascading, accumulating, unattended-to death. As with so much in their history and development, once again women arrive too late at the fair.

Such reasoning won't sit well with my two principal fellow female contributors, I know. But as neither of them has stepped forward to contribute anything toward righting this balance, let me once again try a bit myself.

Beginning in the nineteenth century, friendship among women was an accepted and increasingly fervent activity, commencing when the women were still girls. "Such friendships were viewed as an innocent outgrowth of the emotionality of adolescence and as a way of preparing girls for the emotional bonding both of the adult female community and of marriage," says Lois Banner, the eminent University of Southern California professor of women's history, in *Intertwined Lives*, her riveting dual biography of Margaret Mead and Ruth Benedict, two exceptional woman anthropologists who changed the twentieth century while married to men and yet committed to each other as lesbian lovers.

Banner describes a "vast expansion in interest" in spiritualism and Romanticism following the Civil War, as a result "of the deaths of so many young men on the battlefield." Yes, people were still in grief from that war, now so many years ago, or so many historians find it convenient so to state. Long before the war and emphatically after it, girls and women were encouraged to form special and deep friendships with other females, friendships considered healthy and harmless and actually beneficial in shielding them before marriage from the hungers of men, or from the memory of loves now lost. This "passionate emotionality . . . could be expressed through sexuality or be channeled into spirituality or a drive for material or creative achievement." Such bonding could easily lead "to genital sexuality," or simply to a preference for female company over any further interest in men. Physical affection between girls was not only not frowned upon, it was encouraged outright. Vassar, the first college exclusively for women, was founded in 1865. It was by many accounts (particularly Nutritia Evens-Bell's *Vassar, My Heart, My Home*, 1875) a hotbed of a place. Banner quotes from Cornell and Yaddah college newspapers: "When a Vassar girl takes a shine to another, she straightaway enters upon a regular course of bouquet sendings, interspersed with tinted notes, mysterious packages of 'Ridleys Mixed Candles,' locks of hair perhaps, and many other tender tokens, until the object of her attentions is captured, the two become inseparable, and the aggressor is considered by her circle of acquaintances as—smashed." Smashing also involves much lolling, leaning of heads on shoulders, clasping of each other's hands by the hour, and often fondling and kissing and, one can only assume, much else.

All in all, though, Dr. Banner's work and the work that has been done to claim a lesbian past is remarkable, although preachers such as Jonathan Edwards convey more about sex lives in earlier America than does much that was promulgated afterward. Black and white lesbians continue to fall in love with each other and to be butchered because of it. On another front, I was recently forwarded an excellent college thesis on the tragic story of one Elizabeth Muhwezi, an immigrant from an African country who managed somehow to gain both passage to and disembarkation at New York in 1890 with another black woman, thought to be her "sexual poopsie" because they were holding hands. Immigration authorities conferred and, rather than refer the case for adjudication to any superiors, took it upon themselves to direct the two women to the rear of their boat and throw them overboard; they made certain they drowned by holding them under with paddles from a lifeboat. The two black men there to meet the two women, naming themselves as their husbands, were told that no such passengers with their names appeared on the boat's manifest.

The student who wrote the above thesis is at the University of Oklahoma. Across the front page her instructor had scrawled in huge letters "Not acceptable for credit! GWS." I sent the young student back your Tarpoo section as above. "Give this to GWS with my love! FL."

Ladies, is it not time for all of you to put your houses in order!

FROM GRACE, OF COURSE

Freddie, I shall surprise you by finding your distress with us touching.

It is very lesbian what we do, we ladies.

Let me define what I mean by this expression, "very lesbian." I mean divergent answers being a very lesbian activity. There's a whole line of lesbian jokes that begin with "How many lesbians does it take . . ." "How many lesbians does it take to screw in a lightbulb? Two: One to screw in the lightbulb and the other to sing a folk song about it." "How many lesbians does it take to screw in a lightbulb? Three: One to hold the ladder, one to screw in the lightbulb, and one to process the event." "How many lesbians does it take to screw in a lightbulb? Three: One to screw it in, and two to talk about how much better it is than with a man." "How many lesbians does it take to change a lightbulb? None of your fucking business!"

You get the idea. I cannot believe that you are not confronting similar behavior across the board, across the wide Missouri, as that fucking folk song goes. Houses are rarely ever ever ever put in order, by anyone.

I know GWS at Oklahoma U. She's a closeted bitch and shouldn't be allowed to teach anyone!

I cannot wait for Hermia's exegesis on Harold Ben-fucking-Ezekial. He is a macho pig of the first order. He once made a pass at me at a conference and I was in full drag, i.e., my nun's habit. I was going to say re: Hermia, "I wouldn't fuck her with your dick," but I don't think she would get the joke and anyway, dare it be intimated from her words that she might at last be moving toward our Fuck Central?

You fuckster! You are so fucksome. I love you very much.

FRED UNCOVERS THE LEGEND
OF PETER POWER

Domna Radiance is born in Alhambra, California, of slave parents who have spent their lives one step ahead of danger, from the white man bosses, from the white man rapists, from the white man murderers. In Alhambra, Negro women are raped regularly by white men and thrown dead into ditches to await consumption by the ever-present circling buzzards, hawks, eagles, and, a West Coast specialty, the occasional alligator. Domna does not want to live such a life in such a place.

Domna mourns her brother and her father, both dead in the war. She did not know either of them. Her mother had not wanted another child and murders the man who raped her, a mulatto foreman on the grape vineyards. As he was an unsatisfactory foreman and she was an excellent worker, the owner allows her to stay. He has designs on baby Domna, which her mother recognizes as troubling; she sees him finger-fucking the baby's vagina.

Domna is adopted by a traveling theater group. By eighteen she is one of their leading ladies. These companies tour the West quite regularly. Theater is popular so far away from the larger centers, and Domna Radiance is popular, too. Being a Negro actress makes her particularly exotic. Audiences respond to her startling appearance: she is very beautiful, tall and well formed, with skin as mellow as her voice. Her talent was recognized and encouraged by their leader, Adele Menton Pfizerfield, a German woman of Amazonian proportions and a great tragedienne of her time. Her Lady Macbeth was said to be so terrifying that men everywhere were terrified of her in real life, thus allowing her and her actors to journey safely.

Acting offers one of the few opportunities for a woman to leave home and still eat without selling her body, but it requires a specific talent, the ability to pretend. Many women believe they have this talent, but they don't. Domna does. She couldn't tell you how or why, but she does. She had watched Adele. That had evidently been enough. "The performances of Domna Radiance in the Shakespearean tragedies are imbued with a particular mournful passion to which her audiences, many of them grieving themselves, rapturously respond," writes Joseph Morgandorf Mendell, a critic for *The Wabash and Spokane Bellwether*, in June 1880. Interestingly, women run a number of these touring companies. Charlotte Cushman, Ada Dwyer Russell (a Disciple of Lovejoy "married" to the poet Amy Lowell), the great Eleanore Duse, Adah Isaacs Menken, and the great Sarah Bernhardt are just a few who trek endlessly and in the face of dangers across the western portions of our growing land, where for some reason the audiences are huge and responsive, and hence the profits immense, even when the language they are hearing isn't English. By her early twenties Domna becomes so popular that she is able to run her own company. Here she meets her first lover, Dolly Maar, a Russian Jewess who has also spent her life running away from murdering white men, from tsars, from pogroms (a pogrom is when tsars and their armies march in and murder everyone they don't like, which is usually Jewish people). Neither Domna nor Dolly has been in love before. For both of them it feels right and good and they don't talk about it much.

Domna notices that more and more onlookers seem to disapprove of her lolling with Dolly, and other women Domna has around. These girlfriends are not actresses. They are what today would be called her fan club. They are in love with Domna and she has been known to love one or the other of them back, playing her favorites off against each other, depending on her mood. No one said this star is not fickle.

In Cardo, in the southern Dakota Territory, a band of ugly women wearing kitchen aprons and brandishing rolling pins stand directly in front of her and Dolly to block the audience's view of the stage during a performance of *Othello*, in which they are playing mistress and maid. Just before Cardo, in Tempest, Arizona, Domna has to set afire a bunch of men intent on molesting her. She lights their beards with a torch from her current production of *Burnt Up Love*, which is being performed out of doors at an encampment of Baptist ministers holding their annual retreat in an abandoned mining camp; they had witnessed said lolling during an afternoon rehearsal.

Domna is smart enough to see that it's time to fight. Her civil war is not over. It looks to her that her civil war is just beginning. She recognizes the look of hate in other eyes when she sees it.

She has been looking around for something different and more challenging to do. What does she think she can do that is different and more challenging? Certainly it is challenging enough to perform Shakespeare. She has in all her life only been an actress. She only knows how to act. She can act in her sleep.

She realizes she is bored with pretending to be someone else.

News of the increasing number of murders of homosexuals has reached her ears. The victims have all been men. Domna wonders how long it will be before women get the axe. She knows that several of the murdered men were women in men's clothing. They wrongly believed that as men they would be safe. She also knows of various male homosexuals who are becoming more confrontational. "There are fights to be fought and it is time for us to fight them," she tells her girlfriends, echoing the words she heard Virgil Vindicator speak when he marched alone through the mining camp a few weeks ago, holding forth to the Baptist ministers on his feelings for "my brothers." She heard Virgil Vindicator intone, inspirationally, that he and his brothers were the same as anyone. "Our existence is just as God-given." Her girls do not want to hear any of this, and of course neither do the Baptists who roughly escort Virgil out and away.

She tries to tell Dolly that it is time for their lives to be different. None of her companions want to discuss the dangers of their lives. They have been with Domna through other enthusiasms that waned.

Indeed, what if she were a man?

This is still a new country. They belong here as much as anyone. They must build for themselves as other people build this country for themselves. There is a word now coming into use. She likes this word. *Lesbian*. It is a beautiful word that rings with magic in her ears. She and Dolly, and Dewla and Perla, and Bessie and Mary are lesbians. The world does not want lesbians. Can Dolly not sense this? There are fights to be fought and it is time to join in fighting them. Virgil Vindicator has spoken passionately about how to deal with those against them, those who live with deep-seated prejudice. Combating this prejudice is the great task that must become their life's work. He says it requires the patience of Job, an unceasing campaign to educate the entire populace about the essential and fundamental naturalness of homosexuals. They must advance this passionate claim for all their years to come.

Yes, Domna has heard Virgil speak, and she follows him to several of his speaking "engagements" to hear him speak some more. She becomes transfixed by his words and his courage. She talks to him and they begin a friendship. She misses several performances and Dolly goes on for her. While she is away Dolly and the smashers are abducted. They will not be seen or heard from again. They are taken to Oklahoma, to Nantoo, "farther than hell itself," as the masked abductors of Americans Against Niggers and Nigger Lovers, a cell in the Ku Klux Klan, boast. Oklahoma is not yet a state. Renegade organizations can find safe haven there to do most anything.

Peter Power stands alone. On the evening of Domna's return to her company he is announced as her understudy and performs in her stead. Before the audience applauding Peter's success, Domna can see they are much more comfortable when Othello is played by a man. So be it. She believes it is her duty to make the world better. A woman has never changed the world. It must be a man who can find and protect the Dollys of this world. She sees her beloved and much-missed Dolly in every line of the Moor's that she intones, now more brilliantly than ever. She will be that man.

Domna Radiance is no more.

The change in her is quite remarkable. She has shaved her head. High boots extend her height. Leather chaps and jerkin encase her. Always a master of voice control, she lowers her register and increases her timbre. Her man's voice is convincing. She has learned to cultivate consistent mellow tones.

Domna Radiance is gone.

Peter Power stalks the earth convincingly. Even Virgil, who had met Domna, does not recognize this person.

In some ways she has lived her life as a man. She has made her own decisions. She has played many a man for many an audience.

She may as well be one.

She tries to look into Virgil Vindicator's black eyes. They shine like agates.

Peter is suddenly concerned that if he stares too deeply into the eyes of this towering white man he will be drawn into the man's soul and will never be able to walk away. As with all challenges, he confronts this one head-on. He seeks this man's attention with fervor. They become exceptionally close.

Virgil Vindicator is quite taken with this man before him, who has come to join him, he says.

"It would be a cold heart that did not respond to your warmth. It is an amazing handsomeness that is displayed along with it. Your voice is of a soothing yet firm nature such as is rarely heard from a man. It is a voice that might seduce people into believing. With my own booming voice, so appropriate to addressing vast crowds, and this new voice of yours, I feel that a useful bond is being forged."

"I want us to make a journey together," Peter tells him. "There is a concentration camp for Negro lesbians in northern Oklahoma. I want to go there and set them free."

THE LEGEND GROWS

It takes Virgil and Peter two years to locate Nantoo. They arrive too late. There is nothing there.

Much has happened to them. They have ridden many miles and been ridiculed in many places. They have looked for people like themselves, homosexual men and lesbians. Sometimes they find them, but only a few at a time. And no sooner are they met than they disperse, no doubt from nervousness at what is said to them.

Virgil sadly laments, "Now we are here, but where are we?"

"We must not despair," Peter says, bolstering his friend.

They try a few larger places, like Dallas and St. Louis and Kansas City. Here they encounter more of their people, but with the same result.

"We are here. I know we are here," Virgil says, trying to keep both their spirits up.

They patrol the streets day and night, but it is difficult to put two and two together. They put up posters that are ripped down; they hand out fly-ers, which are thrown away immediately.

"Movements are not built like this," Virgil says and Peter must agree. "We don't even know where to hand out our information safely."

They reach the far part of the West Coast. Washington has recently be-come a state. The men and women they meet here are even more embar-rassed by these soapbox orators.

Yes, it is homosexuals themselves who protest against them. A group of men dressed in extravagant costumes for a party circle the two and taunt them. "We do not want to hear from you! You make us ashamed! Leave us alone! We want to stay indoors. Who are you to preach to us how to live our lives!"

"Oh, my brothers and sisters, how can you cast us aside!" Virgil cries out to the few men and women who have remained.

And so it goes.

Yes, much happens to them. For one thing, they face death many times at the hands of the unfriendly. They always manage to escape.

For another, they have fallen in love. But neither of them wants to go down this avenue. Yes, by now they have each seen the other naked. Have they arrived here too late as well?

We hear no more about them.

They say that she came out of the West and he disappeared back into it.

THE DRIDGE AMPULE

Clarence Meekly wrote Horatio Dridge's life immediately after his death. We do not know how much of it is fact and how much of it is love. While not as highly regarded as Jane Addams's *My Twenty Years at Hull House* and Booker T. Washington's *Up from Slavery*, other classic works by strong indi-vidualists bent on establishing a new status quo after publicly condemning a wretched old one, it is nevertheless of interest to any historian of American disease. Unraveling the history of how the Dridge Ampule, of which Meekly writes so proprietarily, changed history, is one mission of this history of The American People. And at least he is honest about his love, which Jane Ad-dams is not in her own book, which fails to mention her "outlaw marriage" with Mary Rozet Smith.

Yes, Clarence and Horatio found each other at the end of that march of the wandering children in Washington, and not a moment too soon. Many of those kids were rounded up and incarcerated, if not quite imprisoned, in huge institutions for homeless youth. *Institution* was a word coming into vogue, a number of such establishments financed by a new group of The American People who were exceptionally rich and bent on "doing good." The march of the wanderers, as it came to be called, was a red flag inviting the roundup of thousands, young and old, with no beds to sleep in. Put 'em in an institution. Keep 'em off the streets. Don't want to see 'em. Whoever was president? Hayes, Garfield, Arthur, Cleveland, Harrison, McKinley, oh, it is a faceless, feckless, feeble, unmemorable hodge-podgy lot that run our country for the last twenty-five years of this nineteenth century. Quick! Name one important thing any of them did.

Here are some portions of Clarence Meekly's book:

I write this, my beloved's story, just after he has died at only thirty-five years of age. I am overcome with grief and loss. I call my book *The Biography of a Great Man*, because that is what he was. Originally I subtitled it "Only Earth Is Left Alive," because I am so bereft without him, but I then judged this too melodramatic. While I miss him more than I wish to stay alive, there is much for me to do for many years to come. His memory and his gift must be extolled and enshrined.

The world did not want to know about him during his lifetime, which, short though it may have been, was filled with great achievement. After all he accomplished, to be so overlooked! Other rich men, tycoons of other industries, are written of without surcease. It is imperative that I overcome this manifest unfairness. I have had to publish the book myself. No established publisher would do so. I shall now have to go out and sell the book as well, as I once went out and sold Dridge Flakes, making them an international success.

Horatio Dridge was probably from Ohio, as am I probably from Ohio, since we always instinctively knew our way around this state and he chose to accomplish his important acts here, including choosing me, Clarence Meekly, with whom he shared some twenty years of his life. Indeed, for most of our life together, and we met when we were both wandering children, both probably some fifteen years of age, he felt uncomfortable leaving the boundaries of this state. Ohio is the home of many famous Americans and their great contributions. Dridge Flakes, like the cash register and the rubber tire, and Horatio's joining with me, "my soul mate, my inspiration," as he perpetually named me, certainly his goad—all of these have their home in Ohio. Firestone, Goodyear, Goodrich, Tushner, Hanna, Rockefeller, Kroger, Dukavic,

Perk, Duvall, Fester, Allamontano, each lived a history in Ohio. I now add Horatio Dridge to this impressive list.

It is shocking that there exists no full-scale biography of this great man, Horatio Dridge, as lengthy and scholarly as the many volumes on heterosexual American tycoons. There has been no major biography of any homosexual capitalist, to this writer's knowledge. Yes, I use this word *heterosexual* with the same contempt that I have learned of late the world uses the word *homosexual* to discount us. I am new to these terms. They do not fall comfortably from my tongue and from my pen onto this page. But all of us are one or the other, and the latter is what he was, and what I am, and it is why we have been so ignominiously discarded. It is doubly unjust because our fortune has contributed much to enrich this country.

My dear man concocted the breakfast cereal that mercifully brought regularity to a legion of the constipated. He then housed many of the worst sufferers in the chain of homes we established to attend even more specifically to their disorder. Here this emetic was fine-tuned into their principal diet. These achievements were then wed to our growing network of increasingly sophisticated spas that mushroomed to take care of the bowels of an expanding population of the dyspeptic.

But as important as all of this, my history will also reveal for the first time the fortuitous albeit accidental discovery of the mutation of this cereal from flake to pellet to liquid to fermented liquid, and into the true foundation of our enormous fortune, the Dridge Ampule, which is Horatio's greatest gift to the world. The Dridge Ampule is a great discovery, as great as the rubber tire, the cash register, and oil.

Despite the fact that Ohio is farm country and the soil sufficiently providential, he never stopped talking, and movingly so, about his hateful childhood of poverty, a father who abandoned a mother who then sought solace in whatever liquor she could imbibe at whatever homes required a laundress, which, because of her drinking, became fewer and fewer, dwindling to none, after which she too disappeared, during all of which time her only child went hungry and of course unloved. It was not an uncommon childhood, then or now.

He wrote, in his own unpublished "The Struggles of My Life," which I shall also publish and which I am convinced will establish itself as a classic in a new category which I here name "orphan literature": "Very few are aware of how many parentless children roamed the countryside in those days. We were a race of orphans. If we were seen, we weren't cared about, and if we were cared about, it was usually in such brutal fashion as to make us run away to become, in preference, wanderers once again. I sometimes think that more men and women than we know must have met each other as children in dark corners all over America. There we coupled and parted, and if any evidence of pleasure came from those brief moments of release, such evidence, too, had to be denied and put out on the stoop of unhappy memory, like last week's garbage or an unwanted cat. Those children who came to be called 'illegitimate,' I would wager mightily, are the true roots of much from whom this country sprouted. Crime, theft, and larceny, even murder— what separates any of these from the illegitimacy of abandonment? It is all the same package, is it not?"

Horatio writes of eating leaves and branches, bark and acorns and grass. In the winter, he chopped chunks of dirt out of the ground and ate them sprinkled over with sugar he stole when he plunked down a few lonely pennies for a cup of coffee somewhere: "I allowed the earth to warm itself softer in my palms, and the sugar grains to impress their sweetness into it, and I closed my eyes in order to pretend it was something different I was tasting, and swallowing. It was. It was the soil of the whole world, the nurturing sustenance of Nature itself. It made me grow. It made me strong. If I am strong today, and healthy, which I obviously am, then it is because of American dirt."

Some innate gift for survival must have blessed Horatio mightily. I have heard over the years many unkind myths about him, some rather scandalous, suggestions that he was "kept," or of white slavery, or childhood torture, or of being the sex "play toy" of the man whose family founded Akron or the man who invented cough drops, or that he was the youngest and most successful bank robber who ever stuck up Ohio. I can hear him laughing as he told all this about himself. He did nothing to correct any of it, nor allowed me to do so. "I like a little mystery" was all he ever said. "Great men are great because we are mysteries."

Yes, he knew he was great. He knew he was going to be great long before he was great. And I knew it, too.

At some early point before we met he took to researching in libraries what cavemen did to keep alive, "what those hairy-chested, lion-skinned big busters of prehistoric times did to get enough energy to rule the world when farming was unknown and enemies were monstrous carnivorous behemoths." Did diets then comprise only plants and fruits? How could people live on so little? Horatio, at eleven, and having a tough time of it as a traveling salesman trying to peddle cloth ink blotters in an area where many people could not yet write, or had no time to, or no ink to do it with, decided to find out. Horatio, at eleven, returned to the forest "to find myself."

Short of stealing, selling things was the only way to forge a path. Manufacturing, or making something, was expensive. One needed materials that had to be purchased. People had little money to pursue imaginative dreams. People had little money to buy the fruits of others' dreams. People lucky enough to have farms worked the land with their hands, and took care of their animals, and ate what they grew and slaughtered. Or they labored in offices and factories. That was the circle of life. Oh, maybe there was a product like a blotter, or soap, or some elixir in a bottle touted to pep you up and get you going, that needed a representative for the Dakota Territory, where absolutely no one lived. But if you were a go-getter like Horatio Dridge you had to find your own canoe to paddle. Nobody was giving anything away to anyone. There were a lot of children like us, boys and girls seeking and trying and peddling strange notions thrown together mostly with hope. Most of these boys and girls, and most of their dreams, didn't live long. They certainly did not live long enough to see their names up on banners in great big letters like Horty did.

At five feet three Horatio Dridge was a short man, but when he opened his mouth to speak he wasn't short anymore. He was the giant who could sell you a piece of tomorrow. His voice, which was a deeper baritone than anyone so short had a right to house, boomed mellifluously. His hair, and he had much hair all his life, which he attributed to his regularity, which he attributed to his cereal, which he attributed to his "education in the woods," all of which he attributed to his love for me and mine for him, was fluently wavy, always holding itself up high. He never wore elevator shoes, eschewing anything akin to what he called "the city-slicker."

But I digress. In the vast forests and woods outside Petunia, Ohio (recently renamed Dridge, Ohio), Horatio made himself a hut of branches and leaves and started a fire by rubbing "the proverbial two sticks" together. As he quickly discovered, "I am hungry all the time. Leaves and berries are no more than a meal's beginning salad. No man, now or ever, can run wild across a terrain on such a feeble intake. I try to eat twigs and bark, uncooked or boiled or roasted. Each way is wretched. My insides become mutilated from the strain of digestion and elimination. What kind of stomach can digest a tree?

"Yes, I did eat trees. It was the same as what we ate in the war. Oftentimes in war and peace there is nothing else to eat, with ice freezing the earth and trees the only thing visible for miles around to warm up in your hands and gnaw at like chewing tobacco, masticating it into a soft-enough pulp to get down the gullet, in hopes that it will churn itself into enough warmth and energy to get you through a night so frigid that animals freeze to death. To this day there's many a one of us can't believe we're still here. Most thank the Lord. I thank Myself."

Most times there was only earth to eat. Dirt is cold and tasteless on its own. Warmed up, mixed with water, peppered with whatever berries are in season, often isn't enough of a help. What, Horatio wondered, might make earth palatable for consumption, in addition to ravenous hunger?

"Soon it became possible for me to make a flavorful earth. I learned how to make mulch, how to mix leaves and softened twigs and animal droppings with earth and wild berries and fruits and nuts and let it all bake in the sun and be kissed by the rain and churn itself miraculously into sustenance.

"I found that my body responded favorably. My stomach ceased its bark and howl. My bowels gave forth sturdy turds. Most important, my energy was enormous. I had never felt so strong!

"One lovely spring night, as I was lying in a field somewhere near Cleveland, I believe, I looked up at the stars and for the first time, at some fourteen years of age, I clamped my hand on to my peter and pumped it into a fountain of gism six or seven times. I had never known how to do that, and I thanked all the dirt I had eaten for making me feel so top-of-the-world."

There must be minerals and elements in this earth, he reasoned, that have been in it since time began and can be nothing but good for you.

"I thought to give my dirt a name. I thought to bottle it or bag it so I could sell it after I fixed it up. I had an inspiration. I would say it was my First Inspiration, but I think pumping my pecker was that. I fashioned some moist mud into little pellets and flattened them out on a huge sheet of tin and let the sun bake them dry."

And so came into the world Dridge Flakes.

"Tasty, Healthful, Nature's Own!"

Before leaving the forest, Horatio tried several versions to locate more precisely the perfect taste so he could perpetuate it. One day he added a bit of himself. He'd been masturbating again. He did so a lot, now that he knew how. We did it a lot together from the first day we met.

"Pumping your pecker is very healthy, I had by now determined."

And he tastes his semen and it tastes good.

"With Nature's Own Secret Ingredient!"

"I tried selling my Flakes. I'd stand in front of a crowd at a fair, looking peaked and lackadaisical, and I'd chomp on a great handful of my Flakes and perk up and jump high and lift a heavy rock if there was one around. But no one was buying any."

One day I, young Clarence Meekly, walked into Horatio's life and before long Horatio's Dridge Flakes were released from anonymity. How I made Dridge Flakes into a daily household necessity is no more than the story of an enterprising, ambitious young salesman with a promising product, seeking out new markets and never ceasing to believe that my beloved's Dridge Flakes were something Americans in droves must eat. Every successful product I have ever studied has a similar history of a passionate belief in its superiority by its purveyor. Yes, the success of Dridge Flakes is no more than the story of a loved one so consumed for the first and only time by love for a fellow man.

I went west, playing a hunch, correctly, that Dridge Flakes were something cowboys, increasingly known for their constipation, a fact available to a smart young man with his ears to the ground, would eat in massive amounts, such being their appetites. Cowboys took to me and my Dridge Flakes with abandon.

Dridge Flakes were soon consumed in huge quantities all over the world.

It was even estimated that if Dridge Flakes were to be withdrawn from the marketplace the world would no longer be able to shit regularly. The Dridge Flake came to be all about shitting. We had discovered a great American secret. The American People were exceedingly constipated. It was as if, these many years later, all the fare everyone was forced to swallow during the Civil War, just to stay alive, was still impossible to eliminate.

Other cereals soon came along. They, too, were all about regular bowel movements. The competition became so fierce that we could not rise above it. Aspersions were cast about our ingredients. We watched as Dridge Flakes were overtaken and superseded by Corn Flakes and Bran Flakes, Post's and Kellogg's, Mother Maude's and Wilber's, which grew into "brands" more successful than our own. I did not believe they aided regularity more significantly. It was their taste. Our competitors used sugar to make their products sweet. The taste was no longer of the earth.

It was a good thing the Dridge Ampule came along. It would be the Dridge Ampule that made the real fortune upon which Dridge Meekley was founded.

How did this come about?

We owe the ampule to a dog. At the Dayton Spa, I fed our dog, Jasper, his usual Dridge Flakes. I put them in his bowl in the kitchen. Perhaps because he had already eliminated all he needed to for the day, he ignored his food. Late that night a spa patron unloaded the contents of his hip flask of whiskey into Jasper's bowl so his wife wouldn't discover he hadn't been filling it with water to drink when parched. The next morning Jasper was extremely excited. He leaped into the air and rolled around the floor and hurled himself onto Agnes, one of the more attractive of the housekeepers, and tried to hump her with his hugely engorged member. I noted that his bowl was empty and that it smelled of liquor. I suspected a cause-and-effect sequence. I removed the dog's bowl to our room, where I inhaled deeply.

Several bodily changes immediately transpired. First, my heart beat wildly and my head felt giddy and my whole being was as if transported to someplace transcendently elsewhere. I am not certain where, but I very much enjoyed being there. Second, I had an erection, not a regular occurrence anymore by any means, a very firm and large erection. Third, I desired sex immediately. Horty walked in at this propitious moment and I rammed the bowl under his nose. Instantaneously and simultaneously we grabbed each other, stripped each other bare, and fell upon our bed, where we commenced wild sexual experiences of a nature heretofore unknown to either of us. We even kissed each other, many times and in many places. Horty had never been a kisser, despite my deep desires in that area. These timid aging bachelors were behaving like youngsters! When our passions flagged, when our erections sagged, they could be reignited by a further deep inhalation of Jasper's bowl.

Horatio made me, Clarence Meekly, his partner not only in fact but in legal deed.

Numerous orgasms later, we napped, sleeping tenderly in each other's arms. "My Clare, my Clare, my beloved Clare," Horty mumbled in his sleep.

Upon awakening we fell to the floor, this time propelled not by libido but by extreme curiosity. What was in that bowl?

Whiskey and Dridge Flakes was the not-unexpected discovery.

Horatio, the great inventor, pondered.

His flakes were composed of various earthy ingredients, composted together in a secret recipe he continued to toy with. He never stopped thinking about it, or adding a little of this and that into different batches. I had even seen him add some of his own shit. He ate a perfect diet and reasoned, Didn't cow dung cause the crops to grow? Mr. Kellogg's Corn Flakes were said to contain saltpeter to keep little boys from masturbating. Horatio had noticed that when he added a little bit more of his "Nature's Own" to his flakes, the spa guests who were particularly bound up rushed up to him on their way to or from a toilet, in exceptional gratitude. He came to produce various versions of his flakes, and to recognize which of his guests needed what and when and how much, and he gave appropriate names to his inspirations: Dridge Number One (a poor seller), Dridge Number Two, Dridge Number Two Plus, Dridge Number Two Supreme.

We wondered what this new discovery should be named, and exactly how it could be recommended tastefully.

Horatio got up and went to his laboratory, where he did his best thinking.

"Something happens when mud, shit, a bit of piss, and a touch of semen are permeated with alcohol. Something that makes man and beast go wild."

He discovered it was the aroma, inhaled, that caused the fury, and that it was this aroma that must somehow be contained.

He experimented with a number of containers before alighting on a small glass tube encased in a silk sack, which when crushed in the fingers would emit its odor for quick inhalation, quickened heartbeats, speedy passion. It was all quite a miracle and Horty and I, still naked and after sex of course, thanked each other.

The resultant product—the Dridge Ampule—was marketed as "Recommended for those suffering from heart palpitations, physical restlessness, constitutional malaise, feeble desires, hunger and yearnings, and the vapors."

In no time at all the Dridge Ampule was used by everyone from young gallivanters to enfeebled old gents. There was hardly a spinster's clutch purse or a vest watch pocket that was without an ampule. When exhaustion overtook, when those imprecisely named "vapors" overcameth, out with the tiny glass ampule in its little silk mesh stocking, to be snapped in two and deeply inhaled for renewed invigoration.

When Horatio died, he was worth $25 million.

He died, Horty did, in his Clare's arms. We had just made the most passionate love either of us had ever known, and Horty's heart could not take it. His cock was still up his Clare's asshole, and still hard as a rock, when he screamed out his last passionate "I love you!"

N.B.

YRH reminds his readers that this version of the history of the Dridge Ampule might not be . . . all there is. The aphrodisiac that Lucid III carried with him from Fruit Island, and that Pushnow, that mysterious Jew, had pledged that he would capture, and did, and that Messie Too was also traveling with—what has happened to all of these? Was the stuff of Dridge really the stuff of any of these?

DR. SISTER GRACE GOES BALLISTIC

HORSESHIT HORSESHIT HORSESHIT! If you believe Clarence Meekly's dog-fucking version of the "discovery" of the Dridge Ampule you'll believe in the mingy man in the moon! Who is ass-feeding you all this manure? This is not history! Did you not learn from or listen to anything that I said? I told you that I am the one who invented this ampule, which I then sold to Greeting-Dridge Pharmaceuticals. It makes me go crazy to hear that fistfucking fuckpotty name of Dridge. And I am the one who got rich from it. I hold the major patents! There is no Clarence Meekly or Horatio Dridge in the line of patent holders. Clarence Meekly and Horatio Dridge were copulating crap turd charlatans of the highest order. You have pissed me off royally by even giving voice, much less credence, to such arrant lying about this ampule that bears the Dridge name only because a pharmaceutical company was founded to acquire his laxative cereals! And I've been cooperating with you! Go to hell, young man! You are not worth the paper we are piddling on.

I must collect my fucking thoughts and myself.

Oh, what's the use? It's fruitless to fight back. All that does is make everyone think I have something to hide. I do not. I know what I did. History will bear me out. Although I am sick of that useless bugfucking expression. History knows dipshit about ratshit.

For the moment I'll leave it at that.

Fred Lemish, I have known you since you were a child. I held you in my arms and gave you baths. I cleaned up your shitty Fruit of the Looms when you ran all the way home from Franeeda Elementary because you didn't want to use their toilets. I do not deserve this from you.

And which years are you even talking about? The errant timelessness of your roving renderings cascades your telling into fart-bearing fantasy!

HAVE WE ALL FORGOTTEN ALREADY?

Although I find it difficult to say this to her, Grace has a point. As we know, or should remember, or should suspect, Clare's version of the history of the Dridge Ampule may not be completely kosher. (What was in those days?) I defend myself, dearest Dr. Sister Grace, you who tried to clean me up when I was at my messiest, by saying that by including Clarence Meekly's story I am not taking his side, only advancing a chronology. We simply must not fly off the handle so easily with each other. (I know that I myself will come to rue these words of advice.)

Was the stuff of Dridge really the stuff of Lucid? I say not only to Grace and myself, but to my readers: "Clear title" is a term I remember from working in the movies. These are very difficult to prove! That Grace is today's recipient of all royalties on the Dridge Ampule is certainly an indication the law is on her side right now. But even just saying it this way, I see I only step in more potential shit!

Let us continue, as best we can.

HOVES MORE INTO VIEW

OK, back to the proverbial grindstone in attempting to sort out who's who and what's what and who did what and when and why are we here today, if we are here today, if we are anywhere today. I must be of firmer faith that eventually we shall get ourselves somewhere! Although I feel myself toughening up day by day. I must confess to mounting apprehension as I approach the twentieth century. Knowing what I know now and learning more every minute about what we have seen, and not seen, the walls may all still come tumbling down at any minute. It is the Lemish curse to increasingly feel this way.

Now that they have their very own name, will it remain so thorny to follow undecipherable trails through long agos, and not so long agos, to reveal and convey what homosexuals do to protect themselves, to define themselves, what they participate in, allow themselves to do? So few have yet been identified who follow Peter and Virgil, who themselves remain unknown, even to this day. Why, just the other day I realized I could not find out, from anyone, scholar or otherwise, how the word *lesbian* came into general use. Lesbians themselves, still, still, are unable to answer with certainty when their own name came into being! How did anyone in the mid-to-late nineteenth century know about the island of Lesbos, and about Sappho and her sisters? Is a life not diminished when we are ignorant of where we come from? This is a loaded question, to be sure. There are millions of adopted people, unenlightened about their origins, who seem to have lived and live fine lives. But my little tussle with Grace, above, who is most dear to me, only increases my apprehension and the certain knowledge that, from here on in, the ice gets thinner, and being more equipped with a certainty that we can stand up and say, know, and be proud of who we are remains an elusive task. My appeal to my lesbian friends that "it is time to put your house in order" was met with more shrugs than concern, as will be all my similar pleas to men. Coincidentally, a distinguished gay historian has excitedly revealed to the world that he has uncovered a "transvestite" diary from this turn of the century. It is no different from what a similar drag queen might write today. They had different names for themselves then, androdyne or intermediate or third sex, all of which disappear when *homosexual* comes to rule the linguistic roost. The inclusion by the writer of this diary of a verbal attack on him by his employer who, discovering his employee's escapades, fires him on the spot, is included: "My disgust is innermost and deep seated! To begin now to show any mercy to the invert, after having for two thousand years confined him in dungeons, burned him at the stake, and buried him alive, would be a backward step in the evolution of the race! The invert is not fit to live with the rest of mankind! He should be shunned as the lepers of biblical times! If generously allowed outside prison walls, the law should at least ordain that the word UNCLEAN be branded in his forehead, and should compel him to cry: 'UNCLEAN! UNCLEAN!' as he walks the streets, lest his very brushing against decent people contaminate them!" Condemnations like these appear a dime a dozen to this day.

The end of this century finds houses of man and boy prostitutes proliferating in every major city: New York, Boston, Philadelphia, Chicago, St. Louis, New Orleans, and San Francisco providing food for same-sex appetites. Manhattan has a dozen of these. In all brothels there are also women for other women. Western mining towns are similarly equipped, including ones in Utah. The Disciples of Lovejoy's Princely Bountiful Pearl of the World Trust is also landlord to a number of these houses. It should be noted that by this time tens of thousands of teenagers had attended and were attending all-male boarding schools; at the other end of the scale, hobos are becoming an increasingly visible population (there would be two million of them by 1920) across the landscape; they often traveled in pairs, one often younger than the other and in obvious thrall to him. "I didn't do no harm. I minded my own business. I didn't steal or beg. It is an easy way to get by," one of these youngsters told one Edna Squats, an early version of a social worker attempting to study "nocturnal social habits of the single young male." "We take care of each other, we do. In New York, I had to charge fifty cents for my mouth and one dollar for my ass just to eat." Edna's sister, Hedda Squats Berryman, has written a landmark study of the sexual activities of young Disciples of Lovejoy women, which is filled with startling statistics of how much nonmarital sex was going on in Utah and the general unwillingness to acknowledge it, much less punish it. (A third Squats sister, Gretchen, was the seventeenth wife of Brigham Furst, Ezra's successor, Ezra Jr. again having failed at promotion.) When a Disciples of Lovejoy academic, D. Michael Quinn, revealed much of this in the late twentieth century, he was excommunicated.

In 1893, Dr. Magnus Hirschfeld, a physician working in Berlin, travels the world giving lectures and visits Chicago. Indeed, he is to use descriptions of the city's homosexual community in his groundbreaking book, *Homosexuality in Men and Women*.

His appearance in Chicago inspires the establishment of the American Humanitarian Society, an energetic group of voluble young men that grows to include seventeen members who, in the small room where they meet, die of poisoning after eating food "donated by a caring and supportive mother" of one of them.

Also in 1897, following Hirschfeld's courageous lead, which he had learned about on a trip to Berlin, Dr. Trump File starts a homophile (where *did* this wretched word come from?) organization in Vidalia, Illinois. He names it the Abraham Society, for even then word has got around about that original Abe loving men. His intention for this society is for like-minded men to meet regularly in a social setting, no more than that. Dr. File, who is a man with a wife, four children, and a practice in family medicine in this small town, takes his idea to Chicago, takes it to Boston, takes it to Richmond, takes it to Philadelphia, always seeing to it that he's left one or two men in each place to carry on. He's managed, by word of mouth alone, to see his groups grow past the dozens and upward. He decides to take the Abraham Society to Washington, where he stays to set up a "national headquarters." All along the way, he's been accompanied by his best and oldest friend, an important Quaker historian by the name of Reeves Revenue, who has already made a name for himself by writing about what he calls his "clotted theory of historical inevitability." Dr. File and the Abraham Society come to the attention of Eagen Odemptor and Turpa Diamond (who'd cleaned out Nantoo), who attend a meeting with a number of policemen as well as Foster Purview, a leading journalist who delights in performing duties for brother Lovejoys. All is exposed in *The Washington Monument*. Purview details "a perverted orgy" and Dr. File and Reeves Revenue kill themselves that evening. They are found naked in each other's arms by a hotel maid, and it is this photo that makes its way around the world with various headlines along the lines of "Perverted Love Nest Poisons Itself to Death in DC." Purview is given a "heroic behavior" award at the White House by Grover Cleveland, for many years a bachelor but now married for political convenience to a young woman twenty-eight years his junior. The Tally Office is recognized publicly by the president: this very acknowledgment, the first official one it's had, puts it on the map, at least in Washington. It is now all right, officially, to go after perverts. Now we know what they look like. At least a couple of them. On the Fourth of July, the Tally Office marches down Pennsylvania Avenue with hundreds of other patriotic groups, Eagen and Turpa and scattered others from their growing office. Yes, thanks to Foster Purview, Washington now knows what the Tally Office is. They are cheered. "They" are Lovejoys. They are increasingly virulent in their hatred of homosexuals. Why? Like the Catholics, they must increase their membership and eliminate all obstacles.

Back in Germany, Magnus Hirschfeld had formed the Scientific Humanitarian Society in Berlin and publishes what may have been the first gay periodical, *Jahrbuch für sexuelle Zwischenstufen* (Yearbook for Intermediate Sexual Types). The work of his SHS will continue until May 1933, when Nazis and Lovejoy missionaries loot Hirschfeld's institute and burn the extensive collection of books and manuscripts delineating the history of "my people" that he and his followers arduously assembled over many years. This bonfire will be the start of the next chapter of Germany's own hate, leading to Hitler's determined purge of homosexuals, wherein it will be said a million homosexuals are sent to death camps. As we have seen, long before that time and place, such activities are further advanced in America.

In 1899, Dr. Albert John Ochsner (later to co-found the American College of Surgeons) advocates, in *The Journal of the American Medical Association*, for compulsory castration of prisoners to reduce the potential number of, among other awful things, "perverts." Dr. Harry Clay Sharp, who has read the article, performs extralegal medical castrations to cure Indiana State

Prison convicts of masturbating. That he does so attracts much notice. Other prisons follow suit. It is apparently not difficult to locate doctors willing to perform castrations.

By 1890, almost 47 percent of adult men and 37 percent of adult women are single. "Mostly young, these men and women constituted a separate sub-culture that helped support institutions like dance halls, saloons, cafes, and the YMCA and YWCA . . ." (Mary Beth Norton et al., *A People and a Nation: A History of the United States*, vol. 2, 6th ed., 2001). On urban life in late-nineteenth-century America:

> Homosexual men and women began forming social networks: on the streets where they regularly met or at specific restaurants and clubs, which, to avoid controversy, sometimes passed themselves off as athletic associations or chess clubs. Such places could be found in New York City's Bowery, around the Presidio military base in San Francisco, and at Lafayette Square in Washington, D.C.
>
> (Davidson et al., *Nation of Nations: A Narrative History of the American Republic*)

> It is at the various branches of the Young Men's Christian Association around the country that young gay men found each other most readily. It can not be overestimated how important these Y's were for almost a hundred years and continuing even to this day, for the safe harbor they offered gay men, in their gymnasiums, pools, steam rooms, and of course the rooms that could be rented inexpensively and served as hotels for travelers from everywhere.
>
> (Norbert and Noreen Curlue, *A Handbook to America's Most Welcoming Bathhouses*, 1990)

As an interesting example of spreading hate, Cardinal John Henry New-man dies in England in 1890 and by the terms of his will is buried in the same grave in Rednal, Worcestershire, with Father Ambrose St. John, with whom he lived as "husband and wife" for most of their late adult lives. Car-dinal Newman wrote shortly before his death: "I wish with all my heart to be buried in Father Ambrose St. John's grave—and I give this as my last, my imperative will." On their gravestone is a Latin inscription, meaning "from shadows and images into the truth," which some believe is a posthumous coming out. After more than a hundred years of their being buried together the Vatican exhumes Newman's body to be buried on its own, upon his elevation to sainthood. Ecclesiastical hierarchies of every American religion, then and following, vehemently support Rome's determination not to allow this relationship to be viewed for what it was. A New York bishop, Altune Demarest, writes in *The Daily Catholic Lesson*, "The Holy Father has acted correctly, with dignity and Supreme Right on His side."

In 1900 the Census Bureau allowed unrelated persons who lived together, including those of the same sex, to describe themselves as "domestic partners." It was eliminated immediately and not permitted on any following census.

At the end of the waning century, the government distributes pieces of paper listing employment opportunities. There are many jobs and not enough men, still and yet, to do them. The war, you know. Some thirty-five years later and this country still is short of men. Vivo Marpo reads these circulars every time he's handed one. Negro janitors hand them out on the street. Most of the jobs sound boring. He does not know what he wants to do or what he is capable of doing. He once thought he could do anything, but those days are gone. His body is not the same since the war. He wasn't in the war, of course, but his father was, and he was killed at Shiloh, leaving his mother with him in her stomach and no money to nurture him. He doesn't know what's wrong with his body but he has never felt right, in his body or in his head. Doctors have told him he was "irreparably malnourished," and it's true his arms and legs are skinny and his bones break easily. It's a good thing he lives in Washington, because there is now a department that looks after "veterans," and though he's only a son of one, he can go there and get his broken arms or legs reset. A desk job is what he needs, he's advised. He gets angry and is apt to hit people suddenly. A fellow at the new Disciples of Lovejoy local mission tells him he must find some meaningful work "to take your mind off things." The "veterans" doctor gives him some powders for it but he says they don't really help. "Try to stay on top of yourself, son," he advises.

One day Vivo sees a mention of something called "the Tally Office." There is no description of what the Tally Office does or is seeking.

Who today knows that Hesiod Furst, one of the most important of the early Lovejoy more-or-less secret agents, founded the Tally Office? Certainly no one will confess to this, no one in the Sacred Environs of Our Holy Temple, or members of the Princely Bountiful Pearl of the World Trust, or indeed at the Prince of All Waters Central Administrative Headquarters, all of which are now located in Oxonia. But Hesiod Furst was the first person actually responsible for intentionally and consciously ordering legal "removals" of homosexuals on behalf of the United States Government. It was naturally a secret agreement, made by Chester Arthur or Grover Cleveland. (Those years of Cleveland's in and outing—now he's president; now he's not—surely mussed up government records, making it difficult to investigate much with clarity.) And of course Chester Arthur's preference for other men was not so much a secret as he wished it to be, so who knows what he ordered done or undone. In any event, the Tally Office is able to operate.

In 1897 the Dridge Pharmaceutical Company is commissioned by the Tally Office, in an ordinance signed by this Hesiod Furst, to "create" a means by which homosexuals can be quietly and swiftly "put down," as they say of animals. There had been certain conversations between one Furst or another. By now there are quite a few Fursts and quite a few Ezras and Hesiods soon to be joined by a bunch of Brighams running around Washington. Ezra will have eighty-five children by the time he can't get up in the morning.

The president (whichever one it was) and Nigel Rotfeld, the Tally's chief administrator, desired an "end point," which evidently was more fully discussed unfettered by any written word.

Corporate records are still a Sometime Thing. Dridge makes a lot of stuff now, more and more of it each day. Stuff, in these days, usually means concoctions touted to do all sorts of miraculous things they don't really do. "Patent medicines" they come to be called, although no one knows quite why. They certainly weren't all patented. The United States Patent Office is an awful mess, although it was set up by the Constitution and George Washington himself signed the first patent, for an unguent for toothaches. You would think they would be in better shape by now. But people who said they worked for the government issued pieces of paper for all sorts of things, pieces of paper that held no meaning. You'd walk into one office and say, I want to make sure no one steals my cure for the blah blahs, and someone would write a piece of paper saying you were hereby protected for your "discovery." Patents didn't always have numbers on them either; the efficiency of the system depended on who was in charge and how much education, usually not nearly enough, that person had. Education through only a certain number of grades was all most people had. We did not have what could be called an educated working class, or maybe workforce is a more democratic way to say this. Workers are becoming more sensitive to their place in the world, or rather lack of it. If you really looked at the mess Washington and its government is in, you'd wonder how we got this far. Or maybe you'd realize just why we haven't. No one knows that the Disciples of Lovejoy own and run it and that

Hesiod Furst even managed to get the president (whoever it was) to secretly siphon some funds from The American People's Treasury Department.

Vivo Marpo applies for the job of "Master Circulator" of the Tally Office. He is hired by old Eagan himself, who senses the man is like him—that is, someone who genuinely hates homosexuals, or hushmarkeds as they still are called in certain places that do not keep up with the times, or are so behind them that they've just discovered the word *hushmarked* in the first place, and that he will be useful because of it. There is a certain quiet nobility about him, Egan and then Turpa also note.

"Do you know what a hushmarked is?" Vivo is quizzed by Eagan.

"No, sir."

"Do you know what a homosexual is?"

"No, sir. It doesn't sound like I like the sound of it, though."

"It is a man who partakes of sex with another man."

"Oh."

That is all he says, quietly.

Turpa takes Vivo home to dinner where, for his final test to see if he is a homosexual, she tries to seduce him. Vivo is not seducible and calls her "Grandma."

"He has a lovely body," she reports. "But he is very quiet. I do think he is quite noble. He was a virgin." And then, after a long pause, she said, "He wants to marry me. He says he loved his grandmother more than anyone in the world."

Well, quiet nobility is always useful when sent forth to perform the unorthodox. Once again America will send forth a man, in this case Vivo Marpo, a poor, semistunted Italian orphan who doesn't know what he is being sent forth to do. This is not the first time an American man's essential innocence and desire to learn, to please, to fight for his country will be harnessed to the perverse.

THE APPEARANCE OF SIR HENRY GREETING, THE UNION OF GREETING-DRIDGE, AND THE ARRIVAL OF THE DRIDGE AMPULE INTO THE WORLD BIG-TIME

Henry Greeting is not a relative of the Sir John Greeting we met several hundred years ago in the Nearodell, Carolina, territories. But in certain quarters it is a known name, Greeting, and it arouses particular interest in this young man, also named Greeting, an ambitious lad from the Dakota Territory eager to present himself to the world as a pharmacist, a recent graduate of the well-regarded Pittsburgh Dispensary, into whose library and its few books about the history of medicine in this country he has dipped and seen it there, Greeting, why, almost from the very beginning of America's history. He feels blessed, somehow by fate. He will be blessed.

He is born to a missionary father and schoolteacher mother, both of whom have unsuccessfully attempted to help and teach the Dakota Indian tribes, a dangerous and uncaring and ungrateful lot that refuses to believe in God, which actually endears them to Henry, who doesn't believe in Him either. He plays with these Indian boys and they with him. He becomes friendly with the Dakota medicine men, who greatly inspire him with their canny tricks to keep their people "in unity and harmony and bliss." It is the Indian boys who teach him what bliss is. It scares the shit out of him, what they do with their penises and want him to do with his, and theirs. They laugh at him. He does not like being laughed at. By the time he's ready to leave this godforsaken place he's pretty well instructed in a few necessary lessons for that outside world, most important, how frightening sexual excitement is and how he much prefers not to smile and not to be nice. For anyone who grew up anywhere on the plains of America, northern particularly, these are all familiar traits. Wilderness, long winter nights, exceptional cold, all contribute to this, along with more of those unsmiling and unloving parents we've met so often. Few American parents know how to be good parents. You can take this as a rule of thumb, across the board, without exception.

Henry leaves Groyne, North Dakota, for Pittsburgh in 1898. He graduates from its Dispensary in 1900, first in his class. He leaves immediately for England, home of that Sir John Greeting he'd read about. No one remembers Sir John Greeting, but there is all that junk in various museum warehouses that he'd brought back from all over the world. Henry hears about it, goes to look at it, and senses that he knows this man who assembled all this, and why he assembled it, and why it interested him in the first place. And that indeed and therefore he must be related to him. From this moment on he considers himself a true Greeting. There is no one, and no Foundation yet, to say him Nay.

Back home, word of whatever "it" is that makes men feel so good, with such firm erections, has spread much faster than any malfunctions it is being peddled by the Dridge Company to sate and cure (dyspepsia, fatigue, the vapors, catarrh, skin eruptions, gas, depression, loss of appetite, etc., etc.). Not that the Dridge people are silent on what Horatio and Clarence had discovered firsthand. Included with every package is a discreet sealed envelope in which reference is made to such key terms as "potency," and "renewed personal vigor," and "marriage glue." (How generous of Mother Nature, if she it be, that a similar concoction was also "created" in an attempt to cure syphilis. Do you remember those appallingly fervent exercises on Fruit Island?)

"It" of course is the Dridge Ampule.

This word spreads faster than the very blood that not so long ago covered the ground of America from north to south. Rumor, hearsay, and the use of the stuff by many happy consumers naturally spurts out uncontrollably. Never before had a product reached the country with such dispatch.

This Dridge Ampule, manufactured by the Dridge Pharmaceutical Company, Horatio Dridge, founder, Clarence Meekly, president, is the hottest item any place it's sold.

Farrell Pushnow hears from his contact, one Edinburgh Jesus Pushnow, of a young man, now living in England, a graduate of the Pittsburgh Dispensary, who has discovered a way to reduce soft or liquid compounds into tablets and then, by a process he has also invented, dissolve the resultant tablet into an inhalant that has a longer shelf life than the Dridge Ampule, with which, having himself heard of its remarkable efficacy, this Greeting has been tinkering. How did he hear about the Dridge Ampule? He had been to Amsterdam, already a safe meeting place for closeted homosexuals, and been introduced to it. Once again, this experience with another man scared the shit out of him, but even frightened he recognized what a future fortune was being rammed up his nose at the height of his suddenly no longer discomfiting passion, and he took a few ampules back to study in London, where he had formed a partnership with his Pittsburgh Dispensary classmate, Thomas Actim Baxxter.

All Pushows around the world had been alerted to the Dridge Ampule. Farrell's got this tube of salve, you see, and he knows what it does but not how it does it. Henry Greeting sounds like just the kind of man who can tell him. These Pushnows don't mess around. Never have. Never will. They are still around today.

So Edinburgh Jesus Pushnow (he had a Mexican mother, which is a story in itself, how she got to Edinburgh and met his father, etc.) meets Henry and likes the firm resolve and unsmiling nature of the young man. Farrell Pushnow then travels to London and shows Henry the precious salve that has journeyed so far to this historic moment, a salve that must be compounded into a better and longer-lasting product, to rouse man up time after time, effortlessly and without muss. Well, sometimes a little muss. Henry immediately comprehends not only the similarities between the salve and his Amsterdam ampule but also how valuable his own contribution can be to this development.

Farrell Pushnow makes the young Henry an interesting offer.

No fool he, Henry drives a hard bargain with Pushnow. Hence, the launching of the Baxxter-Greeting Pharmaceutical Company. Naturally, Pushnow has been careful enough to know about and take care of Clarence Meekly and *his* Dridge Ampule. In fact, Clarence Meekly has died, mysteriously, leaving rather recently signed documents deeding his company to the "Fehl Trust" in Switzerland. No, there is little that money cannot buy.

Thomas Actim Baxxter commences his partnership with Henry Greeting. They will not get along. In fact, they will hate each other. In fact, they will each wish the other dead, since by the contract Farrell Pushnow negotiated between them the survivor inherits it all. By the time of The Underlying Condition, Baxxter will have been long gone and Greeting will have been long the sole owner and the Greeting Pharmaceutical Company will be the largest pharmaceutical company in the world. You want to know why? Two words will tell you. Dridge Ampule. But you know how unhappy families have a way of carrying on; Tolstoy will tell us all about that. The hate and enmity and jealousy between Baxxter and Greeting is in the genetic blood of this company, and no matter how many times it will rename itself through the remainder of this history, it will be a totally miserable place to work and deal with.

The tablet itself, just mentioned, is a mighty discovery on its own, so Henry Greeting cannot be accused of being a one-trick pony. Think of all the tablets each member of the human race ingests every day and you have some notion of the value of his invention. Thomas Actim Baxxter maintained that *he* discovered the tablet. But he wasn't around to fight back.

Henry becomes so rich that he is knighted. Sir Henry Greeting then marries London's most prominent interior decorator, Syrie Maugham, as cold as he is, recently divorced from another closeted iceberg/genius, Somerset. They will have a son.

The Dridge Ampule is one of the most important products ever launched into the world. It will not only be responsible for more cataclysmic orgasms than all the hookers ever known to mankind, it will also, when it really gets its footing on the ground in the burgeoning homosexual "community," in another fifty or so years, become one of the primary facilitators of the plague of The Underlying Condition. Does Henry Greeting know what lies ahead? Does anyone?

We shall see.

•

I knew what was happening and I was euphoric! If enough people sniff this stuff and then fuck each other I can get a bigger wedge into America. And elsewhere. I know that if I get into enough of them and they keep fucking each other I will survive.

The more people I kill, the longer I live.

Isn't that the way of your world?

DISCIPLES AND ALLIANCES

I should point out the peculiar desire for so many Disciples of Lovejoy to have the same Christian names. There are soon so many Ezras and Hesiods and Brighams that we are forced in our relating of their unusual history to abide by the increasingly astringent regulations set forth by the Sacred Archives of the Princely Bountiful Pearl of the World Trust (oh, this is such a mouthful!), which are out to protect the anonymity of all, and to just call everyone one first name or another. This is a religion based on uniformity and follow-the-leader. But you must remember that every single one of them has talked personally to God and to Jesus and their favorite angels and received reassurance from each that their desires, their way of doing things, as rewards for their . . . well, righteousness, will be taken into Divine Consideration.

Hesiod Whichever is ordered by the Secret Chamber of the Nineteen Men of Superior Wisdom to put more grist into the Tally Office. The efficacy of earlier Hesiodic plans is petering out. It always comes down to the same boring problem: even with a name it's hard to find enough of the guys to go after. They all have wavy arms and high-pitched voices and swivel their hips when they walk. Only they all don't, or so it would appear in Washington. There have been several awful items that actually hit the *Monument*. Swishes were picked up and hustled off to Buffalo (literally) only for it to be discovered they were married men with wives and families and, *mirabile dictu*, got erections big and plenty when tested by the Altheimer Criminally Active Penis

Tester, which displayed naked women and cunts. (See *A History of Biostatistics and Bioethics in the Field of Human Sexuality*, Nuland et al.) Word has been sent from Oxonia, and from its Secret Chamber of the (now) Twenty Men of Superior Wisdom, to get a move on it.

Hesiod decides that the answer is for the Tally Office to find a powerful affiliation in addition to the Disciples of Lovejoy itself, which, a renegade religion, is still a religion distrusted, even with 150,000 members and growing fiercely. As the century proceeds to turn itself into a new one, who can be found to partner in the growth of such an activity as the Disciples desire? Ezra's determination has always been quite clear: "the extermination of all the homosexuals in America." It looks good in print, on flyers. The subtext of all this remains unvoiced: not only will this deed be applauded by the multitudes, which he knows hates the fairies, but also the more concentration placed on getting rid of the homos, the more the Lovejoys can get away with all the polygamy, which they really want. In Ortho, the northern community of the more militant, and even Oxonia, the hunger for polygamy only grows stronger. Many will not give it up come hell or high water. Jesus and God have promised it to every single man among them. Once you've fucked as many women as you want, it's really hard to go back to just one.

Yes, another religious affiliation would be helpful. Does not religion speak for everything in America that is good, and right, and just?

Hesiod wonders if the Catholic Church would be interested in climbing on board. The Catholic Church has consistently spewed enthusiastic hate for homos, as well as, unfortunately, for the Disciples of Lovejoy. "Upstarts," "heathens," "hicks," "parvenus" are a few of the kinder condemnations rained down from what they consider their higher and superior altars. The question for them would thus have to be: Which do they hate more, homosexuals or Lovejoys? Hesiod makes the pitch.

Homosexuals, of course, win by a wide margin. The Vatican itself signals approval to its man in Washington, Monsignor Dmitri "the Angry Pole" Pfaffy. Secret talks commence. These are unsatisfactory. Pfaffy has counted his Holy Beads. On the orders of the pope, Pfaffy instructs the Hesiod he is dealing with: "Come back when you have more million members." When pressed by Hesiod for more details, Dmitri gets up from the gilded throne in which he is sitting in St. Catheter's; he is very tall and stands even taller: "You are talking to a wideworld religion of great portions. You are too poopsy. Come back big. Then maybe Pole tell Poppa talk and we help you deal with poofies."

Ironically (or perhaps not), as the century turns, the idea of using a "lethal chamber" for the removal of "degenerates" begins to grow into a movement called eugenics. Even George Bernard Shaw passionately lectures about the use of such chambers for the unfit. (Much more on this to come.) Hesiod correctly senses the turning of a tide. Why, he and his might be on the right side after all. He and Ezra Jr. join hands in this new crusade to find the million new Disciples so their "poopiness" will be eradicated, they will appear puny no more, and Poppa will come dance with them.

What does Tom Lovejoy think of the religion that bears and bares his name, kills all his brothers, turns against doctrine God had promised him would be sacred, sacrosanct, untouchable until the end of time (not that he believes there is any such thing as the end of time)? "By now I see," he says to Jesus, "that my people are believing wrong things. They forget that the Gospel must truly be known unto each and every one. I have talked to Ezra. Ezra talked to Hesiod. Hesiod talked to Brigham. I ask both You and God why no one any longer talks to me. My principal commandment that makes Lovejoy Disciples different from all the rest is that we are allowed to talk to God and Christ and me directly. I have been forgotten. I am no longer talked to. I am being left out of what one day will be called 'the loop.'"

It's true. Tom Lovejoy is the last person on any Disciple's mind as they begin to grow even more. The Hesiods will shortly give over to endless Brighams (which will be followed by a bunch more Ezras). These stern, unsmiling taskmasters are all one and the same. They all wear the same underwear. In fact, it becomes a no-no not to wear the same underwear. What an unusual requirement to write into your sacraments. Underwear?

Brigham preaches passionately that every male Disciple must take as many wives as he possibly can. More Disciples are required. The bigger their Church becomes, even if they are looked upon with disdain, the more they will meet the deadline of the powerful ally in that Outside World that currently shuns them. More and more young men are sent out into the world as missionaries. Indeed, it is now required of them to go. Pairs of young elders cover the world. The more remote the territory, the more foreign the tribe, the more converts they acquire. People who speak no English are easy to convert. Lovejoy congregations dot more and more of the globe. Catholic missionaries report back to Rome that they are being outconverted. The pope wants to know: What are they giving out that we're not? He is told (more or less): as much pussy as any man wants to eat. Ben-Ezekial points out that this outmaneuvering indicates "the extraordinary youthful potency of this new

American religion that can only lead them toward the fulfillments of all of Tom Lovejoy's eschatological predictions." He is awarded a Sterling Professorship at Yaddah, the highest honor it bestows. With the tenure it guarantees, Ben-Ezra will be a little less restrained in sexually pursuing his pretties, as he calls them, "my scholarettes." Again, we are ahead of ourselves. The juicy stuff just has a way of intruding.

As a sad footnote to the above, Vivo Marpo is sent out by Turpa and Eagan on his first assignment as a master circulator, to distribute, wherever he can, all over town, as many as possible of those flyers that say: "JOIN OUR CRUSADE for the extermination of all the homosexuals in America!" Quite a few of these flyers do manage to paper the city. In fact, he runs out a few times, and Turpa and Eagan have to replenish them with a rush order to their mimeograph operator. After several weeks of this, Vivo doesn't come home. Turpa alerts the police. Vivo is found happily living with a young man his own age in Chevy Chase. He writes a letter to Turpa. "Dear Grandma, please forgive me I have found my very own homosexual and it is fine and ok and nice and I send love Vivo." Vivo and Randolph Geyser are found drowned in the Anacostia River below that old piss hospital, which, also as a footnote, is in use again as an infirmary/reform school for destitute and/or wayward children, one of the first. President McKinley comes to the ribbon cutting. He usually doesn't give two cents for anything healthy but he's lost two young daughters and so he comes to the opening, along with an assistant who conveys to the home's director something along the lines of: "Don't read anything into the president's attendance here today. He will not give you any money."

THE WASHINGTON MONUMENT

Note is made of the appearance on the stage of history of Theodosia Template, daughter of Alvah Schwartz Template, born in 1900 in Chattanooga.

On the day of her birth, Alvah, in celebration, fulfills a lifelong dream he has had since his father settled in Tennessee, a woeful state for Jews, most of whom are reduced to selling furniture, groceries, or clothes. He buys a newspaper. This newspaper, even better, is in Washington, D.C. It is called *The Washington Monument*. It is a boring and uninteresting newspaper and so it will remain until Thea takes over and spruces things up a bit after World War II.

Alvah is a smart businessman. He sees all around him that more and more people now have wealth, often for the first time. He has seen his own father's tailoring shop mushroom into seven men's clothing stores around the South. He sees, in every southern town and city where he travels with his merchandise, other Jews from his and other congregations, Jews whose families had been, only years before, poor and struggling, now building large homes and large wardrobes. Price seems to be no object. The sense of growing prosperity for his people is palpable. And why not? It is time. The Vanderbilts, the Rockefellers (John D. will die in 1937 leaving almost a billion dollars), the Astors, Carnegie, the Harrimans, the Punics—these are already and will remain the hugest of fortunes. These are all gentile fortunes. They like to show off to let everyone see how rich they are. Jewish fortunes have been less visible. Alvah knows in his bones they will become no less mighty, but he will not parade his religion or his bank account outside his front door. His family went through too much Sturm und Drang to get here in one piece. And so far most southern Jews have been able to avoid the lynchings that have so beset the Negro, although it was touch-and-go for a while. (As Dame Lady Hermia would proclaim: Where is the historian of the lynchings of Jews?!) No one has to know the *Monument* is owned by a Jew. He considers removing Schwartz as his middle name. After all, his wife is a rabbi's daughter. "Alvah, my cherished husband and protector, not only must you cease using your full name, but in Washington we will become pillars of the gentile community and go to a Quaker or Unitarian church every Friday night and Saturday morning. With this newspaper we must flaunt our newfound place in this New World the same as Mr. Vanderbilt and Mr. Rockefeller, neither of whom I hear is a very nice man at all, as you are a nice man."

"Are you telling me, my beloved Mesopotamia, that it would be more worthwhile for me to be not a nice man?"

"Do not be so imbecilic! I am telling you that in Washington it is time for us to show our faces outside at last. We can get out of this wretched state of Tennessee. Why should gentile fortunes be more in the newspapers than half-Jewish ones?" No sooner do they leave Chattanooga than seven Jews in their neighborhood are murdered by white men wearing white robes.

THE NITS ARE COMING

Different "historians" have differing versions of the history of NITS. Well, as the English say, "horses for courses." And here follows YRH's.

After Philadelphia, Ontuit, Sagg, and the debacle at Fruit Island, the official Pox, Pus & Sores business takes a detour during the Civil War, then reroutes itself to return to New York City, which, because of its own great growth, has a festering problem that makes Philadelphia look like an out-of-town tryout. It is thus leaping for the opportunity of government payments, regardless of whether the government wants to pay. Is not health a federal problem? New York is now the undisputed power center of our country. Washington may think it is, but it thinks a lot of things about itself that aren't accurate: for instance, they think they know what they're doing, always a big mistake for governments and politicians. There seems to be a lot of foreign involvement with places such as Spain and Cuba and the Philippines . . . well, who even knows where the Philippines are? Teddy Roosevelt, when he shows up, might look like a teddy bear, but he also looks like he should go on a diet and lose a lot of weight. But let's stay with McKinley for a while, before he, too, gets knocked off.

It seems as if everyone wants to live in New York. The city is chockablock, on its way to what it is today. There are many people, and many sick people, especially in Manhattan, where people in all neighborhoods and income classes are not shy about participating in all of life's manifold destinies. A Rose McPherson, who works for the New York City Health Department (a primitive place where as a woman and hence new to the workforce her opinions are disregarded), manages somehow to prepare a map of the city which shows that from lower Broadway to the Bronx there's not a single block that hasn't forwarded to her attention a "representative public health problem" "and, quite frankly, I am swamped." She is unable to release her thoughts of why this is so, that people are fucking everywhere and the syphilis etc. that had almost toppled Philly has just moved farther north. (It isn't that fucking is no longer happening in Philadelphia, but it's a tired city now, trying unsuccessfully to live on past glories as the first home of this and that, and tired people don't fuck as much. Even its Liberty Bell gets cracked.) Rose is also worried about a lot of other things: rampant childhood diseases, whooping cough (pertussis, often fatal), measles (ditto), hemorrhagic bleedings (ditto), mumps, even various paralyses of limbs, though polio as such is not known yet. New York is definitely not a healthy place.

But let us stick with syphilis. Rose doesn't know why more people aren't dying from it since so many have it and she knows it's certainly thought to be fatal. She figures everybody's body's not the same. Believe it or not, this is a relatively new thought and relatively unknown reasoning—that some people get sick and in varying degrees and others don't, from the same fatal thing. She writes a quite impressive report on her thoughts for Newbold Harold Sypress, who she guesses is her superior at a department so muted in its voices of authority. He doesn't answer her, so she decides to write to the president, who doesn't answer her either. She does get a letter from Theodore Roosevelt, who is assistant secretary of the Navy in McKinley's administration. "I know what it means to be unhealthy. I was an unhealthy child. I was called 'sickly and delicate' by my father and told to remake myself, which I did. 'I'll make my body,' I declared to him, and so I did. I have sympathy and sadness for those, particularly the sailors under my department's jurisdiction, who have allowed themselves to decline in health. I suggest that they take up a rigorous program of hunting, fishing, swimming, hiking, and boxing. I shall issue an official order suggesting same. My program certainly did wonders for my asthma, which had plagued me."

Comes to lower Manhattan what is initially called the Clinic for Hygiene, which is built from scratch on a lovely street overlooking the harbor by, yet again, a group of sailors not enjoying the best of health. For some reason sailors as a group appear to be more adept at organizing for their welfare. You never hear of soldiers fighting for their health care. Because, once again, so many sailors use the facilities, it comes to be called the Sailors' Clinic. By 1900, business is so good that a "concerned" local government (i.e., New York City) determines it is time to move this House of Sores farther out. Better yet, as its infected population has grown mightily, it's someone's bright idea to kill syphilis off once and for all. A Captain Martin Reddicher of the U.S. Army Medical Corps, put in charge of preparing a report, "The Disciplinary Problems of Today's Illnesses," determines that enough syphilis is enough syphilis. There are 76 million of The American People now. Enough is enough with them, too. We've been here before, too. The captain is friendly with President William McKinley.

McKinley, thought much less of at the time, has been resuscitated somewhat by biographers who praise his leadership. He took a country in deep depression and turned it into an international powerhouse. Why, United States Steel became the world's first billion-dollar corporation. While he is assassinated by another crazy man, homosexuality does not appear to be woven into this particular murder. He dies before Captain Reddicher can press his case.

Staten Island beckons. Though in sight of the booming metropolis across the harbor, it has been up until now a vast and lonely place, and mostly populated by the stunted, the twisted, the genetically malformed, including an exceptionally large family of Rattlefields. Huge portions of Staten Island thus become home to the wandering, abandoned, senseless, and demented, much as the middle of America has been the home of wandering war-wounded youngsters. Land on Staten Island, so near and yet so far, is cheap and about as easy to acquire as the syphilis most of the inhabitants are running around with. Staten Island is in desperate need of a population change. Rose McPherson knows that Captain Reddicher is talking about stuff she wants to know more about. She is chosen to be in charge of a "new" Sailors' Institute, as a reward for a job well done in New York City.

There is a suitable building already here, called the Great State Hospital for the Destitute and the Wretched. Apparently there were quite a few such edifices around our country, built by nineteenth-century do-gooders to hide their country's unhealthy secrets. Once again, as on Fruit Island, no description can do justice to the horror of its innards—endless smelly hallways and windowless fetid cells. Once again we witness another awful place to hide the sick. How is anyone ever going to get better? The answer, of course, is that no one is, nor is anyone expected to. But who is saying this? What faces and/or forces and/or powers are saying this? All of these are late-twentieth-century questions, fostered by a current plague. People didn't think like this then. People didn't know yet that other people could perpetrate outcomes like this.

To this particular hospital on Staten Island some trace the real beginnings of the NITS we know today. In case you've forgotten, NITS stands for the National Institute of Tumor Science, which has been authorized by Congress and given an annual budget of a very small, tiny, paltry, minuscule, puny amount. Some sticklers trace the birth of NITS, more correctly, to Fruit Island. Neither is a proud place to claim ancestry, which is why neither is ever claimed, certainly not in any "official" history of NITS, when it should be.

This predecessor of today's mammoth, behemoth, gargantuan NITS, under which these hideous Great Hospitals of the D&W fell, is opened here on Staten Island and called the "New Sailors' Clinic," out of someone's misguided desire to do homage to the first Sailors' Clinics we visited earlier in

Sagg and on Fruit Island. Has someone in Washington actually heard Rose McPherson's cry for help? There is no such thing as mandatory reporting, of anything, so it is unclear exactly who is meant to do, on one end, the reporting, and on the other end, the recording, or in between, the caregiving. Oh, a few odd doctors here and there write to their senators if anything interesting or dangerous is seen in their neck of the woods, so it may have been determined, vaguely, by someone or other, somewhere, that by 1901 the cases of syphilis etc. are spreading every which way across, well, every which way. Sorry for the impreciseness of the mechanisms but that's how this country's been run from our get-go. Not all doctors can recognize syphilis, so you can imagine how bad things truly must have been. But this is a country that has already learned to coexist with its sick selves without really knowing what they are doing or how they are doing it. If ignorance is bliss and even if it isn't we're living in it anyway. All population centers just go on infecting all they can.

The "true" story of what happened at this "New" Sailors' Clinic on Staten Island will probably never be known. That big old hospital for the Wretched etc. was burned to the ground in 1858 by a posse of the few residents living in the vicinity. As we have seen time and again, fires are ubiquitous in attempting to change a status quo or to end it. A few matches and a few crazy people to strike them are easy to come by. Indeed, where would this country be without its conflagrations? Or its crazy people? Or their matches? It's time for a commemorative postage stamp for Fire.

This particular fire was set by one Anushkus Rattlefield. We know this because he had so many relatives and they watched him set the buildings on fire and they watched him set his wife on fire and they watched him set his children on fire and they watched him set himself on fire and they watched them all burn to death. And then, all now suitably roasted, the remaining onlookers all ate them. Shades of green-and-goldmonkey days. The American People do seem to have eaten each other a good deal more than has ever been recorded. Mostly in out-of-the-way places. Off the beaten track. We do remember the monkeys, don't we? Anushkus had said, simply, "I tire of living," and struck the match. It was an ugly building anyway. And the Rattlefields were pretty ugly themselves.

Several employees of that same Department of Illness and Disease (DID) (which by the time of The Underlying Condition will be renamed the Department of Disease [DOD]) that sent the Furstwasser brothers to Fruit Island are in fact in attendance at this bonfire. They express to the reporters "by chance" in attendance their "heartfelt" concern for the wretchedness of the destitute, who weren't using the place anyway. Each promises to petition Theodore Roosevelt, who is now vice president and after whom the teddy bear will shortly be named, for a "serious" place where diseases can be studied "once and for all." The *New York Truth* reporter writes all this down. A Dr. Quirky told him his appearance here was "strictly coincidental. DID is making site visits of all its outposts. We must finally establish a new one here to house the poxed." "There is no Dr. Quirky found in any of our records," according to an official NITS historian, Ethel Vance. "We were barely getting off the ground. It's true that Staten Island was to be our launching pad. The hospital standing there was to be generously remodeled as our first exterior flagship."

Miraculously, on the heels of this fire Congress authorizes the purchase of one hundred acres of farmland in the outlying Maryland countryside "for a permanent institution devoted solely to the eradication of diseases most harmful." The bill's sponsor, Congressman Eddie Troeblight (Rep., West Virginia), tells the *Monument*, "it is time to get the heck out of Staten Island and back to a mainland where the disposable are not so free to wander hither and yon and be burned up. Let's bring sickness and disease back to Washington, where it belongs!" So onward to Maryland we go.

This does not mean that the Sailors' Clinic is not built on Staten Island. It is, and it is still there. And the Sailors' Rest Home is indeed most "generous," with comfortable rooms and excellent board. There is a waiting list of the poxed anxious to move in. Captain Reddicher and Rose McPherson move there to run it and indeed become man and wife. He insists on putting a plaque at the entrance, "The birthplace of the National Institute of Tumor Science." Over the years it will become enormously rich from all those "voluntary" contributions withheld from sailors' paychecks that Alex Hamilton set in motion, buying up with these funds huge portions of New York City real estate, which it still owns. The Reddichers retire in great splendor to Park Avenue. Congressional investigations will not transpire for quite some time. Sailors' Cozy Nest still remains an organization with an awful lot of money and more and more real estate but it has little other reason for being and is naturally run by mysterious personages who come and go.

On that land in Maryland (one hesitates to name it "suburban Washington" yet, although that's what it will become) are built quite primitive bungalows to house this nation's first true, real, official medical facility. *Research*, damn it, is still not a term or activity in general use.

One does not have to be terribly intelligent or observant to notice that more and more people are getting sick. Everywhere. In every state of the union. From tons of things. Not just social diseases. Although many diseases are in fact contagious, which means they should be classified as "social diseases." Or else this stupid, discriminatory moniker should be ditched, which it is not. It is too useful, particularly, already, for legislators. It is a scary term used profusely when trying to scare people into voting for or against something that would be for their own good if they'd just shut up. Same thing today. Scare the shit out of people by inferring they are going to "get" something.

It is doubtful that there's a healthy population center anywhere under the sun. Growing populations tend to be like that. Oh, people died in plenitude from hideous illnesses before, but the one symptom separating those earlier centuries from the new one is the mighty one of Hope. Hope is coming into fashion. And when people are hopeful they tend to be, well, more social.

More and more, doctors begin to believe that illness can be cured, the sick made well, the lame less halt. Hope does have a way of disguising, if not downright obliterating, the realities of the moment. Hope also says that contagion can be rendered less ripe and rife. And Hope, for many, is just another word for Truth. Why, if we can only ferret out *the* Truth, truths will come tumbling out of test tubes in torrents! Yes, NITS timidly begins to use the word *research*. It even employs a few doctors who won't ever have to see patients and can spend all their time in new laboratories built especially for this new research thing.

NITS will be The American People's new Home for Hope. It will be our Lourdes. Its first director is Dr. Robert Grant Mellow. "Our land and people must be made pure and clean, as clean as that land the Puritans found and landed on and tilled and turned over to us," are among the first words in Dr. Mellow's fine speech at the official NITS opening. "This Tumor Institute," the now President Theodore Roosevelt announces ceremoniously when officially opening NITS in 1903, "will rid our great land of pestilence and vice." Was he meant to say "lice"? But then, he had sight only in one eye. He lost the other in a boxing match. What a fighter! "How can America fail to be greater still without illness, without sickness, without disease?" Good questions, if not usually posed so publicly by presidents. "We shall be as clean and pure as God decreed." Well, we have heard talk like this before. He polishes his oratory off with a bit of the Bard, shaking his fist at the crowd: "Out, out, damned spot!" Well, we lived through Harrison and Cleveland, we will live through Teddy Roosevelt, a bully, but better a bully than a wuss. So many wusses. My goodness, how we pick them. McKinley, to polish him off, was a wuss: the wife he adored so absolutely suffered from a hideous list of serious ailments, "repeated convulsions, seizures, blackouts, possible epilepsy, certainly depression" (two daughters dead, remember, one from typhoid fever); no wonder the poor woman was always so "sickly, sullen, and withdrawn" (Brinkley et al., *The American Presidency*). Her Billy would sit with her endless hours and through many a night to comfort her. But when Dr. Robert Grant Mellow appealed to him for support for the new NITS, the president summarily dismissed him. "It was a harsh lesson for me to learn so early on," Mellow was to write, "that my President did not care for health. And to be so rude about it!"

The wooden NITS bungalows out there in still-distant Maryland multiply and are joined by larger verandahed hospitals patterned—for is this not a southern state?—on gracious southern models. As new diseases proceed, like the march of history itself, to parade themselves more identifiably, more new buildings sprout over the acreage, which is becoming more manicured and landscaped, a handsome place to dream of Hope. Why, searching for cures may soon become more fashionable than doing the Charleston. One by one the buildings will come to represent differing (and increasingly competitive) interests: eyes, hearts, livers, lungs, blood, children, teeth, aging, and that mighty wild stallion, cancer, and yes, infectious diseases, among them The Underlying Condition. It will not be long before the unanimity envisaged in a congressional charter that heralded "a united crusade in a united land, against disease, all disease, irregardless of color, creed, race, religion" crumbles as each body part comes to fight like a tiger for the same congressional buck. But we are once again getting ahead of ourselves. But know it won't be long before America's lifesavers are at each other's throats rather than looking down them. Saintly harmonies in no time at all become discordant. Competition among the lifesavers comes into being, and remains. This, too, is the American way. So very many unhealthy things are "the American way."

But by now it is official. Since the Civil War it's no longer American for brother to get along with brother.

And we have NITS. NITS will be home to The Underlying Condition. Happy New Year! Happy Twentieth Century!

DAME LADY HERMIA: Fredchen, I must tip my hat to you. You become more and more a true historian. Are you learning how to do this all from me?

DR. SISTER GRACE: No, you biddy bitch, he learned it from me.

ORGANIZED, SANCTIONED, LEGAL, ACCEPTABLE MURDER ON THE WAY?

In 1904 the Carnegie Institute for Experimental Evolution at Cold Spring Harbor, Long Island, opens. Its mission is to document human defects. It begins by establishing the Eugenics Record Office, another of those mysterious places that want to accumulate lists of names. It wants to ascertain the inherited (and hence transmissible) backgrounds of all Americans producing or presenting questionable evidence of absolutely anything unhealthy, "separating the wheat from the chaff." They are interested in bad blood, defective strains, unhealthy everythings and anythings so that these can be nipped in the bud of all present and future generations. They are much more sophisticated than the Tally Office, indeed managing to accumulate many thousands of index cards on ordinary Americans, from which to pounce on those bloodlines worthy of being removed. Hold on to the image of "index cards." They will come back to haunt us, or should.

As a point of interest, Mary Harriman's daughter, also named Mary (who founded the Junior League, that safe harbor and refuge for wellborn gentile white women), donated seventy-five acres in Cold Spring Harbor for this Eugenics Record Office; the land came with a house that contained a fireproof storage addition for all these index cards. Hundreds of young women from Radcliffe, Vassar, and Wellesley, joining young men from Harvard, Cornell, Oberlin, Hopkins, and of course Yaddah, flock here as trainees, going "into the field" to collect all this information for all these cards about all the sick people they can locate. Among other things, they study albinos, the insane in institutions, the Amish, juvenile delinquents, and the feeble-minded, also institutionalized. More than two hundred and fifty young people would participate in this training and fieldwork. Identify those defective family trees and kill their bloodlines! The unfit are so, well, unfit to live among us. Terms like "euthanasia" and "lethal chamber" are heard louder in this land of The American People.

How in God's name did we come to this? What means "eugenics"? Stay tuned. Among those in attendance at their first board meeting are seven members of the Society of the Pocahanti. They are all important people in government and industry, and, naturally, religion. Do you even remember who/what the Pocohanti are? Stalwart, true Americans with noble lineages that they trace back to George Washington is who and what they are. No unhealthy chaps among this lot. And they want to keep it this way. They are pledged to keep it this way, all one hundred of them. They know that Teddy Roosevelt is timid on social issues, and has great difficulty defining exactly what his mission should be, particularly with reference to Negroes and immigrants such as the Chinese and Japanese swarming the West Coast like ants (though Teddy, "to the chap's credit, believes them all 'inferior'"), and he might like women a whole lot, but he won't make any stab at keeping them at home and the divorce rate much lower than it is. The guy's too conflicted, with double standards all over the map. Why are we in Cuba, tell me? What do we want with Guam and Puerto Rico and, God help us, the Philippines? All of them are a recipe for genetic disasters as big as hurricanes and typhoons. *Genetic* is a word coming into lots more usage, whatever it means.

That new guy running NITS, Dr. Robert Grant Mellow, he's a Pocahanti. Garibaldus Mortimer Winthrop, the dean of Washington's National Episcopal Cathedral, is one, too. Terrence O'Dwyer of New York's St. Patrick's is one, of course. A new member is Ralph Zwait, whom Teddy just made head of the Department of Agriculture to run his new Pure Food and Drug Act. A lot of people being poisoned by all kinds of quack medicines out there, not to mention that rotten meat out of Chicago, and we can't have any of either. Lots of things we can't have any more of, and Teddy, even with his big stick, is slow on the uptick. Otherwise we're still mainly a bunch of old farts with a lot of time on our hands looking for something to do, and this eugenics stuff sounds spiffy and right up, or down, our alleys. And Long Island, well, a lot of us live there on the North Shore, so it's convenient to home. Getting harder for a lot of us to travel, you know.

Besides the Pocahanti there are representatives from Mr. Carnegie and Mr. Rockefeller and . . . well, we don't want to give too much away while this whole business is still . . . firming up.

•

In these intervening years I have learned a lot. I have learned that my skills were not yet good enough to infect enough people to make an out-and-out plague, which has always been my desire, indeed my calling, indeed my salvation, for without it I would eventually die. I had to learn by piggybacking along with other carriers, other destructive agents, to learn how they do it. Epidemics of smallpox, syphilis, tuberculosis, dengue fever, Mombasa actoid, typhoid of course; the list is quite long and it has been disappointing to me that so much of my time has been wasted hiding inside other conditions. I have always wanted to stand on my own.

I am uncertain whether I can explain to you why my particular set of features has been so slow in felling larger populations. I was quite surprised myself. Just when I thought I had got going, with several outbreaks in 1723, for instance, in Marenga, Brazil, or in 1860 on Fruit Island, or in 1887 in Malta, or especially back in 1600, in Virginia itself, something happened, or did not happen, to allow widespread infection. I think it has something to do with the "patient load" (as I heard it called). One or two or half a dozen or even several hundred are not enough to start anything big. I suspect many thousands are needed. I keep my eyes open for an outbreak of something in which several thousand are ready and waiting all at the same time, and not just one at a time, which is usually the case with most "growing" epidemics while they get really going. I am very hopeful about a new facility being planned for the wilds of Idaho, where they will be investigating how to eliminate certain populations.

Fruit Island was my biggest lost opportunity. For want of more experience on my part, the patients escaped my grasp and grip.

THE BLOODS

Poor and orphaned, Herman Masturbov grows up in that Southeast section of Washington where all the Orthodox Jews live. He grows up to be a smart businessman who accumulates many highly profitable enterprises before his death at the relatively young age of sixty.

In the earlier years of his wretched marriage, he is also Rabbi Chaimoff's mohel, the man who performs the ritual circumcision of baby boys born into the Jewish faith.

This is a calling just as holy as Herman's duty to make money, money that means freedom from the oppression of the gentiles who have hated him and all like him since time began. Poppa Yissy and Momma Truda were murdered by the tsar or the Cossacks or some other gentiles before they could even get on the boat to America to be free of them. In Washington, where his cousin passes Herman off to another cousin, Herman lives with half a dozen more "cousins" before, at sixteen, he finds and marries Yvonne Jerusalem, yet another cousin, and they settle down to the various challenges he has put to himself. Herman believes that being a mohel will bring him a spiritual return lacking from his important secular investments in land and more land, always more land. He is reaping so many rewards from the New World's earth that he feels an urgent need to give, to do something that will make him truly blessed in God's eyes.

Herman is as obsessed with making money as his second son, Abraham, will be. In this regard Abe will definitely inherit from his father. (No one remembers if Yissy was so ambitious for worldly goods. In Russia there was little opportunity for Jews to get them even if you were energetic and ambitious. In Russia dreaming was all.) In America, Herman comes to believe in a more tangible God, one who might actually make things happen, but still one who must be thanked and that is that. Abe's God, before He abruptly disappears, will be more erratic and unreliable. That is often the difference between fathers and sons, between the Old World and the New, between those who serve unwaveringly and those who, having got what they want, no longer even cross their fingers.

When Rabbi Chaimoff's longtime mohel is removed under a cloud of shame (allegations of latent sadism or possible sexual excitement), Herman pesters young Rabbi Chesterfield, Chaimoff's assistant, for a chance to audition. Rabbi Chesterfield (who will become, and with that name it is better that he does, the Reformed rabbi by the time that sacrilegious sect is truncated from the tribe and more firmly established and Abe's son Mordecai is ready for his bar mitzvah) finally gives Herman the nod. Herman, who has been practicing secretly on tiny kosher salami and pointed baby turnips and carrots, must now perform in front of a rabbinical board, twelve bearded men—no, eleven, because Chaimoff shaved when he moved into his big brand-new Northwest shul, no more Southeast storefront shul for him, and already way over budget—who are merchants as well as rabbis. You cannot make a living from God alone, although Chaimoff, who will become famous with a coast-to-coast Sunday radio program, is on his way.

A mohel is judged by exacting standards. Cutting nice and even. Not too much and not too little. No visible blood or gore. The baby stops crying fast. There is no permanent scar. He doesn't drop the baby, bawling or not. All the guidelines specifying millimeters, instruments, decorum, what you do with the blood, the skin—not only those dozen rabbis are judging but the most famous mohel in America, Schlitz (this is not his real name; no one knows his real name; and no one knows why no one knows his real name), comes down from the Lower East Side of New York, which has never happened before. Herman had gone to New York for lessons from Schlitz, who is very difficult to locate, which means, according to Schlitz, that when you find him, God must want it to happen.

Herman, a tower of a man with light reddish hair, not quite blond but almost, and skin so fair that he must avoid the sun (he is sometimes referred to as "Fikel duster fehl," from a patois spoken in his native village of Grad and meaning roughly "piece of pound cake"), has no nervousness whatsoever that might make this fair skin blush. It is not as if he must perform on the baby of his neighbor. The tiniest infants born of the poorest Jews are used for these tryouts, sons of Jews who don't have so much as an extra dime to slip the mohel as a token of thanks. Thus he can concentrate exclusively on the task at hand, without daydreaming, as poor mohels do, of the tip he will get from a grateful father.

After his first audition circumcision Herman is asked to perform on three more poor screaming tots, understudies waiting just in case the first's father is too busy hauling ice or rags to keep the appointment. On the conclusion of his fourth slicing, Schlitz takes Herman in his arms and embraces him, ritualizing the appointment. Now all the other eleven rabbis take Herman in their arms and kiss him too. Never before have all the judges plus Schlitz kissed a mohel. Perhaps five or six. Eight is the record as far as anyone can remember, and that is held by Schlitz himself after his secret performance on a son born to a United States senator who no one even knew was Jewish. Yes, all twelve kiss Herman, so supreme is his triumph. His hand, a nice-sized hand but which does not look like it has within it such grace, has an accuracy never seen before, particularly around the entire circumference, not an iota of slack overhang. Any Jewish man would be proud to have had such a fine job done on him in his infancy as Herman, from his very initiation, has accomplished, and it will not be long before every Jew in Washington wants Herman for his son or nephew or grandson or cousin visiting from somewhere. A successful mohel can bring in a lot of extra contributions to the building fund. Rabbi Chaimoff's mortgages will be paid off quickly. Herman splits 50/50 with the rabbi, peanuts compared with what he is making in real estate.

By now Herman is thirty-five. He already owns much of that vast empty acreage in what will be known someday as "the metropolitan area." His wife, the beauty Yvonne, hair darkly sleek like a stallion's mane and eyes hauntingly black like the sorely missed olives of Grad, has given him only one son, Emmanuel. That he has no second son and that the first is not the one he wants disappoints Herman beyond measure. Yvonne must give him another. He has tried but she has not complied. Why is she not successfully inseminated by him? After all, God guides him successfully to cut foreskins. Word of his being kissed by twelve rabbis has turned into myth: if you want your boy to be blessed for life, head for Herman. He has swiftly become the most famous mohel anyone can remember, more famous even than Schlitz. Rich parents from as far north as Newport and as far south as Charleston beg him to squeeze the foreskins of their *kinder* into his packed schedule. Desperate fathers slip him fat encouragements to ensure his availability even before their wives are pregnant. Soon he is working around the clock, or at least around the clock on those days permitted by the Vernah, which lays down strict rules governing mohels.

Herman is growing more pious. The performance of his holy calling is giving him something akin to a feeling of saintliness. Every time he performs he feels he can touch the glorious tradition of his people throughout the centuries. He feels that close to God.

By the time he is forty-five, he is slicing every free second of the day, and is richer than ever from his landholdings all reaching out and joining hands to make him one of the biggest landowners in the entire District of Columbia and the surrounding counties too, but he still has no second son from Yvonne. He finds that he can no longer perform sexual intercourse with her. In fact, he is ignoring her altogether, not that they have ever been close. Where they come from, husbands and wives are less friends and lovers than co-workers; if the house is clean and there's food on the table and the tsar's soldiers aren't in the neighborhood, what's to talk about?

But something is wrong with Emmanuel. Herman considers his only son deficient in character, grace, skill, intelligence, and personality. That is what is wrong with him. Herman does not like this boy. So little does Herman think about him that he doesn't even remember that *Emmanuel* means "God with us." He wants another son the way a man with a brown suit decides one day he must have a blue one.

How to reignite his libido again so that Yvonne can produce another suit? In all his life Herman Masturbov has never had trouble getting an erection.

It must be her fault. She smells all the time now, it seems perhaps from her menstrual bleedings. That must be what makes it hard for him to become hard. He once gloried in the aroma of her blood, but that was when he was young, and before God gave him his (and His) gift. He does not have the courage to suggest to his wife that she up the number of her visits to the ritual baths.

He notices one day that she is always wearing the same dress. Why does she not change her clothes? Or have her garments washed? The shvartze cleaning lady and the shvartze laundress tell him she refuses both. He has not noticed that he has stopped inserting himself into her and jiggling himself to a speedy orgasm before turning his back toward her and going to sleep, and he has also not noticed that she is relieved.

Neither of them has noticed that Yvonne is not a woman much in touch with the world. She is a relic of another time and place where women worked very hard, with little time for filling the brain with questions, with answers, with knowledge from books or newspapers, with reasons or reason, where wives, and husbands too, were accustomed to falling asleep exhausted. She has nothing to do now. All day long everything is done for her that she once did herself. She is becoming more and more depressed.

•

Herman starts saving the foreskins. Secretly. Nobody sees him. One day he just starts doing this. Does he think it peculiar? No, he thinks it will prove useful. He does not believe in waste, in any of his businesses, in any of the buildings he is having built all over the place. All these foreskins from all these healthy *kinder*, they should prove useful. He will find a way.

During the service, as usual, he covers them; but one day, when his assistant, who is called the sendek, reaches for the muss to dispose of it, Herman whispers emphatically that he himself will take care of this part of the ceremony from now on. Now after every service Herman extracts the little bits of foreskin, looking like twists of bloody lemon peel, and drops them into a tiny bottle filled with formaldehyde. In his basement he transfers them to a larger bottle, which soon contains many foreskins. When he has a full bottle he starts another. He hides these bottles in a cavelike room in the back of the basement, way under the farthest reaches of his big house.

Yes, Herman has built himself his first big house, moving from the Southeast to downtown Northwest, on Scribbs Place, near where Rabbi Chaimoff has built the first of the enormous Washington Jewish Congregation temples that will appear over the years, a palace to God—Herman's house, that is, though there are many who compare the two, both in opulence and chutzpah—of a splendor even the least conservative Jew finds too showy. The rabbi's temple has an organ more fit for a Loew's movie palace, and a Star of David window high above the pulpit, made from stained glass with colors seen only in cathedrals. Herman's just has a grand piano, though it is a Knoodorf made in Vienna by Beethoven's piano maker, and his stained-glass windows were created by the Meister of Leinwort himself, huge panels that bathe the many hallways in vibrant rays as if God were shining through them, which Herman believes. The joyless cranks who criticize either edifice are countered by Rabbi Chaimoff, who states quietly and firmly that God now encourages such effusive, munificent outpourings or why else would He have scattered money and success upon them so abundantly, His long-suffering people who for so many centuries in so many lands under so many tyrants have been punished so harshly and forced to live such miserable paupers' lives; surely they are entitled to relief. Exactly, Herman chimes in.

Herman's house is surrounded by land, which is unusual for downtown Washington. Space is expensive, neighborhoods are growing crowded, police protection is feeble, and buildings and their builders usually huddle together. That's not for Herman. Russia was nothing but earth and none of it was his. Now he can walk around his land, 80 krechas down, 90 krechas across, a handsome piece of land. When the house is completed it takes up 17 drinels, even more than Rabbi Chaimoff's new temple takes up. It's four stories high, not counting the cellar, with cupolas from which you can see the White House. There are thirty-six rooms. There are seven bathrooms, each with a toilet. There is an attic for Emmanuel to play in, and rooms for servants to sleep in. There is brown shingling all over the outside and rich wallpapers of striped and patterned velour all over the inside. There are rugs from Nekustan and Verlystan and Stanostan and Perkistan, towns near Grad whose populace helped spark the pogroms that sent Herman fleeing to America. Herman and Yvonne cannot look down at the floor without recalling the wretched gentile weavers of Grad. He spends lavishly on heavy furniture: size and weight, bulk and heft guide his purchases, not grace, utility, comfort, or taste. If the sign of opulence is the heaviness of the load, the house of Herman Masturbov weighs a ton.

He has chosen everything. Yvonne was not consulted. He has no idea that everything he has purchased frightens her. Her life in the New World is in all ways overwhelming. She has been married some fifteen or more years by now, but it has all been one long endless night for her.

When he has moved in, when he has put everything in its place, when Yvonne is given the tour and Emmanuel is told not to make a mess, Herman goes outside after midnight and by the light of the moon buries little pieces of foreskin in his back and side lawns. He wants to try out an idea. He has several shelves of filled bottles and over the next nights he plants them all. Then he orders shrubs and flowers and bushes to be planted in the earth. When the ones in front come up less healthy than the rest, he is convinced he knows the reason. He plants more foreskins in the front, too, and more bushes all around the house, though he is careful to look casual as he drops a dollop of skin into its hole in the earliest of hours. His krechas are soon a wonderment of nature's hues and the talk of the neighborhood, where everyone walks by on Sunday afternoon. By the dark of night, way past everyone's bedtime, Herman plops his foreskins into their earth. Fortunately, no one sees him. (Well, perhaps it is not so fortunate and it would have been better if they had.) They come by to compliment him profusely for such glorious results. Even the gentiles have heard of his success in slicing foreskins off the baby yids; perhaps he has some supernatural gift with gardening, too.

One night there is a horrendous storm—almost a hurricane, the newspapers say—and all over town living things are ripped from the earth. Everybody's land is pitted, sad limbs scattered everywhere. But Herman's plantings remain rooted! Nothing's toppled or untimely ripped. Everything survives. And Herman knows why.

Thus he deduces that his discovery is useful for more than just growing little bushes. He can now ensure that his beloved Washington will stand forever. Because of him! The gratitude of a man made holy by his service to the Lord!

Henceforth, whenever an important building is planned, Herman goes to the site after midnight and under the light of the moon plants in these earthly foundations pieces of his foreskin collection. Washington, great new portions of it, is just being built, rising from a small town to a small city. There are many excavations, many foundations. Herman cuts his swath wide. There is probably not a major building going up anywhere in our nation's capital under which Herman does not plant a piece of penis.

When he plants, Herman gets an erection. Night after night through many hours his penis stays hard as he plants and makes his home and his neighborhood and his city strong and proud and tall and unbending and everlasting. When he realizes what is happening in his own pants he talks to God. Yes, he talks to God now. "What is the meaning of this gift in my loins? Is it a sign, Lord, that You want me to make for You my next son?" He talks with familiarity, not in deference. God is his friend now. They are partners in all his enterprises, from circumcisions to nocturnal plantings to amassing krechas.

Herman hears God answer in the affirmative. In the middle of a night on which his plantings seem particularly inspirationally placed and his erection is as hard as he can ever remember it, so hard that he practically falls over, Herman goes to Yvonne, who has her own upstairs room because she never sleeps well, and who is presently sewing a sampler. He takes her hand and pulls her gently downstairs and out into the warm night. He leads her into the backyard and sits her down on a blanket he has thoughtfully spread on the ground in advance. "Is this a picnic?" she asks him in Yiddish. "I haven't made any deviled eggs. You always want your deviled eggs on a picnic." This should be another warning to him that her intelligence is further along on its way toward the unreality that will become her permanent refuge, but it isn't, nor had he noticed any earlier signs. "Stop talking about deviled eggs, my bride," he replies to her in English. He lifts her skirts. He unbuttons his fly. The God who guides his hand in his circumcisions is now guiding his hand as it guides his penis, after so long an absence, into his wife. "What are you doing, my Herman?" she asks in bewilderment. "I have not put any eggs on to boil." Then, as he pumps up and down, she asks him in the voice of a little girl, "How can I devil eggs for you if I have not put any eggs on to boil?" He tries to bring himself to climax quickly because she is smelling even more heady than he remembers.

She screams. A piercing shriek, at a volume he cannot imagine possible from this small person. "If another Masturbov is forming in her at this moment," Herman says out loud to God, "I shudder in apprehension that such geshreiing will mark him for life."

Abraham takes over ten months to be born. Almost eleven. No one remembers such a long pregnancy. This baby's hair is a bright scarlet red.

It is 1900.

●

Emmanuel has from an early age been introduced to the ceremony of circumcision, the bris. At first he is held up to watch. As he grows, he is allowed to assist his father and the sendek, helping to hold the infant on the little white pillows embroidered by some tante especially for this day's event with the ancient design of good luck, the zohrt, the crossed horseradish and leek that symbolize bitterness. Then he is allowed to hand his father the instruments, like a nurse in an operating room, trying to slap them firmly into his palm the way he insists, and then, having graduated in that he has never once fainted or shown an aversion to blood or to the baby's racking screams of pain, he is allowed to help pinion the teeny tiny penis itself as his father lowers the knife and slices away. Emmanuel is a careful observer. He learns which of the many knives his father might want, depending on lengths and widths and thicknesses and whether a slant must be carved in the flesh, and if so in which direction, because there are knives for all directions.

In all this the boy is guided by the sendek, the assistant Herman hired, a big man with furry hands and arms huge from shoveling the dirt he sells to people who need holes filled out Blundenburger way. There isn't much call for dirt, America is still filled with plenty of dirt, but Nate Bulb is a dedicated soul who, once he's made his mind up to do something, does it unquestioningly and thoroughly, as he also does in helping Herman, a man Nate worships for his holy calling and business wisdom, a rare combination rarely seen. Although Nate was hired with the prospect dangled before him that someday he might replace Herman as mohel, both of them know this will never happen. Nate Bulb has huge hands, big clumsy paws whose thick graceless fingers could never cut well enough to please God. When he realizes Nate does not have the gift, Herman tells him so, but his sendek remains loyal to him nevertheless and is particularly good at watching out for Emmanuel. In the early years Nate tries to shield Emmanuel's eyes when the gash is effected and the bleeding commences, but Herman won't have it. He explains to them both, son and sendek, and quite movingly, that such shielding is itself a cruelty in that the truth is simple and beautiful: the pain and blood are there to remind us that from birth we bleed and suffer because of and for God, to earn his love. Emmanuel takes his father's words very seriously, particularly this notion of God's love all wrapped up with the sight and smell of lacerated skin and spurting blood. "Is that why my father does not look upon me with affection and fondness? Must I cause him pain for him to love me?"

"Your father does love you," Nate Bulb answers. "He is only testing you." This is not something a growing boy can understand.

Sometimes after a circumcision, when he is relaxing in the nice room provided by Rabbi Chaimoff for the parents of the baby, Herman reads to his son from the Code of Jewish Legal Ethics for All Occasions, which is always with him in his black bag along with his instruments, much as some parents read aloud to their children from Mother Goose or Grimm's Fairy Tales. He reads it in Hebrew, of course. The boy has been tutored in Hebrew to proficiency. He is ten years old, eleven perhaps, maybe even twelve. No one in the household seems to be certain, because he is skinny and does not like to eat.

Today's selection is this: "An infant who dies before circumcision, whether within eight days or thereafter, must be circumcised at the grave, in order to remove the foreskin, which is a disgrace to all mankind, but no benedictions should be pronounced over this circumcision. The infant should be given a name to perpetuate his memory, and in the hope that Heaven show mercy upon him and include him in the resurrection of the dead. If he was buried without circumcision and there is no likelihood that the body has already begun to decompose, the grave should not be opened. Instead, a special offering must be given to God for His understanding in this error made on earth."

How does a young mind process this? How could he ever have learned enough Hebrew to understand this? Emmanuel's young mind races with questions. What happens to the poor little baby who isn't circumcised properly? Does God grant him peace? Or must he wander the heavens endlessly without a home, without a place to rest? Or must he go to hell? Why doesn't his father tell him all of this in English? What is his father trying to tell him? He has disappointed his father in everything. Is this something he must add to the list?

Almost from infancy the boy has had the habit of playing with himself; his own penis is of inordinate interest to him, which is understandable considering that the penises of the young are the single most important items of interest in his honored father's life. As soon as he can bend over to locate it, he studies his carefully and objectively. When he is old enough to ask, he does.

"Papa, who circumcised me?"

They are in Herman's gardens. Capacious weeping willows gracefully embrace the yard in their comforting arms. The prize yellow Prince of Russia roses are bigger than last year's. (I know why, Herman thinks, smiling to himself.) When Emmanuel asks his question, Herman stops in his tracks and looks not at his son but out into the distance, his face stern with the sturdiest from his wardrobe of frowns.

"You know that it is written in the Vernah that the mohel who circumcises his own son must be careful never to . . . it is so awful I cannot tell you."

And Herman turns away from his son, not having finished this sentence, which would have said: never to do it if he is nervous or his hand is shaking.

This gives the boy the shakes: Why does Papa not answer me? He rushes to the basement and huddles in a far corner where he pulls down his pants to consider his growing penis, an act he's performed many times here, rather than upstairs in his room. He is exceedingly well acquainted with his penis. But now there is a new penis belonging to this new Abraham screaming in one of the upstairs rooms. And there is to be a bris, baby Abraham's bris, conducted, Emmanuel knows, by his father, assisted by Nate Bulb and Emmanuel himself.

Once again, yet again, Emmanuel looks at it. It is such a funny thing. He doesn't understand it more and more every day. Why does it have to be so squiggly and uncertain in its movements? It isn't hard and firm like an arm or leg, which he knows are important. It lacks . . . spine. He wants to be friends with it as he wants to be friends with all the neighborhood kids, but neither seems to be working out. He is convinced that nobody likes him, even his own penis.

The foreskin around his glans (of course he knows the proper names for all its parts) is not even. It looks like Yvonne's skirts, which are too long in front and too short in back or the other way around. It's very sloppy. He's known this, but he's not let himself think about it. Now he can ignore this fact no longer.

If Herman had done such a sloppy job he would be ashamed of it. He would. Yes, he would. Emmanuel, still shaking in the basement, not far from the padlocked room where Herman keeps his bottles of formaldehyde and foreskins, can think of nothing else. My father circumcised me himself and he did a terrible job and he is ashamed of it, and of me, and all my life I will be ashamed too. I will have to hide. No one will ever be able to see me. No one will ever love me. My father made an error and I cannot go to heaven because God is punishing him for not following His commandments. God hates him and God hates me, too.

And now my father is going to circumcise my new brother, his new son. What kind of father do I have? And he wants me to assist him at this bris! This cannot be right, for either of us!

The youngster is getting himself into an awful state of terror from which there will be no exit, at least not in the time necessary to prevent him from writing Herman and Yvonne a note and pinning it to his shirt just over his heart and finding a rope in a corner of the basement and throwing it over a thick pipe traversing the ceiling and then standing on a chair and putting the noose around his neck and jumping off the chair and dangling there until he is dead from hanging in this fine home Herman has finally completed in Washington on Scribbs Place in this new best area where more and more of the rich Jews are now flocking to reside, pushing out the goyim, and buying their land from Herman himself, who has had foresight to buy so much in case it should become the place for Jews to live. Which it now is. For everyone but Emmanuel.

"Dear Momma and Papa, I am very unhappy and I don't want to live anymore. Goodbye forever, Emmanuel."

There is an earlier version, identical except for an additional sentence: "I hate you." This note is found crumpled up in his small fist. It too is found, as is the body, by Nate Bulb, after the bris, which of course has taken place, with special blessings by Rabbi Chaimoff, and from the Elders of the Council of Drenel itself (which is what those now fifteen rabbis call themselves since they have organized), in the huge ceremonial room of the temple. The great Schlitz has come down to perform it as a gesture to Herman. No one misses Emmanuel. Afterward, at the big party in the palatial living and dining rooms on Scribbs Place, everyone is too busy drinking festive wine and eating celebratory food to notice the absence of a young lad whom no one ever noticed anyway.

Nate Bulb goes to the basement to enjoy a secret smoke of opium, which he partakes of occasionally and which accounts for his quiet and benign composure. He leaves the festivities, walking silently through the room packed with guests, feeling the eyes looking at him: Who is this man who never speaks and whose hair is blond with a hue of red? Is he the father of the infant? Nate Bulb is not the father of the red-haired infant, but he finds himself strangely worried that no one will believe him and perplexed that anyone would think Yvonne desirable to him.

Nate comes back upstairs and puts his hand on Herman's arm. "What do you want?" snaps Herman, who is conversing with Schlitz, artist to artist, and is annoyed by the interruption. "Please come with me. There is a tragedy," Nate whispers urgently, pulling Herman away and leading him furtively outside, where they circle to the rear of the house and enter the bowels through a recessed cellar door used by the men who bring in the wood and stack it in neat piles for the fires in the many fireplaces.

It is dark inside the basement, and Nate takes Herman's hand as if leading a small child. "What are you doing?" Herman snaps again but Nate will not let go. Slowly Herman's eyes adjust. He sees. He sees the sack of fleisch swinging gently back and forth.

"Oh my God, what have I done that You have forsaken me!" These are his words. Nate can never remember if they were uttered in Hebrew or in Yiddish. In whichever language, Herman screams so loudly that Nate is certain he can be heard throughout the house and throughout the neighborhood and by God Himself in heaven. Herman would scream louder but for Nate, who stuffs his fist into his mentor's mouth and to this day bears his tooth marks.

The father pulls out his pocketknife and cuts his son down and lays on the stone floor the body of the boy who should have been much bigger for his ten (or eleven or twelve) years.

As he never did in the lad's life, Herman talks to his son.

"I say goodbye to you, Emmanuel. I was not a good father. I was a son too much to God. He would not let me have my own son. God has wronged me. God, You and I are through."

Then he sits on the cold floor and takes the dead Emmanuel in his arms. He rocks him back and forth. He caresses over him and cootchy-coos him under his chin and kisses his face over and over and over. Then he stands up, dropping his hold on the boy. "Take him to Onkel," he orders Nate, referring to the Jewish undertaker. He goes upstairs and announces to the guests, "Please may I have your attention. Please to go home. Please to leave my house. This is no longer a house God blesses. This is no longer the house of the mohel." His eyes are burning with pain and fury and his face is covered with scarlet blotches so that he is both pale and flushed at the same time. He looks like a crazy man. The guests, many of whom are now very rich themselves, or on their way, have always thought this Herman a bit of a stranger, so proud, as if he were the only rich person intimate with God. These Jews look at him now and know that it is time for them to go.

It will not be long before the word gets out not only that Emmanuel has committed suicide, a particularly unacceptable sin in Orthodox Jewry, but that Herman has forsaken his calling, and even worse, thrown God out of his house and his life. And from that day forward commences such a history of our nation's capital as has never been told.

•

Herman takes a screaming Yvonne out of the house and puts her in a nursing home where she is sedated and kept in a locked room. He returns to Scribbs Place and sets fire to his home, starting in the attic and rushing from room to room with ignited wands of Hebrew newspapers and Hebrew prayer books and Hebrew tallises and tefillins, and anything connected to his religion that he can lay his hands on, torching everything as if propelled by some evil spirit. By the time he reaches the ground floor he is barely able to see the front door to get out alive. Oh yes, he wants to get out alive. He is not going to give God the satisfaction of destroying him, no sir. The house is a bonfire, a conflagration so huge and billowing and noisy in its whooshings and groanings that it sounds like a rage from heaven. But he can't leave yet. There is some unfinished business here, with God, for God in some profound way has possessed him and owned him and has now double-dealt him in a way his mind cannot unravel. Instinct, not premeditation, takes him to the basement, where he unpadlocks the room and stands for a moment staring maniacally at the overflowing shelves, almost toppling under the weight of row upon row of jars of all sizes filled to their screwed-on-tight metal lids with snippets of pale pink baby boy flesh. Above and around and beside him the howlings and slurpings of the inferno grow louder and nearer as Herman's temple is consumed. For a moment he thinks he will just sit down and perish here. Where else is there to go? What else is there to do in life? At least he can die among the trophies of his calling as the God who guided his hand so crudely and indelicately when in his nervous chutzpah he dared to circumcise his own firstborn son now takes him, too.

"There is no sin in this!" Nate Bulb has tried to tell him over and over through all these years since Herman performed that bris on his own son. "Where? Where in what book of the Holy Law do you find this prohibition?"

"It is in the Vernah, or the Vishnah, or the Mersh . . . I know I have read it. I know it!"

And even though Nate reads cover to cover the Vernah, the Vishnah, the Mershnah, he cannot find any reference to such a sin.

"I cannot find it, I cannot find such a prohibition, you are wrong!"

"What do you know about how to read the Holy Words! You are not even a Jew."

And since this is true, and since no one but Herman and Nate know it, and since Nate's masquerade certainly crosses the border into its own questionable regulations of sendek-dom, the argument ends here.

Herman watches his jars explode around him from the heat. There it is! He takes in his hands the only small bottle left, the one containing the fragment of his son, this Emmanuel, this Emmanuel now dead. Is his firstborn son now burned up at his feet? Did Nate get him to Onkel? Are these his ashes floating in the air, looking like pieces of black curled tissue paper? Is this Emmanuel now so dead there is nothing left of him but this piece of his tiny penis? His foreskin. He pours all the preservative out of the bottle and holds the tiny bit of skin in the palm of his hand, moving still, as if it has its own life, its scriggly unevenness a taunting reminder of his own ineptitude. As if it is saying to him, I will not die; you must be punished; you must go through life atoning for this.

So Herman washes the piece of foreskin clean of the formaldehyde in the laundry sink. He puts it in his mouth and he sucks on it, to absorb . . . what, he doesn't know. Strength? He doesn't want to be strong anymore. The poor child's spirit? He loathed the weakling. Atonement? Never. Atone for what? I was misled! I was hoodwinked! He chews the skin. Tough though it is, he chews it until it is mush, then spittle, then saliva, then nothing but the taste of bitter rue, and then he swallows it as he walks from the ashes of his house and out onto the front lawn, where he collapses in a fever. With one last horrible gasping whoosh of combustion, Herman's temple collapses to earth behind him. The last tiny bits of what is left in his mouth of his firstborn son now slide into his gut forever.

Oh, the horror of this story is not over. The new son, Abraham Masturbov, has been left by both his father and mother and his nurse, abandoned in the midst of these burning hallways and rooms and corridors and the seven (or is it eight or nine or seventeen or thirty?) bathrooms. Not for the first time in his life, Abraham Masturbov, close to death, in death's immediate vicinity, must save himself. Abraham Masturbov, barely brissed, in his swaddling clothes, is tossed from his layette in the building's turmoil and falls into a cold porcelain bathtub imported at great cost from Ninsky, where no Jew could ever afford such a heavy tub, so heavy that it sinks slowly down, floor by floor, through the weakened timbers, to the very foreskins' storehouse in the basement, to land on top of his brother's black skeleton, now fleshless, with its scorched collar of death. No, Nate Bulb did not get Emmanuel to Onkel. What indeed has happened to Nate Bulb? The infant Abraham Masturbov lies on top of and in the middle of this incendiary horror.

There. There is Nate Bulb, awakening from some bad dream, his head bruised and bleeding, arising from under fallen timbers and stumbling to grab and save the infant and exit with him, just in time.

•

Yvonne emerges several years later from the nursing home, more silent, more taciturn, a white-haired shriveled woman of thirty-five or so.

During these several years, Herman Masturbov has become the richest Jew in the District of Columbia, and perhaps in this New World. He owns— oh, what difference the numbers or the adjectives, he owns and owns, every- where, here, there, outlying, suburban, in Maryland, Virginia, Pennsylvania, West Virginia. People in this New World will live anywhere.

No more the mohel, now he carves up the city itself. He hates God now. No, he doesn't hate Him. He no longer believes He even exists. Herman believes only in evil, and the devil, and the triumph of hate in this New World, no different from the Old World that Jews ran from so fast, in both of which, it is now perfectly clear, God, after such devotion, after such sacri- fice, mows you down in your own tracks.

My own precious son!

No more holy words come to his lips, nor smiles of kindness or neigh- borliness to his face, nor deeds of generosity toward anyone anywhere.

He has been punished for something, and he will never know what that something is.

He had been a good Jew and he had tried to do the good thing and still he had been punished.

Well, he will not lie down and submit. His hands have been too cruelly slapped. Like some petulant child who grabs his marbles and runs to play another game, Herman does just that.

The house Abraham Masturbov grows up in is Herman's second palace, grander, more elaborate, and uglier than its ancestor. This one is out on Six- teenth Street in an area owned mostly by Herman and now becoming most fashionable as this country and its capital city start the long run-up toward World Wars I and II. He does not build this one himself. No, he will never do that again. He buys it from a "developer," a new breed of men who build buildings in groups, on speculation, gambling that at a particular moment in time there will be a man to buy a particular house just like it is. Herman knows this house is the ugliest he's ever seen. That's why he buys it. If the first house weighed a ton, this one weighs ten. It is a monstrosity of red brick and white brick and tan brick with pillars and porte cocheres and caryatids and turrets and minarets and arches and dormers and tidbits of styles from all around the globe and all of architectural history, borrowed haphazardly and ineptly whipped together. It's a gross blight on this neighborhood, his very own neighborhood, and he knows that once he's in it everyone around him will want one just like it.

Yvonne utters no opinion.

"Any room you want," he tells her.

She nods. She climbs to the top floor—the house inside has as many architectural nightmares as outside, stairways up and down and back and forward, rooms tall and odd and paneled, or bare, and all the way up on the fifth floor is one tiny room, no more than a cell, stuck in a minaret, and into this she goes, and shuts the door in her husband's face.

And so continues the hell on earth of Herman and Yvonne Masturbov.

•

After several years in his new house of silence and ugliness—he has furnished the place with greater reckless monolithic tastelessness than the last—Herman decides once more that he must have another son. It is a practical decision. He owns too much now. He must train someone to increase it even more after he is gone. He is fucking not a woman but a city and a country, and his seed, as the Vernah had said when last he read it, must never cease to multiply. There must be Masturbovs forever.

And Abraham is so quiet, so withdrawn as to be almost invisible. He does not seem to be a son to whom a father can bequeath such an inheritance. He rarely speaks, particularly to Herman. Learning Yiddish or Hebrew is of course out of the question, as is any religious education. Besides, the child refuses to go to school, refuses to be taught by anyone except Nate Bulb, refuses to have friends. No one would know that his intelligence is superior, but for some testing done on him by strange new doctors specializing in communicating with the mind. Because he is so quiet Herman thinks his son is soft.

Herman would call him a mama's boy but for the fact that Yvonne is not interested in him at all. Yes, Herman, who is after all a businessman who knows when it is time to cut his losses, decides the time has arrived for another son.

He chuckles to himself as he climbs the five flights to Yvonne's aerie one afternoon. It makes no difference that he's never been up here since she closed the door in his face. It's his house, isn't it? Since he's usually away all day she's come to feel safe in the daytime. That's when she sneaks out into the garden, he's told. He wonders if she still smells and wears the same clothes. She has her food brought to her room, so how would he know? He throws open her door. Her room is neat and bright, painted white before white rooms are fashionable. She has only a narrow mattress on the floor, and a small rocking chair by the window, from which a view of the neighborhood can be seen. Here and there are a few items from Russia: a kerchief of her mother's tacked to one wall; a miniature sewing kit that Emmanuel presented to her one year for her birthday, kept open and displayed on the windowsill, its tiny thimble and row of various needles, its dozen tiny rolls of thread the only bright colors in the room; a small bottle, tightly capped, in which she keeps her wedding ring as a reminder that she is not free, set by her pillow to see last before sleep and first upon arising: it breaks her heart to see this ring, for it is everything and it is nothing. You are my biggest mistake, she mumbles to it. She mumbles useless mantras to herself, too.

She is lying down on the mattress. Her eyes stare at the ceiling. She looks like a corpse to him. How will he ever arouse himself sufficiently? She is thin and pale and white and gray and most unhealthy-looking. The neat spare whiteness of the room makes her look even worse. What is that smell? She stinks. She still stinks. She still wears the smelly black schmata she never takes off. Will she never be clean and smell nice for him again?

He has prepared for this. He reeks of German cologne. He opens a window wide to the crisp afternoon breeze. She shudders as he sits down on the floor beside her. She has wondered how long it would be before he came to her again. He sticks his hand under her dress and pokes around in her vagina. He has not even said hello, how are you, it has been a long time. Her stench has already depleted the erection he carried with him up from his bedroom, where he looked at dirty pictures obtained for him by Nate. He begins to masturbate himself. He has not even removed his trousers, just yanked his penis out through the fly of his tweed suit, so coarse that it abrades the skin of his member. He tries to summon up the images of the women in their black lingerie, but he sees only Yvonne in black rags, a woman looking up at him with the eyes of a prisoner, eyes that say, Are you crazy? Is the world crazy? And answering yes to both. Somehow he gets himself hard. He throws back her dress. She wears nothing under it. He sticks himself into her, holding his breath lest her odor detumesce him. He pumps and pumps. He tries to recall when she was pretty. He tries to recall someone pretty he wanted to fuck sometime somewhere. He is pouring with sweat. She just lies there. She wishes she were dead. He finally feels something arriving. He ejaculates with a pain he's never associated with this act, as if shooting through him is not semen but molten poison. He screams out, "Give me another son!"

The son is a daughter and she is born dead. Yvonne births her on that narrow mattress with the help of Nate Bulb. She pops the baby out of her and she smiles when Nate tells her her daughter is dead.

And so it is Abe who, like it or not, ready or not, will be raised to own the future. Rain or shine, each day, every day, he is driven by Nate Bulb to Herman's office and subjected to an increasingly rigorous exposure to all aspects of money, its accumulation and management, to the ins and outs of real estate, negotiation, borrowing, selling, banking, all the tricks ganifs might put over on you if you don't watch out. Because he loves what he is imparting, Herman is a good if impatient teacher. For the boy, there is not a moment when he doesn't feel his father is saying to him, You are not smart enough. You are not smart enough to learn what I teach you but I teach you anyway. It is difficult for Herman to tell if his son is learning anything, or even listening. Like his mother, Abe is so muted in his facial and verbal expressiveness as to seem retarded. But he's a listener. Even Herman finally sees this.

When he's twelve Abe buys his first piece of property, in Blundenburger. Herman wonders why. It's such a backwoods place. A year later it's worth four times more. Herman buys some land there too, although Abe warns him not to. "I was lucky," he tells his father. Neither smiles, although each would like to.

"This is what you have always wanted," Nate Bulb exults for Herman.

"How do you know what I have always wanted?" Herman answers.

Abe remains a peculiarly passive child. Even though he receives no parental love or affection or attention, he does what he is told, he learns what he is taught; he doesn't complain; he dutifully makes friends with other rich Jewish youngsters placed in his path (to them *he* is the desired one, the one *their* parents command them to be pals with); but of course it is as if he is missing some piece of his insides, some piece that could turn him from the zombie with the crackerjack skills into someone with a heart. For a brief moment in time, Doris Hardware, still some years away from his arms, will be that missing piece. But he should only know now that Doris will be bound to fail him, as his destiny is bound to his birth, at the very beginning of this century, the new day that never quite dawns, and that before Doris, before any woman, there is always the matter of that most egregious missing piece, his mother, Yvonne.

After the stillborn birth Yvonne begins to suffer from an outpouring of blood that suddenly begins to flow, slowly at first but then profusely, voluminously. It does not stop. Much to her surprise she finds that she is frightened. She thought she was waiting for death. Can it be possible that she is regressing to girlhood and periods? Old remedies exert their pull: she takes a taxi, after all these years, to the mikva, the ritual bath off South Capitol Street. Perhaps it is as simple as the God she has not been talking to is telling her anyway that her body simply must be cleansed. But it doesn't work, and when she actually bleeds into the pool she is told to find a doctor and not to return.

When she has the strength she goes out to look for such a doctor. But she can find no doctor who can explain her bleedings, not even her brother Israel Jerusalem, who in a few years is to be celebrated for his solving of the Mercy Hooker bleedings and is thus not yet able to tell his sister, "She had glause. You do not have glause. I need money to understand glause better. Do you think Herman would fund my research into glause?"

When she has the strength she spends whole days going back to the old neighborhoods where the old doctors and midwives and shamans from Russia still live. She goes from door to door, begging for any scrap of information. She sometimes goes barefoot, because in Lastnavatnyia to walk barefoot endows the quest with an aspect of holiness and may improve the chance of success. A sign, a vertov, an omen that over there, there! lies help, an answer, gedugnenheit. Do you recognize my symptoms? she asks old women in the street. Rack your brain. Can you remember anything like this? Some think she has gone crazy, that at last Herman's ill-gotten gains—and in these streets of poor Jews the money of all rich Jews is ill-gotten—have brought him this, a suffering abandoned bleeding shoeless wife. The ever-faithful Nate Bulb trails her at a discreet distance. Some of the old ladies she confronts say they've heard of such an affliction back in the old days, in the old country, in the Old World, in the past, but no, I don't remember what to do about it. Most slam their doors in her face, even when they know who she is, the landlord's wife, what has he ever done for us, but listen, be nice to her, a good deed toward her might give you . . . what? A free month? You are as crazy as she is. Down deep everyone is afraid she has some contagious disease. Plagues have come from less. Some pass on to her names of people who once mentioned . . . or might have . . . or could know . . . but of course know nothing when she finds them. She continues to bleed.

After a while of shlepping to the old neighborhoods and finding no relief she gives in and succumbs to her mattress. She lies on her narrow pallet in the tiny turret room of this mansion in the best neighborhood in Washington owned by a husband worth by now tens of millions of dollars, maybe more, most likely more, yes, definitely more, and she hikes up her unclean schmata so she can rub her privates with thick Turkish towels and clean away the unclean bleedings no one understands. The stench she can't clean away. The stench is awful. It's hard to keep help, to find anyone who will even bring her food, much less remove the growing mound of towels drenched with blood. Sometimes the flows come before she can get a towel in place. She can't clean herself up fast enough and there are puddles on the floor. The mattress is like a sponge. Once, when she passes out from weakness, the blood is unstanched for so long that it seeps through the floor to the room below, one of the maid's rooms, so that the maid quits that very middle of the night.

Nate Bulb brings her new mattresses. He brings her food now, patiently feeding her himself. For some reason her smell doesn't offend him. It is as if he doesn't smell it. He would tell Herman, but Herman doesn't want to hear any of this. As far as Herman is concerned Yvonne is dead. He does not know what is happening to his own wife.

Herman first hears about Yvonne's bleedings from some old harpy who owes him back rent and tears up his eviction notice, flaunting it in his face when he comes to deliver it. Yes, he likes to deliver eviction notices personally now.

"Your wife is a bleeder!" she screams at him.

"What are you talking about?"

"Ask her! Ask her!"

"Ask her what?'

"How she bleeds to death! How she walks around town bleeding at every step! How she bleeds out blood every minute of her life! How you bleed her to death! And take your rent bill and shove it up your heinie. Now put me out on the street! I dare you!"

He returns home late that night, after walking his land, all over the city, in the suburbs, in the Northeast, in the Northwest, in the Southeast, in Franeeda County. He does this every day now, sometimes all night long, again and again, he can never walk it enough, this land is MINE, I own more Washington than any other Jew, than any other man! He slowly climbs all the many steps to the fifth floor to confront his wife, distressed to find that he is panting and winded. How can I walk and breathe freely all night long but when I walk upstairs to see my wife I gasp for air? By the third floor he already smells it, a smell as of something dead. Each step closer, the smell becomes more putrid, until he thinks he will faint. He is forced to put a handkerchief over his nose and mouth. He opens the door. The waves of putrefaction are like some typhoon that swallows men whole and drowns them. He stumbles before he can right himself. He feels her staring eyes in the dark. He reaches for the light switch but no bulb goes on. It is she who turns on a small lamp. She will let him see. She wants him to see, but only by her light.

He sees. Her mattress is crusted with dried blood, the wooden floor stained with overlapping circles in hues of different density. Piles of bloodied towels mass around the room like ancient primitive mounds of dung. He walks around and around in the baby steps that this minuscule space demands, his eyes on the floor, like an archaeologist calculating carbon rings in these patterns of blood. How long has this been going on? No, nothing makes sense. Age brings only more confusion. He throws open the window and sticks his head out to gobble air. What did we do that this should happen? His arms reach awkwardly out the window with his question. Yvonne has her arms out too, to him, as a new tributary of blood trickles down the insides of her legs. He starts to cry. He kneels down in her blood. He sticks his finger in it. He makes an X on his forehead.

"This is all my fault," he finally says.

He picks her up, Yvonne, his wife. He does not know why he made his admission. He cannot tell whether he is crying or sweating from exhaustion, or from fear. But he is carrying them both back downstairs to life. She is light as a feather.

Abe, their child, hears noises in the hallway and opens his door and follows his parents, tiptoeing in the shadows, having learned early on and only too well how to be not seen and not heard. He sees his father lay his mother on the dining room table, light long candles in brass holders, and place them around her. He sees him stick his hand under her skirt and pull it out all bloody. And put his forefinger to his lips. And with this bloody forefinger make an X on her forehead to match the one on his own.

Then begin such moanings and shreiings as Abe has never heard. First Herman begins softly intoning what sound like prayers, in some language unfamiliar, both guttural and high-pitched. Then Yvonne joins the shreiings, her shrill intensity insinuating itself above his, but only for a moment, until the volume of his screeched imprecations walks up some ectoplasmic stairs to reach above hers, only to be joined by her own new cascadings from a higher plane, as if they are making a braid, in and out, over and over, plaiting some crown of hideously painful thorns. It is an awful racket, and frightening to a thirteen-year-old, whose own body is trying to grow up.

When the sun comes up, Abe is still hiding and peeking, listening as his parents' invocations wind down. The shreiings become moans become warblings become soft sobs become daylight. Both his parents look older than he's ever seen them. Herman is almost ethereal; his skin is tighter on his bones, shiny and vaguely yellow like the parchment on lampshades. Yvonne is just a skeleton, without any skin at all.

The parents don't see their son, but Abe is used to that. Not even as Herman picks up his wife, who is no longer bleeding, and carries her upstairs, passing Abraham on the way, is this child seen.

There are smiles on the elders' faces. They have sought surcease and surcease has been granted. In the master bathroom the husband bathes the wife slowly and tenderly, sponging her body and changing the water often so that all traces of red disappear, except for the emerging pinkness of her skin. Then he puts her in his bed and props her up against many pillows and fetches some soup, which he spoons into her with patience and care.

This sounds like a happy ending, and for a while it seems to be, at least as concerns the extreme deprivations Yvonne has endured. When she realizes she's stopped venting blood, of course she's happy. She lies in the master bed next to her husband, both of them waiting to see if good food and rest and a modicum of affection will do the trick. When after a week she ventures to walk a few steps and sit by a window to look out at the garden, which is miraculously in bloom, an actual smile crosses her face, though no one sees it. After a month she dresses in a new dark green robe Herman ordered from Madame Helga in Paris and she goes downstairs to join her husband and son for dinner.

A few days later she is sitting with Abe in his bedroom, both of them cross-legged on the floor, preparing his pants and socks and shirts with name tags for his first summer at sleepaway camp. She's lived for so many years in her silent and invisible world that he feels awkward, pleasantly, being close to her like this. She sees him looking at her and she smiles, covertly, like a bashful girl, and then he smiles back, shyly, and hands her the navy sweatshirt with Kamp Komfort emblazoned in bright maroon lettering, and she takes it and finds a hidden inside seam where she attaches his name, "so you won't get lost," she says. She uses a needle and thread from the little kit Emmanuel gave her.

Abe sees it, the trickle. Suddenly her face is grotesque, twisted by returning fear.

The bloods, as Yvonne calls them in her head, begin again.

"Momma, Momma, what should I do!"

Both of them stare as the floor beneath her becomes a pool of blood. She is wearing a light summer dress and the diaphanous skirt drips blood as she stands to run—where? There are noises from inside of her, rumblings, gaseous quackings, like some rusty machine starting up again. She runs, into the hall, down one flight toward the master bedroom—no, she doesn't want to go back there, so she climbs to her old turret hideout, but Herman has had this horror chamber locked up. She can't get in. Where is there to go? She starts down again, her trail marked only too vividly from room to room, from floor to floor, from son to husband, the poor woman, the poor woman, no animal should live like this, casting its spoor to earth as if to say: I exist.

She collapses on the second-floor landing outside the master bedroom. Abe picks his mother up, the child who years before a bar mitzvah refused to have one, to celebrate that day on which each Jewish boy can say "today I am a man," his answer being, "I already am a man," the mother who is all of 60 pounds, maybe less, as she drips copiously and curls like an infant into his arms. He almost slips in her blood as he carries her to the dining room table, where he lays her down and lights the long tapers in the brass candlesticks. Yvonne tries weakly to protest before she loses consciousness.

Abraham begins softly. He tries to recite the prayers he heard his parents utter, hoping to God that because he had quit Hebrew school long ago the intention is more important than the accuracy of its conveyance. Higher and higher he intones, trying to capture the exact timbre and emotion he recalls from his parents' descants, and then when he reaches as high as he can go without choking or coughing he sticks his hand under her skirt as he saw his father do, poking awkwardly, for what he doesn't know. For the first time in his life he touches a woman's genitals. He feels the burbling blood. He feels the hairy lips that exude this blood. His head starts to spin. He forces himself to be strong. He pulls out his bloodied hand, and as his father did he kisses his forefinger before placing a mark of blood on his mother's forehead and on his own. Over and over, rising and falling, his words rush together into increasing incomprehensibility. He is screaming these prayers now. Or are they cries of horror? What's the difference? He mustn't stop. He must not let the fumes emanating from his own mother asphyxiate him. His father rose above it. Had Herman's first lesson in real estate not been that through consistency, over and over and over, by never stopping, never quitting, always pushing forward, no matter what . . . His voice goes up and up, piercingly up, to a pitch that reaches heaven, and he collapses. By the time his father returns (from a trip with Nate Bulb, to Richmond, a new and farther outpost, where a profit of several hundred thousand dollars was turned on the spot), the youngster has been imprecating for some seven hours; his mother has not revived; his mother has not stopped bleeding; the table and the floor are covered in his mother's blood. No one has heard the son, certainly not God, and Abraham has collapsed into exhausted unconsciousness on top of his mother, convinced not only that he's failed to save her but that her death is on his hands.

Herman finds them thus entangled. Once again he washes his wife and puts her in his bed. She has stopped bleeding again. How? What has transpired? Has the child been able to accomplish this? Has he inherited the gift I once had of talking to the Lord?

Or my curse?

What is the nature of this curse?

What difference?

A curse is a curse.

He returns to pick up his son, who lies still on the table, and carry him to his own room, to the suite of bedroom and bath and study that Herman has made for Abraham and then never once visited, here in his own mansion, a mansion inhabited by three curses.

No. Four curses. There is another youngster somewhere in this house, who never leaves here.

And the dead daughter. That makes five. Five curses.

He tries to think if the number 5 had some ancient symbolic significance in the Vernah. In the Kaballah and the Yohar and the Nitzevehu and the Ahvahdod. In the Kreptz. In the Nidred. When he had read them.

Herman lays his son down on the bed to undress him. There is a spot on the boy's crotch. Fearing he knows what it is, he pulls the clothes from the boy's body, his hands fumbling, his fingers trembling; he tries to yank the underpants off; when they won't come off he buries his face in his son's crotch, sniffing, smelling, even trying to taste with his tongue, knowing what it is, what this spot is; then he peels back the shorts; now he sees with absolute surety: semen sticks both to the little penis and the cloth. He slaps the boy as hard as he can, until there are black-and-blue marks. Finally the boy is brought back from wherever he was. But having resuscitated his son the father as always finds no words. What words are there for this? You have had an emission over your mother? Over your God? He is aghast at either possibility.

Herman begins to cry. I do not know this world or my life or any life. He begins to mumble jumbled words from some old testament, some ancient book of prohibitions. Semen must not be visible before a woman until the marriage vows. Semen spent in vain is semen spent in sin. Semen ejaculated without the aid of woman and without the intent of procreation is semen that pollutes the soul. Semen semen semen . . .

Where am I? He starts walking around the house like some crazy man, a Lear on the heath, abandoned by all yet straining to be heard. From room to room he stumbles, utterances dribbling from him. From the holiest Yablonz. From the most sacred Scrud.

The son lies on his bed awake. His face and jaw hurt. His throat is sore. He tries to speak but can only whisper hoarsely. His penis is cold. The weight of unanswered questions upon him is overwhelming. Where is any future he can understand? He hears his father stumbling through the house. His father's cries are guttural, sudden waves that almost sound like meaning but not quite, followed by plaintive, fervent whisperings and sinister, hollow hisses.

"Papa, Papa, stop! Take my hand! Please!" the naked boy croaks, trailing after the moaning father, who, bereft of his senses, wanders like a driver in a strange country without a map, from room to room, from floor to floor, and finally to the basement. Here Herman unlocks a hidden safe Abe has never seen; his arm disappears into the long dark hole up to his armpit and then withdraws, his fist clutching a leather pouch. He sits down on the floor. No, this is not right. He feels constrained and imprisoned. He stands up and takes off all his clothes, which, drenched with sweat and agony, have been sticking to him like his own skin, and he places them neatly on a workbench. He stands before his son naked. His body is thin and ghastly white, and patched with blobs of hair, some now white, puffed out from his skin here and there with no rhyme or pattern, no grace or symmetry. He opens the pouch and withdraws a hard leather case, and he snaps this hard case open, and there are flashings and shinings as light from the harsh bulb above them catches the silver of a set of tiny knives, the circumcision knives, the knives for slicing this way and that, north and south and east and west, the tools of his former trade, the calling that once called him. He puts the open set of knives down by his clothes. He looks upon them. His fingers hover above them, seeking guidance. He decides on the one he wants. He plucks the longest. He kisses it. Then he lowers it down upon himself and with his other hand parts the blotch of hair that hides his penis.

The son looks upon his father's penis. It is hidden in folds of flesh. It is uncircumcised. The son watches as his father slowly cuts the folds and swaths away, as if paring an apple, his core spurting so much pent-up blood that it should impede any further progress. But Herman's eyes are closed. He is doing it all by touch. He cuts and cuts some more, his fingers darting into the leather kit to exchange one instrument for another, and when he has made it around once he goes around again with yet another blade to smooth the edge. His member is gushing. He is proud. He parades around the room as if to model his new thing. Look, look, look. I am a Jew. I am a Jew.

The stone floor is now slippery to walk on. The father's feet can gain no purchase, nor can those of his son, who, not knowing what to do, does what instinct propels him to do, to catch his father as he loses his balance and slips, as both fall down, as both try to pick themselves up, the father blindly groping, for what? reaching out ahead of him, for what? trying to slither through his own spoor, the son following the trail of his father's dripping penis, to the master bedroom, in which Yvonne is laid in a white gown like a corpse, the ghastly thought still crashing inside the son that he's killed his mother, and now he's driven his father crazy. The follower and the leader, up they go, leaving the mother on her bier, climbing to the turret room, Herman's arms reaching up and up, as if with luck he might bypass this room and reach the roof and from the roof reach heaven.

But it is at the turret room that he stops, and reaches for the key over the lintel, and unlocks it, and forces his son inside. There is no light, for Herman has boarded up the windows against all light and air and memory. He throws his child to the floor and beats him. "Here she would not have me!" he screams out. "Here I burned the house down!" he screams out. "Here she bore me a dead daughter!" he screams out. "Here I now become a Jew!" He is beating his son and beating his son and beating his son, the poundings punctuated by such agonizing cries that the son allows the punishment. In the dark Abraham feels Herman take his young penis into his hand. He feels the growing pain as the father yanks at it and tries to tear it from the boy's torso. Now it is Abraham's turn to scream in agony as he feels the cold steel of the mohel's knife. Now it is his turn to find out if he is able to fight back. Lest he be mutilated for life he fights with all his might, kicking his father's face and pushing him off.

Abraham locks his father in the tiny turret room. He runs the endless flights down to the kitchen, where he grabs towels and newspapers and puts them to the gas stove to turn them into torches. As his father did upon the death of the brother Abe never knew, torching the house on Scribbs Place, so Abraham runs around this second house lighting everything he can touch. In the bloodied dining room he stays the longest, trying to burn up the entire memory, the long slab of mahogany on which she lay, the Oriental rug still damp with her insides. Only the drapes catch fire, but that is enough to ignite the wallpaper and then the wood framing in the walls, and soon the house is a huge pyre, from his father's foreskin in the basement to its owner in the tower.

None of them dies in this new conflagration. Relief from agony on such a grand scale is rare. The house still stands there, out on Sixteenth Street (not, in fact, so far from where Adolphus Fahrt had seen his hospital burned down), the hideous stone caryatids of hugely breasted maidens still supporting the many porches and verandahs. Firemen preserved the structure and luck saved the family, if luck it can be called. Inside, the house is black and redolent of horror, as it always will be now. After a few years it's cleaned up. Yvonne will live here in her turret until she is one hundred.

Herman, after a brief period of institutionalization, is released when Nate Bulb purchases the institution. He is released, only to die the next day crossing Sixteenth Street, run down by an overexcited horse hauling a big load of lumber belonging to his own Masturbov Lumber Company. The horse had been a favorite of Herman's and smelled him coming near. As his will reveals, he does indeed own more of the Washington area than almost anyone else, certainly more than any other Jew. The will bequeaths money enough to support Yvonne, but none for Abe. This boy receives nothing. Everything is left in trust to Abe's first son, whoever he may be, and who in fact will be Mordecai Masturbov, who will become a most important historical figure. Nate Bulb is appointed executor and administrator of this huge estate until such time as Abe grows up and marries and has this son and this son is old enough to understand his great, great wealth.

In defense of his actions, Herman, in his will, quotes the Vernah:

"Sometimes the mistakes of man are so great that a generation must be skipped, if only for the air to be cleared with the fresh air necessary to cleanse history."

History, of course, is never cleansed. Yvonne never stops her bleedings. They will become increasingly rare, true, weeks or months may pass, but one day she will stand at the top of the landing on the second floor in her white nightgown, blood dripping down her legs, and cry out, "Again! They come again!" until the ever-faithful Nate Bulb (Abe will be seldom home) picks her up in his arms and lays her on the table, with the candles, with the trancelike imprecations and shreiings, with the forefinger poked into her vagina to bring forth blood for him to taste and kiss and impress upon the center of her forehead and his own. The sendek has learned every trick in the trade. Then, as if after some sexual act that is completed, its climax reached, the parties thereto exhausted and bored to satiation with each other, with all *this*, she pulls herself off the table and goes upstairs to a bedroom, she cares no longer which, there are so many, and as is commanded in the Vishnah and the Vernah and even the Mishnah, in every long list of commandments ever commanded, she takes her own mikva, the ages-old ritual bath for cleansing, and tries without success to go to sleep.

•

This then is the heritage of Abraham Masturbov, who will soon learn—in a tiny room in a tiny house not far from this house and from the vanished house of his birth just a block or so away—of Doris Hardware's own story, her own hideous history, and her decision—could it ever have been otherwise?—not to marry him.

GOOD BREEDING?

In the richly appointed living room of Mrs. E. H. (Mary) Harriman, widow of the exceedingly wealthy railroad tycoon and early supporter of all things eugenic, a group of people sit sipping tea and discussing what to do about the approximately 300,000 "defectives" of all sorts who had already been tabulated by New York State at the request of Mrs. Harriman, a woman of great energy, conviction, power, and of course wealth. Her husband owned most of the railroads in America. She is also the daughter of a rich man. And she controls a fortune of between $70 million and $100 million. She is sixty-three years old and will live until 1932 at 1 East Sixty-ninth Street. She is a direct woman and minces no words. It is April 8, 1914.

She opens the gathering by welcoming everyone and reminding them, with a touch of pride in her voice, "My late husband's fortune has paid for many local charities, as you know. I cite the New York Bureau of Industries and Immigration, which seeks out Jewish, Italian, and other immigrants to our crowded cities in order to deport them or at the least confine them, should they be candidates, which unfortunately so many of them are, for forced sterilization."

She pauses to modestly acknowledge the polite applause, before proceeding. "The agenda of the meeting today concerns the topic 'What can be done to prevent the continuing occurrence of sexual perversities, including homosexuality, also known as sodomy?' A representative from the Tally Office, Mr. Eagen Odemptor, is present to help direct our discussion."

Edwin Black's monumentally important work, *War Against the Weak*, to which we owe much of our information on the hideous history of the eugenics movement, unfortunately does not deal with the movement's additional interest in ridding the world of homosexuals. This subject, just beginning to interest gay scholars, and just as slowly beginning to appear out of the very wormy woodwork of the groves of academe, is addressed in *Proof Positive: The American Government's Active Role in the Extermination of Homosexuals*, by Waldo Strummer and Mellissa Evinrude, to which much is owed.

"They are mentally deficient, at the very least," Odemptor explains patiently to the group, which is not terribly familiar with homosexuals but has a nodding acquaintance with *sodomites*, a word several admit to knowing, "but only from church and of course the Bible." But once enunciated out loud, homosexuality is nervously added to the list of unpleasant items to attend to.

Has not the former president Theodore Roosevelt himself written just last year that "society has no business to permit degenerates to reproduce their kind"? "I'll know one when I see one," Roosevelt is quoted in *The Washington Monument* as saying to the Temperance First and Last Society at the Willard Hotel for its annual Founders Tea on May 1, 1914. "And so will all of you. Just as we have all come to recognize a drunk." Never one to put down that big stick, Teddy Roosevelt goes even further: "Someday, we will realize that the prime duty, the inescapable duty, of the good citizen of the right type, is to leave his blood behind him in the world; and that we have no business to permit the perpetuation of citizens of the wrong type."

As this movement of "betterment" grows like wildfire and as it's debated what exactly constitutes a degenerate, the definitions do not exactly blur, so much as coalesce into the all-inclusive. Why leave anything or anyone out? As long as we're getting rid of them, let's get rid of them all. Whoever they are. One has the sense that these well-meaning people are eager to get riled up about something awful simply because in their febrile imaginations the world must be filled with awful things to get riled up about and hence get rid of. Money does strange things to people who haven't had it before, or even when they have. There is a terrible impulse to "do something." Is it not the same today? And if a Harriman and a Rockefeller and a Ford are doing it, it must be okay.

"I would like to introduce Mrs. DeWitt Waldschein from our sister organization in Milwaukee," Mrs. Harriman says. "The topic of her remarks, as I understand them, is 'How to Define the Disastrous.'"

"Thank you, Mrs. Harriman. Wisconsin is honored to be represented here. I bring with me today a noble gentleman, an inspired mind, Mr. Jeshua Brinestalker, of the Brinestalker Ranches in Los Angeles—"

"San Diego County, actually, Mrs. Waldschein," Brinestalker interrupts.

"I am so sorry. San Diego County, of course. It is all so . . . large out there that we east of it are often geographically deficient. Do you have as much degeneracy in San Diego County as we have in Milwaukee and Mrs. Harriman speaks of here in New York?"

Brinestalker nods. "I come to you today to speak about the very same. I come to you today to speak about ending all across the country the bloodlines of people deemed unfit. In my position as president of the Western Breeders Association I have noticed that people are not so dissimilar to horses. These are strong words. It is not so important for us to waste our time describing precisely what degeneracy entails. We have higher minds to guide us on this journey. Where I live we just go out and do it, get rid of them. We shoot horses, don't we?"

There is more and more talk like this, and there are more and more meetings like this. The Hearst syndicate of newspapers, never known for its humanitarian concerns, proclaims in September 1915: "14 million to be sterilized!" It suggests first trying it out on "the sons of the billionaires." Are they being facetious or serious?

It is difficult to believe in hindsight what furious stupidities are masquerading as intelligent discourse, much less science. Major intellectuals, corporations, and institutions—Yaddah, the Carnegie Institute, Cold Spring Harbor, Alexander Graham Bell, Rockefellers—are endeavoring to rid "the race" (the Yaddah economist Irving Fisher—Philip Jerusalem, Amos Standing, and Nehemiah Brinestalker all take classes with him before they graduate in 1920— actually calls himself a "raceologist") of everything from too-small Jewish infants to ships' captains prone to shipwrecks caused by an inherited love for the sea, identified as "thalassophilia," or "captain's curse," the riddance of which would increase navigational safety on the high seas and, according to Professor Fisher, "save so many lives." Check out the minutes of this very meeting, located in the Harriman archive at the New York Public Library, also a major recipient of Harriman funds.

Yes, the list of those deemed worthy of riddance surfaces and coalesces as an all-inclusive "only for the moment. We promise you more." The blind. The deaf. Deaf-mutes. The "socially inadequate." German, Polish, and Russian Jews. Negroes. (Don't Negroes already have a death rate twice that of whites?) Mulattoes. American Indians. "Mountain" people. ("The white race in this land is the foundation upon which rests its civilization, and is responsible for the leading position which we occupy amongst the nations of the world. Is it not, therefore, just and right that this group decide for itself what its composition shall be, and attempt, as Virginia has, to maintain its purity?" in the words of a Virginia State Health Bureau pamphlet of 1924.) Illegitimate children. Interracial married couples. Unmarried couples living together in sin. The maimed and malformed. Immigrants. Political malcontents. Dirt-poor debtors. The "strange-colored skinned." Men dressed as women. Women dressed as men. And of course, now that there is a word for them, homosexuals, although this word is spoken softly, being so new and uncomfortable to palates.

Vasectomies, tubectomies, castrations proliferate in their execution and in the widespread locations of their execution. The wholesale removal of sexual organs is championed and celebrated and actually performed in remote parts of our country. Grange, Arkansas, a town in the Ozarks, has a hospital that advertises, "You tell us to take out what you want taken out and point him out and we'll take it out," as attested in *Arkansas Traveller*, the memoirs of Dr. Abraham Vorgessenin, published in 1935. Yes, we must not forget that our very president had proclaimed, "Society has no business to permit degenerates to reproduce their kind."

Single men now find themselves suspect wherever they go and wherever they live. It is only natural for a man to be married. A Dr. Sanis in Grange specializes in castration. Several of his male "patients" have died, and it is thought the good doctor murdered them when he suspected homosexual proclivities, quoting Teddy Roosevelt's permission, our very president's "permission."

•

In 1910 the Eugenics Record Office had been launched by the American Breeders Association. "Its first mission was to identify the most defective and undesirable Americans, estimated to be at least 10 percent of the population. When identified, they would be subjected to appropriate eugenic remedies to terminate their bloodlines. Leading solutions will be, at the least, compulsory segregation and forced sterilization" (Black, described later).

Jeshua Brinestalker is one of the founders of the ABA. He is a California rancher and horse breeder, the owner of the monstrously large Brinestalker Ranch. Jeshua is a handsome man. A large portrait of him hangs in the statehouse in Sacramento. Jeshua, who is a relatively young man, neverthless maintains that he has painstakingly learned to develop and breed horses of great perfection, endurance, intelligence, and beauty. "I can do this for man, too, now that I have thought about it and new organizations are raising this issue of getting rid of the defective," he says in his acceptance speech upon being made a first vice president. "I'll get to work on it right away. I own a great amount of land to try out a great many things."

In 1909, California adopts forced sterilization, segregation laws, and marriage restrictions. Why not? Twenty-seven states already have them. But California will be the leader in these policies. Before the visible power of this movement ceases, some 60,000 Americans will be coercively sterilized, nearly half of them in California, a healthy number supervised by Jeshua Brinestalker himself. Why, the very president of Stanford University, David

Starr Jordan, who in his 1902 book, *Blood of a Nation*, originated the notion of "race and blood," declares emphatically that all bad traits are passed through the blood. He is joined by academics at Yaddah and Princeton and every wealthy philanthropist one can possibly name. The eugenics bandwagon is rolling ahead and all the best people are climbing on board.

Who is this Jeshua Brinestalker? Where did he come from, and why? Does no one detect the faint hint of an accent in his clipped, well-composed English? So many from so many places far and near, even if Americans themselves, are learning, as a group, to speak better, cleaner, purer, English unaccented by regional differences. Why, there are schools for it, in New York and other towns and cities: people want to sound "high-class," sound pure 100 percent top-drawer American. Dale Carnegie and Fulton Oursler and Arthur Murray and Norman Vincent Peale and Billy Graham and other "teachers" for fun and profit and God are still a few years away, but this self-improvement stuff has been around in one way or another since the Bible, and the Wynotsky Schools for Elocution and High-Toned Betterment ("We are in a town near you!") are certainly part of that trend. Why, after Wynotsky you could sound like Edwin Booth.

In 1911, Peter Evelyn Ruester is born. His childhood hero is General George Custer. "He had the courage of his convictions and took a 'last stand' and he got killed for believing so strongly that he was right." Ruester, who speaks admiringly of Custer until his death, is never to know that Custer was a homosexual and was in love with an actor. Peter Ruester is to become an actor himself before he becomes a president. He brought his own crusading background with him into politics. He was a man who adhered strictly to the Bible as interpreted by his mother, who even took him with her to proselytize in prisons, "so that all may see the world as Christians." He taught Sunday school, went to a Christian college, and tithed 10 percent of every dollar he ever made to his church until his death. Or so it's said.

Yes, this is a Pay Attention moment, to this birth, this man.

In 1913 the Eugenics Research Association is founded out of the Eugenics Record Office on Mrs. Harriman's land. Charter members only are allowed, each a generous benefactor "determined to escalate our work into action." A list is made of the particular topics of concern on which these charter members, numbering sixty-three, wish to concentrate. One of the top items of interest is labeled "Sexual Abnormalities." At the next tea in her lavish home, a representative from the Tally Office, the aging Eagan Odemptor, is again present. "This is a moral issue of the highest order," Eagan declares. "I have devoted my entire working life to dealing with it. My devoted associate of all these years, Turpa Diamond, gave her life to it. I have been sent to tell you that President Taft approves of your sincere activities, although of course he will not say so publicly. He has also quite humbly requested that you remove 'the obese' from your categories of concern for rectification." A representative from Nordic Race Supremacy, Hirst Gillie, says in his remarks, "It will be a hard job turning everyone's skin white and everyone's hair blond. It will be a harder job locating those males who persist in using their most personal of instruments on each other. I have no doubt that we can succeed on this latter if not the former. I bring you word from Angstrom, North Dakota, that they have terminated the lives of twelve sodomites and twelve niggers of light skin passing as white."

None of this is a secret. The records of the ERA and the ERO are housed in the Willis Collection at Yaddah.

Jeshua Brinestalker also accepts the first vice presidency of the ERA. "Might as well keep my eye on everything, not just horses," he writes to Gillie. "I think we're on to something grand, don't you?"

Where *does* this Jeshua Brinestalker come from?

We don't know. Much of this country consists of people to whom this curt statement applies. One day they are not here and another day the land records of San Diego and Orange counties list Brinestalker holdings of more than half a million acres. Inheritance? But from whom? Theft? Corruption? Forgery? Probably, and possibly all three. It was easy to perform—or should we say arrange—deeds of any sort in California in those days. California was far enough away from eastern morality, if that is what it can be called, or from eastern watchdogs at any rate. Really quite amazing, all this land owned by someone no one knows much about. One wonders how much of America is this historyless. Or stolen, or out of the blue. That's why historians wind up finding ways to put their own view of things front and center. Pay dirt is often just that, dirt, for lack of anything cleaner. Well, as we're seeing, there is never anything cleaner.

Does no one wonder how such stalwart stock of such an Aryan disposition should appear in advance of World War I? Are Jeshua and his son, Nehemiah (there appear to be only the two of them), establishing some sort of American beachhead, should America win, or lose? We know now that this certainly is a trick much utilized, particularly in advance of wartime. A trick to do what? To achieve what? For whom? But who could have been this farsighted? So early on? Farsighted about what?

In any event, Brinestalker, the father, is also in attendance in 1912 when Dr. John Harvey Kellogg of Battle Creek, Michigan, founder in 1906 of the Race and Betterment Foundation, organizes the First Race Betterment Conference to lay the foundation for his version of a super race. "We have wonderful new races of horses, cows, and pigs. Why should we not have a new and improved race of men?" Kellogg demands. At the Second Race Betterment Conference, held the following year, Brinestalker is there to hear the Yaddah economist Irving Fisher say, "Gentlemen and ladies, you have not any idea unless you have studied this subject mathematically, how rapidly we could exterminate the contamination of this country if we really got at it, or how rapidly the contamination goes on if we do not get at it." A particularly stirring and insidious oration about "race-suicide" is delivered by David Starr Jordan, that first president of Stanford University, a virulent anti-Semite and a "major influence inflaming Henry Ford's 'insane prejudice,'" according to Neil Baldwin in *Henry Ford and the Jews*. In his book *Unseen Empire and the Reversion to a Hideous Past*, Jordan writes about the necessity of ridding the world of "splintered men who claim to be men, but who are not men, and cannot be men." Yes, life was like that. Christians spoke like this. You could say things like this out loud then. But let us return to Mrs. Harriman.

•

At Mrs. Harriman's next gathering, Odemptor from the Tally Office denies government involvement when questioned by Mrs. Ianthe Adams Strode, a young relative of Teddy's married to a rising government official, who raises her hand to "modestly" say that she finds "much of what is transpiring here today distressing." She leaves after she realizes there is no support for her position. Mrs. Adelphia Heinz, another rich woman, this time from Pittsburgh, cries out, "Whoever she is, let that heathen unbeliever go! We must not be put off our mission! We must purify our own midst." There is much applause and Adelphia, a handsome woman beautifully dressed in the latest from Paris, actually gets up, smiles, and takes a little bow. "Thank you," she says. "It is good to know and feel that we are all in this together."

Then the crowded living room adjourns to the handsome dining room to partake of another one of Mrs. Harriman's famous teas.

Intelligent people flock to jump on board with one group of eugenics "experts" or another. "Wholesale reproductive prohibition" becomes the widespread battle cry, the goal, the activity, the act.

Slowly and quietly the euthanasia of newborns has begun across the country. It had always existed, of course—how could it not?—but now physicians and obstetricians are taking the initiative, feeling more and more that right is on their side. Get rid of all those unwanteds. Kill them! Murder them! What are you calling murder? We are doing God's will. And Teddy's, too, of course. It is all so wholesome and wholesale.

Edwin Black hurls this at today's reader:

> The men and women of eugenics wielded the science. They were supported by the best universities in America, endorsed by the brightest thinkers, financed by the richest capitalists. They envisioned millions of America's unfit being rounded up and incarcerated in vast colonies, farms, or camps. They would be prohibited from marrying and forcibly sterilized. Eventually—perhaps within several generations—only the white Nordics would remain. When their work was done at home, American eugenicists hoped to do the same for Europe, and indeed for every other continent, until the superior race of their Nordic dreams became a global reality.

Strummer and Evinrude get more grimly to the point:

> Seventy-three male bodies were uncovered buried in a mass grave some one hundred miles north of Witchita, Kansas. Add to these the twenty-seven female bodies found buried twenty-five miles further north. These graves were staked out with visible black crosses, dated March 1, 1913, and labeled "These sexual perverts are dead courtesy of the Kansas Eugenics Institute." Similar gravesites are found in Alabama, Michigan, Long Island, California, Washington, Oregon, and Louisiana. According to research done by the Magillis Foundation, documents found in the archives of forty-seven states indicate complicity in similar acts. In Detroit, in 1918, there will be a massive rally of more than ten thousand against "all sodomites in this city and anywhere near us." Ten thousand!

Homosexuals probably owe their relative obscurity for the time being to the simple fact that people are still unfamiliar with this word and don't know what homosexuals look like. Effeminate men and masculine women have been a part of the social fabric forever; everybody's family probably has one. Up to now few have given them much notice. Certainly they have not been considered as dangerous as the descriptions now beginning to be their lot, descriptions not fit for family newspapers, though that is where they now appear. Witness this editorial from Tulsa's *Oil Derrick and Advertiser*: "Now we know a lot of families have got an old maiden auntie living upstairs with her old girl friend Tess, or an old Uncle Albert swishing around the house with his old pal Buster, all of them kissing everyone 'Hello, you cute thing, you' with their sloppy lips. What we didn't know is that these people are doing things *with each other* behind our backs that are degenerate and dangerous and we got to get rid of them fast or our city and our country is going to go to hell like our preachers tell us. They are sticking things into each other, unnatural things, and that is all we can say."

So it has not been long before numerous vicinities and states, beginning with Virginia, pass laws authorizing sterilization. Get those homosexuals while they are still in the mother's womb. Over these years extraordinary energy is devoted to locating "the targeted." One can do no better than to again quote the stalwart, vigilant Black:

> At any given time there were hundreds of field workers, clinicians, physicians, social workers, bureaucrats and raceologists fanning out across America, pulling files from dimly lit country record halls, traipsing through bucolic foothills and remote rural locations, measuring skulls and chest sizes in prisons, asylums and health sanitariums, scribbling notes in the clinics and schools of urban slums. They produced a prodigious flow of books, journal articles, reports, columns, tables, charts, facts and figures where tallies, ratios and percentages danced freely, bowed and curtsied to make the best impossible impression, and could be relied upon for encores as required. Little of it made sense, and even less of it was based on genuine science. But there was so much of it that policymakers were often cowed by the sheer volume of it.

Thus are laws passed and acts acted upon. And many are the bodies of men hauled out of their beds by vigilantes in the middle of the night to be sterilized, or to disappear entirely. And of pregnant women, unmarried and poor, who also disappear entirely. Kill two birds with one stone that way.

What they would not know then, anybody, is that the world's population has now reached 2 billion people, more than enough to encourage their crying out in alarm.

DAME LADY HERMIA'S RESEARCH ON BRINESTALKERS

Brinestalker, the son of Jeshua, is a big child, as he was a big baby, and then he is a tall youngster, a tall teenager, soon a tall young man. He is always the tallest in his class, the tallest among those his age, who cannot be called his friends because he does not appear to have friends and he does not appear to want them. His father, Jeshua (there does not appear to be a mother), pays little attention to his only son, whom he says he had while much too young; there are only twelve years or so between them. The son appears to like himself the best, which is perhaps a good thing because there's no one else around to like him, including his father, traveling as much as he does for his eugenics concerns. The son appears perfectly happy by himself. The ranch does have other young boys and girls, but they are the children of the worker cowboys, and his father's offhanded, almost dismissive treatment of them indicates clearly that they are not good enough. He dislikes his first name, Nehemiah, and so from the age of twelve until his death he calls himself only by his last name. Brinestalker he now is.

When he is thirteen, Brinestalker murders his first young man, Owen Rivera, who is his own age and very effeminate. His father has quoted the president as giving him permission to get rid of trash. He chokes the boy to death out in the wilderness where he has ridden him on his horse. They have had sex in distant Trocadero, far from the Brinestalker Ranch. "He made me sick, he was such a sissy. Why can't I find boys to do it with who are not such sissies? I am a man! I only want to do it with other men!" He keeps notes on all of this, as he does until he dies. From this time on he wants to do something about what he believes men should be. Does he have hopes and ambitions, the son? He does know, as he realizes when he has choked to death his fourth or fifth sissy after they have had sex in the wilderness, that he cannot go on doing this to every young person he has sex with who he thinks is a sissy. There appear to be too many of them and besides he will get caught, not that anyone appeared to claim their sons. In fact, he senses that he's doing them a favor, getting rid of what they don't know how to get rid of but would like to. He must find masculine men. He will believe all his life that somehow, perhaps by divine intervention, he saved himself from an awful fate when he came to "my senses" and stopped actually killing the kids. He felt better about himself then, even though his father often instructed him: "Do not be fooled by a belief in the future. Remember Horace. 'To be forewarned is to be forearmed.'"

Horace! That is very touching. I was not shown that touching addition to our joint notes when they were redacted for my perusal. Mr. Carpe Diem Seize the Day Horace. Mr. Most Virtuous Man in the Ancient World Horace. Mr. I Owe It All to My Wonderful Father Horace. Quintus Horatius Flaccus was his real name, which of course he used while we do not. Jeshua as a classicist? Poo.

I bring up this issue. Why is all this being related in such a leisurely, nay gossipy, fashion! How long does it take to cut to the chase, as you people say! A plague is growing in our backyard! Why don't you include right now that Jeshua Brinestalker was a perverse freelance spy, for Germany, for Russia, Poland, Austria-Hungary, Lithuania, Estonia, Latvia, the Baltic states, for all those cold harsh countries nervous about The American People, which many northern countries are. He was planted in this country with his newborn son years earlier, probably around the turn of the century, when he was no more than fifteen, and that the wife you casually ignore was, like Benjamin Franklin's, a perfectly fine woman who was robbed of her son and left where found, in this case some small town in Germany, and never seen again, and that Hubby, once he got to America, proceeded, out there in the wilderness, to "eugenicide" one by one every woman he ever brought there to sleep with, and he was insatiable. They are still, one hundred years later, digging up newly discovered bodies on the Brinestalker Ranch. Where are your notes that would speed the narration of this horrid tragedy along while you keep clip-clopping around without a plan of action? At this rate we shall never get to The Underlying Condition! Great-Uncle Silas insisted that one flaunt the knowledge one acquires, and I am proud to show off my Brinestalker discoveries.

It is this father who will funnel all of this eugenics information to the young Hitler! WHAT ARE YOU WAITING FOR? Hitler will be most impressed by what he learns from his friends in America, chief among them Henry Ford, who probably financed all the land acquired for those damned horses on the Brinestalker Ranch, a cover if ever there was one. God knows what kinds of experiments were being performed on those women before

Daddy murdered them. Now can we get our asses in gear, as you Americans also say? These repulsive gentlemen, the killer father and his killer son, with their peculiarly repellent name, are not worthy of a quote from my beloved Horace!

Did you seek out the most estimable Ianthe Adams Strode, who knew Brinestalkers *père et fils* and was an attendee at Mrs. Harriman's, proudly antagonistic in the face of so much opposition?

If we are all going to work together on this we are going to have to get our ducks in order. You do know the world has a way of ending before it begins!

OVER THERE

World War I is a waste of time and lives. "The most futile slaughter in the history of warfare," says the historian S. J. Taylor in *Stalin's Apologist*. "It was generally agreed that the press's performance during the war had amounted to one of the most thoroughgoing cover-up jobs in the history of wartime coverage." Millions die. Little is accomplished. Little is learned. There is no interruption in the back-and-forth flow of nasty secrets, illicit desires and schemes, bald and bold determinations to do ill. It doesn't get us anywhere, this war, and it doesn't help anybody. Time just stands still for the longest while, during it and after it. It is about a lot of foreigners who hate each other and can't get it out of their system without dragging in the whole neighborhood, which just happens to be much of the "civilized" world. Many who got us into it look really stupid. Enough powerful people manage to employ enough "reputable" historians to write it their way and get them out of the mess with clean hands. The Brits are the dumbest. The Germans, no fools, are the best manipulators in all of history, and know how to play everyone else royally, as they will do yet again in only a few years' time. Nothing that happens during the First World War, the 14–18 War, the Great War as the British still love to call it (Great for whom? Great for what?), makes the world a better place. (But then what war could?) Hate, as it shows itself during this war, is not the true hate that's just down the road. Right now it is only enmity, to be followed in a few years by a most disillusioning and well-deserved Great Depression, which is what we love to call it. Who wouldn't be depressed by and after this stupid, useless war?

In a trenchant article in *The New Gotham*, subtitled "Historians rethink the war to end all wars," its correspondent Adam Gopnik says among many other things that World War I "was an utter and futile massacre . . . that indicted the entire civilization that followed it," "meaningless horror . . . not worth the fight."

Eight million lives were lost.

Seven million days of active duty were lost by the military to sexually transmitted diseases.

In his most pertinent closing indictment, perhaps against all the historians over the years who have "normalized" this war to make it sound worthwhile, Gopnik writes, "It requires a determined mental effort to recall that what happened was not an entry on a tally sheet but the violent death of a human being, loved and cared for by a mother and father, and full of hope and possibility, torn apart by lead balls or shreds of sharp metal, his intestines hanging open, or his mouth coughing blood, in a last paroxysm of pain and fear. And then to recall that any justification for a war has to be a justification for this reality."

The First World War, the Great War, can in no way be justified. Perhaps the only "positive" note that might be entered on the ledger is that it kept the Germans busy enough, for a while, to stop their forward march in partnership with America to killing the world eugenically.

Your Roving Historian points out that for the first time American homosexuals who are in the fighting forces overseas experience the freedom of enjoying each other. It is as if, in leaving home and all that, they are set free. There's no one to stop them from that "on-the-job training" (as the Army will come to call it in its enlistment propaganda by World War II), "where our fighting men learn by doing." You bet. If it meant risking your life to get laid at last, well, since the beginning, life's been a crapshoot for hushmarkeds, hasn't it? When Philip Jerusalem, who will father Daniel and David and Lucas and Stephen, hits France for the war's last year, he can't believe it. No man could. Even for a shy man, it's a movable feast. Whether they were homosexuals or not, sex was everywhere—in the barracks, in the streets—and with everyone and first come first served and all that sort of thing. In this case, when the end of the world feels definitely closer than it does in Oshkosh or even Manhattan, what's the expression? "Every man for himself and the devil take the hindmost." For the first time Philip likes getting fucked. Amos was never as gentle and loving as all the warriors wandering the Paris streets looking for love. He almost doesn't want to go home. He has no idea what he'll do. Here he knows what to do, and is doing it.

•

**It was certainly a waste of my time. I tried my best to suck up their poi-
sons into my poison and spew them back, everywhere from Flanders
Field to the Maginot Line. Couldn't do it. This war *was* a major disappointment. I had to travel so far to come back with so little. Why aren't
I infecting more of them? Is it me? Am I doing something wrong? It's
just that they were being mowed down so fast!**

A TOUCH OF FLU

"Twenty million people died during the flu pandemic of 1918. That figure is
still used in classrooms and textbooks, but as John M. Barry tells us in *The
Great Influenza*, it's certainly too low. Modern experts say that 20 million
may have died in India alone, and they calculate the total number of victims
at somewhere between 50 million and 100 million worldwide" (*The New
York Truth Book Review*, March 2004). It reached America last, where an
estimated 25 million people, a quarter of the population, contracted the disease, some half a million fatally. On October 1, 2005, the *Truth* pinned the
worldwide figure down a bit more: "the 1918 pandemic of Spanish flu . . .
killed 2.6 percent of those who got sick, or about 40 million people." Among
those it took were people we've already met, albert briefly: Mrs. DeWitt
Waldschein, the enthusiastic eugenics crusader from Milwaukee; seventeen
young men working on the Brinestalker Ranch; Noramae Petrie, who worked
at the ritual baths for the Orthodox Jewish women in Washington; and two
social workers—Edna Squats, now working in the Midwest, and Rose
McPherson Reddicher, just settled in on Park Avenue from Staten Island.
President Woodrow Wilson wondered why NITS "let us down; it must
not happen again." His implication, which he spelled out to his wife, the
stalwart Grace, was "If they could all live through it, why couldn't we do
better than we did?" Instead of increasing the NITS budget, he saw to it
that they were penalized for their "less than stellar record," as he quietly told
another new NITS chief, Dr. Alden McDonald, who promptly handed in
his resignation, telling the *Monument*, "If that's the kind of faith our president
is going to display toward us, I thought it best to quit while I was ahead."

Velma Dimly, also in *The New York Truth* (this newspaper dauntless in
getting "facts" on record even after Walter Lippmann's eventual exposure of

extreme ineptitude in this paper's history, see below), will write in March 2006, "It was the worst infectious disease epidemic ever, killing more Americans in just a few months than died in World War I, World War II, the Korean War, and the Vietnam War combined. The virus arrived at even the most improbable places, like isolated Alaskan villages. In one such village, 178 of its 396 residents died during one week in November, after a mailman arrived by dog sled, delivering the virus along with the mail." The flu "struck the United States and parts of Europe hard and traveled to every corner of the world except Australia and some remote islands. A few months later, it vanished, burning itself out after infecting nearly everyone who could be infected . . . [particularly] young adults in their 20s, 30s, and 40s."

•

Vanished, ha ha ha. Vanished, she says. We reckless ones do not vanish. We may take a break now and then, just for you to let your guard down. Not everyone was dying from the flu. They just thought they were.

ONCE MORE INTO THE BREECH

Another soiree at Mary Harriman's. She cares so much. They do go on and on, her teas. Mary loves to invite people over to discuss how to get rid of other people. Someone tried to schedule the discussion to include "Why does Henry Ford hate the Jews so much?" Someone gets up to report that 120,000 Jews have passed through Ellis Island. Mary wishes she could remember every guest's name, but she can't, not anymore, but then everyone appears to be bringing someone else now, and while she has a big house, and has already opened her connecting second living room to manage the overflow, still and all she is wondering if future meetings should be held in a larger venue. Ianthe, still game for being the only one with an opposing view, chirps out with her growing ability to bring irony and humor to the fore ("gallows humor" it will be called one day). "If Henry put half as much energy into his automobile factory as he did into promoting hatred of the Jews and their elimination, he would encounter no competition whatsoever." Of course no one gets the joke, much less the irony, and Ianthe wonders, as she always does, if she should continue to traipse up from Washington for any more of these things. But today she learns that Mr. Rockefeller personally sends a report that he has donated almost half a million dollars to German researchers and $317,000 to build, in Germany itself, an institute for race biology. "A young Kraut scientist by the name of Josef Mengele, still wet behind his perfect ears, has come to extend his country's personal thanks," Ianthe notes in her own notes. (After World War I everyone starts taking notes.) "He speaks with the aid of an interpreter. He himself is from the Max Planck Institute, which elicits applause. Mengele reports that John D., ever on the alert, has placed in charge one Otmar Freiherr von Verschuer, and everyone here ooohs and aaahs when hearing his 'famous' name; Verschuer is evidently already promising 'a total solution to the Jewish problem.' 'We are sterilizing up to 5,000 per month. Mr. Hitler sends his regards and thanks. He is most impressed with your work and what he is learning from you.' A new face claims to be visiting from Michigan, which now boasts of having 875,000 members in its chapters of the Ku Klux Klan. He claims that Mr. Ford is commencing a ninety-one-part series, 'The International Jew: The World's Problem,' for publication in his newspaper and for anyone else who wants to read it."

This new face, a nice-looking fellow, Mary thinks, teaches at Yaddah and reports that the university's president, Lawrence Lowell, is determined to cleanse the school of shameful homosexuals. "A secret nest of them has been discovered and so far three of them have been so shamed they have taken their own lives, and seventeen of them have resigned from the school, before they could be officially expelled, of course."

"Fancy that," Ianthe pipes up. "We must send a letter of official thanks to Larry Lowell for doing our job for us." She realizes that, once again, no one gets her joke when her words receive applause.

Jeshua Brinestalker has sent his regrets and Mr. Odemptor appears to have died. When Mary is about to adjourn the meeting and direct everyone toward her tea and petite cucumber thingees in the adjoining smaller salons, one Henry Gerber, a man with a face and composure that indicate he has been through a lot, speaks up about Henry Ford. "We never did fully discuss this man and his activities and whether they are useful to your cause or not. Why exactly does he hate Jews so much, all Jews, and with such passionate obsession? Is there anyone here who would like to speak to that?" No one there wishes to speak to that. Mary wonders how that Gerber chap got in. She never quits marveling about the wonders of democracy.

But the rush for Mary's famous finger thingees is on.

SOMETHING TO DO WITH TRUTH

I want to get back to Doris and bring Abraham Masturbov front and center, because Mordy will be one of our central characters, indeed one of history's more important ones as well, and Abe's his father. Abe also wants to be Doris's husband, and . . . well, let me try to tell it in a little better order. It's really Lucas Jerusalem who's the expert on Abe's story. Over the years it's been Lucas who's told Daniel Jerusalem many of the little bits and pieces that are put together here. I may be going back further than necessary in laying out the backstory, but if this is the prime complaint against me, I shall remain consistent to my belief that all is better than less than all. (Sorry, Dame Hermia. I remind you once again that this is *my* history of the plague.)

Abe meets Doris Hardware in 1925, on a business trip to Baltimore, where she's living. He sees her on the street. She's walking toward him. He wants her the minute he sees her, with a pain that takes him by surprise. He's never associated sex or desire or attraction with pain. But then he is only fifteen years old—well, almost sixteen—and still a virgin. She has red hair, as does he, and she seems electric, radiating enormous confidence, in her walk, her looks, her clothing, which is of some new fashion, rolled-down stocking tops and skinny skirts that are made of shiny stuff like beads and strips of satin colored to match high-heeled shoes and sequined bags. She looks like everything modern and tomorrow, and she smiles at everyone and the day. She looks wonderful, she looks like she feels good, and she makes you feel good, too.

Abe is walking down this street trying to make a few bucks searching for vacant lots. He's a scout for his late father Herman's old real estate associate, Goldowsky, a rich New York Jew who believes that his money can yield growth only *away* from New York, where all those other Jews, the nosy noisy ones, will see what Goldowsky is buying and beat Goldowsky to the punch. Goldowsky is a quiet Jew. He says there's no room in New York for a quiet Jew to spread his wings and fly. All this means is that the past and present foundations of Goldowsky's fortune are more suspect than those of others, which are often disreputable enough. Real estate is one of those businesses where much can be hidden. Goldowsky believes the future is "out there," away from prying eyes. He would have moved south years ago but for his late wife, who thought the South wasn't kosher.

Goldowsky was also a good friend of Herman Masturbov. They were both members of the Council of Jews, big-deal Jews whose names are well-known. You don't have to be rich to be on the Council of Jews. You have to have done something. Goldowsky did something. He built the synagogue for Jewish lepers.

This was not so charitable as it sounds. (Not that charity affects your membership.) Six Goldowskys were lost in the Fruit Island massacre. Their descendants have convinced themselves that all the Fruit Islanders were lepers, and that this is why they were there, and why they were put to death. Well, Goldowsky is terrified that he is a carrier of the Goldowsky gene, that one day before he dies the gene will assert itself and announce, Bam! Goldowsky, you're a leper.

He owns a lot of land in Brooklyn and Queens. He thinks these are very ugly places, these "boroughs," and even if they are profitable and people are slowly moving there to make him even richer, he isn't proud of owning such ugly land, with belching fumes from plants processing this and that. Jews are supposed to feel good when they walk their land. Goldowsky doesn't feel good when he walks Brooklyn and Queens. Goldowsky doesn't like ugly things, although he is short and squat ugly himself, and knows it.

The synagogue for lepers was really an accident. It's a horrible story. One day his only son, Neil, writes him from the trip around the world that he's been taking, forever, it seems to his father. He has met a wonderful woman and he wants to marry her. He says she is Jewish. Goldowsky, only recently elected an officer of the Council of Jews, is trying to live a life of higher consciousness. He senses immediately that God is finally blessing him. Neil has previously been nothing but trouble. Neil writes that he met Harriette in Hawaii and will pick her up on his return voyage and bring her home for the ceremony.

Goldowsky undertakes to build a small synagogue, a jewel, to celebrate the happy news. He pulls out all the stops to build it before the couple returns. He builds this synagogue in Kretzky Fields, a swamp far out in Queens. He camps out beside it while it is being built. He won't leave the vicinity. When it's finished and consecrated by the chief rabbi, Goldowsky prostrates himself on the stone floor and won't get up. He lies there for days with no food or water entering him and no elimination leaving him. Because he remains so still, and because he requires nothing, and because he is prostrate on the floor of a soon-to-be-consecrated holy place, he is thought to be in some sort of special and holy, if slightly irregular, communion with

Yahweh. Please, God, Goldowsky is said to have prayed over and over, make him a good son. Make her a good wife. His own wife, Neil's mother, disappeared mysteriously after he saw her gallivanting with another man.

At last Neil returns. The daughter-in-law-to-be's name is Harriette Slake. This is both an old Hawaiian name and an old Jewish Hawaiian name, Neil says. Goldowsky didn't know there were Jews in Hawaii. Where did they come from? What kind of Jew would call himself Slake? Evidently, his son tells him, Slake, in the Pertoo dialect of the northern island where Harriette's family settled, and where they now own much land, is a lucky name meaning "to cool or refresh by wetting or moisturizing," which is why the Slakes changed their name from Grebetz when they first came to Hawaii.

Harriette Slake is hideously ugly. Her skin is like the curdle on top of old cream. How could his only child bring him such a hideous living thing? Is this what his grandchildren will look like? Goldowsky returns to lying prostrate on his shul's cold marble floor. God is not rewarding him. God is punishing him.

No matter how long Goldowsky lies on the floor, Harriette doesn't go away and Harriette doesn't get any prettier and his son doesn't change his mind. At least Neil is keeping her inside the house as they prepare for the ceremony. With no cosmic movement and no sign coming from God, Goldowsky finally gets up from the stone floor, brushes the specks of debris from his best-Jewish-tailor-in-the-city-made clothing, looks up at Heaven, and asks out loud, "Why did you do this to me?"

He gives the bride away. The synagogue is filled for the first time. Harriette is heavily veiled. In the entire synagogue, only Goldowsky and his son have seen her face. (The dressmaker will talk! I must pay her off. And the shvartze cleaning lady! Who else?) All Goldowsky's business associates and their wives ooh and aah over the lovely bride. The son, even though he is handsome, certainly a god next to his father, is shorter than Harriette. Why is he marrying such a tall woman? He is smiling happily. Goldowsky is saying to himself, God only knows what is going on inside his head! How can he shtup her tonight? How?

The wedding is over. The guests are gathered for the breaking of glasses and the eating of food. Naturally, Goldowsky waltzes Harriette around. Out of deference to the bride there are young women in grass skirts doing the hula. He dances her around and around. He dances her faster and faster. She must be getting dizzy, because he is. He dances her out of the nitzvah.

He dances her through the holy platkes. He winds up with her, alone, in the vitz.

He strangles her dead. He puts her body in a waiting coffin. The coffin is spirited away by hired henchmen, into the dark night.

Goldowsky walks back to the festivities, beaming like a new father.

He takes out an envelope from his custom-made cutaway.

"I must read to you a letter from Harriette. 'Dear New Friends, I have an important confession to make to you. I am not Jewish. Since I did not wish to be condemned by God in this handsome new synagogue that was built by my kind and generous father-in-law, Mr. Goldowsky, I think it best to admit this important fact and bid you all goodbye until we meet again in Heaven.'"

The son is beside himself. He suspects immediately that his father has tricked him and done an evil deed, even before the son could trick the father.

For what the father does not know, even after he chokes her to death, is that Harriette was really a young man, and that she was so ugly because his face was made up poorly and the hairs yanked from his skin had brutalized his complexion. Only the sheitel, the wig that all orthodox women wear in public, had managed to disguise him under his heavy veils, which he wore unto his very death.

Goldowsky believes his son will now return to being a son, that he will stop traveling to far-off places where there are Slakes, and come into the business like all sons are meant to do, particularly when there is so much money. But no, the son goes off, never to be heard from again. He had wanted very much to marry a man in a temple. Perhaps he has.

"Who cares? Who cares?" Goldowsky asks himself many times over the years. "It was my bargain with God. I had to lose a dumb son or gain a hideous daughter."

This is why and how he comes to be so fond of Abe Masturbov, who is, no doubt about it, handsome and intelligent and ambitious and going places. Like a shipbuilder with a new craft, Goldowsky wants to send his vessel out into the stream to see if it floats. Soon Goldowsky can't remember what his own son looked like.

(In a short while, there being no Jewish lepers in this neighborhood requiring a place to worship, this whole building plus an outbuilding becomes a small hospital. But with no money to support it or local politicians with any interest in it, it will be transferred to New York to become the acorn from which springs Rubin and then Table Medical Center, more important for our concerns. You want history; here is history.)

In these earlier days of our country, there are many stories like these of Neil and "Harriette" and Abe and Doris. Men and women, often in the most unlikely combinations, meet and pick each other up and sleep with each other and marry each other, all within hours or days. It's such a big country, everyone is in a hurry to catch up with an America that's running ahead of all expectations. It's endless and open and so promising, and anyone with half a dream wants to get started immediately now that the Great War is over.

Besides, there may not be much time. People die young. There are always epidemics no one understands, coming out of nowhere, and natural disasters, too, and accidents, and of course wars. It may be the twentieth century, but life is just as mysterious and health just as ephemeral as it always was.

Doris sees Abe seeing her and wanting her. She is twenty, and almost a virgin. She is so full of confidence that she usually scares young men away. Young men rarely have such confidence at that age, or for years later, indeed in many cases for their entire lifetimes. She has confidence galore and nowhere to put it.

But Abe has confidence equal to her own. Her smile meets his smile, which has been infected by her so. She sees his confidence. She sees, too, that he is quite young. It doesn't bother her. She is surprised to discover she feels maternal toward him. She wants to take him in her arms and protect him. These are new feelings and reactions for her. Oh, he is cocky, staring at her, then coming straight up to her, bowing, offering his hand, giving his name, which she doesn't catch.

"Miss, please, you . . . you are . . . you are most attractive to me." And then he says quickly, "I know that must sound cheap."

"It's honest," she answers.

"I'll always be honest with you."

"Do you talk like this all the time?"

"No."

"You're very young."

"I'm young. And I'm poor. So far. But I have a future. I will be rich."

"Just like that?"

"It won't be just like that. Times are hard now. And will be for a while, I think. But I believe in myself."

"How do you know so much so young?"

"Being with you is telling me what to say."

"What a combination of truth and malarkey you are!"

"It's not malarkey."

She laughs at herself for a moment because without even thinking about it she has boldly put her arm through his. Her new dress has streaks of red and purple beads sewn into streaks of yellow, which she thinks of as sunbeams, and she loves this dress and feels like flaunting herself to the world. That is what a lovely dress is meant to do, make you kick up your heels and toss back your hair. He is tall and strong, with bold features, nose, ears, brows, and an awful lot of that red hair that tumbles in all directions. He looks very winning. Yes, she will flaunt herself. Why not?

Her family is in the West, in Denver, and in the outlying cow towns. They have sent her east to study, at Goucher in Baltimore, where a girl can learn without having her head filled with the kind of notions westerners think ruin anyone who goes too far east and/or north. She's finished four years of study in two. She studied economics and wants to go into business. She was bored and boredom worked her harder.

The Jew—she knows he's a Jew, Baltimore is filled with Jews, even Denver has a few, and they seem exotic to her if for no other reason than that you aren't supposed to like them—is handsome to her, certainly, but that isn't his appeal. He has opinions. He's strong. He can defend himself with his mind, in argument, in discourse. She approves. He sees all this.

By the time Lucas knows the whole story, Abe looks upon him as more his son than Mordy. Funny how sons get switched around among various father figures, like clothes that are handed down from the rich to the poor and sometimes fit them better. Lucas, who's been Abe's lawyer for as long as he's been a lawyer, has come to love Abe a lot, certainly more than Mordy, his own son, loves him. Mordy has trouble with love. Grandpa Herman's fortune doesn't help. Do all the Masturbovs have trouble with love?

Fifteen-year-old Abraham Masturbov marries twenty-year-old Doris Hardware outside Baltimore in a town called Jepsom, where almost anyone can get married quickly and legally. On the same day they sleep with each other for the first time, in a modest inn where almost anyone can get a room. Something is happening between them that they both realize is exceptional and probably won't ever happen with anyone else. It can't. First times are first times, and good first times are as rare as inheriting rubies and emeralds at birth.

"It wasn't just sex," Abe will later tell Dr. Shmuel Derektor. "We felt solid and united together. We said if we felt this way from the start, then it was a worthwhile gamble we'd do better together than apart. You know what she told me? She said she felt Jewish even though she wasn't Jewish. And I said what she felt was the part of Jewish that wasn't the bullshit part. The emotional. She felt stable. I wasn't so stable. Then or now. Not in business: there I'm a rock. She felt whole. Most women in my life never seem whole to me. I feel they've only got part of them to give. Most women I've known make me feel like a freak, like men are some sort of peculiar species. She made me feel equal."

Abe has to lie about his age. He has a forged birth certificate, not so difficult to get in those days. He's caught. Not by the justice of the peace or the clerk in the license bureau or any police or civic authority. By his mother. Who does not approve of the unseen and unmet and gentile Doris. Goldowsky tells her. Yvonne Masturbov sees to it that the marriage is annulled and that Goldowsky threatens to fire Abe if he continues with "such heathen fleisch." Having experiencd a slightly more dramatic version of the same story, Goldowsky plays his part well.

"What?" Abe sputters. "I just found you land that made you a profit of forty thousand dollars in three months. Where's my commission! Give me what you owe me."

"Honor your mother."

Abe can't bear it. There had been not one single thing standing between him and lifelong happiness. Now he holds a piece of paper from some lawyer that says he and Doris are not married. A piece of paper! Goldowsky has worked fast.

"We are flesh and blood!" Abe screams.

"That was then and this is now," Goldowsky says, although he cannot bear to meet the young woman's eyes. She looks lovely and she looks sad. So what if she's a shiksa. What is he saying! Abe is crying. Goldowsky walks past them both.

"I will see you in my office in the morning," he says to the air behind him as he leaves them.

Doris says little. Abe assumes, automatically, that he will find a way to make happiness return.

"You must not be discouraged at this, our first test," he says.

Again, she is surprised at her reactions. Never a quitter, always strong— why is she different now? She feels in the grip of some controlling force. She

waves her arms around, lifts her elbows up, as if to free herself from cob-
webs, or perhaps chains.

The operator in Abe takes over. "What you and I do is between us. No
one else needs to know. We'll live together until I'm legal. I can make money
without Goldowsky. You'll move to Washington. I know Washington block
by block. It's time for me to strike out on my own." He goes on describing a
future that sounds entirely plausible to him, and probably is.

She doesn't seem to be listening. Her mind is somewhere else. He recognizes the look. Yvonne. For a second he's frightened, but he shakes it off. He
can outsmart early misfortunes and confound past evils. He can dream.

Doris leaves a note for him at her rooming house. "I love you and I'm
sorry. Stay with Goldowsky." She has gone away, the landlady says.

Why did she walk out? Why did she walk out without talking? He can't
understand or accept the why, whatever it might be. He only knows to nego-
tiate, to hondel, to make deals that will please both sides. Goldowsky can see
his heart is broken. Goldowsky tells him all gentile women behave like this.
They don't know how to talk. They disappear in the middle of the night.
"Jew dames do nothing *but* talk. Forever. You wish they shut up." He feels
bad enough for the kid that he gives him part of the commission due him.
"I give you the rest when your momma says okay." Since when has Yvonne
got so much strength? Abe wonders. "You are all she has," Goldowsky answers
for him.

Through all the streets of their hand-holding the rejected suitor trudges,
imploring buildings, begging bricks, beseeching the empty night. Where are
you? Why, when perfection arrives, is it wrenched away? Love is holy and
precious and forever. How could she leave me if she loves me?

He never doubts for a moment that she loves him.

Wondering if he's come upon an unyielding characteristic of the gentile
mind, he vows he'll do business from now on only with Jews. And marry
only Jews. But he will fuck gentile women over and over and over. Gentile
fucks will continue to haunt him until his death. He convinces himself they
are better fucks. As Claudia will later plant her own seeds of perversity under
Stephen's skin, and under Buster Punic's, Abe has been infected by his own
first shiksa.

He thinks he can put her out of his mind. He thinks he can keep his
mind on vacant lots. He thinks lots of things that aren't possible. This infu-
riates him—that he is not master of himself, worker of his will—and so he

rushes out into the streets of every city where he goes on business for Goldowsky, New York, Philly, Wilmington, Boston, Richmond, Charleston, Savannah (he is afraid if he goes back to Washington he will murder his
mother and he will not go back to Baltimore either), and he grabs any shiksa
he can find, and he fucks until his cock is sore and then he fucks some more
until he thinks it must fall off and it should fall off if there is any justice in
the world, if there was a God it would fall off, for he is hurting himself and
he is hurting others. This is not even lust, it is escape, and there is no escape.
He fucks three, four, five times a night, in doorways, in strange smelly beds,
in putrid toilets, in back rooms of offices, on or under desks while bosses are
out and even sometimes when they are in but occupied elsewhere. He learns
to do it fast. He learns to do it endlessly. He fucks so many women he can't
remember if he might be doing it a second time with some of them, which is
something he never wants to do, lest he give them, and himself, some hope.
Only one per customer, ladies. As if he is working his way through all the
gentile women in America until he either finds Doris or punishes himself
enough for having failed her. Finds her? Every cunt he enters is Doris's
cunt. A few of the women enjoy the brutality, but it frightens most of them.
Some of them fight him, clawing his back until it's covered with welts and
sores and scabs, some of which never leave him. He is one battle-scarred
cocksman.

Finally, when he thinks he has no semen left inside him, or that he cannot be disappointed that yet another cunt isn't Doris's, he commits himself to
a plan. A simple plan. He's heard about some land in Northwest Washington, bits and pieces that everyone else thinks are not contiguous, and he
makes himself go back to that city and he uses the few thousand Goldowsky
has paid him to buy this land on instinct and hunch, convincing the seller to
give him a month's option. Then he turns right around and sells it to the
schmuck Isidore Schmuck, for a hospital yet, a medical center "bearing my
name."

Abe makes for himself an unbelievable sum, $100,000, and for a kid barely
sixteen, and he buys the biggest, most beautiful house he can find, a mansion
overlooking all of Washington from DesVrese Circle, a mansion built by two
lovers, Horatio Dridge and Clarence Meekly (the widow Meekly is old and
the house is too much for him). Abe signs the papers and makes the payment and he goes back to Baltimore. He stays in the Y and once again walks
the streets all day and all night, looking on mailboxes, in stores, offices, bars,
restaurants, asking, looking, seeking. He realizes how little he knows about

her life. All she told him was that she was from Denver and that she went to Goucher College, which won't even give him a clue on how to find her.

Denver! He is such a schmuck.

He rushes to a library, finds the Denver telephone directory, looks up Hardware, and is amazed to find seventeen of them. He runs to the railroad station, where there is a phone operator to help travelers with long distance. He calls the first Hardware, who tells him to call a second, who has no information but passes him on to a third, and finally there is a Hardware who is closer kin to Doris. The man tells Abe that Doris is living in Washington.

"Washington!"

"Who is this?"

Abe hears his own voice yell into the phone, going clear across this great wide country, all the way to a Denver that he is certain is a town fresh like honeysuckle blossoms and smelling sweet like Doris, now so close herself: "The man who loves her!"

"That so," the voice in Denver says. "Well, she's a very nice young woman."

"Yes. Yes, she is. She's wonderful."

"What's your name, young fellow?"

How do they feel about Jews in Denver?

"Please, could you give me her address?"

"If you love her, how come you can't find her?"

"We had a terrible mix-up! It's all right. It's going to be all right! Please! Please could you give me her address?"

He could only have sounded convincing in his youthful ardor.

The voice comes back across this great wide country. "It's 708 P Street, Northwest. Now, what's your name, young fellow?" The voice is a touch impatient.

"Thank you, sir. Oh, thank you! My name? My name is Abraham Masturbov."

Denver hangs up.

Abe rushes back to Washington, to the address in downtown, not far from where he himself grew up. It's funny, he thinks, that she instinctively found such a neighborhood. There is even a synagogue next door, one of those small ones in a tiny house, where a few families who don't get along with other families, or can't afford to, find their own place to pray. Hers is also a tiny house, fairly neat. There is no answer from the bell. He sits on the stoop. It is midafternoon. She comes home close to midnight. It is so dark outside he can't see her well. But he can smell her, and he can see her shadow walking like Doris. Oh, she is beautiful and desirable still, more than ever, dark or no dark.

So is he to her. She cries and cries, both outside, in the darkness of the night, and inside, in the darkness of her small rooms, a bedroom like a cell with a bed and a window overlooking the backyard of the synagogue, strewn with garbage, and an only slightly larger living room and kitchen where she makes him tea without saying anything as he just looks at her, speechless too, and turns off the lamp so the ugliness of the situation is not so harsh as to defeat them. He tries to gather her into his arms, but she pulls away.

"I'm sick," she says.

Abe finds Doris but he's not listening to her. She says she's sick but she looks even more desirable than his imagination allowed. She senses his hunger and she wants to say, Please don't be hungry, I said I'm sick. She tries. She plows ahead: "It's called a breakdown. Have you ever heard of a breakdown?" He just stares at her as her words come more swiftly. "I'm not quite certain what breaks down. I stare into space a lot and for a long time I couldn't leave this room. This is an awful room not to leave, but I didn't notice that. I was afraid to go out. I wouldn't eat and the landlady brought in a doctor, Dr. Israel Jerusalem, isn't that a lovely name, who got me to Dr. Shmuel Derektor. You Jewish men have all been so kind to me. Do you all try so hard to take care of your women? Dr. Derektor said . . . he said . . ." She is having difficulty with the lingo, which is like a foreign language. "He said I have trouble in my subconscious, underneath my ego . . . Have you heard of Dr. Sigmund Freud?" Abe shakes his head. If he is listening he is not liking, certainly not understanding: Does she want him back or not? Three doctors in one sentence (outdoing even his mother) and he is still only sixteen years old. Almost seventeen. "Well, he has revolutionary theories and he has a representative right here in Washington, Dr. Derektor, and Dr. Jerusalem says I am very lucky to be in on the ground floor."

"Dr. Jerusalem is my uncle," he says.

Now she isn't listening to him. She is on the couch at Shmuel's. "I lie down on a sofa and say whatever comes into my mind and memories keep coming, I'm flooded, I can't keep up with them, they pour out so fast, just from lying down and . . . it's called free-associating." She almost sounds like a little girl, except the words are very grown-up.

"Free?"

"I'm remembering terrible things. Awful things. Abe, awful things I haven't let myself think about ever." Now she is sounding like she's fifteen. "And I'm afraid." She comes to a dead stop.

"Like what?" He's shivering, a little afraid of what she might say.

She notices. "You're afraid of me now."

"Me? No. Never."

"Yes, you are. If I had a sore on my arm instead of in my head it would be different."

"No, it wouldn't."

Whatever is keeping her from accepting his answers as truthful upsets him. He doesn't like to have to beg people. They should just believe him.

Now he doesn't want to know what she found out. Why doesn't he inquire or at least sympathize? she wonders. All he really wants to say is, I have bought us a fine home. But he doesn't say anything. He wants some comfort too.

Suddenly she is screaming. "Stop looking at me as if I'm a freak! Why don't you take me in your arms? You should be longing for me as I have not for one second stopped thinking of you."

He can't speak. She stares at him staring. He doesn't know what to do. He wants her. He does the wrong thing. He takes off his clothes. Nakedness, he has discovered, is his best armor. Her eyes fill with tears. He feels cold and shrunken. He imagines his penis is the size of a baby's. He comes to her and starts to take off her clothes. Why do men think fucking is the answer to everything?

Abe fucks her, at first with great force and fury, trying to beg her with his insistent actions: Don't go crazy, don't do this to me, don't! Please let me have you the way I had you. But of course she doesn't understand, women don't understand reasoning like this, which can serve to make the other-worldly so mundane. She just lies there, not responding, trying not to let her memories completely destroy her. She must get herself to Dr. Derektor tomorrow.

Then his fucking turns to gentleness. He kisses her everywhere, softly, his cock turning from stone to a magic wand that wants desperately to bring her pleasure. She holds him close. She wants to say, Why do you think I am here, in your city? I came to look for you after I ran away.

They are both crying, blubbering, sucking in and out huge racking foul heaves of yesterday's uncollected shit.

"Every day is too precious to lose," he says to her. "I won't let you have a breakdown, again or ever. I'm angry you ran away. Promise me you'll never run away." He is simultaneously shaking and holding her, and hoping she will look at him. "I'm sorry," he suddenly hears himself say.

"For you or for me?" she asks him.

"I'm sorry, I'm sorry, I'm sorry, for you, for me, for both of us, for this world which could embrace two such wonderful people as you and me and instead does nothing but make us unhappy."

"I have never heard you talk so much."

His eyes are filled with tears. He is naked and he looks down at his cock, which has shriveled and now seems unimportant. "It even looks funny," he says out loud. "A redheaded Jew. We're very rare. Did you know that?" This for some reason makes them both laugh.

"So then why are you crying?" she asks.

"Because I think when we both know everything about each other, we'll scare each other to death. There's no virtue, so far as I can see, in honesty. The biggest crooks are the richest men. That much I can tell you for certain."

"How do you know so much so young?"

"You may think just because I'm so young that I don't know much about awful things. I do. And I'm going to tell you before you tell me. Not because I'm impolite, because I am not, but because I know your story must be awful. My story is awful, too. I want you to know that. Up front I want you to know that whatever you tell me I will still love you. That's why I want to talk first, not because of any selfishness but because more than anything I want you to still love me no matter what I tell you. Okay? May I put my story into the kitty first?"

He talks for several hours.

Abraham tells her the history of his family, the story of Herman the mohel and Yvonne the bleeder and Emmanuel the brother never seen who hanged himself. He gets lost in the telling: he is back in time witnessing many events he's only heard about, from Herman, from Nate Bulb, from Yvonne, on her better days, who now can't shut up about every symptom of her strange illness, and who regales her son each time she sees him with detailed descriptions of each bloody manifestation since his last stay at home, whenever that was, and from talkative old synagogue Jews he's met on Goldowsky quests, bearded ancients with little plots of land to sell, so that Abe puts the pieces of his past together as he assembles huge parcels for the likes of Isidore Schmuck. Sometimes he can't believe it's true, his patrimony.

When he finally finishes, when Herman is put into the earth and Yvonne returns to her tower, Doris, her back to him lest he see that she is ashen, takes her turn. It is the bleak quiet blackness now of just before the dawn, just before the question is answered: Will the sun come out? There is no light in the room, so perhaps they cannot see each other's face anyway, only hear each other's words.

"Now I think I understand why I respond to you so violently," she whispers. "We are the same. And perhaps there is some fateful force that brought us together. I believe it is this same force that will say we can never marry. Please . . ." She holds her hands over her ears lest he begin to protest. "Please hear me out."

And then she tells him her history. She tells him the story of Turvey, all of it. And then some more.

•

Horace Jr., my father, wasn't much of a talker either, and he was filled with hate as well. But his targets weren't so specific as Turvey's. Horace Jr. didn't think much about his country or his town; he hated himself. He didn't want to run this business, and maybe that was to his credit, except it wasn't for moral reasons that he wanted out. He had no compunctions about enslaving women or providing sex. No, he wanted freedom. He had the wanderlust, but his wife, my mother, Urvah—she was a Disciple of Lovejoy—enchained him with even more women he couldn't be free of. She made him marry half a dozen more. They all bore his kids. That house of a hundred rooms was pretty filled up, one way or another, by the time Urvah and her brood of Lovejoys got through with their moving in. I have no notion how many siblings I have. All this was against the law in Colorado and one day the law said No! and Urvah packed everyone up and went further west to where they came from. Horace and I stayed. Urvah tried to take me and I wouldn't go. Like Turvey, like Horace Sr., I'm the one kid who doesn't follow the rest.

I don't know how it all got so mixed up in both our heads. Perhaps because he was used to having so much sex with so many women, women who were at his disposal in the eyes of some church somewhere, a church that was sanctioned by a God he believed in as much as he believed in any god— perhaps because of all that, *something* said to him, Reach out your hand and take your daughter. And something inside of me said, Reach out your hand and take him back.

And I did reach my hand out and take his into mine, and hold on to it, not letting go.

I was smart. I loved being smart. I loved knowing all the answers to all the questions any teacher asked. I loved doing my homework and reading any book I could find. I loved being the only child. No, Poppa wasn't the most talkative man in the world, but we were all alone, just the two of us, and I was really lady of the house. I was ten years old when Momma left. I was eleven when she sent her first emissary to kidnap me and take me to Utah. The kidnapping almost worked, too. After that, Poppa saw to it I was properly guarded all the time. There were thick bars on my bedroom windows, and all kinds of trick traps all over the place. He took me out of regular school and hired me private teachers, and my classroom was in what he said was the safest place he knew of: one of his whorehouses. He moved me around from house to house; even I didn't know which week or day I'd have my lessons where. The net result was that not only did I get a thorough education and one to be grateful for, but I know whorehouses inside out, and women, too, let me tell you.

In the end I came to cry for most of these women. I came to love them, almost all of them, even the mean bitches. All those "whore with a heart of gold" stories told since the beginning of time—clichés come from truths. Every single woman was there because she felt she didn't have a rightful place anywhere else. The law doesn't protect women. Men don't protect women. Oh, they think they do! But it's only some male dream of dominance and it flits away in a breeze. These women, hundreds of them over the years, gave me more love than I'll ever have again. And I saw firsthand courage as great or greater than that displayed by any soldier on any battlefield, and more consistent too. Some went away, but they'd come back, if not to hook then to do anything that would allow them to stay inside the house. The house was safe. Hardwares from the beginning had made it safe. And this safety inside brought them together. I can't find the words to describe this feeling they all shared. Even though many of them hated each other's guts, each of them would fight like a tiger for each of her sisters against any impropriety from the outside world. I never saw such tenderness as when the girls tended someone who was sick or ready to give birth, or had to part with the baby after nursing, or was heartsick in love and ill used by a man who didn't care, which few of them did. I think it was because the act was so . . . *loaded* with implicit bravery—I mean, giving your body and being invaded by strangers for a fee is a violent striptease, of soul and flesh, a kind of nakedness and vulnerability that no one who doesn't do it can ever fully comprehend—that I came to have so much respect for all of them.

And I came to have respect for my poppa, who held it all together. This was his empire, as much as Mr. Rockefeller's oil and Mr. Vanderbilt's railways and Mr. Ford's automobiles. He was probably richer, too, though you won't see Horace Hardware, Jr., written up in any financial histories. Poppa was God the Father to these girls. He never let them down, which was how he earned their worship. He was always on their side. There wasn't a man, even if he might be right in an altercation, with whom Poppa would publicly side over one of his girls. Oh, I was proud of him! Wherever I was I ran to hold his hand the minute he showed up. And I reported to him, not about anything new I was learning from my schoolbooks, but about house news, who had said something so funny we'd all laughed for the entire day, or who had received a letter from the outside world and what was in it.

•

The telling is becoming increasingly difficult for her. Abe sees this and tries to comfort her; but she pushes away the arms trying to encircle her and warm her. "I am going to do this my way, calmly and without hysterics. You are my test case," she says, moving away from him. "When I see Dr. Derektor I am going to be able to look him straight in the eyes and say, 'I told Abe this whole story, the whole harsh and unlovely lovely story, and I didn't cry one stinking lousy second. I did it like an adult.'"

"It's OK to cry" is all he can get out before she puts her hand over his mouth to quiet him so she can proceed.

•

I said he violated me, my father. Yes, he did. He took me to bed as soon as I made up my mind that's exactly what I wanted from him. All the other girls had their special men, and Poppa was my special man, and it made complete sense to me that I would do with Poppa what they did with their favorites. Maidie and Ruta and . . . I guess most of the girls saw it coming and watched with caution and care. It wasn't that they thought it was wrong—there's very little that's "wrong" in a whorehouse or a whore's history: a body is a body and it's used in many different ways by many different people. Maybe God comes along for some and says such-and-such, but God is a superimposed morality that's got little to do with the here and now inside a whorehouse. No, they weren't concerned for the wrong, only for the potential hurt. They were forever protecting each other from hurt. Because the potential for hurt, for everyone, not just a little girl, is enormous. Tears are shed just as air is breathed and scent put on to cover the smell of sweat.

They saw I wanted it to happen. I wanted the physical love of my father. To me it was the most natural, sensible development in the world. He was the boss and I was one of his girls, the highest placed of his girls. I don't know if he saw it coming like they all saw it coming. I suspect one of the tougher ones—Alice or Pearla, Stutie, Matilda, there were quite a few who had the nerve to stand up to him, now that I think of it—pointed out to him what was happening and told him to give it some thought before he gave it some action, but he continued to let me hold his hand tightly when he showed up, and to let me dress older than my age when he took me out to a fancy restaurant downtown or to go shopping at the Emporium, where I could choose anything, *anything*, I desired. Can you see what a magical childhood I had?

•

Abe can't, but he says nothing. He thinks only of screams from upstairs rooms, and of blood, endless blood, and of what can happen when the wrong men and women chain themselves to each other for lifetimes of hell.

Doris isn't really looking to him for an answer. Her story has taken her to another time and place; she isn't with him; she is back in her father's arms.

•

I am twelve years old. That's not too early. (You weren't all that much older, with me.) I choose my birthday night as the night I will lure Poppa to my bed. He's given me a huge party, in the afternoon, on the lawn, hundreds of people from everywhere. The mayor is there. The sheriff. The governor of Colorado. An emissary from the president himself! My poppa invites all the important political people and I wonder if they know that the beautiful women they're mingling with, each in a new dress I've asked Poppa to buy them for my party, are all his lovely whores! They must know! I want them all to know!

Because this beautiful party is for me I am in heaven. I am one of my father's women. Oh, I know what their fortune is. To be on loan for the afternoon. To serve men, to be at their beck and call, and to be faceless, to be without a last name. It seems more important to me than ever that I be their savior, that I give them a last name and restore their pride. I don't know if I can explain it. I just know I've been given things that can prove useful to all of us, and that it's my responsibility to do all this, though I don't have a notion beyond bedding down the power that possesses all of us. That's the first step, and I know on my twelfth birthday that I want it to be this very night, for there can never be a night that completes a day on which I've been so happy and felt so pretty. I know how all the girls prepare their men, how if they're nervous, or worried, the answer is always champagne. I see to it that my father is champagned and ready, when everyone has gone, to carry his tired little daughter back to her suite and lay her down on her canopied bed. That's when I open my eyes and look at him, as a lover and not as a father. I reach up and brush his lips with mine. He grabs me in an embrace so hungry and so forceful that I know he wants all this, too. He comes into my bed and he stays in that bed with me for five years, until I come east to Baltimore and go to college there and meet you on the street, staring at me with the kind of hunger I understand.

•

Just letting all this out of her system again (the first time was for Dr. Derektor) makes her feel there is a certain comprehensibility to her story—that it can make sense, that it does make sense if she looks hard enough inside it, that she hasn't done anything wrong, and that, indeed, she can even find within it a pridefulness and courage and nobility.

Only . . . only . . . she is the only one who takes these qualities away from her experience. Abe doesn't say a thing.

SHMUEL

In 1910 a doctor opens a practice in Washington specializing in what are then referred to as . . . well, they aren't discussed out loud, so there probably isn't a descriptive name that's taken hold yet. *Nervous disorders* is too modern and *vapors* is too yesterday.

Freud has come to America on that famous visit to Clark University in Worcester in 1909; many of his disciples are now in place, mostly in New York, where else? Washington, as usual, is behind the times when it comes to taking care of personal business. Dr. Shmuel Derektor is Washington's lone pioneer. He studied with Freud in Vienna and went to visit him in Worcester, where he received the great man's permission to don his mantle in D.C.

Most people don't even know that emotional problems which are all in the mind exist. Exactly, Dr. Shmuel Derektor responds. Pioneers must proselytize, if not with facts then with convincing evidence of some sort via the cathartic guidance of words.

"There have always been illnesses whose symptoms are mental, not physical. For centuries doctors have been aware that not all maladies stem from physical ills. So why has it taken so long for someone to come along with help? Particularly here in Washington, where in some areas modern work is actually under way. The National Institute of Tumor Science is a good example. But then tumors are more specific and visible than diseases of the spirit. Is it, then, as if these inside-the-head things are not to be cured? Precisely how to treat the nonphysical has always been in dispute. You cannot just direct an X-ray at it and zap it from existence. But now, these new 'psychiatrists,' or 'psychoanalysts,' which is what I call myself, we doctors of the mind, now we are beginning to say that yes, that is exactly what you do to get better, zap the neurosis, for that is what the problem is called, with an X-ray, only in this case the X-ray is not radiation but words. Jokes are made about us and those who visit us are suspect. We are distrusted men. No, Mr. Abraham Masturbov, even though I know your intentions are honorable, I cannot discuss with you the problems of my patient. No, do not hate me. I am too weak and powerless to be hated. Why is that? I don't know why. Didn't our forebears, for centuries, lock helpless people up, or drown them in tubs, or shoot them full of poisons? But I am contradicting myself. Which is, of course, the essence of my treatment."

•

Abe is undeterred. First he finds them a bigger apartment. She isn't ready for the fancy mansion yet. Then he buys another parcel of land, which he quickly turns over for a profit. In this area he can do no wrong. Each potentially profitable deal is like a hunk of raw meat hanging in front of a voracious tiger named Abe. He is going to have more and more, and buy more and more, pieces of earth and devour this city. He is going to be so hugely rich that the word *rich* will no longer have any meaning for him, it will be so paltry in comparison. Money will make him feel good in a way that nothing else can. He fucks the land as he fucked every woman he could find looking for Doris. The old rich Jews smile. They smell a winner, for weren't they once like Abe themselves? They want to make deals with him. He scorns them. He only makes deals with himself. "In all my years of practicing law," Lucas told me, "I have never seen such hunger and determination for the absolute control of real estate and its nonstop acquisition. Do I think he would have amassed such wealth without Doris? I asked her once. She laughed and said of course Abe would have been Abe. But I know a softness to Abe, the softness she came to see and indeed rely on every day. They say that behind every powerful man there's a strong and influential woman. Doris certainly was and remains that to him."

Yes, Abe asks Doris to marry him. She says no. She must first finish her "analysis" with Dr. Derektor. She has much to analyze. She does not want it to stop. Finally, by the time the war comes along, she feels she is analyzed. She asks Abe for enough money to buy a big house in the best neighborhood in town. Yes, he tells her, it's time they bought a huge house in the Northwest and what she wants sounds perfect, with acres of gardens behind high walls protecting it from the outside world, though with a terrace overlooking all of town. Here they could live an idyll. He asks her again to marry him. He buys all the land surrounding the house so they can be in a completely private paradise. She asks him to put it all in her name. Everything. He gladly does so; in fact, it isn't such a bad idea, for the taxes, which the government is learning about and he senses will learn a great deal more. She is touched by his compliance with her requests. He does not tell her that he is selling her his own house.

And then she tells him that she is going to open a whorehouse. Here. In this new house. Her family has been in whorehouses for almost a hundred years by now.

Then she tells him that she and he are never to marry.

•

After the sessions with Doris, Dr. Derektor is overwhelmed by so many emotions. When she at last finishes telling him her story, he asks for some time off. She runs to him, tugs at his jacket, begs him to tell her for once what *he* is thinking, what comes into *his* mind! Finally he turns to her and raises his fist to threaten . . . what? God? The gods? Freud himself?

"Please, please," he says in a voice that whispers in its uncertainty, "I must think, I must consult, I must . . ." Dr. Freud and his many writings have somehow not prepared him for the stories of Doris and Abe.

For weeks he cancels his appointments with her. At first she thinks she will fall apart for good. He has been her life preserver. She fell apart and he put her back together. As his daily absences continue, she wonders if she'll break down again. She doesn't. Instead, she grows stronger, so strong as to become, she realizes, enormously proud of herself. In fact, it's not so long before she has no desire to see Dr. Derektor ever again. When he finally contacts her, not even with the courtesy of a phone call, just a curt note stating that he is prepared to resume their daily meetings at three, she tosses it in a waste-basket, and thinks no more about it.

•

So there you have the beginning of what will sarcastically be called the Sexopolis Case.

THANATOPSIS

Well, we have not exactly been paying much attention to health and hospitals and disease and plagues, have we? Or have we been paying too much attention to them, only not knowing it?

Dame Lady Hermia Bledd-Wrench contributes the following from her growing arsenal of irrefutable evidence of the evil that is afoot:

I was certainly too young to remember any of this. But that I was alive by the mid-1920s while this was going on has caused my blood to boil today. So many of intellect and caring had no inkling that any of this was going on!

Between 1912 and 1932 there are not only three major International Eugenics Conferences but a plethora of smaller ones. Eugenics is all the rage for People Who Want to Do Something for Humanity. (Am I beginning to sound too much like you, Frederick?) The Mary Harrimans, mother and daughter, are indefatigable with the generosity of their bottomless pockets, along with those of Mr. Rockefeller, who has taken a special interest in funding all things German.

American eugenicists have longed for twins to advance their research. Mr. Rockefeller funds this, and research on twins in Germany explodes, with Americans in this field crying out in alarm that "Germany is beating us at our own game." By now John D. Rockefeller and his foundation have donated almost $4 million to hundreds of German researchers to investigate what he does not see advancing fast enough in his own country. One of Mr. Rockefeller's favorite beneficiaries, that Otmar Freiherr von Verschuer, evidently a beloved eugenicist in both countries, who, even after all his hideous deeds, lives until a ripe old age in Munich and is even given distinguished medical and scientific awards, predicts that his work would yield "a total solution to the Jewish problem." Verschuer's longtime assistant is Josef Mengele, whose own new assistant will shortly be Gottmarr Grodzo. When eugenics will be declared, at last, a crime against humanity, those guilty will cite in their defense the "progressive" California sterilization statutes in operation since 1909 and subsequently expanded under the "leadership" of Jeshua Brinestalker.

The exceedingly cordial relationships between the American and the German eugenics movements and organizations are cemented by the publication in America of the two-volume *Foundation of Human Heredity and Race Hygiene* by Bauer-Fischer-Lenz. (It is only in Germany that Professor Fisher uses the "c.") The contributors are all major eugenicists, all intensely racist, and all filled with admiration and grateful acknowledgment for the inspiration from their dear fellow American friends, particularly Charles Davenport, the horse- and dog- and cattle-breeder founder of the American Eugenics Society, now run by . . . Jeshua Brinestalker and located only blocks from Yaddah's main campus in New Godding. Jeshua Brinestalker is aided by two prominent Yaddah faculty members, Irving Fisher, the influential political economist, and Ellsworth Huntington, a geography professor. The AES claims thousands of members from America's most prestigious universities and its ranks include some of the top thinkers of the era.

"Some people are born to be a burden on the rest" is a motto often used at their gatherings.

At one of their conferences, a speaker says, "There is a great human desire for purity—blue eyes, yellow hair, pink cheeks, tall stature, long head, long narrow face, high narrow nose . . . The only law worthy of consideration is one defining a white person as one with no ascertainable non-white heritage, and classifying a Negro as one with any ascertainable trace of the Negro."

Eugen Fischer, this two-volume tract's co-author, even becomes a member of the Carnegie Institution. It is these volumes that Hitler particularly admires. Someone sends a translation of them to him in prison. It will not be long before he will be writing, in *Mein Kampf,* "The demand that defective people be prevented from propagating equally defective offspring is a demand of the clearest reason and, if systematically executed, represents the most humane act of mankind. It will spare millions of unfortunates undeserved sufferings." By the time Hitler gets rolling in a few years' time, American eugenicists will be "intensely proud to have inspired the purely eugenic state the Nazis were constructing" (Black, p. 277).

By 1934 the Germans are sterilizing more than 5,000 a month, slightly outdoing the American states. (California alone had performed 9,782 sterilizations by 1925, Virginia, Kansas, and Michigan each more than 1,000, and twenty-nine states had eugenics laws permitting same.) "I have studied with great interest the laws of several American states," Hitler will tell a fellow Nazi. Even Mussolini joins this band, hosting an international conference in 1929.

No one appears to protest the exceptionally anti-Semitic statements that the Bauer-Fischer-Lenz volumes contain. Even Supreme Court Justice Oliver Wendell Holmes, Jr., beloved to this day (and according to Frederick having already had sex with Henry James), proclaims: "It is better for all the world, if instead of waiting to execute degenerate offspring for crime, or to let them starve for their imbecility, society can prevent those who are manifestly unfit from continuing their kind. Three generations of imbeciles are enough." The Nazis at Nuremberg will constantly quote Holmes in their defense.

And Frederick, you particularly should know that AES conducts tests on college students, particularly from Yaddah. Huntington believes that Yaddah students stand for the ideal eugenic society—one where the best students reproduce most successfully and create superior offspring. Yaddah was quite literally a breeding ground for the AES's master race. Breeder Brinestalker arranges for all Yaddah students—soon to include his own son—to be photographed naked so that "a record can be kept of both the good and the bad now passing muster as acceptable in our nation's youth."

Oh, Frederick, the bridges of this hateful philosophy are being stoutly built and the traffic flows both ways. How did we, who cared, not know! Where were we all who could have saved the world to come!

And you are all over the place. You are indeed a rover.

YOUR ROVING HISTORIAN WELCOMES ANOTHER EXPERT

"You continue to raise excellent questions, my dear old friend, Fred. It is not so difficult to look back now, though few do, and see the various handwritings on the walls. I know you are doing your best, which I am proud to tell you is not bad at all, to weave the various threads of your own great disillusionments into an account of the monstrosity that is the present day. I salute you in this attempt. The good dame, Dame Lady Hermia, has shared your work with me. I am here to help. Love, Ianthe Adams Strode."

Oh, my dear Ianthe, where are you? Where have you been? That you have been with me in this world all these years and I have not had the benefit of your wisdom breaks my heart. These increasingly horrid years are so pain-ful to write about. Forgive the telling if it fails your standards. Some of it has been so awful to capture that I doubt anyone on earth could write it with continuing sanity. I will see to it that you are kept in the loop from this moment on and I await your reactions.

MERCY HOOKER

Another fucking Hooker we have to deal with. For fuck's sake, it never fuck-ing ends. She fucked up her fucking life. I am getting fucking fed up with fucking Hookers. Doesn't anyone in this fucking family ever do anything fucking right? I can see I'm back to only using "fuck" again. I'll work on it. Variety is the spice. I just get so . . . pissed off how much waste my family represents.

Mercy Hooker is an heiress. Her particular pot of gold, which also dates back to Puritan Massachusetts, is from glass, and is still intact, and is larger than ever because nine out of ten Americans drink from a fucking Hooker glass, whether they know it or not. I have no idea why Mercy doesn't share in Massachusetts Waste. She is from another part of our fucking forest and to this day I can't find any family historian who can tell me precisely where. It's a knee-trembler.

Good old fucking Cousin fucking Mercy. No wonder she never wanted to play fucking dolls with little me. I leave it to Israel himself to tell us more.

In 1925, when just seventeen, and having finished medical school in Palestine, I arrive in Washington and save the life of Mercy Hooker. It be-comes a very famous fucking case of its day.

Mercy Hooker is a beautiful middle-aged woman who is brought into the emergency room of Mater Nostra Dolorosa, the Northeast hospital where Israel is an intern. (Northeast Washington is Washington's Catholic strong-hold and will be mine, too.) Cousin Mercy is hemorrhaging dangerously.

Everyone at Mater Nostra makes fun of Israel because he is so young and so smart. And, of course, a fucking Jew. "Oh, how a Catholic hospital makes fun of yids and kikes and hebes from Palestine. From anywhere. The goyim doctors make jokes about me not even being a doctor, for who is there who can vouch for some Misch Fehl University in such a faraway land. Jews must be pretty desperate over there to make a doctor so young."

It is mid-Saturday when Mercy is brought in by her chauffeur. He drives up in a show-off pissy Quadrata limousine and carefully lifts her body, and gives her like a precious package to the only person in sight wearing a white coat, who is here only because the gentile supervisors made him do weekend duty, on the Sabbath no less, because he's a Jew.

"Please save my mistress," the chauffeur says. He is a handsome fellow with a shaved head and sexy leather riding boots. "Please," he says again, and this time his voice cracks and his eyes fill with tears. His skin is a soft brown color, telling me either mixed blood or a recent vacation. Perhaps the latter, because his mistress is tanned as well, though fading fast.

"I pull on some rubber gloves and take the armful and lay her on the long wooden examining table with the white enamel top. The room is filled with crucifixes. There is one in every patient's room, but here, no doubt because God must bless the occupants more in order to ward off the evil emergency, there is one on every wall and in every nook and corner. There is even a crucifixion mural painted on the ceiling. I counted fourteen Jesuses. I remove item after item of the woman's expensive clothing, handing each to the chauffeur—there is no nursing assistance this afternoon—who folds everything neatly, trying not to look at his mistress's naked body. I commence many jabbings and liftings with my hands. There is no apparent reason for the bleeding. She does not appear to have been hit or to have fallen. I can find nothing broken. The chauffeur says she hasn't eaten anything poisonous. (How does he know?) She is suffering from no evident malfunction, and yet blood oozes from her lips and nostrils and issues from her vagina and rectum.

"The woman is alive; there is plenty of breath inside her. For a brief moment, when I find a crucifix around her neck, there crosses me the thought that something might be transpiring, a stigmata of some sort. You never can tell with Catholics. I turn the body over on its stomach. I ask the chauffeur to leave. Her anus is oozing blood. It runs in dark and heavy trickles down the inside of her leg and onto the white enamel.

"I stick my finger into the blood and rub it against my thumb, testing the texture, the viscosity. It seems more thick than blood should be. Inserting my finger inside her, I find her anal wall is very . . . pitted. The flesh is torn and ragged, like rose thorns can rip smooth fleisch. Has something brutish been introduced into her anus forcibly? And then into her rectum?

"Why am I suddenly supposing another person is involved? Maybe she deliberately sat on something? Perhaps it was an accident of some sort. What kind of accident? I am only seventeen years old. My parents are dead, themselves from a freakish act performed by freaks.

"Then I think I am being too much the detective, too much the psychologist, and not enough the doctor. Why am I concentrating on her rectum when she is bleeding also from her mouth and nose?

"I turn her on her back. The chauffeur comes back and asks if his mistress has been made well yet and when they can leave. I recognize his voice is peculiar, like someone who learned English too . . . precise. I speak sharply at him, 'Don't touch her.' He's reached out to touch his mistress. His hands are strong and hairless. They look Nordic. Does this chauffeur have anything to do with the woman's condition?

"The chauffeur steps back, as if threatened, and moves into the shadows, away from the hard medical lights hanging over the table. I change my gloves and now stick my fingers into the woman's mouth, prying it open. The flesh inside is the same as in her rectum: like ripped . . . meat. Are her nasal passages the same? They are. Is the fact that the blood is only trickling out an indication that the lacerations are surface, and not deep? Her blood pressure is relatively normal. How can that be? She is losing blood. Something medically crazy is happening. What have I read about loss of blood and OK blood pressure?

"I step back to look at her. There is what appears to be a small smile on her lovely face. No, it is lovely but also hard, perhaps mean. This is a woman who gets her own way. Her hair is long and like silk. It falls on the enamel nice and even.

"I turn to the chauffeur. 'Do you know what happened?' I am hoping to take him off guard, and get a truthful answer. The chauffeur shakes his head no. I remove my gloves and scrub my hands. Then I study all her garments, all her pockets. I open her large leather purse. The chauffeur leaves the room again.

"Had I not opened the purse—and most doctors probably would not have opened the purse, or inspected the garments so thoroughly—much less stuck a finger up an anus—I would not have solved the case and thus would not have become so renowned and had my first moment in the limelight. I hate this. The story begins to unwrap by itself, at first through whisperings from staff and then from the mouth of the chauffeur—his name is Aalvaar Heidrich—to whom *The Washington Monument* has paid sufficient money.

"In the large leather purse are numerous penises made of ivory. Each is wrapped in its own linen handkerchief. The penises are spiked with many tiny barbs. On their sharp points are bits of dried blood. There is a small penis that might fit up a nostril. There is a large penis that might fit a vagina. There is a larger and longer one that might reach a rectum. There is a wide one that might stuff a mouth.

"Reporters don't know how to write about penises, to put two and two together. Until Aalvaar Heidrich steps forward and tells the world that his mistress is addicted to pain. 'I am hired to pain her.' It is not easy for him, he says, because he is a gentle soul. Often he has to restrain her from holding her fingers over dinner candles. He claims to have found her many times on the floor of her bedroom, weak from having flagellated herself with a whip. In his estimation, it is not a penance or anything of a religious nature. He says he never saw her indicate any interest in God, though he understands her to come from a religious family. He says she says it's something pleasurable. He believes her because he's heard her scream her orgasms out. 'The chauffeur heard her passion explode,' one newspaper writes. How does he know it was an orgasm, a reporter from one of the even more dirty-minded tabloids perseveres. 'Because I was paid to clean her off. With my tongue.'

"Mercy is dead within a year. Heroin. Her nose was like a rock, almost crystallized. I thought it was the drugs, but perhaps it wasn't. Her body had turned all purple. No one figures that one out.

"Heidrich is her heir. He lives in her mansion, deep in the Rock Creek Park, alone."

EVVILLEENA STADTDOTTER

FROM THE NOTEBOOKS OF DR. ISRAEL JERUSALEM, ADMIRAL MASON IRON VAULTUM LIBRARY OF NITS*

What is there in Mercy's story that causes a middle-aged lady like Evvilleena Stadtdotter to seek Israel out and beg him to be her doctor? The newspaper photographs of Israel make him look unwelcoming.

She does not tell him the truth, which will turn out to be complicated. What she says is, "It iss the youngsters who know what iss new in medshin and schience and reshearch. The old fartss, they are too tired to learn. They cannot understand new wayss. They never learn passht a shertin point. But

*Israel often writes in the third person in his notebooks.

the old never believe the unbelievable until it iss too late. And it iss the unbelievable that musht be inveshtigated. When shomting new kommst, the old fartss pooh-pooh. Every time. Are these good reashons, Dr. Ishrale?"

Yes, she speaks like this, with much slurping and sshushing. It sounds like her mouth is at the dentist's. She sounds more MGM movie-German than the real Germans he knew in Germany. He could understand them and he can hardly understand her, but she says she is German so maybe she is. It's not fashionable to be a German in Washington.

He is not certain what there is in the Mercy Hooker case that's brought him so many single woman patients so quickly. He is the new doctor of the moment. People are reading about him on the bus, if you can believe.

Five, six, seven times in the next months Evvilleena Stadtdotter comes to the private office he's set up in the basement of a neighborhood residence. He is stern with her, which is not his nature, but she provokes it in him with her phony-sounding accent and her batting eyelashes and her invitations. Kommst. Kommst. Kommst! To mein haus. Fur dinner. Fur luncheon. We make spazieren in park. He hates it when her appointments come around. It isn't long before she begins to offer him money. Whatever he wants. Do du not wisch to reshearch? Ssoooo? He becomes gruff and harsh with her, which had not been his nature at all, but she provokes this nastiness in him.

Once she attacks him. He has paid all her offers no attention! He accepts not even a lunch in some safe outdoor café when the weather is nice!

While he is sticking his fingers under her breasts, she throws herself from the table to the floor. Quickly he kneels to help her up. Just as quickly, she pulls him off balance to lie beside her. To her surprise, he stays there, saying nothing, just staring at the ceiling, confused with being confused.

She begins to undress him. He is on his back, his eyes now closed, and she peels away his heavy tweeds like a maitre d' in the fancy restaurant dealing with loose skin on a poached fish. Under all the layers of clothing—it is the summer and yet he wears a jacket and vest and shirt and undervest—he is all bones. He is pale and thin. She runs her jeweled fingers all over his chest, as if he's rare and precious. As her hands descend, he begins to whimper, like an unhappy puppy. Tears come from under his tight-closed eyelids. He is as lonely as she. He's never been touched by a woman. He's never been in a position of intimacy, of any kind. He shivers. She's moved by his shivering. She bends over to kiss him, little pecks all over his bony chest, like a mother hen scavenging the bare earth for something to eat. He pecks back, incompetently. These useless kisses thrill her.

He is becoming aroused. "My skinny pecker that is like a turkey leg is getting hard." He tries to will it down. He knows what will happen almost immediately. Aagh. It has happened. It is always this way when he is masturbating. The very thought of the act causes the finale. His tears come more plentifully. "I will never be able to satisfy. Not even myself."

She has watched as his skinny pecker progresses from flaccid to erection to eruption. It is pathetic, and she knows it, but so what. How many things at her age thrill? She has caused him to become excited. With speed she bends and sticks out her tongue and licks up his semen. She savors it, rolling it around in her mouth, and then she swallows it. She sucks on him, hoping to extract a further drop. This tickles him, and he giggles, and jumps up, and quickly puts on his heavy wardrobe again, his underwear, his tweeds. She shrinks, unattended to, ignored, overlooked on the floor, an old pile of flesh, as he clothes his nakedness. Finally he offers her his hand and yanks her up.

"Israel, will you marry me!"

He runs from the office. Outside, in a garden of macabre statuary, elves and gnomes and fairies and angels, he smokes a cigarette and calms himself down. She is gone when he goes back inside.

He had found nothing wrong with her. Why does she keep returning to see him?

At eighteen years of age, Israel had received the Marcus Dridge Award for studying menoma in Chile, in the Iwacky Indians, a small tribe living high in the Andes Mountains where it is very cold and often freezing. He takes a leave of absence from Mater Nostra to go there and observe and record much that could eliminate their scourge. Diseases come and go. They ravage tribes and tributaries, Babel and Berlin. Entire populations and cultures disappear just like that and soon no one can even remember the name of whatever it was that killed them or who they were.

There is little money in poor Chile to carry out Israel's recommendations, most of them having to do with personal hygiene—don't shit where you eat, that sort of thing—and the Iwacky disappear from the face of history. These are Israel's first on-the-job lessons: you could find the cure to almost anything but rarely the wherewithal to pay for it. It's cheaper to let people die than to save them and anyway there are always more people.

Underneath the Iwacky menoma (a menoma is a like a fedema, only with a crusted surface) there is something usually purple, though it does not look like blood itself. Can there be different kinds of blood? How can that be?

His study is written up in *The New England Journal of Primitive Peoples*, an important journal that makes him feel good.

Yes, he wants to taste more fame. While he is young. You can't traipse through the freezing heights of the world when you are sixty asking Indians to open their mouths and say ah.

You have to discover while you're young!

He discovers something else among the Iwacky. Young boys. Rather, they discover him. The cultural and anthropological heritage peculiar to this tribe, so high above the world, insists on a rite of passage involving gentle indoctrination to sex through anal penetration by an older man. Like in ancient Greece, male youths are required to bond with elders of their own sex. Indeed, young boys push themselves on older men sexually in their eagerness to be initiated. It is considered rude to refuse them. There has been nothing in Israel's life to compare with his Iwacky experiences.

Next, Israel is given some money by Greeting to study the sexual customs of "naïve" populations never seen before by white men. He has been provided with a supply of the company's ampules, informing him that they "boost energy in distant and foreign climates and at unusual altitudes." He is asked to distribute them liberally and to note any reactions. He is appalled by what he does note and withdraws the ampules, causing a riot among the first and only tribe, the Hares in Melanesia, to receive them.

The young Hares (pronounced Hare-eeze) boys also foist themselves on older men sexually, and again it is the custom to allow it, not to be rude and refuse to initiate them. So again he allows it. He does not let himself consider how much he is enjoying these encounters.

He also discovers the cause of a strange disease that is killing these people. The Hares call it "ga-unh-laa-ooze," which Israel takes to be "glause." He had seen it too among the Iwacky but it had not registered, no doubt because it had yet to become as widespread as here. He believes it comes from their eating the brains and the penises of their dead, something they do as a token of great respect. It is horrible to witness the physical devastation that accompanies these deaths. He has never seen anything like it. He tells them to stop. They do not stop. They call this disease "utz."

I am a scientist now researching how boys become men. If they are approaching me and offering, how can I as a scientist not experience it, not research it? But I will not eat the brains and penises. Would a scientist purposely infect himself with a poison he is studying in his research? Perhaps the scientist *should* infect himself, if he believes enough in what he is doing.

His writing is getting better. Maggie Mead will call Israel Jerusalem a hero for his observations when she reads his paper in *The New England Journal of Indigenous Naïve Populations*. "Your journal article is beautifully conceived and written," she says.

It is for his observations about the appearance of glause and utz that years later, when he is an old man, he will receive the Nobel Prize.

When he is nineteen he almost receives recognition for tracking down turbow in the Atlas Mountains, among a Moroccan tribe that eats berries and plants mixed with mud and the flesh of mountain goats, the combination of which is found to contain high Mesirow titers of raw aluminora (the Iwacky also had high Mesirow titers) and an equally unhealthy level of gorge wahs. (Gorge wah is the mineral of the moment. Have you had your gorge wahs today? It is the vitamin rage of 1927.) But this tribe won't change their mud. The entire tribe, the Angastingees, dies, in a sudden plaguelike sweep. He writes a definitive report of their demise, also for the *NEJINP*.

Israel always keeps notes. Travel harbors many strange and valuable sights if one is only able to see them. The consumption of poisoned brains and penises during burial rituals is more prevalent over a wider range of indigenous naïve populations than he imagined. Dementia, severe memory loss, raving sexual appetites, fingernails that drop off—it is a peculiar mixed bag of symptoms, upwinding in hysterical deaths preceded by gasping and enormous bodily heaves. The agonies can take many years. Native medicines don't work. The brains of the kids, who are the main eaters, are peculiarly heavy, he notes about an autopsy, as if something inside them has solidified. He is reminded of Mercy Hooker's rocklike nose. He also notes that he, who has eaten only mud and goat, is still alive.

YOUR ROVING HISTORIAN

It is sweet to note that from all his mountain schlepping, Israel was a real hunk à la Indiana Jones, well prepared to search out germs and poisons anywhere in the world.

ISRAEL LEARNS MORE ON HIS JOURNEYS

I share with you now the discoveries of a young acquaintance, Mike Quinn, who was excommunicated by the Disciples of Lovejoy religion for telling the world this important new information about our joint field of interest. It is cited in *Same-Sex Dynamics Among Nineteenth-Century Americans* by Dr. D. Michael Quinn, University of Illinois Press.

In South America, in Peru, in the tribe of Cashinahua Indians, it is customary for males to greet each other by squeezing softly each other's penis. They sit side by side when they talk to each other, holding each other's penis.

In New Guinea young boys are initiated into sucking an elder's penis and swallowing all the semen if they want to grow up big and live a long life. The boys do this on every willing man they can find until they are twenty, when they marry women, whom they have avoided up till then.

Among these tribes, and others in Melanesia, anal intercourse is believed to be necessary for boys' physical development. Disciples of Lovejoy missionaries, most of whom are men, who converted these tribes by the thousands and participate in these initiations, discover this.

In East Africa boys leave their parents and move to villages inhabited entirely by other young men.

In the South Pacific men-men marriages are common; even if they also marry women, the male partner is preeminent and permanent. When Lovejoy missionaries try to stop this, they are asked to leave and not return.

Among the Lovejoy missionaries writing about his experiences is Charles Warren Stoddard, a Disciple whose passionate prose describing his many love affairs with the boys and men in the various tribes he is sent to convert is to affect Samuel Clemens when he reads these reports as published in the *Overland Monthly* out of San Francisco. Asleep in a bed "big enough for a Lovejoy, the naked teenager "never let loose his hold on me . . . His sleek figure, supple and graceful in repose, was the embodiment of free, untrammeled youth . . . If it is a question how long a man may withstand the seductions of nature, and the consolations and conveniences of the state of nature, I have solved it in one case; for I was as natural as possible in about three days."

Charles Warren Stoddard will also be excommunicated by the Disciples of Lovejoy and become the lifelong friend and a continuing lover of Samuel Clemens.

TOO MUCH TOO SOON AND
NOT ENOUGH TOO LATE

Noggalichee Oba, a young man visiting Birkenstat, Illinois, from the Zoltar River basin in the Upper Vedurnas region of his country, still called, but not for much longer, Upper Volta, in (still called, but not for much longer) French West Africa, cuts his finger off on Saturday afternoon, July 4, 1931, while slicing pork sausages in an effort to help make the communal spaghetti sauce at the annual Fourth of July retreat of the All Nations on High Southern Baptist Redemption, to which church Oba claims a fealty in Africa. Unfortunately, he is a deaf-mute and is unable to make anyone understand where his finger is before he's rushed by an ambulance to the emergency room of what is no more than a clinic, where he dies. Some two hundred people eat the pasta. The next day, as a special holiday event "to introduce us to our community responsibilities," American Red Blood arrives to solicit donations, something new being tried out by the Cook County Hospital in nearby Chicago. Three hundred and eighty-three of the four hundred in attendance roll up their sleeves and give their pints of blood, which are collected in glass bottles. The blood is then rushed by American Red Blood to Herbert Hoover Field for an emergency flight to Rio Grande Tita (on the Del Rio–Paso Dobles Fault on the Texas border with Mexico). Noggalichee Oba, finger or no finger, is dead from something or other. His cadaver scabbed in twenty-four hours into a medley of purples that had not been originally noticed because his skin was so very black.

It is pathetic how no president considers health, medicine, well-being worthy of espousing. One after another of them is too busy somewhere else, overseas more than likely after Teddy starts that trend. He promoted segregation and believed in Negro inferiority. Taft had hated the job and was out to lunch on many things (in 1910 he declined to give his support for a national laboratory devoted to the research of cancer, already very noticeably on its destructive march; it would be 1937 before FDR would set up a National Cancer Institute, which would not be joined to NITS until 1944, and still Congress wouldn't give it any money despite more alarming increases of its incidence; in 1950 *The New York Truth* would still not allow the use of the word *breast* or *cancer* in its pages). Wilson is called great by many for thinking in United Nations–y terms, unsuccessfully, but even after he had his secret stroke, his government was busy elsewhere, notably with the aftermath of World War I, which certainly brought more than its share of health problems to The American People, not that anyone paid them much attention. Great discoveries are made, but only bit by bit, as coordinated research across boundaries, even across the street, is not anything anyone considers doing. In the case of blood itself, other countries are way ahead of us, even Russia, in trying out new approaches on how to use it, how to keep it. The history of American interest in its physical self is appalling in its minginess, its out-to-lunchedness. Why is this? There really is no person visible on any horizon to put this question to. NITS itself has such a turnover of staff on every level that nothing can be undertaken for fear who's in charge won't be there tomorrow, which he probably won't be. In 1918, when Rep. Tobias Arndt from South Dakota inquires why NITS is in such disarray especially during a war, he's forced to write the same letter of inquiry twenty-six times because one after another is returned to him stamped "No longer a NITS employee." He brings this up on the House floor and a committee is formed to investigate. There is no record of any further action by or history of this committee. This is true of a lot of committees. Congressmen are learning this effective tactic for looking busy without having to follow through: form a committee. When Woodrow Wilson has that stroke, Mrs. Wilson imports her doctor from Virginia and overrules all his advice anyway. She jokes that since she was a descendant of Pocahontas she knew more about taking care of men. No one remembers enough about Pocahontas to correct her and anyway Edith kept the old boy alive while she ran the country from the White House, and then for three years afterward, so she was obviously someone one had to contend with. To this day no one knows how much work Woodrow actually did. Shades of Hamilton doing so much of Washington's and no one knowing it.

From here on it's like a bad newsreel. The administration of Warren Harding, a handsome man who is from a small Ohio town called Blooming Grove, harbors more scandal and corruption than's been witnessed so far. He wound up president and took a mistress who bore him a daughter. The Ku Klux Klan continues to grow in numbers and, as mentioned, five million of them march through Washington in their white hooded robes and with their crosses in 1925. Harding dies in office after only two years from an embolism. The feelings of his nonentity successor, Calvin Coolidge, are simple: "Nordics deteriorate when mixed with other races." Prohibition comes and takes away the main pleasure increasing numbers of new immigrants require to keep them in their place. When the out of control Teapot Dome scandal erupts, what with all those valuable oil leases given by Harding to cronies in his cabinet, it's probably just as well he has that heart attack and dies. Neither his embolism nor the death of Coolidge's own much-loved son at sixteen from blood poisoning fuel money for NITS to pay attention to public health. "The chief business of the American people is business" is another favorite expression from Silent Cal, who honestly thought that the United States had attained "a state of contentment seldom ever seen."

Comes 1929 and the Great Depression to bear out the folly of these guys. Once again we have to wonder what it is about The American People that, time after time, we elect these men to—in essence and fact, in their ignorance and unsuitability—do their best to destroy us. De Tocqueville was right: the masses will destroy each other. Ben Franklin was right: democracy will not work. During these years from 1909 to 1929 there are some 257 epidemics claiming some three-million-plus lives. Twelve of these can be classified as plagues. Increasingly during and after the war the number of syphilis cases surpasses any ever recorded or known to mankind. Nowhere is this reported or indeed made much of. Whatever that relatively new Sailors' Home on Staten Island is dealing with is a big secret. (By the way, a historian will finally come along and prove syphilis is an American disease, started on Hispaniola from where Columbus took it out into the world. So what? Who cares? The historian's name is also lost to history.) There will, in these twenty years, be fifty-four different directors of NITS. These names are lost to history for the very reason that when NITS finally puts its house in some sort of vague order, new officialdom will be so ashamed of the old order that they will literally destroy many of the records that detailed it. So much for the much-heralded inclusiveness of that Library of All Libraries at NITS.

THE THIRTIES ARE STUPID AND SILLY. AND MESSY.

Everything is getting messier. A little out of focus. The country is getting stranger. It has always been strange. Where have you been? Nobody has really noticed. And it has always been messy. No one noticed that either. What house is always neat? But up till now nobody has minded much that everything is a little messy. Dirty. Unclean. Soap isn't everyone's Eleventh Commandment. People are accustomed to everyone and everything being smelly. Women don't shave under their arms yet. People take baths once a week, if that.

The economic news continues to be bad. New lows are achieved each minute of each day. The claws of the Great Depression are still causing men to jump from buildings. They also disappear in other ways. They don't come home at night. Mothers tell their children, "We must thank God Daddy comes home from work." When they come home from school to an empty house, children kneel down and pray for Daddy's return from the office. Children don't understand the nature of the new awfulness except that it has something to do with money, which Mommy and Daddy don't have any more of. This is a difficult concept to grasp. "But why?" brings unsatisfactory answers. "Because the president is doing a bad job" comes to be an answer that's acceptable. Bad jobs are understood by everyone. President Hoover's doing a bad job. Everyone comes to hate President Hoover. Everyone knows everything is awful. Everyone doesn't know how to go on.

Every official indicator—and the Treasury tries to create a number of them designed to prove to The American People that nothing's as bad as it's being made to sound—still sounds awful. Parabolas have curved back on themselves and off the chart. Several are in the cellar. The new Heindinger Marker goes up and down so fast it makes people who monitor it dizzy. Hoover goes on the radio and tries to explain that this up-and-downness of the Heindinger "is a good sign, a healthy sign. If it stayed flat, or only went up, or only went down, we would be in severe economic trouble." But since not so many people are eating two much less three squares a day, severe economic trouble is not only already a guest in the house but the man who came to dinner. Treasury executives sit around big tables and discuss new ways to tell the people that, as the president says over and over, "the economy is essentially healthy." Some commentators, like the young Alsop brothers, Joseph and Stewart, ask in one of the many newspapers that publish them, "Is this not the first time that the American people no longer believe in their elected officials?" (Joseph is gay. When he retires in 1974, their column is believed to be the longest-running nationally syndicated opinion column, appearing three times a week in three hundred newspapers. Joseph never lifted a finger to help anything gay, and there were, as we shall see, lots of gay goings-on that could have used his finger.) But as always there are other commentators who differ with the Alsops, like Hudson Pacific, who writes for *The San Francisco Goldmine* that "The American People has never believed an American president since George Washington."

By the time Hoover leaves office in 1933, the Depression is worse than ever. America has become a nation of transients. Almost a million hitchhikers, hoboes, and bums roam the country, some 200,000 of them adolescents. Women dress in men's clothing to avoid trouble and molestation. But then, women are now doing a lot of things, in any way they can, like being breadwinners when those daddies truly don't come home. In the years 1932–1933, 57,908 men all across America take their own lives. It was no longer just a New York thing.

OPEN FOR BUSINESS

Doris Hardware opens her whorehouse. It sits along with the other good-as-gold real estate in this Dumbarton neighborhood. Behind ivied walls and huge oaks and all the extra acreage Abe has padded the place with, it is more than a home away from home for the weary man in Washington. It is akin to Shangri-la, where cares are shed and dreams are worn instead. The women are very beautiful. They are also nice. From the day it opens until the day it closes, it flourishes. From day one, Doris knows her business.

To keep himself busy, very busy, Abraham Masturbov continues to assemble major parcels of land. Bigger and bigger and more and more. He dreams on a larger scale than ever. He's got a great deal to get off his mind. Not for him a mere apartment house or office building. Now he's interested in what up north are being called "developments." In New York there are Sunnysides and Morningsides and Forest Hills and Locust Valleys, even a Tuxedo Park, huge swaths of living quarters for those unable or unmotivated to build for themselves, which is almost everyone. Doris tries to point out to Abe that they are both pioneers in their own ways. He nods, but says nothing. He sees nothing heroic in anything either of them is doing.

Developments should work in Washington, although no one but Abe sees the place as a growth area. Abe also sees more. How can the capital of what he believes will be the most important country in the world not become important itself? Doris, of course, is banking on her own growth industry.

"Besides," Abe says, "there's going to be another war."

How can he tell so far in advance that there is going to be another war? Just when we'd managed to forget about the last one. "Anyone with half a brain can see there's going to be a war. The rest of the world is crazy. Take a trip to Germany, or even to places like Belgium, where people are so poor and so brutalized that there has to be an explosion. I traveled and I saw. And I came back home to America and I could see America was too calm and placid and I just said to myself, It can't last. People who don't have so much get jealous. Like Japan. Listen to people who've been to Japan."

While she was busy making her house, Abe had traveled around the world. If his heart still was broken before he left, it certainly was when he came home.

"It's going to get really bad," he tells Doris. He tells her about all the unemployment he saw wherever he went, "with armies of little hungry children living on the streets."

Doris is impressed when he talks this way. Maybe she should marry him. She peppers him with questions. He loves when she does this. Why won't she marry him?

"Jealous of what? Surely this is a new theory of warfare, Abe. More? We have more? No one here would believe that."

"Wars are always about jealousy. The parents and the neighbors get jealous someone else is better off. Only, the parents are all the countries of Europe—it doesn't make any difference which side they're on—and we're the kids, still trying to please, still trying to find our way, still trying to stand up without falling down and instead tripping over gold in our streets. Compared to them we got gold in our streets. How can you not see a war is coming? Don't you talk to your foreign 'clients'? You really should, Doris." Abe pays no heed to the hungry and the unemployed here. "Things like that pass soon enough in America. If you hold on long enough things get better. The stock market is falling apart? Now's the time to buy!" He loses friends because they think he's crazy. Good. The crazy man buys more of the land they're happy to sell him.

Although Abe already has more money than he'll ever need, he is unhappy. How could he not be? Because of Doris, how could he not be? He's mortified about the house for hookers. How could he not be? But he knows he and Doris are together forever. To live without her is not an option. So he buys more land. That's what he always does to keep his mind off things. He's rich? He'll be even richer. It's the same old recording. For a rich man there's never enough. Ask any rich man and he'll tell you it's so. Ask any poor man, too. But that's another history. This is the history of a very rich country that doesn't know what to do with it. He, of all our cast of characters, knows this from an early age. He knows he doesn't feel any better about Doris no matter how much land he buys. But he knows he musn't stop. He actually is reading *The Decline and Fall of the Roman Empire*, unabridged, a little each night that Doris doesn't come home. When it's apparent she's not going to come home at all, she is going to live in her house full-time, he reads many nights until the dawn, when he gets up and goes out to buy more land. He can't stand her not sleeping beside him. It is the most yawning emptiness of his life, that empty space in their bed beside him.

Ironically, the decade of the thirties is one of the biggest eras of growth for Washington's Jewish fortunes. Jews have been living here since before the Civil War, and only land has been considered a good investment. But where Abe is now buying, it's swampy. It's buggy. It's hot as hell. It's too far from something else. Or what if you have to suddenly up and run? You couldn't unload this land fast. Jews know about running and are always on the lookout for the next time they'll have to leave in a hurry. They're always on the lookout for newly fulminating forms of hatred. Dr. Abner Swartschild, a preeminent pediatrician, is turned down to head a new division at NITS for childhood illnesses. His mother, Sara-Elisabett Swartschild, quietly gives NITS a handsome donation for this new division and he's still turned down. "It should not work this way," Joab Swartschild, whose rich wife is one of those that goes back to before the Civil War, says to Abe. Abe listens and nods and says nothing. This has become his default position.

He has also seen on his trip around the world what is brewing in Germany. Nothing surprises him anymore. Once again, how could it be otherwise, "if you had half a brain"? This becomes a favorite expression. He does not see many full-brained people. When Abe starts buying in Georgetown, a few smart Jews follow, including Joab. "You have to think ahead." Abe always changes the subject. "There will be a machine to keep us cool. Best buy even the swampy land now which seems too hot to handle or by the time this machine comes the best empty land will long since be sold." Indeed, Abe has already bought a lot of it.

Jewish fortunes in cities are being made all over America. Gronsky, Todtmacher, Vergessen, Anstersh, the Gilders, even Bigger Below (a Lopp cousin of Ephra's father who makes tennis racquets and all kinds of other sporting goods) are already on their way to greater wealth before the Depression ends. Many Jews did not lose money during the Depression because they did not do what the goyim did. "Don't follow the goyim," old Herman Masturbov had always advised. "Brokers and bankers on Wall Street won't make us partners—then fuck 'em. We should get down on our knees and thank them," Bigger is fond of saying. "Who wants to be a banker, such pisherdicka returns on your money?" Denver, Chicago, Los Angeles, Atlanta, Richmond, Baltimore, Detroit, Kansas City, The American People don't have any idea how many Jews there are with so much money. Maury the Jew, for instance, left an estate of $100 million when he died sometime around 1890. No one saw him make it and no one saw him leave it. In fact, no one saw him period. When Commodore Vanderbilt died in 1877 he left $100 million, which was more than America's Treasury held. When John D. Rockefeller dies in 1937, he dies America's first billionaire. There is a Jewish billionaire by then too, more than one in fact, but only gentile money gets talked about in histories of American wealth.

That somewhere there are also homosexual multimillionaires is still not widely known, even among other homosexuals, who don't know each other yet, as a group. Yaddah's principal benefactor, James Sterling, also the founder of the enormously successful Wall Street law firm Shearman & Sterling, dies an unrepentant homosexual who's lived with his lover for some forty-plus years. Why, half the buildings and professorships at Yaddah are named Sterling. Yaddah should only know this, like they don't know Elisha Yaddah himself was one too. Who were the wealthy homosexuals? We don't know for certain even now. No one's doing the research yet. Why is it so hard for homosexuals to learn about themselves? Clarence Meekly Dridge left a billion dollars to the Dridge Trust "to find out who we are and where we came from and the names of others like us." What happened to that money?

Southern Jews are quieter and amass their riches with closed mouths. They bury their treasure. No gentile banks for them. That's no place to keep a secret. This is a European trait. European fortunes are not open to the public. Only New Yorkers feel the commandment to be visible. A New York Christian, like a New York Jew, wants everyone to know it when he's rich. The bigger the wealth, the bigger the house. Washington is a southern town. When you rise in wealth you do it quietly. Except for Herman. Except for Abe. What's it gotten either one of them? Abe really wants just to live in a tiny apartment in a development with Doris and raise a family.

Abe buys a huge amount of land in a place called Franeeda County. Hardly anyone lives there. He quietly starts building this first development.

He is actually going to call it Masturbov Gardens. When it's finished it will have three hundred "garden apartments," a phenomenal number. His competitors make fun of him: Who will want to live so far from downtown? But increasingly, housing in Washington is becoming more difficult to find. It must be all those prescient people getting out of Europe. Masturbov Gardens will fill up quickly.

HOORAY FOR HOLLYWOOD

Oliver Wendell "Binky" Krank, a young lawyer fresh out of NYU, arrives in Hollywood in 1934, about the same time sound is getting perfected. He succeeds immediately with his first self-financed movie, *The Accordion Man*. So as to be beholden to no one he determines to finance all his movies with his own money. He is still some twenty years from meeting and marrying Dr. Monserrat Schnee, who will be important to our history. By then he will be one of the most respected film lawyers in the world, as well as an adviser to presidents. Right now he's just a funny-looking, rather short but well-dressed young man searching for a life. Where did he get the money to make *The Accordion Man*? He represented Clarence Meekly and set up that gigantic Dridge Trust.

Also in Hollywood in the thirties are Peter Ruester, Manny Moose, and Buster Punic, who meet and form a three-caballeros-type friendship that will actually endure through time. They go to whorehouses, they pass themselves around to both rich men and rich women for money, they have sex with each other. Caballeros do devil-may-care kinds of things. You come to Hollywood from the sticks where you don't do things like that, and the minute you see other young guys your own age doing them, why you do them too. Buster is rich and Peter is poor and Manny is in between. They are all young studs in Hollywood, and California, if not the rest of America, is filled with hope and promise, and thus much devil-may-care. Where anyone comes from is unimportant. No one has a real past, only one for today. Most good friends don't remember where they first met each other. It was at . . . ? As the gay Cole Porter, who was there for much of it, writes, "Anything goes!"

Anne Edwards, the indispensable historian of much of this era and its "celebrities," including Peter Ruester, writes openly what others fear to utter. She says this, for instance, about Katharine Hepburn: "She told me, 'I don't care what you write as long as it's not the truth.' She was a woman who fictionalized her life to the public. She romanticized and fictionalized her relationship with Spencer Tracy, a bisexual, abusive alcoholic . . . She was not honest about her life. She lived a bisexual life most of her life. She and Spencer were great beards for each other throughout their lives." Gary Cooper and Randolph Scott are living openly as lovers. Clark Gable's face was all over the map. Erroll Flynn would fuck anything that moved. If you think stuff like this is unimportant, you're wrong. As the great "walker" of First Women, Foppy Schwartz, will be fond of proclaiming, "Gossip is Life!"

Peter Ruester is noticed naked in somebody or other's pool or bed and is screen-tested and wins a contract with the Brothers Krakow Film Studio. His test is directed by Fenton Borriss, an extraordinarily talented and exceptionally ugly man. He wants Peter Ruester in his bed and in his arms and he gets him into both. He tells him to his face that he wishes he were a better actor, "but stick with it, kid, you may just bluff it through." Borriss also gets Spencer Tracy in his arms and his bed on a number of occasions over a number of years. He even gets Spencer and Peter in for a threesome, but only once. Anything goes, indeed. Ambitious young actors will do anything for a good part, a good script, a good director. That's why there's no such thing, really, as a heterosexual actor. As Hollywood makes us what we are today, whichever "today" you're living through, we shall have occasion to revist its denizens as a matter of history. When an actor becomes president of the United States, do we have any other choice?

ME, GERMAN?

Between the two world wars hordes of doctors fleeing Germany and Europe flock to America like the endangered lemmings they are, seeking a safer harbor. Because most of them are Jewish they are not welcomed in America with particular warmth. Welcomed only marginally more are the non-Jewish Germans who don't like the smell/sound of things in the Homeland either. No sooner does each group land than each tries to protect itself from the other. Associations of German physicians spread the word that the newly arrived Jews are just as bent on poisoning the blood of gentiles in the New World as in the Old. Do they not mix their own blood with that of their patients while they are under the knife? Do they not fuck all their non-Jewish patients? The Association of Doctors from the Homeland, in Grand

Rapids, Michigan, sees to it that 260 Jewish doctors, or some 35 percent of the state's entire medical establishment, are removed from membership. The Moses and Abraham Association of Doctors in Chicago is no less energetic in whispering that German doctors were butchers there and are butchers here.

From the moment of their arrival neither group considers itself German. The closer we come to war, the less German it is copacetic to appear. Everyone becomes American pronto. Teachers of elocution are in widespread demand. Out-of-work actors find a great deal of employment as English teachers. German is not an easy accent to unload. Women console themselves that they are sounding like Dietrich or Garbo.

Given half a chance, will more people start hating more people the minute they have the freedom to do so? Will this eugenics thing actually accomplish this?

HERMIA NOODLING

"The man who stood at the apex of the German Reich on 30 January 1933 believed himself chosen by providence to be the redeemer of the Germans, indeed of the whole Germanic race," writes Heinrich August Winkler in *Germany: The Long Road West*.

> . . . the Fuhrer intended his National Socialist movement to be . . . a worldly *ecclesia militans*, outside of which there could be no salvation, a totalitarian political religion. [His was] a regime in which political life was defined in terms of a struggle of friend against enmity; that violently repressed any manifestation of opposition and intimidated all dissidence by means of an omnipresent secret police; that eliminated every kind of separation of powers for the sake of a one-party monopoly; and that fostered through ideology, propaganda, and terror the acclamatory mass approval it needed to legitimize its dominance, both domestically and abroad.

It should be obvious, it must be obvious, but it was not obvious, that there is no room in such a movement, in such a country, in such a totalitarian regime, for the homosexual. Is this the true modern beginning of the *elimination* of your people, Frederick? Though this word itself is not visible on the surface of this radical new philosophy, of everything that Hitler and his minions are now saying out loud and propagandizing so furiously everywhere they can (they are not subtle about any of this by any means), it is implicitly embedded in the total rejection of anything that does not comply with what they are now identifying as the norm. It is almost incomprehensible that from the very beginning of this man's rise to power this is not seen by those who do not represent this norm, or fit into it, or want to be a part of it, or by most Jews. This blindness will abet the horrors that are shortly to arrive. It is the classic case of no one listening to what is actually being said, and out loud. It is the classic case of total denial by those who do not want to hear what they do not want to hear. Most people have an unquenchable penchant for sleepwalking through history, despite all that has preceded them. Sir Geoffrey Wrench almost called off our wedding over my growing outspokenness about this. "Hermia, you will get us both murdered in cold blood."

I shudder to place on the table the realization that I do not remember where I was or what I was, or more important, was not, thinking when all of this was accruing to the history of evil in this world, which is to be my chosen field. Yes, this is the field that I was already "noodling" around. Noodling! Even now I attempt to lighten my load of responsibility, lest I take myself too seriously. England was full of Jews *and* homosexuals. Many were friends. Evidently they absorbed the coming of the furies silently; they certainly did not share them with their gentile countrymen, no doubt because we were and always have been such an openly anti-Semitic and, less so, anti-homosexual nation. I was just finishing Cambridge, I was a madcap intellectual running around drinking champagne with young Communists who were then the most romantic of young men to dash around with, and if you could find one for your very own, why, that was the king's knickers. God knows how I wound up with Geoffrey, who can be such a bore. (But then almost every Englishman I have ever known can be a bore.) There were now so many riots beginning to occur everywhere in Europe and in the UK that I moved to the States. Sir Geoffrey got himself attached to our Foreign Office somehow and stayed home. There my new husband became a spy. At least that's what he told me.

BY AND ABOUT KORAH LUDENS

The Manhattan Society for Freudian Analysis was founded shortly after Freud himself came for the first and only time to America, in 1909, to Worcester, of all places, plain then as now. There is a picture in the society's headquarters on Fifth Avenue and 103rd Street of Freud standing amid his children, what looks like hundreds of them, all solemn, unsmiling men and several women. The implication is that he is standing in front of their building. Of course he is not. The building wasn't ever a building but suites of offices, and then not until the early thirties, and it would be a long time before the number of his American "children" was this large. In fact, he is standing in Berlin among his German, Austrian, and Swiss (a few from other countries too, such as Italy) associates, indeed many dozens of them, in 1934, after a long and uncomfortable secret meeting during which no consensus can be reached on "Is There an Oncoming Storm?" Hitler had already had Freud's books burned publicly, and still their owner stayed there. Freud is the only one who is smiling, as if to say we are here despite the world. If you look closely, you will see the faces of all the biggies. Globule. Mestrict. Fehshreif (Mr. and Mrs.). Drehdul. Arramomoniker. Tilsit. Krebs. Ogonquit. Nehrdewehl. O'Fannah. Rinahldie. Jones. Smith. Hopkins. Gillespie (who will analyze YHR in London), Ferenczi, Adler. Brill. Korah Ludens. Yes, I am one of the women (along with Nesta Nehrdewehl Trout and Polly Smith). I am already in practice in New York and I travel safely between the countries to see my own family, not so endangered because I am not Jewish. My hair is cut in a Dutch-boy style even then. I was Ogunquit's analysand in Vienna. Rivtov (who will also analyze Fred at Yaddah) was always jealous of this. Look how Harvey Ogunquit stands beside me so protectively. My theories of Female Child Abandonment, Mother Responsibility, Therapeutic Distancing, and Idealized Imagination will one day be considered seminal; today they are, as they say, "in the literature."

My banishment occurs shortly after this photograph is taken. In December 1934, Dr. Korah Ludens and her acolytes are expelled from the Manhattan Society for Freudian Analysis by a vote of 200–2. There is a photograph of me and a few followers marching down the middle of Fifth Avenue from 103rd Street, in the snow, in the late evening, after this traumatic meeting, singing and celebrating at the top of our lungs, with arms up and legs Rockette-kicking (the Rockettes have recently been introduced at Radio City

Music Hall), faces confident (too confident, it will become evident), eyes shining and mouths open wide saying "cheese" for the photographer.

What has little me done to so anger her elders that an expulsion is in order? It is difficult even today to get surviving society members to talk. Indeed, "the literature" has been pretty well expunged of any mention of my once-upon-a-time membership. As with any nonkosher information on the Master himself—for instance, his passionate, consummated homosexual love for his good friend Wilhelm Fleiss, an ear, nose, and throat specialist who believed in a strong connection between the nose, the genitals, and sex (which will be borne out in the next century with the arrival of the Dridge Ampule); his introduction to Freud of the notion of man's innate bisexuality, which Freud incorporated into his theories (Freud ordered their correspondence destroyed); and of course his own beloved daughter's lesbianism (which he knew about)—the Freudian annals still continue to be under constant microscopic nitpicking. "Disputatious information would only confuse the issue," Ernest Jones, the annointed "biographer," has written. I knew otherwise. I knew that Freud had no trouble with homosexuality and even harbored homosexual fantasies about Jung, big strong tall gentile handsome Jung, who towers above him in height, in prominence (his theories have taken off far more successfully), in authority and fame. Jung confided in me about Freud peeing in his pants on that 1909 visit to America when he and Jung were visiting Columbia and looking across toward the Palisades in New Jersey. They had spent several days and nights in deep discussion about many things, and then, on this afternoon, Freud suddenly had the insight that he could not control this younger man, he could not control America, he could not control psychoanalysis (had not the very meetings in Worcester with dozens of American and European doctors verified this: the Americans particularly were not going to go along with Freud's beliefs whole-hog). He then peed in his pants, like the little boy who has been chastised by his powerful father lest he get out of line. Jung had talked about it and he had predicted that "all his and my children will come to hate homosexuality as an awful illness. They will not allow themselves these feelings of brotherly warmth for each other."

I had put all these pieces together. Freud and Jung both kept notebooks and long analyses of their dreams and their meetings with each other. Oh, those dreams! Filled with either Teutonic visions or, in Freud's case, dreams of Austrian soldiers and of Prometheus. He often woke up having wet his bed. He denied no truth to his diaries. Jung said he had helped Freud out in this situation at Columbia. I always wondered how. Did they both go into a toilet (Freud had complained constantly how difficult it was to locate them in America) where Jung helped clean him off? Both of them had frequent out-of-body experiences in the presence of each other over the years, if you can include, along with the enuresis, which is what peeing in your pants is called, fainting while together discussing theory. Once at lunch in Germany, Freud fainted in the restaurant and woke up in Jung's arms, and Freud said, "How sweet if this were death." Jung, still in awe of Freud at that time, like-wise realized on this trip to America that Freud was not all that Jung had made him into, or needed him made into, hence freeing himself up to march on alone. He was a vicious ladies' man anyway.

One wonders if being so in touch with your inner being makes your outer being more fragile and difficult to control.

These two great men carved up my world. I will just have to rise above it and say what I have to say with even more fervor and volume.

•

Your Roving Historian is particularly interested in all things Freudian. This is what Korah Ludens said that all these men would come to find so upset-ting: that women are the same as men. That women's hates and fears and loves and experiences are as men's. Women are not subject to the envy of penises, or to reverse Oedipus complexes, or to the Rivtov Scale, which says that homosexuality can be changed into heterosexuality (Rivtov will later reverse course, but not until after he has done much damage to Fred). Women can be as ambitious as men. They can be as greedy for power and success and fame. They possess qualities that can take them to the moon as well as to the kitchen. They experience hungers and sexual needs. For writing all this in her book *The Female in Her Time*, Korah Ludens is cast out. For writ-ing about loving your parents, for writing her book *The Patient as the Lover* (and the Analyst as one, too), she is cast out.

At that same meeting which expels her, it is decided by unanimous vote that homosexuality is to be officially considered an illness and that no homo-sexual can be considered for membership. The preceding year, the Ameri-can Psychiatric Association classified homosexuality as a mental illness, which it remains until 1974 (when there are coincidentally now 4 billion people in the world). The Hollywood Production Code fashions its fullest flowering sniffing out all things "distasteful and immoral and averse to the sensibilities of the general public," under the leadership of Peter Ruester, the powerful president of the Screen Actors Guild.

Korah sits in the back of the society's main meeting room, called too cutely Sigmund Haus, while the voice vote is taken.

"Concerning the expulsion of our member and colleague Dr. Korah Ludens, please vote aye in favor or nay against." The voice is that of Dr. Abraham Abraham (the first name is pronounced like Lincoln's, the second is pronounced starting with Aaahb), her orginal Manhattan Society "trainer," the man who was analyzed by Freud himself, the man to whom she has told her dreams.

She smiles, as she will smile in the photograph marching down Fifth Avenue, as she listens to the man who has been, along with Rivtov, who supervised her at Yaddah, and of course Freud himself, the most important man in her life, including Barnett Ludens, Lessie's brother, whom she has just married, who will prove an even bigger disappointment, tallying the votes against her. "I have unfortunately married unwisely for a second time," she had said only last week at their Yaddah student seminar, to Dr. Abraham Abraham, then, softly, asking him: "Why did you not warn me? You saw it coming. You know me. There is a story that one of your trainees is homosexual, though married, and you have met with him every day for seven years and neither one of you has ever mentioned homosexuality. That is a travesty of what we are meant to do, no?" He did not answer her.

"Dr. Tilsit?"

"Nay."

"One hundred and eighty-seven Aye. One Nay."

"Dr. Krebs?"

"Aye."

"One hundred and eighty-eight. One Nay."

"Dr. Rivtov?"

"Aye."

She sits listening, smiling, in the back of that room in 1934, asking herself why she has to endure this, like some complete and total masochist—yes, smiling, though each Aye enters her flesh like a bullet. How can I come out of this and not hate? she asks her journal. Each of these great men has said he loves me. Each has done important work. I must not discount this, just because I think differently about some things. I am ahead of my time. It is always difficult to be smarter than others. I must remember that new thoughts take time to digest. Women are not only the same as men, they are better than men. This she will never be able to say or write, only think in her heart. It is Supreme Blasphemy even to think that the sexes are equal. The last time she saw Freud he still had not left Vienna. What is the man waiting for? How smart can that man be?

"We shall start our own institute," Korah tells her followers at two o'clock in the morning when their march reaches Washington Square.

There will be a large practice, and fame, and her home with Barnett, who will go off to war and go crazy, but there will be no institute. Korah will be sent overseas to work with Dr. Spencer Lure, at first in London, then in North Africa, then in Haiti, then in the Everglades, studying the emotional problems encountered by soldiers engaged in germ warfare. When she returns to civilian life, in 1945, she is no longer interested in institutes. She has seen too many men kill each other and she is tired of men. She does not want to help them. After the war, and for the rest of her life, she will believe, again in her heart, she will not say it out loud, or write about it, or teach it, she will never be able to summon that kind of courage, that man is too far gone to help. She will only witness it every day, day after day, as she does try to help. But gone are the days when she thought she could make any difference.

She is exceptional. She is a woman who wants to change the world. She almost will. She will certainly be on her way. She is actually too wonderful, which means that awful things will happen to her, especially as a woman. But she is just starting out now, seeing patients, trying to locate the ones worth saving.

YOUR ROVING HISTORIAN TELLS US
ABOUT THE STADTDOTTERS

"What are these spots?"

Israel knows he's looking at something peculiar and rare and something inside him is saying that, as with the Iwacky, as with Mesirow titers, he has seen this before and no one is going to believe him. Recently some doctor even asked him about his degree. "I never heard of your Misch Fehl University. Why should I believe you?"

"It is a fine school in Palestine. My teachers were from Russia and Poland and Germany, places of great discoveries. I have been well educated. Better than you." He hates himself for even bothering to answer.

Israel is holding once again the hands of Evvilleena Stadtdotter. She is no doubt thinking, once again, What are huge hands meant to indicate? Doesn't that mean something? It is nice to be touched by Israel's hands. The huge soft hands of Israel Jerusalem are inspecting the skin of Evvilleena Stadtdotter, on December 15, 1933, in the Mount Thymun Pavilion of the Isidore Schmuck Medical Center in Northwest Washington, D.C. Her skin is aging, shriveling, drying up, and it is covered with tiny purple spots. What has happened to this woman since last he saw her?

She is Danish or Austrian or German or "something sort of Baltic," he was told by someone or other. In Washington there is always information available about anybody from someone or other. She says she is concerned about the purple spots. They can be seen, she says, through the thickest powders from the Haus of Destinee, a Belgian firm of which she's fond. "Deshtinee hassh failed." Is he incorrect in discerning that her schlurpings have improved a tiny bit? He seems to comprehend her better.

Evvilleena Stadtdotter is rich and lonely, and no one understands why she doesn't buy herself another husband after the first one disppears. Where the Stadtdotters arrived from, no one knows. Washington is like that. People just appear, and if they have money to pay their way they are accepted. No doubt other major world capitals often require additional, more substantial, credentials. Mr. Stadtdotter was thought to have been a Baltic diplomat (because of the new movies being made, the very word *Baltic* conjures up dark streets and mysterious shenanigans in port cities where strangers are clobbered on foggy docks) from some country or other. And Baltic embassies are notorious for requiring little in the way of representation beyond a body-in-place. Poor governments can't afford to be fussy. So desks are situated in rooms or houses, occasionally mansions, all over the Northwest, and heavy-stock stationery is embossed with eagles or something in Latin, maybe both. Mr. Stadtdotter disappeared a few years ago when the stock market disappeared.

Mr. Stadtdotter, when he was around, was one of the German Germans who oppose assimilation into American life. When he disappears he's been writing a learned philosophical tome entitled *Extermination of the Worthless Life* (he is much under the influence of both Kant and Heidegger). He is mistakenly believed to be a eugenicist. He had written and submitted to his neighbors on Massachusetts Avenue questionnaires with such queries as "Would you agree to ending your child's life if he was incurably ill or an imbecile or possessed of unchangeable qualities that others considered abnormal and abhorrent?" The answers that came in, anonymity guaranteed, were 90 percent in the affirmative. His book poses this question: "Given half a chance, will more people start hating people the minute they have the freedom to do so? Will this obsession with eugenics actually accomplish that?" Hadn't Nietzsche posed similar questions? No one in America knows all the names he's reading. "This country is not interested in philosophy," he writes. "Who and where are the American philosophers?"

Yes, they are a strange couple and are about to become even stranger. Like Germany itself, no one can figure them out. In any event, he was unable to obtain a publisher and had asked his wife for money to do this himself and she had refused.

Between 1929 and 1930 the population of Washington diminished by 13 percent. That is not a piddling amount in such a short time. A further 8 percent disappeared between 1931 and 1932. It was scary seeing so many "for rent" signs. You could even see there were fewer people on the streets. People just went somewhere else. We weren't, it seemed, all going to be millionaires or prominent . . . well, anythings. Foreigners—individuals and governments—came and went. Mr. Stadtdotter just went. No one can remember the Stadtdotters ever arriving. No one can remember Mr. Stadtdotter's first name. What kind of last name is Stadtdotter? One day he just wasn't here. Evvilleena doesn't seem to care, though she doesn't take down from over the front door the plaque with the crest of whatever country he came from (presumably she's from there, too) and was meant to represent. No one questions her. Washington is like that. People come and go. All the time. What was his name? What was her name? What was their name? I can't remember. No one's giving any info away. When they go, they go. The police can't keep up. Since diplomats are exempt from American laws, there isn't much point. These are days before blood types and medical and dental records exist to track down the absentees. Hermia mentioned that her husband is a spy. Sir Geoffrey will have a hard time with all this no-real-name business. Everyone in Britain has a name. He finds himself going after all sorts of people who aren't worth going after. Someone should have started with Evilleena. No one knows who she is either. "She was one fucking snot of snatch," Grace says when Israel tells her about her.

Evvilleena throws lavish parties in her mansion on Massachusetts Avenue, where she's ridiculed behind her back for making passes. She gets drunk and gropes crotches. Even before whatever-his-name-was disappeared. Whash wrong with that? They're my parteez. I do vat I vish. Her crotch-groping was all over town. Men, diplomats, State Department, went there to get groped by Evilleena, so they could tell they'd been groped on Mass. Ave. in a great big mansion. Whether her gropes led to their gropes is unknown.

Mr. Stadtdotter did have one hobby while he was here: black women, Negroes, the darker-skinned the better. He spent a great deal of time in those sections of black Washington where he might locate them. In those days it was relatively safe to go there and safe to purchase a woman at one of the Negro whorehouses or just right off the street. These proclivities are also known around and about. It's hard to keep secrets in this town when they're so . . . specific as this one.

We don't know if he procured one of those women for someone else. There's always someone or other to say that's what he did. For someone high up. It's usually someone high up. Or else why would someone or other say anything at all?

What has any of this got to do with glause?

YOUR ROVING HISTORIAN FILLS US IN ON SOME IMPORTANT INFORMATION ABOUT AN UNIMPORTANT PRESIDENT

According to *The Secret Sex Lives of the Presidents* by Marmora Hecht, Ph.D., Herbert Hoover required colored women to wash his clothes. He demanded that these women be matronly and maternal. He required them to wash his clothes while he still wore them. He would stand in a huge tub and they would stand beside him, two or three of them, and they would pour warm water over his head and take their big bars of soap and rub his clothing up and down. It is an unusual way to have an orgasm but not so harmless an unusual way as might on the surface appear. After each such washing the women would be sent away and punished. Hoover would do the punishing. He would summon Hevander Stadtdotter (Dr. Hecht finally provides us with this man's first name!), who had found the women for him, paying them each two dollars in advance. Both men would take them to a field in the remote Franeeda countryside where they would hang the women from tree branches until they were dead. Stadtdotter was a tall and very strong man. He could string up even the heaviest of the women without too much effort, but Hoover liked to help. He liked to kick away the stool supporting their feet. When the women had choked to death, President Hoover would break down in tears and Hevander would take him in an embrace and comfort him. Then they would sit down and eat some sandwiches and drink some beer from the picnic basket the White House kitchen sent along. Hoover never said out loud that he felt sorry for the poor but he did say to one dangling woman that the economy was sound and everything would get even better for everyone soon and she might mention this in Heaven on his behalf.

This is a man who does not see in what misery his people are living now, all across America. The stock market has crashed. Fifty-one hundred banks have already failed. He would not pay benefits to the unemployed. "It will damage their characters." His wife urged the Girl Scouts to do volunteer work to help out. Soldiers were still waiting for payments for service during World War I. What did he do wrong? The answer is another question: "What did he do right?" Waiting in the wings, Franklin D. Roosevelt is outraged. "There is nothing inside the man but jelly." FDR becomes president in 1933 at the same time Adolf Hitler becomes chancellor of Germany.

Stadtdotter disappeared when the colored neighborhoods became suspicious that his regular reappearances presaged the nonreappearance of a woman from their midst. He was captured and tortured with hot pokers in an underground chamber beneath the new Felindus Max Graves Cathedral of Our Holy People, after which he was torn limb from limb and roasted into cinders in the church's big new oven. (It is a very small "cathedral" and it will be outside Fred's bedroom window.)

When the ashes were taken from the oven, Felindus Max Graves said a prayer over them.

"These are white ashes. These are the ashes of hate. These are the last bits and pieces of someone who hated us. In his hate he performed such acts as our God would not permit us to tolerate. Our God is not his God. That is our sad secret. Our God is not the God of any white man who performs on our people such acts as this man performed. Let us pray for our dead sisters. Let us not pray for the soul of this white man whom our God consigns to Hell. O God, in the name of the only white man we revere, Abraham Lincoln, we have burned up this murderer of our women."

The ashes are then given to Madame Dretta, who has a special formula for a paste she sells as a foundation for colored women's makeup. "White men's bones are good for this," Madame Dretta says. "They're hard and they don't yield. You can pile layers of the thickest gunk on top of your black face and my stuff holds its grip." Madame Dretta becomes very rich and lives in a big house out on Sixteenth Street not far from the Masturbov mansion. As she lives with a white woman, the neighbors' lawyers cannot get her evicted, although they certainly try.

After Stadtdotter's disappearance, gossip comes from the White House servants about Herbert Hoover's roving taste. Always trust the valet and not the historians. It is said that he is able to let his hair down publicly only at the annual two-week Bohemian Grove encampment on the Russian River, which he calls "the greatest men's party on earth."

Bohemian Grove is where all the old rich queens of America's ruling elite go to get drunk, dress up in drag, feel up the giant redwoods and each other, and somehow get their rocks off without women. From its founding in the 1870s, it attracts many a president, including Herbert Hoover's distant cousin, Richard Nixon, another poster boy for sexual repression. In the 1950s, Nixon is seen perpetually in the company of his friend Charles "Bebe" Rebozo, a Florida businessman, in Key Biscayne, where they share a villa in its hotel, and without Bebe's ex-wife, who claims their marriage was never consummated, and without Pat and the girls. When the two first meet, Bebe tells a mutual acquaintance that Nixon's "a guy who doesn't know how to talk, doesn't drink, doesn't smoke, doesn't chase women, doesn't know how to play golf, doesn't know how to play tennis . . . he can't even fish," but soon enough they are so close that people begin speculating about the nature of their relationship, which lasts for forty-four years. Many decades later, on the Watergate Tapes, President Nixon is heard to say, "The Bohemian Grove I attend from time to time is the most faggy goddamn thing you can imagine. The San Francisco crowd, it's just terrible. I can't even shake hands with anybody from San Francisco."

Stadtdotter could and did before his disappearance. He was there with "the Nixon party."

GLAUSE?

With her husband, without her husband, Evvilleena parties on. It does appear that she hasn't got anything else to do. Free feeds bring in crowds of freeloaders. There are always plenty of hungry, dry-mouthed somebody-or-others with big-enough crotches lurking in oversized diplomatic pants. She grabs their crotches. She sticks her hand right in there. She goes for the balls. But she goes to bed alone. It's assumed she's rejected. It never occurs to anyone that she just likes to get smashed and grab dicks and maybe get fucked in a closet because she doesn't like to muss her bed. Yes, she feels sorry for herself in her loneliness. No town is nice to be lonely in. With so many men with such disdain for women, Washington is especially bad even if you speak English, which she doesn't really.

She's in love with Israel Jerusalem. He's twenty-five; she's somewhere way over sixty. She is slender and blond, with coy, flirting eyes that try to pretend they're a young girl's. She has a proud long neck that's always choked with pearls. Israel has stooped posture and tiny owl spectacles and those heavy tweed suits, no matter what the season. "You musht shvitsz profushely in your privatsh," she once ventures. His feet are huge, wide, and long; they are beginning their lifelong habit of always hurting; soon he's taking off his shoes and padding around the halls of Mount Thymun in the soft slippers old men wear.

While he again explores her body carefully with his huge soft hands (these are still the days when the eye is a doctor's most important diagnostic tool) she chatters on to him about her parties, about her crotches (a few choice items from her arsenal: "I am shurtain she padz with falshies"; "Kleine, Kleine"; "Hiss government should know wass ich know"), about her loneliness, "which only you can cure."

She is not shy about her goal.

"I am a rich woman with no one to share my riches with."

"I look at you and you never look back to me. Shame!"

"Israel! I want you for mine! Why are you giving me hard times!"

She told him that late at night, in the dark, in her bed alone, she asked herself if there was any way in this world that he could love her back. "It happenss. It happensss! You did not answer me." That was when she went away for longer than usual and now she's back. She can see his expression. He's not happy with her.

He's never seen her looking so poorly. She always had a pride that buoyed her spirits, a grace that gave her glamour. Now she is too thin and her makeup is too thick. Her spine seems no longer to support her correctly.

"My subconscious says to me: Why?"

She won't look him in the eye. Her confidence is waning.

"I have not been feeling well for a while now. I was feeling wonderful.

For some time. Euphoric. I felt better and better. I was planning to come and surprise you."

Where are all her sshushes?

He waits for her to say more.

"Your office is still too small for such a smart man."

"It is big enough."

He is holding her hands and looking at the purple spots that the last time he saw her were only dots. Up her arm there are more of them, some quite raised and bumpy, of a deep purple color, like some Victorian shade of ink. Yes, he recognizes them.

Without his asking she stands and slips off the white robe. She stares into space as she does so, like someone who already knows the worst, or is preparing for execution. He prays she will not jump him.

He writes in his medical notes: "She stands naked before me. Her breasts have been removed. The scars are still healing: bold black stitches like two jagged zippers slashing her chest. On her trunk are clusters of small raised purple bumps. She bows her head. My eyes fall farther downward.

"There is a penis of sorts, and some kind of sack sagging behind it, weighted down."

His reflexes take over instinctively: Israel's fingers feel all the many spots, one after another, darting from here to there as fast as his eye locates one more, kneeling down to face it head-on, jumping up to reach a farther one, turning her around, poking, sticking, prodding, until his fingers are sore. Some spots are hard, some seem soft, as if there's swelling beneath them, something liquescent.

Finally he takes the penis in his hand. It is a cold thing, and quite large.

He's heard talk and read for years about sex switches. People masquerading as something else is not new. But what she has done, this is new. He feels the testicles. One is hard like a marble; the other one feels pliable. Could they indeed be real testicles? To judge from her wincing when he presses them even lightly, they just might be. One of them at least, the pliable one.

Now she looks at him. He hasn't the vaguest notion what to say. What is this over her eyebrow? Another swelling. Also soft. Also malleable. It is a raised fedema.

Israel takes a syringe and extracts some liquid from the fedema and excuses himself. "I must study this liquid under the microscope. Please to wait."

As he walks from his office Evvilleena Stadtdotter cries out, "Israel, I did this for you!"

"I walk quickly to the Feutra Lab. The Feutra is an old machine, so no one is around. All rush to use the Moneckulir, which I have no desire to master. The Moneckulir is another fraudulent German technical 'wonder' to bankrupt hospitals. It counts faster but I distrust the results. I release drops of her liquid on a slide and place it beneath the Feutra's Quotrum, which I set at a cervicular heft of twelve. Slowly something comes into view. What is it? What is it? These moments thrill me; I prefer laboratories and test tubes and microscopes to people. So why aren't I with *these* all the time? Do I run away from all exciting things?"

As he waits for the smear to expose itself fully he waits for his unconscious to talk to him. There is all this new stuff with the unconscious. He is becoming friendly with his unconscious. He has been reading Freud, who is beginning to be talked about more and more, and learning about an inner self he never knew existed. "Herr Freud writes beautifully. I can actually hear his pure precision that can only come in the German language. English is too . . . squishy, like loose stools. Perhaps there is such a thing as a good German! Well, Dr. Freud is Austrian. Freud is very rational. With such an outpouring, such a plenitude of *newness*! The unconscious. The subconscious. The id. The ego. The . . . Where am I? What says the smear? What is the thread between the smear and . . . Mercy Hooker? I do *not* want to think about mutilated Frau Evvilleena Stadtdotter. What am I to do with her? Him? It? Will the blood tell me what to do? A dim image is swirling in the back of my skull, trying to focus itself. Why is it taking so long? Please, God, will one day someone who is not a German invent something faster than the Feutra? Word is beginning to filter through and I am not listening to those words like I am not listening to my unconscious that could tell me why Mercy Hooker."

"I want to win awards," he also writes in his journal. "Not when I am old and hardly able to schlepp across a podium to mumble a few gracious words to a gathering of faces whose names I can no longer remember. If I fail, will I rationalize? Freud wrote about *die Rationalisierung. Die Rationalisierung* seems to be something mature to do when it's too late to do anything else. As if to say, I did not do better because the world is so imperfect it's impossible for it to change. What a strange thing for an ambitious Jew to write. Perhaps I am not ambitious enough."

This Quotrum is taking forever!

One hour later the Quotrum is still counting. Why is this blood so dense? He cannot leave Evvilleena much longer.

Glause.

He doesn't want to go back to that office. Israel doesn't know how to deal with crazies. (Washington has too many of them.) Is not the world—*anywhere*—organized in a more *coherent* scheme of things? I must read Dr. Freud more swiftly!

Glause.

His pace quickens, not to get to Evvilleena but to his files. Which are in the office. With her. For *me*? She did *what* for me? Yes, he does not want to go back into this office. But he goes.

He is about to say, I think I have a clue; there is something the Iwacky called . . . glause . . .

She is entirely purple. One big spot on the floor. The purplenesses have all coalesced into one consuming blotch. She is dead.

"Also, her penis has fallen off. She is holding it in her hand. There is blood coming from her crotch. Did she pull it off? No. There is a bloodied scalpel near her. My God. Like some Iwacky.

"There is a note on the floor. Beside the penis. 'I thought you wanted to love another man.' "

He is sick to his stomach. He vomits. He cannot stop retching. His vomit meets her blood in pools.

He never forgets the sight of blood and vomit circling the hand holding the mangled penis. The mass of fibrous fictitious flesh fashioned into a male member. He later studies it. Part of it is human skin and muscle; the rest is surgical meshing wired and soldered firmly together. There are people who will do anything to you if you have the money and can find them.

"Why did she think I'm something I'm not?"

"Where did she get this done to her?"

Had these questions been answered, or at least raised more publicly at this time of Israel's asking them, might they have stopped a plague?

Was Evvilleena Stadtdotter the first case in Washington, or anywhere in America, or anywhere in the world, of The Underlying Condition, on June 25, 1933, almost fifty years before the plague of UC is finally named UC? Of course not! Was Mercy Hooker some eight years earlier? Of course not! Was Israel a conduit between them? There is much history yet to learn.

Glause.

"I hear the word *glause* in my ears and in my sleep and in my nightmares, and I sees a grisly mutilated counterfeit penis. Last night I had the shivers. There, in *The Secret and Its Parabola*, were the words 'If it is inside, it will come outside, but only if the dredge is willing to dig up its fulcrum.' I wrote them down. I wrote down the voices I hear also. 'Vasvistuvenu haroror nay vintna ovedembar goi lin fu.' What language is this? I think maybe for this moment I am having some breakdown of communication with all these new parts of me Dr. Freud says I have."

Can he find sustenance, a reason to go on, somewhere in all this?

MORE FROM ISRAEL'S NOTEBOOKS

There is something wrong with her blood. (This I need a Quotrom to tell me!) It is not yielding. What do I mean by yielding? I am making it sound like bread and yeast. Well, blood can be like that. Its secrets must be *raised* out of its depths. The Quotrum isn't working, isn't doing this. And I do not think it is the Quotrum's fault. I study my Mercy notes. Mercy's blood, too, had not yielded. At first.

I saved liquid in bottles. I noticed its smell was awful. Like rotten eggs. Like a particularly gaseous bowel movement.

Some numbers are finally appearing on the Quotrum. I discover they are slightly different from Mercy's. Evvilleena's are higher. None of this is helpful or reveals to me anything useful. In neither case, of course, are the numbers what they should be in normal people.

Evvilleena is dead on my floor. This is unfortunate, because the hospital does not have good arrangements for the removal of deads. You cannot just wheel them out with a sheet over them, because people in the corridor faint. So she is staying there for a while. On my floor. Until the early a.m. shift. That is how they do it. I try to tell them this is exceptionally unsanitary. We are together, Evvilleena and Israel. I almost hear her say, At last I have you.

I pick the penis up off my lab table with big forceps. I must have squeezed too hard, because suddenly there is a squirt and squish and there is blood all over the place. My hands, my clothes are covered. What is this? What is this!

I do not even think of possible contaging. I fall on my knees and look at Evvilleena's crotch. It is bloody and now drying, the brutalized flesh, so that it looks like . . . like what? Like tomatoes in the sun too long in Italy. And it stinks to high hell. Underneath whatever surgery was done to this Evvilleena to make a man of her I see some residual labia! This area is greatly engorged. Just like Mercy was swollen! What is in their blood to do this? To both of them? With Evvilleena I perhaps make a guess it is because of some infection from the operations, perhaps something tropical. I do not know what country she gets butchered in, but no haser who does this for a living is clean wherever he is.

Then I remember what I don't remember, something about Mercy's crotch. There were tiny purple dots all around her crotch, like a rash. They were so tiny I remember thinking she was having a reaction to something, like to medicine or drugs. The rich use lots of drugs.

As I poke around in Evvilleena's privates, now with a small flashlight— yes, yes! I find purple spots there, too. They are not so easy to find because her whole body has turned purple, but there they are, tiny raised bumps, hard on the outside, soft on the inside.

Now I am getting into tricky water because I did not do a thorough study of Mercy's crotch. I didn't have to. I discovered she was bleeding because of those spiked ivory penises and I stopped her bleeding and she went home and took heroin for a few years and died. Heroin? No, I think that is not useful to me. It could have been a bad dose, but that would not cause skewed numbers.

After washing as best I can I go on my hands and knees and scrape Evvilleena's crotch with my Rohl blade and smear the skin and flesh and blood onto more slides. This time I go to my own tiny lab. I have here my favorite tricks. I take some diluted solution of Abner, which is something I learned about in Palestine. Abner is one part alcohol and one part fizemidine, and this, sprinkled on the slide, tells me poison is present. (Of all the doctors in the world, only doctors in Palestine do this trick. Why is that? It is so much faster and so much less messy and complicated than using Divosidol. But then Greeting makes much money from Divosidol. You make Abner for two cents.) The stuff from her crotch is, I would guess, 90 percent poison. The woman is dead, not from slicing off her phony schmuck, but from some poison in her.

It must be some poison she herself is manufacturing. What else could it be! Mercy must have had the same poison in her. Only not so much as to kill her.

Now I must go back a little to those spiked ivory penises of Mercy's. I still have some of her dried blood on some slides, so of course I do the Abner business immediately. Her blood is full of poison, but not more than 50 percent, I would guess. Is that 40 percent difference why Mercy lives until the heroin kills her and Evvilleena krechs immediately on my floor?

I wonder: Can this poison come from sex? Were these women poisoned by having sex? How did I even think this thought? How can I investigate it, and prove it scientifically?

That would mean this comes from what the man inserts into these women.

I sit in my tiny lab. I look out the window at some meshuggener statue in some pretty garden in the moonlight.

"From the distance comes the rest that will protect you."

This is from the Vishnah. It is not helpful. Lately I read all the time Dr. Freud and not so much from my religious heritage. Dr. Freud teaches there are no accidents, so I am recalling this passage for a reason, from out of my subconscious and into the light. It is like a remembered dream. There is a reason, both for the dream and for the remembering, for the dredge digging up the fulcrum.

"From the distance comes the rest that will protect you."

Rest? I do not wish to rest. If anything I am throbbing with excitement. I have so much energy even though it must be the middle of the night and I don't want to rest at all.

But wait. "Rest" is meaning different things. Rest is also meaning "the other part."

Throbbing? Why am I using this word? This is a strange word to come into my head. What does it mean, Dr. Freud, throbbing?

I am having an erection. My penis is very hard and it is, yes, throbbing. It is like another part of me that I am hearing from and it is telling me that it wants to get out from its captivity. Why now? What has been working inside me to make my penis hard? I have been dealing with the poison of two dead women. One of them I had some sort of sex with on the floor. That is the last time my penis was erect and the last time semen came from me.

I am always frightened of my penis. It's always seemed to be another person. How can it be that a man in his mid-twenties looks upon his penis, if not as his enemy, certainly not as the friend it is to most men? It is a war. Not a war with anger, a war with stalemates, with stand-offs. I leave you alone if you leave me alone. You don't cross my borders, I let you live in peace.

Hands off!

I stare out at the garden, the Mathilde Eiker Schmuck Memorial Garden. In the moonlight, the grass looks almost black, like a velvet blanket on the lawn. Snow begins falling gently, creating a lovely sight. I am happy here in America. I say this out loud. I am surprised by the thought and surprised I allow myself to say it out loud. Why are the thought and the thinker two different things? They are one and the same! A whole!

I find myself unbuttoning my fly and burying my hand through layers of shirt, undershirt, underpants, until it finds the center of the warmth. It *is* bigger. It feels so warm and nice. That everything is all right, that there is such harmony in the snow scene of nature outside and the warmth I feel for myself inside, brings tears to my eyes. Hello, hello. Hello to you. The soft, bushy blond hair. The smooth skin on my flanks. The strength of the thing as it pops out to say hello to the night and to its master, now massaging it gently and in a friendly manner in the New World. Hello. We are friends, yes? You become so big! You are happy in this New World also?

We do this nice and slow. So it will feel nice for a long time. I stop every so often, just in case. Then I decide it would be nice not to have my clothing on. To be naked in the night, and free. The room is too hot as it is. So much heat in this New World. I giggle. When have you giggled last, Israel, eh? I cannot in truth remember. I cannot.

I feel my naked body in space. Now, freed, my penis is even bigger, sticking out like some signpost pointing a direction. Why have I not been aware that mine is of a noble proportion? My giggle turns into a laugh.

I've looked at myself so little!

"*Unscrew the locks from the doors! Unscrew the doors themselves from their jambs! Through me forbidden voices, Voices of sexes and lusts, voices veil'd and I remove the veil, Voices indecent by me clarified and transfigur'd.*"

With Mr. Freud I am reading Mr. Walt Whitman. How can he say so much as he does in print? In America is anything possible? I don't think so. Then I begin to masturbate in earnest. I send down some spit to help. I learn this trick from the Iwacky youths. How can a grown man not have remembered how somewhere along the road of life to spit on his dick brings more pleasure when beating off? Well, whatever the reason, I have not remembered it. And now I do. It is filled with life! It, too, wants to stay alive!

Finally it's time. I am ready to explode. I sit down in the middle of the floor, cross-legged—like an Indian!—and I place beside me several glass slides for the Quotrum. My wonderful ejaculation that spurts up to my face, to slide down my chest, so white it's like that silly marble statue outside, along with my happy tears of gratitude.

I want to lie back and enjoy the after-waves of tremors still shivering through this skinny body. I am a scientist! I must know what is in this stuff, this semen.

Under the Quotrum, my semen quickly reveals abnormally high titers of sindel and abnormally low measurements of fane. I am still unclothed and though a moment ago I'd felt cool and refreshed, suddenly I begin to sweat. Low drittal fane is not good and not bad. But combined with sindel it is an indicator that a poison is loose in the body. I prick my finger, rub a drop of my blood on a slide, and put it under the Quotrum. Right away something is wrong. The huge apparatus indicates it is going to take a long time to count something unusual. My sweat is now profuse. I dress myself while the counting proceeds. My heart is racing. While the soft click of the Quotrum's abnometer registers higher and higher readings, I rub my pricked finger onto the marble slab where I mix my tinctures. I squeeze out a big blob of blood. I find my jar of Abner and douse my blood with it. I smear another slide with this mess and rush to my old faithful friend, the small microscope given to me by the shul in Hortz bei Todstadt, as a good luck present when I went off to Misch Fehl in Palestine. Even by a rough calculation I suspect my blood contains something that shouldn't be there. When the Quotrum finally finishes its own calculations, and I look into the microscope, my semen and my blood both are revealed to be at least 50 percent poison. My blode count is off the meter.

I am going crazy. Inside me, I am very sick. I am almost too frightened to consider what is obvious before my eyes: that somehow I have been infected by either Mercy or Evvilleena. But how? Did I cut myself when I investigated Mercy's insides? A small prick from one of those spikes? When Evvilleena and I were on the floor and she kissed me and licked me, did she transmit something? And then her penis exploded all over me. Is *touching* blood enough?

I must not be so frightened. I must get hold of myself. I am a scientist. I am a doctor. I am here to place my intelligence and instincts in the service of humanity. I am here to save people. If I am to be sick from this, then that is part of the highest sacrifice God can require.

So, now I am friends with God again. Where is Dr. Freud? What is Dr. Freud saying about any of this? At this moment, perhaps God is talking louder.

Now I stand tall and become the research scientist. I utilize every strength I can call on to repress my fears.

I make slides of my blood and Mercy's blood, and of my blood and Evvilleena's blood.

I discover that in both cases the poisons have canceled each other out.

What does this mean? I thinks it means that although I have been infected by either Mercy or Evvilleena, or both, something in my own blood has neutralized the invading poison and protected me from death.

My body is beginning to feel ill. I am dizzy.

From what?

I make a cut in my arm. I place a slide on which I have smeared some of Evvilleena's blood against my open flesh. I choose Evvilleena's and not Mercy's because I believe Mercy has less poison and my exposure to Evvilleena is more recent.

Then I sit down on the floor again, cross-legged like an Indian again. I want to see if I will live or die.

•

I am worried about this Dr. Israel Jerusalem. He is sniffing too close. One of these days he could find me. I go weeks at a time feeling very under the weather, without killing anyone. I am thinking that there must be something really smart that I can do to get ahead in this world.

ADMIRING GRACE

This is when I came as close to loving a fucking man as I ever would.

By exposing himself to the poison in Mrs. Fake Prick Stadtdotter's blood, Dr. Israel Jerusalem has unknowingly vaccinated himself against the plague that is yet to come. But that he exposed himself—on purpose—to what he was researching, well, the heroism inherent in this action simply took my breath away when he told me about it and it still does. I know of few scientists so willing to go this far in their fight for knowledge. I sure as fucking shit wouldn't. (Although after Partekla some will say I already have. And they would be right.)

At this point, we are unable to guess which of those two grotesque women infected him. Or if anything placed him in danger of contagion. When he recovers from the fever that lays him low for a few weeks and perplexes the entire staff, he longs to try the same experiment on another human, but of course the fucking ass-dragging medical review boards, something already in place to make all our lives miserable, would not allow this.

Science often smacks of parody or silliness when it can prove to be neither one shitty thing nor another shitty thing. This will not be the last example of the ridiculous parading as the truth it is. Or the truth parading as the ridiculous. This is one reason I cuss so fucking goddamned much. Life is profane and should be honored as such.

DAME LADY HERMIA PECKS AWAY AT HER INVESTIGATION: EVIL IS COMING CLOSER

In 1934, Reinhard Heydrich, who in a few short years will become notorious as the architect of Hitler's plan for the Final Solution of the Jews, prepares and delivers a number of policy papers concerning the Jews and "other unwanted populations." "It is the aim of the State Police to encourage immigration of Jews and homosexuals out of Germany and to discourage in every way possible any desire to remain in Germany . . . Activities of these people should be restricted in order to force them to abandon the idea of remaining in Germany."

Little attention is paid to an ancillary report prepared and delivered by Jeshua Brinestalker in various locales around America, outlining an equally stringent plan to go hand in hand with Heydrich's, to rid the world of homosexuals. "It must be made known to this undesirable element that they too are unwelcome from this time forward and their determination to remain will be dealt with in the harshest terms. It must be made known that they are being identified and their whereabouts identified." There are many German-American associations of one kind or another, and Jeshua tries to visit as many as he can. Many Germans feel conflicted over this determination by "foreign elements" to dictate their moralities; these are the ones who now feel American; but there are of course German Americans who do hate Jews and homosexuals.

Membership rolls in German-American organizations begin to decline rapidly. No matter which their bent, these members realize that it is no longer any time to be a German in America, no matter what. So this pushes Jeshua's activities underground, unlike in Germany and his other client countries.

YRH FINDS MORE SHIT

Brief mention was made of a Dr. Gobesh Table, a Moroccan Jew who opened a small hotel in a remote part of Florida around the time of the Civil War. He was interested in trying to convert human shit into food. By the 1930s, Hi and Meyer Table have opened two "family-style" hotels in rural New Jersey, on Lake Windham, an hour or so from New York. Presumably this is the same family, as the name is a bit unusual, but the New Jersey brothers claim no knowledge of any Moroccan ancestry. What they do claim is an ancestral arrival in America long enough ago to entitle them to membership in the Society of Early Americans, which would welcome them but for their Jewish religion, a rebuff that will increasingly annoy the Table women, who, the richer they will get, the grander. In any event, there certainly is a dark cast to the pigmentation of the skin coloring of all direct Table descendants to this day.

Hi and Meyer run the two adjoining hotels, which cater to Jewish families seeking inexpensive holiday accommodations and decent food, cooked by their mother, Nettie. There is a third brother, Nookie, the strange one, and of course his mother's favorite.

Since childhood, Nookie has been inordinately interested in dirt, the earth. Everything goes into the earth. It is the earth, the very soil, that we build on and in, the earth that absorbs our eliminations and those of our animals, the earth in which we grow our food. What amazing thing dirt must be to accommodate so many contributions. But what can it give back to us? Nookie wonders. Surely there is something valuable it can give back to us, beyond its ability to grow our food. Nookie wants to know the secrets of dirt. In this he follows in the footsteps of the early Hookers that Grace told us about.

At ten, Nookie begins to perform what he calls "screening the soil," which is just what it sounds like: he takes a screen from one of the hotel windows and sifts dirt through it, rubbing it with his palms to get as much through the mesh as he can. What remains is usually nothing more than pebbles and worms and bugs, but sometimes there is thicker dirt, dirt with more clay in it, for instance, or thinner dirt, like grains of sand. He begins to see that there are different grades of soil. He wonders if there is anything to these different grades. Over the next few years he classifies some dozen consistencies. He feeds each of these to the cows and chickens, the cats and dogs, and observes the effects. They come down with occasional maladies, usually diarrhea or its reverse, constipation. Nettie begins to worry about the increasing frequency of these bowel malfunctionings all over the backyard, but before she knows it, Nookie dies from something the family doctor cannot identify. His vomit looks like crimson mud dirt, and he is covered with purple scabs.

Hi and Meyer come across their brother's notes. Evidently he had been testing a "cure-all" on the farm animals. His notes indicate that various weak and faltering animals all "sprang back to life" after he fed them his "cure-all."

He had written down his recipe. It involves nothing more than taking mud from the edge of the lake, putting it into a bottle with some water, and spooning it into the animals. The edge of the lake has been a favorite spot for household pets and farm animals to unload. Hi and Meyer gather up some mud and try the elixir on an ailing calf, and indeed it does work. They try it on an elderly horse, which springs into a gallop. After a number of like experiments the brothers begin to peddle Nookie's No-Nonsense Animal Cure-All. To their surprise, it grows into a substantial success, so much so that they lose interest in the hospitality business and close the hotels.

The success of their product comes to the attention of Clarence Meekly Dridge II. He has its contents studied. Interesting. He is not unaware of the ingredients contained in Dridge Flakes, which is made by the company that his adopted father started. He determines to copy Nookie's No-Nonsense Cure-All for human consumption. After all, he reasons, if it's good for the animals it will be good for the people.

The resultant elixir, Virulea, is released in the Midwest in 1935. If mortality records for this year and in these states were to be studied, it would be revealed that they record 725 deaths from an unknown cause believed to be related to "the ingestion of an unnamed 'patent medicine' manufactured and distributed by 'The New Home of Well-Being,'" which, upon further investigation, would be discovered to be owned by Greeting, which, when the number of dead human consumers of Virulea surpasses several thousand, quietly removes the product from the marketplace. However, Nookie's Animal Cure-All continues to be sold to the agricultural market, and continues to be an important part of the Table family's increasing wealth. As the Tables are unaware of the Greeting Virulea, Hi and Meyer begin thinking about their own version of Nookie's for humans. They buy two more hotels—these are on the edge of the Everglades—where even higher effluvial deposits of ancient shit are stacked up and packed down along the shores than in New Jersey. One of these Tables, probably Meyer because Hi isn't very smart, knows what he's doing. Gobesh Table is not heard from again.

NU SHIT (IN WHICH A BRILLIANT YOUNG SCIENTIST IS FORCED TO SOUND LIKE CHARLIE CHAN)

The history of Catholic medicine is a special one. As I am a Catholic this section falls to me by default or squatter's rights. I am going to try to relate it without resorting to one tidge of profanity, with two hopes, one that God will forgive His Sister Grace for telling it like it is, and the second that its profanity speaks for itself. I shall try to get the sound of Nu, but that's a toughie.

Over the centuries the Church has preferred to tend and minister rather than to investigate or to cure. This attitude has naturally made life miserable for many of us. But cures are tricky matters. If one is intent on proving the existence of a loving God Who heals, then it is a problematic occurrence when a cure might possibly be attributed not to miracle but to medicine. Pope after pope has felt it best to stay out of irony's way and stick to miracles, which, in Catholicism (and perhaps in lay life as well), have about as good an average as unguents, ointments, pills, and invasive lacerations of the flesh.

Washington has never been thought of as a particularly Catholic town. Compared with Boston, say, or Florence, it isn't. But those committed to the True Faith have a way of making their powerful presence known, no matter where. At this point in the District's history, much of its Northeast quadrant is, to all purposes, owned, controlled, and pervaded by my Church. Here in the Northeast can be found the many institutions of low, middle, and higher learning, the cathedrals, grottoes, shrines, and relics, and the enormous hospital and medical center, Mater Nostra Dolorosa, where I am myself enshrined in all my glory so worthy of respect, and of course the Great Shrine itself, the Epostes of the Most High Regard, where St. Trusst is said to have said her last prayer and died (and where I had my first visions of the Virgin Mary and my first orgasm).

In May 1937, *The New England Journal of Feces* publishes the findings of

Dr. Flo Hung Nu, of the Laboratory of Fecal Hematology at Mater Nostra Dolorosa. To coin a phrase, the shit hits the fan.

Dr. Flo, in her own practice, which is confined to nuns, has noticed that when withdrawing blood from several sick sisters, this blood is exceptionally dark, almost black. (She is never to know that this blood matches the fedema fluid Israel has drawn from Cousin Mercy and Evvilleena Stadtdotter.) You almost wouldn't think it was blood. It is also extremely toxic. Dr. Flo's version of Israel's Abner trick, involving a Burmese tincture of beet mixed with ordinary tonic water (or anything with quinine in it), shows the blood to be about 65 percent poison. Nun One dies shortly after her blood sample is taken. Within hours, Dr. Flo has the dead religious under autopsy. She sees nothing she recognizes. Both *The New England Journal of Blood* and *The New England Journal of Poisons*, not to mention *The New England Journal of Feces*, to all of which she reports this, refuse to publish without more information.

The Laboratory of Fecal Hematology deals exclusively in the study of blood in feces. Feces is viewed as the barometer of the body's health. Many parts of the world, particularly those most distant from America, hold firmly to such theories and it was only because of pressure from mushrooming Catholic outposts in Southeast Asia and South America that this small lab was set up in Washington for Dr. Flo. Dr. Flo finds the just-dead nun's intestines were ready to explode from impacted shit. Nothing life-threatening, under ordinary circumstances, but certainly something to keep an eye on if the patient were still alive and hopefully dosing with milk of magnesia. But the nun is dead. From what? The second dead nun's shit is 25 percent poison, which is just short of fatal and would probably not have killed her had a heart attack not presumably done so first. The 63 percent poison in the third dead nun's feces is obviously what did her in.

Very mysterious. A bit too mysterious for the archdiocese, which does not view feces as a barometer of anything but unpleasant. Particularly when it is Catholic shit that is written about in *The New England Journal of Feces*, a publication heretofore unknown to the Church.

Since she's reporting from a Catholic hospital, Flo's research should have been submitted first to Mater Nostra's Board of Procedures for approval before she released it to the outside world. Naturally, such approval would have been denied. As one of the monsignors remarks, "The Church does not desire the world to know it deals in shit." Dr. Flo, smiling, always smiling, as those uncomfortable with the American language often do, nods energetically. "Yes, yes, shit," she grins. The monsignor realizes he's not getting through. Dr. Flo realizes he's going to be trouble. How can she convince these holies of the importance of her discovery when she doesn't speak their language and when she does she sounds like Charlie Chan?

All this medical research business is new for Mater Nostra. As well as for the Mother Church in Rome. Hospitals, yes. The sick must always be tended. But twentieth-century medicine is becoming vastly too incomprehensible. How to justify paying for shit is a question soon on the agenda of covert ecclesiastical powwows. Experiments to find answers that the Church must condemn, by doctrine writ in stone, seem a big waste of money, a public relations nightmare, a pain in the holy asses.

It makes no difference that most of this era's prominent doctors and researchers—all advocating *progress* (a word the Church is coming to dread as much as *condom*)—are men (except for Dr. Flo and me, not that long out of Masturbov Gardens).

Dr. Flo, whose entire education since her birth in a missionized distant land has been financed by Catholic money, understands the monsignor. "You are hereby forbidden to study any more shit!"

"Ne, ne!"

With a piercing cry of protest Dr. Flo runs from the board's convocation room inside the Quadrangle of St. Catheter's Cathedral and out into the quiet streets of this part of the Northeast which in some ten years' time will turn even darker.

"Dr. Nu! Dr. Nu!" The young monsignor, who has been so thoughtless with his tone of voice and who is quite handsome and who (for a change) is attracted to the young Oriental lass, runs briefly after her.

But she runs on. (Americans do not understand that it is quite rude to address her as Dr. Nu, because she is from that part of New Chang where the first name is really the last name.)

She writes requesting a dispensation from the next higher recourse, the Jesus and Mary Board of Oversight.

Jesus and Mary reject her as well. There remains the archbishop of the city himself.

Dr. Flo is not a quitter. "I find way. I not come to New World to be flunky."

The chief residence of the Washington Archdiocese adjoins St. Catheter's Cathedral on the corner of Guam Street and Perth Amboy Place, N.E. (not far from the Most Holy Soul Junior and Senior High Schools where Mercy

Hooker went and Grace did, too), a huge, four-story pile of irregularly shaped stones and boulders stuck together with various centuries' mortars, dark red in hue from the roof's dissolving lead. It is a forbidding place and children in the neighborhood refuse to play nearby. This house was many things in past lives—a rich man's palace, a gangster's den, a whorehouse, the headquarters of an international theosophical society—until the Webb family deeded it to the Church in 1920. Earlier Webbs always had reasons to want God on their side; they were usually leaving town fast but wished to be well remembered in higher places. Daniel Jerusalem will be very smitten with the Webbs' granddaughter, Claudia, who was not yet born, nor was he, when this mansion had to be unloaded. In any event, picture Dr. Flo Hung Nu, her tininess and skin color all peculiarly unexpected in a visitor making her way up the long landscaped driveway to lift the heavy knocker.

This would now be a cardinal's residence if Rome liked Washington more, but Rome doesn't much like America, so an archbishop lives here. He is said to be a flaming queen called Missy, and perhaps he is, though there are those who say as much of every prelate in a dress. Missy or not, some business on this occasion has sent him out of town. Although the curt letter strenuously objecting to Dr. Flo's research bears the signature of His Holiness, Cardinal Nerr, of the Vatican itself, her appointment is with an underling, Bishop Sheeney. He, too, is said to be a flaming queen. He is.

In truth, Bishop Sheeney had smelled something funny and written the letter over the fictitious Cardinal Nerr's name. Discolored blood in shit was not a matter the bishop thought any cardinal would like to hear about. Forgery is nothing when it comes to covering one's ass.

"We do not wish to concern Ourselves any further with your findings," the bishop, also a small person, says to Dr. Flo after she kneels and kisses his ring. "Oh, you needn't go down so far . . . oooh, that's sweet."

She misses in this new world the less insistent Catholicism of her homeland, where the poor people live with God because they need Him, not because rings require kisses. Before she was born, her parents were converted to the Church by French missionaries sent to their tiny village (now deep in Communist territory and renamed), and she remains a grateful Catholic because they made her a doctor. She is not unaware of the many medicines derived from the plant and animal life of that homeland, which have benefited all mankind, and she is motivated mightily to repay her benefactors with the certain fame her discovery will bring. While there is no medicine inherent yet in what she's found, one never knew, one never knew. Feces as a fecund foundation for fostering a future free from famine, well, many are the people in her part of the world who live on some form of bodily waste made into patties and stews and soups.

"Your Bishopship," she says, still with her head bowed, "what is being found by Dr. Flo is something the Church will someday make me saint."

"Do not succumb to the sin of Pride, my child of yellow skin."

"My discovery honor Him!"

"How can that be! The bloody . . . fecal matter . . ." He quotes from the issue of *Feces* clutched in his hand. Something must have gone very wrong with the catechism of her homeland. He always knew it was a mistake to cast the net so wide. No grocery is required to sell every brand. Perhaps he should quote Scripture. If only he could think of something relevant. "My brother is a hairy man . . ."

She says simply, "Bloody shit kill them."

He replies swiftly, "You must cease and desist!"

"Something in bloody shit *contagious*."

Contagious? He steps back. "Nevertheless."

"If contagious then homofruits all kill each other."

This is shit of a different color. "Please, my butterfly, come sit on the floor, as I believe is your custom, and we shall have tea in the tiny cups of your homeland, with no handles. And you shall tell me what you mean by . . . homofruits."

He rings a tinkling bell and sits down on the floor in the middle of the room, crossing his cassocked legs, which are shapely and recently waxed. She wishes to tell him that, among other things, he has his countries confused, not to mention his cultures. After the old female retainer, at first flustered by serving tea at floor level, departs (for some reason she exits the room after serving by crawling on her hands and knees backward), the youngish bishop, putting aside the offending publication, assumes his most unctuous smile and takes her tiny hand in his tiny hand.

"Homofruits?"

"Poofters."

"I know what they are. What about them?"

"This blood shit come from them. This blood shit poison. It pass all test for killers. My cat die from eating this blood shit."

"How do you know that . . . homosexuals—we *must* call them homosexuals . . . much as we dislike them, of course . . . still, that is what they are to be called—how do you know this is happening only to them?"

"I not say only. Contagious is contagious. I say only that my samples come from nuns."

"Nuns!"

"Nuns."

"You consider nuns . . . homofruits?" He seems relieved.

"Yes! Yes!"

"Very interesting." The bishop wonders if an investigatory purge of nuns might be useful to his advancement. "Please continue."

"I see them . . ." She blushes and waves her free hand meaningfully. "They use man's penis made of wood. All covered in shit. They die soon later. I take blood from them and shit from them and shit from wood penis. All poison. One kill other." She shrugs. She makes a face, scrunching up all her features from chin to brow. "My cat lick. Bye-bye, pussy."

Suddenly, at this moment, Bishop Sheeney, who is not Irish, and who is sick and tired of the wisecracks about his name, among other things—no, only one other thing, his correctly suspected homofruitiness—and who has never before sensed that he had a calling or would ever be called, succumbs to a summons. He knows that this yellow-bellied wog, er, child of the Holy Father, is the messenger. He asks her to wait a moment. He rises and goes around a corner and up a few steps to a small chapel where he gets down on his knees. He is going to speak to Mary but upon reflection thinks he might embarrass her. To Jesus, then; but his love for Jesus is too complicated sexually as it is. There is no alternative but to speak directly to HIM.

"Our Father, if what Dr. Nu has discovered is true, the Church is now in possession of a capacity to kill off the dreaded sin of . . . You know, once and for all. Everything You have always wanted can come in one good shit. The only thing that is worrying me, Lord, is that . . . I know that many of Your Personal Servants are among the . . . So, in killing off the sin, You would be killing off the nunhood . . . our sisters, I mean, Tell me what to do!"

He waits for a sign. He is on his knees on a cold marble floor and the incense (Heavenly Scent #5) is being distributed automatically throughout the mansion by the Dial-a-Smell machine, a recent gift from the parishioner who makes them. It is a noisy machine but it saves much work. He farts. The machine clunks off. Is this a sign? He is prepared to accept it as such. He reasons that without the incense the farts can be smelled. This may mean that God wants Flo's shit discovery to be smelled. (Catholic mysticism is complicated.) He locks the door. He crosses himself. He prostrates himself. He turns over on his back. He lifts up his frock. He has a huge erection.

Ah, the cause and effect of it all! He begins to masturbate. Now God speaks to him. As God always does (if he only waits long enough and isn't such an impatient puss) when there is a pressing urgency.

God says: "Do both. Kill 'em and save 'em. That way I can't be blamed for heinous deeds, only for Noble Attempts. Tell that slit-eyed doctor to carry on with her work. Give her some money from one of our nameless funds. Let her publish any findings. The fights which ensue will leave plenty of time for all the fruits to get poisoned. Then our famous Catholic charities will step in to take care of the dying. But it will be too late. Heh heh heh. It will look like I'm trying to save them. But it will be too late. Too late. Yes. Yes. Those who play with shit must die!"

Bishop Sheeney ejaculates generously. There is semen all over his pubic hair. He is messy. He wipes himself off with his handkerchief, which he must remember to throw away, into the incinerator, where it will burn! He doesn't notice the tears in his eyes. He smooths down his dress and gets up, walking awkwardly: the pubic hair all stuck together with dry semen hurts. He unlocks the door to go help Dr. Flo up from the floor. He tells her that her request to continue her research has been granted.

Billy Sheeney, now in one of our retirement homes, replayed this scene for me with great gusto.

•

Yes, darling Grace can be right. Matters *can* look silly.

Dr. Flo extracted the poison from three nuns. The important leap (of faith, as it were) has been made. Whatever is happening with this blood, this poison, this fluid, this shit, is happening to and in homosexuals.

These were days long before epidemiologists and epidemiological studies were plying their wares, days that some still hark back to with a longing for the relief of their innocence, a longing for that naïve ignorance. The likes of Drs. Ekbert Nostrill and Elmo Tabernackle and Stuartgene Dye are mercifully still some years away. In days to come, studies would prove that, if you took enough polls and completed enough questionnaires and tallied enough answers and jiggled enough numbers, why, anything could be proved. But in those dog days of the summer of 1937, scientists are way behind in their less ecclesiastical but just as worshipped determinations of the Truth.

What Dr. Florence Hung Nu (she is to Americanize her name in 1942 so people will stop thinking she caused World War II) of the Laboratory of Fecal Hematology has discovered (not that she knows it) is that what will become known in the 1980s as The Underlying Condition makes its first home in the bowel (as will be confirmed for the first time, by the remarkable Dr. Donald Kotler of New York's St. Luke's–Roosevelt Medical Center, in 1983). The blood she isolates in the feces can spread throughout the rest of the body, causing massive deterioration and eventually death. This is clearly contagious and transmissible.

Dr. Nu (she succumbs to being so addressed although it goes against five thousand years of her heritage) does not hypothesize *how* the blood gets into the stool. (In fact, she assumes, incorrectly, that it is deposited there by malfunctions in some other part of the body.) That remains to Dr. Sister Grace and not Israel Jerusalem, still shilly-shallying somewhere in the wings, hearing "glause" in his head and unaware of Grace's devotion to finding out all she can, particularly from him.

As of now, there is no disease, nothing that anyone can see. We are still decades away from people dropping dead all over the world from The Underlying Condition, which is still a little too underlying. Of course, Dr. Flo is not exactly on the right track (which is why Grace will be able to claim credit): she is only interested in the blood in the feces. She has gone in the wrong direction (and it will not be until 1983 that Dr. Dodo Geiseric comes along to redirect this wrong direction, only, however, then going off in another wrong direction, thus robbing himself of a Nobel Prize). But what's a little thing like a wrong direction? Discovery is all! "And I shall make it *and* prove it!" Grace says out loud to her empty laboratory, aching to work on something juicy.

Flo will never know she played an important role in the history of a plague. She dies in 1943, speaking English rather well. She is pushed into the Mediterranean from the back terrace of the Grand Casino in Monte Carlo, a death any good sissy will recognize as not dissimilar to Moira Shearer's in *The Red Shoes*. Moira's, however, was a suicide. Flo (it is still hard to think of her as Florence) will leave an illegitimate baby daughter, and it is suspected that it is this baby's father who does the pushing. But let's say so long to her now, and thank you from a one-day-to-be-grateful-but-won't-be nation.

Now I think I am relieved of this religious obligation to explain my sisters and am free to go back to cussing my fucking twat off. What a relief. I felt like a constipated nun.

SHMUEL

Dr. Israel Jerusalem goes each day to Dr. Shmuel Derektor, the psychoanalyst. Israel had written directly to Dr. Freud: "As one doctor to another I must tell you that my dreams are of disease and plague and a cataclysmic overwhelming of the earth. It will happen. I do not think I am delusional. Experiments in my laboratory indicate that, should certain forces spin out of control, and there is no reason whatsoever to believe they will not—*indeed, it is my estimation that certain activities cannot be controlled*—then the result will be a plague of monumental severity."

Dr. Freud sends Israel Dr. Derektor's address and scribbles beneath it: "Gehst du, schnell!"

Later Israel receives a short note in that unmistakably firm, bold, and noble hand:

"May your prognosis for the New World be not so gloomy! Although, certainly, the Old one has always been in great trouble. Have you started with Dr. Derektor yet? You must not waste time."

And then he writes in big letters, underscored:

"Zeit ist kostbar!" Time is precious.

Dr. Freud's methods are not taking root in America as quickly as he would like. He had been here in 1909 and found it very hurtful and unwelcoming. "Why are you so slow, you Americans?" Freud writes to Dr. Derektor. "You take too long. Get them in and out!" A psychoanalysis in Vienna takes only months. Dr. Freud gets bored easily. "I require a fast turnover to stay awake." Also, the Germans are just across the border. There is need for faster speed in manufacturing mensches.

"But not so many people in America know they are sick in the head," Shmuel jokes. "Thus 'Tell me what comes into your head' is stretched longer and longer with each patient. A doctor has to eat."

Dr. Derektor has become Dr. Freud's Man in Washington. Shmuel, a roly-poly, tallish, bouncy, well-dressed man (he particularly favors snappy patterned socks) with bad posture and a smiling face is a happy person: he believes he's found the secret of life. Twice. Once in Judaism and once in Sigmund Freud. There's no point in even broaching with Shmuel the black cloud of a possible conflict of interest between Freud and Jewish teachings. Both are interested in freedom of the soul and spirit and that is that. Neither of them has been in Hortz bei Todstadt.

Israel knows that in his own files he has written down enough bits and pieces of information to formulate "an important piece of work," of the kind Dr. Derektor keeps pushing him to birth. But it is as if he cannot break through to what he wants to say—that he has seen glause before as a young doctor in the Andes and he is now seeing it again. He does not want to unleash this awful truth to the world, not even to Shmuel. If he was called crazy before, now he would be called an idiot. Or worse. He could lose his license for spreading false fears. He knows how nasty doctors can be about each other.

On the couch, in Free Association, he relives to Shmuel every bad dream of his life. He vomits out poisons even he didn't know he has. He cries for pains he does not believe hurt him anymore. And still . . . And yet . . . His chains of bondage are not loosed.

Israel realizes down deep that he is not becoming the doctor his brains and abilities, skills, perceptions, should have made him by now. His early successes have been forgotten by the world. No one points to him in corridors or at conferences as one of Schmuck's famous doctors, who are being treated more and more like movie stars. He is now some kind of joke, padding around the corridors. He is known as the famous doctor who never became famous.

"Who is telling you no? What is your place? To be a second-rater?"

Shmuel is afraid he says too much. Freud said shut up and listen, otherwise how comes the transference, that first and only rule of this modern catechism, wherein you take out on me what you have been unable to take out on others?

He continues. "To be a puny? To be a mealy-mouthed follower when you are a leader!"

Israel looks up to Shmuel as a savior. This can be dangerous, Shmuel knows. *Savior* is a dangerous word to Jews.

Shmuel reins himself in and sits back in his armchair, slipcovered with thick-waled hunter-green corduroy, the fabric of a rich boys' youth he never experienced, and awaits the words from Israel's kishkas that he knows are in there. Jewish men always have trouble shitting.

Israel says nothing for a while. "Sigmund said there is nothing that exists without cause, no mental state or act, just as there is no physical state in the universe without its cause. Am I just and forever a tortured Jew who has seen in every possible way how horrible man can be to his fellow man and that is that? How do I not let this stand in my way?"

So he is back at square one. Again he has checkmated his very self.

Finally, *finally* (despite the fact that hardly a night has passed in which he has not dreamed of purple spots, purple germs, purple people), and then only because Shmuel has dared him to put up or shut up, Israel disappears from view for several months and writes a short paper, "The Appearance of Glause." It is all about Mercy Hooker and Evvilleena Stadtdotter and the many perplexing questions their cases raise. Shmuel is impressed. "This is very interesting," he says. So Israel gets his treatise published. It is his first really important scientific publication in the New World. Of course he does not give himself credit for having done anything at all.

"What does it take to make you like yourself even a little bit?" Shmuel asks him, nodding his head both sagely and sadly. "This paper is seminal."

Thus, mention of glause first appears in print in *The Washington Titlement*, a journal distributed among doctors and scientists who do not work for the government and are concerned that the government doctors and scientists increasingly being brought to Washington will upset the balance of power between what is beginning to be known as "the private sector" and what gives every sign of becoming as entrenched and possibly dangerous a bureaucracy as any government agency. The *Titlement* is a peculiar journal: it is difficult to figure out which side it's on. But whatever it is, here is where Dr. Israel Jerusalem's seminal piece of work appears.

VAMPING TILL READY

I had never heard of him or the goddamn glause. The *Titlement* article, long and a pain in the ass to read, is in an almost incomprehensible jargon. But interesting. If wrongheaded. But written by a good mind at work. Fedema liquid is a false trail. He obviously can't see that, this Dr. Jerusalem. I'd already discovered that in my own experiments. This Jew is too simplistic, which Jews always were and are. And he doesn't keep up with the goddamn fucking shitty literature. He should have known of my work, which I published in *The New England Journal of Blood*. I wonder where he went to medical school. His name is unfamiliar to me. Should I have known who he is? I sense from his writing that his mind works somewhat like mine. Though, of course, he is not as smart as I am. They never fucking are.

The fedema could be just an infection, maybe from somebody giving the patient a sock in the stomach. Did nobody follow up on Nu's work? Do I have to do fucking everything? You could make a case for mismitosis, which I certainly recall from my own lonely and hurtful experience with this disease when I was very young. Yes, what about mismitosis, I find myself asking myself. I still cannot think about mismitosis without a few slobby tears.

I want to cry for my own never-ending possibilities. I can cure the world of everything! I know I can! I must! We must not let the Jewish men of the world take over!

Don't be greedy, Grace.

My fat body is shivering. Israel's article, and the rereading of my notes on mismitosis, are telling me loud and clear that there is a Nobel, certainly a Pituitary, in all this, somewhere, and that I know more about it than Israel. He doesn't know where he is going.

I will beat this Jew!

Dr. Jerusalem and Grace must meet.

FROM YOUR ROVING HISTORIAN, BURGEONING SCIENTIST

After Israel's article appears, Dr. Sister Grace Hooker asks for and receives from him a pus sample from Evvilleena Stadtdotter's fedema and a blood sample from Mercy Hooker. Yes, amazingly, Mercy was a distant cousin. Grace dimly recalls meeting at a Hooker family reunion. Grace was a toddler and Mercy was a teenager and quite beautiful. Grace remembers that, her beauty. Her laboratory, or rather one of her laboratories (at this point in time she supervises only three active working labs, scattered over Mater Nostra Dolorosa Medical Center; "Mother Superior promised me she would consolidate me, but she never has"), is one of the few places capable of doing a Kreitsch (a sort of test tube high colonic) on dangerous fluids. A Kreitsch (as against an Abner or "one of those beet/quinine jobs") isolates poison. Mercy, Evvilleena, and the three nuns all had a similar poison. Maybe also Israel.

Aren't I getting good at this?

So Israel and Grace, both sniffing around like two dogs nosing the crust of frozen earth, are, along with Flo, who's about to be dead shortly, at a standstill. Without knowing it each is waiting for the other. And, as always, important discoveries have to be replicated by others using other means before the world can really say wow! In other words, Grace, or Israel, could say two plus two equals four, counting on fingers, but in science you can't say, Yes, that is true! until some stranger somewhere else also says two plus two equals four, counting on toes. And there's another war coming. And scientists all over the world have other things on their mind.

So while we have glause and shit on the table, we don't really have the table.

After getting off to such a fine start, with purple spots and subliminal voices screaming to be heard—"Glause, Glause, Glause!"—Dr. Israel Jerusalem has allowed his attention to be swayed by . . . who knows what? Building a practice? Forcing himself—for self-protection, indeed his survival there—to become more involved in the administrative problems of Isidore Schmuck? Fear from having actually done something identified by Shmuel as important? Whatever, Israel pursues not the many interesting leads fate has so generously poured over his head like cold water, almost handing him an engraved invitation: in this lies greatness—take it or leave it.

Currently he's leaving it. It is not so unusual in psychoanalysis that when something has been achieved the very fear of success shuts things down for a while. There is nothing to be done but to sit it out and hope something will open the door again.

People die because other people take too long. And when they look back, there's no sensible reason for it. And this is not yet driving the world as nuts as it should.

In years to come, Dr. Hoakus Benois-Frucht of the Table Medical Center in New York will testify as follows before the first (or is it the second or third?) (Ruester for the first; Trish for the second; Vertle for the third) Presidential Commission on The Underlying Condition: "Glause was only the herpes of the thirties, some minor disturbance that swept through the sexually active population. No one remembers it now. It came and went. Only a few hundred died. Israel Jerusalem was nuts."

Like the famous scientist he is, Dr. Benois-Frucht conveniently fails to mention that all these discoveries of Dr. Israel Jerusalem's—that glause was a sexual disease, that glause was contagious, that glause killed people—were revolutionary discoveries that might have staved off an eventual plague had anyone paid attention to them. Israel told the world all this. It's all there, on the record, published in the *Titlement*, if you can find any old issues of the *Titlement*. Nothing happened. No fellow scientist got on the phone and said, "Good work, Jerusalem!" No one even called to say, "You're full of shit." *Nobody noticed.* The world did not listen.

ISRAEL WRITES TO YRH FROM THE FEDERAL PENITENTIARY IN GARTH, ALASKA, AUGUST 1990

Dear Fred,

I don't know what I expected. I thought perhaps my article in the *Titlement* would provoke somebody wanting to corroborate my work. Or prove me crazy. There are lots of doctors and scientists who like especially to prove others crazy. There were plenty of people at Schmuck who did not like me, and here was a golden opportunity for them.

What I really hoped was that someone with money would come forward. I missed my chance for Stadtdotter's money.

Nobody wanted me.

I tried. I went to every rich old lady I could find. I pursued every patient I ever took care of. My practice was growing. You do not have Mercy Hooker and Evvilleena Stadtdotter for patients without word getting around. Rich people are crazier than other people. They believe more in the impossible. Poor patients don't believe. Poor people most of the time don't even hope. Poor patients expect to die. Rich patients think each new doctor has the secret of eternal life. That is why they flock to the doctors of crazy people like them. They think that Mercy and Evvilleena found out something with this Israel. Even if both die, that seems to make no difference.

But the rich patients don't last long. They don't like me. They come to me once or twice. They see this funny Jewish man with no nice smooth style, with no bedside manner, with no jokes to make them smile. With no magic pills they must take every fifteen minutes on the half hour before drinking two tablespoons of his special elixir. They wonder what Mercy and Evvilleena ever saw in Israel. They go home and next time they go to the new doctor they've heard about who took care of Missy Mellon or Vera Vanderbilt or Sissy Astor or Prissy Loeb or Helen Hayes's mother.

Yours truly,

Israel Jerusalem, M.D.

GRODZO VISITS AMERICA

On November 9, 1937, Gottfried Grodzo makes a speech, in German, in the small and predominantly German town of Inventa, in Northeast Washington. He delivers the same speech several days later to the German population in Milwaukee, a much bigger crowd.

I would not like to be a homosexual in America after we, and we hope you, attend to our duties. They must be driven to the forests with the animals they resemble. They must be expelled from all areas of our lives, from our schools, from all public places, from their work. They must be eliminated from participation in all aspects of the economy. They must be excluded from all trades, crafts, agencies, from managing firms and management of any enterprise. They must be stigmatized in every way possible, placing them removed from the ranks of society as the pariahs they are, degrading them at will, placing them outside the universe of moral obligation so we can degrade them more. They must be ripped out of their existence on American soil by the roots. They must be excluded from using public transport, from appearing in public as shoppers, patrons at the movies, or visitors to the beach. They must be refused driving licenses lest they drive even further into your midst.

Then, once and for all, we must face up to the necessity of exterminating them, so that the eventual result will be the factual and final end of homosexuality in the world, its absolute annihilation, once and for all and forever. If we do not accomplish this riddance of these infectiously diseased vermin then we ourselves are in danger of perishing from this homosexual infection that I predict will come to them.

It is an extraordinary outburst, an extraordinary statement. Judging from the size of the crowd assembled to hear him in Milwaukee ("in excess of five hundred," the press reports), and from the "exceedingly frenzied response," the feelings he is expressing "must be releasing an enormous amount of pent-up hate."

He actually does not like himself for saying all these things. He has been sent over by the commandant of the regiment of Brown Shirts that he's been required to join in exchange for his appointment to study with several famous doctors at home, doctors involved in secret experiments that interest him. More and more, that is how things are working now at home. You have to give in order to get. He is known to be a good public speaker, he speaks perfect English, he is good-looking, and unknown hands wrote his speech for him. He would get a free trip to America. So why not? He is surprised his reception is so thunderously positive. Somehow he did not expect that from America.

BLOOD MARCHES ON

The first blood bank in the United States finally opens at the Cook County Hospital in Chicago on January 15, 1937.

The award-winning medical writer Laurie Garrett tells us, "Blood is made up of a solid part and a liquid part. The solid part is composed of red blood cells, white cells, and platelets, each with their respective function of transporting oxygen, fighting infection, and aiding coagulation.

"In the late 1930's, evidence begins to link hemophilia to a defect in the plasma, the liquid portion of the blood.

"Plasma is composed of proteins, salts, sugars, and water. Fourteen different plasma proteins have been found to effect clotting. These are referred to as clotting factors. Seventeen recognized disorders (coagulopathies) result from deficiencies of these clotting factors."

THE HUSHMARKED SOCIETY

The Hushmarked Society is officially established in Los Angeles, or rather in Pacific Oranges, a small village twenty-seven miles to the north, on January 8, 1938. Five men are its founders, only one of whom remains with it after its first harrowing year, during which all five of them are arrested several dozen times. The lone stalwart's name is Virgil Vindicator, which of course is not his real name, nor, as we have seen, is he the first to carry it.

The beginning of an official and organized homosexual movement in America is currently dated from this event at this moment in time, though there have been numerous earlier events that might quite as correctly claim the honor. Such being the vicissitudes of homosexual history and its record keeping, it's the Hushmarked Society that now wears the mantle. It won't last long.

Not much is ever known about this Virgil. He writes a lot of pamphlets and he hides behind a long beard and in front of a ponytail. He always wears dungarees and boots and he chews tobacco. He has a high-pitched voice that diminishes the effect of the wardrobe. People know what he is the minute he says hello. He gets beaten up a lot, particularly when he gives out his pamphlets, which are all about male love. He looks different in different photographs, probably because there are different Virgil Vindicators the way there are different Betty Crockers, except that the Virgils are different because different men of that name keep getting murdered. And no Bettys are known to have been murdered.

One or two gay histories list this Virgil Vindicator of 1938 as "the true founder of the American homophile movement," which is what it's called for a while. *Homophile* is just another ugly word for *homosexual*, itself not particularly sonorous. Throughout history homosexuals have had bad luck with what to call them.

PETER IS INTRODUCED TO ADOLF

In 1939, twenty-eight-year-old Peter Ruester becomes fascinated by Adolf Hitler and the methods that have taken him from obscurity to growing notice, even among a few in America. Ruester, soon to become an important Hollywood union leader, wonders how this was accomplished, how an unknown bumbler becomes a national leader, a man of whom people are frightened. Who is this man? How does he create this fear that he is hearing about from a few of his Jewish friends? Ruester comes across remarks by Werner Walter Willikens, secretary of the American-Prussian Ministry of Friendship, made to his fellow members in 1934.

"It is not always possible to wait for orders from the top. Too many bureaucrats are unable to obtain decisions from an all-powerful but absent chief. It was discovered quite by accident that if the workers are deliberately set in competition with each other, each would struggle to fulfill the chief's desires, unspoken though they might actually be, and it soon becomes the duty of every person to attempt, in the spirit of the chief, to work *toward* him."

This will be elucidated more clearly in coming years by the British sociologist Zygmunnt Bauman and the British historian Ian Kershaw. This process of "working toward the Fuhrer" becomes the leitmotif to explain, during the entire grisly era beginning, the mass obedience a willing German society shows to its new Fuhrer as the Third Reich progresses.

Before Hitler, bureaucrats usually reined in politicians. But under this new, Nazi system of government, ambitious bureaucrats in no time flat begin to fall over themselves to be even more ruthlessly radical than their boss. Launching spies and counterspies against each other seems to be the trick. And pretending you never knew anything or ordered anything at all. Get them all to spy on each other! And to turn each other in! Naming names is always All, or at least a wonderful place to start.

"That is what we feel the Fuhrer desires whether he has actually voiced it or not." Functionaries of all kinds in defense of their actions make this statement, in various versions, when the time comes for them to explain themselves.

"I have been sent here again to talk to you, my Deutsche Brethren in America, and bring you the news that you need no longer be ashamed of your homeland, which perhaps you left too early. Our new Fuhrer has commenced a methodology that will reunite us and give us back the world." So sayeth this Werner Walter Willikens.

Peter Ruester, long before he will need any of it, or really comprehend it, senses that "methodology" will become useful to him sometime, somewhere.

HANDS ACROSS THE OCEAN

Since the Great Depression, more and more is smelling really awful. Too much of the air blowing through the world is foul and curdling. Who smells it? Where does the stink waft from? Why is it vague and faceless? Well, we do know where it wafts from. And it isn't vague and faceless if you have the kind of eyes that can see.

The first homosexual prisoners were taken to Dachau starting on July 7, 1934. Edwin Black tells us that in Germany, in 1937, according to IBM's man in charge, one Brinestalker, the production of punch cards for the Hollerith machine totals 74 million per month, production of horizontal scanners would double from 15 to 30 a month, tabulating machines would increase from 18 to 20 per month, multiplying punches would double from 5 to 10 a month, and counters from 200 to 250 a month, and that by 1939 Germany is covered by 750,000 census takers to use all this.

By May 1939 virtually every Jew and homosexual in Germany has been located, registered, numbered, surveyed, and sorted. Each can now be located on a moment's notice.

"At the height of the Third Reich, IBM was leasing, servicing, and upgrading two thousand sorting machines across Germany and thousands more across Nazi-occupied Europe, and manufacturing 1.5 billion custom punch cards each year in Germany alone" (Brad Thor, *Black List*, 2012).

By September, World War II has begun. The ovens are on the drawing boards.

Yes, the American eugenics program is being appropriated in Germany. Brinestalker is in Berlin, in charge of IBM's European markets.

Yes, this is still the history of The American People.

•

Adolf Hitler did not have sex with his roommate from art school, August Kubizek, in 1909, even though Gustl, as August was called, clearly desired it. He idolized Adolf and knew he would go far. But August was shy. He did, however, warm Adolf up for someone else. They lived in a bohemian rooming house where many of the inhabitants were homosexual. Gustl and Adolf of necessity slept in the same bed, and warming up Adolf meant just that. It was a cold room and Adolf was not interested in Gustl's body although he was interested in Gustl's friend, one Josef Neumann, a dark and handsome young Jewish art dealer, who bought several of Adolf's watercolors. They disappeared, the two of them, Adolf and Josef, in Vienna, for the five-day period June 21–26, 1909. Hitler was then twenty, without that mustache, and not bad-looking at all. When Hitler reappeared he was a changed man. And Josef Neumann was never heard of or from again.

According to one of Hitler's major biographers, John Toland, these five days are the only days in Adolf's entire lifetime that are completely unaccounted for. Toland, in a personal conversation with YRH in 1974, confessed to "not disbelieving" the "possibility" that Hitler was or had been a homosexual.

In the summer of 1934, Hitler disposed of Ernst Röhm, who had been his friend and a top officer. He was also a raging homosexual queen. Shortly thereafter a terrified man comes to America. His name is Joe Newman, and he goes to live, first, in Milwaukee. He travels over as much of the country as he can gobble up, riding freight trains, hitching rides, learning English along the way. Because he is handsome, he discovers his body can feed him.

Many a man who picks up a hitchhiker is willing to pay for a meal or two, and often more. Joe is not greedy or sinister. He wants love like everyone else he meets.

It is important to him to keep on the move. He can be a hobo or a dishwasher or clean libraries or clean anything. Just don't expect him to stay put in one place. Because of his accent, the law eventually catches up with him: war is approaching, posters are everywhere warning everyone to beware of the person next to him, and he is "offered internment." In one of a growing number of internment camps (inhabitants are shuffled around in case they form dangerous alliances) he meets many Germans, including another immigrant, Henry Gerber, a budding homosexual rights activist who attempts to give Joe a better sense of himself, and to try to keep him from shaking so much when he hears anyone speak German. "Can't you see how lucky we are to be in a camp," Henry says to him in German; "we get three square meals a day." Joe's terror has of course returned in these camps: What if another German recognizes him from the old days? Hitler is now Reichschancellor, the Führer. Joe has never forgotten Adolf's lustful bragging that "I am going to rule Germany," and the streak of terror that swept over him. Adolf has now been capturing and exterminating homosexuals. Joe reasons quite understandably that the one person Hitler does not want alive is a man who has had sex with him. Names of homosexual friends in Germany who have disappeared reach Joe. Soon his fear becomes so overpowering that it's difficult for him to get a sentence out without shaking and stuttering. So marked is his behavior that it is not long before he is indeed recognized by a fellow inmate, who informs the camp's director, an assimilated German American, of his suspicions. "The man was Adolf Hitler's boyfriend." Rather quickly Joe Newman is disappeared from the camp.

In 1937, in the first part of a three-part profile of Adolf Hitler in *The New Gotham*, Janet Flanner (a lesbian) will write, "In spite of the worldwide rumors to the contrary, there seems no reason to believe that Herr Hitler is homosexual, outside of the fact that, until he finally had most of them shot, there were pederasts among his Party friends and file. But in Europe, where, as one of the frantic postwar phenomena common to capital cities of both the Allies and the Central Powers, homosexuality paraded in all walks of life, that is not sufficient reason to substantiate the charge. There is a rumor that Hitler was wounded genitally in the war. Whatever the cause, his real abnormality apparently consists of the insignificance of his sexual impulse, probably further deadened by wilful asceticism. Emotionally, Hitler belongs to the dangerous, small class of sublimators from which fanatics are frequently drawn."

•

The three-nun shit fucking freaked me out. There is no answer to the many fucked-out questions it raises. The "official" numbers of UC cases are said to be pig-ass males. But in nuns—that is, women pledged to celibacy—in what way did the fucking virus (I am the only one bold enough to call a fucking virus a fucking virus out loud) participate in its transmission? My class-act nose smells something and is twitching to tell me so.

I am bored. I have been prized to death for my various discoveries. It is not that I can think of nothing Superwoman to do. But these are all minor-league out-of-town white-trash time killers not up to my par. When I know going in that I am already better than any result I can suck from what I am engaged in, I am not frigging, rat-fucking interested. I am hugely rich (doesn't that sound like a prissy pussy) from Hooker shit and Vel, my poison detector, which Greeting markets desultorily. Money is not a motivating force for this Sister to get up off her fat ass and waddle forward. Sir Henry, his stiff upper lip more encased as he ages in a turgid personality akin to cement, implores me to change sides and hop over to his shitty side of the fence. He said to me, "In my humble opinion some of these ideas on your list look to me to be possible reapers of interesting returns." He was talking about a facial skin cream I dreamed up that peeled off dead turdy skin and refreshed the complexion with the smile of beauty and the glow of health. Sir Henry has discovered advertising can sell his roster of wretchednesses. Greeting has no major product or lifesaver. The Dridge Ampule is what keeps them up and at 'em, but they can hardly sell these to soldiers. He has nothing for Greeting to market during this coming war. "It makes me feel rather unpatriotic," he uncharacteristically announces.

Mother Superior has already turned down my request to use Mater Nostra's girls for researching my nose twitches. "I think, dear Grace, that you'd best seek out women who live more varied and active lives." Then she added, holding my hand, "Stay with us, dear. Stay close to home."

Fred and Ianthe and, yes, Hermia, I have followed with vivid interest all of your contributions, many of them good and gutsy. None of them quite ring my bell. It isn't so much that Fred has logorrhea, as it is that science is less interested in history than all of you are. But you are evidently writing a very long and involved mystery story, and I do like mysteries. But I prefer them when they involve spies.

So I went off and made the skin cream and Henry marketed it with Mr. Walter J. Thompson and it has made me an additional fortune and I can't recall what we named it. A piece of cake. A fucking piece of fucking cake. As Mother Superior then said, "Next."

Dear friends, send in your shit-spitting spies!

MASTURBOV GARDENS

AN AMERICAN BOYHOOD

OK, Fred, here goes.

I was born on the wrong side of the District Line. The District Line is what separates Maryland from Washington, D.C., which is as far away as the poor are from the rich. D.C. means District of Columbia, whatever Columbia means. Everyone knows that "The District" is another name for Washington, which is over there. Across that line. It's just a line on a map, but it's very real when you live on the wrong side of it. Nobody wants to live on the outside looking in. Washington may be a sleepy little town on the other side, but it's Washington and it is the capital of America and that makes it a bunch of things that Franeeda County isn't. Even buses didn't cross over until they had to. Until Claudia's father bought both lines and put them together, Maryland and Washington had separate bus lines. You had to get off at the end of the line in Washington and change to another bus to take you home. Washington cabdrivers used to say, "It costs extra over the District Line." I was born in the still-smoldering embers of that Depression, from which The American People were told to pick ourselves up, dust ourselves off, and start all over again. I was born in Masturbov Gardens, in the town of Punic, in Franeeda County, Maryland. Washington is divided into four quarters and Punic is like leftover intestine from the Northeast quadrant.

The building of Masturbov Gardens begins in the mid-1930s when few have the money for even the low rent it costs to live here. Abe Masturbov worries he's committed one of his rare errors of business judgment. He impatiently awaits the housing shortage that he alone is expecting and that has found him, in preparation, ordering new brick tributaries to flow over this hill and that. This place is some kind of dream come true for him. Lucas says this is because Abe proves himself right again. Tenants are moving in and he's building faster. No sooner are families living in what was only a hole the week before than another hole is dug for us to play in. We play constantly in these excavations. With such a canvas for our imaginations, we kids, and there are soon enough of us for me to be part of a gang, create new games, of hiding, of domination, of inspection, of capture and victory. New families arrive every day. New playmates to love and hate. Everyone's background is as modest as my family's. *Poor* is not a word anyone uses, even if it applies. But where we are living now is new, and there's a sense in the air that there's beginning to be work, and hope, for all.

When asked about his youngest days, Lincoln curtly answered, "It is a great piece of folly to make anything out of my early life." When pressed for a more definitive answer, he said his entire youth could be condensed into one line from Gray's "Elegy": " 'the short and simple annals of the poor.' That's my life, and that's all you or anyone can make of it." He was asked if that meant he had been unhappy. "It is not easy to be both poor and happy," he replied. "Why does everyone always want to know if someone is happy? Is it that rare—happiness—that a person who claims it is like a talisman others need touch for good luck? Yes, I suspect it is." I know you've researched Lincoln, Fred.

There was a battle here, in Masturbov Gardens, on a hill so low and little that a battle on it of any size and importance seems unimaginable. The hill was called Fort Drue, and it was down the street from where we lived. The battle was part of the Civil War. Not much happened, no one was killed, no victory was claimed. Evidently a bunch of lost, straggling Union troops found themselves commingling with lost Confederates. Maryland was a no-man's-land then, between Pennsylvania and Virginia. Abe Masturbov, who knew little American history and cared less about it, nevertheless put up a commemorative marker and refused to dig any holes on this little hill. He said it was an important place, an auspicious place, because neither side attacked the other. The sign still stands, though now it is more elaborate and bears an official government seal. There's no record in any history of any Fort Drue or of any altercation taking place so far out of the way. Abe, who was the least religious of men, said he had put up the sign so he could kiss it for good luck, like a mezuzah, every time he passed it. "I think he might have made the whole thing up just so he could say he owned some land that Lincoln walked on," Lucas said. The most violent thing conclusively known to have happened on this hill was the suicides of Grace's parents. She laughs when she sees the seal.

Yes, I played constantly in these new excavations of Masturbov Gardens.

Why, from the very beginning, did I want to be somewhere else instead? How did I know that I have always wanted to be someplace else?

Masturbov Gardens was and is a vast sprawling warren of two- and three-story apartment buildings snaking over the low hills of northeastern Franeeda County. On the other side of the District Line, in Washington, there's finally a housing shortage. In Masturbov Gardens there was plenty of room. Here our father, Philip, housed us in a "development" built and owned by our cousin Abraham Masturbov.

I want to describe Masturbov Gardens by saying it was like an organism, an amoeba slithering under a microscope that's slightly out of focus, an amoeba sucking all things in its path indiscriminately to its membrane as it ingests their exudations and excretions, every bit of the pus of life. That's what it seems like now. We all lived in some kind of pus, and we all lived in it together. And we didn't know it.

But it was wrong to think of it that way then. Then was innocence. There's no accretion that adheres to innocence except experience, and experience for the young should be a different set of germs not yet quite so fatally contagious. The sun must have shined then once in a while, even though I recollect it always rained.

When I go back to wander the streets of Masturbov Gardens my memories quickly yield to a disheartenment that I ever lived here. Here I learned too much. Here was the unhappiness that was the first disease that almost killed me. If others think Masturbov Gardens was bucolic, red bricks on green grass under huge ambitious trees sharing their ground haughtily with cowering thorned rosebushes and timid lilacs and droopy forsythia, they're right too. But if they claim that with a thousand places to play Masturbov Gardens could not have been an unpleasant home for any child, a dangerous place to grow up in, I'm here to say that they're wrong. Here I did not have a dog, here I did not take the piano lessons I longed for, here my brother Lucas spent every waking and sleeping minute he could away from home, here my brother Stephen turned from happiness to anger to darkness, here none of us had much love for or from either parent.

And here my identical twin, David, left me.

My, what a heavy load of upset and dissatisfaction and distress! Surely the world doesn't need another unhappy record of yet another unhappy life.

Why do I desire so strongly to tell this story to the world? Why do I desire to tell it to you, Fred, or more to the point, why do you want me to, since you lived in Masturbov Gardens too, although you were younger and we barely knew each other back then? As a physician I learned long ago that it is a certain fact that most of mankind is unhappy. But we both know this history is more than just unhappiness. That must be it.

Yes, as we both know, this is a murder mystery. I will write it as I lived it, hoping that answers will reveal themselves to me as well. Isn't that what's meant to happen in a good mystery story, even though there is nothing good about this one?

Yes, it always rained in Masturbov Gardens.

By the way, for the record, my name is Daniel Jerusalem.

•

The economic news remains dire and hateful. The Depression's never really gone away. I'm in kindergarten when Lorna May Drift's father kills himself. Mrs. Drift is my teacher and Mr. Drift is found dead sitting in one of her schoolroom's little desks. He is holding a note to the children that says, "Don't ever believe your president again."

Washington is still a sleepy town. If it's the capital of a country, why's it been asleep for so long? People aren't polite, they're just bland. Personality is frowned upon. Everyone speaks in the same tone of voice. If people didn't identify themselves, everyone would sound the same on the other end of the phone. There's no sense of power, no sense of a world out there, just waiting to be defended. Moderation in everything is all. Few are those who sense that futures shouldn't be fashioned from such emotional stinginess.

Quietly, fortunes are being made. Bad times for some are ripe times for others. There is no fairness. Huge parcels of land are being bought up, usually in outlying areas. Smart men are out there busily sniffing suburbs that might sprout. The smartest nose belongs to our cousin, Abe. Abe has had a son with Doris, Mordecai, Mordy, my best friend for a while.

In the Washington area, people still know other people, if not by name at least by face or business or place, white and Negro alike. Washington is still small neat houses side by side near woodsy parks. There's never much traffic. The roads are good because congressmen like to drive on smooth roads. Congressmen keep Washington in good shape. It's their little toy city to play with, and they enjoy building big marble museums and blocks of triumphant offices and erecting equestrian memorials to heroes on horses. The glint from the sun off all this celebratory stone is dazzlingly white.

Washington is also white in a less dazzling way. The Negroes say nothing about it. They know there are more of them, that this city should be theirs if democracy knew how to count, but they don't think that way yet. Political figures who, for a brief moment in time, might actually make a reputation by caring for those less fortunate are still a ways away. Critics of the status quo are considered uppity. Negro preachers like Felindus Max Graves, in his Cathedral of Our Holy People, preach each Sunday, and each Sunday hundreds too many come. The overflow crowd stands singing on the one plot of earth Herman Masturbov, Abe's father who was rich and hungry before him, couldn't buy around their small wooden church, this little bit of ground that I can see and hear from my bedroom window where Felindus Max Graves and his flock sing out passionately surrounded by where the whites are living. Felindus Max is famous for his stirring rhetoric. He preaches devotion and duty and discipline, all the D words, he calls them, "that if you don't follow you get the final D word, which is Damnation." He can make *damnation* the longest word you've ever heard. He talks a lot about someone by the name of Jesus Christ. His worshippers come from far away, all over the District and Maryland and Virginia, and line up for hours on Sunday morning, everyone all dressed up. My goodness, how obedient everyone is. Every Wednesday night is choir practice and the music is wonderful and almost makes me happy when I'm sad. Yes, the Negroes are obediently in line, and a good many of them think life is good. The government is hiring a lot of them now, at last, to clean the endless corridors and ten thousand toilets. If they clean them well, they might get to file papers and empty wastebaskets. I write in my little diary, "I wonder if their Mr. Christ has a black skin so any Negro boy can see his own skin on his God."

But mostly, on both sides of this District Line, Washington's dreary. It's never been anything but a town, and towns don't provide much to cheer people up. All the people who work here are paid to worry about people somewhere else. No one has much money. Including the government. America is poor and Washington is the capital of a country having the worst of times and still not admitting it. When Rockefeller dies he leaves more money than is in the Treasury. How can a government, or a country, admit *that*? The rest of the world thinks America is recovering from its depression fine. They're wrong. And the rest of the world isn't even thinking about Washington. Yet.

That doesn't come until much later, although FDR starts them noticing. It will take another war before things boom again. But that, too, will come soon enough.

•

Yes, here in Masturbov Gardens our father, Philip, houses us, for do not Cousin Abe's rental billboards posted at the District Line promise "One Hundred Acres of Heaven"? Like almost everyone else in "the Washington area," then and since, my family has moved here from somewhere else. My great-uncle Israel somehow got here from Palestine. My great-aunt Yvonne, Israel's sister or half-sister and Abe's mother, whom none of us has ever seen, got here from Moscow, "but so long ago she won't talk about it," our mother tells us. My father just crossed over from that part of downtown Washington where all the Jews once lived, huddled in their ghetto, but my mother is an outsider: she comes from New York, that huge city I haven't seen yet, but which lures me with the sound of its magic when she tells me about it. "My maiden name is Wishen," Rivka says, making it sound like royalty instead of the name of another grocery store like the one Philip's mother has. I wonder if anyone in America would have eaten if it weren't for all those little neighborhood Jewish grocery stores. But I was born here, and my brothers were born here. My twin was born here. We're not from anywhere else.

"You had no more than we did! Why do you lord it over me so la-di-dah?" Philip complains to Rivka when she hurts his pride, as she often does. He is sensitive not only to her occasional taunts, albeit truthful, that others of their friends have fared better in the world but also to her constant implications that New York is higher on some scale than Franeeda County and that on both counts her marriage is beneath her. Permanent employment has just found him, in 1941, in the form of the job he will keep (except for several mysterious interruptions) until he dies, a job in a small backwater of the National Institute of Tumor Science, where he devotes himself to investigating "important procedures." He is never more specific, and none of his sons presses him. He's a lawyer, we know, and he went to Yaddah, we know, and to Yaddah Law School, we know, and he finally gets this job after the Depression kept him unemployed, or so we thought, for so long we wondered if he'd never work again, and what's more probably didn't want to, so feeble were his visible attempts to rectify this situation. As a young man, Philip had loved ships and had become an expert on the law of the sea. Sometimes he can be found looking at old picture books from his youth, almanacs of sailing ships, running his hand over the shiny surface of a rotogravure as if he were touching some priceless and delicate object. At work he says he has a staff of several to supervise. At work he is presumably listened to, obeyed, as he is not in Masturbov Gardens, at 4212 Mordecai Avenue, which of course is named after Mordy, my playmate, my first love. Though Philip knows it is a backwater of a job, and beneath the prestige that Yaddah is meant to bestow on all her sons, Philip never wavers in his gratitude to "our country" for landing it and keeping it. Each day of the many years remaining to him in this capital of our country and the world, he will travel one hour to work, one hour home, standing each way in three crowded buses that are freezing in winter and sweltering in summer, to fall asleep right after dinner, exhausted after his day of labor, a repetition of its predecessor, each week and month and year the same, Philip surrounded at the office by a sea of unfamiliar and constantly changing faces as co-workers come and go, and surrounded at home by sons and a wife who do not love him. He is not a fool, and often come more tired complaints. "For this I am an educated man. For this Grandma Zilka saved every penny." Although I discover at an early age that I hate him, for his failure, for his not loving me, for an endless litany of other charges, I wonder, almost in admiration, particularly now that I'm grown and wonder the same about myself, what kept him going for so long, rather than simply disappearing like his own father (and like his other youngest son) and simply not coming home one day. But I'm getting ahead of myself.

·

Several years ago I decided to try to find out what exactly Philip did at NITS. I knew by now that no ships or seas figured in any enterprise of the place. It's not easy locating old records and piecing together the history of anything in this town. Believe it or not, there are no official rules or guidelines or even suggestions for the preservation of ordinary records past a certain date. Washington, amazingly, is not interested in preserving itself for history. Or perhaps it's not amazing; perhaps evaporation, all tracks covered, is the point. I discovered that there had been warehouses holding tons of cartons arranged by years and decades until President Ruester closed them down. Everything had, like Atlanta, been burned.

However, because NITS is concerned with living and once-living human beings, there are congressional mandates that require certain precautions. If a person died from a contagious illness, for instance, or a questionable one, or because of any criminal act, or by suicide, or through any contention with a religious organization or government, foreign or domestic, or of course by "any sexual perversions, irregularities, and/or abnormalities," these records must be kept in perpetuity under penalty of fine. The only question was where.

It took a lot of inquiry and phoning, and then more time for me to be properly investigated and fingerprinted and certified, with pass and badge, before I could get into the Federal Storage Facility (Vera Section), Building Stanley, located almost all the way to Fille de Maison (Velvalee Peltz was from Fille de Maison), which is just about as far as you can go in Franeeda County before entering West Virginia. God, what a monstrous place Vera Section turned out to be, miles and miles of plain wood shelving under a ceiling as high as an airplane hangar's, with no ladders or employees in sight. An old sergeant gave me a sort of electric golf cart and a map of the place and wished me good luck when I asked about the last time anyone had come to look for anything here, and he said, "I honestly can't remember."

After several hours I located what appeared to be the aisle by year and division and finally office. I had to stand on the golf cart to reach the sagging high shelves covered by the dust of decades. I found the old cartons with peeling labels: Inheritance Office, Mr. Philip Jerusalem. Inheritance? Choosing a carton at random I yanked it open to see it packed with neat files, all carefully labeled "In the case of U.S. v. . . . ." I opened one file, then another, then a third, then pulled out another carton and another. In each I found more of the same. My father's signature had confirmed a death and authorized the disposition of estate and remains. In each and every case the person had died from an unusual or communicable disease, often unspecified. The deceased was almost always a resident of—I assumed incarcerated at—government institutions like St. Elizabeth's or St. Recta's or St. Goth's or St. Purdah's. I know all these crumbling places and I know what horror shows they were and, in St. Purdah's case, still are. In many cases my father had made a notation: "Visited the patient on the premises to witness his signature, hereby verified," or some such. That he'd visited those hellholes of dying people so often was news that he never brought home to tell us, unlike Rivka with her running catalogue of her world's misfortunes. Why hadn't he told us any of his?

I spent much of the day studying these files, finding nothing to vary their simple messages, their inexorable parade of disease and death, the depressing monotony his routine must have offered as he recorded these never-ending horrors. Many of the deaths were attributed to diseases long gone, rare and unfamiliar. Nerduze. Atrophied triumphans glans. Heart valve redumtavitis. Fallker's syndrome. Elevated butterfly dirt. Was there ever a fatal illness called elevated butterfly dirt? Granted many of the dead had been incarcerated for many years in these ancient "hospitals" more akin to crazy houses, prisons of soul and body, still . . . elevated butterfly dirt? I left marveling again at how much of his life Philip never shared with us. "Today I certified a death from the last case in modern medicine of Nerduze, a disease from the Middle Ages!" We would have been electrified with interest and would no doubt have looked at him in an entirely different light. But once again I realize that he never really lived with us at all.

And since I'd become someone rather expert at dealing with complications just as uncomfortable as many he faced, how much we turned out to have in common.

•

Rivka journeys in the other direction, into the Franeeda countryside, on uncrowded transport, to small rural Hykoryville, the county seat and biggest town, which means all of several thousand, every one of whom is white. Here she is at first a volunteer, then a paid worker, talking to patients, spreading cheer and her version of worldly wisdom. She will soon be asked to run this local outpost of American Red Blood.

American Red Blood has been around for a while, but it takes a colored man, Dr. Charles Drew, with his really pioneering research on blood transfusion, to popularize the idea of blood banks and bloodmobiles going from neighborhood to neighborhood to collect blood on the spot. This is all very new (no one knows that a colored man is involved—if they did, no one would give blood), and Rivka is in on the ground floor. A lot has happened in the blood world. Landsteiner in Vienna got a Nobel for determining types A, B, AB, and O, and later in New York, of the Rh-factor in human blood similar to one found in the red blood cells of monkeys and thus relates us to them. (He also showed that polio could be transmitted to monkeys by injecting into them the ground-up spinal cords of kids who'd died from it.) Drew was from Washington and wanted to try out his ideas for the bloodmobile in some small place out of sight, and ARB hit on Hykoryville and asked Rivka to oversee it in addition to running the office. (Rivka actually worked by Drew's side until he was taken off the project for objecting that white blood and Negro blood were being segregated from each other.)

Thus she now commences, with great delight, to begin taking charge of as much of the world, and the upcoming crises that are being whispered about more loudly every day, as the world will let her, which turns out to be more and more as the weeks and months and years pass by. It's only a few more years before husbands and daddies begin to be reported dead or missing in strange-sounding faraway places, and wives suddenly are made widows, and children fatherless. Blood comes to represent the answer to it all. Everyone has blood to give! Dying bodies can be made whole and daddies will come home to wives and kids. The current prewar catastrophes, with which Hykoryville Hospital is filled, involve merely unattended children getting sick, a surprising number of fires, and things of that sort. Rivka can manage it all. Blood. Burnouts. It's all the same to her. Like Greer Garson in *Mrs. Miniver*, Rivka bears any and all harrowing news. She helps everyone with advice, like Rosalind Russell in *Sister Kenny*. Over dinner she tells us all the details, every single one, like gossipy Billie Burke. Does anyone besides a lonely kid who lives too much in the dark, in the movies, remember great performances like these?

I confess to a never-ending fascination with Rivka's bulletins. As the war comes at us with fuller force, each day brings Rivka home with tales more grisly than yesterday's. Philip harbors little sympathy for her job, even from Boston, where he and David are now living. "I'm sick of hearing of it!" he writes in one of his few letters home. Perhaps that's why I can't get enough of it. The husband is unhappy that his wife can talk about her work with such pleasure! He's jealous of her growing importance in the world, at least to hear Rivka tell it. He could not have helped noticing his wife and my mother might even be loved by so many others.

Perhaps that's why he went to Boston. Taking David, my twin brother, with him.

No, that's not the reason David went away.

•

Pearl Harbor brings Philip back home from Boston. David doesn't come back with him. This is the third time this has happened. "He didn't want to come home" is the most informative response offered by either of our parents. I understand that, and so do Lucas and Stephen, so we don't ask questions. After all, we've sort of adjusted to life without him, as we certainly adjusted to not missing Philip. Whenever I tell Rivka I want to write to David, she looks out into space dreamily, in that way she has—I'm an adult before I realize it means she's lying—and says, "David is not doing well in school and has to spend every moment working with a tutor at a private school in Boston near Aunt Grabele." David is smarter than I am. I know instantly that this isn't what he's doing. And cranky Aunt Grabele has never given us the time of day.

At dinner one Sunday, Lucas asks out of nowhere, "Is David sick?" Rivka and Philip exchange swift glances, which they rarely do. Rivka says, "He's fine." "Then why doesn't he write or call?" Lucas, who always thought David clumsy and uninteresting, and Stephen, who always did Lucas one better by putting his older brother's thoughts into words and throwing them in David's face—"David, you're such a drip," that sort of thing—both join in persisting in their questions, each inquiry met by an answerless and obvious discomfort. "I think there's something we're not being told," Stephen says, slamming a palm down on the table, as if he cares. He's the most handsome of us boys with his dark curly hair and swooping lashes that win you over when he blinks at you, and a body that's not inclined to the pudgy, like the rest of us are. Stephen can eat anything. "Yes, it sounds like there's something we're not being told," Lucas agrees. "Are you calling us liars?" Philip uncharacteristically hurls back at Stephen. He rarely confronts his older sons. When he explodes it's always at me. No one ever accuses Lucas of anything. Lucas is the saint. Lucas gets up and leaves the table and the room and the apartment, in a quiet dramatic exit, one he uses often; of all of us, he's here the least. I've never been certain why Lucas never fights back in any ordinary way. I marvel at the serene effectiveness of his exit and wish, as always, that I might emulate it someday. Years later he tells me, "There was no use fighting with words. They had no knowledge of the world or of themselves. It was before Freud. They were helpless and sad." But it's Stephen who continues Lucas's cross-examination of Philip: "Why did you come home without him again?"

At this point, I feel compelled to hurl a dramatic statement of my own. "Something terrible is happening to David! Isn't it?" "Do you miss David?" Rivka asks me. "If he does, it's the first I've heard of it," Philip retorts, finding a truth to wound with. I don't miss David. In fact, I'm glad he's not here. And this is the truth that's bothering me. "I hardly remember what he looks like," I say meekly, which after a moment of stark silence strikes us all as silly because David and I are identical twins. And so we laugh. Everyone laughs. You would think that in a happy family a laugh would heal the breach, but this isn't a happy family and the smiles die on our faces. Philip and Rivka seem almost ashamed to have laughed. "But I didn't know he wasn't coming back," I suddenly scream. I hadn't planned on screaming. "Who says he isn't coming back?" Rivka cries out as she goes back to the kitchen with our dirty plates. Now Philip leaves the table; he will listen to some ball game for the entire afternoon.

I feel Stephen look at me. "What are you thinking, kid?" he asks me. "I don't know." "Don't know because you don't want to talk or don't know because you don't know?" He sounds like a lawyer from an early age. "I don't know don't know." He continues to look at me. "What's happening!" I hear myself cry out. Stephen nods in understanding. He gets up and goes. "I don't know don't know, too," he says.

I help Rivka with the dishes. "Can't you tell me anything, Momma?" I surprise myself by asking her. Her response is as numbing as one of Philip's outbursts at me. "Life is hard. Leave me alone. I have too much everywhere to contend with." She washes another few dishes. "Everyone needs me now."

•

Yes, our mother, the formidable Rivka, is saving lives to beat the band. Her bloodmobile is already achieving records for donations, and she's been photographed in the local paper. There's talk that if she continues so successfully she'll be asked to join "the home office in Washington." One day at the Masturbov Safeway a woman comes up to her and grabs her hand and kisses it. "My grandson's life was saved by a blood donation!" My mother embraces her. Bystanders give Rivka a little round of applause. "I saw your picture in the paper," another woman says. My mother beams in pride.

All my life I'll be distrustful of those, including myself, who devote their lives to taking care of others. The world regards this as selfless and admirable, but my mother is as selfish as they come. She does "good deeds" because it allows her to play queen, to lord it over her subjects, to be the purveyor of handouts, all strings attached. She bestows, and her hand is kissed in gratitude by a never-ending stream of her constituents. Her ego is constantly massaged and assuaged by her work for American Red Blood, where she is an important person. Which she is not in our apartment in Masturbov Gardens, where her husband is as weak and inattentive and unhappy as Rivka is strong and effusive, ceaselessly proclaiming the wonders of her world and her useful deeds. "This week I saved one hundred and six lives!" Yes, she's the star of her movie, and I don't mean to slight her contribution to the world. For every unhappy me I'm sure there were hundreds, thousands, millions whom Rivka's good deeds cheered into a happier place.

But not one of her sons ever believes she loves him. Four out of four is a perfect score. If anything bonds us, and we are certainly a foursome disunited in many things, it's our resentment of Rivka Jerusalem, our mother.

I never met a person who didn't admire her. I said that at her funeral. Except her sons. I didn't say that.

•

I'm the only son who really hates our father. In varying degrees, the other three put up with him. I think Stephen is actually fond of him. But then Stephen is perverse. Lucas ignores Philip completely, as if his father didn't live here. Lucas can ignore people completely even when he's asked a direct question, "which is like talking to air, I don't know why I even bother," I say to him often enough, even though I know that Lucas loves me perhaps above all of us. I'll never stop loving Lucas. That's really the way I should feel about David. But then Lucas, whom others would call withdrawn and I call someone thinking about deep important matters and thus not readily available to waste time over chitchat with the common man, has always been unavailable on a pretty broad basis to anyone who needs his emotional support. Like his own children. And his wife.

The resentment I feel toward Rivka is nothing compared with the tangible hate I feel toward Philip. Hate is less complicated than they tell you. He beats me up when he's angry with his wife, which is often. It's Lucas who points that out to me. "It's when he's angry with her that he goes after you. There's a James Joyce short story in *Dubliners* where that happens." I don't know who James Joyce is yet and he tells me that, too, on one of those rare occasions when he's home. Long ago he established his own schedule, only coming home now and then to sleep. He's captain of school teams and editor of the newspaper and an officer of his class. He has a lot of friends to spend the night with. It was only recently that I asked myself why Lucas never did anything about Philip beating me up. He wasn't afraid of Philip. And why did I allow it myself? I was home more than my brothers, who'd learned the simple trick of staying away, so perhaps I must take some blame for being abused. I could have followed Lucas's lead and stayed away. Why didn't I? I have no idea. Perhaps because I didn't have many friends and the few I had were with me here in Masturbov Gardens.

Was I happy when David went away to Boston? David was almost beside the point.

Years later Lucas said to me, "I had long since realized she was of no use to me. And while I had his approval, which you never had, I couldn't stand watching him take all his antagonism out on you. And her allowing it." He said that's why he stayed away from home as much as he could. I cherished Lucas's apology, never realizing it certainly came very late in the game.

Philip hates me right back. Our interactions are belligerent and violent and constant. He yells. I yell back. He yells louder. I yell back louder. He starts to hit me and I try to hit him back. He slaps me. He gets me into a corner while I hold my hands up against his blows. He slugs me and I start to cry. He punches me. It doesn't really hurt but it hurts a lot. Why does he have to do that? He punches me with a hand that's part hand and part fist. Do we recognize each other's unhappinesses? That we are both powerless weaklings? Which is what neither of us can abide. Yes, it is obvious to me from too early a time that my father is unhappy; and as I grow and watch him—surreptitiously, like the incarcerated citizen of the occupied territory observes the enemy, or like the good doctor I try to become observes the perennially dissatisfied patient—I put together the pieces of his life. I see that he's never been happy, as a child, a son, a student, a lawyer, a man, a husband, a father, an American. Another perfect score.

While Rivka extracts a certain satisfaction from her work if not her children (who take an almost perverse and retributive pleasure in ignoring her until she dies, something she will not accomplish until she's a very active ninety-eight), Philip, in his whole life, never has success, or recognition for his considerable intelligence, or a wife who enjoys him, or children who run to him happily. He never has any of this and he dies. As I write this pathetically sad and short summation of a life that encompasses some seventy years, I still cannot find tears for him, my own father. He never gets an iota of what he wants. We, his sons, must at some point have sensed all this, even though we never knew what it was he wanted. But we never asked, and he never told us.

From as long ago as I can remember I wish my father dead. And when he is dead—still some thirty years from the beginning of this war—I am, if not glad, not uncomfortable with this happening. I certainly do not mourn.

I realize that these observations of both my parents speak poorly of me.

•

What does it mean, twins? People often think that identical twins are re-markable, of note, interesting to contemplate, but I don't believe it goes fur-ther than that. I don't think people fantasize having another person alongside them just like themselves. I fantasize *not* having that person beside me. That tells you something, doesn't it?

She didn't dress us alike, mostly because we wore hand-me-downs and they didn't come in twos. We talked to each other in our own made-up lan-guage for a while until it just stopped, the fun of it. We didn't play tricks on people, each pretending we were the other. I wanted to but he didn't think it was nice. She said things like, "You're each your own person." Everyone in the family knew which of us was which. Our brothers, well, they were older and tended to ignore us. They were always tripping over us, it seemed. "Get out of the way, kid." Four kids in an apartment with one john. When David left it was still crowded. I can hear Philip saying about wherever he went to, "Thank God it's not crowded there." Nobody missed Philip when he was away. I don't think any of us even thought about him.

But when David left I felt horrible.

I've said I was lonely. What makes me think he spoke much to me—the other one—or was as nosy as I am about everything and everyone and we laughed and giggled about things? What makes me think he loved me at all? I stage-managed all the attention paid me, negative though some of it was. If I hadn't yelled back at Philip, he might have left me alone. David longed for attention and like our father he couldn't put this into words. Now I see how lonely this made him. That's why he was so quiet. He didn't hate Philip like the rest of us did, and somehow he figured that if he wanted Philip's love he'd have to have it elsewhere. He had to go away to save himself. I think he even worked it out that he had to go away so I might save myself. Had he stayed home we'd both be dead by now. That's a gross exaggeration, but twins do figure in so many horror movies.

I don't know how he figured out how to save himself (which of course is not what he accomplished at all), and I don't know how I figured out what I just said, except to say that—hey, we're twins. After all is said and done, we're twins.

The world thinks twins are loving and united by invisible instinctual bonds, psyches wired together so that each knows what the other thinks and feels and if one should be having distress halfway around the globe the other senses it and immediately picks up the nearest phone. Yes, we're closer to each other than to any other living thing. Does all this, any of this, bring . . . what am I trying to describe? Togetherness? Do we love each other as deeply and desperately and necessarily as twinned flesh is often meant to do? Is that, or the lack of it, or the interference with it, the problem? What is the problem? Nobody is picking up a phone. Some static interference has definitely broken the connection.

Like the scientists I'll come to hound and pester, men who match a second piece of "truth" to a shard discovered decades earlier, I finally realize that my twin made the greatest sacrifice in our family, but by then it's too late for the discovery to do either of us any good. He who most longed for familial love gave his own family away because he knew almost from the day he was born that we couldn't give it to him. And he thought he was the cause. That it was a better family without him. No, I didn't see any of this.

But I'm getting ahead of myself again. I was talking about her. She who performed for me the most interesting drama in my life. When did my worshipful adoration turn into the resentment that colors these pages? Perhaps the day I sensed—no, I knew!—that David wasn't coming back. The day half of me left me and those who made it happen never confessed why. My father I didn't love already; when my twin left, there remained only my mother to blame.

•

Rivka's busyness pours over into weekends, when she teaches at Rabbi Chesterfield's Washington Jewish Congregation. It's an expensive congregation to belong to, and she teaches here so her children can "be instructed in the spiritual wisdom of your ancestors." She "sacrifices" in order to make us "grateful." These words are the jewels of her vocabulary.

I'm the only dutiful one. Stephen plays hooky the third week and is rarely seen in temple again. Lucas becomes devoted to the more Orthodox Rabbi Grusskopf and elects a more rigid wisdom for a couple of years. I, who have already heard insistent whisperings in my ear that there is no God, spend my time at WJC observing the sons and daughters of "the best Jewish families of Washington," as Rivka identifies them exaltingly. The rich. They have so much I want. They arrive in their chauffeured limousines. They live in grand palaces far from Masturbov Gardens. I am a very hungry child. To be in their presence, to be so near to plenty yet so far from it, becomes a sort of hell. My clothes are shabby next to theirs. Their mothers wear fur coats in winter while Rivka shivers. They are always taking vacations to places that are warm. They all go to schools that cost a lot of money. They dance and swim at a country club we can't afford to join. How could Rivka think that all of this was something to be grateful for? Yes, WJC is how I am first thrown in with these chosen people. Through God. A God who wants me to know them but doesn't want me to live like them, only worship Him with them. And then only one day a week. No wonder I refuse His help from an early age. I know a bad bargain when I see one.

"You don't have to work so much! I make a living, for Christ's sake," Philip invariably moans when she indicates that what he's handing over to her every other Friday, on payday, in fresh new bills, is not going to cover "quite everything" this week. "I want you home!" She just as invariably answers, "I like getting out!" Their fights are so predictable. Stephen even mouths their words behind their backs: "You're such a stick-in-the-mud."

It's Lucas who first puts it into words. "They don't really love us, you know," he says dispassionately, as if he's learned this golden rule from a schoolbook for a test and committed it to memory.

Our parents are out for the evening and Lucas is playing Chinese checkers with me. I'm in my pajamas. It's never completely dark in my bedroom because light from the streetlamp just outside my window filters in even through closed Venetian blinds. Lucas and Stephen share another bedroom. For some reason Stephen has recently decided not to bathe. "I like the smell of my own schvitz," he says, saying the word like Philip would, making sweat sound ugly. "I stink so much everyone stays away from me." That's why Lucas is sleeping in the next bed. I can reach out and touch him. Instead of David.

Lucas is more my father than our own. He's my protector, my Galahad, my guide through life. He's the only person with enough patience never to get mad at me. Since he's rarely to be found in any bed in our household, it's a treat to have him home at all. He spends the night with friends "because they fight too much." "They" and "them" are what we call Rivka and Philip. So I love the times when Lucas and I can be close. I can feel his warmth and breath and his special smell, the smell of comfort. I'm safe. Trust is sparse in my life.

"They don't love us?" I don't want to believe him.

He says, "Just watch them and you'll see."

"How long have you known?"

"Every minute of my life."

And then my voice springs out of me: "Every minute of my life too!"

I jump onto him, knocking over the Chinese checkers. He cradles me in his arms as I lean against his chest. He's never embarrassed by my sudden outbursts.

"Are you unhappy and lonely too?" I ask him.

"Shhh. Go to sleep. We'll talk about it some other time."

"Yes. Some other time."

So it's now been said out loud. We have harsh, unloving parents. Children aren't supposed to hate their parents, but we do.

I have just one great terror: that I'll never be able to leave this place, that Masturbov Gardens is where I'm meant to be, that I'll never get away, that my dreams will never be anything but dreams.

As I reread this so many years after living it, it doesn't seem all that sad, does it? Not so wretchedly sad that you want to take these kids in your arms and chastise the parents with a sharp word before embracing them, too, for the sadness of whatever happened to them. No, we just fought back and they fought our fighting back, so it was like following the ball in a tennis match. No sympathy is required, only attention: keep your eye on the ball. Why am I trying to sell myself this version of what is so less truthful than the truth?

•

Lucas has the middle name of Standing. Neither Rivka nor Philip will tell us where it comes from.

Does it occur to Lucas and Stephen and me that the number of unanswered questions we are living with is mounting up?

Evidently we're not on very solid ground with our last name either.

My father's mother, my grandmother Zilka, throws out her husband, Philip's father, whose first name was Teddy, when she catches him in bed with another woman. This happens when Philip is a little boy, and he never sees his father again. Grandma Zilka throws out Teddy's last name, too, whatever it was, and goes back to her maiden name of Jerusalem. She is another relative of Cousin Abe's mother, Yvonne. Jerusalems, it would appear, are everywhere. Philip won't discuss this either. When Philip courts Rivka, there is concern in the ghetto community that all is not right with the genealogy side of things. Zilka's actions are not unknown, and there are those who have been waiting a long time to see that she is punished for her spirited defense of herself so long ago. There are Jewish councils that meet late at night just to discuss problems like this. Family names must be honorable and honored, especially in this New World. You have to be careful. You don't want to roast in hell. Zilka is the one out of a hundred who said go shove it in your face. "My son wants to marry the Rivka, he marries the Rivka, no matter what kind of trouble you make up. You want worse? He never existed, the husband, his father! I make him up. A bad dream. Philip was born by—what do the goyim call it?—immaculate conception."

Philip marries Rivka. He loved her. He did. We kids discover and devour hidden love letters, full of his outpourings, all written before any of us were born. Now we see no displays of affection, only constant dissatisfaction and disappointment. Rivka says he takes after his mother, whom we, as little boys, much against our will, are required to visit once a year in her dark rooms over her grocery store in the Northeast.

From the first time I look up at her until the day I look down at her in her coffin, Grandma Zilka makes me uncomfortable. A large woman, tall (how did Philip turn out so short?), heavy, lumbering, endlessly unsmiling, hair knotted tightly in a severe bun, clumpy thick-soled shoes, and heavily laced layers of stiff dresses smelling of her aging body and the conflicting odors of what I call "Jewish things"—stuff she sells downstairs, gefilte fish, salmon and lox, and varieties of pickles and herrings—overlaid with the wafts of her own medicinal unguents and ointments she swears she can't live without. She is a cacophony of odors.

She is always, every minute, terrified of death. That her heart might stop beating. Her eyes stop seeing. Her feet fail to carry her bulk. She drinks canned carrot juice with such a strong belief that it will preserve her eyesight that perhaps it does. Even in her coffin they can't close her eyes.

The other woman Zilka finds Teddy with is a Negress and she is sitting on Teddy's cock, which is larger, according to Aunt Grabele, than Zilka recollects it ever being for her. Like Hamlet behind the arras, she watches the performance from behind a screen as the Negress, evidently most adept with her mouth and her hands and her vagina, simultaneously intones imprecations of "some native sort" while she sprinkles aromatic spices around and about, all serving, again according to Aunt Grabele, who by the way is Philip's sister, who told me all this after Zilka's funeral (she hated her mother because Grabele was the girl and Philip and an older brother named Fedel, who is news to me, had, at her expense, whatever there was of Zilka's love), to arouse Teddy to tremendous heights. "And she was not only a shvartze but a cleaning shvartze who only twenty minutes before had been down on her hands and knees scouring out the toilet with Old Dutch Cleanser."

The funeral occurs when I am going through puberty. My body's doing things to me I don't think that I want done to it, I've refused to be bar mitzvahed, and I wish David were here to discuss all of this. I tried to ask Aunt Grabele about him and how their lessons were going. "What lessons? I'm not teaching any David how to sing!" is her reply, which makes as little sense to me as I figure my questions do to her. I've never heard some of the words, certainly never imagined any of the acts, that Aunt Grabele, with much relish, is now getting off her chest. Aunt Grabele lives in Worcester, a town of such distant-sounding dissonance that when she ventures forth from it for one of her rare visits, she seems utterly exotic. A divorcée three times, a dilletantish teacher of "classic voice" to whatever budding opera singers Worcester might be home to, she too is tiny, and from such a large mother! Teddy Whatshis-name must have been a shrimp. She is petite and dresses always in navy blue, with white gloves always on her hands, the actual skin of which evidently no one is meant to touch.

What happened to her husbands? She doesn't know. Where is Fedel?

"Who?"

"Fedel. Your brother."

"Oh, him."

She doesn't know. Goodness, how people lost people in those days.

"Your grandma Zilka waited until your grandpa Teddy and the shvartze reached orgasms, which were loud and explosive and in her bed. Her husband lay there, still inside the colored woman. From behind the arras, Zilka made her entrance, a butcher's knife in her hand—a cleaver, the kind that hacked the kosher meat to pieces, still sharp from the grocery—swinging it, aiming to bring it down on just that space between the couple where Teddy would be dismembered for life."

We are sitting in a morose antechamber at Pecker's Funeral Parlor. Grandma Zilka is laid out in the adjoining room. For all I know, at thirteen, she's looking straight at us from Heaven and listening to her daughter run her mouth. Zilka's few friends are dribbling in to pay respects; she was not well loved by the neighborhood because she refused credit and the people are poor. The sobs I hear are Philip's. I've never heard my father cry. My brothers are not here. As usual they've found reasons to be elsewhere. Once again I'm the only one to show up.

I watch my father crying over his dead mother, to make sure those chok-ing gasps are his. Rivka's eyes are dry and her expression stoic. Aunt Grabele continues, not missing a beat. "Just in time Teddy pops out, flops over, and the cleaver slashes the mattress, releasing a crescendo of goosefeathers. The Negress runs naked out into the streets—we still lived downtown in the

Northwest, a shul to the left, a shul to the right. Neighbors stand outside looking in, riveted, as the husband runs through the house evading the hatchet his wife has reclaimed, slicing the air in fury and in the general direction of his dingus, which is now swinging, dangling, bobbing wildly up and down. Suddenly Mama hurls the weapon again! It strikes the cornered husband and fells him. It opens a huge gash in his stomach. His insides are slithering out. He lies on the kitchen floor, bleating in terror, his hands trying to hold everything in. He screams at Zilka to get a doctor. She roars with laughter. He screams at neighbors to call the police. He screams at God to get ready for him. Mama just lets him scream. She goes into our bedroom down the hall and grabs your ten-year-old father—I, of course, am left behind to fend for myself—and yanks him back to observe the kitchen floor. 'Say goodbye to your papa.' Still yanking Philip, she goes outside to address the neighborhood, first putting on an expensive hat. 'I pray I killed him. He screwed another woman in the very bed this son of mine was born in.' All the women cluck-cluck sympathetically. Zilka with Philip and me then walks over to the Northeast, where some Jews have staked out another little neighborhood, and sees a corner store for rent, with some rooms above it. Here she opens and runs most successfully until yesterday a grocery store of her own. She's died a rich lady. Now let's see who gets the gelt."

"What happened to the shvartze?" I ask, having kept track of the cast of characters.

"The shvartze? What happened to your grandfather?"

"Okay, what happened to him?"

"No one ever knew." Another one lost? "I'll never forget the sight of him, on the floor, his innards guzzling out, the bloody blade Mama threw lying only inches away from his huge schlang."

"What's a schlang?"

"How old are you now? And you still don't know what a schlang is? It's your penis, your wee-wee, your wanger. Philip hasn't told you? Of course not. He probably still doesn't know himself. She'd better have left me some of that money. For the life of misery she made me live taking care of her all these years."

"But you live in Worcester."

"So? She sent messages. She almost killed me with her demands." Then she asks me, "Do you know what your real last name is?"

"What are you talking about? It's Jerusalem."

"Is it?"

That's as much as she'll say.

•

Just before we think he's dying, Philip answers me as we stand around his bed, "We're not Jerusalems."

We're in a veterans' hospital, Soldiers and Sailors Memorial, it's mercilessly called. Because Philip fought in World War I he's entitled to free care from his country. This is the only Washington hospital he can have it in. All around us are other old men dying. Or trying to. The place is monstrously steamy in the worst of the Washington summer heat. There's dirt and dust everywhere. There are holes in everyone's sheets, sheets that are rarely changed. The man in the bed on his right never stops wheezing and the man in the bed on his left is always trying to vomit. Philip introduces us to them both. "My friends," he calls them. This from a man who never seemed to have any.

"Then who are we?" Stephen asks him.

Lucas and Stephen and I and Rivka are by his bedside. Lucas and Stephen are now successful lawyers, in partnership with each other and Sam Sport. I, after several false starts in other fields, am about to . . . well, let's leave that for a while.

"Our name is not Jerusalem."

"What is it, then?" Stephen persists.

We all wait, suddenly rendered nameless, to be named anew. What are we? Who are we? What had been Philip's last name?

Three of his four sons are there, naked, waiting for clothes.

"I don't know," Philip finally answers.

"And Standing?" Lucas asks. "Where does my middle name come from?"

Rivka looks like she knows more than she wants to know. I recognize this look if the others don't. Philip gazes at Lucas's hand, without taking it—which it would be nice if he did before he dies, to show at least one of his sons some visible affection—before saying, "Standing is a special name that was given to you for a special reason. Only David can explain it to you."

"Pop." Lucas is trying to reason. "You can't do this to us. If you know something we should be told, then you've got to tell us."

"David? Who's David?" Stephen tries to make a joke. He can be really gross sometimes.

But Philip's eyes are somewhere else. He never was a dreamer, so far as I could see (how blind I was); since I've always been one, I thought I knew a dreamer when I saw one (how wrong I was). But now he has the eyes of a dreamer. Does dreaming come just before death? Does this new look in his eyes mean he is about to begin his journey, the one we are all frightened to take, the one we hope really is a journey to some safe place at last, where wishes come true and there is no agony and pain, no longing unfulfilled? For a second, in my naïve sentimentalizing, I feel sorry for him.

He reaches no hand up to Lucas, nor to Rivka, who is biting her lips in distress, a distress I bet has more to do with practicalities: Should she move into a smaller apartment? Nor to Stephen. Nor of course to me.

I take Rivka back to Masturbov Gardens. On the way home—we're taking the requisite several buses, changing in dark neighborhoods, waiting for connections that year by year take longer to arrive—it begins to pour with rain. There are no trees or passenger shelters, we have no umbrella, and we stand there in this unknown neighborhood with midnight approaching and no choice but to get drenched. For the first time in our family's history we have a little money, enough to afford a taxi at this late hour. Or one of my brothers could have driven us home; they both have cars. But despite the fact, or because of it, that Masturbov Gardens is a very long ways away, Rivka becomes the martyr as we leave Soldiers and Sailors Memorial. "You both go to your own lives. Daniel will take me home. We'll take the bus. The long ride will give me time to think." Is she expecting at least one of her sons to protest, to make a fuss over her, not to allow her sacrifice?

"Good night, Mom," said Lucas.

"Good night, Ma," said Stephen.

"Don't ask me, because I'm not going to tell you," she warns us as she leads me toward the bus stop.

And I am left to escort her home.

She says not a word during the endless trip and downpour. Once, on the first bus, she reaches over and takes my hand and clutches it and runs her fingers skittishly over it, then sets me loose. I consider starting a conversation, but it's almost as if I can feel her shake her head no. The connecting last bus comes, the rains continue, and we are back in Masturbov Gardens.

The apartment is flooded. We left the windows wide open on this hot night, and now there are inches of rainwater over the entire living room floor. The thick dark gray chenille carpet purchased once upon a time for a bargain price at some "fine" store emits sopping groans when we cross it.

The moment she surveys the damage, Rivka looks at me and speaks: "You never loved him." Then, looking at the floor, she begins to cry. "It's gone forever," she sobs, wading through the water to study for damage at closer range various other items purchased on sale at other "fine" stores somewhere. Then she leaves me and changes her clothes and comes back looking like a cleaning lady, in a schmata and stockingless, and she gets down on her hands and knees with a bucket and sponge. I find some old clothes and join her. It's almost dawn by the time she proclaims, "Enough." No sooner does she empty her last pail and squeeze out her exhausted sponge than the telephone call comes. We stare at the ringing instrument. We know what has happened. We actually hug each other in fearful anticipation.

Her tears return, becoming moans, then wails. Her cries for advice— "What shall I do?"—punctuate her gasps for breath. I try to comfort her, but she won't allow it. "You never loved him," she repeats, pushing me away. Her wails continue as the sun of another blistering day comes up.

But her husband and my father is not dead. In fact, his doctor is sending him home.

I take the buses and return to his hospital and attend to the details of his discharge and journey back with him to Masturbov Gardens by ambulance.

I have written more about my father's death in life than I have of my own beginnings. My father and I shared this earth, and share this story, for some thirty years yet to come.

And our questions—Who am I? What are our names?—remain to be excavated. What fun!

•

Down near the bottom of Masturbov Gardens are the remains of a railroad track. They say Pearl White, the silent movie star, filmed several of her cliff-hangers here, the ones where she almost gets run over by the oncoming train that doesn't see her tied to the rails. That movies were once made right here is very exciting to all of us kids growing up, Stephen especially. He likes to play director and order everyone around. He gets Lucas and me to pretend we're criminals holed up in a bedroom while the cops are closing in outside. Lucas isn't good at making stuff up. I'm an expert. "Sometimes I think I can imagine almost anything," I boast. "I can imagine everything!" Stephen says. "Can't you let the little guy win a round?" Lucas says to Stephen, frowning. "Why can't you let me win one myself?" Stephen says. Suddenly it's not a game of pretend. Lucas turns beet red because he doesn't like to answer to anyone. Stephen's almost as tall as he is now. Stephen's gorgeous, like Clark Gable or Farley Granger, one of those dark-haired love gods. Lucas looks like Spencer Tracy, kind and trustworthy. "Aren't you going to fight back?" Stephen keeps trying to bait him. Lucas starts to say something, but doesn't. "Always so tight-assed," Stephen says, shockingly. "Where did you hear that expression?" Lucas demands. "I get around." "Where to?" Lucas asks quietly. Stephen doesn't answer.

These two—so different—plan to be law partners "when we grow up." They're the twins, really. They're the ones joined at the hip. Stephen never lies to Lucas like he lies to everyone else.

"Why should I tell the truth? It doesn't make any difference."

"That's a terrible thing for a lawyer to say," I cry out.

He never stops saying it, by the way, from then till now.

•

When I am a baby and young boy, my grandmother Libby is more my mother than my own. She loves me, holds me, tends me, while Rivka is out there taking care of the world, and she's the one who not only tells me I'm strange but advises me to glory in my strangeness. Often I look up and find her looking at me, smiling. Then she says something to her daughter, if Rivka's near, and Rivka translates: "She says it gives her pleasure just to look at you." I run to be in her arms. She's the only person I give pleasure to, so far as I know.

Even though she can hardly speak English, I understand her gibberish, but only her daughter can penetrate her Russo-Yiddish. In many fruitless attempts to teach her how to speak English, her excuse is always "I wait things get better." As a kid I wonder if this means she's going home to Russia if things don't. Since she steadfastly refuses to learn America's language, I assume what she spoke in Russia is the language of her mind, where she can think her thoughts in words she need not struggle to translate. If there are genetic origins for personality characteristics, I think this is how I begin to live inside my own head. I see Grandma Libby do it. No one is listening, she seems to say; it doesn't matter: talk to yourself.

She teaches me this lesson and she leaves us. Grandpa Herschel, her own unsmiling husband, has a heart attack and they move west to Los Angeles, where his doctor promises more heart attacks won't happen. Uncle Hyman, my least favorite uncle, drives them there and changes all their names from Wishenwart to Wishen. Herschel is Libby's third cousin. He took her from

Russia to a new world and a new life in a strange country and a strange city in the East; now he is taking her to a strange city in the West. On their departure she envelops me in her arms. It's one of the first times in my life I remember crying. Suddenly, Grandpa tries to tell us all goodbye. His words are a salad of Russian and Yiddish and German and Polish—Herschel must never have known where he was, he'd been on the move all his life, escaping this and that with never much to pack. We understand him to say he's sad to be leaving, sad to be moving on, yet praying that we will all meet yet again, if not in the promised Jerusalem (he resents his son-in-law for having that name), at least in Southern California. Such remarkable thoughts from such a remarkably silent man. He's been about as welcoming and as scary to me as Grandma Zilka.

Her departing words to me? My grandmother, in whose embrace I am crying, says softly, with more words than I have ever heard her string together in English before, that no one will ever understand me, and that because of this I will be alone, but that it must not make me sad, because I will view everything—the entire world and all that happens in it—with a third eye.

The strangeness of this thought stays with me, and when, some thirty years later, Herschel long dead and Libby brought back years earlier by her children to be put in this home, she says the same thing to me again, I bob my head up and down like a Jew in a synagogue, in agreement with the word of the Lord. She is one hundred years old now, and withered beyond recognition, in a crib, mewling and wetting her pants, and seeming not to know any of the family of faces, Lucas's and Stephen's kids and even some of their kids, that lean over her, smiling down, trying to cheer her up, elicit some flicker of familiarity from their beloved Nana, as they try not to vomit from the smell of urine, farts, runny shit, the putrid odor of her advanced senility. She simply will not let go of life. She knows nothing and no one and she will not let go. She is in an old people's home that has taken every last cent of her money, for this tiny crib, for no nurse to come and clean her up, for the chance to be surrounded by a sea of the similarly cribbed and drooling. The sounds of screaming, in all registers, is like a zoo, and I can still hear it, particularly late at night when I'm scared of death.

But when I lean over, she smiles and says, "Hello, Danny," as if she's come to take care of me and I am her willing charge. She stretches her hand out for the young child to take, for safety, as we cross a street.

On that day, the day she dies, she becomes fluent. She talks smoothly in English about places she's never been, Phoenicia and Alexandria and Thrace and Mesopotamia, places perhaps from some bold children's tales of ancient times that her own mother told her. She holds my hand between her palms, which are as soft and white as Mary in Michelangelo's Pietà, and she presses my own palms with her thumbs, her hundred-year-old thumbs, as if to punctuate her thoughts, as if her jabbings can metamorphose instinct into words into truth as she brings forth her English sentences just for me.

"Nothing is so sad, not even dying, as the dying of love. You suffer too much the bad, so you can turn around and make it right. You think, like your mother, that you must play the savior. But you are an artist, and you dream, all your life I have seen your eyes dreaming, and for this you will be punished, because there is no room for dreamers. The world must always punish the creator and deny his powers. As the son denies his mother to find another to take her place.

"Your mother is a frightened woman. Her husband is confused in his sex. Men have never been our family's strong point. We women are too strong for them. You, my Daniel, will grow into strength you cannot dream you even have. There is too much blood and war and survival in our past lives for you to fall down, become a victim to . . . I do not know what to call it— punishment, everything in this world comes to punishment, a never-ending plague. That is this New World as it was the Old World, my mother Russia. We run and run."

The gurgling and the slobbering return. She cries out like a baby and then she is quiet, letting go.

How did she sense so much? With her own third eye? I don't understand until I'm helping you write this history of the plague, Fred. There are the facts and there are the opinions and then there is the truth, the true places few can see, that only the special few are cursed with seeing. For why else make Tiresias blind and Cassandra unbelieved?

I wrote down her words as fast as I could leave her bedside and find pencil and paper. It's only now, when I'm a lot closer to death myself, that I realize her prophecy is rather hopeless.

You will be very strong, she also says, and you will not allow yourself to be punished.

Well, perhaps it's not quite so hopeless.

She also says: You will not be loved until you are old.

•

The buildings of Masturbov Gardens are all connected underground by basements tunneling into each other, dark, sinewy, cement-encrusted bunker pathways apt to veer unexpectedly right and left, lit only by tiny bulbs that remain dead for weeks until tardy maintenance men brave these frightening nether routes. On particularly nasty days, when youngsters are instructed to "play indoors," it's possible to start at Mordecai Avenue, where my family lives, in the very first section of the Gardens completed, and journey entirely underground, building by building, all the way to Doris Drive, the farthest point, which takes twice as long to walk to out of doors.

In these tunnels Claudia Webb dares me to play You Show Me Yours and I'll Show You Mine. She does and I do, and it's enormously exciting—the act, not the vision, because in some bulb's last flickering glow, in that brief moment before terror at what we've done propels us both to hike up our drawers, I think I've failed to see hers. What I see is smooth and slit and penisless. No, I mustn't have seen hers at all.

But she's seen mine. She's managed to get a good look, stooping and inspecting me so closely that I get increasingly worried I'm deficient. Has she seen others that are better? Has she seen Mordy's, or Dodo's? Arnold's? If she's seen Mordy's I'll die. I can't compete with Abe's son, the heir to all these buildings and the "probably millions" of dollars Rivka says Abe's worth. Rivka and Philip have made it clear that money buys the world.

Claudia reaches out, her fingers coming close to touch. I'm frozen with apprehension. Just then we hear a sound and Claudia runs away.

I run with her. Up, out, into the wet gray daylight of the miserable outdoors. Our lungs gasp for fresh air and we grab each other and hold on to each other, as if we've seen a ghost.

Unexpectedly, unpredictably, Claudia tugs me. "Come on," she orders me.

She leads me back down into the tunnels, into that maze beneath our homes, I hardly seeing, stumbling behind her through these concrete caverns. When she finds a place that suits her, a slim indentation in a wall, just enough to hide us, she gives another order.

"Drop your pants."

I obey her immediately. I not only drop them, I step out of them.

"Those, too."

I forsake my underpants.

"Keep your eyes closed" is her next command.

The cool air around my crotch is thrilling. I scrunch my eyes up tight, though I peek and see her kneeling in front of me, studying me. Again. She touches nothing. She just looks.

"Turn to the side."

And I turn, profiled for her ceaseless observation.

Finally she stands. We face each other. I wait for her to speak. Have I passed her test?

"I did it," she says.

"Did what?"

"I didn't run away."

What has this to do with my penis?

"I did what I wanted to do."

"What's that?"

"Look at a cock."

"Look at a what?"

"Where have you been all your life?"

"You mean my schlang?"

She laughs out loud and the sound booms in the underground caves.

"Did you like it?" I demand sharply. Why is she teasing me?

"I don't know. I guess so."

I am overwhelmed with disappointment.

"You don't know?"

"I haven't seen anybody else's. I'm experimenting on you. You can see me . . . my cunt. Do you want to?

I nod in the affirmative, if apprehensively. I'm not certain what a cunt is, but I have a good idea.

"Ask."

"Pretty please may I see your . . . cunt?"

She lifts the skirt of her pinafore and yanks down her pink panties and takes my hand and rubs it softly over her smooth vagina. Our breathing seems thunderous.

Then I sink to my knees and study her as she studied me. At first I find the sight upsetting: yes, it does look like she's been amputated. But then I'm overcome with the sense that she is different and this difference is eloquent and poignant: she's vulnerable in a way I'm not and I want to protect her. Of course I can't put any of this into words. But I feel . . . tender toward her. She's sharing her difference, which is not so much less than mine as more mysterious. I feel so . . . obvious. So up front and out there. Why does it make me want to protect her? Is this love? Claudia, were you my first love?

My knees aren't getting sore at all. I look up at her. She's smiling down on me.

I bend forward to kiss her vagina. And I stay there, my lips brushing hers back and forth. Then I kiss harder, more fully, as if these lips are kissing me back. I lay my cheek against the slit. Her smell is sweet and I think of Hershey's kisses, which I love. Then I gently touch it with my tongue. She shudders and instinctively I pull my tongue away and put my arms around her legs and lay my head against her crotch. My tongue can still feel the memory, her softness, yes, but also her slash and cleft and the dividedness of her body into halves. Is one half in touch with the other?

I want to taste more.

I stick my tongue into her. How do I know to do this? A greedy hungry child who'll eat anything? When he catches me raiding the icebox and ravenously stuffing myself with cold baked beans and leftover chocolate pudding, Philip always yells at me, "You'll put anything into your mouth!"

I hear her say "oooh" in a strange way, a sound from deep in her throat. Suddenly everything we're doing makes me sad. It comes from nowhere, this sadness. Why has it come? I feel different. And that I don't belong here. I can be no home for her or she for me. I miss my twin brother, I want to tell him about this. Why is he here with me now? And why isn't he? And why am I thinking any of this?

Claudia kneels down beside me. Does she sense my mood? She holds my head in her hands and looks me in the eyes and kisses me on my lips. It's lovely. I'm back with her again. I feel good inside again. I wonder again if what's stirring inside me is love. Then—what is she doing?—her hand is in my crotch. "You're supposed to get stiff and hard." There's that determined bossy tone, her command spoken with such authority. Her fingers are poking at my tiny bobbing thing. "My mother says you're supposed to get stiff and hard. My father does. Sometimes. She says she plays with him when he doesn't." She's playing with me and I'm becoming what she and her mother talked about. I smile in pride. Do my mother and father talk about these things? Much less do them?

Then she pushes her body against mine. She leans into me and I fall backward and she's on top of me, keeping her skirt up with her hands, her body pushing and pushing against mine. "You're supposed to go into me," she orders. We're lying on the cold harsh floor now. I'm getting dizzy. Her hand is down on my penis again. "Your penis isn't hard at all. You're not doing what you're supposed to be doing at all."

I try harder to comply with these increasingly strange new marching orders. I summon all the energy I can and try to direct it to my cock, like when squeezing hard aids recalcitrant bowel movements. I pump and thrust and push and grunt. I grunt so hard I worry something will come out of my bottom. But it's no use. I know it will be no use. It is no use at all. How I know, or why, I don't know, beyond some unconscious fear that destiny is all. This time it's me who runs back up to the daylight. I think I hear her laughing behind me in the dark.

•

I want to say more about Claudia, Fred. Her presence hovers over these early years of my life with unnatural weight.

In less charitable moments I've called her evil; now I look more to myself to wonder how I ever saw her that way, and why.

I could almost say I've loved her all these years—it's almost sixty years by now—but I stop short of saying this because it sounds as sentimental as it is, a homosexual claiming to pine for the young girl from his youth, the particular homosexual having been a young boy and young man and older man who's had much trouble with love, with finding it, with keeping it, with knowing it when it's there.

I know that in her own way Claudia loved me, perhaps more than she loved anyone else, perhaps instead of anyone else, perhaps only me and no one else (no, that suits my role in this drama too much). Would I have been so impractical as to continue so long in her thrall without *some* return in kind? I did dream that we might live together in some attempt at partnership.

I know—and this is my heartbreaking realization, one reason I must write about her is to get some sadness out of my system, even though I've long since learned there's very little in life that's cathartic—that she learned an even sadder lesson of our age: once you've actually partaken of fantasies, from that moment on there's little chance realities will ever be the same. I don't believe there is one fantasy that Claudia did not live out in her years, or one that she didn't tell me about and I didn't experience vicariously, usually to the detriment of my own heart and soul.

My goodness, what heady stuff.

I've come painfully to realize that she never believed, as I did—and, God help me, still do—in the touching innocence of romantic love that we've been brainwashed, by every conceivable coercive device from mothers to media, into longing for and aspiring to. I wanted her to have that, if not from me, then someone. And of course I failed. As did Lucas, whom she did love and who wouldn't leave his wife for her. And it was for this she took Stephen away, to punish him for all the Jerusalems' failures. Stephen to this day is still a mess.

So no, I can't let go of her, even now. Indeed, she is even more the symbol of what I wish would change about the world, of why the world always looks the other way, time of plague or no.

She always said I was the silly Jew who must invent hope, and if not hope, then anger to destroy. "I insist I am a complete pragmatist" was her answer to all my protestations. I replied, "I watched you grow from a young girl who seemed to hold so much promise into a woman without imagination, expectations, hopes, or dreams." She answered, always, "Precisely my definition of the complete and modern woman." The irony is that she had more contentment in life than I'll ever have with all my quests and dreams. How do I know? How could she get contentment out of *that*? Well, she was that perverse. She said she'd already lived her life, which she called a life of loss; she said she wished I'd get to work on mine and bring it to some sort of conclusion: the death of dreams.

"I will never not believe in dreams!"

"How can you dream now!" she often asked me, long before the plague.

I'm sorry, Fred, that she never met your Edward, who finally came along to disprove all she said and stood for.

She went to live and work with Doris Hardware. It was a pleasant sunny morning in spring.

Claudia walks the few miles from her house off Military Road. She locks the door and casually drops the key to her home of ten years down a gutter, not even waiting to hear it plink against the bottom. She isn't concerned with what's in that house any longer, who will pay the bills, or what will happen to her MG convertible illegally parked in front. Another gutter, plink goes the MG key. Now she carries nothing, not even a handbag holding phone numbers or cash. She carries only herself and the light summer clothes she's wearing—a navy-blue skirt of rough cotton, a pale pink blouse that makes her skin look whiter than it is, and a pair of squeaky sandals from a trip to Mexico we took together. Her hair, which is jet black, is cut short around her round face. She always looks like a very pleasant person, except for her eyes, which either look through you or are sad, though she doesn't seem to know this, or care. It's as if she's never with you. Which, for some, certainly the likes of Stephen, makes you want her more.

She is not a woman given to memories. Each moment is each moment. Oh, she remembers things when asked. "What happened to you in San Antonio when you were nineteen?" and she recalls quite precisely, sounding like a footnote in a history book or an entry in a particularly dispassionate diary: "That was when I was in love with Chipper. Reems." Then she goes on to say how they went to Houston and had a fight on top of that revolving monument erected to commemorate a world's fair. "I warned him I was going to leave him. He somehow got himself outside the tower, on the roof, and threatened to jump off. I left him there." "Did he jump?!" "I have no idea. I never heard that he did." And that's the end of the entry as far as she's concerned.

What were you thinking that day? What were you feeling that day? Oh, I used to pummel her with questions. It was as if I were a writer and she my best character and I couldn't let her go.

She gave me a gift. She showed me how the achiever can become a prisoner. This also made Stephen love her more. Lucas recognized the dangers and stepped down.

People write whole books on any of these sentences. What am I trying to say?

"You simply don't understand me at all!"

But I think I do. And it hurts. Which is what she wants it to do.

The day she walks south to Doris Hardware's she's twenty-one years old. She spends her birthday the night before with Stephen.

I know she's with him. I know about their affair. I asked her all about it; she told me nothing. Do you tell him all your history? I demanded. No, of course not, she replied. I believed her. Her history—and that I'm the only one who knows it—is what joins us at the hip.

When she's twenty, she flies to San Francisco from Los Angeles, where she's living with a young carpenter, to join an older man she met only briefly at a party in Malibu, who offers to indoctrinate her into what he calls "realms of sexual excitation within yourself which I think you have been unaware of." He meets her at the airport and takes her to his home on Divisadero Street, and there he instructs her, and she becomes his total slave. After several months in San Francisco, she has experienced what it means to be a slave, all the implications, the crawling around on the floor and being tied up for hours and days and ordered to perform acts on him and others, and being totally without wishes of her own, except as they please him, her master.

"I realized I had never been without wishes of my own. It was a novel experience. Now I had the general idea. Now, what to do with it? What did it mean to me?"

"Why did you want to do anything at all with it!"

"Life can be so miserable if all you do is regret all the time." She says that to me the first time I enter her, the first time I have an erection with a woman, the first time I have an orgasm with a woman. She allows me to make love to her, ten times in all, during a monthlong period when we're both in our early thirties, many years after she goes to Doris's and twenty years after I first try. I make wonderful love to her, she says so, and she cries out in pleasure each and every time. We climax together each time, and I don't know then that this is an accomplishment of sorts, having an orgasm together, or Claudia having one at all. I'm thrilled with the joy of succeeding at something I never expected I would even try, and though I know I don't want to repeat it with any other woman, I also know I am more than happy—at that moment—to have done it, and with Claudia.

That day, as she walks toward Doris's, without so much as looking at them, she passes several men she's slept with. She's been a memorable person in their lives, too; this compliment (that they look at her, that they remember her, that they hope she'll acknowledge them) means nothing to her. They nod to her anyway, not with any particular relish, because they were all rejected by her or hurt by her in other ways, but because they'd hop into bed with her again in a second should she so much as raise an eyelash of hope. But she doesn't see them. And she doesn't see me, because I'm hiding behind a house, a tree, a car here and there, scooting behind her to see if she's actually going to do what she told me she was going to do. "You have no idea what you're getting yourself into!" I cried; but of course that in itself makes it all the more entertaining to her. She has a very low threshold of boredom. Yes, she's smiling to herself, because the commencement of any new activity, particularly one so startling in its conception, its bravura, its gall, is all.

When she arrives there, at the great garden of the great house that is Doris Hardware's, she stands there, among the green trees and blossoms. She actually looks full of repose. "Here it feels good, here I can rest. Just walking through the gates, everything is finally fine," she tells me later.

Those years ago in San Francisco . . . she showed me a photograph. She is bound up. Her wrists are tied together and then tied by an only slightly longer cord to a knobby protrusion that passes for the leg of a sofa, short and stubby and weighted down by the heavy Victorian plush above it. Her ankles are similarly corded, to each other and to this knob. Thus she is forced to remain for many hours in a slightly curled position, lying on her left side, unable to maneuver much. For an hour or so, there is a certain amount of sexual tension that pleases her. She is alone; he has left her; when will he come back and claim her, what will he require her to do when he does come back? Will he come back? He'd told her that once he'd flown off to Hawaii for a long weekend. While she feels comfort in the subservience, she knows he will come back and not go to Hawaii. He is strong and rich and his house, of which she pretends she is mistress, is filled with expensive items and a bedroom in which she is pleasurably fucked and wishes to be again. His body, that of a forty-year-old man, is firm and yet softening into something comfortable and no longer the hard, intractable one of youth. "His chest is covered with lightly graying soft hair and his arms have a defined musculature I feel when I'm allowed to hold him. His eyes are kind, when they wish to be, and his hair is brush-cut and bristly. He brushes it across my stomach like some sort of porcupine mop, which tickles me and then excites me. When he finds that this arouses me, he continues to do it again and again for a long time, until I come." She tells me all this. She tells me everything in great detail. She looks out into space and talks to a far-off place. Will I someday tell it all to Stephen, or to Lucas? Is fitting them into this piece of the puzzle worth those encounters? Any finer points I feel deprived of I request, and receive. Coming in so extraneous a way—in that their sexual organs never touch—amuses her: "I am doing this in a way that no one else can." That she doesn't know his full name, or maybe even his real first name, and refuses to scout among his papers and mail to find out, that she doesn't know what he does for a living, or with any certainty who he truly is, amuses her as well. That she is where she is, and doing what she's doing, is the totality of the excitement.

"Don't you see, Daniel, that was it, that he had this hard cock of his inside me, and his skin was hard and soft and his head was covered with that brush cut and my skin was like his skin, which made us almost like brother and sister, and that he might have me tied up but I had him tied up too, because he needed my cunt for his cock to be inside, he needed me to climax, otherwise he could only do it in some second-best fashion by himself, with his own hand, he couldn't be a part of something, of us, so I had him tied up too." I've taken her clothes off by now, and have an erection of my own as I envision the two of them in San Francisco, that man with his hard cock, their skins alike, he inside her, she letting him. This would have been our eleventh time. This time she said, "No. No more."

Once she invites me to a party at her house, by then (her father having hit one of the jackpots he's in the habit of winning and losing) in the best neighborhood of Northwest Washington—the third alphabet—Albemarle, Brandywine, Chesapeake, where the grand houses are, nestling in the outer edges of Rock Creek Park east of Connecticut Avenue, down elite tributaries haughtily bereft of public transport. To travel to that august locale takes at least ninety minutes on another set of three different buses from Masturbov Gardens, and then you have to walk because you're only dropped off at its border. I'm in junior high school. I can feel the little boy in me reacting as closer and closer toward Mecca I come, my eyes growing wider and my imagination wild with unbounded hope. I will fall in love tonight. She'll live in a house like that one or that one! This is where we'll live, with maids and a chauffeur, I guess a gardener, too, and in all these other mansions will re-side my friends. Oh, how I want to be rich and not have to worry about how much everything costs, as we seem to do every single second in Masturbov Gardens, where everything costs a great deal. I don't know if the bus route is still the same today. I suspect it must be. The big houses are all still there, as is the park that so often protected us as it enveloped us in darkness on our walks at night when she let me hold her hand.

I don't know why Claudia invited me. I thought when she left Mastur-bov Gardens that was it. She had found out about Mordy and Mordy had found out about her and I had found out about him. Tic-tac-toe and we all canceled each other out.

Claudia says she invited everyone she knows. Most of the other kids are driven here by parents or staff; a couple of them probably drive themselves in their own cars with fake IDs. No one else takes three buses from the Other Side of the Park.

"Do you think I invited you because I found you interesting and attrac-tive and different?"

"Yes!"

"Well, I did." This is years later, when she also tells me she always knew she could tie me around her finger and make me obey her wishes.

"What were your wishes that evening?"

"That you hadn't arrived so early."

Her house is mock Tudor and sits on a small rise, filling its large plot amply. I stand on the street looking up at it. Claudia is going to private school now, and her guests will be dozens of kids I don't know, which frightens me. They'll look at me, and at my brown sharkskin suit bought on sale at some downtown store like Hecht's where the rich never have to shop. I feel that both the suit and the self belong somewhere else. We are intruders. I am now an intruder in Claudia's life.

But up the flagstone steps I softly march. A black butler opens the door. I don't know whom I expect to open it, but I don't expect a butler, black or any other color, or a black maid to take my overcoat, another sale item from Hecht's, in a dark pukey green "so it won't show spots," a working mother's highest recommendation.

Claudia appears. Is it from down a curving stairway or from beneath an arching portal, or does she spring full beautifully reborn from some god or goddess's head? How many thousands of times have I seen her before? But have I really noticed her? She stands there surveying me from afar, as if she's never noticed me either. It's like a scene from one of the romantic movies I've already seen too many times.

She is all in dark violet, looking old enough to be in college; as she approaches I can see her eyelids are dark violet too, and my heart stops from the awe of this exotic touch. She comes to me and takes my hand and kisses my cheek and says, "Janet Mesirow thinks you're very cute and I'm telling you this in advance so when we play Spin the Bottle you can arrange to kiss *her*."

"I don't know Janet Mesirow."

"She's seen you."

Why is she fixing me up with someone else? Have I been summoned all the way from the other side of town for this?

Still holding my hand, she leads me to a small, dark den and sits down on a plaid-covered sofa, assuming I will do the same, sit beside her, uninvited, which I do. I can still feel the embrace of that room. It was like a womb, like that thrilling moment of being held for the first time in a lover's arms, like stowing away in a closet playing hide-and-seek. Somehow it was also somber and magisterial and ecclesiastic: I am courtier to her queen. If there had been incense burning I wouldn't have been surprised. She lets go my hand and leans forward to kiss my forehead—I am being knighted!—and touches her tongue to my nose.

"I'm going to let Janet Mesirow have you tonight but someday, when you and I have both accomplished what we're meant to accomplish in the world, we're going to be very good friends."

"I don't want to be good friends," I answer, fighting even then for the whole hog.

But she ignores me and continues: "I've slept with many men already. Does it shock you that I should say this at a mere fifteen? I think I've been in love with several of them. Why doesn't it last, do you think? I liked sleeping with them, but I don't think it's all it's cracked up to be, do you? But then, you haven't slept with anyone yet and that's another reason why I like you. You're not sad yet."

"Oh, I am sad, I am," I hear myself say.

"Then you're sad for other reasons." Her tone tells me that she will not be matched in accomplishments she considers her special province. But then she must have decided it's okay for me to be sad too, for she brings her gaze back from outer space to see and be with me (she is as adept as Rivka in utilizing those I'm-not-really-looking-at-you looks). "We sad people must stick together," she says, "for we're the only ones who will ever understand . . . so many things. My mother is always saying I'm too grown-up for my age. But I've got nice tits and I've got a cunt that's well broken in and I don't see why everyone makes such a big secret of it all."

I certainly think she's mature. I am also hurt that someone—from the sound of it a number of someones—has been with her so intimately already.

It's easy to smile about what a precocious child she was. It's not so easy to smile that she's stayed that way. Just before her murder, as Claudia and I are having a late afternoon lunch on Doris's terrace overlooking all of Washington, for some reason she tells me of the time—only months after her purple dress on the plaid sofa—when she fucked with a couple in a hotel not so far away from where we're sitting.

"He said they were brother and sister and could I get off on that."

Again, still, I listen nervously. Yes, these tales of her sexual exploits are sad, but they make my penis tingle and I worry why such experiences—from which I was obviously excluded—excite me.

She continues. "I nodded I could get off on that, and he fucked me while she watched and it was only later I realized they were husband and wife and that's how they got their kicks."

She can see that I'm fascinated, that she can work her tricks on me. She runs two of her fingers up my knee, like two tiny people running after each other, and she rummages around in my crotch to see if my penis is paying attention, and so help me, even after years of being homosexual, it is. She can still make it hard. And of course, the minute she discovers that, she takes her hand away.

Once, we go walking in her neighborhood, down a couple of blocks, across the street from a brick house with small windows. She takes my hand and starts running across the street, where we position ourselves in front of various windows to try to look inside. To no avail; heavy drapery is in our way.

"Mr. J. Edgar Hoover lives here. He is trying to put my father in jail. But Daddy is smarter than he is." Even more mystery wafts around this girl. I guess "girl" is no longer the correct definition of her. And of course she will tell no more. My own twin brother will fall into Hoover's grasp but I am not to know about this either until many years pass.

I kissed Janet Mesirow that night. I closed my eyes and pretended she was Claudia. There's a scene in *The Magic Mountain* where Hans Castorp remembers taking a pencil from the young man he worshipped when they were boys together. They never exchanged anything beyond that pencil. But that boy haunted him, and when Hans falls in love with the divine Clavdia, it's because Clavdia reminds him of the boy with the pencil. I've always thought it of minor literary interest that Mann does not delve into the sex change that transpires over the intervening years. (But then, we've since learned Mann loved men himself; what a sneak to so slyly keep it out.) That my Claudia is so close in name? Well, that is man's coincidence.

I don't see Claudia for over a year after that night of her party.

"I just didn't want to see anybody, so I stayed home and was tutored," she tells me when she surfaces and summons me to her home again. "I'm in high school now, just like you."

"Janet Mesirow is married. And so young. You should have carried on. She's very rich. You care about that."

We're both in bathing suits, because I've been invited to come and swim. She once told me that she liked my body, "sort of," but it would be better when it had all the hair that was on its way to growing in. Now that it has I'm anxious to see if it meets with her approval. She pulls my suit off underwater (no one else is at home), and she submerges to have a look, treading water a foot or so away from my crotch. How much progress have we made, toward anywhere, since she kneeled in front of me when we were hairless in the dark basement tunnels of Masturbov Gardens?

"It's a nice dick," she says, surfacing, her face, tanned and beautiful, breaking through the blue clear crystal water.

I lean forward and kiss her. "Dick," I repeat.

"You still don't get around much," she says, kissing me back, though she won't let me hold her.

I feel the rejection awfully: one kiss is not enough. My cock is much bigger than when she submerged to see it. I try to put her hand down there to feel.

"We're not going to do any of that stuff with each other. We're friends. We're best pals. We're brother and sister."

But her hand is on my penis.

"Brothers and sisters don't get like this," I say.

"Oh, of course they do," she answers.

"Is that supposed to give me hope for the future?" I ask plaintively.

"I just don't think people ever really change," she says.

"What does that mean?"

"I can tell you'll never be able to give me what I want, so I don't want to get started with anything."

"How can you say that?" I'm still a few years away from hearing my grandmother Libby's prophesies about my various strangenesses, but eerily, as if in some precognition, I sense something's coming. "Why not? What's wrong with me?"

"Why do you automatically assume it's you?"

"Because you're perfect."

"I'm not perfect."

Then she won't talk about anything sexual or personal anymore. We have our lunch in that musty, seductive study and talk about other things. After lunch, we're sitting on that plaid sofa, and I lay her back and unbutton the pinafore she's changed into and look at her body. We have watched each other bud. I'm shaking with fear and stage fright: what I'm doing now feels different. I know what men are supposed to do to women. Which I think I want to do to her. She is suddenly very . . . alien. I know I'm looking at a perfect body: her long arms, her breasts like the ones in paintings and on statues in art galleries, the dark hair between her legs. I lean over and kiss that. It smells sweet, perhaps of soap, a smell I can remember still and perhaps remembered from when she was smooth and there was only that slit so perversely different and divisive. She lies there. Her eyes are closed. My boldness makes me bolder. I begin to kiss her all over. "I enjoy your kissing me," she says, opening her eyes and looking at me. We both see the bulge in my bathing suit. "I told you no," she says. "I don't want to," I say, looking down at my penis, my hand on it. "I think I could, but I don't want to." "*I* don't want you to," she says; "I told you that. I told you I don't want us ever to do that to each other. What does it take to make you listen to me?" Then she lays me back, and she takes off my bathing suit, and she looks at me, then kisses me all over, as I have done to her. She goes nowhere near my penis, which stands up like a flagpole, too ungraciously inelegant for this touching scene. When she finishes, she says, "Please remember how my kissing you all over felt, because it will have to last you a lifetime. No one else will ever have so many of my kisses."

"Why not?"

"You do insist on asking unanswerable questions. If you give people what they want and what you want . . . you don't get anything. You'll always be the giver. I don't want to be the giver. The trouble is that I don't want to be the taker either. I still have to figure that one out. When I do, I'll tell you."

I don't have the vaguest notion what she's talking about.

I don't think I'm being frugal in relating these events. Yes, I know that I've related them chaotically. Yes, I know there's a feeling of something missing. But that is Claudia exactly.

"Sex is like heroin," she once said to me. "For some people it's an addiction. Sexual obsession. I'm not one of those. You are. And I can't satisfy you."

"I am not obsessive about sex! What are you talking about!"

"I don't think people can change."

"Stop saying that!"

"They just have to learn to accept themselves."

I vehemently protest that people can indeed change if they want to change, that it's just hard work, but worth it, and that nothing important ever comes easily. And I still have no idea what she's talking about. Or how I already knew how to answer her as I did. My sexual obsession?

"Where in the world did you get all that?" I almost explode.

"It just makes sense! You wait and see!"

"See what!"

"In many things, in all important things, I think we have no choice."

"Stop saying things like that!"

And so it goes. She pooh-poohs me and I pooh-pooh her and then we get angry and then she reaches out and puts her hand on my crotch that's frightened of her and then we don't make love and then I go home and she leaves town again and who knows where she's gone to now.

And I stay home, wondering why I didn't take her in my arms and possess her so fiercely she had no other choice but to love me back.

But if confronted with this question she would reply, "But Daniel, I already do love you back."

So these are a few scenes with Claudia, out of their proper historical order as memories are. The underground tunnel in Masturbov Gardens I followed her into—neither of us came out of it the same.

•

"Mommy, what's a penis really?"

Rivka and I are carrying heavy bags of groceries up the steep and winding hill from the Safeway. It's the summer before Pearl Harbor. Many unknown things are in the atmosphere. You just know it and feel it. Life seems off balance, strangely imprecise.

Surely, with a father and two brothers—no, three—somewhere along the way I must have noticed a penis. Or two. Or three. Or four. And wondered. No. Not wondered. Known. Why is it important that Rivka tell me? Was I looking for some common sense after Claudia? Or verification? "Why didn't you or Daddy ever tell me?"

Rivka doesn't bat an eye. "It is the male sexual organ," she explains in her schoolteacher voice, the one she uses when she tries to instill facts in me. "It is what you urinate with and when you are a man you will use it to insert yourself into a woman's sexual organ, which is called the vagina, and which is not at all like your penis but is flat and with an opening, like an envelope— or my pocketbook—in order to receive you." We don't miss a step in our heaving up the hill, which is suddenly steeper, and the summer day more sweltering. No, not for one second does she cease her riveting discourse, and I feel myself sweating inside my underpants, mysterious driblets dripping and sticking my little penis to the cloth. I didn't know that daring the gods or tempting the fates made your crotch behave so markedly.

"This insertion, which requires that the man's penis is erect . . ."

Erect? Is that the same as hard?

". . . will result in the deposit of male seed, or semen, into what is called the uterus, and if it is the proper time of month, conception will occur, resulting in pregnancy and, nine months later, a child."

My little penis?

I am stunned by her forthrightness, and what certainly sounds like an honesty not witnessed since David's disappearance somehow changed the rules. She who once held and cuddled me, she who once made me feel safe, is now telling me about erect penises. Her words provoke a hundred further questions. I sneak a look at her but she's looking straight ahead, as if all she'd told me was the time of day. The silence continues. Am I meant to respond? Will I disappoint her if I don't? I fill the air with lots of panting and heaving as we work our way to the top of the hill with our formidable loads.

"What do you mean, the proper time of month?"

She then tells me about menstruation and sperm swimming upstream to fertilize eggs. Eggs? Like the eggs I hate that she makes me eat for breakfast? I'm way more unsettled than enlightened. Usually, when we discuss "current events" or right and wrong, she asks me, "Do you understand?" She's not asking me now.

Instead, I ask her, "What are we having for dinner?"

She answers that one too, and we are home.

•

There's a war creeping up on us, isn't there? When its rages finally start perking more violently into our consciousnesses, it will seem like it's been here all along. And like everyone was already working on it beforehand, weren't they? People slip into rhythms fast. Many parents are doing "important things." Express buses now run daily into the District.

All the fathers in Masturbov Gardens now want to be seen doing something important downtown. Their sons and daughters, my playmates, endow them with important-sounding jobs. New families are moving in all the time to ride those express buses. And the rental billboards posted at the very District Line, which once promised One Hundred Acres of Heaven, now announce, "Live Where the Important People Live!" Both Rivka and Philip remark how "important" everyone now looks. She says it's because people now have a purpose in life, "like I do."

If food will soon be rationed all over the country, if people will have Victory Gardens and be eating carrot and beet tops and kale, and pour their rendered fats into tin cans for surrender to the butcher, how come we in Washington will be able to eat so well and suffer so little, especially in comparison with the little boys and girls our parents now start telling us about who are starving overseas?

Where is David? Is he eating properly?

Like the mysterious "war effort" no one precisely defines, not the newspapers or the radio or our teachers in school, not Philip or Rivka, though they are both apparently busy working for it, life appears to move onward unquestioningly.

Something's happening. Isn't it? Somewhere?

But I don't remember people asking, What's really happening?

We're all playing Follow the Leader, aren't we, and rather well.

•

My uncle Hyman is a traveling salesman, of books more legally salable than the one I discover while secretly investigating his suitcase. He's also the first "free man" I know, someone who is his own boss and goes from city to city anytime he wants to. Philip hates him, and I don't like him either.

He looks sly and greasy. He never looks you in the eye. He smells of body odor and endless cigars. He has a waxed mustache, of a kind seen in old movies on villains and untrustworthy French lovers: pointy and itchy for those like me who are forced to kiss him. "Kiss your uncle Hyman hello." Yuck. Hello, Uncle Hyman. His mustache sits over a narrow mouth, a pursed slit when closed and a maw of tobacco-stained teeth when not. Does he know he's so repulsive? He must! (And if he knows, how does he live with it?) He doesn't have any friends he ever talks about. He never has a girlfriend. He wears elevator shoes with heels so high they pitch him forward, and he's still a shorty. And his hair! So gloppy with grease, from a jar labeled Lilac, though certainly unlike any lilacs that bloom in Masturbov Gardens, stinky, with a cloying sweetness. Oh, everything about Uncle Hyman is so disgusting, how can we be related?

Uncle Hyman arrives regularly in Masturbov Gardens twice a year.

"Why doesn't your cheapskate brother spring for a hotel?" Philip twice a year complains.

"He's my brother! I want him here with me!"

This exchange transpires in loud whispers as Hyman heaves his suitcase onto David's twin bed.

He gives us our gifts. Philip receives something like an old accounting text; he can never fathom the workings of a mind that gives him, in 1942, a book copyrighted in 1927 and as out-of-date as auction bridge. "The man is so cheap he's nuts."

And for me, similarly archaic works in biology or chemistry or math, their publications all preceding my birth. Perhaps he's giving us something valuable, perhaps he knows something we don't, that if we hold on to the books for years and years they might be worth untold dollars, like the Gutenberg or a first edition of Proust, to those devoted to collecting such earlier examples of knowledge.

But I soon discover these are not *the* books. How I come to ransack, at every opportunity, every outpost of the unknown (Uncle Hyman's suitcase is by no means an isolated gold mine), I'll never know. Are lonely children always nosy children? How far does "nosy" extend before "trespassing" or "against the law" is more descriptive of the act? To this day I dislike anyone who isn't filled with questions. How can people *not* be curious? What's wrong with being nosy? I've discovered that most people, when confronted, will tell you almost anything. Why are questions rarely asked? Why are people always so infernally polite? What do you gain by being so polite? Certainly not knowledge. I fervently believe that truly interesting information must most often be excavated and extracted rudely. Given half a chance, I still investigate drawers and desktops, closets and shelves, suitcases, old trunks and packing cases, cartons, coat pockets, refrigerators, cupboards, no matter where. I am a scavenger of other people's secrets. These are much more important caches than the places we usually turn to for "truth."

I don't think I would have become a doctor but for Uncle Hyman.

I am lying in bed. Lucas, who comes home late if at all, has been moved back to his own twin bed with smelly Stephen. Uncle Hyman's suitcase lies where David would. Mom and Hyman go for a walk. It's a nice night. Pop's listening to a ball game. Pop never comes in here. So what am I waiting for?

My heart thumps like a kettledrum. I am stealthily opening Pandora's box.

What's making me do it? I *hate* Uncle Hyman. All the more reason!

I press the two lock releases and they jump to attention. I swing the two halves of the giant suitcase apart and they lie back, awaiting me. I gently raise the top layers of clothing. Item by item, layer by layer, my delicate excavation reaches the bottom of side one. Nothing. Onward.

I flip over the dividing panel. Socks and handkerchiefs and underwear. What's this? "Sold for the prevention of disease only." Prophylactics. Yes, I have seen one. I even put one on, one night when I was babysitting for the Droods. Mickey Drood's bottom drawer was filled with them. I had to figure out what it was for. I figured it out. Of course it fell off. But it was exciting anyway and I looked forward to growing into one. What's this? Phooey. More books. But these are slim and slickly shiny. I open one up. Photographs. I suck in my breath.

Here, before my eyes, on my very brother's bed (or should I say on my very brothers' bed), my hands are holding pictures of every imaginable combination performing every conceivable act. Here are thin pamphlets of naked men and women. Here are naked women and women. Here are naked white people and naked black people and naked Oriental people. Here is a naked woman with a German shepherd. With an erection. In her. Here are group scenes. Here are children with other children just as naked of pubic evidence as I was. Here are naked children and naked adults. And here (almost a relief at last?) are naked men and naked men.

So this is what it looks like.

How do I know this is home?

I feel all fluttery inside like the time I was in a play awaiting my entrance offstage. I feel giddier by the moment, positively dizzy. As I turn from page to page of the several volumes devoted to my sex, I feel faint in my head and stalwart in my underpants. A throbbing turns to a surge. The men are good-looking. One of them reminds me of Lucas, and another's chest hair is just like Stephen's. Everyone's penis is hard and thick and huge. I have never seen penises like these. Certainly not on anyone in this household when I've covertly peeked. Some of the penises have skin on their ends that looks strange, and anatomically new to me. Oh, God, am I somehow deficient here as well?

Some of the men are playing with their penises with their hands and/or playing with the penises of others. Some of them are in a circle, each holding on to the penis of a neighbor. That looks like fun, although their faces are all unsmiling and stern. One of the men has his penis in another's mouth. One of them has his penis in another's rectum! The picture I like best is of two men just holding each other tight and kissing. Something in my pajama pants explodes. (I wear my underpants under my pajama bottoms. Why?)

I never felt like this before! I throb and tingle. But the strangeness of it suddenly scares me more than the wonderfulness of it makes me feel so good. I yank down both bottoms. I must look at my small thing to see if it's still there after such a throbbing. I am relieved to see it is. What are those sounds from the front of the apartment? They're back! They're back and Uncle Hyman is coming to bed!

I jam the books back into the suitcase and the suitcase back to its closed position. I jump into my bed and pull up the covers and turn off the light and scrunch my eyes closed just as the door opens and I smell Uncle Hyman come in and walk near and what is he doing now? Have I successfully covered my tracks? Have I left evidence at the scene of the crime? I hear him heave the suitcase down to the floor and take off his clothes and sink into bed. Soon he's snoring. I guess everything's all right. I guess wrong.

Uncle Hyman offers to take me on his round of Washington bookstores. I have nothing else to do. Summer vacation is boring. His accounts are all dusty ground floor and basement secondhand places in the poorer neighborhoods, off the beaten track, with high stacks of old books, long aisles between them, and dim lighting. I am left to wander while he takes orders for his "special line" on the occult and how to perform card tricks and recognize the value of old coins. First one store, then another; there is little difference between them; I come to recognize similar stock, the same old bestsellers trying to find a home again.

Each store also has unmarked sections for sex.

How swiftly I find them. No matter how small the type, SEX jumps out from the spines. I pause nonchalantly, pretending to look at some neighbor, health or diet or eugenics (whatever that is), my fingers inching closer to pounce on something that says, Take me! I come to recognize that the books with titles like *A Manual for Modern Marriage, What Every New Bride Should Know*—I discover that marriage stuff always has drawings of men's "sexual organs"—*The Bachelor's Handbook, Sex and Today's Man* are the ones I want. Homosexuality. That's what it's called. *The Bachelor's Handbook* tells me so. Now I know its name from what are called "Case Histories." Young boys having sex in a school dormitory is a Case History. Old men locked up in institutions for playing with young boys outside of school dormitories is a Case History. I sniff the odor of disapproval. The whiff—hell, the stench. How quickly I adapt to it. The insatiable hunger of the voyeur is stronger than the stench of societal condemnation.

Driving home from his last stop, Uncle Hyman puts his hand on my knee.

What is this greasy, smelly uncle doing? Now his hand is in my crotch! Now he's trying to unbutton my fly! What am I supposed to do? I'm terrified.

My windbreaker is on the seat between us. I push his hand away and pull it over my lap.

"What don't you want me to see?" he asks.

I don't answer. I can't answer.

"Let me see," he says matter-of-factly, trying to pull the jacket away. "Men shouldn't be ashamed to let other men see them."

He pulls it off. I pull it back.

"Did you enjoy my picture books?"

His hand, now under the windbreaker, has succeeded in unbuttoning. He's poking for my penis. His fingers are darting around, seeking, then finding it. I'm having what I don't know is one of my first grown-up erections and I wish I wasn't. He's driving, looking straight at the road. We aren't on the way home at all. We're on some country road. We must be way over in Virginia. "Do you like this? Doesn't it feel good? I'm going to keep doing it because your little cock that you don't want me to see is hard. That means you like what I'm doing to it. I wish somebody had done this to me when I was your age. Nobody enjoyed me while I was young and cute. In a few seconds your little cock might squirt white gism all over my hand. You're going to shake because it feels so good. There it is. Keep it coming, Danny boy. Keep shaking. Learn how to make it last and last. Now, isn't that the most wonderful feeling in the world?"

He takes his hand out. It's covered with something slippery. He undoes his fly and pulls out his own erect penis and slowly starts gliding his hand back and forth, back and forth, while his penis gets bigger and bigger, like some magic toy that does things like get bigger and bigger before your very eyes. He does it slowly, all the while mumbling, "Don't want to do this too fast, want this to last and last." His breathing comes heavier until he's panting and the car is swerving from side to side, and then he lets out a scream of agonizing release just as a huge spurt of white shoots from his penis and sprays all over everything, the steering wheel, the dashboard, the clutch, him, even a little on me. He's visibly shaking as he pulls the car over to the side and stops. I think he's going to clean things up a bit, but instead he pinions my wrist to the seat and with the most sinister look, his eyes boring into me, he commands me, "If you tell your mother about this, I'll tell her how you ransacked my suitcase and opened things that are none of your business and secretly read the dirty books in the bookstores and . . ."

I start crying.

"Shut up!"

I shut up.

That night, in the middle of the night, he comes into my bed. He's naked. He feels cold and clammy. He tries to take me in his arms. He tries to kiss me. His breath smells awful. I push him away. He stuffs a pillow over my mouth and turns me over on my stomach. I feel his hard penis poking at my bottom. It finds what it's looking for. I shriek but only the pillow hears me. He pumps me and pumps me. I feel his hard penis inside me. It hurts. I feel when he has his orgasm. I have one too. This time I don't shake, I choke.

"Shut up," he hisses again.

He goes back to his bed, my brother's bed. My brothers' bed.

He leaves for another city the next day. He stays at hotels on his next trips to Washington. He never stays with us again. My tushy is sore for weeks. When I have a bowel movement I see blood. I want to tell someone, but I'm afraid. I'm even afraid to tell Claudia, though I'm sure she'd love to hear about it.

·

The first time I hear the words *camp*, preceded by *concentration*, which I thought meant thinking deeply, and *gas* followed by *chamber*, which isn't a term I know at all, I'm in the really swell Chesterfield house on Verbena Street, N.W., to which I've been invited but probably not to observe what I'm looking at first thing in the tiny bathroom right by the front door, into which I'm practically hurled by Tibby Chesterfield, Rabbi Norman Chesterfield's son, who's the same age I am, thirteen or fourteen, and who stutters, and who's showing me his exceptionally long penis, at which I look with wide-eyed amazement. I wonder why he's showing it to me, why I can't take my eyes off it, why mine's not the same size, and any number of other things.

"I don't have to go to the bathroom," I protest.

"Well, I-I-I, ah do," he says, locking the door. We're in the same class at Washington Jewish but his thing looks ten times the size of mine. I think that he must be a freak.

Tibby's the joke in our class. First because he's son to that phony father who talks with that phony hoity-toity accent that's sort of British. Second because along with his terrible stutter he has a pretty bad twitch in his eyes, and also his lips, and every once in a while an arm springs up like a turkey's wing. He's a mess. In that cruel way kids have, Tibby's laughed at behind his back, and because he never fights back or even objects, sometimes to his face. The only reason I've come here to his house is that I feel sorry for him.

"You-you-you are the only-only person who d-d-doesn't laugh at me-me-me-me. T-t-tell them abbbout th-th-th-this!"

Tell them? I'm a bit further along from that little kid asking his mommy what a penis is. I certainly know what one is now. But tell them?

"T-t-t-tell th-th-th-them th-th-th-this is nothing to-to-to laugh at."

Why is he showing me his penis the minute I enter his house? His mother called Rivka and said the Rabbi said I was very smart and would I consider having cookies and milk with their son. They wanted to send their driver to pick me up in Masturbov Gardens, but Rivka said, "Oh, no, we'll drop him off," and later I heard her say to Philip, when he asked her why she declined the offer of a ride, "I don't want them to see how we live."

"How do we live?" Philip asked.

"We live in Masturbov Gardens and they live on Verbena Street."

"So what?"

"They live in a famous house that's all glass and was designed by that world-famous architect. Didn't you read that article and see the pictures in the *Monument*? They're rich. Mrs. Chesterfield is a wealthy heiress!"

I wait for Philip to respond to this, but he doesn't.

And so I'm dropped off. A block away. I insist on that. I don't want the Chesterfields to see our crummy Dodge that Philip finally broke down and bought. I'm in league with Mom on that one. I leave them at the corner and I find the number on the gate. You can't see any house at all. You have to ring a bell and a servant comes and opens the gate and leads you down a long approach through lots of trees and plants and flowers. I see the glass house. It's huge. Much bigger than any house I've ever been in. I ring the bell, and the next thing I'm in the tiny toilet by the front door.

"D-d-d-do-do-do you th-think w-w-w-we c-c-c-could b-b-b-be friends?"

Is it more painful for him to speak than to listen to his efforts? He spits a lot, and I'm now a little wet.

"Yes, we can be friends. Pull up your pants and let's go have cookies and milk like your mother said. If you want to show me something, show me your house. I've never been in such a large house before. Do you like living here?"

"N-n-n-n-n-n-no!"

"Too big?"

"T-t-t-too lone-lone-lone-lonesome."

I nod. "You come home from school and there's no one here?"

He nods.

"That happens where I live, too, but I don't mind being alone. That way I don't have to see them. They don't love us, my brothers and me, so we don't love them back."

Tibby's eyes grow huge in disbelief. "Th-th-that's the g-g-g-g-greatest thing I ever heard."

He takes me by the hand and leads me into the glass palace that's the Chesterfield mansion. You can see photographs of it in those Great Homes of the Ages art books you find on sale tables in bookstores. It was designed by Franz Heimlich Gluck, who evidently changed the history of domestic architecture by figuring out how to make a living room with three glass walls float over a waterfall. The Gluck Cantilever. It's very dramatic, standing in your rabbi's house with an actual waterfall gushing inches underneath your toes, spurting straight out into the future before it crashes on the rocks at the bottom of the hill. Who knew rabbis lived like this? God is in these details. But then, I don't have any more experience with rabbis' houses than I've had with enormous penises on my peers. How do I manage to notice that I can't see any stars of David or mezuzahs anywhere?

I feel very small and I'm glad Tibby's still holding my hand. The ceiling's very far away. The whole outdoors, a beautiful park of trees with that waterfall gushing out from under the house, seems like it's inside. It's all one big room, and I'm way up on top of a mountain looking out and down. Be careful! You might fall! I automatically take a few steps back. Tibby catches me in his arms. He kisses me. He kisses me all over my face like he's licking a lot of stamps on a lot of envelopes.

We hear voices from another room behind us and Rabbi Chesterfield comes in. I've only seen him in his flowing robes in temple. He looks skinny in slacks and jacket. With him is Mrs. Rabbi Chesterfield, whom I recognize from the *Monument* spread. She looks like Maria Montez or Ava Gardner, one of those dark-haired, husky-voiced, sultry types, with long red nails and luscious red lips and very high heels and a slinky black dress even though it's only afternoon. The main difference is that she has a big nose, so you know she's Jewish.

Behind her is one of the fattest, shortest men I've ever seen. He looks smooth and polished and fine-tuned and shiny all over. His eyes gleam in concert with his shoes.

"This is Mr. Yidstein," Mrs. Rabbi says to me.

I offer my hand. "Good afternoon, Mr. Yidstein. I'm happy to meet you."

"It is pronounced Y'Idstein. There is a Y. There is an apostrophe. There is then a capital I small d-s-t-e-i-n. There is a pause after the Y. There is before the apostrophe a suck of air. I am descended from the kings of Israel.

Goodbye to you, Rabbi Chesterfield, Mrs. Chesterfield. I am certain this is the beginning of some very rewarding work. I shall be in touch."

Rabbi and Mrs. Rabbi accompany Mr. Y'Idstein as he waddles to the door. They are whispering and that's when I hear "concentration camp" and then "gas chamber." A maid hands him his coat and hat and opens the front door. He turns and bows before clicking his heels and leaving.

I try to describe Mr. Y'Idstein to Lucas when I get home but he isn't interested. He certainly isn't interested in Rabbi Chesterfield. "A phony," he calls him. Lucas wants me to come to his synagogue and "see what a real rabbi is like." I don't tell him about Tibby's stutter or his exceptional penis.

•

You don't just drop a penis like Tibby's into the narrative and let it go. I can still see it. It's not the size that makes it large; it's the relationship it has with the rest of him. He's short and thin. I notice that when I think about his penis my own penis feels warmer, as if it wants to meet a friend. I notice these feelings and I don't know how to deal with them. They trouble me, vaguely, imprecisely. Images of Tibby's genital area seem to stray in from the cold, from their rich glass house. Where I can't live.

So I have these thoughts and feelings and that's all I can seem to say about them. I think that I should mention them. But to whom?

It does not occur to me yet that I am acquiring a collection of penises in my life and will have to decide what to do about them.

•

"Dear Daniel, I am sorry if I scared you. I scare everybody. I scare myself. I showed it to you because I want you to tell all the kids in Sunday School that Tobias Chesterfield has something that is really important. I know they laugh at me. I can't help it that I talk this way. I try not to. I have a teacher every day but he doesn't help me. I like you. You don't laugh at me. I think someday I could have talked to you okay. Please remember me."

•

"Thank you, my dear boy, for coming. It is very kind and good of you to come. It has been a trying time for Marguerite, and for me, too, of course. A painful, trying time. I understand he wrote a note to you before he left us. There were many versions of the letter in his room. He tried many versions. My wife is in deep distress. She has had to enter a hospital for rest. I am left alone in this house. I have never minded being alone before, but then there was always someone who would eventually be coming home. Did my son show you around this vast palace of glass? No? Not entirely? Come, let me show you some of our treasures. Marguerite has an extraordinary eye. She can enter a country completely foreign to her and spot the treasures to be plucked and pluck them. By Jesus, she can. Here, let me open this door. It's too heavy for you to push. Close your eyes and I'll lead you into the room and you shall be totally amazed at what you'll see. All right, now open your eyes! Isn't it amazing? These are all ours; of course, only for safekeeping. Only until this war is over. Only until their rightful owners are able to return and reclaim them. It is perfectly dreadful what is going on in Europe. There is not much said about it out loud. People are actually disappearing. They are simply disappearing. One isn't quite certain where. There are notions held by some that are quite sinister. Tell me, what exactly did my son mean by showing you 'it'? Of course you don't have to tell me if you don't want to. Ah, I can see that you don't want to. This is a Rembrandt. Do you know what a Rembrandt is? There are thirty of his canvases here although most of them are quite small. And I would estimate by now, oh, seventy-five other paintings by . . . Well, it is not of interest to you. Children are not interested in art. Why should you be? Rembrandt was a very great painter and this larger one is one of his great masterpieces. It is properly called *The Removal of the Intestines of the Wife of Ghent*. It is not an attractive title, which is why it is known as *The Burgher's Wife*. These gold candlesticks are from the synagogue in Belgium that is perhaps the oldest synagogue of medieval Europe. Forgive me if I can't recall its name. Mr. Y'Idstein will refresh my memory. They are solid gold. Feel how heavy they are. It's actually impossible to lift one of them comfortably. The synagogue seems to have suffered a mysterious conflagration but these were miraculously saved. The conflagration seems to have come out of nowhere. I hope this house isn't set on fire. That is why I had it built of glass. Imagine, losing all these great works. Mr. Y'Idstein would be very upset. As of course would I. That is why we are trying to help. Mr. Y'Idstein and myself. 'It'? *It* is such an imprecise word. Was he showing you something from our house? From his room? Could you give me a hint? I am sorry for these tears. They come upon me quite suddenly and without explanation. Oh, there is explanation enough. He wanted you to have something of his. Come, his room is off the lower salon. We can go down this way. He left it for you. Careful as I close this door. Ahh,

I almost caught my finger. I often do that. Marguerite said she might not be coming back. No, it is the doctor who offered that as a possible outcome. Then I shall be here in this house alone. I am afraid I shall be afraid. God is here with me, of course. God is always with me. I could not live otherwise. I am not so certain that a rabbi is meant to live in other ways alone. We are commanded by God to share our knowledge with the world. We spend so many years acquring this knowledge. Where can I go? This is a very large establishment to just leave. Who would buy it? What would I do with all of our treasures? I must not say 'our.' That is incorrect. The ones I am holding here are for safekeeping. Are you certain you won't tell me what he wanted to show you? Perhaps he did show you? What did he show you? We are missing several quite valuable pieces, all very small, all eminently capable of being held in a child's hand. Yes, there are missing jewels already. Huge ones. Worth many millions, many millions. No doubt they will turn up. Here we are. His room. I leave the lights on all the time now. He said he was afraid of the dark and I didn't believe him. You will forgive me if I just send you inside alone. There is a package for you on his desk. I took the liberty of having it wrapped. It is a photograph of him in a nice walnut frame. He signed it with his love. I believe you were the only friend he had. Had you known each other long? Don't look up. The rope is still there. I can't imagine why the police haven't returned to collect it. They said they would."

•

I've read lots of books about the mood of hope and optimism said to pervade our city on the eve of war, and during it, and after it. That's not the way I remember it. While I don't think any of us kids actually look up at the sky at the sound of planes, fearing that an enemy is about to drop a load of death, it's hard not to be aware of the mounting talk that peppers dinnertime conversation and the evening news about various foreign "fronts." Philip seems particularly concerned about how much money, which our country doesn't have, a war's going to cost us. And how we won't be able to travel freely from our country anymore, a peculiar notion for him to dwell on. Parents working in the District come home each night looking increasingly nervous and bearing terrible reports from their agencies about what is sure to happen. Their days have been filled with "preparedness" courses. Nobody knows what to do. "We had an important strategic planning meeting today," fathers tell their families at dinner. *Strategic* is a newly popular word. They have these meetings but they can't tell you what they're about or what they decide. "What are you going to do, dear?" every mother is asking. Heads shake in bewilderment. Shoulders shrug. "Actually, we've been told not to talk about it."

This atmosphere becomes a part of our lives very quickly. Rumor and fact merge. If there's little that's trustworthy, there are plenty of Rivkas around, naïve and accepting, never-endingly hopeful, bleating that "it" will all work out just fine. In no time at all no one remembers what it was like before. How can you remember yesterday when so much is happening today that no one understands? Life, for the Jerusalems and others, was precarious enough before. The future is too foreboding. That's the word. Pasts became past very quickly because they really weren't that great, so there's no comfort remembering what used to be. Now everyone's the same age and in the same place, for probably the first time in our history. We're all going to become a little frightened all at once. "Try not to think about it, dear" is heard in every home and from every parent.

The movies identify our rumors and focus our fears. The movies at the Masturbov are now about foreign spies living right here in our town, men and women who speak funny English and are blond and belong to a "master race" engaged in a massive effort to take us over. Peter Ruester is a young actor we watch being trained in the army for "fighting the unknown enemy." He poses without his shirt on in photographs with his producer, Oliver Wendell Binkington Krank. Mr. Krank, though quite young himself, is said to be the friend of "powerful men in industry" and indeed of the president himself. Great things are predicted for both the producer and his new young star.

•

Rivka tells us that Rabbi Chesterfield has called his staff of teachers together to announce "everything is now more spiritually challenging than ever."

Thus Lucas and Stephen and I must go to Sunday school every week without fail. No more visits to other rabbis. No more "I don't feel like it." "This is not the time to test God's patience," Rivka warns us in that tone that says don't test hers. Tibby Chesterfield's suicide has joined David's disappearance as a subject we don't discuss. Then Donald Shapp across the street accidentally kills his father by hitting him on the head with a golf club for coming home in uniform and announcing he's going off to war. And then Karl Adroita immolates himself in the boys' toilet of Franeeda Elementary School after he hears that a favorite cousin of his in Chicago did the same. Soon there's nothing we can't and won't talk about. A psychoanalyst specializing in children opens an office on Connecticut Avenue downtown.

I put Tibby's photo on my bureau. It's a wan face, too young for melancholy but terribly glum. No one else likes to look at him, so he doesn't last long on the bureau top.

Young men start champing at the bit, ready to go. But until war's declared they're like a bunch of runners waiting for the gunshot before the start of a race. It's amazing nobody's saying, "What's the hurry?" That's certainly what they'd say now. Why are we so ready for war? Doesn't anyone remember the last one? We can hardly wait! We're so cooped up we're ready to explode.

Before we know it, of course, it comes. It's just there. It's happened. It's happening. I don't remember the president's famous speech. I don't remember Pearl Harbor. I just remember one day we're not at war and one day we are. My cousin Barry comes back with one leg only months after he signed up. I meet him at the bus stop to help him find our building. I pretend I don't notice anything as he hobbles slowly with his canes, dragging his stiff artificial leg. He went off to war so talkative and smiling, and now he's staring wordlessly at the ground. Rivka talks endlessly throughout dinner, trying every trick in her repertoire to put him at his ease. Out of nowhere she suggests I sing a song. I never sang a song to her or anyone else. It's a painful meal. Barry's bitter and sour he got shot so fast. He's failed and he believes everyone else thinks he has too.

Rivka takes to inviting "tragic cases" home to dinner. Wounded soldiers whose wives left them for another man or disappeared because they couldn't face a husband with only one arm or leg. Blind young men with their attendants, worshipful nurse's aides mooning with cow eyes, saintfully grateful to be doing something "for the war effort." One soldier, Bradley Purvis, marries one of these young women and they move next door on Mordecai Avenue. I watch them grow older over the years. He has a twin brother who's also blind now, who comes to visit with his own wife. The two brothers walk down Mordecai Avenue holding hands, being led by their adoring beloveds. Where is David? Oh, where is my twin?

One thing the war brings to our home is a sense of its coziness. What with Rivka's tragic cases and Philip appearing to be a bit more important because his work is keeping him "even busier" and Boston not mentioned and Lucas and Stephen sleeping at home because their friends' mothers now say things like, "Don't you have your own bed to sleep in, young man? There's a war on and your parents need you," our little apartment actually seems warm and full.

It's become increasingly difficult for kids to play games. Shouting "Bang, bang, you're dead!" isn't much fun after Cousin Barry loses his leg. I beg Rivka to let me help her but she won't. "You're too young to work on the bloodmobile." She's in charge of a growing number of them, deploying them daily to different "collection points." Her "quotas" keep getting increased "and I keep meeting them!"

Claudia is the first to peel off from our gang and say she no longer wants to play in the excavations for the new buildings going up faster than ever. Day by day she is more beautiful. Her black hair is clipped even shorter around her scalp like a cap. Her sweaters reveal two blossoming breasts. Sometimes I find myself looking at them like a traveler who wants to go back to a spot he visited years ago to see if he feels the same about it. How had I felt? How did I feel now?

Claudia's father, Mr. Webb, is making a fortune removing government wastepaper. It's turning out to be an enormous contract. You see trucks all over that say "The Webb Company." Empying wastebaskets seems like such an isolated small task until you realize how many wastebaskets there are in the government. (That's what it's all called, where all our fathers work, collectively, "the government.") The *Monument* says so much paper has never been removed before on such a grand scale. The *Monument*'s never heard of Mr. Webb and wonders who he is and where he comes from. Philip says, "They make Claudia's father sound suspicious. That isn't fair." The emptying of wastebaskets is a sensitive matter because valuable information might fall into enemy hands. Mr. Webb's built big furnaces way out past the Bladensberg dumps to burn everything up. In a few years' time, just as Hitler's marching into someplace else and the Webbs have moved into a grand mansion in the District, Mr. Webb will be arrested for not burning all the wastepaper. He's invented a method of turning paper into cardboard and he thinks he'll be congratulated, but instead he's accused of profiteering. His lawyer gets him off by saying he has a bad heart, which is news to everyone. By then Mrs. Webb has redecorated the mansion that the *Monument* calls the "House of Cardboard," but Rivka says, "It's on the right side of town and they're living in it, so it doesn't sound so cardboard to me." Philip naturally takes this as a criticism of his own earning power: "So I should come up with some great idea and break the law?" Lucas points out to Pop that "not so long ago you thought Mr. Webb was innocent until proven guilty." Stephen mumbles that Philip wouldn't know how to break the law even if he wanted to.

No, I don't remember all that much optimism.

The Webbs used to own a huge house in the Northeast before Claudia was born; they were forced to give it to the archdiocese when Mr. Webb bought the bus company and raised the fares so high nobody could afford them. He was threatened with prison for that, too. "He sure gets a lot of opportunity to cheat and break the law and live so high off the hog," Philip complains when he sees Mr. Webb in his Cadillac, its backseat packed with clothes they're moving. "Mrs. Webb has always hated living in Masturbov Gardens," Rivka says. Mrs. Webb has never been Rivka's favorite since the time she tried to pull Claudia away from playing with me and the Schwartz-bach sisters and Claudia screamed at her, "You go to hell!" The sisters, shy girls from France and very polite, were shocked but I thought it was great. Imagine having the guts to yell at your own mother like that. Mrs. Webb just stared at Claudia, with an icy coldness that said she hated her daughter, then turned and left us, but not before we all heard her spit, "Why must you always play with Jews?"

"Imagine talking like that," Rivka says when I report to her. "And with Mr. Hitler killing so many of us."

Yes, the enemy is now personified and his name is Hitler, and his secret is out now, at least in this house.

Mr. Schwartzbach, or Monsieur Schwartzbach, gets transferred back to France. They haven't even been in Masturbov Gardens for very long. Everybody promises to write. I wonder what will happen to them.

Mordy and I are the only Jews in our gang. Dodo, Arnold, Billy, and Orvid are Christians. Mordy's very rich, but not the rest of us. Money's difficult for Rivka to discuss with us. She won't talk about it when we boys wonder why some fathers are making money and our father is not. I know she wants too much for us that we can't afford. In the dark through the bedroom walls you can hear her saying, "There simply isn't enough coming in, Philip. I simply cannot make ends meet. You are very lucky to have a wife who knows how to stretch a dollar. Why do you constantly criticize me for having a paying job that helps us make ends meet?" Lucas is determined to make tons of money. I have daydreams too, but they're usually about how to spend it.

It's after Rivka says things like this privately to Philip that he's apt to haul off and slug me. I'll have bought a comic book he doesn't approve of, or a new fountain pen. "You have absolutely no consideration for money and how hard your mother and I work to put food into your mouths!" Slam slam slap clang ouch. I refuse to cry. Fred, you told me this is exactly what happened to you with your father. Well, my list of the world's grievances against us was certainly growing.

Rivka's always trying to impress on us that it's Jews who have a special, heavier burden, "particularly now that we are being killed somewhere far away." When she first says this, it's news to us. Stephen doesn't believe her. "It's just another example of her never-ending know-it-all that makes me nauseated." I, of course, believe the worst immediately. Avid listener to all tales, I press for more. She switches to one of her off-into-the-distance looks and says nothing. Then she admonishes us yet again to be even more grateful than we were before that we're American, and alive. She stops peeling a carrot dead in her tracks. "I could be holding you in my arms as we are herded naked into a freezing cold warehouse and slowly gassed to death," she whispers. What? What's she talking about? Boy, this is big-time stuff. Where does she get her info?

"They're only stories. Why are you scaring us?" Stephen asks.

"Rabbi Chesterfield has heard!"

"Well, Rabbi Gribden says they're only rumors and if we spread them it will only make Hitler angrier." Since Stephen's never been known for any interest in world events, much less Jewish ones, Lucas and I turn and look at him.

"Since when are you hobnobbing with Rabbi Gribden?" Lucas asks. Like Lucas's Rabbi Grusskopf, Gribden is a breakaway rabbi who split off from Rabbi Chesterfield to start his own temple. Unlike Grusskopf, he's even more liberal than Rabbi Chesterfield, who himself is held by the old Jews to be so liberal he's more gentile than Jewish. The three rabbis hate one another and take opposing stands on everything as a matter of course.

"It is amazing that on certain topics there should be opposing points of view," Rivka says, quite sensibly.

Grusskopf is successor to the late Rabbi Martashevsky. After his death his old shul mysteriously burns down and all the most religious Jews feel homeless. To go to either Gribden or Chesterfield is anathema. Grusskopf does his best to carry on in a converted storefront. No one knows that he is presiding over the end of the old ultra-Orthodox Judaism in Washington.

Since putting people into warehouses and turning on the gas is a pretty tall-sounding story, seriously topping "all the starving children in Europe," Rivka lays on us that we have to eat our kale that she's now growing "for the war effort" in her Victory Garden on the other side of the Masturbov River on land Abe has allowed his tenants to use. I do have strange bad dreams about what she told us, as if it's more connected to me than I know. Philip, whose family roots are German, doesn't want to hear about it. At least we think that's his reason.

You'd think that stories of the murder of Jews, or even rumors, would elicit an outpouring of concern, especially from the Jews for other Jews, but it doesn't seem to work that way. Most of the stuff on the radio and in the *Monument* is about how very expensive the war's becoming and how everyone's going to have to help pay for it. American Jews don't want to be blamed for costing everyone money, just as homosexuals today don't want to feel guilty, but do, every time a serial killer comes along who victimizes little boys. This may seem a strange comparison to insert right here, but at the time, in the woods not far from the American Red Blood office in Hykoryville, there was a small mass murder of little boys, some seven of them, all by the same person, a college student majoring in anatomy, "such a nice-looking young man," as Rivka said when she saw his photograph in the papers.

It was the face of a young man I'd met. He took me back to an empty apartment in Masturbov Gardens. He had the key. He said he and his family were moving in and we'd be neighbors. He gave me several comic books, embargoed from my life by Philip. (You, too, Fred! God, did all our fathers study at the same penitentiary?) How did he know I wanted them so much? All I had to do to get them was let him stick his finger up my anus. He said he was a medical student and was studying this part of the body. Courtesy of Uncle Hyman, I was an experienced hand in the anal penetration department. I let him and he had an orgasm. He pulled down his trousers and underpants and tried to make me suck his dripping penis, but I grabbed my comics and ran, or waddled, really, as I was pulling up my shorts at the same time. Yes, my list of homosexuals was growing longer.

The murders were spaced over several weeks, during which time little boys in Franeeda County were practically quarantined at home, which didn't make me feel any less guilty. Yes, I felt guilty for this drama, for these murders, for this murderer. Should I have spoken up after our meeting? If I had, would those other boys be alive?

I could have been one of those dead little boys. Why was I spared? Was it destiny? *Destiny* was another of that era's favorite words. Mr. Churchill was always talking about our rendezvous with it, and Mr. Churchill was as big a star in Washington as Clark Gable was in Hollywood. When The Underlying Condition is finally identified and gay men are terrified of being scapegoated, Arnold Botts, always a hisser, spits out overactively to some reporter on the evening news, "These sinners sent this destiny down on their very own sinning, sinful heads!"

Of course, words like *homosexual* did not appear in newspapers, or issue from people's lips. What words *were* used for us in those days? "Homosexuality," as a distinct concept, didn't appear until the late nineteenth century, and *gay* evidently became an underground code word in the 1920s, but what the world was calling us out loud for most of history is a mystery. Did I know what I was? Did I really have any sense, all of Uncle Hyman's books and bookstores notwithstanding, of what my feelings amounted to? When I heard about the murdered boys, did anyone or any paper or any radio commentator say anything like "sexual pervert" or "sick fairy" to make me feel swell, like I'd found my name?

In the Jerusalem household, the main outcome of the murders is that the ARB office in Hykoryville is closed "temporarily" and Rivka is transferred to District headquarters and given a raise, at least in authority. She's now in charge of several bloodmobiles in the districts. She'll be working directly under Miss Theodora Von Lutz, evidently a well-known name in government service, who is being brought back from her retirement, along with her sister Eurora. They are written up jointly in the *Monument*, which also runs their picture. They both look very forbidding. They had been involved in something called the Tally Office before their early retirement. "Everyone must give their blood so that the living may live," Miss Theodora's rallying cry, comes to be one of Rivka's constant refrains. I told her she should have been in that photograph in the *Monument* too, and why wasn't she?

No, I don't remember all that much optimism.

Mostly it seems everyone tries to pretend there isn't any world out there, to close out the bad and find a safer place inside. Everything is "home front" this and "home front" that, as if it's a real and comforting place. We listen to the radio a lot to laugh; nighttimes are filled with comedians. There isn't a real world after the evening news. While some of the war movies we sit through at the Masturbov are filled with dead bodies spewed all over beaches, others are filled with songs and dancing. Sailors sing a lot on the decks of their battleships, and this, at least, seems jolly. And we can all imitate fat, jovial Kate Smith singing "God Bless America" as if what she's singing about is a big jolly presence like she is.

President Franklin Delano Roosevelt is an actual person, a palpable presence in our lives. He is our protector and he lives with us, even if he's in that big White House downtown. Every kid no matter how dumb knows how to spell his entire name. We can identify his dog, and Mrs. Roosevelt, who is accorded a mighty reverence even though women think she's a bit too pushy. Nobody knows about their bad marriage, or her lesbian girlfriend, or his lady friends, or his gay assistant secretary of state, or even his polio and crutches. God has no blemishes. The president and his city and his country and his government are all the same. "Does your father work for the government?" is invariably answered yes. There isn't any other employer in town. We're all told what to do and think and eat and no one questions a thing. We are all one big happy family, in spite of Mr. Hitler and Mr. Mussolini and Mr. Tojo—the cast of characters keeps increasing. We might be way out here in Franeeda County in Masturbov Gardens but—at last!—we're now a part of Washington too.

We've crossed over the District Line.

•

Mordecai Masturbov is the first person I know I want to fall in love with and have love me back. I want to touch him all over. He has skin like marble. He has skin like velvet. He has skin I desperately want to touch. He looks like the Greek statues in the Mellon Gallery downtown, which I pretend is where I live, walking regally down the majestic staircases in the empty mammoth halls, going into rooms to stare at Roman and Greek men with lost penises.

I can't remember the first time I saw Mordy. His father is our landlord, of course, and his grandmother Yvonne is a sister to Uncle Israel Jerusalem, the other sister being Grandma Zilka, who threw out her husband and took back her maiden name. So I guess Mordy's been in my life all along. One day he just appears in my consciousness. Another day, in some boring class, I start doodling the letters of his name over and over in my notebook, the scrawls and curlicues taking over entire classes. And another day my constant thoughts about him start to hurt. I realize he isn't thinking of me back, and I don't know what to do about it.

He really isn't like a relative. He's rich. That whole side of the family is rich, so our side of the family never sees his side. At least that's why my brothers and I think we're kept apart. We weren't to know yet that they had secrets as well.

Mordy has the only father who doesn't work for the government. Is that why he wants to play with us? Kids so want to belong, and God knows Mordy, who's driven everywhere in a chauffeured limousine, doesn't belong. And Abe Masturbov hates Franklin Roosevelt, which is like not believing in God. "Everybody on Sixteenth Street hates everything," Mordy says about the fancy rich neighborhood where he lives. "Franklin Delano Roosevelt and Winston Churchill and Betty Grable." He gets into the limousine, his head down because he never wants to go home. "They never mention Hitler. It can't be possible that they *like* Hitler." The car pulls away from Yvonne Street, and I see him looking back at Claudia. I've never seen her look at him at all. I sigh. Claudia's growing breasts and I'm growing pubic hair. Is Mordy growing anything? I sigh again. I am having fantasies of gods with their penises not broken off. Sneaking peeks at dirty books in dark bookstores or in a hated uncle's suitcase is different from looking at Mordy in the daylight. I sigh some more.

None of us kids in Masturbov Gardens knows what to make of Mordy. He's the landlord's son, hence of a higher class, and this landlord, we know, is more than just any old landlord, he's fantastically rich, owning huge portions of Washington and Franeeda. He, too, is driven around everywhere in his long black Lincoln limousine, which drops Mordy off to play with us. Mr. Abe Jerusalem waves hello. He doesn't smile much. Why doesn't he smile more? Maybe he doesn't like his son playing with us on the wrong side of the District Line.

Mordy doesn't seem to have any other friends. He joins us as soon as he can be driven from St. Anselm's School for Boys, which is way far away, almost to Wisconsin and Alhambra, next to St. Fewgh's Episcopal Cathedral. St. Anselm's is the best private school in Washington. (Many years later, some St. Anselm's boys and a few St. Anselm's teachers and some St. Fewgh's priests all have sex with each other, and it comes out only because one of the priests gets upset that one of the teachers has a kid he won't share. The kid will be Stephen's son, Brian.) It takes an hour to drive from St. Anselm's to Masturbov Gardens in a limousine. Mordy doesn't even stop off at home on

Sixteenth Street, the House of Mystery we call it, because we have no idea what it looks like inside since we're never invited over there for cookies like we are to each other's apartments here. The limousine drops Mordy off on Yvonne Street, at Abe's office, which is on the highest hill, looking down on all the buildings his father has built. From there Mordy comes racing down to find us.

We have a gang that always plays together. Yes, for all my feelings of loneliness, I have friends. We all have clumsy bodies, unformed things that are trying to become something, but are still between here and there. There aren't many kids our age in Masturbov Gardens, so we're kind of stuck with each other. We don't play with dolls or jacks or bubblegum cards; we don't know our warplanes or our latest-model cars. Instead, we pride ourselves on outdoing each other in what we can pretend. All of us are powerful and mighty pretenders, which suits me just fine, since I don't want anyone to know how awful I really am inside.

There are so many places to play! Excavations and incomplete buildings and little forests that haven't been chopped down yet. We go from one playground to another. We are Kings of This and That, Hardy Boys and Nancy Drews, indefatigable sleuths solving the most elaborate conundrums and protecting our world. I'm particularly adept at dreaming up scenarios that feature runaways determined to get to the big city. Arnold Botts never likes my plots. "How can it be a mystery when they leave because they want to and we know where they're going?" Arnold is always belligerent. I don't want to see Arnold naked at all.

But I want to see Mordy Masturbov naked, and kiss him all over, and touch his skin. I'm so very hungry for him. These are my secret thoughts and I haven't the vaguest notion how to act on them. There's no one I can tell about them. I can hardly tell myself. I am too young. Isn't that what every adult you ever knew said when they couldn't explain something "too grown-up" to you? "You're too young."

All these thoughts and feelings—it seems I've always had them. Always.

One day I take the requisite two buses to the Masturbov Mansion on Sixteenth Street in the high second alphabet, which is where the big old houses are. (Washington is crisscrossed north to south by numbered streets, east to west by streets that begin with a letter of the alphabet. The first alphabet—A Street, B Street, etc.—is poor and downtown and government. The second alphabet—Alton Street, Byron Street, Calvin Street—is halfway uptown and blends at its farthest end with the third alphabet, Albemarle, Brandywine,

Chesapeake, the richest part, by far, and so far away.) Though it's broad daylight, the sun blistering hot and the heat so vile there's nobody on the sidewalks, I tiptoe as I circumnavigate the block on reconnaissance like a true Hardy boy. The house sure is big and . . . ugly. It pains me that my nice new friend lives in a house I'd never want to live in. It's built of some sort of dark-hued strips of timber like you see in Adirondack lodges inhabited by outdoorsy people like Theodore Roosevelt. It has a funny little one-windowed turret poking out of the roof, short and squat and entirely out of scale with the magnitude of the big boxy house it sits on. The verandahs on all four sides seem much too narrow to have much fun on; even if there were rocking chairs you'd risk rocking right off the edge. All in all, with those verandahs like wings tucked in close and that tiny turret of a head up there, the place looks like some giant prehistoric vulture. It certainly is *there*, this house. It seems to have a lot of confidence. But I wonder if it knows it's ugly, all its bravura just for show.

And what about those breasts! I've never seen columns with extremely long legs and gigantic breasts. I later learn this is very Egyptian and ancient Greek, but gee, this is Washington.

The lawns are being sprinkled. They're covered with parched patches, but so are everyone's during the torrid Washington summers. Branches try hard to hold up their wilting roses and lilacs, the tall bushes planted symmetrically at the corners of the house. There isn't much else in the way of plantings, no tall hedges to separate this house from the ones on either side, big stone piles with shaded windows, maybe embassies of foreign countries you've never heard of. An old man comes out of Mordy's house. He's big and burly and has a huge head of pure white hair. He wears a black suit and tie, even in this weather. He stares at me sternly, and so I run. He's the one who drives Abe and Mordy around. I hope he hasn't recognized me.

Why am I so interested in so many things that I'm not studying in school? Is such hunger natural? I have an awful lot of secrets. I'm collecting them at much too fast a rate. Should I stop? Why would you ever want to stop accumulating secrets? Anyway, even then I sensed that stopping wasn't an option.

The practical answer to every question I can't answer now is: Get out of Masturbov Gardens! But I can't just yet, not while I'm having these feelings I don't understand for Mordecai Masturbov. I've been planning to run away and look for David. Well, not a real plan, just a thought I've been considering every time Philip hits me.

Our gang is pretty hard to describe, except for Arnold Botts. He's a shit. Nobody likes him, he knows it, but it doesn't make him self-conscious, apologetic, or eager to please, it just makes him keep being a shit. And we keep putting up with him. He's the perpetual player of dirty tricks, the one who sneaks up and screams in your ear or tries to pull your pants down or throws ice snowballs at your head in the dead of winter. He has a quick temper that can be set off by unknown forces, and then he explodes with rocks or sand or sticks or words. He has a ferociously precocious imagination that leaves the rest of us in the dust, a repertoire of perversities we've never heard of or imagined. I'm still trying to sort out what he made up.

We're frightened of him, so we try to please him. We the tormented have yet to learn the lesson of standing up for principles and beliefs. If we retaliate in any way, he runs to his mother, who in scant moments is on the phone to ours, embroidering some story he's told her. Mrs. Botts has an imagination as perfervid as her only child's, and our mothers are always prepared to believe the worst about us. Each of us has been bawled out mightily for something awful her son told her: that Dodo stuck a stick up Billy's rectum, that I ripped a bloody Kotex from under one of the French girls' dresses (causing Rivka to render unto me another of her peculiarly unemotional descriptions, this time of what a Kotex is). This go-round, I sense she's disappointed in me, either because I didn't know what a Kotex is or she thinks I do indeed do things like this.

When Arnold blabs that Claudia and I were having sexual intercourse that day underground (Had he been there? How could he have seen us?), our parents are so upset that they meet in the Webb apartment to discuss what to do.

"How can you be so *delighted* about it all?" I ask Claudia as we're awaiting the verdict. We're walking through Masturbov Gardens and she's humming songs and playing with my fingers and mock-punching me in the belly. It's one of those summer twilights, soft and warm, with darkness lowering so gently that it's late at night before it gets dark.

"I'm sorry you think it's so funny," I say.

"They think we've had sex."

"I'm sorry you think *that's* so funny," I say, without much of an idea what having sex means.

"Silly billy. It's not *us*. *They* probably haven't had sex since we were born. They'll be too embarrassed to even talk about it. How I wish I were under the sofa listening to them. Have they even asked you if you did it?"

I want to answer, "Did what?" but I know that's really giving it away. "Rivka just asked, 'What did you do with Claudia Webb underground?'"

"And you said?"

"I told her you were frightened so I held you in the dark as I led you out of the tunnel."

"I am never frightened!"

When we arrive at the new excavation on Emmanuel Crescent, the gang is there. "Our little lovebirds who screwed!" Arnold announces gleefully as if he's Gabriel Heatter on the evening news.

Mordy looks very upset. I don't know yet that he and Claudia actually went much further than she and I, and only hours after, on that same rainy day.

"We didn't!" I protest, mostly because of what I see in Mordy's eyes. Why am I protecting *his* feelings? Do I really think he's upset because he'd wanted to be with *me*?

"I don't know why you're so ashamed of it," Arnold retorts. "If I'd screwed Claudia I'd tell all of Masturbov Gardens."

"You'd tell them even if you didn't," says Orvid Guptl, a journalist even then.

"Stop picking on Daniel," says Billy, a blond boy I remember very little about except that he was sweet and docile and kind, qualities calculated to make anyone forgettable.

"I didn't know you had it in you," Dodo says softly, slapping me on the back.

We know already that Dodo Geiseric is the genius among us. He has the thickest eyeglasses you ever saw, he can instantly figure 123×1234 without even closing his eyes, and he never has any idea what's playing at the Masturbov. Because he can rarely remember a movie's plot or the names of its stars, we tend to overlook his brilliance. Genius in young lives is never appreciated.

"Daniel screwed Claudia! Daniel screwed Claudia!" Arnold singsongs, rushing among scattered bricks and pieces of lumber, deftly maneuvering along the edges of gaping holes where basements will be, leading us across precarious bridges where basements already are. Why do we follow him?

When he's led us up to what will be a two-bedroom second-floor apartment but is now only a vague wooden outline in space, he stops in the middle of a plank and turns to confront us. He puts his small hand outside his fly and wiggles his thin hips like a gyrating hula dancer, licking his lips and rolling his eyes and grunting and groaning and sighing, as he pretends to be jerking off. As he comes close to me, thrusting, I put up my hands to keep him away and he almost falls from the plank to the cement basement three floors below. But he's a great balancer, Arnold. He's a trapeze artist. "Oh, no you don't," he says, smiling, his own hands up as if to keep me at bay, to make me think I actually tried to push him off. Then he's back to his orgiastic oscillations until all five of us boys—Mordy, Dodo, Billy, Orvid, and I—corner him against a wall and jump on him and hold him down until he stops. It takes us a long time. He's like an active volcano with a lot of lava in it.

Orvid looks down on him. "You really are an inferior human being."

Arnold doesn't seem to care. Insults don't insult him. As always, we let him stay. We're incapable of getting rid of him. Once we try not talking to him for weeks. He keeps talking to us as if he hasn't noticed, and before too long we're answering.

Physically he's small and moves covertly, like he's sneaking around trying not to be seen while trying never to miss a thing. His eyes are pathetic: they look at you defiantly, but when you stare him down something isn't in there looking back. He's like some nasty pet you keep even though he destroys your house, even as you're muttering, "He gets away with murder."

I see Mordy whispering to Claudia. He looks on the verge of tears. We've reached a new section of Masturbov Gardens that up to now has been a forest but will be three stories ready for new tenants in a matter of weeks. We're in a living room with holes waiting for windows and floorboards waiting for shellacking. The walls are up but the doors aren't in, so I nonchalantly try to listen to Mordy and Claudia, who are on the other side. Arnold, having escaped his torturers once again, has led the rest down to explore the new basement and how it feeds into the underground labyrinthine network over which our entire world is built.

"Oh, Claudia, how could you?"

"Don't be so pathetic, Mordecai. I simply do not want to entertain this discussion." I recognize that tone. When Claudia doesn't want to entertain, she does not entertain. She walks around the wall, takes my arm, and leads me away. It makes no difference to her that I've been listening; she probably expected me to. She waltzes me right under the nose of a forlorn Mordy.

The punishment handed down by the Jerusalem-Webb summit is peculiar. Rivka confesses they didn't know what to do. Philip actually left the meeting and went home to bed.

"Did you . . . do . . . what Arnold Botts says you did?"

"I tell you all the time how Arnold Botts makes things up. You never believe me. You always believe him. I am beginning to lose faith in you."

"Don't say things like that."

"You never believe me!"

"Mrs. Webb says Claudia said it was true."

I screw up my face in thought. It hadn't occurred to me that Claudia and I would brazen this one out as truth. How like her to neglect telling me this vital piece of whatever scenario she's playing. In her own way, she's as untrustworthy as Arnold.

Claudia's defense? "I didn't tell you because I automatically assumed that of course you'd want to tell your parents we performed that miraculous act. How could you not want to tell them? Oh, Daniel, what am I going to do with you? Still. Yet. Forever."

"How could you not?" she says again, years later, when we're in her room at Doris's discussing the past. In Doris's whorehouse. Where Claudia is a hooker. Full-time. High-class. And I'm still her friend. Full-time. Yes, I'm still looking for truths to pinpoint. And she's still laughing at me.

"The interesting thing is that they believed we could do it," I say.

"You couldn't have but I could."

"Did Mordy?"

"That's none of your business."

"Not even today!"

"Not even today."

"Did you? You did, then?"

The punishment for our sexual act, whatever it was, is that Claudia and I must visit a priest and "have a discussion on the matter," as Rivka presents it to me. It's obviously the Webbs' suggestion. "I certainly don't know any priests," Rivka says, concentrating too hard on shelling peas. "And I don't want to involve Rabbi Chesterfield."

"So this is a Christian punishment?" I ask her.

"Don't be so grown-up. Christian, Schmistian. Your father and I didn't know what to do. And Mrs. Webb is so . . . pushy."

Wearing a black suit and a hat with a veil, Claudia looks twice her age. In my summer short pants and short-sleeved plaid shirt, I look half mine. We will make an unusual sight for Brother Dana. Mr. Webb is driving us in complete silence in the first Cadillac I've ever been in. "It belongs to the company," Claudia says. Mr. Webb, who never speaks much anyway, drops us at the huge Church of the Most Holy Mother, where we are shown into a study paneled in nice warm wood and with a thick maroon carpet on the stone floor. There is incense, and a choir is practicing in the distance, and Brother Dana looks like Bing Crosby in *The Bells of St. Mary's*. I have trouble taking in what he says or what he means. I'd no idea priests were so attractive. He has his hand on my knee. I know now what that means. Well, better Bing than Uncle Hyman. I note that I'm beginning to find some humor in all this. I smile to myself. Claudia's elbow jabs my side. "Pay attention!" she whispers sharply.

Brother Dana is very serious as he says things like, "We must remember the sanctity of the marriage vow and how Jesus Christ wants everyone to be married before procreating." I ask him what procreating means and Claudia pinches my hand, which she's holding as part of her act. I can see her, under her dark veil, sticking her tongue out at Brother Dana and me, and trying to cross her eyes and touch her nose with her tongue. Brother Dana rattles on and on; he's beginning to seem less attractive. After a lengthy passage filled with lots of Catholic terminology, he seems to be winding down. He asks me if I have to go to the toilet and I say no. He asks me if I'm sure, he'll show me where it is. I decline again, which provokes him to inquire if I want to take confession. I say I don't know what that is.

"You are not of the faith?"

"He is of the Hebrew extraction," Claudia offers in her plummiest voice.

"Then why in the world did you bring him?"

"So you could feel his knee and take him to the toilet."

Brother Dana shows us out.

Back in the sunlight, I ask Claudia if we can lie down together sometime in a soft bed, and hold each other close, and kiss and cuddle.

"Wherever do you get ideas like that?"

"Because you make me laugh. It sounds nice, doesn't it?"

"It sounds icky."

"It does not sound icky. It sounds wonderful."

"It sounds icky."

"You were really funny in there," I say.

"Funny peculiar or funny ha-ha?"

"I just thought what we did was . . . special."

"It was one of the most special things ever," she says, touching my cheek again in that gesture she has so often used with me, or should I say on me, through all these years. "Now let it go at that."

At this point, she stumbles; one of her mother's high heels breaks. She has to hold on to me as we head toward the car. She refuses to not play the part she's dressed up to play. She is going to walk to that Cadillac erectly and dramatically, and she does. My arm hurts to prove it.

Mordy doesn't play with us again for the longest time; it must be months. I wonder if word got back to his father about naughty exploits among the children, but it turns out, as I learn when Mordy reappears and we are walking alone late one afternoon, that Abe remarried. For a third time. Or is it a fourth? And when Abe gets married, he always requires Mordy to come on the honeymoon.

"I don't think this one is going to last either."

"Why do you have to go with them?"

"Because he hates to be alone."

"So why does he marry her?"

"I don't know. I don't think he actually gets married. I think it's only pretend. For me."

"Really? Why?"

He just shrugs.

There was no way I could know about Doris Hardware at the time; I've discovered only recently that Mordy knew about her even then; and he knew about Yvonne's "bloods," and the fires. That is some set of stories for any kid to carry with him.

By the time Mordy returns, Claudia's left for some fancy finishing school in Switzerland, according to the rumor. Or she'd run off with Rupert Chesterfield, the rabbi's new stepson, who, unbelievably, also stutters and has a huge penis (according to Fifi Nordlinger of the Jew Tank, which I'll get to later). "Nah, it's because she screwed with Daniel," Arnold sneers. "She's having his baby and had to go away in secret." Funnily enough, nobody talks about her when she's gone. I walk around keeping my thoughts of her to myself, but I must confess that, like David, she leaves them after a while and it's a relief. Life is less complicated. Perhaps it's the same for the others. Now we can all return to being less mature and less aware of what awaits us.

And now I can pine for Mordy without interruption.

Mordy and me.

It seems almost a relief, after Claudia.

Yes. Mordy and me.

We spend summer afternoons walking farther and farther into the country, observing how far out Masturbov Gardens is pushing. It's amazing to hear him say, as he walks his future land with me, "This will all be mine someday." The farther beyond Masturbov Gardens we walk, the closer I feel to him, like we're friends now, really buddies.

I'm happy being with him. I look forward to him and miss him when he's left me, when all I can do is think about him. How he really looks me in the eye when I talk to him. How he seems so interested in my opinions. How he isn't snooty and snobby at all, which, as the son of Abe Masturbov, he's certainly entitled to be.

I haven't the vaguest notion why he wants to be my buddy and I don't question it one bit. He's here. We're together. Good enough.

My growing friendship with Mordy coincides with Lucas going through a strange period in his growing up. Suddenly he won't talk to me; he's silent in general, but he would always talk to me. When I try to make him talk now, he just sort of grunts back. "Answer me!" I hear myself demand. He doesn't. "Please talk to me!" I plead. "What do you want me to say?" he finally responds. "Are you unhappy?" I ask him. This he certainly doesn't answer. "Tell me! What is it?" I go and stand right in front of him on tiptoe and stare into his eyes, just stare and stare. He just looks at me, perplexed. He picks me up and stands me somewhere else, and then he leaves the apartment. I feel exiled by my brother's behavior, and I try to explain this to Mordy, on a walk that will take us even farther into the wilderness his father owns.

"I'd give anything to have a brother or sister. You're so lucky to have two brothers."

"Three."

"You have three brothers?"

"I have a twin brother."

"You do? More than anything else I'd love to have a twin."

He looks at me as if I'm the luckiest person alive. Then he shakes his head in amazement, whispering, as if a hidden fortune lost for eons has just been dug up at his feet, "A twin."

We jump over a rusty wire fence. "This is the end of Poppa's land," Mordy says casually as we hit the other side and he stalks forward like an early pioneer.

He wants to know everything about David and why he's away and do I miss him so much it hurts? Since I can't remember the last time I thought about David, I'm a bit taken aback that Mordy finds such mysterious glamour in him.

"He's away living in another city, going to school there."

"Why? Why is he doing that? Why does he have to go away to school? There are plenty of good schools here. He's your other half!"

"He is not my other half! I'm whole by myself."

I owe these words to Stephen, who was furious when we first learned— has it been over six years already?—that David wasn't coming back for a while, and I screamed out in terror, "How can I ever be a whole person?" (Rivka had once explained what twins were by drawing a circle and slicing it in half.) Stephen took me by the shoulders and shook me: "Don't you ever say you're not a whole person! Do you hear me?"

"He *is* your other half!" Mordy's eyes are huge. "He's your same-aged brother! He's your twin! Do you know what's happening to him at this very minute? If I had a twin brother we would be together every single second of every day and night!"

I suddenly begin to feel guilty and tears come to my eyes. I want to say, You don't understand! I don't know David very well. We were so young when he went away. I don't think he wants to come home. He doesn't want to see me. So I don't let myself think about him. But I don't say any of this. It all sounds too shameful.

Mordy sees my tears and stops walking to put his hand on my shoulder.

"I'm sorry," he says. "I'm sorry."

Now I really start to cry. I'm not accustomed to sympathy. His concern touches me more than I know how to handle. I'm wailing and shaking, which elicits more sympathy. Mordy takes me in his arms.

"He moved away to Boston when we were about six. My father, he didn't have a job and he found a job in Boston and he took David with him be- cause . . . because . . . And when Pop got a job back here, David didn't want to come home." I'm blubbering into Mordy's arms now. "I miss him. Yes, I miss him, but I don't let myself think about him because it hurts too much!" There. That should do it. I haven't been aware that it hurts, but now that I've said it, why not? Why not?

As soon as I say it, it's true. I miss David terribly. I want David back, and right this minute I could run all the way up to Boston to get him. No. Not right this minute. Right this minute Mordy Masturbov has his arms around me and I don't want him to let go.

"Aren't families the worst?" he says, one of his hands cupping my head, the other smoothing my hair, over and over, like a mother comforting a suf- fering child.

By now, we've walked so far from home that neither of us knows where we are. Evening is falling. We're surrounded by dark trees and tall green weeds waving in a tender summer breeze. School is out. We're free till fall.

He bends forward and kisses me. I must be dreaming. I kiss him back, and he's still there. I kiss him and kiss him and kiss him. I can't stop. He laughs, and then he grabs my crotch so roughly it hurts. I don't care. I do the same to him. I start to pull off his shirt, but he pulls me down in the field beside him, rolling on top of me, laughing, he's laughing, it must be all right! I can feel a bump in his trousers. Now he's pumping me like I do to my mattress sometimes in the dark because it feels good. My hand undoes his fly and I grope for his penis. How do I know what to do? Today as I write this my head is hammering with this thought: How did I know so ably what to do? Did Uncle Hyman teach me, or did Uncle Hyman just show me what I would know how to do anyway, when the time came, when the right person came?

I find it! I have it in my hand—the penis of someone my own age, someone I want so much. I can't begin to describe the overwhelming release of need I feel. A lifetime—and for the young time is much longer than for the old, when days pass much too quickly—a lifetime of desire has suddenly been released, the painful pressure of what's been hermetically sealed now freed to escape. I shiver as I'm being borne aloft and off this earth. I'm dizzy. He's holding me tightly now, because my penis, which he has pulled out, is jumping with a life of its own while he hugs me tighter and tighter as I find myself screaming out loud, some guttural noise unfamiliar to me, as if from another person, frightening in its hunger, its sheer uncensored pleasure.

Then something happens. I watch it. I'm terrified by its strangeness. Something spurts out of me and it falls to earth.

And then I'm aware I don't feel as good. I'm tired and timid and frightened.

Why did it end so quickly?

Why do I overlook that most important fact: he kissed me. *He* kissed *me*. He kissed me first!

He lays me back and looks down on me and gently kisses my nose. "Be quiet while I take care of myself." And he lies on his side, eyes clenched, holding me in the cradle of his left arm while he uses his right hand to masturbate. It takes him a very long time. He grunts and groans so. His face is pale white and covered with perspiration. I want to help, so I start kissing him again. His exertions take so long that the kisses turn from ardor to arduous. Finally, he too has his release. Now we are both experienced young men!

But now it's Mordy who's crying. Or is he? Is it just accumulated perspiration? No, I'm convinced it's sadness. Despair isn't an emotion that boys tend to recognize, but it's the word I think of. I don't know how I located it in my vocabulary, but I'm filled with an overwhelming sadness for both of us because . . . No, not because we've done what we've done. I just sense he's vastly troubled, Mordy, though I can't tell why or how. But then, I'm vastly troubled too.

Far from anything being resolved for either of us, it just gets more complicated.

"What's wrong?" I ask, knowing that something is the moment I ask.

"Nothing's wrong!"

He rolls away and sits up, and if I don't do something he'll stand up and walk away. I grab his shoulder and pull him back down. At first he resists, but I'm stronger now, or he lets me be. What difference does it make? He's back and lying with me.

I use my shirt to wipe his face dry. I kiss his chest through his shirt and I kiss his stomach and where I think his belly button is. I kiss his thighs and his knees and his feet. I silently but certainly declare my love. If he kissed me first, then I more than return his invitation.

I'm all naked. How am I all naked? I don't remember taking off my clothes or his taking them off for me. If I am like this, how can he be so fully dressed?

I don't expect the question he asks.

"What was it like, with Claudia?"

I don't want Claudia here.

"I'm in love with her," he says.

I don't expect this either.

"Are you in love with her?" he asks.

"We're very close."

He nods, accepting this.

Has Mordy done with me what we've just done because of Claudia, because he wants information from me, or wants to share me because we shared her, or for some other indirect reason, and not because of *me*, because he wants me, because he feels the same about me as I feel for him? Well, I don't let myself think any such thoughts.

I think them all.

Here in this field I discover how adept I am at automatically absorbing yet another new kind of pain. I don't even wander the usual route: from rejection to depressed acceptance. As much as it hurts, as much as Uncle Hyman hurt, I go on, smile plastered on my puss. It's frightening that I stomach pain so well.

"Can't you tell me anything?" He's begging now, so I guess I'm in some sort of vague contol.

I'm still holding him in my arms. I'm still wiping his face off, now with my handkerchief, though he's dry and cool. Why am I still holding him in my arms? He's just said he's in love with *her*. Rich man, poor man, beggar man, thief . . . I beg you to love *me*. Is my body ugly? Am I too poor for you? I know something, Mordy. Something you don't know. Claudia will never love you! She isn't in love with me either, I know that now, but I don't care. Oh, I'll always be her friend, because she's too interesting not to stay close to. But she'll never make me feel like I've just felt with . . . this young man like me.

I could also tell him, though I certainly won't, that Claudia prides herself on not being in love with anybody, ever, and that I'll bet a million dollars she'll never change.

Yes, I've written off her entire romantic life. How could I know back then? Well, I could and did and I was right.

"She's so beautiful, especially naked. We . . . she . . ." He's telling me a story I don't want to hear. But I guess I'd better listen. The doctor-to-be in me is now enduring this scene of rejection in order to extract every ounce of dirt for the records, toward any diagnosis. "It was just great."

Is that it?

"You're not telling me the whole story."

He nods and he stares out into the night. I wait and watch as his eyes fill with tears again and he finally says, "I have such trouble . . . You saw how long . . . I can't seem to . . . And it hurts so . . . and . . . besides . . ."

He's sobbing like a beaten man. He stands up and starts walking, farther out into the country. I run after him, and we walk quietly for a while. Then he starts talking.

He talks (I'd say he tells me, but he's talking to the air, the space out there, perhaps to her, but certainly not to me) about the time he and a bunch of his friends from St. Anselm's went downtown to some whorehouse. "I was last. I'd been hard for so long, watching the other four do it, that I was dripping and throbbing, and when the last guy did it and he . . . ejaculated, I ejaculated too. Right out into the room." We keep walking. I don't say a word. Then he starts up again. "I found a book. I can't tell you where. It wasn't a book. It was typewritten. It was all about a bunch of soldiers off at war without any women around. None at all. Just them. They didn't know what to do. They were real bored and had a lot of time on their hands. One of them said, 'Let's cover ourselves with honey and lick each other clean.' And that's what they did. And it was the most exciting thing for all of them." He's got me excited again, but now I can't kiss him because he's in love with Claudia. "Let's do it again," he suddenly says. And this time he lays me back and undoes my fly and pulls out my penis and puts my hand on it, and I sense that he wants me to masturbate, which I do while he watches without doing anything to himself, which makes me think he must still be sore from his first time, and I ejaculate—how swift my facility—and then he jumps up and starts back toward home. I clean off with some leaves as quickly as I can and button up my pants and jump up and run to catch up. I'm the beggar again. We walk home in silence, and he leaves me at my front door. I guess he'll walk up to Abe's office, where there's always a limousine, no matter what time it is, to take him across the city to his house with its columns of women with big breasts.

Just as he leaves to go, he says: "I think next time we want to do it with chocolate syrup, not honey." And he winks at me.

•

When I come home Philip is sitting in the dark in his undershorts and T-shirt, his slippers on his pale feet, staring at a television program. It's hot indoors and he's got a towel hanging around his neck. We're been living alone together for a few weeks. Rivka's off at some conference of her fellow saviors, and Lucas and Stephen are working on a farm in Maine for a woman named Dorothy Thompson.

He comes into the bathroom without knocking just as I'm ready to take a shower. So far as I can remember he's never seen me naked. He is going to take a pee.

"What's that?"

He's eyeing my crotch. Am I too small? What now?

No, he's staring at the dried white gook embedded in the growing black tuft of my pubic hairs. Mordy's and my dried semen. There seems to be a good deal of it matted into a peculiarly protuberant clump.

"What is that?" His voice is louder. He looks me in the eyes, a terrified expression inside his own.

"Where have you been? What have you done? What's . . . what is *this*?" His voice is hoarse and squeaky and trembling, and almost macabre. His fingers dart in swiftly and yank a hairy glob out of me.

"Ouch! What are you doing?"

"What is this!"

I can't answer him. He knows what I don't want to tell him. Or enough of it to hate me even more. How do I know he knows? How *does* he know?

However he knows it, he does.

He smacks me hard. He slaps me over and over. It hurts more each time. He doesn't stop until I somehow get past him and run into my bedroom. I expect him to come after me, but he doesn't.

•

My body is sprouting chest hair, rivulets heading north and south from my navel, black whispers on my nipples, all still subtle with innuendo but filled with a foresty foreboding. I find what's happening to my body terrifying. I liked myself before, or so I tell myself; I don't like myself now, that I know for a fact. I have no idea why being hairy should produce such self-hate and discomfort, but it does. Stephen is very hairy, and there's something about Stephen that troubles me. I'm never completely comfortable with him. Philip is hairless except on his chest. His pale unclothed body is not a pretty sight. Lucas is sort of in between, a nice balance of hairy and hairless. Lucas is nice to look at any which way. With my little clumps of dense black scruff, I'm beginning to look like a spotted cow. A big Dalmatian. An ape. I don't want to look like an ape. I want to look like Lucas! I want to look like Lucas and I'm going to look like Stephen. Mostly, I'm just afraid. My body is trying to tell me something.

I loathe my body hair and violently wish it away.

Ponzo Lombardo! What a tuft of pubic hair *he* has! He eyes mine in gym class and confides to me, with *pride*, "We're the only ones growing into men!" Why don't I accept Ponzo's invitation to grow up? "Come on in the shower and let's show off!"

Dickie and Jimmy and James and Billy and Orvid and Arnold and Dodo and Patrick and . . . *all* the other boys—not a *hint* of hair! All possessed of the unsullied marmoreal smoothness I'll always associate with gentile-ity. The state of being Other than I. No brushy black Brillo for them. I look at

Ponzo's equipment, already fully embraced by a muff of celebrity, and I look down upon mine, smaller but haloed by fibrous fluff, and I realize in despair that I'm on my way to joining Ponzo and I can no longer hope to be like Dickie or Jimmy or James or Billy or . . . Mordy.

Of course. That's it. Mordy is as hairless as a Greek statue.

I want to be like Mordy. I want Mordy to like me.

So I sashay away from Ponzo, my towel my armor as I sneak my underpants on, vowing never again to shower in school. But I can't help casting my eyes down at Ponzo's huge hairy thing. Yikes, am I going to be as big? I'd like to be a good size, but I don't want to be like Ponzo or Tibby Chesterfield. Get dressed! Slam that locker door closed!

Why has no one said a word to me by way of preparation? Do I want to be a Peter Pan all my life? How else to get out of Masturbov Gardens if not by growing up? Isn't my constant wish, the one I make on birthday candles and lucky pennies, Please get me out of Masturbov Gardens?

I don't know why Ponzo, whose three-piece suite in a few years' time I would be more than happy to accommodate in my bedroom, is the object of my disdain. Daniel, the guy's cock is huge! And gorgeous! Can't you see?

So many confusions!

Why do I have so many "erections" of "engorged blood" without warning? I find these terms in my own first dirty book, which I've bought for one whole dollar off of fat Grace my once babysitter, and which is forthrightly called *Learning to Live with Sex*. Looking at Ponzo. Thinking of Lucas. Dreaming of Mordy. No one has told me *anything*. When the shadows first appear, then the fuzz, then the actual tentacles sprouting around my thing, I think I'm coming down with a case of what happened to Mr. Hyde. When the incessant, uncontrollable throbbing of my "member" first starts, I think I'm plagued by some incurable illness that must be bathed with the compresses I'll note in a few years' time are used by Nurse Rosalind Russell on kids with polio in *Sister Kenney*. I might just as well have polio. Nurse, it won't go away; it just stays hard, no matter where I am. I'll be walking down the street and then—my crotch breaks out! Lest I be seen, I have to resort to some protective shield—a jacket, a schoolbook carried jauntily, a sweater tied around my waist. Imagine comparing it all with polio. When will I pause to make note of how . . . disorienting all this stuff with boys is becoming?

Soon I learn in *Learning to Live with Sex* about "nocturnal self-mutilation"; this is a nighttime lesson, taught to me in my own bed by my wet sheets; the two plus two of it all scares me no end, not only that something so . . . personal could transpire while I'm asleep, but also that Rivka will notice my dirty deeds. I rush to purchase multiple sets of underpants to sleep in, one for each encounter with the Unknown Night, and then I dispose of them the next day in the garbage room, via the long, dark, winding underground tunnel I know too well. When it becomes apparent that I'll go broke buying new ones (even combining my own babysitting money and Philips's allowance), I take to washing them myself and hanging them in the back of my closet to dry. Stephen discovers them while searching for an old tennis racket and gives me a look. Life gets more complicated by the minute.

How do I free myself of these new torments? I have no idea. What would Claudia say? She'd make fun of me. Can I bring a touch of levity to the situation by myself? Apparently not, because as I stare down at Ponzo's effluvial and effervescent penis in its copious black nest, bigger and bolder and longer and thicker and wider than any I've ever seen, in or out of Uncle Hyman's suitcase, I realize I want it in my mouth! I want it! And I don't even love him. Mordy at least I love. Further complications abound, and it was complicated enough already.

And Mordy hasn't even called me. Why hasn't Mordy called me?

And how can one mouth want the penises of two such different boys? Well, why not? Every leading man in every movie musical has a batch of girls. Ah, but what I want is not exactly girls.

No, I decide I want only Mordy. Ponzo is just a wicked temptation, Linda Darnell when what I want is Katharine Hepburn. And in no way can I jeopardize my precarious social standing with the hairless. Dickie and James and Mordy are the elite, not Ponzo. Will their Grand Hairlessnesses shun my emerging animal self when they see it? As I do so often these days, I flagellate myself almost to the point of enfeeblement.

I've been thinking about my missing twin. Mordy has opened this particular well of loneliness. I write David a letter. I figure he must be going through all this too. Lucas comes and sits on my bed one night. "Why are you crying?" "I'm not crying." "You are so crying. Tell me why." "If I tell you, will you tell me why you're so strange?" "I'm not strange. Strange how?" "You don't talk to me anymore." "You're strange too. You don't smile anymore." "Then why are we both strange at the same time?" "You first," he says. Where to start? "I want my brother," I hear myself say. A long pause. "I am your brother. You mean David?" I nod. I hope I haven't hurt his feelings. Another long pause. I guess I have. "I can't help you there," he says. Yes, I've hurt his feelings. My only friend in this household. I learned only later that he'd been so sour because he'd found out where David was. Rivka had "confided" in him.

I ask Rivka for David's address. "He's away this month." "He must be *somewhere* I can write him." "He's traveling. He's on the road." I guess I sound like a fool, letting her get away with this, not once but a number of times. I'm such a nosy person in all other respects, why do I let myself be hoodwinked about my own twin brother? I can only say in my defense that from their moods and tones and the glances Rivka exchanges with Philip every time David's name comes up, I know instinctively something awful's going on that no one's going to talk about. It's been this way for a long time now and still no one ever talks about it. I try to shake my head back and forth to make some sense of this.

Finally Mordy calls me. He's never called our house before. Rivka is impressed. "The landlord's son is calling my son." "The landlord is my cousin," I say. "You hardly know each other," she says. "It's another branch of the family." Mordy's voice is matter-of-fact. "Wanna go for a walk?" My heart begins pounding. He wants to do it again!

We walk and walk. We walk to the exact same spot under the exact same dark night's summer sky. Silently. He doesn't speak and I don't know what to say. We sit down in the weeds. He lies back. I watch him unbutton his fly and pull himself out and start to masturbate. It's a thrilling sight. I watch him, hoping he'll look into my eyes and give me permission to adore him. But his eyes are closed, tighter as he increases his speed, pausing every so often to spit on his hand. Again the act looks like an awful lot of effort. "You don't seem to be enjoying it much," I hear myself say, wondering what on earth prompts me to intrude with such a harsh observation. How can I help him? Well, I can help by sticking my face in his crotch and putting him in my mouth.

The minute my lips touch him he grunts and jiggles himself over a few inches to continue his work alone. His face is covered with sweat.

"Let me see *you*! Let me see *you*!" he orders.

My master has spoken! I yank my own out—of course it's as hard as a rock—and get to work on it. I come way before he does. It's not very exciting or much of a release. Suddenly Mordy's hand grabs hold of my depleted penis, grabs as much of my semen off me as he can, and uses it as lubricant on himself. How resourceful. Where did he learn that?

"Hold me! Hold me!" he cries out.

I hold him. He's sweating bullets and pumping himself so energetically that I ache in sympathy. I keep waiting for his orgasm. So does he, I guess. Time and again it seems to be almost arriving, any second now. When I kiss his cheek for encouragement, he heaves out the words "Don't do that!" as he carries on with his manual labor. Is there something wrong with him, or with his penis, or with his plumbing? Or with his liking me? Could it all be my fault?

Finally—finally—it's over. He cries out in a gasp that's certainly more relief than grand finale. Some modestly gurgling liquid caps his penis's head, like water from the spout of a fountain with exceptionally low pressure. He's angry with himself. His fists pound the ground. "What's wrong?" I dare to ask. He turns his fists on me. My chest hurts but I let him carry on. Then I grab his fists, prying open the fingers to make them into hands I can hold. He falls back again, heaving huge sobs. "I don't know what's wrong!" "Let me look," I say, trying to inspect him. "NO!" And he jumps up, and again we walk back home in silence. I want to put my arm around his shoulders as if we're buddies in one of those war movies we all now constantly watch.

•

Mordy and I are sunning ourselves in the protected courtyard behind the building where I live. It's sort of weird every time I realize his father owns where I live and weirder because his son, on whose penis I've been concentrating so much, will one day own it too. Will his father evict my family if he finds out what I've done? How do I know that I've done anything wrong? I just know. It's in the air of life.

His father's buildings form a rectangle all around us. In the winter, tenants can look out their windows and see everything; but it's summer and the Carolina willows are full, and protecting us as we lie on a blanket in shorts and jerseys, ostensibly to do our summer reading for school. We've now made that long trek out to those lonely weedy fields six or seven or eight times for a repeat of what I've already described. By now I feel paternal toward him. He's talking less and less. He must be struggling with it more than I am.

Ever since I saw Ponzo, I study myself carefully down there on a daily basis. It's now impossible to overlook the evidence that if things keep up at their current pace I'm on my way to becoming a hairy freak just short of a baboon. What to do? My body's doing something I don't want it to do!

Late last night, with moonlight flooding our bedroom, I made myself look at Lucas as he undressed, thinking I was asleep. My heart almost stopped. His body is so handsome. He stood in front of the mirror inside the door and studied himself, posing shyly like a body builder, flexing his arms and puffing out his chest.

I don't think I'm going to look like he looks.

I'm staring at Mordy's legs and noting yet again that they're smooth and unshadowed. No darkening ode. We did it yesterday. Usually it takes him a few days to cheer himself back up again. He needs longer than I do for the hunger to renew itself. I masturbated thinking about him this morning, on the toilet. I masturbate a lot now. It isn't nearly as interesting alone, but it's better than nothing, and I don't feel as unsatisfied as Mordy makes me feel when we're finished. Each time we part I'm convinced he doesn't want to see me ever again, that what's happened is my fault and he's holding it against me.

"Your legs are getting hairy," he says. We're pretending to read. At least I'm pretending. Maybe he's doing it for real.

"No, they're not. They've always been this way."

"You're going through puberty."

"What's puberty?"

I know fucking well what puberty is. I've scared myself shitless any number of times covertly reading volumes in Uncle Hyman's bookstores, just happening to be in their neighborhood, pretending to be a customer, "just looking, thank you." *Psychopathia Sexualis, Sex in Marriage, The Sexual Manual for Today's Married Couples, Learning to Live with Sex*—they are all terrifying. They are books written by nasty doctors to scare people to death. Puberty leads to girls. Girls lead to babies. The cause and effect of body hair is marriage!

I fucking well know what puberty is and I fucking well know that I'm "a homosexual," a.k.a. "an invert," i.e., "sick." Dr. Krafft-Ebing in his book, which has the lengthiest descriptions, incarcerates people like me in sanatoriums and prisons. But that apparently doesn't stop people like me. People like me ejaculate just from descriptions of ejaculations. On the day I discovered the name for the sprouting of my body hair and it's called puberty, and that when you reach it you have orgasms, which are uncontrollable emissions of white fluid, I ejaculated just standing in an alcove in some ratty bookstore reading the goddamn book, and it ran all down my leg. The printed word is certainly powerful.

"Puberty is when you get hair everywhere," Mordy says, sighing. I'm getting wet inside my Fruit of the Looms.

Mordecai Masturbov begins to cry. And this time we aren't even having sex.

"I don't have any."

"What?" I ask.

He hoarsely whispers a word: "Hair."

He's crying and his eyes are cast down. I want to comfort him, but I can't put my arms around him out here in the middle of his courtyard, even with the willows.

I hear myself say, "I don't have any either."

What a strange young man I'm growing up to be.

"Yes, you do."

"No, I don't."

"I've felt it in the dark. Don't lie. My father told me to expect it, and that was a year ago. We went to France so he could take me to a famous doctor. In Switzerland. Oh, please don't lie."

"I'm not lying. Wait right here and I'll prove it to you."

I rush upstairs. I grab Rivka's sewing scissors. I step out of my shorts and brutally hack off my pubic growth, snipping and chopping and trimming the black explosion, surveying the results in that full-length closet mirror. Stubble, black and ugly, is still too evident. Shaving cream! Philip's razor! Some fast alcohol and Johnson's baby powder to disguise my clumsy nicks! The final statement is cleaner. I'm a virgin again. I carefully preserve the black puffs of hairy evidence in a Kleenex, tucking it into the back corner of my bottom bureau drawer. I put my shorts back on. I go downstairs to show Mordy we're both alike.

He isn't there.

The next day our gang is playing in what will be a huge basement of already poured concrete when Mordy joins us. He comes over to me and says, quietly, lest he be overheard by Arnold Botts, he who is everywhere, "I have a confession to make. I really don't like doing what we do. I wanted to try it. I believe in trying everything at least once, but now I've tried it enough. And I know you like it more than I do. Thanks for trying to make me feel better by saying you don't have any pubic hair. That was very nice of you. I always want you and me to be friends. I'll see to it that we are if you will too. Will you?"

"Yes." My heart is broken on the spot. My crotch hurts where I cut myself shaving.

"Guess what?"

"What?" I can hardly utter the word.

"When I went home, I got a magnifying glass and I looked and it's coming! I found my first hair!" And he hoists me up on his back and gleefully runs around this new excavation of his father's. Arnold, for once, looks startled: something's going on that he doesn't know about. Mordy and I have a secret.

So Mordy doesn't want to do it anymore. Because he doesn't like it. I want to do it forever and ever. So what am I going to do?

•

I enter the world of service. Rivka finally lets me volunteer for the bloodmobile. "We're at war and everyone must do his bit." Since everyone now wants to do his bit, our bloodmobile trailer's always a madhouse, and it's fun. My fellow workers include wisecracking nurses like Eve Arden and Joan Blondell. Each Saturday we try to beat last Saturday's record. That a youngster like me should be a helper impresses every donor. I give them cups of orange juice and I collect the used syringes for boiling and I alphabetize the completed paperwork into an accordion file. Little Mister Helpful. What with two or three bodies always being drained, and the snappy ladies, and the driver (somebody's husband who's retired or with the day off) doubling as "our big strong man" carting the iced containers that hold the blood, plus little Daniel exuding so much sanctimonious enthusiasm that you want to slug him, it's a busy little space. No one says boo about my age.

This is before the days of strict sanitary precautions. Donors bring dogs and donors get sick and there are bloodstains from occasional spurts. The trailer's scrubbed down each night, but we're always far too busy for anyone to be a constant cleaner-upper.

After a Miss Trudy McNab faints on the floor and her head accidentally plops on a batch of full vials that Mr. Homolka hasn't yet refrigerated, my Washington Red Blood career is over. Trudy gets some shards of glass in her eyes and somebody's blood gets in there too, and before you know it she loses her sight, which doesn't seem to be coming back.

A district supervisor is summoned to supervise.

"Why is someone so young performing in an official capacity?"

People are not so litigious in those days, but there's no doubt Miss

Trudy McNab's lawyer wants compensation to make the rest of her life less miserable.

I'm the one who's blamed. My mother, to save her cherished unblemished record of continuous devoted service, does not defend me or point out that Trudy couldn't possibly have fainted and bonked her bean because of me. A scapegoat is needed and I'm it. "There's also a legal technicality involved," Stephen tells me. "You're underage. If the fault can be pinned on you, you can't be sued. Blind she may be, but she's got less ground for a lawsuit. And there's no law preventing ARB from allowing you to help." I want to write Miss McNab a letter saying how sad I am for her, but Stephen says I mustn't.

I feel abandoned by Rivka. I miss my Saturday bloodmobile. I work up the courage to ask, "Momma, do you think I was guilty somehow?"

"Of course not, darling. It's just the way Washington works. I've found you something else just as helpful. I've heard the most awful news from Miss Theodora Von Lutz, who has confided in me that American Red Blood has had a secret meeting and determined that Negro blood will not be collected. Isn't that awful! And to make matters worse they have also determined at their International Headquarters in Geneva not to confront or even in any way allude to the horrible things that Rabbi Chesterfield says the Germans and Mr. Hitler are doing to our people. I don't know what the world is coming to. I'm not sure I can continue working in this field. Miss Von Lutz says I must not despair. That it's just the way the world works. Miss Von Lutz is certainly plugged into the right sockets. Now, I have a lovely new volunteer job for you! I was talking to Rabbi Chesterfield and we have pulled a rabbit out of his hat."

•

The day I'm meant to be bar mitzvahed is the day I learn where David is.

When Rivka asked me a few years before if I was ready to begin my Hebrew lessons, I put up a stink expecting her to insist, which amazingly didn't come. That I just wouldn't do it didn't seem to bother them at all.

I had made the monumental philosophical decision that I don't believe in God the night Uncle Hyman fucked me, stuffing the pillow over my mouth and silencing me with threats. I still remember that feeling, not so much of being fucked, because I've been fucked many times since, symbolically, literally, with both pleasure and pain, but of being both checkmated and being silenced, being forced to participate in an act against my will. I remember lying there, a child, with my smelly uncle snoring on top of me, my ass sore, some kind of fluid—his semen? my blood?—trickling down inside my thighs, and thinking, What kind of world is this that allows such things to happen? I felt older than my years, very old. How can there possibly be a God watching over this and me?

I said earlier I date my desire to become a doctor from that day and night with Uncle Hyman. It was a decision that grew slowly as piece by piece it was building up.

But I have to go to Sunday school anyway, even though I think it's a joke. I'm shipped off each week to Washington Jewish so I can be thrown in with all those richest kids in the city. Thumbing my nose, I pride myself on a new rebellious act every few weeks or so. When the ark that holds the sacred Torah is opened and everyone's supposed to stand up, I stay seated. When a teacher's back is turned, I sneak out to Murphy's Five and Dime across the street and return blowing my just-purchased bubble gum or looping the loop with my new yo-yo. When I am finally caught, I'm called up in front of Rabbi Chesterfield himself, more than ever looking and sounding like a phony Ronald Coleman rip-off in flowing robes, in his study lined with signed photographs of world leaders. Now he has a radio program to tell his opinion of world events. Philip goes for a walk when Rivka insists on listening to it. "He's the first Jewish leader broadcast coast-to-coast!"

Rabbi Chesterfield leans back in his enormous leather swivel chair and asks me why I'm behaving so badly.

"I don't believe in God."

He rocks a few times, nodding to himself, and he twirls slowly around in his chair.

"Can you tell me why? On the basis of what information?"

I realize he doesn't remember me or my interaction with his dead son. I shake my head no. Now I'm not even sure he knows I'm the son of his prized teacher.

"Well, we shall discuss this further when you are older. You may return to class."

My announcement elicits nothing more remarkable. I'm not struck dead or otherwise smitten. The rabbi does not broadcast my momentous news to the Jerusalem home front. After a while, tired of my rebellious acts, I just sit through temple activities bored out of my mind. When the time comes for those Hebrew lessons to prepare me for my bar mitzvah and I refuse, Rivka's only fear is that the news will kill Grandma Libby. "Don't tell her," I say. "She lives in Los Angeles. How will she ever find out?"

"Are you suggesting I lie to my own mother?"

When thirteen arrives so does Grandma Libby's bar mitzvah present. It's addressed to Daniel and David Jerusalem. It comes by special delivery. I open the door and sign my name for the parcel. I rip it open. Inside is a letter and a dirty strip of canvas cloth with a yellow Star of David on it.

Rivka comes home from work looking very tired. I show her Grandma's letter, afraid it may make her fall apart. But when you think Rivka is going to do one thing, she doesn't. She is presenting a stone jaw and a tough face.

Grandma Libby's letter (written for her by Uncle Hyman, evidently presently peddling his wares on the West Coast) says, "I send you this because today you are men and men today must fight. The world is more awful now than ever I remember. I send you this awful thing so you always remember and make your grandma proud as I always am of you and always will be. More than ever you must be good Jews and fight for your people. Do you know what this is I send you? It is an armband from the camp at Todstadt, worn by a Jewish little boy just like you, Daniel and David, who was sent into the gas chambers to be exterminated. The rabbi from our shul brings this back from a conference where rabbis from all over the world discuss this terrible problem. They kill us and kill us. But with bar mitzvah men like the two of you I never lose hope."

I go walking by myself along the banks of the creek—the Masturbov River it's called, a stream barely a foot wide and dry most of the year—viciously kicking pebbles with my feet, feeling increasingly chained to this culvert and this town and this life. In the eyes of the Jewish religion, I should officially be a man now, but I haven't been bar mitzvahed. Is a bar mitzvah some sort of passport without which you can't be a man? If so, it isn't fair. Either you're a man or you're not a man. I do not feel like a man. And I do not feel like I am surrounded by men in our house. How many years has David been away by now? I have to count on my fingers. Six years? We certainly don't hold family remembrances of him on our birthday. I start thinking about Lucas and Stephen. They have been so silent and passive all these years. I am really kicking the shit out of the pebbles in the culvert now. I am furious with my brothers. I am furious with everyone and everything.

When I had declared my atheism to Philip, he looked at me as if I were a crazy person and he had no idea where I sprang from, "certainly not from my loins." *Loins* is a new word for me. And he sits down and turns on the radio, shaking his head. "He's not my son. He's not my son," he mutters. This is not a new refrain to me. I am used to it. I thought I was used to it. I thought I didn't care if I was his son or not.

"He's your son," he announces to Rivka, who's preparing dinner as I return home from my pebble-kicking.

"What are you talking about? He's your son, too."

"No, he's not. He's your son."

The dirty armband with its wrinkled Star of David is still laid out on the dining room table where I'd opened it. I go to my room and write another letter to David.

"You know we don't know where to send this!" Rivka yells, crumpling up my letter when I bring it back and hand it to her silently. She runs into the living room, where Philip sits inebriated by one of his baseball games, in near-dissolution because his team is losing. He always takes it personally; he yells at the team and he yells at the Philco just like he yells at me. "Philip, I can't take it anymore," she cries, in a voice more pained than usual. "You must tell him! You must tell him *something*!"

"Leave me alone," he says in Yiddish. They speak Yiddish when they don't want "the kinder" to understand, which of course by now we do, at least the basics.

I am suddenly aware that I feel naked, that neither of my brothers is ever around when the gathering storms are, well, gathering, as I know, sure as shooting, one is gathering now. How do they know when to stay away? I wonder if they are leading double lives, having another family to go to so they can be fed and not have to get stomachaches from all the awful things going on in this family that are never talked about.

"I won't leave you alone! Doesn't anyone have any consideration for me? I can't take it anymore." She uncrumples my letter and reads aloud a few lines. "I miss you and wish you were here. I'm going through such a tough time and I wonder if you are. You must be, because we're two parts of the same whole even though Stephen says we're not. It bothers me not to be sharing growing up with you." Then she skips to the part about my puberty problems. "My body seems to be changing more than I want it to. Is this happening to you? No one has told me anything about any of this and I'm frightened a lot by these changes that seem to come out of nowhere."

"Give me that!" I lunge for the letter and grab it.

Philip speaks. "Are you yelling at me to tell me that this sissy who lives with me in this apartment who doesn't believe in God is afraid he's becoming a man, or are you yelling at me because David is in a concentration camp in Germany where they don't have daily mail service?"

She lets out a piercing scream. Then she's bawling, repeating over and over, "That's not the way to tell him! That's not the way."

Have I stopped breathing? In a concentration camp? Where they gas people to death? I stare at my parents in horror. My mother is blubbering. She reaches for me and I pull back instinctively and she stands in the middle of the room not knowing where to go, with her arms reaching out unplaced like some puppet on broken strings. In no way does Philip relinquish the ball game's hold on him. "Shut up," he says. "I can't hear what's happening." Rivka goes and kicks the radio, the solid floor-model Philco, which doesn't so much as burp. So she yanks out its plug. He sits there looking into space. Her foot hurts and she sits down to massage it.

I stand in front of the low armchair where Philip sits in his underwear. I stand there glaring at him. *"Tell me what!"* I scream.

He isn't talking. He isn't that kind of fighter. He's never been a fighter. All he can do, and only when provoked by Rivka, is bully me. I hate him more and more for his passivity and his cowardice. Sitting in his armchair, the chair no one else is permitted to sit in, not that anyone ever wants to, and staring at the Philco as if waiting for it to resume beaming his ball game at him, any ball game, he's pathetic to me. Whatever's happened to David, I'm sure it's Philip's fault.

Terror such as I've never known overtakes my body. I'm gasping for breath. I'm boiling hot but I'm shivering. Who are these two people in this room with me? I don't know them. Aren't they supposed to be my mother and father? Why is it hard to breathe? I have to run, but where? If I run to my bedroom, I'm still here. If I run out into the street, where do I run to next? I'm frozen to the spot.

If I leave, how will I find out the truth about David? If I stay, how will I live with it? And them?

I shake my mother. I grab her and I shake her in and out and back and forth. She stares at me in horror, her face comes closer and then recedes, only to return, like she's swooping down on me on a roller coaster.

"Stop it, stop it, stop it," she says, not so loudly at all. "Obey me! I'm your mother!" she then cries out plaintively. "What are you doing to me?" Her words pierce a hole in my anger and we hug each other, crying into each other's shoulder. "Mommy, Mommy, please tell me!"

And we sit down on the sofa and she tells me. Some of it, anyway. When she starts to speak, Philip gets up and goes to the bedroom, only to emerge moments later, fully dressed. He leaves the apartment.

"Your father was out of work for the longest time. He just couldn't seem to find a job. It was the Depression. It went on and on. It wasn't so hot for most people but it was particularly hard on professional people like lawyers. Who had any money to hire a lawyer, no matter how great the wrong? Finally, he read in the Yaddah alumni magazine about a classmate of his, a Mr. Standing, who owned a large Boston company that evidently made film, and even though it was the Depression, this business was booming. I thought, How could it be booming, people don't have enough money to take pictures. But it was film for movies. Everybody was so poor and wretched that they spent their last pennies going to the movies. Movies made people laugh and feel good. They helped people escape. Philip wrote Mr. Standing a letter, not expecting much to happen. Lo and behold, after a few weeks, an answer comes. Yes, there is a job for a qualified lawyer, particularly one who, like Philip, speaks German. Mr. Standing's company is partners with a German company. The salary is such and such and can Philip report to Boston for work on such and such? He doesn't even want to meet Philip or interview him. So Philip packs his suitcase.

"You know how you and David never got along particularly well? You seemed to be the artistic one and he the opposite. You liked to pretend and he hated that . . ."

I nod. When I would put on my little playlets in the privacy of our bedroom, David always looked embarrassed. He was too polite to say anything so I plowed on, hoping I could entertain him enough to overcome his disapproval, but I never did. Soon he ran out whenever I wrapped a towel around my head like Carmen Miranda or clomped around in Mom's high heels or paraded in Lucas's jockstrap pretending I was a big-deal athlete.

For his part, by the age of four or five, like Dodo, David had a home chemistry set and could concoct every one of the formulas in the thick book that came with it. It wasn't pretend to him. It was what his world was made of. I didn't like the smells, but I enjoyed the magic, and I wanted him to enjoy my pretend games in return. But it was obvious that I embarrassed him more than he could bear. He was quiet by nature, so it took a while for this to sink into my consciousness: that he felt uncomfortable in my presence, that my own twin felt uncomfortable near me. When it did dawn on me, we started fighting. Some of what he was really feeling came tumbling out. He thought I was silly. *Frivolous* was the word he used, a word I'd never heard. Then he started using a word Philip used a lot. *Sissy*. That word I knew the meaning of. I hated sports and I hated that Philip monopolized the radio to listen to his endless contests, and I had the guts to say so, I am proud to recognize now. I think it was a pretty gutsy thing to say, "I hate baseball, I hate football," knowing that I was flying in the face of all that in Philip's mind defined a man. It wasn't that I was siding with the feminine—Rivka was for both David and me a true pain in our asses, someone we jointly complained about, someone we knew from our earliest comprehension was much too busy to be our mother. If I was learning that I'm a rebel by nature, I was also learning that I enjoyed the role, and that David wasn't like this at all. He had withdrawn from our world, and it seemed I was here to remind him of it.

I couldn't stand those "sissy" implications, though, and I started fighting back. I'd short-sheet his bed or put some of his chemical stuff into his food so he'd piss blue. When he hit me for the first time, I started to cry. I ran out of the bedroom, I was so shocked, but I ran right back in and clobbered him with all my strength. We were both surprised by that—that I had it in me to do something like that at all, and he that I had it in me to do it to him. Things went from bad to worse after that and for months on end we didn't say a word to each other, not one single word.

No wonder he went away.

For those who are always wondering if twins ever do it with each other, I offer only this: on that night when we were really fighting physically, I sucked his penis. Doesn't that make me sound like the aggressor? Well, to this day I'm convinced he put it in my mouth. Why should we have been so angry with each other? We shouldn't have been. In a concentration camp?

My mother continues. "You used to sleep in the same bed together. Do you remember? In each other's arms." We did indeed. Once upon a time.

"He started to cry when he saw Daddy packing up to go away. 'I want to go with you!' he sobbed. Your father and I held a conference and I said, 'Why not? It would make life a lot easier for me,' and you two weren't getting on at all by then, you mustn't forget that, so off David went with Philip. They always got along better. I have no idea why. You both always looked so alike to me.

"He went to school there and Philip's job was very interesting—wasn't it, dear?" (This to a Philip she thought was still staring into space, traumatized by listening to her; hadn't she seen him leave?) "And before you know it Mr. Standing was actually sending him back and forth to Germany. Imagine that. On a ship, a big fancy liner, back and forth, in a stateroom. Philip was his trusted assistant. He knew how to deal with the Germans in their own language and everybody on both sides appreciated it. There was no trouble because of Philip's Jewishness. Why should there be? He was the emissary of an important American company. Soon he was even taking David over on his trips. We didn't tell you for fear that you'd be jealous.

"One day Grandma Zilka decided she wanted to go find her birthplace in Drensk. She was old and she wanted to see the place one more time before the war made it impossible. Who knows, she said, maybe I stay and die over there. She bought herself a stateroom on A deck. Nobody knew she had so much money. That little grocery store in Northeast, she'd been raking it in. She sails over to see her son and grandson. Isn't that right, dear?" Her "dears" were not dears of love. They were like poison darts.

Philip, to my surprise, has returned. He just stands there, in a corner, near the doorway, like a little boy. He listens to her tell his story.

"When she gets there Zilka takes David and they go schlepping around asking how do you get to Drensk while your father goes to the moving picture studios and to the factory where they are processing the films that the producers are making in the studios for—"

"Mr. Hitler?" I interject. Where that came from I don't know. Maybe from David at last talking to me after all across time and space.

The name makes her scream so loudly that I know I've hit some truth. Then she starts shaking her head, as if trying to jiggle something into place.

This story is taking forever, and I want to cut to the chase: Where is my brother and how can I get him back? I will not consider the possibility of his death.

"For Amos Standing," he finally says from his corner. "Don't say the name Hitler in this house."

"Who's that?" Then I remember. "Lucas's middle name is Standing."

Philip, with an enormous sigh, hauls up his shoulders like a heavy burden and shuffles from the room like a beaten man. We hear him go into their bedroom and close the door. I think I hear sobs from inside, but perhaps it's my imagination, always troublesome.

But she's heard it. She jumps up and runs to their bedroom, hurling open the door. Indeed, Philip is sobbing mightily, his bulky body heaving on their double bed like some giant bellows. "*NOW* YOU CRY!" she screams. Rivka the yeller—God knows I've heard her yell often enough, but she's never raised her voice to such a pitch. She throws herself on the bed, kneeling over him, and pounds his back over and over, as if he's some big swollen pike that Grandma Libby is pummeling into gefilte fish. He takes it all. He sobs and she clobbers him and I want to run out to the street and get as far away as I can. But not knowing David's fate keeps me riveted in place. David, cast out of our shared world because of our discomfort with each other, cast into some other hell—oh, how I long for him now more than ever. Oh, what a supreme instrument of guilt he is for me now! That I have let so many years go by without him, all allowing this!

It would be presumptuous of me to try to tell David's story. I'm not trying to back out again, or justifying its delay. He should be permitted to describe his own hideously wounded self. Let me just say, for the sake of carrying this history forward, that Grandma Zilka disappeared in Drensk, where she'd taken David. She found her birthplace, a tiny home and adjoining barn where her father once made bricks, now turned into a movie theater of all things. What had been the outskirts of town was now the center; there was a small inn across the street, and she checked herself in with David. That evening they went to the movies. Then David went to bed and Zilka went out drinking at a club in her old hometown. When David woke up in the morning she wasn't there. David was all alone in this remote outpost on the eve of war, with no money, a limited facility with the language, and no idea where Philip was, just a note from his grandmother saying, "I go out tonight to find my youth."

And where was Philip? Philip was with Amos Standing, he who provided Lucas with his middle name. With Amos Standing in an inn on the Wannsee. In a romantic inn on the Wannsee. In a bed with Amos Standing in a romantic inn on the Wannsee, under one of those famous German comforters stuffed with down. My own father, once upon a time, actually found love, with a man. That inn on the Wannsee quite possibly held the only happiness he ever knew. He had told Rivka. He had little choice. She cross-examined him so furiously trying to piece together the minute-by-minute scenario of this trip of David's to Germany that he finally confessed. She knew.

"Oh, I knew." She is still pounding him violently on their bed, in their bedroom, blaming him for everything gone wrong. "I always knew."

"But where is David?" I plead.

"Today is his bar mitzvah day too," my mother wails helplessly.

"Can he be saved?" I bellow. "What are you doing to save him!" I scream even louder.

"He's safe!" Philip blubbered. " I always promised you he's safe!"

But she isn't having any of this.

"And I don't believe you!" She tries to strike him once again but this time her heart isn't in it, and her arms fall to embracing herself as she sobs.

I look at them both. She's now collapsed on top of him and he's lying there like a slug, a sack of potatoes, albeit one with tears streaming down his face. Her sobs have clogged her throat and she coughs and coughs. If they know more, which I am fearful that they do, that they *must*, it's not going to be forthcoming right now. I leave these two people to their bed of pain.

•

I see the gang playing on the concrete bank that funnels the "river," or would if there was ever any water in it. But I don't want them to see me, so I cut to the left, running along the grass that's been planted at the top of the culvert and around this newest section of Masturbov Gardens, which will be receiving its first inhabitants any day now. This place is growing like Topsy. Abe can't build these warrens fast enough. The war is crowding out the District and we're no longer such a small faraway place. All of us used to know this terrain inside out. Now we get lost. Now there's no end to basements leading to garbage rooms and laundries leading to endless new miles of underground tunnels we haven't mapped out. Still, in my desire not to see or be seen, I plunge underground.

I wish I'd come upon a dead body, say, which would have been much less awful for me. But let this day be marked down somewhere as the day of days for Daniel Jerusalem. There can't be worse to come, but the day isn't over.

I sit down on the floor of a laundry room filled with brand-new Bendix washers and dryers, all lined up ready for the tenants. The floor is cold and I soon feel numb. I'm staring into space and it makes me wonder if this is how Philip feels when he does that, just stares out at nothing. If you took a piece of string and stretched it from his eyeballs to the point on the wall you think he's staring at, you'd discover he wasn't looking there at all. Vaguely I feel I'm becoming a prisoner to powerlessness. Will I be like my father? I've hated him as far back as I can remember and I thought my anger would protect me, but now some new element lurking in the shadows in the back of my head is making hate less cooperative. Philip seems like a prisoner too.

Amos Standing. Does Philip long to see him every minute and kiss him all over and hold him in his arms in his sleep and waking up kiss him again, and be kissed, oh God yes to be kissed, as I still want Mordy, Mordy who has left me? What happened to Amos Standing? Do they still meet secretly somewhere? Or has he left too, walking away forever? My father is so physically unattractive, but I don't know what Amos looks like. Maybe he's not so hot either. Is Philip as uncomfortable with his body as I am with mine? I sense a growing war between me and me, between the me I want and the me I am. Does Philip have the same problem? Does everyone? I think about all this as I sit on the stone cold floor. Why would Mordy want me? Why would Claudia want me? Why would David want me? Why would *anyone* want me? I'll wind up someday on a sagging bed in a benighted suburb with some unhappy spouse beating me in fury for failing her. Her? Him. Him!

Why am I thinking about Philip and Amos Standing? Why am I not thinking about David Jerusalem in a concentration camp? Because I can't bear thinking about David Jerusalem in a concentration camp. That way lies total despair and madness.

I'm staring up at Arnold Botts. I am sitting backed up, leaning against the cement wall. He is walking closer and closer to me. He has his penknife out. When I move to the left or right, or forward, he feints like a boxer to imprison me.

"If you can do it to Mordy you can do it to me."

Does Arnold Botts shadow the entire world?

"Open your mouth."

His delivers his orders in a low, sinister voice.

"I'm going to put my dick in your mouth, so the faster you open it, the less I'll have to hurt you."

"Didn't you get in enough trouble for lying about Claudia and me fucking?"

His knife darts forward like the tongue of a poisonous snake. I scream and jump up to evade him. But he pushes himself right into me and a streak of blood appears on my arm. I feel the tip of the knife against my stomach.

Just then, just like I'm Pearl White on railroad tracks, Mordy, Billy, Dodo, and Orvid run in, summoned by my scream. They were scouting out the new underground tunnels, too.

Arnold turns to face them, like a hoodlum cornered, his shiv out in front of him as he weaves back and forth. We all circle him. "Why are you defending this pervert and his dirty, filthy, disgusting acts!" He hisses, lunging at me and slashing my other arm, more deeply this time.

"Botts, have you gone crazy?" Dodo yells.

"Not so you could see, you blind Coke bottle!" Arnold spits at Dodo's glasses.

"You want to know from dirty, filthy, disgusting acts!" Mordy yells, grabbing Arnold from behind. "I'll show you dirty acts." And he twists Arnold's arm so that the penknife falls to the floor, to be claimed by the quiet Billy.

Mordy is in command. He's fighting to protect *me*!

Arnold is screaming "Fuck!" and "Shit!" and "Prick!" and "Cunt!" all strung together with our names, but we're a long way from where anyone can hear us. Even so, Billy instinctively puts his palm over Arnold's mouth and Arnold bites him viciously. Then Dodo just yanks Arnold's pants down, and his underpants, too, just tears them right off and hurls them in a ball out the window, which still lacks glass, and into the Masturbov River. Billy then rips off Arnold's shirt and undershirt and pitches them out as well. Orvid, a big, strapping, dirty-blond farm boy whose father works for the Army, holds Arnold's arms while Mordy instructs Billy to take off Arnold's shoes and socks and get rid of them, too. Arnold is stark naked. Orvid pinions him against the cement wall with his back to us. He's actually kind of pretty, arms and legs and trunk in nice proportion, and his behind looks white and soft and round; I wonder if anyone has violated it and made him cry uncle. I'm angry at myself for allowing his pretty nakedness to interfere with what should be my anger at him.

Mordy spins him around, taking his waist like a dancing partner and yanking him away from the wall. Arnold screams holy murder and we see why. We all stare in rude awe. He has an exceedingly tiny penis, more like a little bump. It almost isn't there. Not that we're so accustomed to seeing bigger ones, but we recognize short shrift when we see it. Dodo, who wants to be a scientist, bends closer to study the little thing more critically. He's about to speak when Billy says, "The poor kid."

Arnold, much to eveyone's surprise, collapses in a heap on the floor, almost as if he's fainted. He lies there looking helpless. We stand above him, staring down, less at him than at that little thing and the tiny bit of pubic fuzz around it. I look up to trade glances with Mordy—some sort of conspiratorial exchange that might bring us together—but his eyes stay down.

Arnold's passivity turns to ruse. When he sees our attention is elsewhere, that no enemy arms impale him, he slithers through our legs to make a dash for freedom.

"Oh, no you don't!" Mordy says, tackling him easily. "You don't get away!" We hear Mordy's body go splat against the concrete floor as he gets a hold on Arnold's legs.

Like some grand entrance just before the final curtain, Claudia arrives. She is back, presumably from Switzerland. "I don't like him. I've never liked him. And he's never going to be likable." She says this like the lady of the castle dictating with a wave of her wand that her knights dispose of the unwanted body in the moat. She looks around at all of us. "I just don't want to see it." And she departs.

Billy, Mordy, Dodo, Orvid, and me. Against Arnold. It's hardly a fair match. But when is such a crafty enemy subdued by fairness? We have Arnold pinned to the floor. Five of us to control his thrashing fury. Each of us has part of him in check. Dodo, like a doctor at a patient's bedside, keeps looking at that almost invisible bump. "Have you been to a specialist about this?" he finally asks. "Modern medicine does wonderful things. If it doesn't improve, look me up when I get out of med school." This provokes an awful scream from Arnold. Again Billy clamps a hand over his mouth, only to be bitten again. "Jeez," Billy yells, curling his bleeding hand into a fist and slugging Arnold's jaw. Billy has never done anything like this, and he looks sort of proud. "Good work, Bill," Mordy says. "Thanks," Billy replies. "He's a fairy too! Billy's a fairy too," Arnold screams. "Shut up!" Billy commands, slugging Arnold again, and Arnold, midway into formulating another insult, shuts up. Dodo pokes unbelievingly at Arnold's penis with his fingers, sticking his face in closer, his thick glasses magnifying his eyes. He tries to stretch the penis, but it jumps back like a tiny rubber band. After a few more tugs it begins to get a little bigger. A few more and it begins to have an erection. We all stare at it. It looks like a pencil that's been shortened to a stub. Mordy, who has a knee placed on each of Arnold's shoulders, suddenly leans forward and takes Arnold's tiny erect penis in his mouth. Why is he doing this when he said he didn't want to anymore? And why to Arnold? Does this mean he's got it in his makeup after all? Does this mean he just doesn't want me? Does this mean he's still one of . . . us? Who else is us? Billy? Somehow I doubt it.

I feel my own penis start to get hard as Mordy sucks and sucks, up and down in slurpy spurts. He never did that to me. No, he never did that to me.

Doesn't he care what the others are thinking? What are the others thinking? They're all staring at Mordy with bulbous eyes. Mordy smiles at them when he sees the effect he's having. (It will be a while before I figure out the clue to Mordy: novelty is all. He'll try anything.) When Arnold tries to take advantage of this lull in his captors' concentration and squirm away, Billy tightens his hold on Arnold's ankles, his eyes glued to Mordy's mouth. Dodo hasn't lost his professional expression of "Very interesting." Mordy, coming up for air, stares straight into Billy's stare and clamps his hands on either side of Billy's head, like a vise, pullling it down, slowly, because Billy is resisting, until Billy's mouth is right on Arnold's penis. Billy's lips are locked tight, but Mordy keeps the pressure on the back of Billy's head with one hand while he sticks the fingers of the other into Billy's mouth until the penis goes in. Then he moves Billy's head up and down. After a few up-and-downs, Billy starts to do it on his own, and Mordy relinquishes his tutelage. Arnold has stopped struggling by now and is moaning softly. I guess he's beginning to feel something. Billy performs for a long time. Finally, breathless, he sits up and smiles at Mordy as if he's been dared and has answered the call.

Dodo abruptly springs into action, yanking off his glasses and going down on Arnold now himself. Arnold screams out, "Don't bite me!" and Dodo slurps out, "Sorry," and must have readjusted his mouth and lips because Arnold seems to relax.

It's Orvid Guptl, whom none of us knows much about, who now takes over for the finale that causes all the trouble, not that what went before it wouldn't have been enough for Mrs. Botts.

"I thought you were angry at the guy," he says from the sidelines. "I thought you wanted to teach him a lesson."

Nobody says anything.

"You're just pleasuring him," Orvid continues. "Shit, I wouldn't mind that myself."

"So what do you want to do?" Mordy finally asks.

"Hey, Dodo, get up! Now everybody stand in a circle around little Arnie."

Dodo's head stops bobbing. We all stand up.

"Don't stop!" Arnold yells. When nobody returns, he starts masturbating himself.

"Let him finish," Orvid commands, and we do.

Or try to, but soon Mordy pulls out his penis and starts masturbating too. Billy follows, then Dodo, then me. The only one who doesn't is Orvid, who stands to the side waiting.

One by one, everyone ejaculates, including Arnold. Even Mordy. Everybody's semen shoots all over Arnold, who screams in protest. I'm amazed that Mordy climaxes so quickly; I guess this is all more exciting than being in some distant field with me. Still, it's exciting for me to watch him, and everyone else. I shoot a second after he does, then Billy comes, and Dodo finishes. His penis is actually quite large, and he has as much pubic hair as Ponzo Lombardo, but since he goes to a Catholic school, I haven't had the opportunity of noticing. Billy seems the most polite and well-bred. He uses his handkerchief to wipe himself off, and then he bends to wipe off Arnold.

"Don't do that! Shit!" says Orvid. Billy immediately steps back.

Then Orvid unbuttons his fly and pulls out the strangest penis. It's uncircumcised, with a foreskin that's hugely long and dangles, like a big sloppy sock off a small foot. Almost everyone in gym is circumcised; there are one or two who aren't, but we all have a good idea what we're looking at, and what we're looking at is freaky. We know it's freaky and Orvid knows too, but he's proud of it. He gets a kick out of showing it off. So there's Orvid acting as if he owns the best cock in the world while the rest of us are looking at it as if it belongs in *Ripley's Believe It or Not.* The only person uncritically fascinated is Mordy. (I hear him ask Orvid a few days later if he can take a picture of it.)

Suddenly Orvid urinates on Arnold. All over him. He directs his penis like a fire hose. When Arnold moves his body, Orvid moves his stream. He gets Arnold in his crotch, in his mouth, all over his face and hair, in his eyes. He must have been drinking water for days, because he seems to have an awful lot in him.

Finally he finishes. Arnold is drenched. We're all standing in pools of Orvid's pee, staring down at the concrete basement floor. Arnold appears to be in shock.

There doesn't seem to be anything else to do. One by one we leave. Billy goes first.

"See you."

Then Dodo grunts in departure.

I wait to see if Mordy wants to walk out with me, but he doesn't even look at me, he just leaves.

I give Orvid a weak smile wave and take off. I don't even wonder how

Arnold's going to get home all naked and smelly, or what he's going to tell his folks.

Some dividing line has been crossed but into what kind of territory, I have no idea.

•

Though I'm afraid to go home to the family drama, I want to take a hot shower that will wash me clean of piss and blood. I feel dirty all over. The apartment is deserted, thank God, and I stand under the shower for an eternity, looking into the steam trying to decipher feelings and reactions and discovering only more questions, attempting to sing a few of my usual shower anthems, only to discover that my voice cracks. When I finally step out red as a beet, I find my shower's water has flooded the floor. I stand in it and it's like standing in Orvid's piss. Indeed, the tile on the bathroom floor is a sort of sickly yellow color. I nod my head in understanding at these coincidences. I am talking to myself a lot now. I have a new memory to add to the rest of my life. I use my bath towel to sop up the water.

I walk to the kitchen to get something to eat and I find a note from Rivka taped to the refrigerator. Philip's ulcer started to bleed and she's taken him to the hospital in an ambulance. She'll be back when she can, she says; she's left me some money for food, just in case she has to stay.

The information that my father is bleeding in a hospital passes over me like the hot shower. I pause for a moment to wonder what his death might mean in my life. Since I've been fantasizing about it for so long, it's not a new thought, nor does it summon any new emotions beyond willing acceptance. What I'm really thinking more about is the sight of Orvid pissing on Arnold. And Mordy—Mordy doing everything, egging us on like a cheerleader.

David, wherever you are, you are going to get out! Do you hear me?

It turns out to be just as well that Philip chooses this day to have his hemorrhage, and that Rivka stays with him at Soldiers and Sailors intensive care for a couple of days, because Mrs. Botts has a field day with this one. The next morning, all of us kids are summoned by phone to some lawyer's office. Mordy's there with his father, Abe, who nods a lot but looks uninterested and unsurprised. Billy's parents are high Wasp and buttoned-down. Dodo has obviously been chastised, to judge by his discomfort in sitting down; his parents, his mother wearing an enormous crucifix and his father fingering rosary beads, alternately glare at their son and offer beggarly smiles to the man Mr. Geiseric keeps calling "Avvocato." Neither Orvid nor his parents are present. The lawyer says in a tone of sad regret that Mr. Guptl refused to appear without a legal summons.

Then the lawyer begins a long speech condemning the acts of yesterday afternoon; he states that Mr. and Mrs. Botts do not wish to press charges, though in his estimation they certainly have more than sufficient grounds to do so, and that they will be moving away from Masturbov Gardens shortly—

Abe suddenly grunts. "It's about time. Six notices. They owe six months' rent."

—but they wish us to know that these acts were "very ugly indeed" and have no doubt scarred their "precious, beloved, and peace-loving" son forever. We all want to smirk at this description of Arnold, but we don't. There's something frightening about the lawyer's sanctimoniousness. Is this how justice is dealt out in the grown-up world?

Now Abe speaks up strongly. "I won't have this! That kid is a monster. He destroys property all over the place. You been inside their apartment? No? You should go look. It's a stink bomb. Everything's defaced or broken. Filthy. They live like slobs. They want to use this as an excuse to move away? Good! It's going to take me hundreds of dollars to fix the place up. They want to threaten and accuse my son? Screw that! I piss on all of *them*!" And he grabs Mordy's hand and pulls him out of the office.

The rest of us are about to leave when the lawyer tries to return to the severity of the matter. He reminds us that Mr. Masturbov has changed the subject, the subject being the sexual molestation of a child. Oh, I thought as I walked out in the middle of this sentence, is that what it's about? I'll be sure and remember.

Outside the office, which is in downtown Washington, on Connecticut Avenue, Abe Masturbov turns to me.

"How is your brother Lucas?"

"Fine, I guess. He's going to go to Yaddah Law School in the fall."

"I know. I told him I'd be his first client. Mordecai tells me you weren't bar mitzvahed."

"No. I didn't want to be."

"Why not?"

"I don't believe in God."

He nods. "That is very perceptive of you." He has his limousine take me home after dropping him and Mordy off on Sixteenth Street. Nobody says anything. For the rest of the trip I pretend it's my car, my chauffeur. Going into our apartment brings me back to earth. Masturbov Gardens is the death of any fantasy. For a few days I eat all the cupcakes and doughnuts and candy bars I want. I get sick to my stomach.

I go and visit my father in the hospital. I told you about that visit and all the rain and the mess in our living room and what Philip told us about our not having a last name, not being Jerusalems.

A week later Billy moves to North Carolina. His parents decide Masturbov Gardens is no place to raise a young boy. The problem is that Billy doesn't want to move, so he makes his way back on foot, sleeping who knows where until he comes down with pneumonia and is found dead trying to keep warm in that laundry room behind that Bendix dryer that still isn't connected. No one really knew Billy. He was a small blond kid, quiet and eager to please. Evidently his parents punished him for the Botts debacle by not talking to him and he missed us a lot. So he came back to talk to us. But when he got here, he didn't know where to go, whom to go to, and he was too polite to ask anybody for anything, like food or a warm bed. He was still carrying Arnold's penknife.

When he was found, his body was entirely purple and his anus was mutilated and caked with blood. That's what Arnold Botts said. He found him.

Billy is the first person my own age I know who dies. No, the second. Tibby Chesterfield committed suicide. Well, Billy's the first friend I had whose last name I didn't know.

This seems like the end of childhood. I would say innocence, but what a stupid notion an innocent childhood is, don't you think, Fred? Who thought that one up?

And if I'm not a Jerusalem, who am I?

WHAT'S COMING NEXT

Yes, the war is going on and people are killing each other all over the place. Yes, of course that's important. Yes, but more important is what's going on to facilitate the killing of many millions more. Yes, it's all coming closer and we're not talking about the war. There will not be nearly enough of us dead from just a war. Wars don't always kill enough of the right people. Now, as with so many seminal events in history, Major Important Things are happening, many of which are not going to be discovered until some future date, if ever. A perfect case in point is David's story, which follows next in our chronology, although David will not share it with anyone for many years.

DAVID'S WAR

Our father was awful to Daniel. He yelled at him and called him names. He called him a sissy in front of people. Sometimes he hit him. He never talked to him like he talked to me, like a son. He never talked to him like a human being. Philip either ignored him or yelled at him at the top of his lungs. Philip was only interested in me. Lucas and Stephen could see this. They had little interest in me because they didn't like Philip much, or Rivka either. I think all my brothers felt I was not on their side. I wanted to be. I wanted to be part of their closeness. I just didn't know how. I only knew how hard it was to live and feel like this.

I can remember Philip taking me in his arms when I was still a baby. I can remember his warmth and his love and his kisses all through my childhood. One day he asked me, "If I could arrange for us to go away and live all by ourselves, away from your mother and your brothers and your twin, perhaps never to see them again, but we would always have each other, would you like that?" I was six years old. I had nothing else. Philip was the only one who loved me. I said yes.

When he took me with him to Berlin he entered me in swimming contests. I was an excellent swimmer, as I'd I discovered when I was three years old. I accidentally fell into a pool. Rivka screamed but I instinctively started paddling. I loved it. I paddled to the other side of the pool and before she could yank me out I turned and flapped myself back. I was laughing.

My father was proud of me. He had me taking lessons at the Jewish Center in no time. I won my first race when I was four. The other contestants were all between six and twelve.

Daniel didn't like my new skill. I don't think he was jealous. I think he was afraid of losing me. I certainly was afraid of losing him. At night we slept together and hugged each other close. He would come into my bed. I was too shy to go into his. He was smarter and nicer. Everyone liked him. I seem to have different insides in me. They are full of suspicion. Daniel believes everything will work out. I believe nothing will, and I don't expect it to. Nobody liked me. Nobody liked Philip either. I assume that's why we were close. Daniel never wanted to come swimming with me.

Philip and I would go for long walks around Masturbov Gardens and into the country. One day he started talking to me in German. It made me laugh. The words sounded funny. "This is how I learned German from my mother. We made it a game." He got me to repeat what he said. It became our secret. At first that I was learning it at all. And then our secret language that we could speak to each other when no one was around. It made me feel important to have my own language with my father.

I went to the Jewish Center every chance I could. Lucas and Stephen played basketball there, or Philip would take me in the evenings or on weekends. I swam until I was exhausted. I loved to swim underwater particularly, making myself go faster and faster beneath the surface to the far end, coming up only when my lungs said I must. Only then would I reluctantly surface, gulp every bit of air I could without losing my rhythm, and go under again. I would do this over and over. Until I swam my last race in Berlin I won every race I was ever in.

The Jews of Berlin were well organized athletically. Grandma Zilka had written to some distant relations and they all came to watch me win my races, even though she'd gone back to America. Philip discovered there was a Jewish Junior Olympics at the same time as the regular world Olympics. The winner got a gold medal and a chance to compete in the All-City, Jews and gentiles together. Father was eager for his American son to show these Germans up. This would be the last race Jews were allowed to swim in.

Some of our relations were being moved into different neighborhoods. There were people crossing the city day and night. I wasn't accustomed to big cities, so I didn't question these movements. Philip's friends lived in big houses in rich neighborhoods. These were the people I spent my time with. I was only seven, and who talks about such things to children?

I won both big races, the Jewish Olympics and the All-City. Since I was younger by far than any of the other contestants I became a little celebrity. My photograph was in the newspapers. I was interviewed on the radio. That I could now speak German made me more of a novelty. Other children asked for my autograph.

At the Jewish Olympics I met Pieter. He congratulated me with a smile that told me he meant it. That never happened in America, where people got angry at you when you beat them. We became friends. He showed me around his Berlin. His school. His house. His grandparents' house where he was born. His family was rich. We looked a little alike. We both had blond hair and blue eyes. Even though we were the same size, he was older. I could see in the locker room that he was already growing hair around his penis. When I stayed overnight at his house he told me that he was ashamed of this, and of being so short.

"I'm a freak!" he said, with tears in his eyes.

I put my arms around him. "No, you're not," I said.

One day we're waiting for the Jewish swimming pool to open when a man pulls Pieter and me out of line. We're frightened and hold on to each other. The man says he prefers identical twins but fraternal twins will do. We're taken to a clinic of some sort. When we're alone in a small examining room he tells us in a kind voice that he is Dr. Grodzo and he hopes to prove that physical and psychological characteristics are inherited. He tries to explain further but it goes over our heads. He asks us if we love each other. We are silent. "But do not brothers, particularly twin brothers, love each other?" I catch on. "Yes, we love each other very much. Isn't that always the way with twins?" And I take Pieter's hand and give him a big kiss on his cheek. Dr. Grodzo laughs. Pieter catches on.

Grodzo makes us strip. When we're naked he says sternly, "You must tell me why your twin brother, who talks so little, has hair around his penis and you do not." I want to cry. I don't know how to lie yet. "I guess I'm backward," I try to joke. "Yes, you must be backward." The doctor smiles. I feel sick to my stomach from the horrible smell everywhere. No one has given us anything to eat. I'm shaking because I have no idea what's happening except that I know I'm not safe. When Grandma Zilka first disappeared, I was taken to a police station and men with the same brown shirt as Dr. Grodzo were unpleasant. "Don't be upset, little one," Grodzo says. He gives us chocolates. Pieter refuses his. Dr. Grodzo takes me and Pieter in his arms. "We are a threesome. We are a family," he says, hugging us tightly. "Come, lie down." He takes us into another room. We are still naked. He lays us side by side on a wooden platform so that he can examine us more closely. "So one of you has pubic hair and one of you does not and you are Jewish fraternal twins and so we must try to discover what has happened to you." Here he pulls my penis. "And to you." He pinches Pieter's penis. "We must discover how you are different when you are meant to be alike."

He leaves us. The room is cold and the platform is hard and uncomfortable. Pieter and I cling to each other. "Help me, help me," he sobs. "No, no, not here." I put my hand over his mouth.

A flashlight wakes us up. Pieter and I have fallen asleep in each other's arms. "So you are lovebirds too," Dr. Grodzo says. His expression is very stern. "This is not right. But perhaps for the history of science and medicine it is good that I am noticing your affection for each other. I must discover if you love each other because you are twins or because you are homosexuals." A nurse comes in pushing a cart with instruments on it. I don't know what a homosexual is.

Several guards bring in four older twins. They're naked too. They're ordered to hold us down. They're shaking so much that a guard slaps one of them across his face. Overhead lights suddenly make the room like day. I now see there are perhaps a dozen sets of twins in beds around the room, all shivering in fear. They are all ordered to stand around our platform. "Do you not notice, David, that these twins are identically developed? Both twins in each set have pubic hair, or do not. Except you. I must understand you more thoroughly." Men in white coats now circle our platform too.

Pieter screams out violently. Dr. Grodzo drops Pieter's penis and his scrotum into a bowl. Pieter's crotch is a pool of blood. I don't faint like a few of the other twins do. I lie there beside Pieter. I watch Dr. Grodzo watching me.

The nurse hands Dr. Grodzo an enormous needle with thick thread. He sticks his hands into Pieter's bloody pool and starts to stitch up his flesh. Pieter has lost consciousness. I hope he's dead. "I am making Pieter into a woman," Dr. Grodzo says. "I am giving him a hole." One of the guards vomits on the table while Dr. Grodzo finishes sewing. Pieter's crotch looks like raw liver. Dr. Grodzo roughly lifts me up and puts me facedown on top of Pieter. "Now you must fuck your sister," he orders me. What does he mean? I lie there not moving. He grabs my waist and lifts me up and down against Pieter. I feel our crotches sticking together. Many of the boys are crying loudly.

"Bring me Heimat," Dr. Grodzo orders. I will learn that Heimat is one of the camp idiots. He walks around with a constant erection. He wasn't an idiot when he arrived. He was kind and gentle.

A guard pulls me off Pieter and shoves Heimat into my place. Heimat pumps away. He's laughing like a baby playing in a bathtub. He pumps and pumps until he screams out happily and pulls out from Pieter. He sits up on the table, looking sad. He is looking down at his bloodied penis, which is still erect. He hits it to try to make it go down. Strings of white semen connect him to Pieter like a cobweb. Dr. Grodzo pushes Heimat aside and sucks up liquid from Pieter's hole with a large syringe. "For my specific protein studies," he says to me. I've been holding Pieter's hand but it's let go of mine. Please, God, let him be dead.

Dr. Grodzo takes my arm and injects me with Pieter's blood. I am numb so I don't seem to mind whatever he is doing.

The guards who have vomited have been taken outside. I hear them being shot.

•

I believe I am eight years old. I no longer know how long I have been here. By now Dr. Grodzo knows I am American. He speaks perfect English. "Dr. Mengele and I have been to America many times." He tells me there are three kinds of camps. The first is the ghetto, where unwanteds are isolated, "for the time being." The second is the labor camp, which "is far away where they cannot be seen, is just what it says, a place where harsh physical labor is imposed rigorously without stopping." Then there is the concentration camp, where everything is devoted to torment and extermination. Mungel is one of these. I am in Mungel. It is near to Drensk, where Grandma Zilka was born and where Dr. Grodzo will tell me that she died. We are just outside Berlin, although I will not know this for many years to come. By now my body is scarred from the many needles and experiments they have performed on it. My back is particularly bumpy and feels like my favorite corduroy pants I used to wear to school. It looks worse, my back, than it ever felt, whatever they are doing to it.

When Dr. Grodzo believes any of his twins are homosexual he sends one or both of them for special experiments. He wants to find out what causes homosexuality and he wants to find out how to get rid of what causes it. He invites me to have dinner with him one evening because he wants to explain these experiments to me. His quarters are located in a distant part of Mungel, requiring a long ride in an automobile with armed guards. I live in a tiny room in a dormitory where the twins are kept. I have my own room. No one else has his own room. He lives in a very nice brick house with a garden. Rivka would have admired the furnishings.

"I believe it is thought that camps are only to kill people. Camps are the laboratories where changes in human nature are tested."

He talks to me as if I am a grown-up and can understand everything he says. I have not been a participant in a lot of these experiments. But I have been made to watch most of them, placed in front of them to see what is going on. I am also aware that a long line of people is always walking slowly past the room where I sleep. The window is high and barred and the glass is thick, so I can only hear them slowly marching, and their crying. I can't see them but I can feel them through the wall. I know they are there and I know that for some reason I am not with them.

I have watched Grodzo in action day and night and I have watched him watch me watch him. I have watched everyone I have met here disappear.

He has demonstrated the effects of electricity pumped into a body. "Will this locate the cause of your homosexuality?" He is looking at me as the boy screams and tries to break loose from his restraints. "Will this kill homosexual cells?" The boy has fainted. I have seen him "washing the bladder" and "massaging the rectum." I have witnessed several "lobotomies." I watched him drill into skulls. I watched as twins were sewn together back to back, or face to face. I watched as eyes were removed and sorted by color. He removes many testicles, dropping them all into the same large container. He removes whole bowels. I have watched him attach electric prods to every part of a body, particularly penises. I have seen semen from many injected into many others. I have watched as bodies were inoculated "with various strains from all over the world." I have received a number of these inoculations myself. He talks out loud to me, explaining what he is doing. I have watched as bodies died on the table and were taken away to an incinerator. I have watched as many "medicines" were administered, by mouth, by needle, by enema. Many bodies go into spasms and die. Rarely does a body lie down on a table and get up from it alive.

Boys are made to masturbate all the time. Semen is collected at all hours. If someone fails to ejaculate often enough he is taken away and shot. Doctors watch everything without expression. There are many other doctors and nurses. I begin to notice that often there are bulges in the guards' trousers when they watch Grodzo at work.

There are no female twins. They have their own building. "Dr. Mengele is more interested in the female and I am more interested in the male," Dr. Grodzo tells me.

During every act I witness I feel him looking at me, studying me, as if he wants me to learn quickly. Once he says, "This is what life is all about." Another time he says, "I am happy to be your teacher."

"What is going on here at Mungel is evil," he told me at that first dinner in his house. "You do not know much about evil yet. You have only seen it. Evil comes about when hate becomes so strong that no longer can it be contained. Each instance of evil is like a new strain of poison from a virus that was thought to have been tamed. But it escapes and grows. It becomes increasingly *actual*. It becomes its own event. If you know what you are looking at, it is an amazing thing to witness. Properly done, it inspires deeds and accomplishes them. What you have witnessed thus far reflects only a certain amount of what interests us here. One can learn only so much from cutting off penises. We have come to a certain end of the road with what our experiments reveal to us. We must locate a way to move faster toward the more useful knowledge that is awaiting us. That is what research doctors do."

I realize that I understood what he was saying. It had not occurred to me to question how and why his English was so good. He told me he had visited America often. "I toured when I was a Brownshirt. I should like to live there someday. I do not believe the pressures put upon one are so extreme."

I was fed beef with a delicious sauce for dinner, and chocolate ice cream with melted chocolate over it. I did not know that food could be so fine. It was brought to us by handsome young men in tuxedos who would not look me in the eye.

"Do you believe that there could be such a thing as a particular gene or germ you are carrying that makes you infect others with what you have or what you are?" he asked me with excitement, looking directly into my eyes, as if he might still find an answer there, inside me. "No, of course you do not have any idea how to answer such a question. Just know that you are of particular interest to me. You are Jewish and homosexual and of course a twin. Although I did not believe that young man was your brother, it is no longer important to me. You say you are a twin and I believe you. And there are other reasons to be interested in you."

I still did not know what a homosexual is, much less how he knew I was one.

After dinner he stood up and took my hand. "I find you quite sympathetic, which is unusual for me. I have never been personally interested in a young boy before, most especially a Jew. Jews have different kinds of bodies, different kinds of bone structure. And of course different kinds of brains and different kinds of minds and thoughts. All this interests me. You are going to live here with me. You are going to be treated well and studied carefully. You have my promise that you will be kept alive. You fascinate me because what you witness does not frighten you or make you ill. This is what Mr. Hoover told me. You also appear to have a remarkable tolerance for witnessing cruelty, a tolerance equal to mine. What has happened to either of us that we should be this resilient, in the face of the horrid tribulations of others? What a gift to humanity it would be to the world if we could find out! Do you understand me at all?"

I did not.

•

I don't know how long I lived with him. I had no sense of time. I had been put to sleep many times. My arms were sore from needles and my body continued to be covered with more spots and scars. All this time Dr. Grodzo studied me carefully. He measured and calibrated every part of my body, sometimes from day to day. His hands were very gentle. Then he neatly made entries in a journal. He seemed particularly concerned with my head, my skull, which he would hold between his palms as he searched for any changes. He would smile when he finished. Once he said, "I cannot believe such excellence in a Jew." Once he took me to a room filled with skulls lined up on shelves and tables. They all looked alike to me but he pointed out one table. "These are the perfect ones. Here is where your skull would be."

I would wake up in the middle of the night and find him staring down at my body. He would hold my penis and try in vain to make his get hard. One night he masturbated me until I had my own erection for the first time. He didn't explain the shivers I had, or anything, as he usually did when with me. When a tiny bit of hair began to show on my legs, under my arms, around my penis, he shaved it and sent it away for study. Periodically he would carefully collect my bowel movements and urinations. He was always very affectionate toward me. He performed on me like a housewife doing pleasant chores. He kissed me often, though never on my lips. He would study his own skin constantly, to see if he was catching anything from me. "No, not yet," he would say, smiling. "We can stay together a little longer." We were sleeping in the same bed now, both of us naked. I came to realize that his body was not unattractive. He was not circumcised and his foreskin was long. He explained these differences to me. He would put his fingers on my eyelids and close them. "Shhhh," he would say. "Go back to sleep." Then he would kiss me good night again.

Each morning and each afternoon I was taken to a classroom where a woman taught me the subjects I would have learned in school, mathematics and science and literature, even philosophy and history. She was a very good teacher. I could see that she was a prisoner by her number and her Jewish star. She was terrified of me and fearful that she would say or do something to provoke the guards. One day, like almost everyone, she was no longer there. There was a new teacher for me. Over the years I had a number of other teachers, always very smart and always shaking as they replaced the one before, but that first one was the best. Much later I would see photographs of world-famous scientists who died in Mungel. I recognized several of them as my teachers. I am indebted to this strange group of schoolteachers for whatever formal education I have. It will turn out to be a far better education than I would ever have received in America.

As I get older I'm taught higher forms of mathematics and science and chemistry. Grodzo helps me with my homework. He is a doctor and a surgeon but he is a chemist most of all. When we work on my chemistry assignments I can tell from his excitement how much he loves it. He says he dreams that after the war he will invent medicines. "I believe that medicines can be invented to accomplish almost anything!" He will not talk about his life before Mungel but he makes me talk. He is constantly interviewing me about my family, about all my relatives, about everyone's health and physical characteristics. We were never a close family and I didn't know many relatives. This doesn't stop him from trying to get me to remember things. He is particularly interested in everyone's teeth. It will be discovered years later that Dr. Mengele was obsessed with teeth because his own were bad and he was ashamed of them.

We live a very orderly life. I am at school much of the day and when I return he makes our dinner. He enjoys cooking and is good at it. Then we do my homework. And then we go to bed. It's cold at night, so it's good to have a warm body to sleep with.

Never will he talk about what we both know is going on elsewhere in Mungel. On many days and nights, even where we are located, the sounds are hard to ignore and the smells can become awful. The names Adolf Hitler and Josef Mengele are never heard. Dr. Mengele is not at Auschwitz, which hasn't opened yet. Whether he was here at Mungel I don't know.

I am put to work as an assistant to Dr. Nyiszli. He's a surgeon. He's a British Jewish prisoner too. His job is to do autopsies on all the twins Dr. Grodzo thinks are homosexual. There are hundreds of sets of twins in Mungel. Each day guards wheel dozens of dead bodies in on flat carts and place each set of twins on a white marble slab with channels for the blood to drain into holes in the concrete floor. Then Dr. Nyiszli begins his work. As he carefully enters each body he dictates his findings to me and I type them. He talks out loud to me as he works, like Grodzo does. There are always guards with us, but never the same ones. It is hard for many of them to do this duty and they are often taken away in the middle of the day.

Grodzo says to me over dinner one night, "Pay attention, for there is much you can learn from autopsies. I am always amazed by autopsies. Bodies opened and exposed reveal subtle and grotesque transformations. Ghastly cancers perforate tubes and organs. These are part of the mystery that causes death. We always want to know what causes death. Autopsies can be our key to finding out why we die."

Dr. Nyiszli works quickly. "It is important that these twins have died at the same approximate time. Otherwise we would not be able to compare them accurately. These bodies have been killed by different means just before they come to me. Most of them have been gassed to death. Their skin falls from their bones most easily. Some of them have been shot in the back of the head. Their bodies are the most tense. And some of them have been killed by injections of chloroform into their hearts." He points to the tiny dot. "Many of these young men had syphilis." He shows me the tumors in their hearts.

Once in a while someone who was shot is still alive. We hear a groan or see a movement in the pile of waiting bodies. Dr. Nyiszli injects their hearts so death comes. Then he teaches me how to do it, explaining that we are giving this one a gift by helping him finally to die.

Dr. Nyiszli dissects them quickly. He studies them with great care. There are receptacles for all the parts he removes. Brains. Throats. Tongues. Lungs. Hearts. He washes them. He studies them closely. He throws them in their buckets. He studies penises and testicles particularly.

One day I am allowed to help him. Grodzo comes to watch. I make the initial incisions myself. Blood spurts all over me and down my body's side and into the channel below. I remove the lungs of a young man who is going through puberty like I am. I remember when Dr. Grodzo had first said this word. I can feel him watching me intently, but I'm used to that by now. "I am proud of you," he says. That night he finally gets an erection with me and inserts it into my rectum until he has an orgasm, as do I.

But mostly I type reports. They're for the Biological, Racial, and Evolutionary Institute and they must be neat. I ask Dr. Nyiszli again if he sees anything different in the bodies classified as homosexual. He does not answer. I help him do more than two hundred autopsies.

Twin boys lying side by side in each other's arms make me think of Daniel often.

I work for Dr. Nyiszli for a long time. And then he, too, is gone. After the war I learn that Dr. Miklós Nyiszli went to work for Dr. Josef Mengele at Auschwitz. He wrote a book about it: *Auschwitz: A Doctor's Eyewitness Account.* In it he does not discuss his work on homosexuals prior to Auschwitz, at Mungel.

●

One night after dinner Grodzo stands up and takes my hand. "I shall not see you for a while. You are a smart young man now. I hope one day you will appreciate how fortunate you have been. I am sorry you must go out into a world that hates you so much."

He has tears in his eyes.

"You may wonder why I remain a true believer. A true believer in what, you have every right to ask me. In almost every town and village of my country you will find some kind of prison or concentration camp or labor camp, all indeed death camps, all until very recently filled to capacity. We are finished here for the moment.

"You will now be sent out to see 'the real world.' You will be sent on the next part of your journey, where you will find the world no different from what you have seen here.

"Your father's files are filled with interviews of dying people. That has been his job for many years. He does not know it but his ability in this area has become well-known in certain quarters. His reports are excellent and moving. He has a gift for this particular work. We hope he has many years left to do it. There is a world filled with people burdened by the awful experiences of their lifetimes. To record misery and unhappiness on the widest possible scale is a necessary task. There really are few happy memories, and those who delude themselves with them must be shown how little there is to believe in. That is the true state of man. I hope you have learned that here. That is what we have been teaching the world. That will be our lasting legacy.

"Some will think that you have been spared. And so you have. You have been dealt with in a different way. You are being ushered into strength. When we meet again perhaps I can tell you more. Perhaps we shall know more by then. If any of us are still alive."

With that, Grodzo leaves and the next thing I know I am being taken to a bunker. There is a network of them all over the country so that you can go underground from one place to another. The German leaders have been expecting trouble, so years ago they began preparing for it. The rooms in the bunker are not unlike prison cells but they are not for prisoners. They are for important people. I sense as I walk down endless corridors that I am in the presence of some great frightening power waiting behind these walls.

Hankl, the man who's escorting me, asks me if I would like to stay here. "Why, should I want to?"

A few minutes later he says, "You would be safe here."

That night I leave the bunker and walk out into the dark streets of some place I don't know. Just being outside makes me conscious suddenly of the many years I've been inside.

Light is dim. I'm tired. I can't remember when I've had a peaceful night's sleep. Not sleeping enough can leave me unprepared for whatever the daylight may do to me. I am feeling something else. When you're isolated and alone, it's difficult to be angry. I'm beginning to feel I should be angry. My stomach aches as always. My stomach will ache for the rest of my life.

Grodzo told me someone would meet me at the gate. Someone is following me. I stop and wait for him. It's a boy my own age. I've seen him on the inside, always in the distance. I don't think he was a prisoner but I don't think he was free. There were a number of people in this category. Like me. There were different levels of torture and of prisoners, of participation.

I greet him and try to get him to talk. He shakes his head. I don't know if this means he can't talk or won't talk or won't talk yet but he stays with me and I let him. He's handsome, and he would be more handsome still if there wasn't such sadness in his face. When I ask him how he got out, he just looks at me. I look back at him and realize he's beautiful to me. He reaches out suddenly and grabs me in his arms. We kiss and I feel another boy's lips and tongue. There's an air raid going on around us but we don't seem to notice all the people running for shelter. We're in a field kissing and discovering each other's penis. We're crying out uncontrollably, as if our bodies are acting on their own. And then we realize what we're doing is good. Neither of us understands anything, but for these moments we think we do and we smile in happiness. Indeed, we laugh out loud. Then he tells me his name is Klaus.

•

During my years in Mungel I knew I was being watched, and not just by Grodzo. There was a small windowed room in the back of my classroom where faces could be seen watching through it. In fact, there are observation rooms in much of the camp. I always tried to see if and when anyone had come to look at me. Perhaps my father. Perhaps Mr. Standing. Or their friend Brinestalker. Once, I saw Mr. Hoover. He nodded a tiny bit as if to say, Not now. Tonight, as I'm seeing the dawn of the city with my new friend, a man appears from some basement's rubble. I recognize his face, from watching me through that window. He pulls us apart, me and my new friend. Then he takes me aside and talks to me very sternly.

"I've come to lead you out of this collapsing city. Don't you remember me? I'm your father's friend, Amos Standing. No, I am your father's lover. You probably don't know what that means. It means we love each other and can't bear to be separated as we are now. He's gone back home, to his wife and to your brothers. I want you to know this because our trip will be dangerous and if something happens to us, it's information that both your father and I want you to have."

As if to underline this, more airplanes fly overhead and drop more bombs. Immediately there are more giant fires. He grabs me to him.

Amos Standing is an ordinary-looking man. I remember that about him now, from having seen him with my father and Mr. Brinestalker just after we arrived. You couldn't pick him out in a crowd. But I can see he has become much older-looking than when we were all together at Wannsee.

"The Brits have been bombing Berlin regularly. Hitler has decided it's time to evacuate nonessential people, which means you and me. He sees what is happening. Hamburg is almost destroyed. Half of Berlin has been destroyed. He is not a person to trust even when things go well. Tomorrow he could change his mind and we could both wind up in a camp. You must not stay with this young man. He has run away from Hitler."

I go and take Klaus's hand and won't let go. Mr. Standing shrugs and we walk to a gigantic film studio that's withstood the bombing. Mr. Standing calls it UFA. "It's the biggest film studio outside Hollywood." The place is scattered with scenery for movies waiting to be filmed. "Everyone who was anyone worked here," Mr. Standing says. "Ulrike Ferme, Lotte Weimar, Lauritz Lorengau, even Greta Garbo." Then he explains that the studio is still set up for the filming of the story of Sodom and Gomorrah, which he outlines to me in a way that I don't understand. He tells me he's worked here on many movies. "It was a part of my job." He takes us on a tour. The hanging dead bodies aren't real, he tells us. Most of these "dead" people are dressed in leather and chains, and wear masks and carry whips. Penises and breasts are naked. There are naked people piled on top of each other everywhere. Mr. Standing says it's all meant to convey "debauchery and eroticism," two words he defines for me. After all I've seen these past years, it seems almost funny. When I say so, he laughs loudly.

"Oh, my dear young David, you will do just fine."

Klaus doesn't understand why we're laughing. Mr. Standing doesn't understand why Klaus is still here. "Leave us alone," he snaps, and Klaus goes off into the studio's darkness. There are many places to hide inside this place.

"Don't be cruel to Klaus," I say, but Mr. Standing has been called away by an assistant who appears out of nowhere.

I walk on. I trip over a body. It's an old man with a full white beard and watery eyes, and he's alive.

"Sit down and talk to me. I am waiting to die and God is not taking me. I pray He will. You do not recognize me, I am certain. My name is Gotz, Stiller Gotz. I know who you are. I have heard about you. You are the American boy who remained unharmed at Mungel. Someone special protects you. Do you know who it is?"

I admit I do not. The thought hasn't occurred to me.

"How can you know so little? Have you no opinion of what you have seen and endured?"

I admit again that I do not.

"Then I have no hope for you, young man, as a human being."

My eyes fill with tears. After all this time of questioning nothing in case something worse happened to me, this old man makes me cry. He, too, takes me into his arms.

"There, there, my child, sudden safety, or something that is perceived as safety, can do this to you. Now that you are free you must promise henceforth you will look at everything directly and ask yourself, 'What is going on here?' Will you promise me this?"

I nod uncomprehendingly. I ask him why he's here.

"I was directing the greatest film this studio ever made. It is destroyed now in all this rubble. Each visit by the Royal Air Force destroys more of our culture and heritage. I will stay here to die with it. Five years we were shooting this film. Until this month of November 1943, fifteen years of work is destroyed in a few nights and days. I directed a cast of twenty-seven hundred actors." He grabs my hand, pulls himself up with great effort, and leads me to the canteen, which is filled with boys my own age, all eating canned goods right out of the tins.

"These children have been brought here from Golsterhauf, my ancestral family home just inside the French border. The French are as repellent as the Germans. These sweet harmless youngsters were imprisoned there because they were students in my theatrical school and because they were . . . not masculine enough. I left two hundred sweet young men in Golsterhauf dead. Imagine murdering youngsters because they bend their wrists the wrong way. These you see here are all I could lead away. We shall all be dead soon enough."

I notice Mr. Standing and Klaus sitting at a table, apparently deep in conversation. Gotz follows my gaze.

"Everyone knows who the pretty youngster is. He is one of Hitler's boyfriends. I cannot imagine how he escaped. The situation must be very dire in the Führer's bunker. I wonder if the Americans are near. They certainly have been taking their time. They are probably fucking all the women along the way. Women are so desperate for men they even jump on the enemy's soldiers. People are so desperate for any kind of affection they fuck strangers anywhere. In the hallways of the packed hotels. In the subway cars. In the air raid shelters. No one cares if they are witnessed. The Americans must hurry or everyone will have syphilis by the time they free us. The Russian soldiers will be worse and it is said there are more of them. Most of these boys that you will see here have syphilis, so be careful.

"Your people own this country already, so you should come and get us and take us to America and truly get your money's worth. I would be most happy to direct a film in Hollywood. You do not know that America owns Germany? It is true. Many of your richest people have been investing in us for years. They thought we were going to win the war. They want us to win the war. Can you imagine that? Our studio here is run by Americans. From Hollywood. Your friend over there. We are part of an industry controlled by I.G. Farben, the most frightening business in the entire world. How do I know this? Because I am the son who knows too much and must run away. I do not expect to live to tell what little pieces of truth I know. I tell everyone with the hope that they will float in a magic bottle to tell the world the whole hideous truth of the hatred that is Deutschland. But there are too many little pieces of truth, blowing too fast in the wind and too far and wide in the land to be gathered up. There is no direct journey to truth. I do not know why I even raise the possibility. Germany will never be capable of truth. Promise you will try to remember what I say and that you will tell what you remember to whomever you can if you ever get out of this prison that was once a great country. My name is not Gotz. That is my masquerade name, my runaway name. My name is Schmitz. My father is Hermann Schmitz. He is the head of I.G. Farben, the largest chemical company in the world. It manufactures everything that is bad. The gas in the ovens is I.G. Farben gas. One day no one will remember the name Schmitz. The bad history is always erased. Without Schmitz there would have been no Hitler. Without Ford and Rockefeller and National City Bank and Chase Bank and Standard Oil and DuPont and Alcoa and Dow and IBM and . . . there would have been no Hitler. Do you have a court of law to condemn your industrialists for treason against their own country? Without them there would be no Schmitz. Particularly Henry Ford. Because of Ford they all climbed on board. Ford convinced them that Germany would win and to place bets on both sides just in case. Henry Ford would destroy any place on earth as long as there was a Jew still living in it. The world will never know or believe this, that Henry Ford hates Jews even more than Hitler does. That there should be a God who gives the miracle of the automobile so everyone can drive around to say hello to everyone else, that this miracle comes from such a monster! When the war is over everything I am telling you will be buried just as I will have been buried, under all this rubble, with my masterpiece that will never be made or seen. Why does no one know that without my own father, without these American companies, this war could not have been waged, the nightmare dreams of this monster could not have been made real? That is not too much to remember. All your Jewish people have been murdered by my father, Herr Hermann Schmitz, and my father's company, I.G. Farben, and my father's mad puppet, Herr Adolf Hitler, and their friend your Mr. Henry Ford. I repeat it and repeat it. Every bit of evidence will have long since been destroyed. Can you remember? I do not want to hear your answer." He has seen Mr. Standing coming toward us. He moves off quickly into the jumbled scenery of his unmade film.

"I see you have met our crazy man," Mr. Standing says. "There are a lot of crazy people wandering around everywhere spouting insane messages."

"He said he was a famous film director."

"Well, he was that."

"Did you work with him here?"

"That is a long story I will tell you at a more propitious time and in a more suitable place. But yes. I ran this studio for Mr. Adolf Hitler."

"And my father helped you?"

"No, your father's hands are clean. That is enough for you to know for now."

•

That nighttime there is a wild party. Dozens of costumed young men appear out of the cracks, their faces and bodies painted crazily. They make me laugh. Gotz rushes among them, trying to embrace them all. "It is too late for me to make you a star," he cries as he kisses one after another. They lift him up and parade him around. They sing rousing songs from their film. I didn't know such fun existed. When the music becomes soft and romantic I find myself in Klaus's arms as we move in time to the music. The other boys are all kissing one another. Klaus kisses me. Mr. Standing comes to separate us. "I do not think it wise, David, for you to continue this friendship." He pulls me brutally away from my new friend. I don't like this, and when I make it known Mr. Standing slaps me hard across my face. "You don't know what you are talking about!" He pushes me out of this room of dancing and fun and yanks me along until we're back in the small room where we've been waiting for someone who doesn't come. "You must trust me. If it weren't for me you'd be dead. There is no one else to lead you to freedom except me." He doesn't let me out of his sight from now on.

He tells me the next morning that in the night two SS men had come to take Klaus back to Hitler.

"Don't ever think that you'll be safe anywhere, perhaps for the rest of your life."

"What do you mean?" I find myself grabbing him. "I thought I was free now. And that you'd come to save me."

He grabs me in return. "I'm sorry. We must hold on to each other. We will get back to our country and find our new lives."

There is much confusion from the party. A bomb, several bombs have ignited in the studio and Gotz has been set on fire and is now dead.

"I don't think it was an accident," Mr. Standing says softly, still holding me. I feel him shiver. It occurs to me that he must know as much as Gotz and perhaps there will be an accident to set us on fire as well. I am amazed to realize this doesn't terrify me as it does him. I am used to being frightened, so much so that it makes me not frightened. I have been told this now several times. I wonder what use this will have for me.

•

The planes come throughout the night to bomb again and again. We are forced out into the darkness. The studio isn't safe. I try to watch as it goes up in flames but Mr. Standing picks me up and carries me. He's bigger and stronger than I thought. As he dodges great pieces of destroyed buildings and roadway he breathlessly mumbles things about my father. He tells me that he and Father have been lovers for many years, since they were young men at college. He tells me Father is afraid to leave Mother and come live with him, even though he's miserable at home with her and my brothers, who ignore him. He tells me how tender my father is in bed when they make love. He has tears in his eyes. He tells me that safety is still a long way away but he will get me back to America.

"Isn't this the end of the war?"

"Good heavens, no. Not by a long shot. The Brits fly over and do this to us every week."

"Then why are we free to go?"

"Because I asked Hitler to let us go now."

Then he suddenly starts to cry.

"I tell you this because if we don't live I beg your forgiveness in Heaven. You have been here because of me. When your father threatened to go back to America, I was so afraid he was leaving me for good that I went crazy. I had you kidnapped from your grandmother and abducted to Mungel, where I could keep an eye on you. I knew Dr. Grodzo, and he promised to watch over you in exchange for an American visa. And Philip left me anyway. He said he had to check up on things at home and would be right back. Now, of course, he can't come here and let us hope we can still get there. Your own father left you because my love frightened him. But when I went to get you, I couldn't get you out. Mungel had been transformed, almost overnight. All avenues of escape from Germany were closed, even for me. I was stranded here too. Hitler had me at UFA making his propaganda films. I'm talking like a crazy man, trying to tell you everything in ten minutes. I work for Hitler. I've been in charge of what we in America call his public relations. I really work for an American company run by a man named Ivy Lee who took care of Hitler personally. I was his protégé, Ivy Lee's, but now he's died and I've had no instructions from America. His work with Hitler was his secret. Now it's mine, and it's never good to be alone with such a secret."

And then he mumbles over and over again into my neck.

"If I don't get you home will you forgive me? Will you? Will your father forgive me? If I don't get you home. Safely. To Philip. You do love Philip, don't you? As I do? Why did he leave us here? I want to go home. Like you."

Now he is bawling. Bombs and explosions and huge bonfires punctuate every word and thought and moment. How are we ever going to get out of here? He is acting like a big sissy.

DAME LADY HERMIA BLEDD-WRENCH LAUNCHES *MY HISTORY OF EVIL*

With some trepidation, I fear it is time for me to take further hold of our history. Young David's history should alert us all to the necessity of this, of *focus*, of *direction*. I know that British Greeting wants its history of UC, that Hadriana Totem wants hers as well, and that Fred also expects something erudite and convincing from us all. But I now see that this one must be for me. I don't believe I've ever written anything for me. Everything has always been to please or convince or educate someone else. Am I saying I am un-educated in evil? I confess I am. Everyone is. It is time to rectify this failing, if only for myself. Did not Virginia Woolf say that the best writing was usu-ally done for oneself?

It is getting much too complicated for the layperson (excuse me, Fred) or for an American (excuse me, Fred and Grace and now Daniel) to carry on from here alone, and in such a nonunified fashion. You all should know— and embrace this fact—that America is unaware of the rest of the world. This has been both one of your gifts to yourself and your failure to others. But then, you guys never do know that, and you're certainly not looking at this truth foursquare in the face.

As an example, some fifty years on from Hitler the confidences that David Jerusalem has gifted us with will have proved quite accurate, in that what he said did indeed happen, yet they will still be ignored by too many, and intentionally so. Much of it was there to be seen while he endured it, and you and yours and mine as well elected not to. The truly grotesque facts of Hitler (and Stalin; for some reason your country always overlooks Stalin) are by now enshrined in a god-awful plethora of your (and yes, my) historians' histories that tell you everything ad nauseam, except for whom, who, really, and why, really, and what, really. Modern history is a fairy tale told by idiots. I refuse any longer to stand by while others discuss this in an equally make-believe fashion.

I have been dilly-dallying and I should not have been, but for not wanting to spoil my thus far impeccable manners by rudely barging in. I am a guest in your country and a guest in this history. But as we have got caught up in fleshing out The Underlying Condition to its necessary ignominy and as this Second World War was the true jumping-off point for UC, someone from another part of the forest must obviously be summoned to show you which of the trees that you planted must be pulled up and out by their roots.

Forgive my brutal honesty. David is giving me courage. The great German social philosopher Hannah Arendt, whom I've just discovered, is giving me courage.

Increasingly, all of humanity's leading poisons were slowly being run up flagpoles in locations distant to your own present spheres of concern. Hate, extermination, "scientific" researches into unheard-of means of killing each other—they simply must forthwith make a more furious entry into this history. I can see now that they interest you insufficiently or you lack a belief system that can make room for the evil I am talking about.

I believe that Fred is much too personally involved in living this history to be able to write about it objectively. The pain that resides in him must prevent him from attacking it full force, and certainly with greater speed and authority, now more necessary than ever. We are many hundreds of pages in, and where are we? Having lived there, and then had the courage to finally chuck it ("it" being the island of my own people who also congenitally travel wrong byways). I am henceforth going to put my money where my mouth is, as you so quaintly put it.

I am going to lay out my assortment of goodies that I've so far gathered. Just read them, please, and take them into your ken for now. After all, it is your history, too.

In 1924, Adolf Hitler is released from prison (for being an agitator) and commences planning ways to put into practice all he has learned from America's eugenicists and their movement. Imprisoned, he figured out that, compared with the States, his has been a namby-pamby movement, many ideas, little action, too many people without any power to do anything, and a lack of focus and direction. Yes, he was smart enough to recognize in

American eugenics the making of a German world order. His "Nazis" can dispense with the niceties of democratic rule. American eugenicists actually welcomed the idea. Churchill's great history of World War II begins with a volume entitled *The Gathering Storm*.

In 1928 the Nazi party publishes a pamphlet, "Anyone Who Thinks of Homosexual Love Is Our Enemy," which contains its response to the idea of repealing the anti-homosexual law known as Paragraph 175. On February 23, 1933, twenty-four days after being appointed chancellor, Hitler bans all homosexual-rights groups. On October 24, 1934, the Gestapo secretly orders local police to collect the names of all homosexuals in Germany. On June 28, 1935, Paragraph 175 is amended with broader language, so that a mere touch between men can be interpreted as an arrestable offense. On October 26, 1936, the Reich's "Central Office to Combat Homosexuality and Abortion" is established. (By the mid-1930s, Stalin follows suit, copycatting Hitler, whom he recognizes as another man who gets what he wants.)

For Hitler, a most important event is the Third International Congress on Eugenics, held at New York's American Museum of Natural History in August 1932. Even Italy's Fascist government sends a representative. The proceedings are dedicated to Averell Harriman's mother, she who paid for the founding of the Eugenics Record Office back in 1910. Harriman himself arranges for the Hamburg-Amerika Line to transport Nazis to New York for this conference, including Dr. Grodzo. The Hamburg-Amerika Line is owned in part and controlled in all by founders of the Trish dynasty, George Walker Trish and Prescott Trish. "We must do my dear late Momma proud," Averell said in his opening speech. Unfortunately, as with all the documentation damning IBM, what happened at this international congress has so far been kept from history.

In 1933, Hitler's interior minister calls the Germans a degenerate race for producing feebleminded and defective children. A plan modeled on sterilization laws in Virginia is placed into effect.

In 1934 comes the "Night of the Long Knives," and then the destruction of Röhm's SA, the first against the Jews and the second against the gays. Röhm was a raging homosexual and surrounded by same. So Hitler has his former best friend, Ernst Röhm, murdered.

The Hollerith machine, an American invention owned by an American company, is forbidden by U.S. laws to be manufactured and sold and serviced in Germany by 1938. These prohibitions will at first be ignored and, if and when caught, circumvented, and then when challenged in court, flaunted.

Mr. Thomas Watson of IBM cares only for money and more money, no matter its source. It is a rueful story, Mr. Watson's uncontrollable greed.

You have reported some of this. I repeat it.

At least a thousand people are being executed every day in Russia, including many Jews and homosexuals. This bloodiest period of Stalin's scourges is now known as the Great Terror. Hitler wanted his targets eliminated; Stalin wanted his starved to death so he could utilize their food, and feed their flesh to the animals. The end results of course were the same.

By 1940 some 40,000 Americans had been legally castrated or sterilized. These included 8,000 suspected homosexuals and lesbians. They were identified by the Tally Office. Leaders in the eugenics movement are pleased with this progress although word is reaching them that Germany is forging ahead in more forceful fashion. The information you gathered about Jeshua Brinestalker and the Tally Office is obviously deficient. If you are going to be a historian, be one! Brinestalker, the son, will soon be (as you people so charmingly put it) "up for grabs."

By 1940 there are some three thousand concentration camps in Germany. By the end of the war there will be ten thousand.

•

No one wants to believe me when I say that The American People also have concentration camps. Before America even enters the war, there will have been some dozen of these camps. Fred has told us about two of them. The most cruel and top-secret of these will be the development of Partekla in northern Idaho, established by the American government itself. Idaho was the last of the states to be explored, and its isolated northern "panhandle" has become a home to America's misfits and malcontents. Not dissimilar to Mungel, it will now be home to incarceration and punishment and experimentation of and on homosexuals. Dr. Grodzo will be brought by Rockefeller, Harriman, and Trish money to America to participate in Partekla's administration. He is given American citizenship, facilitated by J. Edgar Hoover. And Dr. Stuartgene Dye will make his entry to our history at Partekla.

If anyone in the Jerusalem family knew anything about any of this, he or she certainly wasn't saying anything. You are correct, Fred, in citing your country's numerous failures. You might add this one to your list.

•

By October 1941, as my chum Zygmunnt Bauman of Sheffield University has written:

Himmler orders the stop to all further Jewish emigration. The task of "getting rid of the Jews" had found another, more effective means of implementation: physical extermination was chosen as the most feasible and effective means to the original, and newly expanded, end. The rest was the matter of co-operation between various departments of state bureaucracy, of careful planning, designing proper technology and technical equipment, budgeting, calculating and mobilizing necessary resources: indeed, the matter of dull bureaucratic routine. The Holocaust was clearly unthinkable without such bureaucracy . . . the ability of modern bureaucracy to co-ordinate the action of a great number of immoral individuals in the pursuit of any, also immoral, ends.

Every stricture applied to the Jews is also mandated to apply to homosexuals and gypsies, and a hodgepodge of other unwanteds. Six million Jews were eliminated during World War II, but 20 million is the sum total of all those murdered. Buried within this figure are a monstrous number of homosexuals.

Starting as early as 1915, and with Rockefeller funding, the Institute for Brain Research becomes bigger and stronger and eventually Hitler's medical center for experimentation on the human body. By 1935 a revered eugenicist, Otmar Freiherr von Verschuer, also, as noted, a hero in American eugenics circles, leaves this institute and, again with funding from Rockefeller, forms the Institute for Anthropology, Human Heredity, and Eugenics. Beginning in 1940, at first thousands and then, with the aid of the Hollerith machines' tabulations of the interviews conducted by 750,000 soldiers, hundreds of thousands of Germans, and eventually those six million Jews (the only number that "scholars" toss about), are able to be easily located and taken from their residences and, when of interest, first studied at institutes like this, but eventually murdered. Verschuer's assistant is Dr. Josef Mengele. Mengele's assistant is Dr. Gottfried Grodzo. Grodzo's assistant will be an American, Dr. Stuartgene Dye, there on a Rockefeller scholarship.

By 1943 the Germans, now with a list of every Jew in a Denmark they've invaded, start to round them up. The important words in this sentence are "with a list." Lists would have been impossible without Mr. IBM Watson's Hollerith machine, illegally manufactured and easily available abroad, certainly in Denmark.

My chum Alec Wilkinson has told us that in the fifty-four days between May 15 and July 8, 1944, 434,000 people were put aboard trains to Auschwitz—"so many people that the crematoriums, which could dispose of a hundred and thirty-two thousand bodies a month, were overrun, and bodies were thrown into pits dug by prisoners and set on fire." The Holocaust scholar Michael Berenbaum described 1944 as the year in which "'Auschwitz became Auschwitz.' Before, it had been merely one of several death camps." My (and Fred's good) chum William Percy III from the University of Massachusetts has written, "In every shipment to the camps and to the ovens there were among those sent off numbers of homosexuals approximating at least twenty percent or more of the total dispatched, or more." It has been exceedingly difficult to obtain figures about how many gays were eliminated for many reasons, not the least of which is that gays who survived the camps were very reluctant to speak out because homosexuality remained illegal in Germany until the 1960s.

One should be able to say—without qualification or hesitation, and proudly—that The American People are at war.

Well, some people know this and some people don't. How does one hide from a war? Many people stop reading newspapers and listening to the radio. Some families move to remote locales, as if this would keep them and the kiddies from learning of hideous matters transpiring far away. What is going on "over there" becomes gory so quickly that newspapers are nervous about telling too much. American newspapers with their comic strips are read by the entire family. So no one is going to report that Goering is going around Europe screaming about the eternal Jew devils. A man named Anton Schmutzer, who travels with him, says that Goering is also "proclaiming" that homosexuals are worse, and that Goering's scream is often at such a fevered pitch that "it breaks crystal goblets." No, no one in America is reporting that, and yes, it's reported in Britain, even the bit about the goblets. Prague, Vienna, Budapest, Munich, the Sudetenland, Chamberlain, what about them? You don't hear about these, you see. No, you don't see. Even to this day, you don't see. To this day Americans still don't want to know that a hideous war was transpiring somewhere else that you weren't told about by your very own newspapers. *The New York Truth? The Washington Monu-*

ment? Their steadfast determination not to tell The American People the truth about what was happening is quite remarkable.

How could it be that your major publishing families, the Dunkelheims of the *Truth* and the Templates of the *Monument*, both families riddled uncomfortably with more Jews and homosexuals than they will ever wish revealed, choose instead to worry over this conundrum: If we tell *too much,* will we be accused of . . . ? Or *too little,* could we be accused of . . . ? Of which accusation are they more afraid? And what has amount got to do with truth? And humanity? And responsibility? And this will not be the first time they behave with such complete contempt for others. I repeat myself.

On October 14, 1942, in Geneva, representatives of all the Red Bloods and Red Crosses and Red Crescents and the newly founded and private International Bank for Blood vote *not* to speak publicly of what they're learning about the Holocaust. Even the pope won't open his mouth. (And speaking of the Catholic Church, that Sheeney who was so concerned about Dr. Flo Hung Nu and her shit has become Archbishop Sheeney and is performing his own services during wartime, and I do mean servicing. Word gets around how skilled he is, and discussions are held about whether he should be sent to Rome, where the pope is having so much trouble sleeping. He is sent to Rome.)

"Our story is simply not getting out," Rabbi Josef Dreitzel reports daily to his board of World Jews for Zion, which communicates to some several hundred thousand members across the country. "Tens of thousands of our people are being disposed of each and every day and Adolph Arthur Dunkelheim and Alvah Schwartz Template, the owner-publishers of the two most powerful papers in the world, are too ashamed of being Jews to let their reporters report it." Theodosia Template, the daughter and heir, who will take over the *Monument* mid-war, will prove no better. She marries a gentile and more or less becomes one. Their excuse is if they report this with the strength and regularity that this story demands, then the country will turn against Jews, "and make our situations, both here and in Europe, even worse."

American Jewry's most revered rabbi, Stephen Wise, already knows about German plans for the complete annihilation of his people and also says nothing. By the time he speaks out, some four million Jews have been murdered. This figure will appear in the *Truth* on page 10. Three million Jews had rated page 7. President Roosevelt does not talk about any of this publicly for another fifteen months, until 1943, by which time half of Europe's Jewry is already dead, and only God knows how many others because it quickly becomes the habit everywhere to enumerate only Jews. Even the now almost totally worthless League of Nations acknowledgment of what the Nazis are up to fails to make a front page anywhere, including Britain. And if the *Truth* and the *Monument* aren't reporting, the rest of America's papers follow their lead. Jews are rarely referred to as Jews, but as refugees.

If you find all this difficult to believe, I refer you to my chum Laurel Leff's *Buried by the Truth*, a gold mine for haters of *The New York Truth*. Everything you need to fully comprehend that newspaper's infamy is here. It joins David S. Wyman's *The Abandonment of the Jews* and Arthur D. Morse's *While Six Million Died* as indispensable for every historian.

As mentioned, homosexuals aren't reported anywhere at all.

"Our story is simply not getting out," Virgil Vindicator reports in the mimeographed bulletins issued irregularly by the half dozen or so Homosexual Rights Now! (formerly the American Association of Hushmarkeds) chapters struggling against extinction as Mr. Vindicator and others try to press these bulletins on uncaring recipients outside covert gathering places from coast to coast. "Large numbers of our people simply disappear daily from the streets of Central Europe, where they are being kidnapped and mowed down with machine guns." It's all too melodramatic for any American homosexual to believe. It is always the most threatened who turn their backs from truth. My new chum Hannah makes this very clear. It appears that not knowing makes people feel safer. The more people murdered, the more people don't want to know. You would think it would be the other way 'round. I have spoken earlier of your people's perversity, both as Americans and as homosexuals, your dance with the destiny of death.

One thing is certain. The American People are not developing a sense of the truly monstrous. (I doubt you ever will.) You have not learned how to be cruel. Millions of people are being murdered "over there" and you go to the movies and listen to the radio and laugh at Dagwood Bumstead and Jack Benny. We did the same, too, of course. There is nothing wrong with laughing. As long as the laugh's not on you.

Let me continue to provide examples.

The first wartime Perdist Poll is conducted as the Germans are occupying Poland. Not many of The American People are noticing either event. The Perdist Poll is supervised by Rep. Ti Perdist (R., Montana), who wants to prove statistically that "The American People are in favor of deporting all Americans of German descent back to Germany." Representative Perdist is less concerned with the Germans invading Czechoslovakia and Poland than with a large German population invading Montana, sneaking in from their enclaves in neighboring Idaho, and Minnesota and Wisconsin, and even via Canada. Perdist deploys such slogans as "The American People don't like Germans" and "The American People don't like Roosevelt" to skew his poll's results. He represents a rural area with a voting population, should it ever be honestly tabulated, of fewer than 60,000 and he conducts the poll entirely in this district. When *The Washington Monument* reports for the second time that the Germans have invaded Poland (important events occurring overseas have to be reported more than once before they might sink in), twenty-three other congressmen join Perdist to co-sponsor the Perdist-Nyer-Phail Bill, which proposes acting on "the irrefutable conclusions of the Perdist Poll." The bill is defeated, but only by three votes, not because of its contents but because at the last minute Representative Phail (R., Arizona) tacks on an amendment permitting legal prostitution in any district with a population comprising "more than 500 people of Negroid persuasion." By now the Germans have occupied Poland and Austria as well.

Yes, The American People are at war.

Franklin Roosevelt is the first of your presidents to realize that numbers can be manipulated into lies more useful for rallying support than any truths. According to Breckenridge Winesap's biographer, "FDR immediately grasped Perdist's methodology: just ask the people questions the way you want them answered and put the answers out in the morning papers as facts. He set up SIC to do just that."

The newly established Department of Statistical Intervention and Control (SIC), under Stuart Symington, along with the Bureau of Abnormal Acts (BAA), is under the supervision of Winesap, Roosevelt's invaluable traffic cop in all matters of discomfort, such as stateless Jews and homosexuals in high places. This latter is on its way to becoming a big problem for Roosevelt, Washington, and the government. Exposés like *Washington Confidential* are about to be written by the score about how many fairies and queers and pansies and poofters work for Uncle Sam. This new ammunition will prove to be of enormous help to Jeshua Brinestalker and his Tally Office, into which BAA has been subsumed.

As Robert E. Sherwood tells us in his wartime memoirs, when FDR faces reelection in 1940, SIC "invokes" the Phail-Dridge line, which "proves" that at the start of any hypothetical war there exists a market value of .89 percent, which means 1 out of every 1.3 of "The American People" (now coming more and more into use as a term of bureaucratic endearment) will be better off than before it. Every study after this Perdist one proves that people are happy and Roosevelt can pretty much do what he wants to, which of course he would have done anyway. Gods don't have to have reasons. Another Winesap rule of thumb learned by smart operators: Confuse 'em enough and they won't be confused. He told me that one himself.

Hitler by now has invaded Russia. Does anyone in America know that Hitler invaded Russia with more than four million soldiers, the largest invasion in the history of warfare? No wonder the *Monument* doesn't report this; it's difficult enough when Edward R. Murrow broadcasts for CBS from London for many to figure out where such places as "the European theater of war" are located.

At any rate, in plain English, there is no money for "supererogatory budgetary items," meaning the Jews, who already want their people rescued and they don't even know yet whom they're missing. So pushy, the Jews. So expensive, rescuing them. Homosexuals, who are also missing, of course do not exist, and you cannot rescue people who do not exist, can you? Hence the only thing to do about them is to continue to collect their names, which, as we have seen, a number of you are doing.

Who has noticed that for the first time an explicit prohibition against homosexuals is inserted into an official government regulation? "The entitlements of the National Abundance Stipulation, and any of its current or future Perdist-Phail-Dridge extensions, shall not apply to those who traffic in hushmarkedry" (Footnote 21987, Appendix G). That this by now archaic word for homosexual is deliberately utilized conveys one thing: someone used it knowing full well it would go unrecognized and unchallenged by the majority of people reading the regulation, if any. If, as has been trumpeted by gay historians, nobody knew who these were, somebody still knows what they are.

We are conducting a war, aren't we? Of course we are.

The American People are at war.

•

Did you pick up on that name dropped in above, Partekla? Its complexity will overwhelm you.

The American People build and maintain a secret camp in northern Idaho where members of the armed forces known or discovered to be homosexual or caught in homosexual activity are imprisoned. It is authorized under the Perdist-Phail-Dridge Extension Act 21987, Appendix G.

Partekla is under the supervision of Dr. Stuartgene Dye.

It has several sections, each involved in different tasks.

It is open for business just as the war begins. How thoughtful of someone to take an old tin mine and turn it into such a fortress and just in time. Who in your "killing apparatus" (to use German terminology) has such foresight?

THE PAST IS A FOREIGN HARBOR

They meet as freshmen at Yaddah, where they are assigned to live in the same rooms. It's 1916 and there's a war on, another war where young people are trying not to pay attention to an outside world that doesn't pay any attention to them anyway. They bond immediately, evidently recognizing in each other something that each was finding in himself and hadn't quite known what to do with. Each had puzzled privately with these feelings in a hometown where no one else seemed to notice them either. Philip, of course, is from Washington and Amos Standing is from Cincinnati and Brinestalker is from somewhere between Los Angeles and San Diego.

"We shall just have to give the world something to make them notice us."

Who said that, Amos or Briney? It certainly wasn't Philip. He was happy not to be noticed, although he didn't say it. He just smiled his yeses. He hadn't had friends before. Zilka, it turned out, had saved so diligently her son could make them here.

Together they see a silent movie about three friends on the battlefield, three handsome German actors more interested in each other than the war, the world, or any woman in it. The movie is an international success, less so in America, of course, but it plays in New Godding. It was made by Studio Babelsberg, the German studio that was to become UFA (which Amos will one day run), and there is some resentment on campus that a German film is even being shown. Our threesome takes to pretending to be one or the other of the leading characters, Heinz or Heinrich or Helmut. They discover they're good pretenders, a complicated skill to deal with emotionally if they were to think about it. Each can pretend easily as long as the other two are around as an attentive audience. Alone or in twosomes they are left more revealed, with less protection, less pretense, and what is pretending if not camouflage, a safer place to be? Three is their perfect number.

It isn't long before they are having sex as a threesome. Yes, they are having sex with each other quite regularly, each unquestioningly accepting the others' bodies as if it was meant to be. "We weren't even drunk when we fell into each other's arms spontaneously at the end of one of our sessions of pretend," Amos will say later. They claim there is no favoritism of one over another. They all state definitively in letters they exchange when they're apart that their threesome is historic, like nothing ever before, "a love of equality, each for each, all together as one. Three against the world!" These are Amos's words. He appears to have been their cheerleader. One marvels that they have fallen into this love so easily and with such celerity (an early indication, should anyone be noticing, of how movies are able to seriously affect lives).

One wonders what they knew of homosexuality. There must have been similar fellows, even groups, at Yaddah. New Godding has always been a town of feverish sexual activity, of all sorts, going back to colonial days, which history YRH spoke of when we were there several hundred years ago. But wasn't the world a bit more innocent in the seventeenth century, and its youngsters more naïve, than in 1916? On the other hand, Philip had already seen his father disappear after almost being emasculated with a meat cleaver by his mother. Perhaps what is naïve is to believe that just because the world was once younger it was concomitantly simpler, a stupid mistake historians fall into. We know now that Brinestalker's father was a murderer. Did the son witness his crimes? Perhaps he did. Or not. He was briefly a child murderer himself. But in the wild west he came from, murder was not unusual.

Amos has pleasant looks that are set off by the excellent traditional clothing he alone chooses to wear. He believes himself handsome. His family has for many generations been a principal builder of ships and canals and railroads and wealth in Cincinnati. Philip is of medium height, with the stocky frame he will have all his life, and the white skin that makes him look like a sheet when he's naked. Brinestalker is the most unusual-looking, in that he's taller by a head, with protruding jug ears positioned unevenly on his skull, and terrible posture that finds him always leaning forward, as if listening for something. It is his awkwardness that makes him attractive. California is a faraway place not many at Yaddah hail from yet, and his father, Jeshua, who is very rich, provides horses for the silent movies now be-

ginning to be filmed on his enormous Brinestalker ranch. This land is said
to have been "Coronado land" that once belonged to Spain. Like Briney's
ears and posture, the history of this land, and indeed of his forebears, is a
crooked one. Only one thing is for certain: there is an awful lot of acreage,
swirling in and out of several counties, all of which at one time or another
have claimed it unsuccessfully. Jeshua knows how to fight back.

Early in the friendship Amos falls in love with Philip alone, so much so
that the more Amos blossoms into it, the more confused Philip becomes in
his identity. The threesome's activities originally seemed so carefree: kisses
and cuddles at night, with swift ejaculations and then a gentle slumber in
each other's arms, all three jumbled together in sleep. In his growing passion, Amos's extreme determination to have Philip at his side all the time
requires harsher measures if Philip is not obligingly there, so that Philip becomes even more afraid of him, which Amos enjoys. Orders and commands
soon fall from Amos's lips with regularity. Philip obeys quickly, often from
fear rather than politeness, and his subservience becomes a habit both pretend to enjoy, particularly when it consummates in an exciting new kind of sex,
now only when Brinestalker is away. Amos ties Philip up and Philip finds
that this excites him. Then he gets frightened, both of the act and of his excitement. That this all leads Amos years later to actually kidnap Philip's son
in an attempt to pressure Philip back into his arms—well, it is a strange act
for the lover who professes such love, which Amos believes sincerely that he
does. And why does Brinestalker withdraw from active participation in the
threesome? How does he abandon an extremely active homosexual life and
insist to the other two that he's not a homosexual anymore?

By the time of Partekla it will be some thirty years since their Yaddah
frolics. Amos is still formulating plans to get Philip where he wants him. He
is perhaps the strangest of these three, to hold on to his fantasy for so long,
with so little satisfaction, particularly after Germany, after watching Philip
not only abandon his son but run away from Amos as well in his growing
terror. And then Hitler interferes and even Amos can't facilitate any movement for the moment, a moment that lasts six, seven, eight years.

How often did these three see one another between college and their
wartime reunion in Berlin, between youth and middle age? More must have
been going on than each wished the others to know. Mustn't it? You would
think so. Or to be perverse about it, perhaps less, as with most men in middle age and bored. According to Daniel, Philip was pretty much on view

before he went to Germany (or was he?), so one can only assume it was Brinestalker and Amos Standing who kept in touch. But why assume anything? Partekla will be open for business.

BRINESTALKER'S DEFENSE

I had long ago begun to find it increasingly unpleasant when I had another man in my arms. Most of them were not men at all. They were silly girls. They got all giddy when they were kissed, and even sillier when the question of who was fucking whom was up for grabs. They either rolled over giggling to indicate there was nothing to discuss, or they put up strong opposition, a fortress not to be breached. I met few homosexual men who were men. After a while it repelled me. Amos and I spent many hours debating the question "What is a man?" I gave up and turned to celibacy. It sickened me that a man could turn into a silly, simpering schoolgirl so fast. Yes, that a big hairy-chested man could become such a fairy now made me ill. In the beginning I would say to them, I only want the hairy-chest part of you if you don't mind, and they wouldn't know what I was talking about. Too, I began to have trouble fucking another man up his asshole. I did it to Amos and did it to Philip and they certainly did it to me. But when we left each other to go out into the world, something inside me changed. What we had done together was spontaneous; we were learning from each other and we loved each other. Without that love, sex changed for me. Everyone I met wanted it up their filthy assholes, and that made them women in their own minds. God, how they screamed and groaned. Still, when I think of cocks and holding cocks and rubbing cocks together, I remember the masculinity in the nature of being homosexual that appealed to me in the first place, that hairy-chestedness of it all.

I was able to come back to America before the war was over because Hoover summoned me. I felt like a bitter middle-aged man who had lost too much time and had too little to show for himself. I had a great deal to make up for. I was looking for something that excited my interest. I was sick of drug companies! I was sick of IBM! I had delivered enough information on both.

What should a homosexual man be? And how can he be made that way? It seemed as good a new cause for me as any. It was actually Hoover's idea. He was a remarkable man. He was not only determined to make America safe, but he was open to creative means to change our lives in other ways.

We have a hundred young men lined up and ready to go. Dr. Dye has said, "Get cracking!"

DR. STUARTGENE DYE

Stuartgene is not a graduate of a prestigious medical school. He is a "hick" from the dirt flats of rural Maryland. You'd have to be a "dirt-poor" kid to be named Stuartgene. Dye is another matter. It's American Indian, from the Pottawattamie Senecks. It doesn't mean death or to change a shade of color. It means "Unusual Son," but only Stuartgene knows this. In the outside world everyone hearing it thinks to himself, What a peculiar name. You think he doesn't know it? Do you think he cares?

His skin is light tan. He's of average height and weight. His hair is black and slick. He's quite good-looking.

Stuartgene knows how to kill. He can look at all things living and determine the best way to end them, or make it look like they've ended themselves, or to bring them back from the almost-dead. It's an odd gift, but a gift it is. He knows how to string lives out as well, although he much prefers to figure out new and better and more invisible ways to not extend or even delay. Stuartgene knows without question that what he has in mind is not only not immoral but will be blessed, in the end, not only by the Nobel committee, but by his god, the Seneck god of gods, Hymos Eleckro.

Death is all Dr. Stuartgene Dye is interested in. He has killed from the earliest of ages. Bugs. Rats. Cats. Dogs. Mules. A horse or two. As a boy he was fascinated with finding ways to make them die at differing speeds. A slow death for a cat could be achieved by mixing potassium salts with mondicaridal drops. A fast way to get rid of a horse: three injections of mynth, a wild mountain herb. He voraciously read ancient books wherever he could view or steal them, and stole as well medicaments, herbs, and unguents with greed from drugstores in the bigger towns, all the while working for Doc Rebbish, who wasn't a doctor but a medicine man, a good one, famous among the many tribes still scattered around the country, living in small towns or sequestered on reservations or just wandering around like gypsies. There are still medicine men wandering the back roads, though they are harder to locate as there are fewer back roads, but you can find them if you really want to. And there are always people who want to. The disenfranchised and the distrustful and the fatally diseased will wander the back roads of the world forever.

Stuartgene's parents were wandering gypsies. He was dropped from his mother's womb in Fairchild, Maryland, and left there, never to see her again, never to know who she was or who his father was. He was brought up more or less by the whole town, a few hundred folks who sheltered him and shunted him to whoever had a spare room. It's not as bad an upbringing as one might think: people in "the sticks" are generous with food and affection and interest.

One day when Doc Rebbish came to town, Stuartgene gravitated to him as if pulled by a magnet. (The life stories of so many seminal—there's that word again—forces in history often begin with the words "one day.")

Doc Rebbish was the first person to show him how to kill humans. To put them out of their misery when the misery went too far. People came to him in such pain that they begged to be put to sleep. Doc was pretty good at telling who would snap out of it, but mostly he obliged. When someone wished to die "so bad," it was a mercy to grant it. These were mighty poor people who got all tuckered out and had had enough. Doc Rebbish tried to impart to this smart kid all the lore from all the tribes to back before Columbus so there'd be continuity in these particular tasks when he himself got too tired. Yes, he taught Stuartgene everything. "You'll kill me, boy, just when and how I'll tell you, and then you'll get the money I'm leaving you to get the fuck out of this dump full of mud and shit and puke and germs and hooey. I'd have gone a long time ago, but what can a half-breed Seneck do in the white man's world? Nothing but drink himself to death. I'm trying. I'm drinking as hard and fast as I can, but I must have a liver made of steel." He wrote this "to get it down on paper."

When the time came, Stuartgene was seventeen years old, tall and lanky and the heartthrob of every girl in town. Doc Rebbish stumbled into the bedroom they shared in the back of Ferla Peltz's Deltoid Barbecue, and nodded to Stuartgene. "Get the stuff." He was doubled over in pain from his gut; a white-man doctor would have diagnosed it as pancreatitis from unknown causes, but Doc knew it was pancreatitis from chewing too much snalfa, the bark of a local tree that everyone knew made you feel too good. Doc knew that eventually snalfa knocked the life out of the liver and the pancreas, worse even than drinking yourself to death.

Stuartgene must get to medical school. Which is exactly what he does after shooting Doc Rebbish full of "the blue stuff from the locked green trunk" and burying his body out back in the earth by the creek. Also in the green trunk is a letter bequeathing all of Doc's money to him, more than $200,000, a mighty amount. Stuartgene has no idea how this man who never seemed to have enough for a hamburger could have amassed so much money. Doc Rebbish's big thick book of knowledge is in the green trunk, too—cures and possible cures and ideas for combinations and failures that just might work if you tinkered with them. Also, in a thick bundle is a wadge of receipts "for services, goods, and knowledge rendered" to someone called Boris Greeting.

There aren't many medical schools that take kids at seventeen, much less kids who haven't even gone to college, but Stuartgene finds one called Southern Towser, not all that far away, over the hills and into West Virginia. Of course it isn't accredited, but it teaches the nuts-and-bolts stuff well enough, all in a couple of years. And if you have some extra money Dr. Ishie Ferse, who owns and runs the place, will give you a diploma under the table stating that Dr. Stuartgene Dye has graduated with honors from the Medical School of the University of Florida (or your choice of any large state school where it's hard to check the records). Stuartgene got another one from the University of Michigan just in case. From there he will answer an ad in the *International Journal of Poisons* that will take him to Dr. Otmar Freiherr von Verschuer and his brain research in Darmstadt, which will develop into the opportunity to study with Mengele at Auschwitz, where Brinestalker will locate him for Partekla.

Stuartgene is charged with turning Partekla into a camp for the confinement of "the ill and diseased," where it is legally in his power not only to admit patients but to keep them incarcerated. These patients can be given various drugs, under provisions established by the Department of Food and Drug Supervision (FADS) that allow for "the testing of treatments which in the estimation of the Director and his staff might lead to the betterment of the health of The American People." There are also still in existence various provisions of the Wartime Powers Act that Truman had been advised by Winesap to keep in operation, which empower almost anything.

In addition to being in charge and the administrator for the growing Partekla complex, Stuartgene is in charge of that specific program which is "treating" hundreds of (early UC?) patients. Are he, and it, intentionally infecting young men with what he, or it, knows to be a lethal new disease? Yes, he is. But he will claim that he's seeking certain historic breakthroughs in virology, still a subject little understood. So whether it's intentional or not that he's also going to kill a lot of young men in this research that's the effect of what he's doing. He's using questionable "potions"—for want of a better description of all the pills and infusions and lavages and enemas and unguents and nostrums being stuffed and injected and coerced into all his charges—provided to him by Brinestalker, Levy, Coro, Kokoh, Feltrin, Sasauer, Grodzo, and yes, Dr. Sister Grace Hooker, and of course Doc Rebbish, many names David might recall as among Philip's and Amos's visitors in pre-Mungel Germany, except that David was too young then to remember any of these. As noted, German scientists from the German pharmaceutical industry are becoming the American scientists of the American pharmaceutical industry. Partekla is a godsend for them and for all the potions in their suitcases that they've been working on, some for many years.

On the other side of the wall, still here at Partekla, are the laboratories Dr. Dye has established "to harness some of the best scientific minds our century has given birth to," as he says to Hoover, who has arranged for them to be legally invited and absorbed.

On one side you have the guinea pigs in residence and on the other side you have those who are experimenting on them. All this is in one compound, Partekla. In a more orderly, dare we say civilized and democratic, world, much of this should have fallen to a place like NITS, but then NITS itself is still somewhat of a joke, a few more directors having come and gone.

In other buildings, still here at, yes, Partekla, we have Brinestalker and his Ferdinand Kursie Institute of Greek Warriors and we have the hard-labor boys, the American soldiers Aalvaar Heidrich punishes for being homosexual. He punishes most of them so strenuously that they die. Their next of kin will be sent letters announcing that they died performing "magnificent service to their country." There are, of course, no records of these U.S. soldiers, or of these Greek Warriors, of how many there were, of even their names.

Yes, it is a busy place indeed.

Why should there not have been a concentration camp (or camps) in the United States? There is a substantial group of people here, not exclusively Germans, who believe that Germany will win the war. There is a smaller group of people here, again not only Germans, who know that concentration camps have been in operation in Germany for some time. There's an even smaller group of people here who have memories of earlier deadly incarcerations in America, of Negroes and of gay men and lesbians, at such places as Nantoo and Abbator, and Tuskegee.

Another reason Idaho is chosen is that Canada is just over there for fast escape. FDR and Truman are not the first presidents to worry about invasion via Canada, an unprotected border. Get some soldiers up there fast, any kind of soldiers. Even if some of them are sentenced to solitary confinement or hard labor, others are not. The verdict of how exacting the punishment was left to the sentencing officer, from whatever "theater of war," and might be punitive or lenient depending on whether he hated homos or just wanted the fairy out of the way on a battlefield.

Aalvaar Heidrich. Do you remember him? He was Mercy Hooker's chauffeur, the keeper of the spiked dildos. He was also a cousin of that Reinhard Heydrich who created Hitler's Final Solution. Just prior to the war Mr. Hoover summons Aalvaar to discuss this question of what to do with homosexuals. Aalvaar has already made a name for himself as warden at St. Purdah's in Anacostia after he was hired by the D.C. penal system. It is Hoover who charges him with turning part of Partekla into a place of extreme punishment for homosexuals "in our fighting forces." Aalvaar is given the rank of major general in the U.S. Army and assigned several armed platoons. Partekla resembles a regular army post except for that underground mine, now converted into cells for various confinements of "a scientific nature." Aalvaar is not a man filled with love for his fellow men, particularly if they are homosexual. He most certainly hates himself for being one.

Aalvaar is familiar with the Nazi belief that homosexuality can be cured. At Partekla he designs methods to do just that, mostly involving ridicule, humiliation, flagellation, and hard labor, all after Nazi models. Rudolf Höss, the commandant of Auschwitz, believes that homosexuals should be segregated to prevent their "disease" from spreading to other inmates and guards. Naturally, Aalvaar and Hoover follow suit.

But Dr. Dye is fervent in his belief that people can be made to disappear via chemical means.

Much in the history of The American People is accomplished with few questions asked.

Heidrich's armed forces, Brinestalker's hairy-chested sissies, and Grodzo's sacks of infected potatoes are administered various drugs, all under the supervision of Dr. Dye. Doctors at NITS and elsewhere are invited to provide whatever they are working on for testing. Heidrich, Dye, and Grodzo also lend their "patients" as guinea pigs. Prisoners to this day are still utilized in this way. There are always doctors and hospitals and laboratories and drug companies needing guinea pigs. There can never be enough guinea pigs. Or else how would we ever learn anything?

Brinestalker, with his connections to German scientists in the pharmaceutical industry, is of enormous additional value to the entire enterprise. Using IBM as a cover, that is why he was in Germany. His father had many influential contacts with German drug companies. These contacts and this industry will thrive in America. A few are given labs at Partekla. The fruits of their labors—i.e., the suitcase of German patents and discoveries they've brought with them as house gifts—must be tested too. Dr. Grodzo brings with him many things from Mungel.

"Protocols," "controlled trials," "peer review" are for some future time. Underground cells are perfect for the testing of the toxic on the tainted, so to speak. Hoover certainly believes that these men are tainted. Hoover, like Brinestalker, and as we'll see, others like Vulcan Greeting and Sam Sport, doesn't like effeminate men. Each in his own way attempts to contribute to their elimination. There probably aren't enough psychoanalytic theories to dissect why they behave like this. If, as the head of the FBI, Hoover is America's strongest of strongmen, then, also as a homosexual, does he not wish other homosexuals to be like him and Clyde? That sounds too simplistic—or, as Grace might say, a shitty pisspot. Hermia will try to get to this in due course. Much of what's written in these paragraphs is stuff YRH has uncovered so far.

None of "our side" has responded to my charges. They're too overwhelming for an immediate response.

FROM *MY HISTORY OF EVIL*

A Dr. Grossvatter has brought over with him a trunkful from the German-Dutch-Belgian foray into "germ warfare." It's amazing how such disparate nations managed to collaborate so adroitly on such top-secret stuff, all of it unpleasant. Why, among a certain set it's as if there's no enemy, as if research is all. Even the Japanese wanted anything to do with germ warfare, and they found a way to get it, even if it meant actually collaborating with countries with which they were at war. There appear to be no enemies among such determined investigators into the life of poisons.

Experienced German scientists were worth a lot of money in certain American markets long before the war even started, and even more so when it did. You didn't want to know about this then and you don't want to know about it now. To be sure, there are books and exposés galore on the German infiltration of America before, during, and after the war, but they're kiddie stuff compared to what's actually going on.

"Concentration camps are the laboratories where changes in human nature are tested" is a much-quoted statement from these times. As David told us, he heard it uttered by Grodzo. In this country it's attributed to Aalvaar Heidrich, in what's become a highly regarded textbook in his field, the study of prisons. "There is nothing wrong with concentration camps. They are very useful and perfectly logical. They do just what their name suggests: concentrate. Everyone's life concentrates on one thing or another." Aalvaar Heidrich was sent over to America in the 1920s to infiltrate. Sent by whom? How did he wind up looking after Mercy Hooker? Did his own sexual needs (or theirs? whose?) determine his attachment to her? "Homosexuals are useful because they can be infected and allowed to die. Since their sperm will never play any part in procreation, no one in fact is killed," Heidrich also wrote. In fact, homosexuals are far more useful than Jews for wartime, and soon peacetime, activities. Actually, there will be money in dead homosexuals, or more precisely phrased, in homosexuals whose demise no one will care about. Partekla is actually catering to a potential market.

Aalvaar Heidrich is one of those who believed Germany was going to win the war and take over the world, so why not get started here early, and secretly of course, with a staff of spies who speak perfect English, and with no small amount of American help from American companies working in and with Germany, including Greeting? And especially many are represented by that most "eminent" of law firms, Sullivan and Cromwell. J. Edgar Hoover, like Roosevelt, does not object to the participation of the private sector. Many talk of Hoover as if he were president, with so much power. He does have this much power. Over the years little by little he learns how to just . . . take it. Do these companies know what's going on? Somewhere in their bowels can be located proof of concerted efforts. It is increasingly difficult not to wager that.

And what about Project Paperclip, the effort by the Office of Stragetic Services (OSS) to recruit the scientists of Nazi Germany for employment by the United States? The Joint Intelligence Objective Agency (JIOA) worked independently to create false employment and political biographies for the scientists, expunging from the public record any Nazi memberships and affiliations. Once "bleached" of their Nazism, the scientists were granted security clearance by your government to work in the United States. America, of course, being the richest, gets its choice of the cream of the scientific crop.

THE SON ALSO RISES

Yes, it's a play on words but a necessary one. It's my turn up at bat now. I've read this novel by Hemingway about a man who doesn't have a cock that's in working order. Well, mine is, at last. And I've finally got a way to smite the old geezer, bite the hand that feeds me, and direct my feet to a sunnier side of the street. Jeshua's said I can play in part of Partekla.

I obtained funds to go full steam ahead. Old Ferdinand Kursie, whom the geezer put me in touch with, set up the South African gulag at the beginning of this century. Mengele's teachers came from there, hell, Goering's father ran the place, and I remembered Mengele telling me in Berlin about Kursie, the rich South African who financed it. There was a lot of money to be made from workers imprisoned in that gulag and Kursie made it. And old as he is he wants to make some more. "How much du you vant!" he spat out at me in his Afrikaans accent. "Tell me vat you do vid it." He roared with laughter when I outlined my ideas. "I give you dubbel. You ask not enuf. Learn to think biggest! Build building and put my name on it. I vant vide vorld to know." And so comes into being the Ferdinand Kursie Institute, Partekla, Idaho. I had no idea that perversities could be so profitable so fast.

All of Partekla was Furstwasser land that somehow wound up in the government's hands during World War I instead of being returned to the Partekla Indians, from whom the Disciples of Lovejoy stole it. Amos insists our division will revert to us in due time and that Edgar will protect us and not allow otherwise. Because of our intended activities Edgar doesn't want there to be any visible connection with him or his department.

One part belongs to Amos, too. I guess a third belongs to Philip as well, though I don't know how a college pact (even one we sealed in blood) that "we shall be together in what we do forever" can be binding, but Amos is insistent on Philip's continued inclusion. I still keep wishing Amos weren't a fairy. I thought he might grow out of it like I did. I can't believe his feelings for Philip are so strong after so many years of hardly seeing the guy. I wonder what will happen when they are back together again.

Brinestalker, did I tell you you're a genius? It's all beginning to fit together nicely.

I located someone outstanding in Berlin to oversee all of Partekla. His name is Dr. Stuartgene Dye. The more I learn about him, the more that I can't wait.

YRH

The first thing Dr. Stuartgene Dye does upon arriving for his first day in his private laboratory at Partekla, with its fresh paint still not dry, is to pierce his nipples and thread them with bands of gold. It's his own celebration, his own gift to himself, for being back in his own country, for being *here*. He is the new director, its first, of this top-secret "Ennoblement," a word supplied by Philip when Amos asked for a distinguished name "for when the ball gets rolling." Philip always obeys; this was an easy one. In response to Philip's querulous demands concerning the whereabouts of his son, Amos told him that David would be safely returned. Yes, Amos and Brinestalker confided in him their plans for Partekla, and even promised him a financial participation, should whatever it is be profitable.

This has all been conveyed by mail. Philip is terrified Amos will turn up at Masturbov Gardens. Amos can be very sinister, and when he is, Philip is truly frightened of this man who professed such great love for him, "why, since the first time I saw you freshman year in New Godding, across the Yaddah campus, when you and I and Briney became such comrades."

Amos has been "in like" a hundred times with another man, and both he and Brinestalker have separately traveled the world and consulted every quack and read every "medical" volume on the "sickness," for that is what everyone says homosexuality is. Why has Amos come back to focus on poor Philip? It would seem to be an act of a most sadistic and/or masochistic nature. Indeed, when they first met, sadism and masochism were being investigated, in Vienna, in Berlin, in Oslo and Stockholm, in Adelaide, in Philadelphia, all places Amos and Brinestalker visited to pick up pointers. Briney now claims to have turned straight immediately after Yaddah, which as we'll see is not quite true. Philip still tells himself he'd forgotten all about both of them until in his financial desperation he reached into this past and applied to Amos Standing for a job and was reminded. Philip understood nothing when he arrived in Boston, and then went with Amos to Berlin, experiencing a returning hunger so strong and consuming that now he remembers that he married Rivka to escape it, a mistake just as torturing as the obsession for his two friends' bodies. In Germany, after Briney left, taking with him the leavening he peculiarly provided for the threesome, there was only the harsher reality of Amos alone. One did not say no to Amos. And once again Philip is increasingly troubled by his realization that he does not want to say no. He wants to be bound, beaten, and demeaned as much as Amos delights in doing all this to him.

So Germany for him was a bad place at a bad time, as it was and will be for others and for quite some while. Philip found one long-lost lover and loses one newfound son. He runs away from both of them. And now he can't go back. Amos's big client shut off all entrances and exits to his country. "Amos promised to watch out for David as if he were his own son," he'd told his wife, not voicing the real reason he had come home, which was to firm up his decision to leave her for Amos and return to Berlin, until he saw his three other sons, and yes, even sour Rivka, and was overwhelmed with guilt about how he had been avoiding his responsibilities on the home front. He sits there and awaits the return of his son, fearing for his own future. He does not want to go to Partekla to claim it.

The second thing Stuartgene does is to anesthetize a young man who has been watching his nipple procedure, and to puncture this young man's foreskin, threading through it a chain he clips to a metal ring. When the young man, who was walking among the evening shadows in downtown Boise when Dr. Dye picked him up, wakes and discovers not only that he is in great pain but that he's being brutally disfigured, he begins to cry. Because of the chain, he cannot comfortably move on the metal lab table. He would scream but for the effect of the anesthetic, which has left his throat numb. Indeed, this young man is a prisoner of this moment in time, this place in time. He sees no future and recalls no past. Dr. Dye approaches him again. He smiles at him. He runs his hand across the young man's face. It's a nice face, a kind one, the eyes so trusting only moments ago.

"Here, let us take some of the pain in your cock away," Dr. Dye says, producing a ready hypodermic and injecting the penis. The young man hardly has time to consider screaming. He is fast asleep. He is dead. It works again.

Dr. Dye then severs the penis, the scrotum and testicles. He flips the body over and eviscerates the various canals utilized in anal sex from the kid's rear end. He labels the parts and freezes them and locks them in a thermal chest.

With the formulas and chemicals and potions and poisons that are now his to use freely in his research, Dr. Dye, just commencing his work in this new laboratory, proceeds to dispose of the remaining flesh and bones and hair, easy tricks he learned from Dr. Mengele. He has concocted his own more advanced recipe that results in the complete, utter eradication of bodies. No need to put ashes in an envelope or to bury them or to flush them down a toilet. It takes a while, but it works. He will learn to make it go faster. Stuartgene is perfecting a method that the Nazis only dreamed of.

Doc Rebbish had been an inspired teacher, as of course was Mengele.

Stuartgene will win a Nobel for the results of this work.

This nameless eviscerated young man from Boise, for a brief moment before his demise, fantasized that he'd found the man of his dreams, at last, his perfect love, a doctor.

THE SON RISES EVEN MORE

I've just performed my latest interviewing of two young men from northern Minnesota who according to their applications are without parents or next of kin. It's all been ridiculously easy. Even in Germany nothing was this easy. My arrangements so far are really impeccable. It was an excellent idea to advertise for young men unable to pass their army physicals and who would thus be glad for the chance to serve their country after having been rejected by Uncle Sam.

I've been interviewing all the boys. I call myself their "proprietor," "an archaic legal term" Amos claims Philip also came up with. (It sounds to me like Amos is telling Philip too much, and I've told him to think about this.) The Kursie Foundation had advertised for one hundred young men, offering to pay them a modest sum "to free yourself for the adventure of a lifetime, no questions asked." They all had to sign papers pledging their "exclusive services" to "Partekla Kursie Institute" for the "protective entirety." They came from all over the place geographically, these youngsters, and were requested to report to various locations to have blood samples taken and toss back cups of "elixir" like shots of whiskey in a saloon.

I travel around the Midwest witnessing these blood tests and libations.

"Not long, not long at all!" I say heartily to keep spirits up when the impatient ones ask when their big adventure is going to begin. I've always been amazed how gullible people are.

•

I think I've finally found friends on the other side who don't appear to want to destroy me. It's almost as if they are saying: Let's see how far we can go with this. I count at least five hundred full-fledged infecteds in America, in various places and pockets, though they're still too scattered to what your Dr. Itsenfelder calls "meld."
The war effort, the war effort, what does that mean?

ISRAEL AND GRACE

Dr. Sister Grace Hooker finally calls Isidore Schmuck and arranges to meet Dr. Israel Jerusalem. Each has declined to approach the other's turf. Israel distrusts anything Catholic: a religion that has as its symbol a man nailed to a cross says it all. Grace, not all that experienced with Jews, puts her foot down on Schmuck, which she can't even bring herself to say. So these two peculiar people agree to meet in the small park across from the White House. Until she knows better, Grace tells herself to keep her mouth in check. For his part, Israel attempts to accept that a woman in such strangulating attire can be a decent scientist.

Small bits of information continue to trickle in from the battlefields about peculiar new maladies. From knowing something of each other's work, each of these protagonists has fortunately and instinctively recognized in the other an excellence that could challenge them to greater heights.

Israel knows of Grace. She wrote to him after his *Titlement* article appeared, requesting fluid samples from Evvilleena Stadtdotter and Mercy Hooker. He's read her many articles in the many journals. She is some hard worker. She puts him to shame. He knows he's stuck, somewhere, somehow. He is not *acclimatizing*. That is what Shmuel said. He is still and unendingly having trouble in the New World.

At home—he lives in the fancy Waldbaum Towers out Massachusetts Avenue also built by his brother-in-law—he stares into space night after night and on weekends. He isn't clinically depressed. He's just . . . unacclimatized. Often he just sits in the lobby and watches the many people come and go.

What is my life in aid of? What am I doing? Why am I not doing what I should be doing? I thought I was doing what I should be doing!

Oh, it is a curse to be so steeped in Dr. Freud. Israel has read *everything*. A little knowledge is messy. Like the battlefields over there, like the hospitals over here, Israel is a mess.

I now see how discontented civilization must be for anyone who reads Sigmund Freud. I am very angry with you, Sigmund, for teaching me this. Before you, I thought I could function.

Waldbaum Towers is filled with Jewish families with growing bank accounts. Everyone in this New World prospers. The Depression was *gestern. Heute bist* fabulous. War is good for business. Sons are leaving, fathers too. Who will run the business? May I request an exemption for my son so that he can take charge? No, you may not. So wives and grandparents take over the business, and they do better than ever. Here in Waldbaum Towers women leave every morning in business suits, often in town cars driven by female chauffeurs.

Do you remember Mr. Y'Idstein, whom young Daniel encountered at Rabbi Chesterfield's house? He lives here. In a penthouse. He can look out over all of Washington. His closets are brimming with European masterpieces. Mr. John Foster Dulles, who goes to Germany so often to speak to Hitler, comes here often, to speak to Mr. Y'Idstein. Mr. Dulles runs the big New York law firm Sullivan and Cromwell. Many Jewish lawyers whom Mr. Dulles visits also live in this building. The last time he was here he joked to the Negro doorman, who doesn't get the joke, that there were as many Y'Idsteins in Waldbaum Towers as in his firm in New York City. "But not as partners, of course." For those interested, this firm's wretched wartime activities and the wretched involvement of its chief partner, John Foster Dulles, are chronicled in *A Law Unto Itself: The Untold Story of the Law Firm Sullivan & Cromwell*, by Nancy Lisagor and Frank Lipsius, which states unequivocally, "Many clients of Sullivan and Cromwell are responsible for many bottlenecks in the war effort."

The owner of *The Washingon Monument*, Alvah Template, also continues to visit Mr. Y'Idstein often. In the lobby one day, Mr. Y'Idstein tells Template to continue not writing about Jewish problems in his paper. "It is not good for the Jews, continues to be my advice." The Negro doorman, whose name is Bill C. Panama, hears him say this. "Mr. Y'Idstein sure must be one powerful man to speak to Mr. Alvah Template so," Bill C. Panama says to Claudia Webb, who is here to drop a package off for Mrs. Gertrude Jewsbury, who is in Europe and is rumored to be having difficulty returning. Bill C. Panama recognizes Claudia Webb because she visits with several of the gentlemen in the Waldbaum Towers tower.

"Good afternoon, Dr. Jerusalem," says Bill C. Panama, trying to conceal his surprise. "It's good to see you out of your apartment on a weekend."

Yes, Israel is happy when Grace calls him.

"Great minds think alike," Grace says when she finds him on a bench in the park.

"So wast thinkest du?" Why am I talking to her like this?

She forges ahead anyway. "I have studied the fluid you took from over the eye of Evvilleena Stadtdotter. It is not a new poison."

"I believe I have seen it before. In the Andes Mountains. Young people ate each other and died."

They both look across the street. Somewhere inside that house, Mr. Roosevelt is taking care of America, with his fine wife. I hope he knows what he's doing, each of them thinks privately. Grace crosses herself out of habit.

"You too are frightened of this?" he asks.

"I have studied a sample of blood from a nun, Sister Fidelma Mae Chinchillie. It was sent to me by Dr. Flo Hung Nu."

"These are unfortunate names."

Grace nods. They both smile.

She plunges in. "I have done further tests. I consider her blood to be a false trail and not worth pursuing."

Who is this woman calling false? Israel is surprised at how much her finding stings him.

"Why are you frowning?" she demands. "You really did not complete your work. You found something interesting and you abandoned it. The work I did was work you should have done. I'm tired of cleaning up men's slops." She almost chooses harsher words.

He stares at her. When confronted, he gets tongue-tied. When confronted, he walks away. He stands up to leave.

"Where are you going! You uncovered something important and I am trying to discuss it with you and you walk away! A new possibly transmissible poison discovered as men all over the world are killing each other and spreading their blood is something of great significance. I have already had reports of the increasing appearance on the battlefields of regurgia, which is another name for hepatitis. Is this how men become famous? By walking away? Come back immediately!" She heaves her bulk up and waddles after him, with her good right arm pulling him back to the bench.

"What is of such great significance if you are calling it false and myself an idler?"

She smiles kindly and shakes her head. Men have to be coddled at every step. "But surely you must know that in research the mistakes, the false starts, are as important as the successes, and that . . . You . . . fool!" She is suddenly angry that he's so naïve.

But then she notices his beard, all brown, has no gray in it. He's still a child, and her voice softens. "You are brilliant to have done what you did so young. And it shows great instinct to take the samples along the way. Great discoveries come from great hunches."

Words will not come to Israel. Inside him are many notions he wants to express. He is so thirsty and yet he cannot drink. Here is a fellow scientist who would understand. He has never had anyone to talk to before. She takes him seriously. At Isidore Schmuck, they laugh at him.

"Talk to me!" She sits there in Lafayette Square, a huge rock in a black frock, shouting even though he sits beside her.

His eyes fill with tears. Tears are often a leavening agent. He takes her hands, which she is holding out to him, and they go to sit on another bench, this time with their backs to Mr. Roosevelt and his fine wife.

"Glause," he says.

"What is glause?"

"I have seen it before, the poison. And it was called glause, but I have what Freud would call a repression. The Iwacky knew how to treat it! There are no more Iwacky. I cannot locate my records." He takes back his hands and presses his palms fervently against his forehead, as if to squeeze pus from a recalcitrant pimple. "Explain, please, my failure, as you called it."

She goes over in great detail her findings. She stops suddenly and asks him, "Do you remember mismitosis?"

His brow wrinkles. The word is not unfamiliar. Again, his eyes gleam with tears as he realizes that mismitosis is somewhere back inside him with glause.

She thrusts her right shoulder forward for emphasis as she goes on. "I obtained your prehectral slides. I studied them in many ways. You could make a case for defouled mismitosis. But then I think it is my own self-serving nature to consider it. I have longed for any information on what caused my own deformity."

They sit silently, looking into space. Then Israel asks, "Are you family to Mercy Hooker?"

"Yes, she was a distant cousin," Grace sighs. So much tawdriness in all this and so much poison. So much that belongs in the tabloids and so little that comes from the laboratory. When can she say "Fuck it all" out loud?

"They are preparing new laws," he says.

"They're always passing new laws. What kind of new laws? What are you talking about?"

"Senator—one of my patients. He tells me. There is to be a new division of NITS with much power and authority to regulate what treatments we may prescribe and what the manufacturers of pharmaceuticals can sell and indeed our basic scientific research itself. The Department of Food and Drug Supervision. FADS."

"FADS?"

"And FADS will become part of a new enlarged Center of Disease. COD."

"Don't be such a defeatist! What do you care anyway!"

"We shall be forbidden much that we are now permitted."

"The great ones always break the rules!" She wanted to add, "You asshole, haven't you learned this yet!"

She finds herself disgusted with him again. Now it's her turn to leave, without so much as a goodbye.

"When can I see you again?" he finds himself calling after her.

She turns and addresses her manifesto more to the park and the White House and the world than to Israel Jerusalem, who calls himself a doctor.

"You fucking asshole, I have no use for stupid laws requiring scientific certainty when no such fucking thing exists! Laws are to keep the fart-faced idiots in check, to keep dumb dildo dickhead doctors from murdering puking patients who got sick doing something naughty-naughty they shouldn't have. Fervently I believe that I, Dr. Sister Grace Hooker, with all my discoveries and prizes, am exempt from these lewd lily-livered laws and that every discovery I have ever made, including my love of another woman, has been made because I broke the fucking goddamed shit-eating failure-guaranteed rules."

"You loved another *woman*?" And such foul language she uses!

"I did, yes. That's how I caught my mismitosis. Everything good and fine has its price. That's a law of life that never seems to change. You should know that by now, you who have called yourself a scientist."

Again she walks away. In her hurlings, she lobbed the word *scientist* at him. As a dare? As a threat? As a noble calling he has shamed?

"No, no!" He runs after her. The words pour out of his mouth, out of his brain, out of the knowledge and instinct that he is overwhelmed to discover are still preciously his.

"Sometimes diseases, viruses, bacteria, plena, run their course. Like an illness running through a flock of sheep or a group of children, they come, infect, cool down, and disappear. But sometimes they come back next year, next season, next heat wave or cold spell. Sometimes they come back slightly mutated, last year's flu slightly reformed, renamed, and out to find new converts to its way of damage, even death, especially death. Sometimes they seem to disappear for years or decades or centuries. Sometimes medicines, what I hear called 'wonder drugs,' appear to eradicate a disease, we think forever, when they only suffocate it until it teaches itself how to reappear and cause a plague."

"I know all that! You speak elegantly when you are angry. What are you trying to say?"

"Glause and . . . aliyahhah—yes! That is what mismitosis was called in Palestine when I was a student there! I will bet money on it—that they are the same. I believe . . . I believe . . ." He finds these next words almost impossible to utter. "I believe that I myself am now a carrier of glause. Perhaps with your mismitosis you are as well! You have inspired me to attempt to find out. You must send me some of your blood. I shall contact you when I have results. You should attempt the very same and contact me as well. Then perhaps we both can believe more in each other."

He bolts off across the park.

"Be careful!" she cries out after him.

She sits down on the nearest bench. She's so tired, and she recognizes the feeling. She is becoming God's prisoner again. A voice inside her head torments her. It's not a strange voice. It's velvet and reassuring and comforting. "To give in to passion is wrong," the bishop says, "and contrary to what makes us human beings. We do not need to have sex. We can be pure. We can be chaste." He says these words conspiratorially, yet with a voice exploding as he pumps her harder and harder, with increasing enthusiasm, and for her, pain. He's mounted her with his purple robes raised over his knobby white legs, and now he's raping her, grunting into the empty cathedral, "We must care about the lives of human beings inside the womb!" She is twelve years old and the bishop is known everywhere as "the hard-liner."

Grace has fallen on the ground of Lafayette Park. She's having her annual fit, and there's nothing she can do about it. She wishes the damn thing didn't always happen away from her rooms. She's glad Israel's gone, and she hopes a stranger will be kind and get her home before she starts thrashing and drooling.

Please, Israel, please discover something that will save us both.

As she drifts off across from the home of the president of the United States, of all The American People, she asks herself once again, Can a cure of cures exist? Why not? I wonder if it already exists and we don't know about it. Scientists since the beginning of time have dreamed of it. There need never be another war. There need never be another illness. Pain will be eradicated. Dangers will be gone. Men will stop murdering each other. Why is it always the men? Why are men always murdering each other?

And my good Dame Lady Hermia, is Fred playing his part a little better now?

THE SKINNY ACCORDING TO FETTNER

PART ONE

Ann Fettner was a medical writer who just appeared one day after the plague had started. She had an impeccable list of credits covering viruses all over the world, mostly in the Third World, which is why Fred had never heard of her although she'd heard of him. A straight woman in all ways, she shoots from the hip and takes no crap, his kind of dame. She appeared at Orvid Guptl's office at the Prick. God knows how she found it: it moved often and was very dumpy. "You guys are going to be eating crap in ever-greater quantities. It's going to be one helluva story. I want to write it as fully as I can. No one else will let me." Orvid paid her zilch (his staff is always quitting for nonpayment). Fettner appeared not to care. "I've got a few ex-husbands keeping me going, more or less." She was about fifty but she smoked like a chimney and her lungs would cave in after four or five years of the plague. Middlemarch will get her lungs a major clean-out at NITS but it won't work. But by then her lungs aren't the only things to have caved. "This is the single most depressing story and the single most helpless story I have ever encountered," she will write for her final story in the Prick, just before it folds as well. Again, we proceed too fast. Fred asked her to contribute some background info for where we're going. As you'll see, she provided some of the best coverage anywhere.

Nobody much ever read The New York Prick. *The New York pricks especially didn't read* The New York Prick. *Fettner might as well have been writing for the man in the moon. She didn't know this yet.* "I was still scallywagging around Washington scratching for scraps of information and thrilled with how much I was uncovering. I think people were actually happy to talk to me. I was what was called a Free Ride. Decent People wanted to tell Someone when they had dirt they knew was really dirty. It was their way, without anyone troublesome noticing, of going On the Record in case someday they got hauled up for not speaking out. Then they could say, But I did! See* The New York Prick *of such and such a date. They knew no one ever read or would read Orvid's rag. So all my superb, if I may say so, investigative reporting was damned if I did it and I was damned (in my own head and heart) if I didn't. It was to take me a few years to figure all this out. That would be the end of it for me. Oh, Fred helped me get his friend Will Schwalbe to publish a volume of my stuff called* The Science of Viruses. *But by then it was old stuff. People in Washington care about old stuff about as much as they care about the truth.*

This plague and its history was the greatest story ever waiting to be told. It still is.

•

Okay, Fred, here's some stuff to start you off.

Regurgia. The ancient word for hepatitis. Yellow skin is the sign of the body's unhealthiness, and yellow eyeballs a top clue. Hepatitis is wildly unappreciated as a bedmate of The Underlying Condition. Like when you say George Washington was gay and everybody laughs, this is another big ha-ha to the boys and girls at NITS and FADS and COD. Oh, yes, and HAD, although they're too ivory-towery to care much about lowly hepatitis. My buddy Laurie Garrett wrote the best stuff on this stuff (I cribbed some of it from her Pulitzer tome, *The Coming Plague*, with her permission), the disease, its implications, its ancient history. I love Laurie. She deserved her Pulitzer. She's the one who first raised this interconnectedness with UC and then she wouldn't write another syllable about it. Even good old Grace won't sign on to what Laurie, Fred, and I figured out. Laurie, gutsy lady that she is, must know something she can't tell anyone.

Yes, hepatitises were known to the ancient world. Several dozen of them have been identified so far. It's a very deadly virus, and for centuries a bitch to trace accurately in the body, yellow body or urine-tinted eyeballs notwithstanding. As my friend Douglas Starr writes in *Blood*, What "struck tens of thousands of soldiers during the American Civil War, and broke out among millions of soldiers and civilians during the Franco-Prussian War and World Wars I and II" carries on mercilessly to this day, which should be to those few who can read between the veins very bad news. I don't know why it's excited the interest of so few. No doubt it's because for the most part it's struck the poorest of the world, or the dirtiest, or those lacking physical stamina or with compromised immune systems (I know you told me you haven't got to immune systems yet, but you will). The immune system per se will not be given more than what Dame Lady Hermia calls "a tinker's damn" until those who have eaten too adventurously, or loved the same, and Geiseric and Pewkin and of course Omicidio come up against its brick wall and are forced to try to understand it, *try* being the operative and very limited word, but just not being good enough, fellas.

Regurgia means, literally, "throw-up," as in regurgitate. (I didn't make this up. See *Methane's Dictionary of Medical Root Equivalents*.) An unhealthy liver provides a lot of stuff to vomit out. That this vomit is top-drawer contagion will not be discovered until World War II, which, Fred says in his chronology, is right about now. But there are going to be a whole lot of mysterious killers saying hello during these war and postwar years. It's a messier war because it's being fought all over the globe and the number of dead is huge and dispersed. It's also the messiest because of concentration camps and gas ovens, an entirely new way to kill people. It gives too many overly imaginative folks everywhere new ideas about pushing the envelope. Gases inhaled can destroy livers (we should have learned this in World War I but didn't) and the masses of dead bodies lying around unburied that have been gassed to death allow regurgia's poisonous stench to be released into the atmosphere, indeed the air of the entire European continent. (I didn't make this up. See Heinrich Holzer's *Encyclopedia of Mass Extermination and Its Consequences*. See, indeed, what happened in early Philadelphia.) Ignorance about regurgia should top the list of what will kiss more boys goodbye. Why, even to still call it regurgia after all these centuries is an indication of what a dumb backwater hick place COD remains. COD is still the gatekeeper of "official terminology."

No one has put two and two together to realize that blood transfusions are a particular culprit. Little enough is known about hepatitis yet, how long it is infectious or contagious. We know now that many would pass it from their systems; we know now that many would not. We knew, then and of course now, that this virus was in the blood supply and we had no way to get it out of the blood supply. And we needed blood very badly. We didn't quite know there were different types of hepatitis (and indeed of blood itself) as well as other foreign strains, for want of a better word, which had different effects on the body.

And then there's hemophilia.

In the second century A.D. rabbis wrote in Jewish texts about what must have been hemophilia, indeed exempting male boys from circumcision if two previous brothers had died from nonstop bleeding from this procedure. Moses Maimonides (1135–1204), the great Jewish physician, extends this ruling to the sons of a woman who had married twice, thus, it would seem, alluding to the hereditary nature of the condition. In the Arab world, their great early physician Albucasis (1013–1106) made note of a family where only males died after minor injuries.

In the United States the transmission of hemophilia from mothers to sons was first described in the early 1800s. In 1803 a Philadelphia physician named Dr. John Conrad Otto wrote an account of "a hemorrhagic disposition existing in certain families." He recognized that a particular bleeding condition was hereditary and affected males. He traced the disease back through three generations to a woman who had settled near Plymouth, New Hampshire, in 1720. The word *haemophilia* first appeared in a description of a bleeding disorder condition at the University of Zurich in 1828.

Recent history has found NITS full of doctors trying to evade the draft and the few left afraid of being caught for doing so. COD was even worse, because it was a young place trying with difficulty to recruit staff to such an inconvenient city, Chattanooga. No one wants to work there, the place said to be so hot with racism that black people can still be shot to death on Main Street in broad daylight. And Paulus Pewkin, who runs COD, is known to be a pain. All of the doctors, whether those gone and returned or those who hadn't left, were, quite frankly, dumb. NITS was the only job they could find. The result of all this, obviously, is that not much gets done at its various divisions.

Hepatitis is bearable in a society when just a few people have it. More and it can be disaster. This country is about to enter a long string of physiological disasters. Hepatitis will be only one of them. A nasty one. With syphilis, that makes two. Two very nasty ones. And then there's hemophilia.

I'll be back in the late '60s/early '70s with the real McCoy.

PEOPLE QUITE OFTEN APPEAR FROM OUT OF NOWHERE

They sneak into places like offices when no one is in them. They look through drawers in desks and file cabinets. It's really quite easy to gain entrance to an awful lot of places. Fern Hetheringay dresses up as a man and does it lots of times. When she writes an article about it for the *Monument* they won't publish it, and Fern is one of their star reporters. There aren't enough men to be guards. Lots of stuff is stolen and lots of stuff isn't stolen so much as looked at, as if to see what's going on, what's being done. Five thousand mostly young new government workers arrive in Washington every month. Not all of them are on official payrolls.

IANTHE'S DAY

I write in this diary because a record of the way we live now is lacking. Like all those antebellum ladies from whom we know more about the Civil War than the ten thousand male historians who've churned their drivel into an enormous waste of trees, so will I, Ianthe Adams Strode, write about life on the home front during this current strife. I shall be the insider with a mouth. Histories, particularly ones by male historians, never have anyone quite like Ianthe.

How do you make men understand? I know this quandary has challenged women since the first gasps of time. I shall not be the one to answer it any more satisfactorily. I am not a big fan of men. Women break my heart enough.

I predict that Frank will not let one Jew into America if he can help it. And every Jew in this country thinks Franklin Delano Roosevelt is God. And *Jew* is not a word to be uttered out loud. We are truly awful.

This is the most hypocritical city in this strange country of naïve bumpkins. It is a joke to think this city is the capital of an important country. It is a joke to think this is an important country. God help us all that this country is now required to save everyone else.

And what about this secretary Franklin is "seeing" and this woman Eleanor is drawn to? It's the first interesting thing about either of them I've ever heard. I don't know why I'm surprised. Each of them, Frank and Eleanor, has at one time or another held my hand too long. They are hungry carnivores unable to understand their lust. There are few things more touching and distasteful than witnessing the faltering, tentative acts of people who want your body but have no notion how to get it. Just for the kick of it, I think I would have gone to bed with Eleanor the first time she didn't let go of my hand if she hadn't dissolved into a stuttering nervous Nelly. Franklin, well, I had to bite his little finger to get my rejection across, although I suppose it's best that presidents are persistent.

To walk down any street in Northwest is uncomfortable because this town is filled with visiting everythings. There are Germans walking around simply everywhere. Why are they here? Who could know they were never to be trusted? Anyone who knew them, that's who. I lived in Berlin before the war and I knew then. How could one not?

One desperately needs amusement. Washington, always a social sewer, has become a deeper one. People actually go to bed at nine. Where else is there to go? Dear Nancy swears there's no fun in Paris now that Hitler's come. "The streets are so filled with his soldiers that often you cannot find your own front door!" And no one has a penny in London. "It's in a kitty for a rainy tomorrow," Lady Austa writes. "It is always raining tomorrow," I write back. "It is not amusing to make jokes about the weather, just at present," she replies. "I am not talking about the weather," from me. "You Americans must always have the last word." Much of that sort of thing. Hardship brings out a certain additional petulance in the Brits. Stiff upper lips? Poo. Also from London, Sir Eric writes inquiring why Franklin installed a nice college professor as our ambassador to Germany as the storms were gathering. William Dodd. A history professor from Chicago. Sir E. wonders now, as did I when Strode was his assistant ambassador there, if this was quite "the demeanor required at that juncture." Sir E. inquires, "Since you know that city," whether I in fact know that American companies continue to sell massive amounts of stuff like airplanes and heavy machinery to Germany while our banks lend the huns money as if they all know something about that country that Sir E. does not. "Your biggest banks and industrial manufacturers!" Yes, I do and did not know that. One wonders what kind of cagey gimpy game Frank is up to still. When I confront him he says that they are all private companies and he is unable to stop them because they can do whatever they want. The second time he told me this, I said right to his face: "You do not sound like a major wartime world leader to me." Do none of his advisers, whoever they might be—henchmen I call them, also to his face, and theirs—have the balls to speak up to him? I am the only person who speaks out loud. "This war is going to last a long time," I said to him. "Even after it's over it won't be over. Do you really think Germany is going to disappear now that we are saying boo back?" I was asked to leave. As always when such unfathomable silence reigns, one can only think: This is the way they want it. Or better: This is the way the world ends.

I know all this because I was there. Strode was assigned to Berlin to work with Ambassador Dodd, who was too nice and resorted to his Bible too often. His daughter Martha was a true hellion, screwed young Nazis and Russians and anyone who caught her fancy. She was very busy. Mrs. Dodd couldn't take it all, Hitler *and* her daughter who actually flirted with the Führer, so she had a nervous breakdown and FDR brought them all home. (Whereupon Martha has become a spy for the Communists against America.) Dodd was the last official American ambassador to Berlin, but Strode, and I too of course, stayed on until '41 when FDR closed our place there down. While it lasted Berlin was the strangest amalgam of fun, fury, champagne, and hate I've ever seen. What one saw couldn't help but change you forever. Strode was never the same. Hitler scared the bejesus out of him.

People look at me like I'm a shark. It's a lonely fish, the shark. Eleanor asked me softly the other afternoon at tea, "Do you ever expect to find another husband?" "A husband!" I screamed, suddenly overcome by a fit of guffaws. "Who would ever want another one of those? Hasn't yours made you miserable enough?" She doesn't like it when I talk about Franklin that way. She gets very prissy, starts to type or make notes or knit, a little tear falling from an eye, her needles quivering. No wonder Franklin is always busy elsewhere. Everyone wonders how he gets away with it until they look at Eleanor. And his gimpy legs. Strode only had a gimpy member. I don't think they're called "members" anymore. I must ask my Jewish kids what a member is called today. I do think of them as my children. I want to protect them from the intense pain that is ahead. I am among the few I know who can remain aghast indefinitely.

I spend most of my days at this sad, sad little enterprise of Heidi Osteroff's. It moves me enormously. I sit in this pool of sweet young Jewish women who "must do something." I enjoy them. They rush to me every time they run up against a brick wall, which is with almost every telephone call. I usually know a few higher-ups we can pester. But what's the point? Franklin is not interested in Jewish refugees. In Jewish anything. No one says this out loud but it's so and that's why I'm here. To say such things out loud. No, I am not certain why I'm with these children. Franklin is my people and these girls are not. I should be trying to help my people, but they are beyond help.

Jews, Jews, everybody hates Jews. It is truly remarkable that all the anti-Semitism of centuries not only has not disappeared one bit but is actually worse now that this—what are Jews? a race? a religion? a people?—now that Jews are being decimated by that monster. Do I think that Christians are hideous enough to be glad? Yes. I do. I think there are many people who are grateful to Hitler for accomplishing what too many in this country, down deep, desire. Why are we even bothering, then, to fight this war? I'll tell you why. So we can continue to be the most hypocritical people the world has ever bred. On this, Hermia and I agree. For a Brit, she becomes more outspoken by the moment. She pleases me. Her husband is as unavailable as mine was.

So I continue to wear large shoulder pads, the symbol, and the burden, of my sisters, and come here each day as I try to be useful. There are few other places around that welcome an aging gal like me. Mariamne's father was an old flame a hundred years ago. I was only interested in Jewish men all my young girlhood. Why in all the world did I settle for a Strode? An Adams should know better.

So I continue to go into these wretched barracks, dreadfully hot, with nary a breeze from the north (the White House), and try to help several dozen sweet Hebrew children who have never before in their lives so much as picked up a telephone for anything more than ordering food, or calling their chums, or chatting up a potentially rich husband. Not one of them has more than a vague idea of who I am or was. I may be a cousin of Franklin's, but I am still a Republican, and Republicans are still unwanteds. I wonder how long it will be before this man, whom everyone worships, dies and the truth is told about how inhumane he is. I actually believe that Eleanor could do his job better. And we all know how I feel about her!

The other morning Fifi Nordlinger rushed in filled with excitement. She announced that she desired to open a catering business. She is a quite handsome thing, about twenty-four, with short blond hair and a rather square but full-figured body. I suspect she likes to be tossed around a bit. I believe she married unhappily—her father is a successful Northwest builder; he put up a good deal of Chevy Chase—but her new husband, who I think was a used-car salesman, is off at war, so perhaps he won't come home.

"What in the world would a catering business accomplish when absolutely nobody is giving parties?" Mariamne quite reasonably asked Fifi. Mariamne is also blond, but June Haver to Fifi's Betty Hutton. I am helplessly in love with American movies. They are so repellently innocent! We shall pay a big price one day for believing in the dreams they indiscriminately dream for everyone.

Speaking of movies, I ran into Amos Standing at a cocktail party at the British Embassy. He is finally back from Germany, looking most strikingly debonair. Though a bit worse from . . . something I cannot quite put my finger on. Perhaps it is no more than being witness to these present horrors so close up. When I blithely inquired how he could stay there so long, he wouldn't talk about it. It was almost as if he's a spy. Amos, as I recall, was somewhat possessed of a soul; but then we were just neighbors and Chevy Chase wasn't yet a suburb of Berlin. He's aged and I should not be surprised if he is homosexual. War brings out so much in men.

Mariamne is a pert, attentive blonde, quite sure of herself. She says if this were not wartime she would become a doctor. I said, "Why not now? What better time?" She responded, "I must raise children first. Jewish girls must work overtime to replace those our rabbi says are being murdered. We don't have time to even go to college. And besides," she whispered, "my two brothers are homosexual." She is pregnant with her fourth. I loathe it when women feel obligated to drop offspring like cows; we are, after all, more than childbearing machines.

"Oh, everybody is giving parties," Fifi told Mariamne, "it's just that Jews aren't invited to any of them. Every gentile friend I know does nothing but go to strings of parties." Fifi moves in a gentile crowd. She's still one of those cheerleader types, quite the fast and loose one, but no longer with a high school football team. I can see her, with her huge bosoms energetically bouncing up and down. She continued: "If I cater some of these parties— and I know enough of the hosts, one way or another, to call in a few favors—I could pick up the sort of secret, unofficial information we could use more of. I'll become a spy!" I do believe she was quite sincere. I tried to advise her that spies don't talk so much. "I'm only talking to my friends," she snapped back. "If I can't trust these girls, who is there to trust?" Indeed.

This molelike gnat of a man, Winesap, Breckinridge Winesap—he wears moccasin shoes with pennies in them and he must be sixty years old—came over from the White House, mainly, I believe, because I yelled at Franklin: "Tell me, Franklin, why do you hate yids so much!" To which Franklin replied, "It is really quite rude to refer to them anymore as yids." To which I replied, "That's exactly the point!" To which he replied, "I'm afraid I don't understand . . ." To which I replied, "You most certainly do not!" He must have asked Brecky to keep an eye on me and us. Brecky has named us the Jew Tank.

I was going to tell him I knew all about Hoover's new homosexual whorehouse, courtesy of Pippy Phipps, my pal at the FBI, but that would get her in trouble. A house of young men for hire by others of their sex, for the purpose of entrapping spies and others who might disclose valuable information. Pippy was fairly screaming with laughter when she told me about it. "Can you believe our chief actually thinks this is the way to win a war? And he wants everyone to know about it—not that he's behind it, of course, but that it exists. 'How can we find anything out if no one goes there?' he demands. J. Edgar is one big creepola. I wouldn't trade this job for a diamond ring!" Personally, I wonder more about who the hookers are than who their customers are. Have we got a bunch of Mata Haris at work here?

Why do the Jews believe that Franklin's helping them? I ask that all the time and every one of these sweet girls says, "My father would disinherit me if I said anything against FDR." Blind blind blind!

So what it boils down to is that each day we come into these barracks and we tackle stacks and piles and bags of mail, each with a list of missing relatives and a plea for help. With each letter we must call an embassy or a consulate and register a formal inquiry. "Please, Mr. Belgium, could you put out an official inquiry as to the whereabouts of the Ashkenazi family, consisting of . . ." Typewritten inquiries must be submitted in quintuplicate. It is quite difficult to type through four pieces of carbon paper. It should be obvious how pointless this all is. We cannot instance one single person who has been located or moved one inch closer to these shores.

Fifi became quite emphatic: "I will cater one of these huge parties of all the kids I was in high school with, who are now admirals and captains or work in the Office of This and That, and I will tell the band to stop playing 'I'll Be with You in Apple Blossom Time' for a second, and I'll grab the microphone and look straight into the eyes of all the men who had their hands up my panties or on my tits, and I'll say, 'Hey, guys, how about a little help?' "

Then she started to cry. "It won't work, it won't work, nothing will work." All very sad. So sad. Tragic, really. Fifi's desk, like the others, is covered with framed photographs of relatives presumably lost over there.

So life goes on. Washington also now has its very own exclusive heterosexual whorehouse! The real kind, not that one for fairies. Actually, we've had it for a number of years, but now so many of the best men go there, we talk about it more. Perhaps it's a sign we might be getting up there with all the best cities at the pinnacle of their sophistication. The peak of chic. The madam's name is Doris Hardware, and I know and like her. Pippy says Hoover has it under constant around-the-clock surveillance, which sounds a little like Berlin was when we left it. Martha Dodd told me that every time she screwed with a Nazi her father heard about it.

I knew Doris's father. Do you remember Horace Hardware? (Why am I asking myself questions in my own diary?) Horace hailed from Denver. He owned a chain of whorehouses, all across the West. They were very important for the growth of that part of our country. They all had raunchy names like Ace in the Hole, Up Your Lazy River, that sort of thing. You got a leather wallet with the name of the particular house branded on it when you spent a certain amount of money, and those wallets are now collectors' items. Horace built himself the biggest damn palace of a house in Denver you ever saw. He invited Daddy and me to lunch when Daddy was in the cabinet. Daddy didn't think it was a good idea for him to go, but I went. It was great fun. I sat at the table with a bunch of his girls. Horace proudly said something like, "These girls are America's secret weapons. They could spread the clap to the entire world if I wanted them to." His little daughter at our lunch that day is now not only the madam but also married to one of the richest men in Washington, Abe Masturbov. I met her at a Jew Tank reception and we nodded to each other in dim remembrance of things past before we figured it out. I am certain we shall get together and become friends.

I constantly forget to make note of sweet young Daniel Jerusalem, who is here every day. He must dearly desire to get away from home. I don't even know where Masturbov Gardens is. His constant smile is quite infectious. Only dreadfully unhappy kids smile so much and want so much for you to like them.

WHAT DANIEL LEARNS AT THE JEW TANK

Everyone at the Jew Tank is obsessed with missing persons. I wonder if that's what David is. "He's in California! He's with Grandma Libby!" is now what we're told, and which we don't believe. What's he doing there? When's he coming home? Why doesn't he write? There are questions our parents still refuse to answer. It's hard to avoid the thought that something fishy's going on. Stephen is the one who says, "I think it's something so awful they don't want to talk about it and it may be cruel of us to force the issue."

I ask Rivka why Jews can't be traced through her American Red Blood friend, Mrs. Algonqua Lemish, a Masturbov Gardens neighbor who works in the home office downtown. "I told you that. You never listen to a word I say. None of you does." It seems that all the blood organizations have made a pact not to deal with the "Jewish problem." And she'll speak of this no more, just as she won't speak of David. She's doing her best to put a good face on the fact that she works for an organization that is suddenly visibly anti-Semitic, and that she feels betrayed by her employer, to whom she's been so loyal and devoted for so many years.

How our family lives in this small apartment with all the horrors of a lost son and a lost marriage—well, it's our own dreadful war, bloodless perhaps, but with definite fatalities nevertheless.

I file a report about David at the Jew Tank. I figure, why not? I saw a war movie where an American spy got inside Hitler's bunker, so maybe someone got inside a camp. I corner Mr. Winesap and beg him to place his special seal on my search application, indicating that Mrs. Strode has blessed it.

"People are getting lost every minute," he says to me. "I'm sorry it's your brother." He's very courteous. I know I'm supposed to hate him because he's supposed to hate all of us.

My country is at war and I'm growing up, faster in some ways than in others. The Office of Alien Immigration is called, not always behind our back, the "Jew Tank." Rivka arranged for me to volunteer here. She knows most of the young women who run it because she taught them in her class at Washington Jewish, where I met them too.

Heidi Osteroff started it. Her father was a close adviser to FDR and talked the president into humoring his Heidi. Her husband, a banker, is one of the most handsome men I have ever seen. Alexei. Alexei Osteroff.

He looks like Alan Ladd with John Garfield's dark brooding eyes. And Clark Gable's wavy hair. And Lew Ayres's kindly face. And Dick Haymes's lilting voice. Every time he appears I stare. Everybody does. It's hard not to. And he loves it, in the nicest way, as if he knows he's blessed with this gift he's going to share with you. He's lovely to everyone and he's lovely to me and from the moment I meet him I love him. If it takes being accused of Trudy McNab's blindness for me to be so handsomely rewarded, then maybe God knows I'm innocent. I shake Alexei's big soft gorgeous hand every single time I can.

I'm so happy when I see him and sad when he goes. Of course, I don't let myself think of this, or anything else that would reveal such a clear preference for my sex alone. Mordy was yesterday and I don't think of him, either. He's gone. Our group is over with. I don't even know where Arnold Botts is, my nemesis who threatened to torture me forever. While I'm discovering as I get older that I have lots of girlfriends at school, or rather friends who are girls, boys are another matter. Boys smell me coming and take off. Boys sense what I sense: I'm not one of them.

Heidi is very unattractive. No one can understand how she and Alexei are married to each other. She has a hawk nose and moles near her mouth and she's about half a foot taller than he is, and also older. Ten years, it's said, although "she's been to Switzerland," whatever that means. She stands proud, though. If she thinks she's ugly, she doesn't let you know. She wears high heels and beautiful clothes and lots of dangly gold jewelry. People think she's the rich one and that's the reason they're married, but Feef Nordlinger, who knows these things, says no. "The money is his." No one wants to accept the idea that these two people might love each other. They do have four children.

Heidi started this office because of Alexei. His family is Russian German Polish Jewish and his father is caught somewhere, whether in Germany or Russia or Poland isn't clear. His mother and siblings are safe in Paris, "with their valuables in Vuitton sacks. They got out of Heidelberg just in the nick of time. However, the books were burning," Alexei tells us. The books were a big library of what he describes only as "something very special." One day Minna Trooble offhandedly asks Alexei, who comes around quite often, what his father was doing in Heidelberg. "Running the special library," he says. "A Jew? In Heidelberg? In 1943? He must be a spy." Sensible Minna. It's now more or less accepted that Mr. Osteroff was on a secret mission for President Roosevelt. But Mr. Breckenridge Winesap, whose name we are all adept at enunciating unattractively, with pursed lips and hissing, tells Alexei that his father "is only one Jew so stop showing off." Then word comes that Mr. Osteroff is dead. "His file has been consigned to 'Unreturnable Citizens'!"

Fangette Berghertz reads the letter out loud. Alexei is called to the White House and a medal is pinned on his handsome shoulder "to honor some unspecified heroic service by his father," Heidi says, "and everyone slaps him on the back and shakes his hand and would you believe that is meant to be that?"

Not for Heidi. She barges into Winesap's office. "I will get them back. All the Jewish lost, the refugees, the wandering strays. From wherever they are. And I'll get them back alive! Before you can label them 'Unreturnable'!" Winesap knows a tough Jew when he sees one. A tough Jew with a tougher grandfather. He says to her, Mr. Winesap does, "I am seeing more people like you these days." He shows her stacks of letters from rich Jews begging Franklin, begging Eleanor, to look into the matter of their beloved So-and-So.

Heidi, a tough Jew indeed, and a potentially noisy one (her grandfather is Alvah Template, who owns the *Monument* and is president of our temple), is given an old Quonset hut barracks building down by the Mall. Heidi and a few friends had been working out of the three-story Osteroff recreation room on Albemarle Street. There are a lot of these Quonset huts abandoned after World War I still on the Mall. The place is empty, awful, dirty, unheated, and Heidi takes it. In twenty minutes she's got a dozen volunteers, all young Jewish wives or eligibles, who by the next day have tables and chairs and telephones and typewriters they've had no trouble getting hold of just by calling friends. It usually takes months to get even one phone connected and we have twelve in a week. Heidi wants to call the place In Search of Lost Jewry, but Brecky won't allow the word *Jew* in our official title. "We can't play favorites. Now and then hunt down a few Christians, will you? I hereby christen you the Office of Alien Immigration but I'll call you the Jew Tank." He makes the sign of the cross and leaves so Heidi can't pester him anymore.

Heidi Osteroff, Ariadne Finkelbaum, Fifi Nordlinger, Mariamne Teitel, Fangette Berghertz, Lynne Mesiroff, Portia Schwartz, Pandora Fleischman, Ellie-Anne Groober, Samantha Sue Dodeck, Dracinda Applebaum, Janet Guelff, Francesca Adderondakz, Natalie Rudoph, Minna Trooble. There are fifteen of these young women, and their parents are all very rich. I don't know yet what the dividing line is between rich and very rich, and Rivka never makes the distinction: everyone else is always very rich. Their ancestors came to this city and made a lot of money. They all know where Masturbov Gardens is and are grateful they don't have to live there or anyplace like it. They are now second- and third-generation Jews-with-money. These fifteen young women become two dozen, then three dozen, and then fifty, and Winesap has to give us another old Quonset hut, then a third, until he sternly orders, "Enough! Find your lost Jews with what you've got!"

I discover the letter on Heidi's desk one Saturday afternoon. All the desks are piled with such heartbreak that reading anything on them is worse than any war movie at the Masturbov. I hang out at the Jew Tank every chance I get, on weekends and after school. It's a long way, those same three buses that take Philip back and forth to work, but who cares how long it takes to get away if you hate home? Here in Heidi's office, Quonset Hut 23, there's a detailed map of Europe all covered with pins. "I am afraid I must now ask you to calculate each pin as one thousand Jews," Heidi tells us before they all go out to lunch. Lynne Mesiroff starts to softly sob.

"Oh, shut up, Lynne," Ellie-Anne says. "We must prove ourselves stronger than that."

"I am not stronger than that," Lynne yells back. "And neither are you. And neither is anyone else." Then she sobs some more, building to a hysterical pitch.

Feef Nordlinger slaps her. "My God, what am I doing? I just slapped you!"

Lynne doesn't stop. "I can't take care of the world! I just can't! My tante Gute is lost in Poland. My nanny's sister is trapped in Armenia. I don't know where Armenia is! Why should she be trapped there? Is there a war in Armenia I don't know about? Some sort of local struggle that the papers aren't telling us about? She isn't even Jewish!"

"What is she screaming about?" Portia Schwartz asks Pandora Fleischman.

"She doesn't read the papers. She can't read," Pandora says.

Mariamne Teitel frowns. "That's not nice, Pandora. Of course she can read."

And Ariadne Finkelbaum gets so upset she runs out of the room, pulling her car keys out of her purse. Ariadne's father has pull somewhere, so she always has plenty of gas.

Then the rest of them go out to lunch, and I read the letter. It's not dated. The handwriting is very tiny, as if the writer is trying to smuggle out a secret. We get lots of letters in tiny handwriting on small pieces of paper. There mustn't be much paper over there to write on.

Heinie, my darling sweet heinie, my heinie, missed and blessed with the good fortune to live in safety, I send you greetings from a dark pit of agony with no escape. I love your hands, I love your feet, I love your nose that seeks and finds. Oh, why did my heart not love your heart! Had I only lied to us both, I would be free, with you, in that New World so far across the earth, free from this monster who chains me in this basement somewhere, somewhere, I don't know where, oh heinie, I don't know where I am! I only know that it hurts, not so much the pain of chains around my ankles, but the knowledge, the *experience*, that we have come to this, where one human being does this to another. I no longer know what means this word *human*, when one human does this to another human. I no longer know what means . . . almost anything. You know the irony of this? That around this monster, that around him one two three four five six of them, his now-trusted fellow conspirators, were all my lovers. That all of them gave of themselves inside of me. That for a brief moment in time I was one with each of them. That with each, with the monster himself, in that moment, coarseness turned affectionate and tender, like your huge paws of hands. I did that for this world! I thought such tenderness as I could give, as I could draw from them, might save us all and alter history. Can you understand such a feeling in such as myself? To turn something so brutal and ugly into something decent? That is better than art. That is my kind of art, the only art I am capable of creating. I am crazy. They have burned the library. All the books collected by so many of us for so long. The history of our people. The testimonies of our endurance, impossible as it has always been. Our bibliothek is gone. When all this is over, promise me that you will start collecting our books again. Promise me! When I see the flames from my window out here in this cold wilderness, then comes my overwhelming shame. I see that my abilities have all been puny. And that I have too big a part in this tragedy. I could have poisoned them all. I could have stabbed each one in his back. Enough! What are you doing to save me? What are you doing to save all of us from the monsters in charge of this enormous underwater dungeon we must swim in forever seeking breath that cannot come in time to keep us from drowning? What are you doing to hold your head up as a homosexual, to say, At least I have tried! For my people! For both my peoples! To be a homosexual is as awful as being a Jew. There is no difference in the degree of hatred against us, or in our inability to combat it. The word must somehow be spread that it is not only Jews who are being burned to ashes. It is those of us who love others like ourselves. But I know that this news does not and cannot reach the world, because we are dismissed and shunned so vehemently, with such regularity, that to put the news out would jeopardize whatever sympathy and support might be raised for the possible salvation of being just plain Jews. I have heard Hitler speak often. He talks always with metaphors of disease, comparing Christianity to syphilis and Jews to a putrid infection. He calls us germs, vermin. "The discovery of the Jewish virus is one of the greatest revolutions that have taken place in the world. How many diseases have their origin in the Jewish virus? We shall regain our health only by eliminating the Jews." I know these lines by heart because two of my lovers were forced to compose them for him. Hateful words about homosexuals were eliminated at the last moment only because people must not be reminded of Röhm, who was a homosexual and also Hitler's lover. He was also popular and is still missed. They say he was the only one who could control Hitler's hate. As he was murdered, so do we expect to be. I send you this via my guard Abner, who protects me so long as I let him fuck me every night. He smells and has rotten teeth but he loves me. Perhaps, for one brief second in time, God is being kinder to Jewish homosexual artists than to just plain Jews and you will receive it. Although what good it will do you I don't know. Perhaps it is better that you don't get it and that we were never born.

I think the writer is saying things in this letter that should be told to important people, but I don't know anyone except Brecky and I'm sure not telling him this. I'm not supposed to be reading it. I'm sitting at Heidi's desk and she'll be back from lunch any minute.

The letter frightens me, not only because I'm Jewish but because, in knowing Mordy, and now Alexei, I've learned, like the man who wrote this letter, what it's like to feel for other men. I've learned, starting with Uncle Hyman, that I'm marked with a double curse. Life will be even more complicated than it already is.

By the time I know the whole story behind this letter (which I will learn from Claudia)—that the Mr. Osteroff who wrote it was Alexei's uncle, not his father (he owned Osteroff's Chevrolet and his own son was in Phi Pi Psi with Stephen), and that he was also his lover—Heidi will have married someone else just as handsome as Alexei, who has committed suicide because Mr. Osteroff reappears one day after the war is over with another man. Mr. Osteroff had also been among the rank of Röhm's lovers and was brought to Germany at Röhm's suggestion and Hitler's request to discuss American distribution of the new Volkswagen "bug" that Hitler believed would be all the rage worldwide. Hitler kept him on ice in camps so that he could use his automotive services when the war was over.

I forgot to mention Ianthe Strode. She is very impressive. She's like one of the movie actresses I love most, Eve Arden, Rosalind Russell, Bette Davis, Joan Blondell, Thelma Ritter, the tough ladies who make us both laugh. She smiles at me all the time and I think we could be friends. Minna told me Ianthe is very wellborn (as with Rivka, there's always a "very" when Minna describes people) and is related to the president even though she's a Republican. Her father was vice president of the United States, I forget whose.

DORIS HARDWARE CALLS THEM AS SHE SEES THEM

On this anniversary, I write this for our records and for anyone who may come to be in my place.

Do you know what it's like to run a whorehouse? A comfortable, elegant whorehouse that has already served the nation's capital for some dozen years, with not a whit of trouble, and is now booming in wartime as never before?

Do you understand what happens to a man when he gets the need on? When whatever he's doing—and it may be the most overwhelmingly important national need, a treaty awaiting drafting, due on the president's desk the next morning, or approval for the launching of a troopship or secret spy negotiations—his cock says, You've got to take care of me first.

It's not difficult to find good whores, especially today when girls want to leave home because wartime makes them restless. Good beautiful whores. Good beautiful loyal whores. Good beautiful loyal trustworthy whores. I used to hate the word *whore*. Now I consider it distinguished. Women have disappointed me much more than whores.

When word got across the country and around the world that my house was a good place to be, women began knocking on my door daily, inquiring.

I always interview them myself, in my study, where everything is unthreatening floral patterns. People feel safe around flowers. I've interviewed thousands and kept their names and my reactions to them in my secret files. If you don't think that's been some valuable network over the years . . . Well, anyway, I mostly hire on the spot if I feel the right feeling, whether I need them or not. It's a huge house and there's always room for one more.

So what's there to understand about providing vaginas for the pricks of Washington? Are Washington pricks different from any other city's pricks? Is anything different required for my cunts? I don't like to use language like this, but that's how most men think of sex, as something involving cunts and cocks. Wives are for the romantic fantasies that are never realized, and are just there to torture both sides. I provide the cunts and they get erections here that they can't get at home. They don't think of anything here as involving love or kisses or affection, which is what I'm convinced women want from men: wells of affection, tons of love, barrels of kisses, gobs of sentiment, but no sex. Wives don't like to be fucked. Which is just as well because my fuckers can usually only get it up for cunts.

So one of the things I look for in a good whore is a woman who doesn't want or need wells of affection. But she can't be a glacial woman, because most men don't want to fuck a complete iceberg (though I've met a few who do).

What makes a woman uncaring to the degree I require? "Uncaring" is not quite correct. A good whore cares. I mean, perhaps, disattached in some primal interior region, perhaps if only for self-protection, which is OK, fine, really. How can I tell this with enough precision? For the whore has needs too, and madams who have come and gone unsuccessfully in the History of Whorehouses have come a cropper on just this shoal: a whore has needs too, and you cannot deny them or ignore them. You may not wish to act on them, but as in any good relationship, they must be discussed.

Actually, it all has very little to do with wanting to get fucked or enjoying getting fucked. It has little to do with actual fucking period, just as licking an envelope has little to do with the writing of the letter sealed inside it.

Do these women get pleasure from pleasing? Some do, some don't. *Abandonment.* If I had to search for one word to pinpoint what I endeavor to sense empathetically from the woman across from me, that's it. The ability to let go.

To let go of many things. The past. The future. Even, in a sense, the present, the outside world. To let go of romantic notions. To let go of worldly responsibility. To let go of the outside world. To some this is a consummation devoutly to be wish'd.

Because romantic notions are breast-fed and force-fed into us every day of our lives from birth, it's not easy to let go of many of them, much less all.

The whores of literature, of movies, of novels—these aren't the whores I want. When any of them show up, I can tell immediately. They're like cheap chocolate creams that you spit out because they aren't caramels or nougats, the more long-lasting ones you really want. You send them away immediately. You don't put them in the active file. (Though you always keep them in a file. Names on lists are precious treasures. You never know when you'll need your lists to fight back with.) These girls are pining for husbands or children, believing they can find love, believing in love in the first place. My girls don't want any of these things. They never believe they can find love.

Which isn't to say that some of them haven't found it. But nonexpectation is everything.

Abandonment of body to sexual pleasure? I've never made up my mind on this one. Whether it's a plus or a minus. Yes, some of my girls like sex a lot. Some like it too much. Some have favorite diversions that are usefully salable. But rarely is sex, or what they do, or their customers, their main interest. Like many good employees who work hard at their jobs, when they're finished for the day, they're finished for the day, or in our case, night.

How can I sense when a woman can let go? Especially in this society of ours, with so many rules and regulations and parameters, a society where women particularly are forced into molds invented by others, invented by men, invented by men long ago?

I know this isn't a very scholarly answer, but I just can. And I'm here very successfully to prove it.

Once I found the following in a magazine article and I clipped it out because it said what I thought: "I seek the courtesan who neither loves her customers nor expects them to love her; yet she waits for them and enacts the drama of love. Neither the artificial love nor the payment she receives truly satisfies her. I realized that all human beings are like courtesans, trying to get the world to enjoy us. But the payment is invariably inadequate, and we're always dissatisfied. Thus I learned to live with dignity and self-respect without expecting fulfillment from this world. The only place I will find it is within."

That's the kind of abandonment I seek.

Abe, of course, doesn't understand a bit of this. That's why I never talk about it with him. He's as bad as the whores I never hire. He believes in love. Even after everything I've put him through. He will never understand that I do love him. It's just not the love he wants. Men!

•

I think events are moving along quite nicely, thank you.

HAPPY BIRTHDAY

Mordy Masturbov was actually born in Masturbov Gardens, even though the place wasn't quite ready to open for business. Doris moved into a large three-bedroom apartment on what she named Mordecai Place, a quiet cul-de-sac, furnished especially for her lying-in, and here she gave birth to the baby boy and nursed him quietly for a while, holding him closely and dearly and touchingly in her arms, looking down at him as if she'd brought something truly inestimable into her life and, God knows, not knowing what in the hell to do with it, before returning to her other life. She did break down and allow Abe to marry her. Yes, she wanted her son to have a decent and uncomplicated birth certificate. He was then sent to that house on Sixteenth Street, the house his father grew up in and now lives in again, the house with the big gargoyles and caryatids with enormous breasts—where he would be brought up by many a nanny, with a rare visit from Granny Yvonne. Yes, as in some never-ending grim fairy tale Yvonne is still upstairs in that turret's tower.

Doris never comes to Sixteenth Street. Mordy is brought to meet her at outings to parks, the zoo, the movies. He calls her Doris. Sometimes Abe comes along. At this point, who knows what his parents have told him, about . . . anything?

The big tits on the columns always make Abe smile. No woman will live with him for long in this place. Although he'll never give up on Doris, he's auditioned a few live-in contenders. "Blanche, Ruba, Sally, Demetria, Allynda, that's only five and there were six before I was twelve. Vi, right. And then Hortencia, Nulla, Flo, Garah . . ." As a kid Mordy shows off by counting them on his fingers. He remembers them all, but he doesn't remember their faces. Mordy takes pictures of this ornamentation with his little Kodak Brownie. At six he knows where to point his camera. He knows because the big breasts excite him. In the rain one night he takes out his tiny penis and massages it with the rainwater as he looks up at the columnar women with those huge breasts and closed eyes and placid unchanging expressions on their carved implacable faces. Yvonne watches him from above and goes to Abraham, with whom she will confer when something upsets her. It looks like Mordy's starting young. All those adult picture books Abe's put in the kid's rooms must be having an effect. Abe is pleased by his son's excitement.

Abe fucks nameless women on the floors of unoccupied rooms in this house and in empty apartments in Masturbov Gardens. He makes a lot of noise when he fucks, unusual for a man so quiet all other times. Mordy comes to recognize these noises, the slurps and screams and heaves and groans and even farts that come from behind closed doors. Abe stuffs his big paw of a hand over the women's mouths if he hears so much as the beginning of an "I love you" forming on their lips. Mostly they don't hang around after he comes. He shows them out right away, jamming a fifty into their hands, he still naked, bits of dripping semen congealing on his cock. As for the two or three who sweat it out and manage to move in for a while, he never fucks them once they're there. They have to listen to his grunting intimacies with others, or they find out about the crazy old lady in the attic, or worse, they run into her in a hallway and are subjected to her Yiddish curses. They move out soon enough. "Yeah, I know I'm not nice about any of this," Abe tells Lucas Jerusalem, with whom he spends a great deal of time. He likes Lucas. Lucas is the son he wishes he had. He doesn't dislike Mordy, he just likes Lucas more, and Mordy knows it. Strangely, it doesn't bother him. Mordy will always have this dissociative streak. The only thing he'll love obsessively, and from which he'll draw all the return of love he requires, will be *Sexopolis* and anything to do with it, which will come unfortunately to include one Velvalee Peltz.

Abe remembers his father bathing him, playing with his penis, studying it carefully, in the huge bathtub in the same oak-paneled room that's always cold no matter how hot the furnace. One day Abe takes the boy's tiny penis in his own hand and says, "I promise you that this is the most wonderful thing in life. Your penis will bring you great pleasure. And that pleasure will cost you pain deeper than any other you've experienced. I know that doesn't make sense. But you'll find out soon enough."

Doris won't sleep with Abe, won't live with him, won't have another kid with him, won't go on vacation with him, but she'll talk to him as many times a day or night as he wants. Doris has been the biggest heartbreak he ever wants to know. He thinks of her every time he fucks. Erections come only with her image in front of him. When he thinks of the whorehouse he gets sick to his stomach. "We do have a life together," she answers to his pleadings. "There isn't anyone else, if that's what you're afraid of." As it was for Herman, life on the only level that matters becomes unavailable to his son. As with Herman, the only thing Abe really understands is money. Nothing else in his entire life will grow. When the war comes Abe thinks of joining up. He has no patriotism, only a desire not to have to answer inquiries as to why he isn't in uniform. He tells the truth. He has a son to raise and a crazy mother in his attic. So he's rejected for active duty.

Abe's only son takes too long to become a man. He's twelve, then twelve and a half, then twelve and three-quarters, and still no pubic hair. Yes, the penis itself is growing noticeably larger, but there's no hair. Abe's hair came before he was twelve. Herman told him it was because they had bathed in the same water. So what's delaying Mordy? At twelve Abe had taken him to a Swiss doctor who said there's nothing abnormal. Mordy's scared by the doctor's poking in his groin and that he seems to have a problem important enough for a medical consultation, and in a foreign country and a foreign language, too. His sleepless nights begin. Early each morning he throws back the covers. At twelve and three-quarters he's still bare. At St. Anselm's he'd seen that all the others have started. Many have even finished! He dreads each shower with his classmates. He feels like a puppy who's punished when he can't control his wee-wee.

Abe knows he's too impatient. He knows the damn hair will grow soon enough. Why is he behaving so? He wants to love this son. What else has he got to show for all his love for Doris? So what has pubic hair got to do with any of this? Abe couldn't tell you. Fathers are meant to worry about their sons. So he's worrying.

Abe hurts for Mordy. He's hungry for Mordy's adulthood. He wants to show him what awaits him, teach him what his own father never taught him. So with or without the hair, he supplies Mordy with more sexual lessons: books and toys and unguents and photographs. Mordy studies them all quietly. He learns what a dildo is, and about the bevy of items for self-mortification, and well, lots of other things. Never does the son ask the father for an explanation, and never does the father offer one. He'd never needed a book. All he needed was his schlang and a hole. He sees that the world has changed. Doris showed him that.

How does he prepare his son for his mother? How do you tell a son such a thing? She wants to take Mordy and show him around as her father did for her, but Abe puts his foot down on this one. "Do we have to tell him every-thing in the world?" he asks her. So nothing's been said yet (often the worst course of action when something's so complicated, so problematic), especially now that the boy's first pubic hair's arrived, and on his thirteenth birthday. He does rush to show his father, and Abe does beam and make the obvious joke, "Today you are a man."

Doris decides to violate Abe's wishes. On this thirteenth birthday, when he, like Daniel, will not be bar mitzvahed by his own choice and his parents' deferral on this matter, Doris comes to the house on Sixteenth Street and asks the boy if he would like to join her for a ride in her new convertible. She drives him to her house and parks outside it.

"I think it's time for you to know certain things. For one, I'm your mother, which I assume you've figured out. For another, I own and manage this whorehouse that I'm now going to show you. And last, I want you to take to heart this thought: that no matter what has happened or will ever happen, I love you and have loved you and will always love you, and that what your father and I have worked out, in our own no doubt misguided but honest attempt to take all of each other's needs into consideration, has probably not been the best way to raise a son. Whew. Yes, that was a long sentence. Both of our families are filled with long histories of attempts at establishing home-steads in unwelcoming locations. Abe and I have survived. You must survive as well. That's an order. From your mother." And she bends over and kisses him as best she can on the cheek closer to her. He nuzzles his head into the crook of her neck. "Good. Now, come on. Let's go take a look. I was younger than you when my poppa gave me a similar tour. I inherited this calling from him and this is yours someday if you want it."

One by one, the girls, nicely dressed and on their best behavior, and all lined up as if visiting royalty were making a state visit, shake Mordy's hand. He is overwhelmed with the beauty of these women, and, yes, warmed by their smiles in a way he's not yet associated with women, or sex, or anything, really. It is all very much "Howdy do." One or two of them refer to him as "young man," which also sounds comforting to him. Doris leads him through the house. He's shown all their rooms, neat and with flowers and sun pour-ing in the windows where the drapery and blinds are open, for a change.

She also shows him her office, where she interviews and keeps her led-gers, and the locked room where she's got all those names. Then she shows him a little room she'd made, filled with all kinds of mementoes of the old days in Denver, of Turvey, Horace, Horace Jr., tintypes of them and of lots of the girls, whose faces and names she could remember. She's overcome with good feelings for all of them, and "that life which you could lead as Denver grew to become strong." As he paged through albums and looked at framed celebrations where the girls were all lined up like the class photos on the walls of St. Anselm's, he told her, "You miss it."

"I miss something," she finally answered, taking his hand. "Life is about missing and trying to find. I just want you to know I think all of this is good and, yes, healthy. It's hard to maintain all of that when no one else does."

"I'll help you," he cries out impulsively, and she breaks into laughter and, again, some tears. She hasn't been this teary in God knows when. She's glad she did what she's done today. She'd thought about it long enough. Yesterday she'd received word that Urvah, that mother that she never really knew, had died in Utah, surrounded by 17 children and 105 grandchildren and great-grandchildren, none of whom she'd known, her family, her blood relatives. It all didn't make any sense.

And then they all go into the dining room, where a birthday cake is waiting for its candles to be lit. Doris lights them. They all sing Mordy "Happy Birthday."

Yes, he does have tears in his eyes. He looks at them all as they all smile at him. He looks at his mother, as she has tears herself. No one, it would appear, has in any way succumbed to the macabre nature of the moment.

Doris then drives him home and comes into that house and faces Abe, who's waiting there, a frown upon his face.

"So now you know?" He looks at them both.

"Poppa, I'm happy I know because at least these are answers to questions I don't want to have anymore. Don't be upset. How is what she showed me any different from the roomful of books and toys and . . . stuff you give me?"

They go out to dinner at Fairmount, the Jewish country club built on land he sold it. It's a daring thing to do, and Abe sees that Doris's eyes are flashing triumphantly. He hasn't seen this in . . . he can't remember the last time. She is making him smile again. So they all try hard to enjoy this new familial togetherness. Doris asks Mordy lots of questions about his school and his studies and his interests. He thinks of telling them about Claudia and his notions that he's tried to spell out to her himself. He suspects they'd both approve, so he tries.

"There is a girl that I love a lot. But she's not having any of me. I write her long letters that she doesn't answer. But she will!"

And they all laugh.

Abe knows that fellow diners are looking at them in their own wonderment. Doris knows that a number of men in this room know who she is. It seems to Abe that she's actually sitting taller, her face radiant, perhaps with relief, or perhaps with something else. Has she been reading Socrates: courage is the ability to know what should be feared and what should not? Has she been smitten by Roosevelt's "the only thing we have to fear is fear itself"? Or Mr. Churchill going on about "This was their finest hour"? Abe's become quite the reader. What else is there to do?

So be it, at least for now.

Mordy's happy to find a mother as welcoming as Doris. They go out together and more and more Abe joins them. Do they all each begin to smile at the absurdity of it all? Mordy begins to get better grades in school. It could not have been this easy, Abe says to himself after Doris comes home to Sixteenth Street one night and they sleep in each other's arms. Easy? What is he talking about? She's not slept with him in twenty, twenty-five years? They don't fuck. They both have the sense to know that's not what this moment's about. "We are taunting fate too much," he said to Doris as they left the country club. She only stood up taller. "Perhaps it is time to fight certain fights with more . . . audacity," she answered. "This is not a city for audacity," he said, so that even Mordy could hear.

Mordy had those perplexing few months with Daniel Jerusalem. Daniel tried to help him in some commiserating fashion. They were both going through bad patches. Mordy sensed that Daniel didn't understand what sex is about and that what he needs from Daniel isn't what Daniel needs from him but what he, Mordy, needs from Claudia. And he's still convinced Daniel's getting it from Claudia. Mordy went along with Daniel for a while. Why not? He'd read about homosexuality and it sounded like fun; he can see where it's useful as part of a repertoire. But Daniel moons and moans so. Daniel goes to great lengths to prove to Mordy he cares. It shouldn't take that much work. How can Claudia be interested in Daniel?

Of course the hair comes. With it comes his discovery that sex is even more complicated than he thought. He will sort out the complications.

Mordy's first experience with a girl, like Daniel's, is with Claudia, at just about the same time.

One day Mordy finally says to her, "I want to talk to you. No, I want to kiss you. No, I want to see your body. No, I want to hold you and hold you."

"So many nos to make a yes, Mordecai," she answers, like a teasing siren in some sophisticated movie.

He wants to ask her what that means, but he decides to concentrate on his desires. The dark tunnels that connect all of Masturbov Gardens are cool in the hot weather. To get Claudia down into one of these snaking tunnels and screw her on the cement floor—Daniel's experience, as "revealed" by Arnold Botts after Mordy bribed him with five dollars—holds no romantic appeal for him. Mordy wants his passion to be gentle. He's read enough pornography where cruelty and bad manners are paramount, and he hated its coldness. He's heard enough doors slammed by his father's departing visitors after the sound effects, the heaves and the thuds when Abe throws the occasional fuck down on the floor. The son desires a different kind of performance. It hurts him enough that Daniel, according to Arnold, has already . . . known Claudia . . . completely. He isn't jealous. He just wants Claudia himself.

Down into the tunnels they go after all, and in the dim light he pulls her into his arms with no finesse. She smiles. Like so many of them, he talks better than he performs, but she lets his hands find their way to her white panties and caress her wherever they land. Finally she shows him what he's searching for and then studies his penis with great interest. "I think it will look very nice." He's throbbing and he starts to masturbate and she watches quietly for a few moments before taking his hand to stop him. "The mystery is better," she says, and he doesn't understand this either.

"I want you, I want you," he moans, echoing sentences he's read. He tells her she's meant to receive him, that he has in his pocket the necessary protection (although during a dress rehearsal it looks so big he's afraid he might fall out of it), and he asks her if this is her first time. She lets him go on with his not uninteresting chatter, deciding to let him think what he thinks. It makes little difference to her. Finally she says, "I'm not a tease. I've done it before, but I'm not going to do it with you, and I don't wish to discuss why. It has nothing to do with you, or how I feel about you. Please don't ask any more questions."

When she disappears, he's forced to think about her more than he sees her. He writes her long letters like this one, but when he mails them she's no longer there.

Claudia, I want so much for you. For me. For us. For this wonderful act called love. How joyous it is for two people to come together, this flying-high, this two-yet-oneness that takes us to the top of a mountain and lets us float into our own heaven, ours alone.

But we shouldn't have to do it in a place that's cold and nasty and dark and underground. We shouldn't have to hide it.

I think what I'm driving at is something more universal, more philosophical. Hey, I'm a philosopher, telling you my philosophy! What do you think?

We have to invent a whole new attitude about sex itself! We have to begin to see it as fun, and everyone has to feel free doing it. If they don't, they're just entering a prison, like the other prisons they enter every day.

I don't think sex is fun for most people. It sure isn't for my father as far as I can tell.

I want every man and woman to feel wonderful before, during, and after making love, just as you and I, Claudia Webb and Mordecai Masturbov, would feel. Oh, if you would only make love with me!

I make a promise to you, here and now, Claudia, my first love: I promise to bring this new philosophy into reality. I'll preach it and write about it and scream it from the rooftops. FUCKING IS FUCKING FANTASTIC! AND DON'T YOU FORGET IT! I'll tell the world! That's what all the great philosophers do!

These letters—and he'll write many more—will turn out to be his first attempts to formulate what will become *Sexopolis*. He thinks about his new philosophy all the time.

War? What war?

YIDS, FAIRIES, WHORES, AND *SEXOPOLIS*

It's not the time to proclaim that one is Jewish. This doesn't trouble Stephen, but Lucas feels shame "for all the hiding." His own Rabbi Grusskopf has told him about the 232 rabbis stranded in France on their way to America when their travel visas are invalidated by the State Department. Appeals to Cordell Hull, with his secretly Jewish wife, and to his assistant, Sumner Welles, with his own secrets, and to Treasury Secretary Henry Morgenthau, also Jewish, bring naught in the way of help for the stranded rabbis. Their plight is leaked to Drew Pearson, a columnist more courageous than others, and a public hullabaloo transpires before the State Department validates the rabbis' visas, by which time they've all been sent to their deaths.

"What do you care about a bunch of foreign rabbis?" Stephen asks his brother.

"How can you even ask me such a dumb question?"

Rabbi Grusskopf also tells Lucas about the 129 homosexual Jews reported by one of his congregants to have been "gobbled up and spit out somewhere south of Dresden." This sad tale, of course, is never written about. For some reason Lucas tells Daniel, who nods and frowns and doesn't respond.

Stephen and Mordy become friends through Phi Pi Psi, a fraternity of rich Jewish high school boys, most of whom go to private schools. Stephen accepts their offer, even though Lucas declines. "It would be like trying to be something we aren't," he tells Stephen. "We live in Masturbov Gardens and they live on Brandywine and streets like that. You know how many buses it takes to get there."

An outing takes half a dozen Phi Pi's to a whorehouse, in fact to Doris Hardware's whorehouse. Six teenagers go into a suite. Stephen is forced to strip down in front of the others. There's a Norman Rockwell on the wall: Mom icing a cake in the kitchen, soldier son arriving at the front door, home for his wedding, which is being rehearsed in the parlor. Stephen stares at the soldier; he does not take his eyes off the soldier as the six boys stand naked trying not to look at one another.

For the first time, Stephen has a body, which he hates, adored. Three girls cannot be getting such joy from this hairy body, which they roll against, over and over, declaring their pleasure. The other boys are looking at him peculiarly. And there's his new friend Mordy mounting and performing as if he's been doing it since birth. At the height of orgasm one of his "brothers" reaches out a hand and Stephen takes it and finds the exchange strangely moving.

The guys perform and perform with the women. After Stephen's fifth orgasm completes itself and what little semen is left inside him dribbles onto the faces of the girls, their tongues licking it up, the boys from Phi Pi Psi clap in admiration, Mordy emitting a soft "Wow!" Then all the boys shower together, and are joined by the girls in a huge tub, "a plunge," one of them calls it, all their bodies once again intertwining. Stephen feels the male flesh of his friends encroaching on him; he feels hands reaching out to run their fingers through the thickets on his body that had always embarrassed him so. He thought he looked like an ape. Mordy submerges in the tub and looks at all the genitals. A few of the guys are hard again, the girls adeptly coaxing them. "You guys are a treat. You wouldn't believe who we have to pretend to like the rest of the time."

Mordy exclaims to Stephen, "We should be able to do anything we want! Without guilt. With pleasure. Do you feel good?"

"I feel wonderful," Stephen answers. "I feel wonderful."

In the steam room, Mordy and Stephen are alone. Mordy outlines his philosophy for him.

"I want to start a revolution."

"What kind of revolution?"

"A sexual revolution."

"What does that mean?"

"I just told you."

"Tell me again!"

"We should all feel free and great doing what we want to do. We shouldn't feel bad. We should feel wonderful. Always."

And so it's in the steam room of a whorehouse owned by his father and run by his mother, in the continuing years of another world war, that Mordy Masturbov describes his plans for *Sexopolis* to Stephen Jerusalem, who in a few years will become his lawyer. *Sexopolis* will become Mordy's own war against the world.

Stephen hates coming home as Lucas hates coming home. Rivka doesn't miss them. Philip doesn't miss them. After a while it seems almost natural to Rivka that they're not there. David takes all the worry time she can spare. She harbors the thought that Lucas and Stephen are actually being considerate, relieving her of their presence. She wonders when Daniel will be leaving, too. She doesn't even know he wants to become a doctor. When she finds out she worries how they can pay for it.

Lucas does tell Daniel where he goes. Abe is taking him to the ball game. Abe is taking him fishing on Chesapeake Bay. Abe is taking him to a movie. Abe lets him stay over too, after Abe takes him out for a really great dinner. "Abe thinks I'll be a great lawyer and he'll give me business. Abe is a really great guy."

"Do you see Mordy ever?" Daniel asks.

"Sure. He's sort of quiet. He doesn't like ball games or fishing. We ask him to come with us. Abe wants him to be more than he seems to want to be. Didn't you two used to be good friends? What happened?"

"I don't know. Ask him."

With Lucas at Yaddah, and Stephen at Franeeda State, and David in a concentration camp, three out of three of Daniel's brothers have left him.

Rivka wonders why it falls to her to be privy to so many strange things. She is told constantly by her boss, Miss Theodora von Lutz, that "the war is a stern master." Rivka repeats it like a mantra that will help her get through each day with patriotism. What is peeking through the letters, directives, and now actual cables, international pieces of paper from Geneva? Why, she even has a code name; she, Rivka Wishenwart Jerusalem, now actually has a code name: Verdingy? Verdingy doesn't sound very reassuring, it sounds a little flippant, but at least it's distinctive, or so she thought until she's contacted by a Verdingy II in Halo, Idaho, and a Verdingy III in Washington itself. She tries to talk to Miss von Lutz about this but she is shushed, as she somehow knows she will be. This is not Rivka's idea of "fighting for the war effort" (Mrs. Roosevelt always makes it sound so noble), with these silly names. Whatever is she doing? Well, she has no idea. Boxes come packed in dry ice from Halo or Washington, or even from Geneva, Switzerland, itself, and Miss von Lutz sends someone to pick them up. Boxes or communications, all labeled "via Hykoryville," which is where Rivka is, and addressed from "Hooker Partekla" are sent out to "Puttsig Geneva" and boxes from "Odorstrasse Washington" are sent to "Puttsig Partekla," and there have been several to and from Hooker Partekla to Odorstrasse. They are all always picked up or delivered by a uniformed armed courier from Perseus Air Freight Services. Hykoryville seems to be some sort of halfway drop-off point, and she wonders why things can't be sent directly. Every once in a while something must have broken inside, because the packages are stained with blood. Miss von Lutz has warned her, "Don't touch it unless you wear the special gloves. Don't let anyone else touch it unless they wear the special gloves. If it arrives damaged, you must immediately dispose of it in the furnace, burn it up, posthaste! You do have the special gloves, don't you? You do leave the furnace burning at all times, don't you?" Had she not dealt with bloodmobile blood almost every day since before the war even started? She's certainly touched enough bloody things accidentally broken or spilled without wearing special gloves or burning anything up. It's hard not to have the notion that something is going on. She misses her bloodmobile. She misses running Home Service. She misses taking care of people, having contact with people, having sad stories to tell Daniel when she gets home. But Miss von Lutz ordered her to cease all patient contact. Many people still call with cries for help. She no longer goes home at night believing she's done some good for America.

Philip seems pleased she no longer enjoys her work. He actually says to her once, "Now you know how it feels." She goes into their bedroom and cries. He comes in and from behind so she can't see him gather her up in his arms. "What's happened to us, Riv?" he coarsely whispers. She wants to let go of the even larger amount of tears inside her waiting to flow out, but she pulls away from him and runs to the bathroom, where she locks the door.

Once she thinks she might be on to something. Someone or something named Dye evidently knows Brinestalker. Brinestalker was meant to be in business in Germany. Philip mentioned his name when she forced his confession. She saw his name written on an envelope that had come to Philip at Masturbov Gardens. The return address was Brinestalker c/o Dye, Puttsig Partekla. She asked him about it and he went into his silent mode, not that they lived by any other. She can finally get through a whole night sleeping by his side in their double bed without waking up feeling sorry for herself. Is she now so accustomed to the peculiar that she can sleep like a normal person?

She really has few friends. And for some reason ARB closed this office down, sent her downtown, and has sent her back here to her old office in Hykoryville, now an empty house where she sits alone in her ARB uniform with its jaunty cap and insignia pins and waits for more deliveries.

Rivka is noticing that more and more she's filled with less and less of the milk of human kindness. If President Roosevelt and *The New York Truth* and *The Washington Monument* aren't taking care of her people, as even Rabbi Chesterfield is now saying out loud, she's feeling less charitable about taking care of theirs. No, no, she mustn't think like this.

Is Philip's "friend" now back on the "home front"? She shudders involuntarily. What does that mean, if he is? Well, the father may be back but his son is not, and the father isn't talking about that either. She tries to consider this a good omen that David is somehow safe. Wouldn't her own husband and the boy's father tell her if it was otherwise? She realizes that she honestly doesn't know the answer to this.

She had recently received a phone call from a Mrs. Purvis, inquiring about a place called Partekla, in Idaho, "where young men are being murdered because they are homosexual. Does American Red Blood know anything about this? I have a young boy who wears my dresses when I'm not at home and I worry for him." Rivka finds herself being impolite. "American Red Blood does not deal in homosexuality or inquire about our clients' private lives." And she says goodbye, almost hanging up the phone before she does. She sits in her office for some time staring into space. It's getting dark outside. Is David in a place like this now? She has always suspected down deep he's homosexual like his father. Does it run in families? She picks up the phone and calls the main office.

"Partekla?" Miss von Lutz exclaims questioningly. "I don't know where such a hideous story comes from. That we in America should be killing our own young, of whatever stripe, is absurd!" And she hangs up just as Rivka had, not wanting to discuss it further.

She prays David isn't there. Don't be ridiculous, she tries to tell herself again; how could he get from Germany to Idaho?

MORE

My dear colleagues:

I have been very busy here at Schmuck because we are seeing so many soldiers and sailors sent home in terrible condition, awful wounds and strange illnesses. And of course much more syphilis. I have not forgotten Grace's and my visit outside the White House and the many interesting and unanswered questions it raised. Several of my sailors (although several could be soldiers; it is difficult to distinguish which in hospital gowns; also their medical records often are lost and missing) are afflicted with symptoms that hark back to my early cases with your late cousin, Mercy, and with Evvilleena Stadtdotter.

I have gone back and made additional slides. I have discovered that all of the cases, Mercy, Evvilleena, the nuns, my sick sailors or soldiers, are *equal* on the Guttman Scale. Yes, this applies to my new soldier (or sailor) cases. *Twelve in one month.*

Grace, when last we met (or should I say when first we met) I spoke of this word *glause* and proposed it might have something to do with your mismitosis. If you consult your *Meritorium Ancien Atticus*, which I suddenly had the instinct to do, you will see that the ancient Greeks make mention of glause as a devastating illness, almost invariably fatal! The symptoms were cancerous skin sores, and "a mismitosis" which means "fatal weakness in the limbs."

From my armed forces, I have also scraped samples. With our powerful Ivanospitch I have discovered infinitesimal dots, like the tiniest of points from the tip of my pen. They look black at first, then red, then their true color, deep purple. The Greeks, using mirrors and rays from the sun, mention purple glause dots.

I still await the blood sample.

PICTURES AT AN EXHIBITION

Mr. Y'Idstein and Rabbi Chesterfield meet with Eugene Template at his office at *The Washington Monument.*

"I have been approached by sources abroad that must remain confidential," Mr. Y'Idstein begins. "Eight hundred thousand of my Jewish Hungarian brethren are in great danger in my homeland. My sources, who are safe and free, have been made the repository of an extremely valuable collection of great art, given them for safekeeping by many Jews from France and Germany and even Italy, who my sources tell me are no longer alive. They would like to use some of the art to bargain for the lives of these Jewish people. You will know that this offer is legitimate because the art is worth many tens of millions of dollars and Hungarians do not give away their valuables so casually even when they do not actually own them. Perhaps you can give me some notion of how to proceed with this offer. On their behalf, of course."

Various plans like this have been regularly discussed over the years, to no avail. This suggestion of Y'Idstein's is made in March 1944, just as these Hungarians are facing a change in their formerly relatively safe status. The War Refugee Board has just been formed to deal with information that Template and Dunkelheim and their newspapers are ignoring. Indeed, Adolph Arthur Dunkelheim is on the WRB, although that has made no difference in the *Truth*'s silence.

Y'Idstein's plan is turned down without discussion. Template won't touch it and bluntly tells him so. Rabbi Chesterfield, well, one wonders what's going on inside his mind or in that house with its closet holding its own stash of great art, including that bunch of Rembrandts. (It appears that Mr. Y'Idstein isn't including the Rembrandts.)

In New York, Virgil Vindicator has also managed to get his own meeting with Adolph Arthur Dunkelheim. In real life he's an accountant and knows one of the *Truth*'s accountants. Virgil Vindicator is perhaps the tenth or twentieth Virgil Vindicator out there trying to fight the good fight for his people. Each knows that all of his predecessors have been eliminated along their way. Somehow more and more is leaking out about his brothers and sisters.

"Richard Otto in Dresden. Does that name ring a bell? And Oskar Petzer. He lived in Bavaria somewhere. He was the son of your cousin Estelle Petzer."

Adolph Arthur stares at Virgil before curtly nodding.

"These two men were homosexuals."

Adolph Arthur does not nod.

"Of the sixteen million 'homeless victims' in camps or some form of incarceration, my sources believe that easily three million of them are homosexuals, Jewish and otherwise. Can you help us get this information out to the world? This number includes your cousins Dick and Oskar, as well as Fraulein Anna-Maria Sorberg, a Swedish lesbian who was loved by . . ."

Adolph Arthur gets up and leaves the room. Virgil remains seated. After twenty minutes or so Adolph Arthur returns. His cold eyes reveal nothing. Virgil thought he might detect redness or a hint of tears. The word is that he and Anna-Maria had been particularly close.

Virgil is ushered out. His mutilated body will be found in the town dump not far from the town in New Jersey where he'd lived all his life.

At the annual meeting of the Association of Newspaper Publishers, this year in Roanoke, Virginia, a young nurse, who is not identified in the program, commandeers the microphone to speak to the several hundred in attendance.

"At an army hospital in Chicago, Illinois, where I currently work, it has been discovered that wounded soldiers returning from action are, in increasing numbers, coming back with something called HSJ, homologous serum jaundice, which is being spread through plasma transfusions drawn from different pools, each pool made up of donations from fifty or more different donors. It's discovered that the larger the plasma pool, the more likely it is to contain this HBJ stuff. Captain Emmanuel M. Rappaport of the U.S. Army Medical Corps, one of my bosses, has concluded not only that transfusions are to blame but also that the pooling of plasma probably increases considerably the incidence of this deteriorating and often fatal illness. Nearly a quarter of a million soldiers inoculated with the yellow fever vaccine, made from the pooled plasma of many donors, have developed HSJ.

"And our COD, our Center of Disease, established to prevent the importation of syphilis into our country by returning soldiers, has prevented nothing, but no one notices. No one notices how many soldiers have venereal disease and the HBJ stuff that indicates hepatitis . . ."

At this point, she's gently ushered out. She's crying. She rushes back to the microphone.

"I know you're all in a bind! I know! I know it must be hard for you to work and be a human being. But what I'm talking about is infectious! And we don't know much about it. This hepatitis shit is now in the blood supply. And we have no way to get it out of the blood supply. And more and more soldiers with it are coming home. And we need blood very badly. And . . . and . . . and . . ."

And this time the guards are not so gentle as they pull her out, crying even more, trying to yell out, "Please help, please help!" but her own tears stifle her words.

IF IT'S NOT ONE THING, IT'S ANOTHER

It is Dr. Korah Ludens's misfortune to have been in love with one of America's greatest artists, who is locked up in a loony bin for yelling about Nazi twats being preferable to kikes'. This sentence, set down, looks awful, but it is factually correct. Barnett Ludens, when he was free, walked down the streets of Washington yelling out such things. His wife finally had to commit him.

Poor Korah. She doesn't have much luck with husbands. Lessie, the first one, was so boring that she didn't notice when he disappeared. He did not return, and after sufficient time she was able to divorce him legally. Barnett, the great writer, is Lessie's, that is Lester Ludens's, brother. They bonded while collaborating on looking for Lessie; she was touched by how much he seemed to care. To her recollection, Lessie had rarely evinced much feeling or sentiment over family matters. Perhaps she'd married the wrong brother. She'd find out. "Shrinks are the worst at looking out for their own lives," she is to write. "One wonders why so many have so much faith in us. But that's our secret, and we keep it."

She's tried to convince herself that Barnett wasn't loony, except about sex. Since that marriage, he's written long novels that are—there's no two ways about it—filthy beyond belief; he'd have them privately printed and leave piles of them off at bookstores to be sold any which way or handed out for free. Many of the plots involve Hitler being "queer as a kike, fucking little boys' heinies and sucking their tiny pee pee wangers as if they're lollipops." The moral of all his plots is something like this: "I encourage all you handsome young women of pure blood to give your services to any man of noble brain and body, blond and blue-eyed and naturally sane, listen to me, listen, it's important, if we're ever going to get anywhere . . ."

Barnett has been in this particular loony bin, St. Purdah's Hospital in Anacostia, his room overlooking that still-filthy muddy river, since 1938. In a sense you could say that his early labeling of Hitler as a nutcase was certainly prescient. He'd lived in Germany and in Italy, where he'd picked up a fondness for Mussolini and fascist chitchat in general. "Benito was a pig but he was a secondary pig, subservient to adorable Adolf, who fascinated me far more because he kowtowed to no one. You try and run an army and then a government and not kiss ass! What a gift, my Korah, can't you see that?" Barnett's paintings from this period hang in the Guggenheim and the Modern. He's particularly praised for his palette, which, as Clement Greenberg wrote in *The New Gotham*, "caught that era dead center. There are few modernists who use colors so effectively as messengers."

In those earlier days, Korah would sneak into St. Purdah's late at night from an embassy ball, wearing, say, the black velvet evening gown given to her in Paris by Colonel Molyneaux that made her look like that Sargent portrait in the Mellon, not all that far from here. She'd sit in his dingy room— it's still the same one—looking down through the iron bars at the garbage the inmates tossed out onto the grounds. She'd bring along a beaded sachet purse filled with money to pay off the staff to treat Barnett nicely, which wasn't easy.

She still wears a gown from time to time, when it's been too long since she got dressed up. By now the guards are used to her. Barnett thinks she's still wearing the same gown. He still stares into space with those piercing eyes that condemn the world. His white hair still spikes up like it's electrified.

"You asleep, Barney?"

"Take me dancing."

"Right here. I'll sing the song."

"I'm composing a letter to Roosevelt and I don't want to lose the flow."

"He doesn't want to hear from you, Barney. Nobody does. They'd just as soon you were dead, but you're too famous and you know too many people, so they don't know what to do with you."

"Let me feel your titties. You used to giggle."

"That's before I met you. What's giggly at '21' doesn't last."

"How'm I going to get out?"

"You're not."

"Can't you help?"

"The general feeling is you're here to stay."

"I encourage you as a young and handsome woman of pure blood to give yourself to any Nordic officer who wants you. Listen. Adolf sucked my cock. If you fuck with a Jew, it's punishable by death. End of September that'll be the law. Got to finish my book by then."

"You're not a Jew. Why'd you write those putrid books?"

"You think I'm crazy?"

"Yep."

"That's a blessing."

He pulls up his pajama top and shows her his chest. He points to one of his nipples.

"See this tattooed number? 1123456. That means I'm next."

"No, you're not." It was when he paid someone to tattoo him that she first knew she'd made another terrible choice.

"Suck, suck, suck," he says. "Twats, twats, twats," he chants. This from the man who once painted as well as Gorky and wrote of love more passionately than Henry Miller. Rothko and Jackson Pollock will bow down to him and Hemingway will call him a genius. Heidegger will call him "the poet in the time of distress." Makes for a complicated case, being so multifactorily gifted.

"Of course I cry," Korah tells Doris Hardware, one of her patients (although "client" is coming to be the more preferred description, just like her whores now call theirs . . . clients), during one of their luncheons at Garfinkel's, as the models parade around in the latest fashions. "Now he thinks the world's being taken over by the masses. He hears them on the radio. 'They come out of nowhere and take my world away. I've lost my power.' He looked at me last night and said, 'I am constantly surprised that you are not hefty, raucous, marceled, minked, and shooting Derringers straight from your hip.' Great poets can get away with talking like this."

Doris pours her more tea.

"Here's looking at us," Korah says. "How did I wind up like this? And I'm a psychoanalyst. At least we know why you became a madam."

And then she asks Doris, as she always does at their lunches and their weekly sessions, "And what's new in your life?" To which Doris responds, as always, "Nothing much." Korah wonders why she bothers with Doris anymore. She never seems to say anything new.

But then, what is she, Korah Ludens, still mentioned in the same breath as Karen Horney, so far the only woman analyst to make a great and respected name for herself in a field dominated by men, what is she, Korah Ludens, doing to make herself interesting, if only to herself? What is it about this woman across from her gently sipping tea that allows her to run such a profitable business so efficiently and safely? What is it about herself, Korah, that draws clients like Doris and Mordy and Stuartgene Dye? Is there one of them who could change a world so much in need of changing? Is this her only true criterion for her choice of clients? If so, she's certainly failed, both them and herself. She can recite the daily palaver of each of them by heart. Each is so different and so strange, and Korah could not tell you, as they could not tell themselves (which is why they come to Korah), what they want from life, what is missing for them. She would like to talk to Dr. Freud about his system. Something is not working, Sigmund. No one can ever hit a bull's-eye. And yet, down deep, that is what you wanted for them, for us, we all want the same. What's the missing piece, Sigmund? Where is it? How do I find it?

What was he like—this Barnett Ludens fellow—when they fell in love, courted, married? She tried—it was and is a desperately hard fight—not to be destroyed herself. She has undertaken many times to shoulder burdens too heavy to lift. She can't seem to help any of them. Could anyone? Why is it so important to help the helpless? Why had she ever thought she could? That is not the point! she yells at herself. The point, always, is to try! And they are all becoming crazier than anything she has ever seen, just like the soldiers are coming back wounded in brains as well as bodies.

Barnett appeared in her life after Lessie had disappeared; he read to her great portions of his new writing, and, yes, she recognized the influence of fascistic thinking in the enormous volumes of his poetry. She thought it was because he was just a man, and men as rulers were coming into their own therapeutic limelight as something not always so healthy. Because he reminded her of Lessie—no, she could not help him either, and felt robbed, deprived because of that failure—she married his brother. She would not admit it— she could not make the same mistake twice!—but he arrived as a crazy man, Barnett did. She never knew him otherwise. Only after he underwent many tests at St. Purdah's under the supervision of Dr. Heidrich (on his way to

Partekla) was it discovered that he had nothing physically wrong with him. He was just . . . crazy. "And I think he has syphilis that is not showing up in his tests." She then told him Barnett had lived abroad for many years before the war. "That might be it, then," Aalvaar said. "I have many memories of my own earlier wild oats, both over there and here." He smiled as he said this in a mock-confidential tone. He is very handsome and obviously muscular and lean in his well-tailored NITS officer's uniform, with a shaved head before it was fashionable, and an indeterminate accent, as so many people in Washington possess. She wonders how he came to St. Purdah's, and what his qualifications are. She makes a mental note to check when matters here calm down.

Barnett was then administered massive doses of malaria. "We do things like this now," Dr. Heidrich explains. "Give people a disease. Give people another disease to fight the first disease." She'd already heard that scores of Negroes were being "given" syphilis. Dr. Heidrich continues, "In the case of syphilis, we infect them with malaria, give them so much of it that they become fevered with high temperatures. It often destroys the syphilis. Sweats it away. Boils it out. Sometimes it works. Many times it doesn't. But I have nothing else to offer." Barnett had been "given" malaria twice and now Barnett is "given" mammoth doses of syphilis via injections of blood from a man very sick with it himself.

After she leaves Barnett's room she walks the endless corridors of this endless place, St. Purdah's, tonight with the lights out and none of the guards she knows around to help her now that she's lost. The cries of crazy people in the dark are always infinitely sad to her. This place was said to be "enlightened" in 1905 when it opened. They bathed people in warm water endlessly. That was considered progressive thinking, to lead the patient back to "reasonableness." God, the place is big. She finally finds the exit, guarded by its gargoyle.

She is called back a few weeks later. Barnett Ludens has turned purple. He is covered from head to toe with purple blotches.

"Baby, what's happened to make me so colorful again?" he jokes. "Ezra taught them all how to write." Now he's nuts again. "Hemingway. Gertrude. Fitzgerald."

He can hardly talk for coughing. He's trying to make light of it but she can tell he's scared. She sort of is too, but she wouldn't mind if he died. She admits it to herself here and now, on this spot. She has never before wished a person in her life dead.

"We don't know what it is," the young doctor from COD admits, referring to the purple color, with Dr. Heidrich arriving and standing by. "Has he been fucking with anyone lately?"

"*Intimate* would be a preferable term, young man," Heidrich says as if it were a fact.

"In here? He's been in here a long time. Barney, what twats have you been licking?" For some reason, she's decided to be brazen.

Instead of answering he lapses into gurgles and mumbles, punctuated by short bursts of loud screaming that convulse him in coughs and saliva drool.

"His penis . . . well, here, look."

It is Dr. Heidrich who pulls back the covers and raises the hospital gown. Barnett's penis has been cut off. Everything under the covers is blood-soaked. Yes, she wishes him dead.

Barnett Ludens suddenly grabs for the sky, loses it, and falls into the arms of his wife, and death.

And she realizes that, really, she had for so long wished him dead. Well, here it is, in her arms.

Later, in Heidrich's office, where she notes that his first name is Aalvaar but has no time to decipher the framed diplomas before he brusquely hands her a report, written by "P.J.," which describes P.J.'s interview with Barnett Ludens, "such as it was," on what was apparently one of the last days of his life. Heidrich nods that she is free to read it and she does, while she knows his eyes never leave her. There is much of Barnett's gibberish, "patient is unable to finish a sentence," and reference to "patient's inordinate usage of profanity." P.J. then apologizes. "I am afraid that I was summoned too late to assess and record much more about anything from his final thoughts." And then, just above his initials at the bottom of the single page Korah's just read, the details of the autopsy, which "reveal that the patient had been penetrated anally so many times his rectum was wrecked beyond repair."

"Presumably it was one of the staff," Heidrich contributes. "Because of the war we're forced to hire many we shouldn't. Director Hoover's office has been notified because he wishes to be informed immediately of any unusual deaths, which this certainly is."

After several more weeks a Negro attendant at St. Purdah's, who is a deaf-mute and who bathes the men, is arrested and charged with Barnett's murder and rather quickly dispatched. Israel, too, had been summoned because of his still-recalled experience with bodily mutilations. He cannot believe what he discovers. Someone penetrated Barnett Ludens repeatedly with a tiny spiked dildo, not dissimilar to the one used on Mercy Hooker, though of metal and not marble, that was discovered in Barnett's bowels. Israel looks down upon it almost as if it were an old friend. He looks up at Heidrich and smiles enigmatically. He does not recognize Heidrich, just as he never remembers enough about glause.

It is never discovered who did any of this to Barnett. It is never discovered who severed his penis. The mute Negro attendant, who for the record held the name of Booker T. Washington Jones, was in fact electrocuted for the murder of Barnett Ludens.

Years later, when she is quite old, Korah writes a famous essay that appears almost at the end of the last volume of her collected works, totaling twenty-three thick and influential books now considered among the most estimable in the field of psychoanalysis. She calls the essay "The Sublimity of Art, the Brutality of Fact." It is the first and only time she writes about Barnett Ludens, whose own work—both his art and his poetry—is by now considered part of the canon of American culture and listed on university syllabuses here and there. It would be on more of them had he not been so weird.

"What do we do with cases like this, where the outpourings of interior messages are so bipolarized and intertwined, incapable of separation, really? His mind was both vile and sublime. His art was both cruel and of a sort that reaches to the angels. Certainly the latter could not have been achieved without the tortuous expense of the former. To be sure, there is no answer to the question: Which ones do we save and protect? And we must stop thinking there is an answer and breaking our own hearts seeking it. As with Siamese twins joined at the brain, we can only witness with awe the incredible energy it must take just to stay alive, much less maintain balance. We are left with the painful injunction to cherish that which reaches for eternity and withhold our instinctive punishment of a torment that we cannot ourselves begin to comprehend. It is far from a perfect solution, particularly in these punishing times, which all times seem to be or we psychoanalysts would be out of business, but it is the only solution a civilized country, which we are far from being or becoming, can attempt."

AFFAIRS OF STATE

The assistant secretary of state, Sumner Welles, is discovered to be, particularly when drunk, a loud and aggressive homosexual, particularly toward

Negroes, particularly toward Negroes who are Pullman porters. His boss, Secretary of State Cordell Hull, uses this information to see that Welles is put out to pasture. Roosevelt is fond of Welles and certainly fonder of him than of Hull, but he dislikes fairies and in the end gives in to Hull, who has always been jealous of Roosevelt's obvious preference for Welles over himself. Hull has his own dark secret: his wife is Jewish. It is Hull, among others, who oversees Roosevelt's covert policy of denying any help to the Jews running in terror all over the globe, desperate for sanctuary. Hull is called to task for his hypocrisy by Joseph Alsop, a popular political columnist who writes regularly with his brother, Stewart, for the *Monument*. Joseph is a homosexual and equally terrified that this information will be used against him. When Joe threatens to reveal Mrs. Hull's heritage if Mr. Hull doesn't help a few Jews stay alive, Mr. Hull retaliates with a threat to reveal Joseph Alsop's homosexuality.

After another Pullman porter incident, Welles is fired by Roosevelt in 1943. Cordell Hull will be awarded the Nobel Peace Prize in 1945.

In March 1956, *Confidential* magazine will run an "exposé" revealing more or less all these same juicy details, but not until 1995—some forty years later—when the Johns Hopkins University Press publishes Irwin F. Gellman's *Secret Affairs: FDR, Cordell Hull, and Sumner Welles*, will the world be treated to this news in an academically acceptable version.

Welles goes on to become a stirring advocate for world peace. He lectures, he writes bestselling books, he is miserable. He is dragged out of Negro bars drunk many times over the years.

Welles does not die until 1961. His being found dead drunk and face-down in a filthy stream in the Maryland countryside precedes his death. Some say he was murdered. He didn't live long after being rescued from this near-drowning.

Emendations to earlier Nazi laws and to the "recommendations" of the Wannsee Conference of 1942 to eliminate all Jews were officially extended to include gypsies and homosexuals, who were and are being killed all along anyway. As a homosexual, how was Welles dealing with this? Or Joseph Alsop? Whatever the repercussions from these emendations, they were never written about, although there are loads of scholarly studies about how many Jews were murdered. Joseph Alsop was one of the great journalists of his time, honest and fearless about everything, it would seem, except himself. It is an old and pathetic story, how "secrets" silence people.

How much did Welles know about the active participation of "his kind"—i.e., Ivy League, North Shore, Back Bay, Main Line, Lake Shore, even Beverly Hills—in the financing of the very Nazis with whom our country was at war? As an assistant secretary of state, how much did he know about Ivy Lee, the founder of Public Relations, dead since 1934 but not forgotten (part of his papers to this day either still embargoed by or stolen from Princeton)? Ivy Lee's job was to make Hitler look good in America. Amos Standing was assigned by Ivy to "run the Hitler account." How much did Welles know of one of America's most powerful law firms, Sullivan and Cromwell, which represented I.G. Farben's American subsidiary, American I.G. Corporation, the largest manufacturer of film in the world?

But why should any of these men talk about any of this? To this day, neither Dredd Trish nor Junior, his son, will speak of their family's relationship with Hitler. Or did Welles know and in the knowing drink himself to death? Or did he just drink himself to death for his uncontrollable unsatisfied longings for love?

FROM *MY HISTORY OF EVIL*

Having still not heard from you, Fred, I feel I must reiterate my calling lest you did not get my message.

I am proud that I am getting so caught up in my enterprise. I was going to call it *The New England Journal of Evil*, but in the end I thought that would be gilding my lily under false pretensions. I shudder to think that it might be your pestering, hectoring, confrontational style, Frederick, a style which I believe is called in-your-face, that has enabled me to see that my role is more than simply to supply a superior IQ for the wireless.

The problem of evil should have been the fundamental topic of wartime among intellectuals. But it wasn't. Nor was it after. Nor is it now. Nor has it ever been in the entire history of The American People. Of any people. Even the Germans themselves. Almost as a matter of course, from war clouds' first dim gathering, politicians ignore evil and historians do the same. I find myself haunted more and more by evil's increasing apparitions. They are so absolute, so total, so everlastingly resonant. So overwhelmingly suffocating. So impossible to overlook, and yet so totally ignored.

I learn something more about evil every day. I have been reading a most instructive volume by Michael H. Kater, *Doctors Under Hitler*. Did you know that Josef Mengele was born with wide spaces, gaps, from teeth missing on each side between his upper incisors, yes, missing on both sides? His own research had determined that such irregularities were hereditary. This knowledge disturbed him greatly and guided his intense study of anthropology. To be able to research hereditary malfunctions in an unrestricted fashion on humans as was now provided to him in various camps was utopia. Auschwitz, his final posting, permitted research and experimentation on human bodies with no concern for life or death. He could now add to his field of interest a growing obsession with pain. Was the administration of or the receiving of pain in any way also an inherited characteristic? Such investigations soon combined into his own pathological predilection for cruelty. To discover what inside of him might exist in others motivated him to punish those others in retribution, his paybacks as it were, for his unwanted physical and genetic inheritance. This, of course, is the genesis of sadomasochism. Mengele's thinking, complicated and confused, was beginning to follow insights formulated by Freud. Germany was already infected by many new unconventional ideas, not only from Freud. German medicine would certainly never be the same, or trusted in the way it was. It will be estimated that as many as 400,000 persons of both sexes were sterilized, most of them involuntarily, between 1933 and 1945. And, of course, that some six million Jews should be exterminated under the supervision of an evil monster in retribution for his absent bicuspids is as historically unforgivable as the twisted contributions that IBM and Hollerith provided, which allowed so many people, Jews, gays, and other unwanteds, to be located so they could be murdered.

I wish you were all on board with me in framing our whole history and discussions in terms of evil. Why is this a leap for you? Is your gay world so timorous of admitting that you are actually hated?

FRED RESPONDS

There comes a time in the middle of the night when one awakens from a troubled sleep and wonders if one has not begun to go slowly crazy. You are all correct about my infinitesimally drip-by-drip slow extenuation of this. I cannot seem to let go of every grain of detail, for each at some moment seems so important that I must scoop it up and slither it into my own voluminous vomit-out. *The world must know everything!* I suppose many journeys can be like this: midway, or even partway, the most relaxed of tourists (and I know I'm hardly that) can punish himself for the such-and-such signpost missed along the route. "How could you have spent so much time and energy and money coming this far," he says to himself, "and be so stupid in not including *that*, of not stopping off to go face to face with *that*, of missing that turn." That is how I feel. I think you're each correct, in what you've called me on.

If this were an ordinary life I'm attempting to lead, I'd commit myself to a shrink's care, if only to start tranquilizing my growing despair. I'm grateful for every single word each of you has said to me, and to each other. I can offer an apology (for evidently disappointing you), but for the life of me I don't know for what. It is my life, too, that this plague and this history is all about. I am trying, as it were, to shit it out as best as any constipated little boy all clogged up can do in his rush not to do it in his pants before he gets home from school to . . . what? An empty household with no arms to hold him, but at least with a toilet to embrace his innards as he squeezes them out bit by bit.

I think, at this juncture, we must each go along our increasingly less merry way. I can see that each of you is now firmly embedded (and emboldened!) in the same search that I am. Good! For the hovering special-delivery man standing in the doorway, I sign acknowledging receipt of your package of disappointments in me, and sign off, and may we all meet somewhere over the rainbow.

In other words, you tell your history, and I'll tell mine.

In love and gratitude, Fred

OF COURSE BORIS GREETING CAN SPEAK

Of course my pal Senator Vurd has not made his fearful reputation by relying upon facts. Thus it is "known with certainty" by Senator Vurd and his "confidential sources," inside first the Tally Office and then the Office of Unnatural Acts, that Greeting is suddenly making a fortune from the sale of its ampules, marketed under the trade name Dridgies, to the homosexual population. Senator Vurd knows "for sure, for goldang sure" that an awful lot of the single men living in Washington are also beginning to stick Dridgies up their noses just before they reach for heaven as they climax during sex. He's even tried it himself once, maybe twice.

In his autobiography that of course no one's ever read, Clarence Meekly says that he watched as the only love of his life was massacred and immolated. And of course he vowed that the world would pay a price for his great loss. This is the part of our company lore that of course I delight in telling at our retreats and sales conferences. I delight in owning a company that can claim its very own massacres.

•

I'm being left out in the cold and I don't like it. Everybody and his mother and brother is making up part of this history. OK, here is part of mine that is useful to Greeting in this time of blame.

A twenty-eight-year-old male is admitted to the Baptist and Jesus Memorial Hospital in Memphis, Tennessee, with a diagnosis of pneumonia. Various tests are administered, as is the current prescribed treatment for pneumonia, Ventt-easy. The fever subsides and the abnormal markers bounce back to normal. The patient is discharged.

He had not been a soldier or served in the war or been overseas. He was ineligible for the draft because of bad eyesight. He was unmarried and lived with his widowed mother. He had spent his entire life in Memphis, working as a gardener. He dies within the month, covered in purple scabs.

He never took Dridgies.

FROM *MY HISTORY OF EVIL*

Who would care even if it were to be discovered what's transpiring? In addition to goodies from Mungel, trunksful from the German-Dutch-Belgian-Japanese foray into "germ warfare" are in this pipeline. It's amazing how such disparate nations manage to collaborate so adroitly. Why, among a certain set it's as if there's no enemy, as if research is all. Even the Japanese wanted in on anything to do with germ warfare, and they found a way to do so, even if it meant actually collaborating with countries with which they're still at war! There seemed to be no enemies among this group of determined investigators into the life of poisons.

Experienced German scientists are worth a lot of money in certain American markets before the war begins. There are books and exposés galore on the German infiltration of America before, during, and after the war, but they're kiddie stuff compared to what's actually going on.

"Concentration camps are the laboratories where changes in human nature are tested" is a much-quoted statement from these times. David heard it uttered by Grodzo at Mungel. In this country it's attributed to Aalvaar

Heidrich, in what's become a highly regarded textbook in his field, *The Study of Prisons*. "There is nothing wrong with concentration camps. They are very useful and perfectly logical. They do just what their name suggests: concentrate. Everyone's life concentrates on one thing or another." Aalvaar Heidrich was sent over to America in the 1920s to infiltrate. Sent by whom? How did he wind up looking after Mercy Hooker? Did his own sexual needs (or theirs? whose?) determine his attachment to her?

"Homosexuals are useful because they can be infected and allowed to die. Since their sperm will never play any part in procreation, no one is in fact killed," Heidrich also wrote. In fact, homosexuals are far more useful than Jews in wartime, and soon peacetime. There will be money in dead homo-sexuals, or more precisely phrased, in homosexuals whose demise no one will care about. Who wants them? Or any of this information?

Aalvaar Heidrich is one of those who believed Germany was going to win the war and take over the world, so why not get started early with no small amount of American help? Help from American companies working in and with Germany, such as Ford and National City Bank and Chase and Stan-dard Oil and DuPont and Alcoa and Dow and IBM and on and on, includ-ing Greeting. Many are represented by that most "eminent" of New York law firms, Sullivan and Cromwell. J. Edgar Hoover, like Roosevelt, does not ob-ject to the participation of the private sector in the war effort. One talks of Hoover as if he were president, with so much power. He does have this much power. Over the years little by little he learns how to just . . . take it.

DRESS REHEARSAL FOR THE GREEK WING

We are lined up naked in a big gymnasium, bigger than we had at high school in Davenport. The blond young men are all together. I'm dark. I have a hairy chest and so does everyone else, including the blond men. There isn't a hair-less man here!

There's no question that we're all homosexual. We're all around eigh-teen or so, no more than twenty. Some of us are having problems controlling erections in the midst of so many good-looking naked men. We've been told not to talk to each other, but there are no guards to stop us. Slowly we move up to the beginning of the line, where men in white coats measure us and weigh and photograph us from head to toe in front and back. The longer we wait in line, the more we are drawn to each other, touching familiarly, smiling, clapping each other on the shoulder, laughing at our erections. When we get to the front of the line, even the doctor laughs. "I don't know what we're going to do with you boys!"

We are taken to an auditorium, still naked, where Mr. Brinestalker addresses us. Standing beside him is a womanish young man with an almost hairless body.

Mr. Brinestalker talks to the young man in his commanding voice. "Warren, listen to me. We do not accept your effeminacy. God made you a man. Being a man is special. Do you understand what I am saying to you? If you do not you will be sent away. If you do not become a man here you are useless to us."

The young man breaks down. He waves his arms and flutters his hands and starts to cry.

Mr. Brinestalker turns to face all of us. "You see! This is what I mean. See how this youngster flaps his wrists and acts like a woman! Why, his body is even hairless like a woman's. When he lies on his back to let you screw him, I guarantee he will act like a woman. Perhaps he thinks he is one.

"The Kursie Foundation has invited you here to become Greek Warriors. You will learn what this means and how fortunate you are to be chosen to be one. Greek Warriors reject effeminacy. Greek Warriors live the truth that one man can love another man without any surrender of either man's masculinity and without turning into a pseudo-woman. You are going to learn a new and different message about yourself and what you can be and should be. And you are going to be sent out into the world to teach our people that message!"

He speaks with such conviction and urgency that we all stand up and give the old man a rousing cheer. Our erections are gone now. I don't think anyone here has ever thought of himself as such a special person. We have never talked about sex so openly or heard it talked about so publicly.

He summons two of the blonds up to the platform, on which there is a bed.

"I invite you to lie down side by side, to touch each other, to run your hands across each other, to enjoy each other." Naturally the two of them are embarrassed. "Tell me your names." Dano and Julian. "Dano, kiss Julian's nipples. Do you know what nipples are?" There is giggling in the audience. "Take your tongue and lick his nipples. Remember how they taste. Kiss him. Julian, kiss Dano. Take his penis in your hand and play with yours." On the wall is now projected a film of two young men on a bed, hairy-chested young men with enormous penises that they are rubbing against each other's hairy chest. Clearly they're having fun, laughing as they roll around. One of them plays now with his partner's pubic hair, twisting it playfully around a finger, then jumping on the bed so his cock waves up and down, his hand on it as it gets harder and harder, and then they shoot, the penises in the grainy black-and-white film and the penises on the platform.

We're happy! None of us here is accustomed to being happy. We have had no information about our sexual desires. We have not been able to find explanations for why we feel the way we do for other men. Life has been mixed with fear, uncertainty, and stupidity. How did they find so many of us who are like this? I do remember answering an awful lot of personal questions at my interview and Mr. Brinestalker making marks on cards.

"Note that they have kissed each other as two men!" Mr. Brinestalker commands. "Note that they have not engaged in anal penetration, taboo in every known culture from ancient Egypt and Greece and Rome to the book of Leviticus to the present day!"

Taboo is a term new to most of us, and so is *anal penetration*, though I'm sure a lot of us have done it, and it was probably messy and painful, so it's easy enough to dispense with if that's what Mr. Brinestalker wants. Clearly he's a decent and caring man who wishes us the best.

"Are you ready to reject anal penetration? Are you ready to reject effeminacy?" he shouts from the platform.

"Yes!" we shout back, and throw ourselves into each other's arms. All of us in the audience are now with someone else, with several others. "Kiss each other as man to man!" Many of us are country boys from small towns. We are the sons of mothers and fathers who do not want to see us again.

I'm going to Yaddah in the fall. A rich man in Davenport is sending me there. He is a homosexual but he leaves me alone.

WHY ARE YOU DOING THIS TO ME?

I know you are back in America. What have you done with him now? I'll be damned if I'll shut up, should it come to that, without clearing my name, at least with my wife, who still hardly talks to me.

Please return my son forthwith. I am not going to come to get him. You would never let me return alive.

IANTHE ADAMS STRODE REPLIES TO DAME LADY HERMIA BLEDD-WRENCH'S INQUIRY

Ah, yes, my dear Hermia, Brinestalker. The strange man without a first name. We met in Berlin just before we entered the war. He looked like he was no picnic, like he belonged in a Bierkeller with a hundred other men just like him chugging from huge tankards and singing those revolting songs with their insidious tunes you couldn't get out of your head. Big fellow, funny protuberant ears, brutish and frightening when he was all dressed up in his black leather overalls and those clumpy boots men wear when they want to look German.

It was my Edwin who introduced me to him, at an embassy party. He was with Amos Standing, my old pal from bridge classes in Chevy Chase, who was working in the Berlin film industry. They both escorted buxom peroxide blond beauties they said were being "groomed" for stardom. The Krauts love their babes like this. The minute I saw them standing side by side ignoring the babes I should have known they were fairies. Berlin was filled with fairies. (I am sorry but I cannot bring myself to call them homosexuals, which I think is not nearly so friendly as fairies.) They gave the city life. Brinestalker talked so rapturously about this new machine and what they were learning with it and how there were really more people in some groups than the census takers were tallying. Fairies, for one. And Jews, of course. Hitler had ordered the census takers to up the numbers of both Jews and fairies no matter how people answered the questions. He was telling me all this. Lots of Jews carted off to the camps weren't Jews at all. Minna Trooble from our Jew Tank actually met the daughters of a gentile couple who'd been exterminated in this way. It started her looking for others, and she found a number of them here in Washington alone. They're still frightened. After all these years there are gentile Germans who are still frightened. Minna told me they'd say things like, "We're not that far away from Germany, you know. Airplanes fly every day. They will punish us for leaving Germany. They have eyes and ears everywhere. My cousin was kidnapped and never seen again."

I didn't put two and two together when we were stationed in Berlin. Smart I was, but still one naïve tootsie. I would dance all night with a mob of men in leather and think, My God, these men are sexy. And when it came near dawn and they were all dancing with each other, I just told myself, Hey, that's what they do in Berlin. Even Hitler came once in a while and did a funny jig that made everybody laugh. (I've since wondered about Hitler. His being a fairy too would cause no end of interest, wouldn't it?) Edwin would work all night at the embassy and we'd meet for breakfast. That's when Berlin was fun. That's when Edwin was fun. Shit, that's when Hitler was fun. He joined us for breakfast a few times. Who fucking knew? I like to say I did, in fact I *have* said it, but I really didn't. I *sensed* things. I *sensed* he was strange as all get-out, and then I went and danced until dawn. I didn't figure it out about Amos until I saw him here in Washington with Brinestalker. And there was a third man, well dressed but short and stubby, who turned out to be Daniel's father! He didn't look too happy to be on whatever voyage they were on together—for they were definitely a threesome. By then I had better antennae. They sort of hung on to each other without actually hanging on to each other, or knowing that this is noticeable because they are trying so hard not to show anything.

I don't know what Amos did over there in Berlin, or does in the State Department now—oh, I asked him of course, but I got a nebulous answer which I knew wasn't true. I didn't think much about it. Spies were all over the place now. I didn't know then about the Ivy Lee–Hitler PR gig. Imagine having Hitler for a client! And I.G. Farben. And that big movie studio, whatever it was called. UFA. Too bad Ivy died in 1934 (the year Edwin was sent to Prague, so we missed his funeral; we knew Ivy; everyone knew Ivy), before anyone could get to him. Amos, it turns out, was in charge of the Ivy Lee German office, this Hitler account, including the movie studio, and Hitler kept him on almost through the end of the war. Edwin had been called home long before. The Ivy Lee organization went on into the '60s. There must be people who worked there who could still talk, maybe even Amos, if he's still around. And Brinestalker, too, of course. He told me all of this on Carlotta's lawn; Brinestalker never stopped talking about himself.

Anyway, Brinestalker collected the names of all the men being exempted from the draft because they were fairies. I mean American men. He had their names and addresses. And he talked about this list of his. There were a lot of these names, he said, almost gleefully. He wanted me to tell Edwin, who was not returning calls (which is another story). Brinestalker had already brought his list to Breckenridge Winesap, that monster of Franklin's who kept any Jews out of America. I wondered if Jews were yesterday's slug of hemlock, with Brinestalker regaling so forthrightly that fairies were tomorrow's. Once Franklin, in the height of all that Sumner Welles mess, actually asked my opinion about what he should do about "these people." He actually said something like, "Ianthe, I believe you move in a more free and liberal set than I do and no doubt know a number of people like . . . these people. I feel uncomfortable with . . . these people. I was very upset about Sumner when . . . Cordell threatened and . . . I had to let Sumner go." I told him to leave these people alone. They were already in enough unhappiness. "I suspect you are correct," he said, which made me impetuously give him a little peck of a kiss. He never knew how to handle that!

Breckenridge Winesap, well, Charlie Higham said this about him in his *American Swastika* book: "No record is blacker in World War II than Winesap's." That is strong stuff, particularly in this particular history. Brecky was in charge of the Visa Division and he left half a million places open on the quota list while Jews died in the camps. All that shit-on-a-smile he was handing us at the Jew Tank! He was also Mussolini's big buddy. How did he get away with all of this, and while working for Franklin?

Brinestalker will try to peddle his wares to Truman next. I know this because of a hideous personal connection to this part of this perverse story. I'm going to tell it to you now, although it's too early; but we both could be dead before I can unload.

Edwin and I were driving to Franeeda Naval Hospital to see Jimmy Forrestal, who was there recovering from a nervous breakdown he'd had after having been sliced to bits by Drew Pearson and Walter Winchell. They were the two most famous muckrakers—liberal, they were called, hah!—of that era and Jimmy had been a noble secretary of the Navy and defense for Truman. He was against the establishing of the state of Israel. He foresaw that it would cause nothing but warfare in the Middle East forever. That's why he was being carved to bits. Truman gave in to all the pressure and Israel was born and Jimmy was out of a job. He was very handsome and a true workaholic, so much so that his two boys never saw him, nor did his wife, who took to booze. Edwin and he had worked together, of course, here and there. I had made a load of cookies and we were driving out Wisconsin Avenue when a bulletin came on the radio that Jimmy had committed suicide by jumping out his window. Sick as he was from his breakdown, they'd put him in a suite on the highest floor, I think it was sixteen or seventeen. No one could ever make that one out. He'd been treated by Menninger himself, the great shrink of the day, who said he warned the Navy doctor to watch out. Edwin almost drove us into a tree. I had to grab the wheel and maneuver us to the side of the road. Edwin was not a crier but he was bawling. In fact, I don't think I'd ever seen him cry. Well, he was an ocean of tears and shudders and moans and I held him in my arms trying to comfort him. He finally stopped. Then he looked out into space and told me that he and Jimmy had been lovers when they first came to Washington. They were both very handsome men. And they saw each other over the years, even when we were in Berlin. And his own breakdown, my Edwin's, started when they broke up, which, come to think of it, was about this same time that Brinestalker was complaining that Edwin wasn't accepting his calls.

I can remember that car scene as if it were yesterday. "Oh, it wasn't too regular," Edwin said, "but it was enough to keep our warmth and affection going, and yes, Ianthe, our love, and get us to our next meeting, which was never easy to arrange for two such busy guys." I'd never heard him use the word *guy* before. Then he told me the rest of it.

Truman had called him into a meeting. There was Brinestalker, trying to peddle his list of American fairies, "to protect your country, our country, my country from becoming a nation of perverts!" Truman was holding a piece of paper, one of the pages of Brinestalker's wad. At the top of this page, headed "Prominent Homosexuals in Our Government" or some such, were Edwin's name and Jimmy's name. After that day in the car at the side of the road listening to the radio, Edwin's breakdown started. Truman asked Edwin if he was ready to retire, and he really wasn't. Poor dear man wouldn't know what to do with himself all day long.

You know, his personal diaries were never found, Jimmy's. He wrote in them every day. I remember a number of times when he excused himself "to go and write *my* history," as he would laughingly say. My friend Pippy Phipps, who worked at Unnatural Acts (and who, it turned out, was married to a fairy herself, "that's why I work here" she told me, "to protect *him*, my own husband"), believes Jimmy jumped because he was afraid he was about to be what you now call "outed." She'd modeled in Florida for a time, and the male models said Jimmy had a gorgeous boyfriend in Coconut Grove and helped put him through college. There was even a rumor that Jimmy was murdered by a Jewish terrorist from the Irgun who pushed him out the window. He was a very decent, loyal, honest public servant, of which there are few anymore. And he and my Edwin had been guy friends. My, my.

It was still a number of years before Sumner Welles died, also mysteriously, in 1961. I don't wish to bracket either of these two fine gentlemen (who were said to suffer from paranoia, with good reason) with Edgar Hoover and Sam Sport, and, yes, Richard Nixon (Bebe Rebozo was much more than Nixon's guy friend for forty-four years, let me just squeeze in here: Why does no one ever notice this?) and James Jesus Angleton of the OSS/CIA (he was a real biggie—someone should nail him as well), who all fit a pattern of repressed homosexuality and paranoia. Serving one's country is no easy task for closeted fairies.

But back to Brinestalker. Why was a fairy going on so enthusiastically about how many fairies he'd located? Before long Edwin was deep in his depression, so I could no longer count on the benefit of his mind. Being in Berlin hadn't done him any good. He knew about the camps, and Franklin did not want to know about them, or anyone else to know about them. And it turned out that Franklin was just as big a shit about fairies as he was about Jews. He knew Edgar Hoover was a fairy and was up to no good about fairies, and many other things as well, and that was just fine with him. And because Hoover knew it was fine with Franklin, he felt free to expand his activities. He was a major monster sprouting there in front of my eyes and, like seeing Brinestalker in Berlin, even Hitler, Ianthe just was not on the ball. I couldn't have done much about it, especially with Edwin about to be bedded down, but I have my mouth, which in its own way was becoming better known. I'm grateful, Fred, for this chance to what my mother used to call "churn my butter."

You know how some people of phenomenal historic importance manage to get through everything, including posterity, clean as a whistle, despite their hideous deeds? Well, that's Brinestalker, mark my words. How did he get hold of those names in the first place? Why, through IBM, of course. IBM had the same sort of setup here, with those same Hollerith machines and punch cards and lists, endless lists, many from the Office of Unnatural Acts, run by Eurora von Lutz, the other Lutz sister, with the help of that strange Arnold Botts and various additional Hoover appointees. Was Hoover our Hitler? Did he really say, as Brinestalker claimed to me, "these particular sex lives are of vital national interest and must be committed to a list"? Harry Truman claimed to not even know what a fairy was, if you can believe it. I don't. You can't work in a haberdashery in the sticks without knowing what a fairy is. Shit, Edwin told me that where he grew up in Altoona it was a well-known fact that fairies went to the local haberdashery on Saturday afternoons to meet each other and try clothes on and jerk each other off in the fitting rooms, or get a blow job from one of the salesmen. How could young Harry have missed out on that? Edwin didn't.

Yes, Hoover was our Hitler too. It may seem ironic that a fairy did so much to exterminate his own. Our Fred gets very upset whenever he hears about such a thing. "But he's killing his brothers!" he rails in sincere perplexity. What he refuses to see is this: Why should Hoover have been nice to "his own" when he was monstrous to everyone? That impressive gay playwright Tony Kushner has written to Fred, "I don't think of me and Hoover belonging to anything shared no matter how much dick we each sucked."

To this day IBM's wartime files are sealed, if they haven't been destroyed altogether, and it is only thanks to the remarkable scholarship by my friend Edwin Black that the ghastly history of this company is known. His book *IBM and the Holocaust* kept me up nights, and I longed to discuss it with my Edwin, but as you know his depression turned into his slitting his wrists turned into my burying him. I've felt very alone without him, and been grateful for your friendship and your work, my dear Hermia, and for our Fred, who has helped me keep my what is now called liberal mind alive by encouraging me, listening to me, and most important, believing me. It sounds as if he's having a little breakdown of his own. He'll come out of it, I know.

That day in the hospital—Brinestalker managed to get in to see Edwin that way—he delivered a diatribe about homosexuals that I shall never forget. "The homosexual population is the axis around which the wheel of world history revolves. Homosexuals in America are now coming into a position where they will undermine our way of life. Too much of our culture will be built on their worldview. I saw this in Berlin before the war, and in London and Paris and Budapest and Prague and Vienna, and even in Russia, where Stalin was getting older and sloppier. I see it now in Washington, now that I'm back. New York and San Francisco are sewers. The homosexual spirit seems to survive every physical assault on the homosexual body. The war may be freeing them up to creep into the open, but it's time to expunge this evil spirit from the soul of our country once and for all before we're poisoned beyond repair!" No, I'm not quoting from memory. I am reading from one of many flyers he hurls around Washington like confetti.

Edwin and I listened in openmouthed shock, and then Edwin looked Brinestalker straight in the eye and said, "Get out," in a tone of such moral authority that Brinestalker turned on his heel and left.

"Expunge!" Edwin said. "God help us."

My Edwin killed himself by the next morning.

DR. SISTER GRACE IS ON TO SOMETHING!

Shitty ass rat fuck!

You can imagine my buzzer when I read in *The New England Journal of Feces* that the important work begun by Dr. Flo Hung Nu was threatened by a cessation of all feces delivery. Then I read an article in *The New England Journal of Digestion* by a young woman at Isidore Schmuck whose research led her to an establishment on the Gulf Coast of Florida, the Table Family Hotel, situated on "unusual" alluvial deposits of human waste. "It is old shit," this Dr. Nesta Trout wrote (they even allowed the word *shit*; what is scientific research coming to!), "historic shit, dating from the Civil War, and it is full of verts and gligs." Verts and gligs! It's not a joke! That is what they used to call shit then. But since I now had shit from the North, that good old trusty Hooker shit, and Dr. Trout's analysis of that prehistoric shit from the South, my stump was twitching.

Fuckheads beware!

Dr. Nesta Trout is a protégée of mine. Chary though I always am of doling out praise to associates for work I've initiated myself—it's not for nothing they call me the Queen of Shit—I publicly congratulated Trout on her discovery of this old shit, which, amusingly, surprised everyone, unaccustomed as all are to a word of praise coming from yours truly. Nesta's article had my stump twitching in a number of ways. The little cunt was on to something although she obviously didn't know what. I had an idea, a good idea, A GREAT IDEA!—one that needed testing of a highly confidential nature, but my instincts told me it was out there, just waiting for Dr. Sister Grace to pluck it.

Fred, I note that you have taken offense at dear Hermia, and even me, your dearest Grace. I guess it was overdue, the stress, I mean, not its inconsiderateness. I would slap you around if you were anywhere in my shitty vicinity. You simply must be made of fucking sterner fucking stuff to fight this fucking fight. Get over it. You are needed.

BACK

I was taken from Germany back to America. I don't know how it was arranged. A man with a pilot's cap came to UFA and took me from Amos to a nearby field that had been leveled by the bombing. He put us in a small plane and we rose up into the air and flew over the remains of this tortured city. Before I knew it I was asleep. I was so tired. It did occur to me that for the first time I might have more hope than fear. I don't think I had ever faced how frightened I have been all these years. It felt good to let that go. If that was what was happening.

When I was there I would count the days since I came to Mungel, but after a while I stopped. So I don't know how long I was there. It was a long time. I don't know how many of the boys I'd started with at Mungel remain alive. I had seen or heard or smelled most of them put to death. I'd had no friends since Pieter. Except for Klaus. My Mungel story begins with one and ends with the other. No one talked to me because after the beginning I was rarely done to. The tests were on others. I still have no understanding of why I'm alive. I will always have nightmares of penises being chopped off and intestines being scooped out and instruments being inserted into the bodies of my companions. Is it a relief, now, to have the freedom to think of anything?

I know a lot has been written about Dr. Mengele and his experiments on twins. People always want to know about Dr. Mengele. He only wanted to work on twins. He would do something to one twin and something else to the other. Grodzo did this at our camp too. As Daniel wasn't there, Dr. Mengele wasn't interested in me, despite Grodzo's believing me that I was a twin. Dr. Mengele slept with me one night when he was visiting Grodzo. "I cannot sleep without a youngster beside me. Usually I am able to have a young girl, but this Mungel is only males. It is very kind of Dr. Grodzo to, as it were, lend you to me." He crawled into my bed and kissed me good night and put his arm around me and went to sleep. He felt and smelled just like any other man.

Dr. Mengele walked around our little house stark naked from the moment he arrived, stretching his arms lazily. He asked me to be naked too. He asked me to open my mouth. "Ah, you Americans have such good teeth," he said approvingly. "How do you manage to achieve it for so many people?" We ate our dinner naked, the three of us, even though we were served by one of the camp's young men. I kept waiting for our visitor to make a physical advance. He didn't try to fuck me, which I expected him to. Even guards were always fucking everyone all over the place. I had to watch him operate a number of times. Grodzo would hold my hand. He and Mengele would smile or frown in disappointment, depending on the outcome of the surgery. I had no idea what they were trying to do.

My nightmares started only when I returned home, if I can call America home. I was back in America only days when I realized how hard it had been to not be afraid for so long, how much energy that took that I wasn't aware of, and which now fell from my shoulders to be replaced by nightmares. Amos would tell me at Partekla that I had nothing to be afraid of. "Then why am I afraid?" I asked each time. I am afraid that I am still afraid.

When I wake up on that small plane, it's flying toward the mountains. In every direction there's nothing but snow. We must be at the North Pole. We're crossing a desert of snow and ice. The sun is so blinding I have to close my eyes again.

When I open them we're sputtering down. I don't know why, since there appears to be nothing here but snow and ice. The pilot lands and motions for me to get out. I jump from the door as he takes off and leaves me in the middle of nowhere.

The same thing happens three more times. A total of four small planes fly me from one icy wilderness to another. Or maybe there are more planes. It all takes many days and nights. The flying is always bumpy, the night flying particularly frightening. I don't know how much I sleep and how much I'm awake. I'm given sandwiches and soup. Perhaps there was something in the soup. The pilots are all middle-aged men who don't talk very much, not that we could hear each other for the noise. I think each speaks a different language as we cross the globe, but I'm not certain. I do know that none of them ever smiles.

Another plane deposits me and leaves me in another icy wilderness. I'm freezing in seconds. I run just to keep warm. There is no indication that one direction is better than another. I keep looking at the sky for another plane to appear, but it doesn't. Still, that there is so much sunshine gives me a small sense of hope, just as through all the awfulness of many years I clutched some hope. Sometimes people press me. What's your story? And I answer, I'm sick of my story, tell me yours. I try to find stories that are worse, as if that might help me. I haven't found one yet.

I keep running through the desert of snow. There is a house in the distance that I see. It seems to be waiting for me. I'm tired and cold and my eyes hurt from the glare. It seems like a nice place. It's made of logs and there's smoke coming out of the chimney. When a man opens the door and says hello and invites me inside I realize I haven't heard English spoken, or spoken it myself, for many years except for those few words with Amos Standing. It's a comfortable house inside but I wonder why it's far away from everywhere. I ask him where we are and he doesn't tell me. Instead he hands me a bottle of whiskey and tells me to drink and get warm. I manage to get a little down. I ask him for some food and he starts complaining angrily about being cheated out of several hundred dollars' worth of something that a Mr. Dridge was meant to send him to sell. He swallows from the bottle and it's not long before he's drunk. He stands up and holds his clenched fists out to box with me. I run around him, trying to make it look like a game, but he's determined to have a fight. When I won't fight back he picks me up and throws me down a flight of stairs. I land on a cold cement floor. I hear him roaring with laughter as he slams the door and locks it. I'm in darkness.

A candle is lit and a woman's voice says, "Don't mind Joe. He gets like this. You must be the lad he was meant to meet and take to Partekla. He's a-frightened of that place. We all are. More people live around here in this godforsaken wildnerness than you think. We all work at the Greeting factory, except now they've stopped production. There's to be a big rally of protest tonight."

"Where are we?" I ask this person overflowing with such information.

"Idaho."

"Idaho?"

"Have you never heard of it? We are in the northern narrow part near to Canada, and near a town named Coeur d'Alene that's very beautiful in the summer, short though that is. It is called Partekla. Many crazy and dissatisfied people come here to live. I married one of those. You can hate America easier up here. You can not pay your taxes and they don't come after you. You can shoot people you don't like and no one cares. All these lands around here—Oregon and Washington and Montana and Wyoming—are filled with crazies. They meet all the time. You'll see. Whatever you're here for. What are you here for?"

"I don't know."

"Then you'll have a lot of friends."

"Do you have to stay down here a lot?"

"I been down here since night before last, I think it must've been. He's not been feeling his best. He does bring me my tea, though. Once he even kissed me right here on this floor. You can't think ill of a man who could do that, can you? At least I'm his only wife."

After several hours Joe comes down and drags us both up to the daylight.

"Make us some eggs, Iris," he growls, and then he sits me down, slamming the whiskey and a pot of coffee in front of me, and commands me to drink.

Why do I obey his order? Why have I obeyed everybody's wishes? I didn't have to go away with Philip. I didn't have to become Dr. Grodzo's special friend; there were boys who refused him and they were allowed to live. He called them *nützlich*. Useful. I guess nothing ever seems too awful to me. I always figure it can be worse.

I drink like Joe said. I puke, on the table, on the chair, into the fireplace. Each time I vomit he makes me drink more. "Only way to get over it." He mixes the whiskey in the coffee, which makes it go down easier, though not for long. Iris comes in with hard-boiled eggs and salad as I'm vomiting again. "A nice plate of salad will do you a world of good."

Joe puts on his clothing for outside. "It's time to go." He piles me into his car. Evidently Iris isn't coming. It's dark outside now, and very cold. We drive off into the night.

Joe drives too fast on the ice and we skid a lot. I try to get him to talk. Eventually we reach a fenced encampment hung with a lit-up banner announcing "We demand fair wages for our labor." People are rushing to get inside the gates, what looks like hundreds of them. There are buses and cars parked in the snow. Most of the people are men.

The crowd is moving in the direction of a huge black building. There must be five hundred people inside, listening to speeches that have already started, screaming their approval, all of them as drunk as Joe. I'm smelly and messy from vomiting, and I still feel sick. Everyone is weaving back and forth, trying not to fall down. The stench in the place is awful. People would be in the middle of a sentence when they would suddenly throw up. Then they'd take another guzzle from the bottle clutched in every hand.

From the speeches and the drunken conversation I learn there's been a hijacking. Several thousand dollars' worth of something called Dridge Ampules have been stolen somewhere. Because of the war, there hasn't been a steady supply of them. Salesmen get a dollar for each packet of six ampules they sell. These men depend on the ampules to make a living. "We would go over to Spokane and down to Missoula and even Anaconda to sell them," I hear someone say on the loudspeaker. "Now we stay home and get drunk. I'm sick of getting drunk." Tonight the manufacturer is making things up to them. They had stopped production with the hijacking but now they would start up again come Monday. A man tries to give Joe a tiny glass tube in a case of white silk, but he slips in a mess of vomit on the floor. When the people near him see that he's dropped the ampule, they dive into the mess after it. A fat woman finds it. She grabs a man and breaks the thing and sticks it in the man's nose and then her own. In a matter of seconds he's ripping off her skirt and she's grabbing his pants. People crowd around screaming and yelling and cheering them on while he fucks her. Now I know what a Dridge Ampule is and can see what a popular product it is.

A fire is burning somewhere near. Loud music drowns speeches out. Men are now tossing little boxes from the stage while other men pass through the crowd giving them out. People grab for them, desperate for their contents. Soon the tiny ampules all fall like snow, hands and arms snatching them. More and more people fall to the ground fucking, sliding in the vomit. No one notices that the moon is now in the ceiling. The sounds of fucking are louder than any noise of burning wood or falling timbers.

"My friends!" The man who has been pointed out to me as "that greatest of great men, Horatio Dridge," is trying to address the crowd, with "my great friend" Clarence Meekly by his side. "We have come to tell you that Greeting-Dridge is waiting for your return." Many years later I will learn that Horatio Dridge has been dead some fifty years at this time and Clarence Meekly would have been some hundred years old and that many products send their "founders" and their "inventors" out on the road to pretend they're still alive, as if this will sell more product.

Men stand transfixed before each other, not accustomed to seeing each other naked. They see themselves in front of each other everywhere. Suddenly some of them are choking and gagging on each other's private parts. Then more of them. The few women start cheering them on.

That night I learned that passion can spread like fire itself, all kinds of passions. Most of the men have already had orgasms, but more sniffs keep their erections going. Then they must realize what they've been doing they've been doing with another man. They turn on Horatio. Their hands are sticky with semen, their shoes dripping with vomit. They start calling him hateful names. They hate him because he and his "pansy" friend beside him are "perverts," doing the things all of them have just done. They hate him so much that they rip him to shreds in seconds, pieces of him thrown in all directions, but mostly into the flames.

The roaring of the fire is joined by the screams of those noticing it at last and too late. The building collapses. Almost everyone perishes in that fire.

But not me. And not Joe. Joe is not letting me go so easily.

SHIT PAST A CERTAIN AGE NO LONGER SMELLS

After Dr. Nesta Trout also announces in *The New England Journal of Digestion* that the Table Family Hotel is built on a foundation of historic shit, the government immediately forbids the hotel to take in paying guests, which is just as well because business was awful. The Gulf Coast hasn't been "discovered" yet, and the hotel is dying. Hi and Meyer are able to force the United States to pay them as if their hotel is filled as long as the government embargoes their shit. They also receive from the government $23,000 each and every month. When, under the Alien and Enemy Reciprocity Act, they receive the government's check for some $4 million, Hi and Meyer burn the place down, collect the insurance, and move back north and start buying hotels in New York City.

THIS IS WHERE I WAS TAKEN

Mr. Hoover came to see me this morning. He said he was happy to see me. He said he wanted me to stay here. He said I'd be safe here.

I asked him why all this was happening to me.

Mr. Hoover said something like, "I am the possessor of many details about the illicit sexual activities of every person in the public limelight, and I'm very proud of it. This information helps me protect America. You will help me, as your father helps me."

He said that Amos would come for me when it's time.

Then he said, just as he said when we met, "Let me see your body, boy." I showed it to him, and he shook his head in sadness, nodded, and left.

Strangely, I am allowed into the daily schedule of this place, which is mammoth. I have a room instead of a cell. At least a hundred young men show up for meals. I come to realize that not all of them are being done to in the same ways, even though we all seem to live in the same small rooms, which are left unlocked. In the shower I see wounded bodies, but the wounds appear to have healed. Perhaps there's no torture here. Sometimes soldiers come up to me and ask where I got my scars.

I hear people talk about what's happening to them. They're receiving injections, or blood tests, or tests of strength, of endurance, of intelligence, of "social skills." They're being done to in many similar ways to Mungel, some of them, the constant jerking off to study their semen, saving their shit and piss, being circumcised if they're not already, and new stuff, like having hair implanted into their chests if they don't have any. All of Brinestalker's lot are given shots to make them have more body hair. Some of the very effeminate men are having their rectums sewed up so they can't be fucked, and their shit is rerouted into bags outside their bodies. They are all in pain and more and more they are no longer willing patients. When they become too noticeable and their pain too loud, they are not heard from anymore.

I recognize little bits and pieces of Mungel-inspired "research." Sometimes I think I see Grodzo in the distance. Quite frankly, I miss him holding me. I realize he made Mungel easier to endure. Then I realize it is Grodzo, here. And he turns his face away when he sees me looking at him. It hurts that Grodzo is treating me this way.

Once again, everyone is getting done to, except me. A German doctor, Oderstrasse, is in charge of the shots and taking blood. I assume he's a Nazi. I see a woman with one arm supervising the collection of shit from patients. She is familiar to me. When I think it is from Masturbov Gardens I begin to think I am having fantasies or delusions or they are doctoring my food, which everyone believes is being done to them.

One day Brinestalker appears with Amos, who immediately tries to take me in his arms as if we last saw each other yesterday. I won't let him.

"David, how glad I am to see you!" he says anyway.

He and Brinestalker take me below. I've heard rumors about "below."

I haven't seen Brinestalker since I first was in Berlin and he and Amos and my father were sharing a house on the Wannsee. We had all been in bed together. Amos, this man Brinestalker, and my father. We had pillow fights and we fell asleep all tangled up. Why are the two coming to see me here and now? Surely not to begin again where we all left off. And where is Philip?

"Where is my father?"

"This is no time for questions," Amos answers.

"When will that time come?" I find the courage to ask him. He doesn't answer, but I see him frown.

We walk down into a vast dungeon in the earth. It's lit by lights so bright they hurt my eyes. Nurses and orderlies are busy tending to bodies in endless rows of cots neatly lined up into the distance. If they are not completely encased in bandages, their inhabitants are hideous to look at, all misshapen and moaning. The bodies completely bandaged are the scariest because you can see arms and legs struggling to get out. Suddenly there is a piercing

scream and "Schline! Nurse Schline! Calling Nurse Lota Schline!" is heard
from a loudspeaker. Nurse Schline appears, a tiny Oriental woman carrying
a doctor's bag filled with tubes and needles. "These are the brain-dead,"
Amos says, referring to the cots of completely bandaged patients. Nurse Schline
is busily injecting a bunch of them, rushing from one to another, unsnap-
ping their openings and ramming a needle down into something. "They are
vegetables. We call them the potato sacks. They would be dead if Dr. Dye
hadn't sought them for our research."

I become bold.

"What would they be dead from?"

"That is a naïve question coming from you. Some experiments work,
but most do not."

"What are they trying to find out here? I don't see any twins. What is
Dr. Grodzo doing here? Why are you showing me any of this?"

"He is doing vital and top-secret research with Dr. Stuartgene Dye, another brilliant scientist. Nurse Schline is Japanese and has recently joined us.
She is also very brilliant and would be called 'Doctor' but for it being forbidden to women to become doctors where she studied, in Manchuria."

When Nurse Schline discovers a man is dead, she raises an arm and orderlies come to remove the body. This room smells of death, a smell I know.

"What can you possibly learn from these men who are almost dead?"

Brinestalker tells me. "Each body is being used to incubate a virus.
And while each virus is the same, each virus is not the same, according to
Dr. Oderstrasse."

Amos looks at him sharply, as if to say, Why are you telling him so
much?

"The boy is right, Amos. It is time to answer some questions for him."

Amos snaps back, "I will be the judge of that."

"Why are you showing me all of this?" I ask.

Now it is Brinestalker who snaps back. "So that you might be grateful
that you're alive. Many of us risked our lives to get you here."

•

I am free to walk freely from one part to another, though no one actually
tells me so. I just start doing it and no one stops me. I attend Brinestalker's
peculiar classes and watch his troops losing interest by the day. Sex can be
exciting for only so long, it seems, and "manly lust" cannot be whipped up on
demand as Brinestalker apparently thinks, with his films of hairy young men

with their big penises waving. I can even visit Nurse Schline's clinic, where I try to talk to some of the men until she tells me not to. "They cannot hear you," she says, nodding sadly. As in Mungel, I am left alone, as if I'm meant to be an observer. Underneath the bandages I will soon recognize faces from Brinestalker's classes and soldiers who'd been condemned to hard labor by General Heidrich. I see dead bodies pulled out of their sacks of bandage, some so hairy they look like faceless apes.

At first I'm not permitted to visit Dr. Dye. His section is off-limits. Then Grodzo himself comes and takes me there. He leads me by the hand, but he won't talk to me. But he holds my hand tightly, like he used to do. It's the only physical warmth and connection I've had since Amos held me at the film studio. I want Grodzo to take me in his arms and hold me. I want to pound on his chest with my fists and scream at him, "Why am I being treated this way!"

Bodies are laid out on tables. Dr. Dye and his assistants poke at them. Dr. Dye says to me, "I understand you are accustomed to such sights. This is how we learn. More than anything else it is important that we learn. There is always so much to learn. There is never enough time in our onward march to beat the devil. Do you believe in the devil? By now, you should. The devil is very interesting. He haunts these walls as completely as God haunts all the churches in the world." His eyes blaze like Grodzo's did when he was teaching me in Mungel. When I try to pull my hand back from Grodzo, he just grabs it back.

One night someone my own age comes into my room.

"My name is Warren. I would like to make love to you." He takes off his hospital gown and stands tall and proud, almost as if at attention. I realize he is displaying his body, which is covered with hair. "I am a new man now. I would like to try out my new manhood with you." Without any response from me, he lies down beside me. He takes my penis and his penis and starts massaging them both. Neither of us becomes hard. Warren starts to cry.

"It won't work anymore!" And he runs away. I hear guards outside capture him for having somehow escaped from his room to mine. I hear his high-pitched screams, suddenly silenced by someone covering his mouth. Or perhaps killing him. Yes, I remember similar things.

Another night Amos comes to my room. He's heard about my questioning of Nurse Schline.

"Nurse Schline's first name is Lota or Lothar. She or he is not at this moment male or female. She is here to become a he. Brinestalker has ordered

Grodzo to supervise sex changes on those of his young men who resist his best efforts to curb their rampant effeminacy. Grodzo is not happy about this assignment. He did not come to America to supervise sex changes. Brinestalker actually slapped his face in front of me. And then he threatened him. 'Perhaps we should have a discussion with your Guarantor.' Anyway, Nurse Schline is a different case. She must become a man in order to return to her homeland and become a doctor. The Japanese are involved in historic germ warfare discoveries and he must be able to steal those for us."

The next day Grodzo goes to Nurse Schline and takes her hand in his. "You must know that even with all we learned in Germany, this operation is far from perfect. We can give you a top without difficulty. We cannot give you the bottom with any effectiveness. Is that good enough for you?" She nods yes. "I can fake it!" Smiling at her use of American slang, he adds, "You know that Dr. Dye is against this because he doesn't want to lose you?"

And then, just as at Mungel, Grodzo turns to continue to teach me. "Schline worked in Japan for Unit 731 led by Dr. Shiro Ishii, who is their Dr. Mengele, and therefore she's brought with her much we can learn. The Japanese perfected a system of infecting hundreds of thousands via viral diseases, much more effective and less expensive than gas chambers. Quite frankly, all their different experiments on how people can and do and don't infect each other are more horrifying than ours ever were. Ishii would not let her perform duties by his side. She's furious with him and has sworn vengeance to go back and show him! And the Japanese are further ahead with their monkeys than our Dr. Bosco Dripper."

"Have you heard from my father?"

Amos doesn't answer.

"I don't want to stay here anymore. Can you let me go?"

"No. I cannot let you go until your time to be let go has arrived. I don't know when that will be."

"Who is deciding these things for me? What are you doing here? You ran a film studio."

Amos finally says something.

"My best friends in all this world have been your father and Brinestalker. I have sent communications to your father telling him about Brinestalker and requesting your father's advice and help because Brinestalker's doing such strange things. I've also told him that I have you here with me. He hasn't answered. It is up to him to provide you with the answers. I can't let you go until he comes to get you. When the three of us were together, he was the only one who could calm me down and keep Briney in check."

Once upon a time in another lifetime I asked Grodzo why Mengele and Hitler focused that hatred on Jews. He shrugged. "Why not? They are as good as any, and there are more of them than homosexuals and gypsies, which they throw in just for good measure, just in case."

"Just in case what?"

"In case people condemn the Jewish extermination. Then Hitler can say to them, But I have rid you of your hated homosexuals, too. Is that not worth something to you, at least a few Jews?"

I asked him how he knows who's a homosexual. By his own admission no one could really tell what a homosexual looked like at Mungel.

"What difference does it make? A certain number of them have to be. That is just good science. How else does one eliminate?"

I suddenly thought I'd never get out of here alive. Brinestalker had said as much. "We're showing this to you for you to be grateful you're alive and to know that your father is an ungrateful son of a bitch."

I do not want to stay here one more minute.

Several days later an armed guard marches me to a door and shoves me out into the freezing winter, tossing heavy clothing and a backpack after me.

In the backpack I discover matches, a road map, two hundred dollars, and a note from Grodzo saying, "I thought we might be safe here. I was wrong. Good luck in reaching your home."

FROM *MY HISTORY OF EVIL*

What David witnessed was just that old tip of an iceberg. Stuartgene can legally not only admit patients but keep them incarcerated, all under provisions established by the Department of Food and Drug Supervision (FADS) that allow for "the testing of treatments which in the estimation of the Director and his staff might lead to the betterment of the health of The American People." There are also in existence various provisions of the Wartime Powers Act that allow activities like this.

Stuartgene is in charge of a program that is "treating" hundreds of (early UC?) patients. Is he, and it, intentionally infecting young men with what he knows to be (a) lethal new disease(s)? Yes, he is. But Dr. Dye knows he's on to something, that he's got *something*, he just doesn't know what yet. But he will claim that he's seeking certain historic breakthroughs in virology, the study of which is still relatively unknown. So whether it's intentional or not that he's also going to kill a lot of young men in this research, an outcome that many of his superiors here and there and round and about would be happy to sanction, that's the effect of what he's doing. He's using questionable "potions"—for want of a better description of all the pills and infusions and lavages and enemas and unguents and nostrums being stuffed and injected and coerced into all his charges—provided to him by Brinestalker, Levy, Coro, Kokoh, Feltrin, Sasauer, Grodzo, and, yes, Dr. Sister Grace. Partekla is a godsend for them and for all the projects they're still working on.

Yes, Partekla is a busy place indeed. On a regular schedule dead bodies are laid out in a surrounding field and Aalvaar's prisoners dig their graves and bury them.

Something should be pointed out. I have been struggling mightily to make the case that what went on "over there" started over here. Now comes Partekla, which is meant additionally to be the equivalent of what various people over here know not only about what Hitler had been doing over there, but what indeed has been going on in other countries—for instance, in Japan, and in Manchuria, where the Russians conducted experiments that started the great bubonic plague that eliminated 250,000 Mongols in 1941 when an infected prisoner of war escaped. Who would want so many Americans made near-to-death? If you were running a drug company and had a drug you believed in mightily, wouldn't you be desirous of the largest possible "patient load" to test it on? It was Brinestalker's father, Jeshua, who as head of Bayerische AG during World War I conceived of such a notion. And put it into operation too. Many more men died in World War I than were killed on the battlefields from drugs tested in this way.

Each country has its own little posse of guinea pigs, and each country somehow manages to know about the existence of this work in the others. The whole category comes to be known as "germ warfare." Since the subtext of germ warfare is kill or be killed, no country wants to fall behind. Cooperating they may be, and to steal all they can.

And lest we forget, all of this experimentation is conducted quite righteously, embedded as it is in concrete already poured by eugenicists since the turn of the century. Why, had not even John Harvey Kellogg himself, whom we still eat every morning, proclaimed to The American People at his 1914 Race Betterment Conference that the United States was already home to some 500,000 lunatics, 80,000 criminals, 100,000 paupers, 90,000 idiots, 90,000 epileptics, mental defectives comprising at least 10 percent of the population?

Partekla is home to many an experiment. Some of them are even well-meaning.

Fred, we've lost Grace in the bowels of that place.

IN WHICH DANIEL JERUSALEM TELLS FRED MORE ABOUT *SEXOPOLIS* AND MORDY MASTURBOV, AND HIS UNCLE HYMAN

Philip and Rivka still won't say David's name out loud. How long can this go on? As if this isn't enough to still be dealing with, good old reliably repellent Uncle Hyman comes back on "home leave" from serving as a medical orderly, to stay with us, apparently looking for sympathy for all that he's going through. He'd been summoned home by his wife, who cabled the army that his daughter was dying, but when he went to their home they no longer lived there. Ironically, I guess, he was assigned to a VD clinic in Germany and took great relish in describing grotesque symptoms over dinner. What sympathy he gets is from my mother, who describes a few cases with hideous deformities on her own, all news to me. He certainly must have heard Philip announce loudly, "Over my dead body." All he gets from me is a kick in the groin that night when he attempts a return visit. So he takes off in the morning to "pick up a flight back to my theater of operations."

He had sold a lot of dirty books and pictures, but now they're from Belgium and France. The etchings and the photogaphs are remarkable in quality but the people in them still aren't very attractive. What they're doing is so perverse that even he can't believe his sales are so robust. I know because he actually showed them to me, "so you can leave my suitcase alone," trying to reach for my penis to see if it's hard, which it became when I kicked him in the groin. Why does it get hard for someone I don't like? He will continue peddling his merchandise for the rest of his very long life. Over the years the people will get better-looking, and so will the animals.

Somewhere along the line Hyman had married a Canadian girl named Ora. It's a dreadful marriage. Three quick children make matters worse. Hyman spent as much time on the road as he could and was grateful when the war came along. Ora asks for a divorce and he gives it to her. He lies about how much he's worth. He never sees her or their three children again.

My source for much of this is my aunt Fran, a really cool woman who hates him too, but has to see him because she's married to Rivka's and Hyman's brother who's his partner in a bookstore. "He tried to get Murray to carry his filth in the store and I said then I'd finally have a reason to murder him."

It isn't long before Hyman's biggest customer is Mordecai Masturbov, who takes great interest in the dirty books, which he finds in one of those downtown Washington secondhand bookstores on Ninth Street to which my uncle had taken me. "I never saw such excellent and imaginative photographs covering the whole range of perversities," Mordy would tell me years later. He said that Hyman was my uncle. I asked my childhood buddy if he ever considered that the overwhelming success of his *Sexopolis* was a major contributing factor to the spread of UC. "But I wanted to utilize this stuff in *Sexopolis*. *Sexopolis* must always be a total inspiration. Your uncle was helping me to feed the world's mind and my imagination. That can only be healthy." Hyman will be proud to help Mordy, who will henceforth always list him on the masthead as a "Contributing Editor (Photography) and among Our Honored and Beloved *Sexopolis* Family Members." Evidently Mordy set it up for the magazine to sell Hyman's photos without anyone knowing where they came from; it made my uncle a millionaire. According to Aunt Fran. No wonder Ora was looking to get him.

When I do come to see Mordy again (and I'm woefully out of sequence here), I wonder what I once saw in him that made me love him so, this tired middle-aged businessman's once-gorgeous marble skin now pallid. "I work too hard," he says almost apologetically when he sees me studying him, "but you look great." And then he flashes me a smile, of a kind he never gave me when we were kids. And yes, that did it, we fucked again. There is something so plaintive and touching about an old love's body come back into your arms. It's hard to disguise the facts of life, we're older; but there are the memories of two youngsters out in the fields under the moon, holding each other for the first time, that come back, that never go away. Today's fuck had been as unsatisfying.

"Let's stay in touch," he said as I was leaving. "Write me something racy about your world and I'll run it if it doesn't frighten my readers." He grins at his joke.

"Did you ever actually watch a German shepherd fuck a woman?" I ask him, referring to a photo that Uncle Hyman published to look like an etching.

He pauses, then says, "I even let the dog fuck me once," and then gives me a bigger smile when he sees I'm shocked. "Only joking, Danny. Where's your sense of humor?" and I swear I would have hopped back into bed with him again. But he was checking his watch. "This guy from New York wants me to buy him out. He owns a faggot modeling agency named One Touch of Penis." He laughed and with the fraternal slap on the back gently ushered me out.

By then *Sexopolis* is bigger and more powerful than ever, each issue pushing the boundaries of taste, further and further. Bare tits are no longer enough. Bare beaver takes over the roost, with men's admiring faces hovering nearer and nearer. Mordy's increasingly florid prose in the accompanying text borders on the lascivious, but he has a rare gift for making things sound amusingly juicy and comforting, just the ticket, first for our returning soldiers, now home again and bored, and then for The American People, increasingly the latter. Mordy does try to make all the far-out sexual activities *Sexopolis* hints at, or even trumpets, sound like good clean fun. The overwhelming number of letters published from satisfied customers ("You have changed my life!") attest to Mordy's success. Give us more, give us more, they implore almost plaintively.

I come to believe that *Sexopolis* will create a sexual revolution; I want to say will create it more or less by itself. Sorry to jump so far ahead of our time line, but this sexual revolution does have its seeds of origin in the era we've arrived at, a country waiting for the boys to come home. Mordy hasn't stopped thinking about his baby for a single minute. He's made mock-ups, he's written reams of prose, he's sought photos of sexual activities from Uncle Hyman and all the sources and catalogues and countries and creeps he could locate. He's carried interviews with sexologists, both respectable and not so. At times his issues seem overwhelmed by the variety of human possibilities. He is amazed, as he will put it to me, by "the myriad mishegas that flesh is heir to." *Mishegas* is a Yiddish word for "craziness." It's a word his father occasionally uses when they meet to discuss Abe's business, and Abe's hope, fast dying, that Mordy might consider taking it over. Yes, I read every issue. Knowing that they contain his heart and soul is of never-ending amazement to me. How could it not be? If he's the progenitor of the sexual revolution—and Fred will come to claim him emphatically to be such—I was his first trick.

I didn't know then that he'd shared all his dreams with Stephen and that indeed my brother would not only be his lawyer but his silent partner. By then my brothers both had graduated from law school, Lucas from Yaddah and Stephen from Franeeda State. All through the war, they'd both been waiting and worrying and wondering when they'd be drafted. They didn't know that Mr. Sam Sport had seen to it that they wouldn't be. They didn't know Mr. Sam Sport, much less why he'd do such a thing for them, and for Mordy, too.

STATE OF THE UNION: FRED GIVES IT A SHOT

Hermia, Grace, Ianthe, Daniel, I appreciate all your communications and concerns about the way I'm fashioning this history. I'm old enough to remember these unfocused years we're up to, confusing years for all of us. I'm glad to note that you have each held on to your sanity, or should I say balance, better than I appear to you to be doing. I'm sorry if I upset anyone. I'm sorry that I upset myself. How do I not do that? I don't know.

This has always been a country where we keep trying to tell ourselves that nothing's wrong that can't be fixed, when of course everything's wrong, and it's always been wrong, and no, it can't be fixed. I'm still not accustomed to being quite as angry as I'm becoming. From all my shrinks I've learned that managing anger is a gift. Some days I have it. Some days I don't. I'm hoping to get it up and running full-time as soon as I can.

World War II is over. War makes even less sense when it's over. War's a very heterosexual thing. It's a funny thought to have had so young, but I had it. I'm aware of this when Rena regales me with all her Red Blood war stories. I now know she's talking about other issues that don't include or concern me. American Red Blood isn't concerned about gay anything, and my mother works for ARB.

I don't have many friends in Masturbov Gardens. A number of fathers have been killed in the war. Some of the mothers remarried and moved away with their kids. My father hits me when I say I don't want to go to Yaddah. I don't know why hitting is his favorite sport. When Daniel tells me what Philip had done to him I figure all fathers take swipes at their sons. I learned how to hit him back. The first time I did this he was shocked and hauled off with a big one, which hurt so much I lunged forward and bit his hand. It just came instinctively. He bled and I thought, That did it, I'll be exiled for life. He looked at his bloody mitt and started to cry. That I didn't expect. In fact, he started bawling. He went into the toilet and put on a couple of Band-Aids and he came back into the living room and he swatted me hard again across my face. And I punched him hard in his belly, so he doubled up and fell on the floor. I could detail more choreography of our fights because this was just the beginning, and anyway Daniel's father and my father were behaving the same way. Rena was never home, of course. So I had to learn not to be home alone with him, because he wouldn't do it in front of her. Or so I thought. But soon he would and did and she screamed out at him, "What are you doing?" And he yelled back at her, "What does it look like I'm doing. He's your son and I want you to see it because I do it to him a lot and he deserves it because he's a sissy." Then she started bawling herself amid many sobs of how she couldn't take it anymore and she was going to leave him. And this would make him cry again and beg her, "Please don't leave me."

That's what it was like and it never varied much and both Mom and I stayed at home in Masturbov Gardens with him and nobody left anybody because nobody knew how to leave for good or where to go, and it goes on like this until it will become time for me to go to college. I haven't told you about my covert experiences with fellow high school guys. I had them, and they had me, and after we did it they'd make fun of me in front of others, as if they hadn't been part of it too. Nope, I didn't have many friends in Masturbov Gardens.

I would get into Yaddah not because of my brains but because my father and brother had gone there and a few uncles on both sides and they gave me a scholarship. Seth, my brother, told me I'd have a hard time there, which I would. I would try to kill myself there, after which Seth sent me to my first psychiatrist, thus beginning a lifelong enterprise of trying to figure out who I was and am and am meant to be.

So the end of the war led to the postwar years led to my going to Yaddah and the start of my own war in that outside world that I'd never seen. It was an awful childhood, but when Daniel tells me about his and David's, mine doesn't seem as bad.

The American People also didn't really know where we'd been either, and of course no one knew where they were going, although many claimed they did. We were told we'd won a war, which more and more made me say (rather boldly, if I may say so), Oh, yeah, who says? It never occurred to anyone that we'd lose. I was not going to lose, no sir!

Did you know that the most common cause of rejection for military service was defective teeth? That's the kind of helpful stuff the papers were full of.

I've read a lot about postwar prosperity, as if all the wounded jump right back into civvies and the playing field is level and everyone has a chance. As if there's enough for everyone of everything, now that we're all back in the same place. Or almost everyone. There is no accurate determination of how many American lives were lost. Troll and Hibernate weigh in first with 800,000, a figure quickly "adjusted" by the Bureau of War Statistics to 500,000, which is quickly pooh-poohed by the National Veterans Association, which insists on 1,000,000, as if it could come out so nice and even. But no one's bothered to refute any of them, mainly because there's no way they can be checked. How could we not know how many of our kids we'd sent off to die? It would be in 1950 before it's finally calculated that America is poorer by 793,560 war casualties. That's the "official figure," from the Gurney Institute of Numbers, now part of MIT, having been siphoned off from the Bureau of Wartime Statistics, now out of business.

As Mr. DuPont tells us, progress is our most important product. GI Bills for this and that, start-up loans for this and that, education, a job, a house. Yes, yes, as Mr. Carl Sandburg tells us, *The People, Yes.* On paper and in the papers it all sounds swell, but a number of the potential beneficiaries are dead, and hence are unavailable to substantiate the statistical good news that Harry Truman, with his Midwestern down-homeyness, is successfully peddling as fact. We should be proud of ourselves! We won! America won! The American People won! And among those who do come back are too many who won't or don't or can't rev up, no matter what's added to the gas. A lot of them come back and kill themselves or someone else. The suicide rates for 1945–52 are among the highest ever estimated for any "civilized" country, and the number of murdered women also breaks all records. To this day these figures are still classified by the Bureau of War Statistics. Harry doesn't tell us any of this. With that kindly face and haberdashery demeanor as comforting as macaroni and cheese (another cozy item, like "home front"), people trust him, even after he drops a couple of bombs that "usher in" (a quaint phrase redolent of theatergoing that now accompanies all mentions of such horror shows as Hiroshima and Nagasaki) the nuclear age.

"They didn't come back like, 'Oh, we saved democracy; so we're happy,' " writes the gay playwright Craig Lucas in *The Gay and Lesbian Review.* "They came back as totally broken people who could barely function. I saw family after family where the mother paid the bills, made the decisions, took care of the children, and was basically the fiber of the family while the guy with an empty shell went off to work every day and drank himself to death!"

Yes, in one form or another, the wounded are what are flowing back. We can actually see firsthand what the war was really about. Cripples, disfigured men still bandaged somewhere, the worst accompanied by a nurse's aide. Hospitals everywhere experience heavy loads. Rena takes me with her when she visits the paraplegics. That's her new Red Blood assignment. She brought home artificial limbs for me to feel and see and Richard went nuts, which made me parade around with them all the more—the fake arms and legs and feet—singing that Andrews Sisters song "The Victory Polka." NITS still isn't ready (it's on its thirty-fourth director) and the half of its medical staff sent overseas comes back just as much basket cases as those they're meant to treat.

And all the stories from overseas about jungle this and tropical that and poison everything—what are all these boys coming home bringing with them? "New cures are coming every day" is an announcement from the thirty-fifth NITS director, Dr. Horace Merman: "I've got all my boys working overtime." FADS can't staff up fast enough and its new director, Dr. Elijah Montrose, announces, "Diseases will be eliminated!" The *Monument*'s happy to quote them both. Penicillin and vaccines and new derivatives of old favorites like sulphur and warjim are reported in all the *New England Journal of Whatevers*. People believe what they read. A soldier is interviewed from his bed in the North Nerts Wing at Sibley General (where I'd had a broken elbow put in its cast when I was six): "Oh, I caught that in Iwo Jima and I almost died until they gave me this new stuff called warjim and it saved my life." Who wouldn't believe a story like that? In six months warjim will be discovered to be worthless and no one's reporting that. There are lots of these new "wonder drugs" concocted by all our new research scientists. Trajan. Apollo. Elgin. Dolphus. Fedrick. Rheingold. (These are all "lifesavers," not doctors' names.) *The Merck Handbook* of 1946–47 lists pages of them.

There are rumored to be a lot of military deserters still at large, or unaccounted for. Where did so many go? Were they killed or are they still in hiding? No one writes about this matter, nor is much written about the savage violence that's erupting in the larger cities because of a huge shortage of trained police officers to keep order.

Here's a doozie. Fewer than a third of American families had a close relation fighting overseas. That's another statistic Harry doesn't let out. We're supposed to believe that America is a country where every family suffered. Well, it's just not true. Fewer than a third? Where was everybody else? It's another one of those Greatest Stories Never Told. Yes, many guys just changed their name and started up somewhere else. Or they were still lying dead on some battlefield like after the Civil War.

Almost everyone who had stayed at home is employed, which means that when Johnny comes marching home he has a tough time of it. His job's taken or gone. He wants to go back to where he left off but he lost his virginity at Pearl Harbor.

In the postwar euphoria, journalists and historians don't notice much amiss, except for a few of the more prescient, like Lippmann and the Alsops and the Blisses, and of course you, dear Ianthe. I've been reading your occasional columns in the *Monument* from those days, and I was particularly moved by the one about "the sorrow abroad in the land," so Churchillian, gently acknowledging those like Daniel's cousin Barry, who came back without a leg or an arm to find their jobs, or their wives, or the girl-friends they dreamed of on Wake Island or Normandy Beach gone with the wind.

But for many, no bad weather's in sight. No one thinks winter is coming. Is there anything more comforting than a president named Harry? Churches are full of people thanking God for everything. People are being grateful all over the place. Archbishop Sheeney is dropping in on more masses than ever to check up on all his boys. Rabbi Chesterfield's radio program is now carried on more national stations. A rabbi broadcasting coast-to-coast on CBS! Let's talk about progress. A Professor Volblade at Notre Dame devises the Serena, a method of calculating just how happy people are, using various measurements that will "usher in" new "disciplines" such as advertising and public relations. According to Professor Volblade, everybody's happy because Serena says so. Who can dispute Serena? Since unhappy people haven't learned how to speak out yet, unhappy mouths stay shut.

Also largely unnoticed at this moment is that Washington is a hotbed of homosexuality. Single men are everywhere. Did they flunk their physicals so they wouldn't be sent overseas? Did they go over in the closet and come back out of it? They won't go unnoticed for very long, though. According to Jack Lait and Lee Mortimer in their 1951 bestseller, *Washington Confidential*, in the chapter "Garden of Pansies," "The Washington Vice Squad had listed 5200 known deviates." Dr. Ben Karpon, the psychiatrist at St. Purdah's Hos-

SEARCH FOR MY HEART 753

pital, believes they are in the tens of thousands. Dr. Kinsey wasn't appalled by the 6,000 "swishes" in government jobs. According to *Washington Confidential*, 56,787 federal workers are congenital homosexuals. This includes 21 congressmen and 192 others that are bad behavior risks.

So if you're wondering where your semi-boy is tonight, he's probably in Washington. The good people shook their heads in disbelief at the revelation that over 90 twisted twerps in trousers had been swished out of the state department. Fly commentators seized on it for gags about fags, whimsy with overtones of Kinsey and the odor of lavender. These 6000 homosexuals on the government payroll comprise only a fraction of the total of their kind in the city.

One of the few who does notice, and long before Lait and Mortimer give their official "Heads Up" to this issue, is Senator O'Trackey Vurd (a Republican from Arizona), a pleasant-faced young "conscientious objector" whose heart is not so smooth as his saintly milk-white skin, which makes you wonder if the fellow ever has to shave. Fearful that he's the only heterosexual man left in Washington who walks around DuPont Circle at night, he almost single-handedly sees to it that the Office of Unnatural Acts is given more money to play with itself, that said new office be declared a "department" instead of an "office" (bigger budget this way), and that said new department be renamed the Tally Department, which of course was its original name, which excited little interest. Senator Vurd is eager for its return to that state of overt anonymous invincibility, all of which he is able to now accomplish legally under Section 21A of the Official Wartime Powers Act (still in existence and will be until—are you ready for this?—2011), which is entitled "How to Deal with Those Men on the Home Front Unfit for Active Duty Due to Social Misinformation," which of course is the parent to the "Don't Ask, Don't Tell" bullshit that Boy Vertle will foist upon the Armed Services in 1993. Vurd is a high-ranking Disciple of Lovejoy (and serves on its Dominion Council of Elders), a covert homosexual (covert is the same as closeted), an alcoholic, a wife abuser three times over, an abusive father of eight children, a pederast, an embezzler from that Dominion Council of which he's treasurer, on the take from sixty-two Arizona corporations and twenty-seven out-of-state ones, a three-time senator, and an evil man. Yes, you could get away with almost anything, particularly in any and all western states. Lait and Mortimer were not writing about Vurd, nor were Lippmann, the Phippses, or the Alsops.

Corruption as a complete and utter way of life has yet to have its Gibbon, its Thucydides, etc. Vurd and many others will get away with similar lives and lies.

Senator Vurd is joined in vociferous lobbying by Senator Joseph McCarthy, his buddy, and also of course by J. Edgar Hoover, another advocate for healthy living, all three of whom will be "discovered" after their deaths to have been pretty socially and solidly misinformed themselves. Eurora von Lutz is now riding a larger tiger with bigger teeth; it's too bad she's lost hers, as well as her life, in a simply dreadful automobile accident on the East-West Highway; the woman has simply been driving too long, thus paving the way for the Tally Department to be up for grabs. Brinestalker is offered the job but turns it down. "I don't want to be so fenced in," "Don't Fence Me In" being a Cole Porter hit sung by Bing Crosby and the Andrews Sisters. Vurd is no doubt aided in his search for more and more fellow travelers by the mimeographed "anonymous" exposé mysteriously handed out in all government cafeterias reporting on "unimpeachable authority" that there are more than 75,000 fairies in "our" government "according to the late 'beloved' Eurora von Lutz." Vurd and Brinestalker decide to leave the Tally Department leaderless for the moment. Eurorah's well-trained minions can still do the work.

Almost overnight more and more new agencies are created to take care of more and more new problems. The Animal Experimentation for the Post-War Effort League (AEPWEL), the Anti-Animal Experimentation for the Post-War Effort League (AAEPWEL), the Hadema Adonai Schwartz Clinical Wing for Severed Limbs (at Isidore Schmuck), the Nelson Punic Foster Home for Abandoned White Children, the Office for Aid to New War Widows (OANWW), the Agency for the Preservation of the Sanctity of Home and Marriage (POSHAM)—if ever a bureaucracy growing with the speed of lightning can be said to be exerting itself real hard to come out of the womb, it's Washington attempting to look after various public thorns in its postwar ass.

Yes, the war is over.

Some figures are just in from Eugen Kogon in his 1947 pioneering report on this subject, *The Theory and Practice of Hell* (to be verified by Frank Rector in his 1981 *The Nazi Extermination of Homosexuals*): During the twelve years of Nazi rule, nearly 500,000 men and women were convicted in Germany for being homosexual. The majority wound up in concentration camps and virtually all of them perished. And German homosexuals, should they have survived, remain silent after the war because being a homosexual is against the law. (In 2008, Professor William Percy at the University of Massachusetts will present evidence that "one million homosexuals somehow disappeared during the Holocaust.")

And while we are throwing around some grotesque numbers, try this one: "During 998 press conferences over the course of his twelve years in office, FDR never sent a word of warning" to Hitler and Germany about Hitler's mass murders, which he'd promised many he would do. (Thanks to Laurel Leff and to Rafael Medoff at the Wyman Institute.) Such a monstrously inhumane disdain for the persecution of some of his people will be repeated by Peter Ruester in his utter disregard for The Underlying Condition and its sufferers, and its potential sufferers.

History certainly requires a lot of history before you can say out loud you're not wanted.

DON'T FORGET TO TAKE YOUR DRIDGIES

It's been a slippery thing, Greeting Pharmaceuticals. It's been plain old Dridge, it's been Dridge-Meekly, it's been Uriah-Dridge (I think I missed out on that one), it's been British Dridge, it's been BaxxterDridge, it's been Greeting-BaxxterDridge, and after that it became what it is at this moment, Greeting Pharmaceuticals. During the two world wars, it was not enough of a player in any market big enough to cause big boards to notice. None of Greeting's pharmaceuticals was useful to the troops. No antibiotic, no anti-anything. Greeting was so useless as a supplier that its executives were drafted. Now that peacetime's back, the only item of value in its portfolio of nostrums and elixirs and balms, all remnants from an earlier era of medicine men hawking "cures" from portable valises set up in traveling carnival shows, will turn out to be what's been simply and innocently listed in their catalogue for ages as the Dridge Ampule.

Why is Fred harping so on the Dridge Ampule? Because it will be one of the most important participants in the plague of The Underlying Condition, as Dr. Rebby Itsenfelder will warn all along. The one certainly helped contribute to the other. Sit tight. As one of the greatest of gay Broadway composers will warn us, "Something's coming!"

The Dridge Ampule is the current incarnation of several hundred years of searching for the perfect aphrodisiac. We had whiffs of it from Dr. Hogarth

Hooker, the Drs. Punic, young Lucid Hooker, the lovers Horatio Dridge and Clarence Meekly, Doc Rebbish, and . . . has anyone been left out? These have snowballed, as the years marched on, into something that will shortly knock all jocks off. Many hands have tinkered. New cooks constantly revise the latest recipe. This is indeed how most drugs are developed. It's difficult to assign credit though many have claimed it, do claim it, and will claim it (until the drug becomes so embarrassing on UC's playing fields that attempts will be made to hide it from view). The formula—Dr. Sister Grace's discovery of Vel had a great deal to do with it all metamorphosing into the current "product," which lasts a little longer (so important in an aphrodisiac), leading her to claim its current patent—has been marketed successfully for almost a century as a "cure for those vapors that come upon a perfectly happy afternoon to cloud the sky of blue." (It did not cure Grace's mismitosial fits, which she thought it might, which was why she got involved with it in the first place.) The Dridge Ampule helps old people revive themselves, having been much used by maiden ladies with a propensity to fainting, or with hearts no longer young and gay but desirous of being both. Ladies, just pinch the little glass bauble in its little silk stocking until it breaks and hold it under your nose and heartily sniff. Don't you feel young and wonderful again? With all kinds of unnameable tinglings in your equally unnameable nether-regioned body parts.

Yes, history does require a lot of history.

DANIEL, AT HOME

David won't speak to us. He's completely silent. He disappears from Masturbov Gardens for days at a time and returns and won't say where he's spent the nights or slept or bathed. After a while I wonder if he's come back just to punish us. His silent presence is a constant accusation. To be honest, it's been so long since I've seen him that I've lost any sense of personal blame for his disappearance.

Mostly I'm struck by how much we still look alike and yet how different we must be inside. I don't understand his silence but Rivka says he's shell-shocked and we just have to wait for him to come out of it. Mrs. Blood Bank has had so much experience in this field that in the face of the obvious fact that one of her sons is acting catatonic, she confidently proclaims, as always, "everything will be all right."

So David's back. He sleeps in his old bed across from mine. He looks at my body and I look at his. He's much more blatant in his observations, open and without embarrassment, and once he's registered whatever he's looking at he gets into his bed and goes to sleep. The pattern of hair on his chest matches mine precisely. He has a lot of marks and scars on his body, particularly his back. I want to touch them but he won't let me.

"Why won't you talk to me?" No response. "It's amazing how our bodies are still so much alike," I try again. I give up.

No, I don't. Nothing would silence me now. Not now.

I stand naked by his bedside, by his sleeping head. "Look at me," I say, so close that he must feel me practically on top of him. "Did it scare you when your body started to grow hair? I got scared. Did it scare you when your penis got hard? I got scared. Do you want to hear what Uncle Hyman did to me?" I keep thinking that each confession will open his eyes and he'll look at me. I suddenly wonder if I'm jealous. Silence has a way of making things dramatic. He's been having a wonderful time all these years and he hasn't had to live with Rivka and Philip.

David is asleep now, breathing deeply, as if he's in some dreamland even further away from me. I reach out and run my fingers millimeters above his scarred skin. The marks seem of several kinds—lacerations, burns, stitches, welts. No, he couldn't have been having a wonderful time. Should I run and get Rivka? Look, Mommy, look what's happened to David. I'm overcome with pity for him. I shake him until he finally opens his eyes and looks at me. Yes, he looks up at me, but he still doesn't speak. Can he possibly be half of me anymore, this David whom I haven't seen since I was six and now we're seventeen? I start to cry. He's still looking at me. He gets up and puts his arm around me and puts me in my bed and pulls the covers up to my chin. Then he goes back to his own bed and turns his face to the wall, and soon enough he's left me again. I have awful dreams and when I wake up he's gone.

DAVID, AT HOME

I want to punish them. Something started under this roof, with this family. You know how people are always saying these days, "He's a survivor"? I hate that word. As if some decide to survive and some don't. It has nothing to do with will. It has nothing to do with anything but luck. All around me boys just like me were getting killed like flies. Better-looking boys, boys with big-ger penises, boys forced to do more than I would to stay alive, like give guards blow jobs or let themselves be fucked. Once, I was standing in line next to a kid who was making faces at a guard behind his back and I did exactly the same thing, and the kid got sliced to pieces like a steak on a carving board. The blood's the same color.

I'm back and I'm doing my best to scare my family to death. I'm thin as a rail, which to a Jewish mother means I'm unhealthy and haven't eaten properly since I left home. Rivka loads down the table with piles of food, "your favorites," as if either of us could remember what they were. She slaps any hand that reaches out. "It's for David! Let him choose first!" This an-noys Philip. If anyone's going to play the martyr, it should be him.

He corners me in the toilet after a few days. I'm peeing and he claps his hand over my mouth. He spits out his questions. "Why has it taken you so long to get in touch with me? Why aren't you talking? Why won't you speak to me?"

He removes his hand as if to release the answers. I flush the toilet. "How is Mr. Standing?" I ask, without waiting for an answer.

I wonder how much he's told Rivka. Everything? Nothing? Maybe they've worked out some story that lets them live with themselves. She must know something. How could she not after all these years? Maybe they never expected me to come back. Now, that's a thought. Rivka never once asks me about where I've been.

Lucas and Stephen are away at college. It would be hard for me to stand up to their questions. It's hard enough with Daniel. When I look at him I still can see myself.

DANIEL, NOT AT HOME

All I am is selfish, trying to get him to look at me and say hi, I'm back, I missed you, I still love you. Why should he say any of that? I haven't said it to him. I didn't miss him. I barely thought of him after a while.

I walk the streets at night after I finish at the Jew Tank. The women still believe they can save people. I like being with them. The war is over and they don't have a very good record of finding loved ones but they don't give up. I have after-school jobs too, ushering at Constitution Hall, where I can hear all the concerts, and working at a record store. I like staying downtown.

Anything so I don't have to go home. I want to see him. I don't want to see him. He's there. He's not there. Sometimes I walk so long that it's too late to go home because there aren't any buses after midnight. I go back to the Jew Tank Quonset hut and sleep on a beat-up sofa and go to school in the morning from there. I go to a Washington high school now. Lucas made me transfer. He says I won't get into Yaddah from the crummy school in Franeeda County.

The papers and the radio are filled with Senator Vurd this and Senator Vurd that. He's naming names every minute. The names he's naming used to be Communists, but now he thinks everyone in the entire government is a homosexual. I read in the *Monument* that Senator Vurd has 112 men fired for being homosexual. There's an editorial agreeing that such people should not be employed in "sensitive" jobs. I've known what a homosexual is since Uncle Hyman's reading class, but something different is involved now. It's no longer being with Mordy way out in the bushes past Masturbov Gardens. Now it's a sensitive job that gets you fired. What is a sensitive job? Does Philip have one? What was he doing with his friend in Berlin? Was it homosexual? Whatever it was, it certainly made Rivka angry. Senator Vurd is now sending men into hiding. There's a story about a man who changed his name and was still found and fired from a job that wasn't sensitive-sounding at all, selling insurance door-to-door. A man down the street from us in Masturbov Gardens kills himself because Senator Vurd names him in the *Monument*. He has a wife and five kids, so now I'm not sure I know what a homosexual is. Now it seems to mean seeing your name in the newspaper and killing yourself. At Constitution Hall, they wouldn't let Marian Anderson sing. There's a picture in the *Monument* of Senator Vurd with his two handsome associates, Sam Sport and Louis Blick. Why do you all hate me? I ask the photograph. Is David homosexual too? Did whatever happened to him happen because of that? Why don't I just ask him? I decide I will, but he's gone again.

IANTHE REMINDS US THAT OLD SPIES NEVER DIE

Forgive me, Fred, for what may appear a digression, but the subject of spying deserves some attention. Just about everything nasty that went on during the war continued after. Brinestalker and Standing were spies, of course, though I can't imagine they were good ones. There were many more, and people receiving government stipends to fight the war in covert situations did not wish to be abandoned for some old piece of peace. You don't get rid of old spies just like that. When people who possess top-secret information feel threatened they can do desperate things.

Men had become accustomed to getting paid for talking, rewarded somehow, but you had to be careful to whom you talked to get it. You could just as easily get fired or somehow disposed of. The Brits were the best at that: they chased their best daredevils all the way to Russia, where they had to spend the rest of their lives or be executed if they came back home. I'd estimate that of the hundred or so men in the "intelligence field" that Strode and I knew, more than half of them wound up stuck behind various curtains, iron or otherwise, and can never come home, no matter how many big kills they brought off for their home team. Spy stories don't tell you about this because it appears unheroic, which it is. I never could understand why men want to spy. The English lot, most of them out of Cambridge, claimed they were doing it for their country, which I never believed for a minute, although I'll be the first to admit that there's a lot about men no woman can ever understand, and I don't think that they undertstand about themselves either. It's all a big game somehow, left over from childhoods of challenging each other over who was King of the Mountain, who has the biggest dick, and going out and using it, metaphorically, of course. Most of the best ones did turn out to be fairies, like Burgess and Maclean and Philby and Blunt and our own James Jesus Angleton. In these cases, I've always wondered if it was some sort of retribution toward their mommy country that didn't approve of fairies, an "I'll show you who's a fairy!" sort of thing. When you get to more recent times, all they were interested in was money. In my day that was considered insulting.

Most spies aren't given but half a picture, if that. Edwin always complained that Franklin had a way of keeping everyone in the dark about his overall picture, which only he had in his mind's eye. That's why most histories of leaders are so full of baloney. No one can ever know what the subject really had in mind, no matter how much he wrote down or said out loud or even whispered. Since things change day by day, minute by minute, you'd better not have had too many drinks, which spies, to a man, love to do, get drunk, which made them, drink by drink, feel increasingly important. Or to get caught up in some other obsession, like poor Sumner and his Negro railway porters. Sumner was a real loss to Franklin because he knew what had to be done and Franklin usually didn't. The more I find out about

Franklin, the more I believe we just had good luck, little of it coming from him but from the fact that the war somehow ended itself and in some way we were relatively all still here. Nobody bombed us for a start. I don't think one single American considered "luck" a part of winning this war. But it was. Big-time. Franklin wasn't smart enough and the men he had around him weren't either, except for Sumner.

I personally believe that Franklin spoke with Hitler a number of times and that deals transpired. There. I've said it. God knows I've thought it all along. What's the point of being a leader if you can't make deals? I'll bet old Franklin got something in return for not allowing Jews into this country. The only question is what, and this we'll never know, no matter how many historians or biographers write their "definitive" works of horseshit. I put it bluntly to Eleanor one day: "Do you realize that you and Franklin will go down in history as the ones who wouldn't do anything to help a zillion Jews and fairies and gypsies survive?" Well, she was a bucket of sobs and groans and protestations. "No! No! No! Don't say that again! I tried! I begged! I didn't know about the gypsies and the . . . homosexuals, but I got down on my knees and I begged for the Jews!"—something that's hard to visualize, but I took her word for it. She had the only heart in that relationship. Once during the war she took me to a meeting of Hadassah ladies whom she was addressing and trying to console, somewhere in Jew Tank territory, North-west, third alphabet, Ellicott Street, I think. They were lapping up her sympathy when I got up and actually shouted at them. "Your relatives and families are in hell, if they're still alive, and you have done nothing to help get them out! They've been living in hell for the entire duration of this war while you've been living in houses like this one, Sara Sue Goldenstein's gilded baroque monstrosity. Sara Sue, how many hundreds of thousands of dollars did your Sammy let you spend on this hideously tasteless morgue? How can any of you face your own blood when they come back? If they come back?" Eleanor ran from the room. The Hadassah harpies just stared at me, speechless. On my way out I saw Emma Liebowitz, whose son, a homosexual, was arrested in Berlin trying to emulate Auden and Isherwood and hadn't been heard from since. We filed a Seek and Search for him. "And you, Emma, what kind of mother are you? The Nazis murder homosexuals right alongside Jews." The poor woman collapsed in a faint on the floor, and I—oh, I am so righteous—stepped right over her body and haughtily stalked out.

Yes, it may seem inapt to digress into something that on the surface appears so alien to the world of science and our plague as spying, but it really isn't and I do think we all must ask, what exactly is spying, or "intelligence" to call it by its more formal and more ridiculous name? How inclusive was it? Spying during World War II particularly attracted faculty members from America's and Britain's elitist educational institutions, no one has ever been able to tell me why. Chief among the American schools, in that it provided some 75 percent of all spies working for America and Britain, was Yaddah. In charge of the most important and confidential wartime initiative (code name: Boola) was Yaddah's Tom Jones.

Tom Jones was, of course, not his real name. We haven't heard much yet about Yaddah since its founding, and I know Fred and Daniel will rectify that in due course. How you two got through four years at that prison, I don't know. Edwin was on the faculty there for a few semesters after we returned, long enough for us to know that the tactics of Stalinism were not confined to Soviet Russia. I don't mean it was full of Commies, although Tom and a lot of others will shortly do their best to convince everyone that all of America could be. I mean you couldn't take a breath of fresh air in New Godding without there being a regulation for where and when you did so, and if you breathed out of sync you were summoned for chastisement by someone you'd not met and would likely never see again. There must have been spies in the woodwork for them to know whatever it was that so never-endingly bothered them about anyone. It was almost a joke, unless you were fined, I mean your salary was actually docked if you talked about the "wrong things" in a classroom. Joseph Grandage, who refused to join the OSS, told me he walked into a dining hall while an officer of the university was eating with the boys and he was told to have dinner elsewhere. And if the boys weren't wearing ties, forget it! Fifty lashes with a wet noodle, they used to joke. My God, but it was regimented! And petty! And as at Harvard, Yaddah students and faculty were booted out very quickly if any whiff of fairylike behavior could be smelled on them. Suicides at both universities for being gay were highly guarded secrets and I'll bet still are.

I'll just bet also that the same charge could be brought against the pharmaceutical industry, that the number of suicides and even murders is numerous and classified. But as Grace is fond of saying, that's somebody else's history to tell.

D. HEWLING DUPPERS REDUX

Hello again. I hope you remember me. I increased that information overload for you with my earlier entries about Comstock and Garfield. I'm the boring queen who managed to keep his tenure at Yaddah. I'm retired now but as I still live locally I go in now and then to pinch-hit if someone in American Studies is out for a spell, sort of the Yaddah version of the substitute teacher you had in grade school. Fred has asked me to fill Ms. Strode in on Tom Jones because number one, I was his student, number two, I was his office assistant, number three, I was with him when he went to England and came back to Yaddah after being a part of such historically important work, number four, he was one of the strangest men who ever walked this earth, number five, we fucked like bunnies, which wasn't easy for him because he was a hunchback and often in great pain, and number six, I really loved and admired him. Because of five and six I'm not going to use his real name, although anyone who was at Yaddah then and involved in its administration or its American Studies department will be able to figure it out. I hope they're all dead and if they're not I hope reading this will give them their well-deserved heart attacks and finish them off.

Tom Jones loved American literature more than any teacher I ever had or heard about. He knew all our great ones inside out as if they were his blood relatives. Hawthorne and Melville especially. He knew they were both gay and loved each other. He'd hold me in his arms as he read to me parts of both their works to point out stuff to back up his theories. "Can't you just read what's underneath these words?" he'd ask me. "Subtext. You've always got to search for subtext. In art and in life." He was a big believer in codes, for everything, particularly art, "where artists aren't able to be as honest as their art demands but they're trying to be honest anyway. Not easy." His friends were all writers, poets, certainly not teachers, "we're too boring, and we need our artist friends like a vampire needs blood to stay alive." When I asked him why he didn't write his own great work—academics are always looking to do that—he said, "Because I'm not brave enough to say what has to be said." I loved him even more for that. He would lecture his classes to "pay attention to what Hawthorne and Melville are *really* saying," that sort of thing. But when confronted to flesh that out a little bit more, his eyes would twinkle mischievously and he'd be silent, and I'm sure no kid had a notion what in the world he was talking about. He could lose his job if he talked gay anything and we both knew it, every teacher at Yaddah knew it. Yaddah was not what you would call a gay-friendly place. It started at the top, with all its presidents, who said in public really awful things.

I was his assistant as an undergraduate and when I was writing my thesis. At first I just filed his correspondence to the many famous writers all over the world that he kept in touch with, like Gertrude Stein and Ezra Pound and a lot of lesbian "imagists," as they were called. When we first fell into each other's arms, it was, or seemed like, an accident. I was on a ladder and slipped coming down. Simple as that. He picked me up and held on and so did I. "You don't want to go any farther with a cripple like me, laddie," he said, as neither of us let go and we kissed. I'd had lots of men by then, and lots of hunky bodies, but I loved his bent and crippled body as if he were Cary Grant. He had some kind of childhood malformation that never healed right and in those days they couldn't do much to fix it, even though his family could afford it. After that, we were together all the time we could be. I told him I didn't want to know if he had a wife and kids, because I figured he did and I didn't want to feel guilty and I didn't want him to feel guilty either.

When the war came he offered his services immediately. It turned out he'd also studied mathematics and was interested in the burgeoning field of computers and collecting information more efficiently, as I certainly knew because I had to deal with his thousands of every kind of literary ephemera his vast collection contained. He was Mister Neat and Mister Organized and Mr. I Must Be Able to Lay My Hands on Everything I Own or You're Fired. The stacks and shelves and file cases in his office were a feat of modern—I don't know what to call it—library-ology. When the offer came for him to go to England, and to Bletchley Park, he took me with him to be his assistant there as well. He told the Brits in charge of Bletchley they couldn't have one without the other. I guess they were used to guys like us. We figured that out when we were given a room with a single bed!

In and out of this stone pile came a formidable amount of everything imaginable to send forth into battle. None other than James Jesus Angleton, who would become head of America's Central Intelligence Agency, was our assistant in our Office of Strategic Services, the OSS (code: XYZ-22). Office XYZ-22 worked with the intelligence divisions of each branch of the armed forces of both our countries as well as our FBI. James Jesus was a dark and sly weasel and sexy as hell and gay as a coot, though trying so hard to hide it you'd think he was trying to keep himself from an onset of diarrhea, trying to hold it in. Wild Bill Donovan, who founded the first OSS, the two Dulles brothers, Bill Casey, who worked for both the OSS and the CIA and will run Peter Ruester's successful campaign for president (and along the way convince him of that worldwide Communist threat that was as fictional as Dredd Trish, Jr.'s weapons of mass destruction), all were then youngsters, wandering about searching for political enemies. Philby, Burgess, Maclean, Anthony Blunt, all had papers of top-secret affiliation. It was like anybody who was or would be anybody wanted to be part of XYZ-22, even though it was considered a British hothouse. The Brits were a seedy, smelly, unfriendly lot, and they were, to use their own terminology, beastly to each other. We were all, Brits and Yanks, also a part of the Fifty Committee, my goodness there were a lot of committees; every committee leader claimed he was trying not to play favorites (we learned fast that down that road lies eventual blame and responsibility for sure), and if there was a committee headed by a Brit, there had to be one headed by a Pole, or a Russian, or of course a Yank. Now, there was no way in hell that each country had the same goals in sight. So the whole system, not only of international cooperation in "intelligence," but of out-and-out spying, was, as Tom and I learned to say, "pretty much of a wash. We'll just have to find a way to do it by ourselves."

Tom, who as I said was a demon for detail and total neatness, became noticed because he managed to compile and input, with the expert assistance of yours truly, some 400,000 entries into what today we'd call a database, the likes of which had never been available before. We chalked up many an all-nighter, just the two of us, in that attic room at Bletchley Park, an amazingly down-at-the-heels once-stately pile, by the way. While we'd played with each other in his office at Yaddah, compiling this true achievement in the UK is what really brought us together. For one thing, there was only that one bed. I got to see how horrid his curvature was becoming; often it was a suppurating sore, and I tended him like I was his nurse, which I was. He didn't want anyone to know that he was in any way infirm. If there was a physical challenge every other man was performing as a matter of course, like climbing five flights of stairs numerous times a day, he would do it faster. From this database, the Brits concocted Operation Gracie Fields, which involved the "turning"—that is, imprisonment or killing—of every German spy introduced into Britain, another amazing achievement that not so coincidentally gave us access to the German codes necessary for us to break the Enigma code, which Tom and chiefly Alan Turing did, which won the war.

Kim Philby, the great spy against his own country, was Tom's counterpart. We went to many an all-night drunken orgy with him and his fellow twits from Cambridge that wound up quite naturally as a sexual orgy too.

People still have no idea how homosexual the world of spying was! Mind you, as with armed forces in the trenches, there's nothing else to fool around with but other guys. But this was more than that. There was such an intensity to our work and its importance that we really became a brotherhood of men, and, like something out of ancient Greece, preferred each other. I can't recall one single time when any of us went into any neighboring town, or even London, to lasso a lassie.

By the end of the war, Tom was a very powerful figure, for good reason, and got lots of medals from various governments. Then Truman decided to close down the OSS and form the CIA and give the leftovers to the FBI. Hoover was in there on the ground floor already, keeping touch with his gay spy contacts—that man's tentacles were sprouting everywhere. Tom had to decide whether to move to Washington with the CIA or come back to New Godding, which he'd left as a lowly instructor. He was offered $8,000 a year from Uncle Sam, a lot of money, and $2,500 a year from Yaddah, and he took Yaddah. He knew he couldn't continue to live our kind of life for the government even if James Jesus was his co-worker, and he thought we could at Yaddah. No, I put too much emphasis on his and my sexual attraction to each other. He had idealistic reasons for electing Yaddah that I didn't know about yet. He wasn't finished trying to change history, and this was when things between us turned sour, as would much of the rest of his life.

Tom's goal was to reconstruct the American Studies that he'd left into something beyond the study of America ("Brits ruling the curriculum have had more than enough time at bat, boy"), into a curriculum that inadvertently would provide ideological ammunition for what soon was being called the Cold War. It was a new American crusade. Rich alumni now appeared who wanted something to show for their money and saw this as virtually a second Civil War and they wanted in. You've got to remember (well, I'm sure Ms. Strode remembers quite well) that this was a secret postwar world then, secrecy being the operative necessity because spies and spying, as she points out, was a bigger deal than it had ever been before. And this was not Mata Hari and Ashenden kind of stuff. This was dangerous in new ways, most particularly in terms of exposure: you were out there in the open air with no government or rules of war to really protect you should anything go wrong. No government, even to this day, is willing to admit it has spies. During World War II, what came to be known as the U.S. Intelligence Community, well, my goodness, it was all puffing meerschaum pipes and

Burberry raincoats, but after it, spies now carried guns. And the rich and powerful Yaddahs loved it.

This new American Studies program that Tom was setting up at Yaddah was not only part of a university bureaucracy but cheek to cheek with that U.S. Intelligence Community, now depiped and de-Burberryed and called the CIA. Tom knew it could be harsh. He didn't know it would be treacherous. "It was our time in our history for that."

The people running Yaddah were a tough lot. Charles Seymour was president and he was related to a handful of previous Yaddah presidents going back to 1740 and Griswold and Devane and Gobus and Mendenhall and Henning and Buck, they were all, well, not one of them was a professor I'd trust to help me in a fix. Mendenhall, now president of Smith, would drive the final stake into the heart of Newton Arvin that put paid to lifetimes of great scholarship by Newton and his gay group.

Mendenhall had taught Fred Lemish at Yaddah, as had Joel Dorius, with whom he'd had sex in the Provincetown dunes. The Smith board member Mary Griswold, wife of Yaddah's new president, A. Whitney Griswold, who was known to make homophobic remarks as was her husband, supported the firings of these scholars, ruining their lives. (See Barry Werth, *The Scarlet Professor: Newton Arvin—A Literary Life Shattered by Scandal*, and Joel Dorius, *My Four Lives: An Academic Life Shattered by Scandal*.) Somehow my Tom had talked President Seymour and Griswold and Dean DeVane into setting up a new program, called, of course, New American Studies. It was so described: "the purpose of this new American Studies program is not narrowly nationalistic [whatever that was meant to mean], but is adapted for American students who desire to study the civilization of our country as a whole with the aim of more effective service in national life." He was setting up a program to teach students to go out and take over the world. It might look a bit, say, overarching in print here. But that's what it was, and what university wouldn't glom on to a gig like that if Yaddah was doing it? In bed (we stayed in my rooms but he had to get home each night), Tom would dream his dreams out loud to me. He felt America was the greatest thing that ever happened period and that it was our responsibility to prove this superiority to the rest of the world. He'd come back from England hating every Oxbridge Brit who ever walked, and he came back from Washington feeling much the same for every uneducated and crude bureaucrat who'd worked for Roosevelt and Truman, "who have no sense of who we are! I'm meant to spy for them!" and Tom being Tom had determined a way to rectify all this, using our country and our history and our culture and our literature that he loved so much as the tools and template for doing so. Yaddah promoted him to assistant professor at a salary of $4,600 and placed him in charge of "his" program. The program was being secretly funded by Angleton's OSS. Tom knew that, of course, "but I had to locate start-up funds from somewhere, laddie." And he thought he could trust James Jesus, we sharing our own personal special secret.

"That's it for us," Tom said to me, when he got everything more or less in order. "We can't continue anything between us except on a scholarly basis." I won't say my heart wasn't broken. He also had a wife and family and that was harder for me to face. We both decided it was better than nothing. At least I did. By this time, looking back, I don't know what Tom was thinking. When I asked him, he answered the same as he did when he was working out codes at Bletchley. "You just take it a day at a time, laddie. You make it up as you go along, if it lets you. And if it doesn't let you, you're not doing something right." And then, as I was literally sticking an American flag in a stand beside his desk, he said, with much more clarity, "I have fashioned a way for America to secure peace in the world."

The university put out this official announcement: "Yaddah believes that it has a special duty to perform not only for The American People but also for common humanity, providing an understanding of American life and culture that will serve the interests of all." Seven of Tom's roster of instructors asked to be transferred to other departments, or found other places for themselves elsewhere. They smelled something and they weren't far wrong. In no time at all came that Congress of Cultural Freedom thing, again secretly funded by the CIA, with Tom as its board chair.

I told myself it all seemed logical and even beneficial. For by the time the Cold War came, the CCF was set up to fight the Communist "menace" to America. "We must utilize all the resources that we can to mobilize to teach our students the facts of Communism and the implications of Russian ideology. The Communist threat must be met vigorously." DeVane and Seymour wrote that. Tom by now had an American Studies department with five hundred guys clamoring to take one of our classes. No need for fundraising now. Every conservative corporation or rich alumnus poured money into our coffers as if we were the Holy Grail. "One comes to a new appreciation of what we are and what we have done, demonstrating it to the world,"

Seymour writes again. This was in 1949, not far from McCarthy and Vurd and Sam Sport and that gang.

An anonymous donor accompanied his million bucks with this warning. "I have become greatly disturbed over the drift in recent years toward a totalitarian governmental and economic system in this country, and unless one of the clearly stated objectives of our, may I now say our, general program is to counteract this tendency, I doubt if I will be interested in further supporting it." And sure enough, don't you love democracy and one vote for all, in a Prospectus of the New American Studies Program, you can find these words: "A program based on the conviction that the best safeguards against totalitarian developments in our economy are an affirmative belief in the validity of our institutions of free enterprise and individual liberty." God, it all sounds so innocent! With the appearance of this Prospectus, eight other faculty members left, not only from American Studies but History and Economics and Political Science, all now also having their teaching programs dictated to them, four of them to Harvard and the other four to UC Berkeley. There appeared to be no official love lost for any of them. The anonymous donor was so pleased "with how things are developing" that he gave another million, identified himself as Boris Greeting, and was rewarded with a seat on the Yaddah Corporation board. In one way or another he will be on one Yaddah board or another until . . . well, Fred says to hold off on discussing this.

Another major donor, one Jeshua Brinestalker, who said his opinions had become "completely turned around by your William F. Buckley and his groundbreaking book, *God and Man at Yaddah*," wrote this. "I further request that the Professor who heads this Program of New American Studies shall always be one who firmly believes in the preservation of our System of Free Enterprise and is opposed to the system of State Socialism, Communism and Totalitarianism and that my funds be used for furtherance of our new System above referred to." Ironically, this, it turns out, from an old spy for foreign powers, now—most of them—Communist and broke.

Tom was appointed to associate professor with no additional raise in salary. You can certainly begin to see what an ungrateful alma mater Yaddah is proving for this man who helped to win the war in the first place. When I tried to point this out to Tom, he broke down in tears and I comforted him, in my arms once more for a moment or two. I think he was beginning to see what damage his dream was creating. When James Jesus came for a visit, and we all got drunk and wound up in bed together like the old days ("My

God, this feels so good again; you have no idea how hard this is for me to do in D.C."), and Angleton then said he was hiring four more of Tom's faculty for the CIA, Tom started to cry again. "I did not start this as a recruitment tool for the CIA. I did not start this to create weapons for the psychological warfare that is going on and that you are whipping up to such a froth and fury and frenzy, James Jesus." Since one of Tom's concerns during the war had been as a trainer of intelligence staff and agents, Angleton didn't understand. Quite frankly, I'm not so sure Tom understood completely either. He'd have had to be blind not to see how guys from the English department, or Music or Art, and History certainly, now passed him no longer nodding hello. McCarthy and Sam Sport and Vurd were big-time on the front pages now, and *Washington Confidential* was on everybody's nightstand. I tried to get Tom to read it, but he wouldn't. Someone had already put it on our official required summer reading list at New American Studies.

It would be 1974, by which time Tom was a full professor, when Marchetti and Marks would write in their honestly groundbreaking *The CIA and the Cult of Intelligence*,

> To spot and evaluate students, the Clandestine Services maintained a contractual relationship with key professors on numerous campuses. When a professor had picked out a likely candidate, he notified his contact at the CIA and, on occasion, participated in the actual recruitment attempt. Some professors performed these services without being on a formal retainer. Others actively participated in agency covert operations by serving as "cut-outs," or intermediaries, and even by carrying out secret missions during foreign journeys.

Tom pressured James Jesus into telling him who was doing anything as "demoralizing" as this and discovered it was pretty much every man in his department, for a start. "Tom, what's come over you, man? I thought you loved your country?"

One of my own students, Michael Holzman, assembled many of the details above that so refreshed my own memory of those awful times. He has written an amazing essay about it, "The Ideological Origins of American Studies at Yaddah."

I want to go back to something I dropped in earlier, Tom's relationship with Alan Turing.

As perhaps you remember, Ms. Strode (I know Fred knows, because he mentioned it in one of his plays), Alan Turing is credited with founding computer science, but also with cracking various German codes, enabling the Allies to win World War II. Both are gigantic achievements, historical ones for all time. He and Tom became quite close at Bletchley Park, and Alan and I had a brief affair. He was a bit of a loner, a bit withdrawn into his own brilliance as he tried to constantly figure out everything that he was uncovering day by day. I adored him. Tom wanted to join us in a threesome, but Alan didn't want to, ostensibly because of his disfigurement but I believe because he recognized in Tom someone as brilliant as himself. They remained good friends after the war, how good I was to learn only much later.

In 1954, Alan picked up a hustler one night in Manchester who subsequently returned to rob his house. Alan reported him to the police. In the course of the investigation Alan acknowledged homosexual sex with the man. They were both instantly charged with gross indecency, the infamous Section 11 under which Oscar Wilde had been convicted more than fifty years before. This man who won the war lost his security clearance and any opportunity to continue his work. He was refused permission to enter the United States. He was offered by the British government the choice of punishment, either imprisonment or castration. He chose the latter, by hormonal treatments, chemical castration—which caused his body to grow breasts. He was found dead from poisoning. A poisoned apple, less a bite or two, was on the table beside him. Tom had come up from London. They had finally made love and, at Alan's request, Tom injected the cyanide into the apple for him and stayed there until Alan's end, holding his hand, before sneaking out and coming back home to America.

"Fucking Brits with their hypocritical snot-nosed culture full of Wordsworth ballads and Keats odes and Shakespeare sonnets. They demand complete fealty from us. They demand we worship their culture as superior as we deny our own! I hate them."

And then he told me, "And I'm going to set up a program to prove that America's talent and culture are superior to any others." It damn near killed him. When we all were asked to sign "loyalty oaths," he retired.

DAVID VISITS AN OLD FRIEND

The first person I go to see when I come back is Mr. Hoover. He loved me once.

Mr. Hoover lives across the street from Skipper, who was my first friend outside of Masturbov Gardens. We met when we were little boys and our mothers took us to the same dentist. We both had bad sinus infections. Skipper liked to take charge of everything. We'll do this. We'll go there. I liked him. He called me up all the way from Chesapeake Street after we met in the doctor's office. "Hello, this is Skipper. Come to my birthday party. I'll have my pop pick you up and take you home." We'd take long walks in Rock Creek Park with his dog, which also had red hair, and his mother would make us peanut butter and jelly sandwiches and great apricot cookies. We would take her cookies over on a plate to Mr. Hoover. Skipper's parents and Mr. Hoover and Clyde, his housemate, played bridge together. Skipper was afraid of him and would run away before the door was opened and I was left holding the plate. Today I ring Mr. Hoover's bell hoping Charles the butler will open it fast in case Skipper is still looking out his window. But he wouldn't recognize me now. He must be married by now anyway.

Mr. Hoover is standing on the upstairs landing looking down. He's short and round and he always reminds me of Philip. He's just got out of the shower and is wearing a bathrobe. It's open and I can see his penis. He had the first uncircumcised penis I ever saw.

"It's good to see you again," he says. "Come on up." He takes me to his dressing room and sits on a little stool, studying me in all the mirrors on the walls. He looks at me a long time before he says what I hoped he would, "Take off your clothes, boy." He takes a pencil and lifts my penis. He lifts up my arms and runs the pencil through the tufts of hair. He runs his fingers over the scars on my back. I hear him sigh. He turns me to look at him. He shakes his head. He looks sad. I want to cry. "Don't you cry, boy. Do you hear me?" I nod. "We're just at the end of a chapter, boy. It's time to start another chapter. That's what life's all about. You end one chapter and start another one. Come now, give me a hug."

Then we do what we always did before I went to Germany. I put my arms around his big belly and give him a squeeze, the way he liked it. He liked to have me run my hand over his stomach, too, like I was smoothing down a big pile of sand. Even his genitals are shaved. He always smelled of soap and powder.

When I was five or six with that plate of cookies, he invited me inside. It was very exciting. His house was dark and filled with lots of furniture and paintings that looked valuable. We went into the kitchen for milk and some of the cookies. He was very easy to talk to. He asked me all kinds of questions about Philip and Rivka and what they did and if I was happy. I didn't answer that one. In fact, I suddenly started to cry then, too. No one had ever asked me a question like that. In fact, I started to bawl. He was smiling, in the nicest way, and I ran to him and he did what suddenly I wanted him to do. He put his arms around me and comforted me. I covered his face with kisses. I wouldn't let him let me go. I wanted to stay in his arms. If he was as powerful as Skipper said, then I would be safe in his arms. He was wearing his bathrobe then as well. "Put your arms around me, boy, and give me a big, big hug." I stuck my arms under the robe and did just that, feeling his soft skin and his tough big belly. "Now give me a big, big squeeze." I did that, too. Then I said, "I want you to do that to me, too!" And I ripped off my jersey and short pants and put his arms around me and told him, "Now give me a big, big hug plus a big, big squeeze." He laughed, and he did so. I can still feel it. I will always remember how wonderful it felt and how Philip never made me feel this way, my own father. Then he said what would become his routine every time we met. "Let's see your body, boy." And I threw off my underpants and yanked off my shoes and socks and he turned me around this way and that way, and then pushed me a few steps out so I could do it as if I were showing off for him, which I really was, which I really wanted to. I turned this way and that way and wound up bowing to him like I was in a play. He really laughed loudly then.

Did we ever do more than this? I am not going to answer this because I've learned he was a first-class monster and deserves to be hated big-time. If I were a religious person, I would think of Jesus, who was always said to have compassion and forgiveness in his heart for all mankind. Mr. Hoover comforted me when I needed comfort most. Someone once said to me that I always bet on the wrong horses. But I never placed bets. Only hope.

Clyde comes into the room. "Yes, another chapter," he says as he helps me to get dressed. He sounds sort of sad, too. Once Mr. Hoover told me about Clyde's penis. "It's like a huge fire hose," he laughed. "All Clyde has to see is a glimpse of stocking and anything goes."

There was devotion there. Some kind of love. Each did whatever he did for the other. I don't think one could have lived without the other. Mr. Hoover couldn't have been Mr. Hoover without Clyde. His act was as much for Clyde as for history. They were great actors, I see now. No star of stage or screen could have played such parts for so long and so well. When I later became friends with Fred and he professed such admiration for the actor's courage in getting out there night after night to pretend, to be so vulnerable, so naked, I laughed in recognition. I had witnessed some of the best acting in the world, and those performances had gone on nonstop for years. Clyde and Mr. Hoover didn't do it out of courage. They did it because that was the only way they could live. If you ask me now, that's not so much courage as cowardice. It's much easier to pretend. It's safer. And I can't blame anyone for wanting to be safe.

I never liked Clyde. I thought he was an asshole. He is a slave and yes-man and is mean and nasty to everyone, including Mr. Hoover. Mr. Hoover ignores him most of the time. Once Clyde took me downstairs to show me "the room." I was taken into one of those basement dens with gallows and stocks and whips and all those props that sadists and masochists use. I looked at it all quite calmly. I didn't know yet what I was looking at, and Clyde didn't tell me. He just took me back upstairs. I don't think you're supposed to like Clyde. I think this is the way Mr. Hoover wants it.

"Why do people hate us?" I ask Mr. Hoover on this visit to him when I come back from Mungel. "You put me in camps where I saw how much they hate us." I'm not sure how I know he's responsible, but that's what comes out of my mouth and he doesn't correct me.

"Now that you're home, what do you want to do?" he asks.

"Why do they hate us? Can you help me?"

"I started your education long ago, and I will continue to do so, if that's what you wish. What you will do with such information—well, this will be interesting to see."

I am never asked about Hoover as I am about Mengele. If people knew about me and both of them, would I be considered a monster too? How in the world do I care what anyone thinks?

WHERE ARE WE?

The never ending story of what's happening is too horrid for most homosexuals to believe, even if they could hear it. It was unbelievable enough to hear all those unconfirmed rumors about Hitler and homosexuals and concentration camps and ovens. A pathetic parade of a few dozen calling themselves the New Hushmarkeds protests outside the White House and then disperses when it looks like they'll get arrested. They've marched from the Capitol to the White House with placards saying "What Is Really Going On at Partekla!" Nobody knows what Partekla is. No one inside the White House even looks out the window. The New Hushmarkeds will only be around for a matter of months. There are few of them. So no one sees them. Or hears them. Or cares about them in the least. Including all other hush-markeds. Correction, homosexuals.

The longer life's lived like this, the more there is to haunt it. "Search for my heart no longer" (Charles Baudelaire), "the beasts have eaten it" (*The Flowers of Evil*).